EVERY SHORT STORY
1951–2012

EVERY SHORT

CANONGATE

ALASD

STORY

1951–2012

TO
THE
GOOD
ANGEL
MULLANE
AND
CHRISTOPHER
BOYCE
AND THEIR DAUGHTERS PETRA AND ANTONIA

EDINBURGH

AIR GRAY

Published in Great Britain in 2015 by Canongate Books Ltd,
14 High Street, Edinburgh EH1 1TE
canongate.co.uk
3

Where & when the following tales were first
printed is given in notes at the very end.
British Library Cataloguing-in-Publication Data
A catalogue record for this book is available on
request from the British Library.
ISBN 978 0 85786 561 8
Typeset in Optima by Sharon McTeir
Printed and bound in Great Britain
by CPI Group (UK) Ltd, Croydon CR0 4YY
The publisher acknowledges support from the National
Lottery through Creative Scotland towards the
publication of this title.

TABLE OF

UNLIKELY STORIES, MOSTLY

LEAN TALES

CONTENTS

LEAN TALES

GLASWEGIANS

TABLE OF

TEN TALES TALL AND TRUE

THE ENDS OF OUR TETHERS

CONTENTS

TALES DROLL AND PLAUSIBLE

UNLIKELY STORIES, MOSTLY

EDINBURGH 1983

They passed through the galleries, surveyed the vaults of marble, and examined the chest in which the body of the founder is supposed to have been deposited. They sat down in one of the most spacious chambers to rest for a while, before they attempted to return.

"We have now," said Imlac, "gratified our minds with an exact view of the greatest work of man, except the wall of China.

"Of the wall it is very easy to assign the motive. It secured a wealthy and timorous nation from the incursions of barbarians. But for the pyramids no reason has ever been given adequate to the cost and labour of the work. It seems to have been erected only in compliance with that hunger of imagination which preys incessantly upon life, and must always be appeased by some employment. He who has built for use till use is supplied, must begin to build for vanity, and extend his plan to the utmost power of human performance that he may not be soon reduced to form another wish.

"I consider this mighty structure as a monument to the insufficiency of human enjoyments. A government whose power is unlimited, and whose treasures surmount all real and imaginary wants, is compelled to solace the satiety of dominion by seeing thousands labouring without end, and one stone, for no purpose, laid upon another."

From RASSELAS by Samuel Johnson

THE STAR

A star had fallen beyond the horizon, in Canada perhaps. (He had an aunt in Canada.) The second was nearer, just beyond the iron works, so he was not surprised when the third fell into the backyard. A flash of gold light lit the walls of the enclosing tenements and he heard a low musical chord. The light turned deep red and went out, and he knew that somewhere below a star was cooling in the night air. Turning from the window he saw that no-one else had noticed. At the table his father, thoughtfully frowning, filled in a football coupon, his mother continued ironing under the pulley with its row of underwear. He said in a small voice, "A'm gawn out."

His mother said, "See you're no' long then."

He slipped through the lobby and onto the stairhead, banging the door after him.

The stairs were cold and coldly lit at each landing by a weak electric bulb. He hurried down three flights to the black silent yard and began hunting backward and forward, combing with his fingers the lank grass round the base of the clothes-pole. He found it in the midden on a decayed cabbage leaf. It was smooth and round, the size of a glass marble, and it shone with a light which made it seem to rest on a precious bit of green and yellow velvet. He picked it up. It was warm and filled his cupped palm with a ruby glow. He put it in his pocket and went back upstairs.

That night in bed he had a closer look. He slept with his brother who was not easily wakened. Wriggling carefully far down under the sheets, he opened his palm and gazed. The star shone white and blue, making the space around him like a cave in an iceberg. He brought it close to his eye. In its depth was the pattern of a snow-flake, the grandest thing he had ever seen. He looked through the flake's crystal lattice into an ocean of glittering blue-black waves under a sky full of huge galaxies. He heard a remote lulling sound like the sound in a sea-shell, and fell asleep with the star safely clenched in his hand.

He enjoyed it for nearly two weeks, gazing at it each night below the sheets, sometimes seeing the snow-flake, sometimes a flower, jewel, moon or landscape. At first he kept it hidden during the day but soon took to carrying it about with him; the smooth rounded gentle warmth in his pocket gave comfort when he felt insulted or neglected.

At school one afternoon he decided to take a quick look. He was at the back of the classroom in a desk by himself. The teacher was among the boys at the front row and all heads were bowed over books. Quickly he brought out the star and looked. It contained an aloof eye with a cool green pupil which dimmed and trembled as if seen through water.

"What have you there, Cameron?"

He shuddered and shut his hand.

"Marbles are for the playground, not the classroom. You'd better give it to me."

"I cannae, sir."

"I don't tolerate disobedience, Cameron. Give me that thing."

The boy saw the teacher's face above him, the mouth opening and shutting under a clipped moustache. Suddenly he knew what to do and put the star in his mouth and swallowed. As the warmth sank toward his heart he felt relaxed and at ease. The teacher's face moved into the distance. Teacher, classroom, world receded like a rocket into a warm, easy blackness leaving behind a trail of glorious stars, and he was one of them.

THE SPREAD OF IAN NICOL

One day Ian Nicol, a riveter by trade, started to split in two down the middle. The process began as a bald patch on the back of his head. For a week he kept smearing it with hair restorer, yet it grew bigger, and the surface became curiously puckered and so unpleasant to look upon that at last he went to his doctor. "What is it?" he asked.

"I don't know," said the doctor, "but it looks like a face, ha, ha! How do you feel these days?"

"Fine. Sometimes I get a stabbing pain in my chest and stomach but only in the morning."

"Eating well?"

"Enough for two men."

The doctor thumped him all over with a stethoscope and said, "I'm going to have you X-rayed. And I may need to call in a specialist."

Over the next three weeks the bald patch grew bigger still and the suggestion of a face more clearly marked on it. Ian visited his doctor and found a specialist in the consulting room, examining X-ray plates against the light. "No doubt about it, Nicol," said the specialist, "you are splitting in two down the middle."

Ian considered this.

"That's not usual, is it?" he asked.

"Oh, it happens more than you would suppose. Among bacteria and viruses it's very common, though it's certainly less frequent among riveters. I suggest you go into hospital where the process can complete itself without annoyance for your wife or embarrassment to yourself. Think it over."

Ian thought it over and went into hospital where he was put into a small ward and given a nurse to attend him, for the specialist was interested in the case. As the division proceeded more specialists were called in to see what was happening. At first Ian ate and drank with a greed that appalled those who saw it. After consuming three times his normal bulk for three days on end he fell into a coma which lasted till the split was complete. Gradually the lobes of his brain separated and a bone shutter formed between them. The face on the back of his head grew eyelashes and a jaw. What seemed at first a cancer of the heart became another heart. Convulsively the spine doubled itself. In a puzzled way the specialists charted the stages of the process and discussed the cause. A German consultant said that life was freeing itself from the vicissitudes of sexual reproduction. A psychiatrist said it was a form of schizophrenia, a psycho-analyst that it was an ordinary twinning process which had been delayed by a severe case of prenatal sibling rivalry. When the split was complete, two thin Ian Nicols lay together on the bed.

The resentment each felt for the other had not been foreseen or guarded against. In bed the original Ian Nicol could be recognized by his position (he lay on the right of the bed), but as soon as both men were strong enough to walk each claimed ownership of birth certificate, union card, clothes, wife and National Insurance benefit. One day in the hospital grounds they started fighting. They were evenly matched and there are conflicting opinions about who won. On leaving hospital they took legal action against each other for theft of identity. The case was resolved by a medical

examination which showed that one of them had no navel.

The second Ian Nicol changed his name by deed poll and is now called Macbeth. Sometimes he and Ian Nicol write to each other. The latest news is that each has a bald patch on the back of his head.

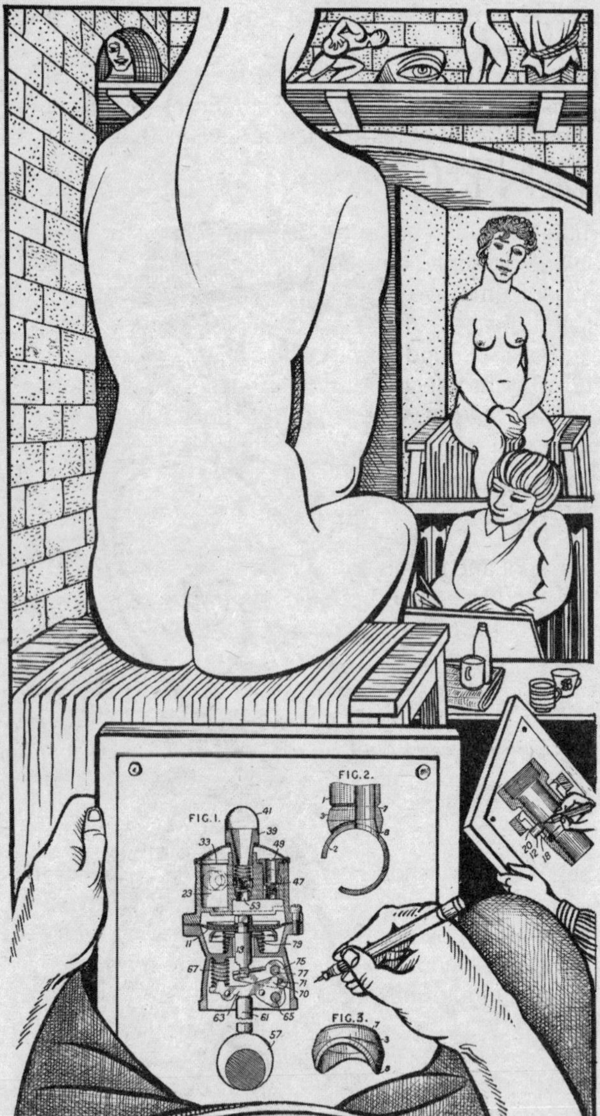
FIG. 1.
FIG. 2.
FIG. 3.

THE CAUSE OF RECENT CHANGES

The painting departments of modern art schools are full of discontented people. One day Mildred said to me, "I'm sick of wasting time. We start work at ten and tire after half an hour and the boys throw paper pellets at each other and the girls stand round the radiators talking. Then we get bored and go to the refectory and drink coffee and we aren't enjoying ourselves, but what else can we do? I'm tired of it. I want to do something vigorous and constructive."

I said, "Dig a tunnel."

"What do you mean?"

"Instead of drinking coffee when you feel bored, go down to the basement and dig an escape tunnel."

"But if I wanted to escape I could walk through the front door and not come back."

"You can't escape that way. The education department would stop your bursary and you would have to work for a living."

"But where would I be escaping to?"

"That isn't important. To travel hopefully is better than to arrive."

My suggestion was not meant seriously but was taken seriously. In the seldom-visited sub-basement a flagstone was replaced by a disguised trap-door. Under this a room was dug into the school's foundation and here the tunnel began. In forty minute shifts boxes of waste were winched up and the waste put in small sacks easily smuggled out under students' clothing. The school was built on a bank of igneous quartz so there was no danger of walls caving in, no need of pit-props. Digging was eased by a chemical solvent applied to rock faces with a hand spray, making them soft as cheese. This was invented by industrial design students who despised the painters digging the tunnel but supported it as a technical challenge.

The tunnel did not fail after a few months like the attempt to start an art school debating society, magazine, choir and outing to Linlithgow. Enthusiasm for it actually increased. The Students Representative Society was packed with members of the tunnel committee who organized dances to pay for the installation of more powerful winches. We all became more tense, jumping at small sounds, laughing loudly at feeble jokes, quarrelling with small provocation. Did some fear the tunnel would open a volcanic vent? Yet the diggers noticed no increase of temperature. Sometimes I wondered how the project remained free from interference. An engineering venture supported by several hundred people can hardly be called a secret. It was natural for those outside the school to regard rumours as fantastic inventions, but why did none of the teachers interfere? Only a minority were active supporters of the project; two were being bribed to remain silent. I am sure the director and deputy director did not know, but what about the rest who knew and said nothing? Perhaps they also regarded the tunnel as a possible means of escape. One day work on the tunnel stopped. The first shift going to work in the morning coffee-break discovered that the basement entrance was locked. There were several tunnel entrances now but all were found to be locked, and since the tunnel committee had vanished it was assumed they were inside. This caused a deal of speculation.

I have always kept clear of mass movements, so on meeting the president of the committee in a lonely upper corridor one evening, I said, "Hullo, Mildred," and would have passed on, but she gripped my arm and said, "Come with me."

She led me a few yards to the open door of what I had thought was a disused service lift. She said, "You'd better sit on the floor," and closed the gates behind us and pulled a lever. The lift fell like a stone with a noise so high-pitched that it was sometimes inaudible. After fifteen minutes it decelerated in violent jerks, then stopped. Mildred opened the gates and we stepped out.

In spite of myself I was impressed by what I saw. We stood in a corridor with an arched ceiling, asphalt floor and walls of white tile. It swept left and right in a curve that prevented seeing more than a mile in each direction. "Very good," I said, "very good indeed. How did you manage it? The fluorescent lighting alone must have cost a fortune."

Mildred said gloomily, "We didn't make this place. We only reached it."

At that moment an elderly man passed us on a bicycle. He wore a peaked cap, an armband with some kind of badge on it and was otherwise naked, for the air was warm. As he passed he raised a hand in a friendly gesture. I said, "Who was that?"

"Some kind of official. There aren't many of them on this level."

"How many levels are there?"

"Three. This one has dormitories and canteens for the staff, and underneath are the offices of the administration, and under that is the engine."

"What engine?"

"The one that drives us round the sun."

"But gravity drives the world round the sun."

"Has anyone ever told you what gravity is and how it operates?"

I realized nobody ever had. Mildred said, "Gravity is nothing but a word top-level scientists use to hide their ignorance."

I asked her how the engine was powered. She said, "Steam."

"Not nuclear fission?"

"No, the industrial design boys are quite certain it's a steam engine of the most primitive sort imaginable. They're down there measuring and sketching with the rest of the committee. We'll show you a picture in a day or two."

"Does nobody ask what right you have to go poking about inside this thing?"

"No. It's like all big organizations. The staff are so numerous that you can go where you like if you look confident enough."

I had to meet a friend in half an hour so we got into the lift and started back up. I said, "Well, Mildred, it's interesting of course, but I don't know why you brought me to see it." She said, "I'm worried. The others keep laughing at the machinery and discussing how to alter it. They think they can improve the climate by taking us nearer the sun. I'm afraid we're doing wrong."
"Of course you're doing wrong! You're supposed to be studying art, not planetary motion. I would never have suggested the project if I'd thought you would take it to this length."
She let me out on the ground floor saying, "We can't turn back now."
"Why not?"
"Too many of us have invested too much to stop now."
"That's a usual, ancient and very bad excuse."
But she stayed in the lift, shut the door and I never saw her again.

That night I was wakened by an explosion and my bed falling heavily to the ceiling. The sun, which had just set, came up again. The city was inundated by sea. We survivors crouched a long time among ruins threatened by earthquakes, avalanches and whirlwinds. All clocks were working at different speeds and the sun, after reaching the height of noon, stayed there. At length the elements calmed and we examined the new situation. It is clear that the planet has broken into several bits. Our bit is not revolving. To enjoy starlight and darkness, to get a good night's sleep, we have to walk to the other side of our new world, a journey of several miles, with an equally long back journey when we want daylight.

Sometimes I look across
the very near horizon
at other chunks
of the old globe.
It seems likely
that the accident resulted
from a chance remark
of mine.
It will teach
me
to keep my mouth
shut,
in future.

A UNIQUE CASE

The Reverend Dr Phelim MacLeod is a healthy, boyish-looking bachelor who has outlived all his relations except a distant cousin in Canada. Though unsurpassed in his knowledge of Latin, Hebrew and Greek his main reading since retirement has been detective stories, but he can still beat me at the game of chess we play at least once a fortnight. I tell you this to indicate his apparent normality before the accident last year. A badly driven, badly stacked glazier's van crashed beside his garden gate as he walked out of it, and a fragment of glass sheared off a section of skull with his right ear on it. I am his closest friend. At the Royal Infirmary I heard that no visitors could be allowed to see him in his present state, but I would be called if it changed.

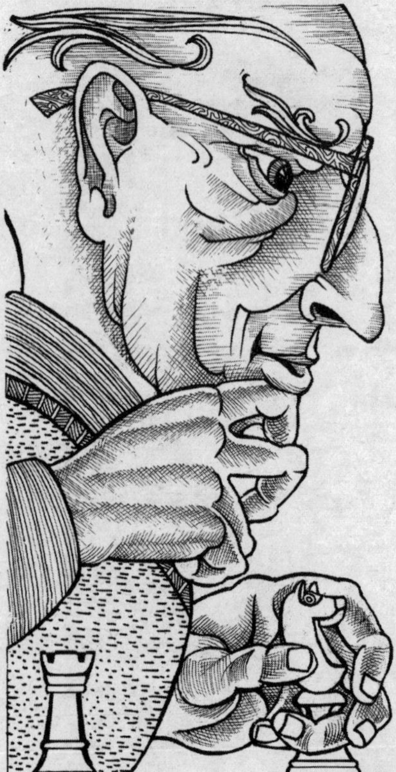

I was called a week later. The brain surgeon in charge of him said, "Dr MacLeod has regained consciousness. We are providing him with peace, privacy and a

well-balanced diet. His unique constitution makes it impossible for us to do more."
"But is he recovering?"
"I think so. Judge for yourself. And please tell him nothing about his appearance that would needlessly disturb him."

In a small ward of his own I found Dr MacLeod propped up in bed reading one of his detective thrillers. He greeted me with his usual calm, self-satisfied smile. I asked how he felt.
"Very well," he said. "You are interested in my wound, I see. How does it look? The staff here are less than informative."

In war films I had seen many buildings with an outer wall missing and the side of my friend's head resembled one. Through a big opening I saw tiny rooms with doors, light fittings and wall sockets, all empty of furniture but with signs of hasty evacuation. There was also scaffolding and heaps of building material suggesting that repair was in progress. I said hesitantly, "You seem to be mending quite well."
Dr MacLeod smiled complacently and pointed out that he would be seventy-six on his next birthday. I asked if he had any pain.
"No pain but a deal of inconvenience. I am forbidden to move my head and am sometimes wakened at night by hammering noises inside it. I sleep best during the day."

After chatting with him about the weather and our acquaintances I returned to the surgeon's office. I told him that my friend seemed surprisingly fit for a man in his condition and asked who was responsible for the improvement.
"Agents," said the surgeon slowly, "who seem to inhabit the undamaged parts of his anatomy, only emerging to operate on him when nobody is looking – nobody like us, I mean. I am carefully keeping students and younger

doctors away from this case. Mere curiosity might lead them to kill your friend by delving into what they understand as little as I do."

"There are obviously more things in heaven and earth," I said, "than are dreamed of in your ..."

The surgeon interrupted testily, saying every experienced medical practitioner knew that better than Shakespeare. A year seldom passed without them encountering at least one inexplicable case. A hospital he would not name recently treated a woman, otherwise normal, for panic attacks caused by her certainty that a sudden shock would crack her into a million pieces. When every other therapy had failed a psychiatrist, thinking a practical demonstration might work, suddenly tripped her so that she fell on a padded surface which could not have injured a child, and she had cracked into a million pieces.

"With tact," said the surgeon, "your friend's case may have a happier conclusion."

It did. A month later the wound had been closed. Skin grew over it, a new ear, also a few strands of the white hair which elsewhere surrounds Dr MacLeod's bald pink dome. He returned home and we meet once more for regular chess games. His character seems in no way changed by the accident. I am sometimes tempted to tell him that he is worked from inside by smaller people and always refrain in case it spoils his play. But maybe it would have no effect at all. Like many Christians he believes that a healthy body is a gift from God, no matter how it works. And like most men he has always thought himself unique.

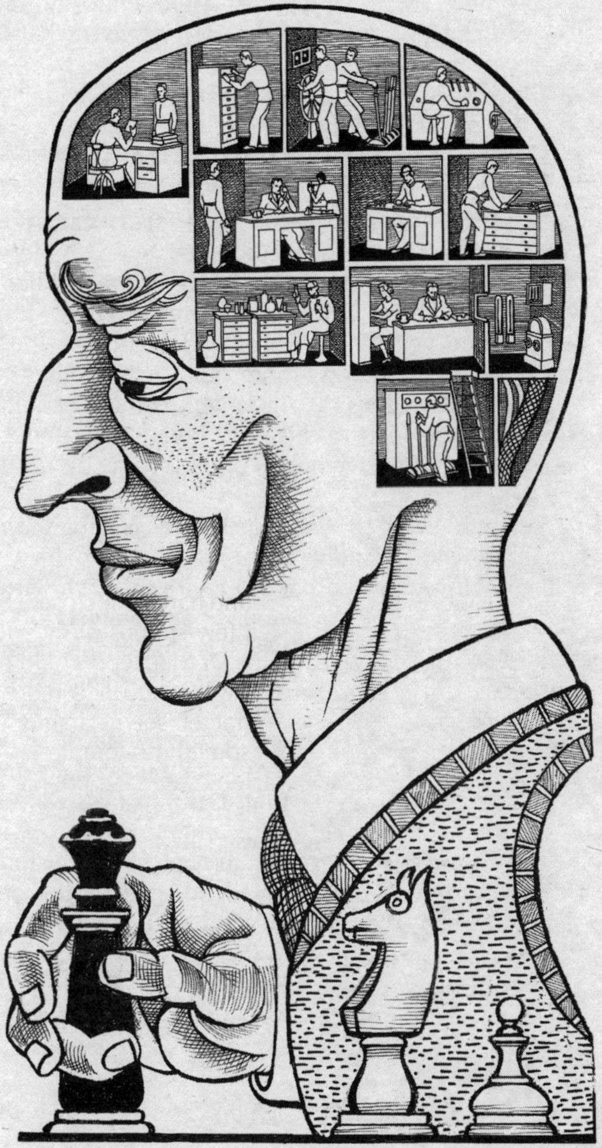

THE COMEDY OF THE WHITE DOG

On a sunny afternoon two men went by car into the suburbs to the house of a girl called Nan. Neither was much older than twenty years. One of them, Kenneth, was self-confident and well dressed and his friends thought him very witty. He owned and drove the car. The other, Gordon, was more quiet. His clothes were as good as Kenneth's but he inhabited them less easily. He had never been to this girl's house before and felt nervous. An expensive bunch of flowers lay on his lap.

Kenneth stopped the car before a broad-fronted bungalow with a badly kept lawn. The two men had walked halfway up the path to the door when Kenneth stopped and pointed to a dog which lay basking in the grass. It was a small white sturdy dog with a blunt pinkish muzzle and a stumpy tail. It lay with legs stuck out at right angles to its body, its eyes were shut tight and mouth open in a grin through which the tongue lolled. Kenneth and Gordon laughed and Gordon said, "What's so funny about him?" Kenneth said, "He looks like a toy dog knocked over on its side."

"Is he asleep?"

"Don't fool yourself. He hears every word we say."

The dog opened its eyes, sneezed and got up. It came over to Gordon and grinned up at him but evaded his hand when he bent down to pat it and trotted up the path and touched the front door with its nose. The door opened and the dog disappeared into a dark hall. Kenneth and Gordon stood on the front step stamping their feet on the mat and clearing their throats. Sounds of female voices and clattering plates came from nearby and the noise of a wireless from elsewhere. Kenneth shouted, "Ahoi!" and Nan came out of a side door. She was a pleasant-faced blonde who would have seemed plump if her waist, wrists and ankles had not been slender. She wore an apron over a blue frock and held a moist plate in one hand. Kenneth said jocularly, "The dog opened the door to us."

"Did he? That was wicked of him. Hullo, Gordon, why, what nice flowers. You're always kind to me. Leave them on the hallstand and I'll put them in water."

"What sort of dog is he?" said Gordon.

"I'm not sure, but when we were on holiday up at Ardnamurchan the local inhabitants mistook him for a pig."

A woman's voice shouted, "Nan! The cake!"

"Oh, I'll have to rush now, I've a cake to ice. Take Gordon into the living room, Kenneth; the others haven't arrived yet so you'll have to entertain each other. Pour yourselves a drink if you like."

The living room was at the back of the house. The curtains, wallpaper and carpets had bright patterns that didn't harmonize. There was an assortment of chairs and the white dog lay on the most comfortable. There was a big very solid oval table, and a grand piano with two bottles of cider and several tumblers on it. "I see we're not going to have an orgy anyway," said Gordon, pouring cider into a tumbler.

"No, no. It's going to be a nice little family party," said Kenneth, seating himself at the piano and starting to play.

He played badly but with confidence, attempting the best known bits of works by Beethoven and Schumann. If he particularly enjoyed a phrase he repeated it until it bored him; if he made a passage illegible with too many discords he repeated it until it improved. Gordon stood with the tumbler in his hand, looking out the window. It opened on a long narrow lawn which sloped down between hedges to a shrubbery.

"Are you in love with Nan?" said Kenneth, still playing.

"Yes. Mind you, I don't know her well," said Gordon.

"Hm. She's too matronly for me."

"I don't think she's matronly."

"What do you like about her?"

"Most things. I like her calmness. She's got a very calm sort of beauty."

Kenneth stopped playing and sat looking thoughtful. Voices and clattering dishes could be heard from the kitchen, a telephone was ringing and the noise of a wireless still came loudly from somewhere. Kenneth said, "She's not calm when she's at home. They're all very nice folk, pleasant and sincere I mean, but you'll find all the women of this family – Nan, her mother and grandmother and aunt – all talk too loudly at the same time. It's never quiet in this house. Either the wireless is on loudly, or the gramophone, or both. I've been to one or two parties here. There are never many guests but I've always felt there are other parties going on in rooms of the house I don't know about. Do you want to marry Nan?"

"Of course. I told you I loved her."

Kenneth laughed and swung from side to side on the piano stool, making it squeak. He said, "Don't mistake me – there's nothing disorderly about the house. Nobody drinks anything stronger than cider. Nan's father and brothers are so quiet as to be socially non-existent. You only see them at mealtimes and not always then. In fact I'm not sure how many brothers she has, or how large this family is. What are you grinning at?"

"I wish I could talk like you," said Gordon. "You've told me nothing surprising about Nan's family, yet you've made it seem downright sinister."
Kenneth began to fumble out the tune of 'The Lark in the Clear Air'.
"Anyway," he said, "you won't get a chance to be alone with her, which is what you most want, I suppose."

Nan came in and said, "Gibson and Clare will be here in half an hour ... er ... would you like to have tea in the garden? It's a good day for it. Mum doesn't like the idea much."
"I think it's a fine idea," said Kenneth.
"Oh, good. Perhaps you'll help us with the table?"
Gordon and Kenneth took the legs off the table, carried the pieces on to the back lawn and reassembled it, then put chairs round it and helped to set it. While they did so Nan's mother, a small gay woman, kept running out and shouting useless directions: "Put that cake in the middle, Gordon! No, nearer the top! Did ye need to plant the table so far from the house? You've given yourself a lot of useless work. Well, well, it's a nice day. Where's my dog? Where's my dog? Aha, there he is below the table! Come out, ye bizum! No, don't tease him, Kenneth! You'll only drive him mad."

Gibson and Clare arrived. Gibson was a short thickly built man whose chin always looked swarthy. At first sight he gave a wrong impression of strength and silence, for he was asthmatic and this made his movements slow and deliberate. Though not older than Gordon or Kenneth his hair was getting thin. As soon as he felt at ease in a company he would talk expertly about books, art, politics and anything that was not direct experience. Clare, his girl-friend, was nearly six feet tall and beautiful in a consciously chaste way. Her voice was high-pitched, pure and clear, and she listened to conversation with large wide-open eyes and lustrous lips slightly parted. Her favourite joke was to suspect an indecency in an ordinary remark and to publicize it with a little exclamation and giggle. Kenneth had nicknamed the two Intellect and Spirit. He said there seemed nothing animal between them.

The tea was a pleasant one. Only Nan, her four guests and the dog were present, though. Nan's mother often ran out with a fresh pot of tea or plate of food. The sun was bright, a slight breeze kept the air from being too warm, and Kenneth amused the company by talking about the dog.

"There's something heraldic about him," he said. "It's easy to imagine him with another head where his tail is. Look, he's getting excitable! He wants to sit on a chair! Oh, I hope he doesn't choose mine."

The dog had been trotting round the table in a wide circle, now it came toward Kenneth, wagging its tail and grinning. Kenneth grabbed a plate of meringues and got down under the table with them. "These at least he shall not have!" he cried in a muffled trembling voice. The others laughed, left their chairs and finished the meal sitting on the grass. All but Gordon felt that pleasant drunkenness which comes from being happy in company. Kenneth crawled about the lawn on his knees with a sugar bowl in his hand and when he came to a daisy peered at it benevolently and dropped a small heap of sugar into the flower. Gibson crawled after him, adding drops from the milk jug. Clare sat with the dog on her lap and pretended

to cut it up with a knife and fork. Actually she stroked and tickled its stomach gently with the edge of the knife and murmured baby-talk: "Will I be cruel and eat oo up doggie? No, no, no, doggie, oo is too sweet a doggie to eat up."

Nan had taken needles and wool from her apron pocket and was quietly knitting and smiling to herself. Gordon lay nearby pretending to sunbathe. He was worried. He really did not know Nan well. He had only seen her at the homes of friends, and had not even spoken to her much. His invitation to the party had been a surprise. Nan did not know him as well as several other people she might have invited. He had assumed she knew what he felt for her and was giving him a chance to know her better, yet since he arrived she had not paid him any special attention. Now she sat placidly knitting, sometimes glancing sideways at Clare with a slight ironic smile; yet he believed he saw in her manner a secretive awareness of him, lying apart and wanting her.

"Ach, the bitch," he thought, "she's sure of me. She thinks she can hurt me all she likes. Well, she's wrong." He got up, went to the table and started piling the plates together.

"I'll take these indoors," he said.

"Oh, don't bother," said Nan, smiling at him lazily.

"Someone will have to shift them," said Gordon sternly.

He took several journeys to carry the table things into the kitchen. It was cool and dim indoors. Nan's father and three of her silent brothers were eating a meal at the kitchen table. They nodded to him. The mother was nowhere to be seen but he heard her voice among several shrill female voices in some other room. Gordon brought in the last table things and put them on the drying board of the sink, then stood awkwardly watching the four eaters. They were large men with stolid, clumsily moulded faces. Some lines on the father's face were deeply cut, otherwise he looked very

like his sons. He said to Gordon, "A warm evening."
"Yes, I prefer it indoors."
"Would you like a look at the library?"
"Er, yes, thanks, yes I would."
The father got up and led Gordon across the hall and down a short passage, opened a door and stood by to let Gordon through. The library had old glass-fronted bookcases on each wall. Between the bookcases hung framed autographed photographs of D.H. Lawrence, Havelock Ellis, H.G. Wells and Bernard Shaw. There was a leather-covered arm-chair, and a round tin labelled 'Edinburgh Rock' on a low table beside it.
"You've a lot of books," said Gordon.
"The wife's people were great readers," said Nan's father. "Can I leave you now?"
"Oh yes. Oh yes."
The father left. Gordon took a book at random from a shelf, sat down and turned the pages casually. It was a history of marine engineering. The library was on the opposite side of the hall from the living room, but its window also looked on to the back garden and sometimes Gordon heard an occasional shout or laugh or bark from those on the lawn. He told himself grimly, "I'm giving her a chance. If she wants me she can come to me here. In fact if she has ordinary politeness and decency she'll be bound to look for me soon." He imagined the things she might say and the things he would say back. Sometimes he consoled himself with a piece of rock from the tin.

Suddenly the door sprang open with a click and he saw coming through it towards him, not Nan, but the dog. It stopped in front of him and grinned up into his face. "What do you want?" said Gordon irritably. The dog wagged its tail. Gordon threw a bit of rock which it caught neatly in its jaws, then trotted out through the door. Gordon got up, slammed the door and sat down. A little later the door opened and the dog entered again.

"Ye brute!" said Gordon. "Right, here's your sweet; the last you'll get from me."
He escorted the dog to the door, closed it carefully, turned a key in the lock, then went back to the chair and book. After a while it struck him that with the door locked Nan wouldn't get in if she came to him. He glanced uneasily up. The door was open and the dog stood before him, grinning with what seemed, to his stupefied eyes, triumphant amusement. For a moment Gordon was too surprised to move. He noticed that the animal was grinning with its mouth *shut*, a thing he had never seen a dog do before. He raised the book as if to throw it.

"Grrr, get out!" he yelled. The dog turned jauntily and trotted away. After thinking carefully Gordon decided some joker must have unlocked the door from outside: it was the sort of pointless joke Kenneth liked. He listened carefully and heard from the lawn the voice of Kenneth and the barking of the dog. He decided to leave the door open.

Later he found it too dark to see the page of the book clearly and put it down. The noises from the lawn had subtly altered. The laughter and shouting were now not continuous. There were periods of silence disturbed by the occasional shuffle of running feet and the hard breathing of somebody pursued, then he would hear a half-cry or scream that did not sound altogether in fun. Gordon went to the window. Something strange was happening on the darkened lawn. Nan was nowhere to be seen. Kenneth, Gibson and Clare were huddled together on the bare table-top, Clare kneeling, Kenneth and Gibson crouching half-erect. The white dog danced in a circle round the table among over-turned chairs. Its activity and size seemed to have increased with the darkness. It glimmered like a sheet in the dusk, its white needle-teeth glittered in the silently laughing jaws, it was about the size of a small lion. Gibson was occupied

in a strange way, searching his pockets for objects and hurling them at the shrubbery at the far end of the garden. The white dog would run, leap, catch these in its mouth while they were in the air, then return and deposit them under the table. It looked like a game and had possibly begun as one, but obviously Gibson was continuing in an effort to get the dog as far away as possible. Gordon suddenly discovered Nan was beside him, watching, her hands clenched against her mouth.

Gibson seemed to run out of things to throw. Gordon saw him expostulate precariously for a moment with Kenneth, demanding (it appeared) his fountain pen. Kenneth kept shaking his head. He was plainly not as frightened as Gibson or Clare, but a faint embarrassed smile on his face suggested that he was abashed by some monstrous possibility. Gibson put a hand to his mouth, withdrew something, then seemed to reason with Kenneth, who at last shrugged and took it with a distaste which suggested it was a plate of false teeth. Kenneth stood upright and, balancing himself with difficulty, hurled the object at the shrubbery. It was a good throw. The white dog catapulted after it and at once the three jumped from the table and ran to the house, Kenneth going to the right, Gibson and Clare to the left. The dog swerved in an abrupt arc and hurled toward the left. He overtook Clare and snapped the hem of her dress. She stumbled and fell. Gibson and Kenneth disappeared from sight and two doors were slammed in different parts of the house. Clare lay on the lawn, her knees drawn up almost to her chin, her clasped hands pressed between her thighs and her eyes shut. The dog stood over her, grinning happily, then gathered some of the clothing round her waist into its mouth and trotted with her into the bushes of the shrubbery.

Gordon looked at Nan. She had bowed her face into her hands. He put an arm round her waist, she laid her

face against his chest and said in a muffled voice, "Take me away with you."
"Are you sure of what you're saying?"
"Take me away, Gordon."
"What about Clare?"
Nan laughed vindictively. "Clare isn't the one to pity."
"Yes, but that dog!"
Nan cried out, "*Do you want me or not*?"

As they went through the dark hall, the kitchen door opened, Nan's mother looked out, then shut it quickly. In the front garden they met Kenneth and Gibson, both shamefaced and subdued. Kenneth said, "Hullo. We were just coming to look for you."
Gordon said, "Nan's coming home with me."
Kenneth said, "Oh, good."
They stood for a moment in silence, none of the men looking at each other, then Gibson said, "I suppose I'd better wait for Clare." The absence of teeth made him sound senile. Nan cried out, "She won't want *you* now! She won't want *you* now!" and started weeping again.
"I'll wait all the same," Gibson muttered. He turned his back on them. "How long do you think she'll be?" he asked. Nobody answered.

The drive back into the city was quiet. Gordon sat with Nan in the back seat, his arm around her waist, her mourning face against his shoulder. He felt strangely careless and happy. Once Kenneth said, "An odd sort of evening." He seemed half willing to discuss it but nobody encouraged him. He put off Gordon and Nan at the close-mouth of the tenement where Gordon lived. They went upstairs to the top landing, Gordon unlocked a door and they crossed a small lobby into a very untidy room. Gordon said, "I'll sleep on the sofa here. The bedroom's through that door."
Nan sat on the sofa, smiled sadly and said, "So I'm not to sleep with you."

"Not yet. I want you too much to take advantage of a passing mood."

"You think this is a passing mood."

"It might be. If it's not I'll see about getting a marriage licence. Are you over eighteen?"

"Yes."

"That's good. Er ... do you mind me wanting to marry you, Nan?"

Nan got up, embraced him and put her tear-dirty cheek against his. She laughed and said, "You're very conventional."

"There's no substitute for legality," said Gordon, rubbing his brow against hers.

"There's no substitute for impulse," Nan whispered.

"We'll try and combine the two," said Gordon. The pressure of her body started to excite him, so he stood apart from her and started making a bed on the sofa.

"If you're willing, tomorrow I'll get a licence." He had just settled comfortably on the sofa when Nan came to the bedroom door and said, "Gordon, promise you won't ask me about him."

"About who?"

"You can't have forgotten him."

"The dog? Yes, I had forgotten the dog. All right, I won't ask ... You're sure nothing serious has happened to Clare?"

"Ask her when you see her next!" Nan cried, and slammed the bedroom door.

Next day Gordon bought a marriage licence and an engagement ring and arranged the wedding for a fortnight later. The next two weeks were among the happiest in his life. During the day he worked as an engineering draughtsman. When he came home from work Nan had a good meal ready for him and the apartment clean and tidy. After the meal they would go walking or visit a film show or friends, and later on they would make rather clumsy love, for Gordon was inexperienced and got his most genuine pleasure by keeping the love-making inside definite limits. He wasn't worried much by memories of the white dog. He prided himself on being thoroughly rational, and thought it irrational to feel curious about mysteries. He always refused to discuss things like dreams, ghosts, flying-saucers and religion. "It doesn't matter if these things are true or not," he said. "They are irrelevant to the rules that we have to live by. Mysteries only happen when people try to understand something irrelevant." Somebody once pointed out to him that the creation of life was a mystery. "I know," he said, "and it's irrelevant. Why should I worry about how life occurred? If I know how it is just now I know enough." This attitude allowed him to dismiss his memories of the white dog as irrelevant, especially when he learned that Clare seemed to have come to no harm. She had broken with Gibson and now went about a lot with Kenneth.

One day Nan said, "Isn't tomorrow the day before the wedding?"

"Yes. What about it?"

"A man and woman aren't supposed to see each other the night before their wedding."

"I didn't know that."

"And I thought you were conventional."

"I know what's legal. I don't much care about conventions."

"Well, women care more about conventions than they do about laws."

"Does that mean you want me to spend tomorrow night in a hotel?"

"It's the proper thing, Gordon."

"You weren't so proper on the night I brought you here."

Nan said quietly, "It's not fair to remind me of that night."

"I'm sorry," said Gordon. "No, it's not fair. I'll go to a hotel."

Next evening he booked a room in a hotel and then, since it was only ten o'clock, went to a coffee bar where he might see some friends. Inside Clare and Kenneth sat at a table with a lean young man Gordon did not know. Clare smiled and beckoned. She had lost her former self-conscious grace and looked adult and attractive. As Gordon approached Kenneth stood, gripped Gordon's hand and shook it with unnecessary enthusiasm saying, "Gordon! Gordon! You must meet Mr. McIver. (Clare and I are just leaving.) Mr. McIver, this is the man I told you about, the only man in Scotland who can help you. Goodnight! Goodnight! Clare and I mustn't intrude on your conversation. You have a lot to discuss." He rushed out, pulling Clare after him and chuckling.

Gordon and the stranger looked at each other with embarrassment.
"Won't you sit down?" said Mr. McIver in a polite North American voice. Gordon sat down and said, "Are you from the States, Mr. McIver?"
"No, from Canada. I'm visiting Europe on a scholarship. I'm collecting material for my thesis upon the white dog. Your friend tells me you are an authority on the subject."
Gordon said abruptly, "What has Kenneth told you about the dog?"
"Nothing. But he said you could tell me a great deal."
"He was joking."
"I'm sorry to hear that."
Gordon stood up to go, sat down again, hesitated and said, "What is this white dog?"
McIver answered in the tone of someone starting a lecture: "Well known references to the white dog occur in Ovid's 'Metamorphoses', in Chaucer's unfinished 'Cook's Tale', in the picaresque novels of the Basque poet José Mompou, and in your Scottish Border Ballads. Nonetheless, the white dog is the most neglected of European archetypes, and for that reason perhaps, one of the most significant. I can only account for this neglect

by assuming a subconscious resistance in the minds of previous students of folk-lore, a resistance springing from the fact that the white dog is the west-European equivalent of the Oedipus myth."

"That's all just words," said Gordon. "What does the dog *do*?"

"Well, he's usually associated with sexually frigid women. Sometimes it is suggested they are frigid because they have been dedicated to the love of the dog from birth ..."

"Dedicated by who?"

"In certain romance legends by the priest at the baptismal font, with or without the consent of the girl's parents. More often the frigidity is the result of the girl's choice. A girl meets an old woman in a lonely place who gives her various gifts, withholding one on which the girl's heart is set. The price of the gift is that she consents to marry the old woman's son. If she accepts the gift (it is usually an object of no value) she becomes frigid until the white dog claims her. The old woman is the dog's mother. In these versions of the legend the dog is regarded as a malignant spirit."

"How can he be other than malignant?"

"In Sicily the dog is thought of as a benefactor of frigid or sterile women. If the dog can be induced to sleep with such a woman and she submits to him she will become capable of normal fruitful intercourse with a man. There is always a condition attached to this. The dog must always be, to a certain extent, the husband of the woman. Even if she marries a human man, the dog can claim her whenever he wants."

"Oh God," said Gordon.

"There's nothing horrible about it," said McIver. "In one of José Mompou's novels the hero encounters a brigand chieftain whose wife is also married to the dog. The dog and the chieftain are friends, the dog accepts the status of pet in the household, sleeping by the fire, licking the plates clean et cetera, even though he is the ghostly husband of several girls in the district. By his patronage of the house in this ostensibly servile capacity, he brings the brigand luck. His presence is not at all resented, even though he sometimes sleeps with the brigand's daughters. To have been loved by the dog makes a woman more attractive to normal men, you see, and the dog is never jealous. When one of his women marries he only sleeps with her often enough to assert his claim on her."

"How often is that?"

"Once a year. He sleeps with her on the night before the wedding and on each anniversary of that night. Say, how are you feeling? You look terrible."

Gordon went into the street too full of horror and doubt to think clearly.

"To be compared with a *dog*! To be measured against a *dog*! Oh no, God, Nan wouldn't do that! Nan isn't so wicked!"

He found he was gibbering these words and running as fast as possible home. He stopped, looked at his watch, forced himself to walk slowly. He arrived home about midnight, went through the close to the back court and looked up at the bedroom window. The light was out. He tiptoed upstaris and paused at the front door. The door looked so much as usual that he felt nothing wrong could be behind it; he could still return to the hotel, but while he considered this his hand was stealthily putting the key in the lock. He went softly into the living room, hesitated outside the bedroom door, then opened it quickly. He heard a gasp and Nan shriek, "Gordon!"

"Yes," said Gordon.

"Don't put the light on!"

He switched the light on. Nan sat up in bed blinking at him fearfully, her hands pressed protectively on a mound between her legs under the tumbled bedclothes. Gordon stepped forward, gripped the edge of the bedclothes and tugged. "Let go!" he said. She stared at him, her face white with terror, and whispered, "Go away!"

He struck her face and she fell back on the pillows; he snatched away the bedclothes and the white dog sprang from between the sheets and danced on them, grinning. Gordon grabbed at the beast's throat. With an easy squirming movement it evaded his hand, then bit it. Gordon felt the small needle-teeth sink between his fingerbones and suddenly became icy cold. He sat on the edge of the bed and stared at the numb bitten hand still gripped between the dog's grinning jaws: its pink little eyes seemed to wink at him. With a great yell, he seized the beast's hind leg with his free hand, sprang up and swung its whole body against the wall. Nan screamed. He felt its head crush with the impact, swung and battered it twice more on the wall, leaving a jammy red stain each time, then he flung the body into a corner and sat down on the edge of the bed and stared at his bitten hand. The sharp little teeth seemed to have gone in without piercing any veins or arteries, for the only mark on the skin was a V-shaped line of grey punctures. He stared across at the smash-headed carcase. He found it hard to believe he had killed it. *Could* such a creature be killed? He got to his feet with difficulty, for he felt unwell, and went to the thing. It was certainly dead. He opened the window, picked the dog up by the tail and flung it down into the back court, then went over to the bed where Nan lay, gazing at him with horror. He began to undress as well as he could without the use of the numbed right hand. "So, my dear," he muttered, "you prefer convention."

She cried out, "You shouldn't have come back tonight! We would all have been happy if you hadn't come back tonight!"

"Just so," said Gordon, getting in bed with her.

"Don't touch me!"

"Oh yes, I'll touch you."

Toward morning Gordon woke, feeling wonderfully happy. Nan's arms clasped him, yet he felt more free than ever before. With a little gleeful yelp he sprang from the nest of warmth made by her body and skipped upon the quilt. Nan opened her eyes lazily to him, then sat up and kissed his muzzle. He looked at her with jovial contempt, then jumped on to the floor and trotted out of the house, the shut doors springing open at the touch of his nose. He ran downstairs into the sunlit street, his mouth hanging open in a grin of sheer gaiety. He would never again be bound by dull laws.

THE ANSWER

Late at night a young man entered a phonebox in the suburb of an industrial city. He put coins in the slot, lifted the receiver, dialled and waited a moment. Later he heard a girl's voice say, "Hello?"

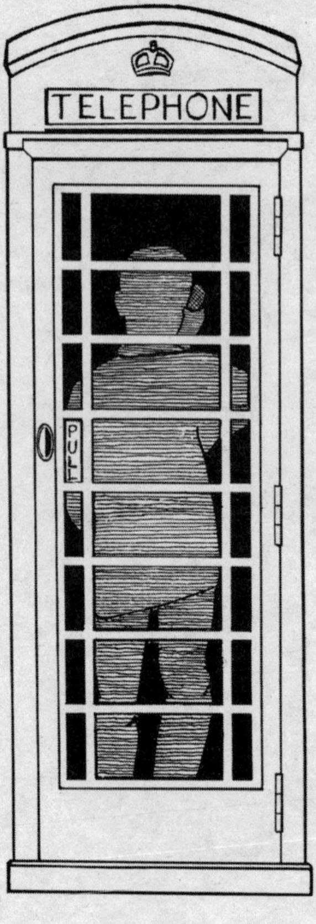

"Hello Joan!"

There was no answer. He said, "This is Donald."

Silence.

"Donald Purdie."

Silence.

"How are you, Joan?"

Silence. He frowned in a puzzled way and said, "I'm just back from Loch Lomond – I've been boating with the McEwans. They asked me to give you their love."

Silence.

"Listen Joan, is anything wrong? … Are you *all right* Joan? …
Joan, is this a joke? …
If you don't want to talk to me you'd better put the receiver down."

After a while he heard faint movements, then more silence.

He put the receiver down. He stood with heart beating loudly and a heavy weight in his chest, wondering what to do. He was too disturbed to go home to bed and it would be hard to live through the next days without knowing exactly what was wrong. At last he left the phonebox and walked through several streets to a place where two roads crossed. A taxi stood at a corner. He got into it and gave the driver an address on the other side of the city. He sat on the edge of the seat feeling excited and depressed. Sometimes the feelings in his chest got so big that he had to breathe deeply to quieten them. At other times he stared out of the window. The taxi passed through tenements, then the larger office buildings of the city centre, and after twenty minutes came to a district of bungalows, fields and petrol stations. It stopped before a bungalow with a garden sloping up from the road. Donald told the driver to wait and got out. The path to the door was made of granite chips and to make no noise he walked on the grass verge. The only light in the bungalow was at a side window, the kitchen window. Joan often stayed up late, reading in the kitchen. He stepped to the lit yellow oblong, struck the glass with a knuckle and called, "Joan! Donald here! Joan!" A moment later the light went out.

He walked heavy-footed on the crunching granite to the front door and rang the bell, waited ten seconds, rang again and kept on ringing. A light went on behind the door's thick rippled glass and it was opened by a girl who looked at him with a welcoming smile. She wore dressing gown and slippers, copious brown hair hung down loosely behind her shoulders, her eyebrows were strong and black, her nose long, her mouth large and humorous, her chin receded. She held the gown together at her throat with a big finely shaped hand and said in a pleased voice, "Donald!"

"Hello Joan."

"I've just been washing my hair."

He looked keenly into her face. She smiled back less broadly. He said, "Look, Joan, I phoned you about eleven. You answered the phone but wouldn't speak to me. I've come to find why."

Joan looked worried and said, "Come into the hall."
He followed her into a narrow hall, shutting the door behind him. She said, "You phoned at eleven?"
"Yes, and you answered."
"But Donald I came home at quarter-past eleven. I've been to the farm all day. You must have spoken to someone else."
"I didn't. You said 'Hello'."
"Then you must have got the wrong number."
"No, I didn't. You said 'Hello' and I went on talking and you didn't answer. I listened a long time. You must have put the telephone receiver down and gone away ..."
He glanced down at a telephone on the hall table beside him. The receiver lay off its cradle on top of a telephone directory. She said quickly, "As soon as I came in I took the receiver off in case any of my mother's boring friends rang up."
Donald said heavily, "I don't believe you."
He put his arms round her shoulders and smiled sadly down at her face. She smiled and laid her hands flat on his chest in a gesture that stopped him pulling her towards him. He said, "Why haven't I seen you lately?"
"I'm sorry Donald, but it's been such lovely weather – I've been working for these friends on the farm and I've been so happy there that I haven't seemed to have time for other things."
Donald let his hands fall by his side and stared at her. After a moment she said uncomfortably, "Come into the kitchen for a little while."

The kitchen was small and cosy with a white tiled grate, an electric fire burning in the grate and a hearthrug before the fire. An open book lay on the rug, as if someone had sprawled there reading. Donald sat on the armchair by the hearth, his clasped hands between his knees, leaning forward slightly and looking at a piece of hearthrug. Joan sat at a distance on a chair by a dining

table. Donald said, "You see I've come to feel ... rather emotional about you."
Joan said gently, "Oh, I'm sorry. I hoped that hadn't happened."
After a while she said, "You see we enjoy different things. You like books and jazz and ideas and ... clever things like that. When I was with you I thought I liked these things but I don't really. I like exercising horses and cleaning out hen-coops and living like a tinker. I realized that quite suddenly last week. Physical things are very important to me. I'm sorry, Donald."
"But I don't see why that should separate us! Most people who ... like each other a lot keep bits of life private from each other."
"I'm sorry, Donald. It's very neurotic of me but that's how I see it."
"You're not neurotic."
"Oh but I am!" said Joan anxiously. "I really am very neurotic! I often do the most silly things ..."
"Like not speaking to me on the telephone?"
She looked down obliquely and murmured, "Well, yes."
Donald stood up and said, "I'd better go."
"It was very kind of you to come all that distance."
"It was not. I had to find out what was wrong."
At the front door he said, "Goodbye, Joan."
She said kindly, "Goodbye, Donald."

He got into the taxi and gave an address in the city. He sat on the back seat in the posture he had taken in the armchair, and bits of thought passed through his head.
"Why did I say 'rather emotional' when I meant 'love'? Why was I so meek and reasonable? I should have struck her. As I left I should have struck her face. The last time we met we seemed to get on very well."
The taxi stopped in a street of tenements with a theatre at one end. Donald paid the driver, entered a close and walked up flights of steps to a landing with a bright red

door on it. He pressed the letterbox open with a finger and whistled through. After a while the door was opened by a young cadaverous man with a straggly red beard and wearing a coat over pyjamas. He stared at Donald, raised his eyebrows and said, "Well, well."

"Can I come in? I know it's selfish of me but I need to talk to someone …"

"Come in then."

They crossed a lobby into a small room containing a bed, a chair, a dressing-table and a television set. The floor, dressing-table and television set were covered with untidy piles of books. The bearded man threw off his coat, lay on the bed, pulled blankets over him and stared at the ceiling, hands clasped under head. Donald said, "A bad thing has happened to me. If I don't tell someone I'll have to walk about all night brooding on it."

"All right, tell me."

Donald walked carefully about the room, talking in a slow, almost hesitant voice. Sometimes he said, "I may be mistaken about this bit …" and sometimes, "She didn't say exactly that, she put it more subtly."

When he had finished the bearded man yawned and said, "That's very interesting, Donald. Were you very keen on her?"

"Oh yes. I thought we were going to marry. She's the one girl I know who didn't make me feel embarrassed when I wanted to be … sexual with her. We were always comfortable together, she was so frank and pleasant and … beautiful."

"No, Donald, not beautiful. Remember, I've seen her."

"Yes, beautiful! I know her face is so individual it's almost ugly, but her body is beautiful by any standard – slender, with wee steep breasts, and a very big backside (she said it made clothes difficult to put on) and fine long legs. And she could undress without looking self-conscious or coy."

"She *slept* with you?" said the bearded man, looking surprised.

"Once or twice. Twice, to be exact."
"I always thought her a quiet sort of girl."
"She is a quiet sort of girl."
"And ... what was she like?"
"Like?"
"Like in bed?"
"Oh, I never fornicated with her – we just slept. I wasn't in the mood for anything more urgent, and I didn't think she was either. She kept her underwear on. But I've never slept so sweetly as I did with her arms round me. I'm usually a poor sleeper."

After a pause the bearded man said, "Don't you think she might have felt cheated?"
Donald sat down, turned the pages of a book without looking at them and said, "It had occurred to me. It's one reason why I can't blame her for her behaviour tonight."
"Still, she could have broken with you more kindly."
"But you can't break kindly with someone who loves you! The right way is to break honestly. By a very honest little act she showed me she was done with me. She put my voice carefully down on the hall table so as not to disturb it, and went quietly away and washed her hair. Her meaning was pretty clear, but like a fool I went to her house and *discussed* it."
The bearded man said sleepily, "A pity you didn't play on her love of animals. If you'd galloped up to her door at the head of a troop of cavalry she would have found you irresistible."
There was quiet in the room for several minutes. Then Donald said thoughtfully, "Why don't I protest more? The last time I was in love and the girl broke with me (that was five years ago) I protested all the time. I did stupid things, like insulting her in public and praying to God to kill her. I thought my condition was unbearable. Now I feel quite calm. I have this ache in my chest, but talking to you has made it less, and it will disappear altogether when I get to sleep. Tomorrow it will come back for a few

hours in the evening, but it will be perfectly bearable. And during the coming weeks it will come for a shorter time each day, and in three or four months I won't have it at all. And that –" said Donald standing up, "is the sad thing. Joan will be nothing but an ache to me, then not even that, and in a few years it will be hard to remember her. I wish this ache would last as long as I lived, so I could always remember her. But even my memory of her will come to nothing and everything we did and felt together will be senseless and useless."

He looked at the bearded man as if
hoping to be refuted, but the
bearded man was asleep.

THE PROBLEM

The Greeks were wrong about the sun; she is definitely a woman. I know her well. She often visits me, but not often enough. She prefers spending her time on Mediterranean beaches with richer people, foreigners mostly. I never complain. She comes here often enough to keep me hopeful. Until today. Today, perhaps because it is Spring, she arrived unexpectedly in all her glory and made me perfectly happy.

I was astonished, grateful, and properly appreciative, of course. I lay basking in her golden warmth, a bit dopey and dozey but murmuring the sort of compliments which are appropriate at such times. I realized she was talking to me in a more insistent tone, so I occasionally said, "Yes" and "Mhm". At last she said, "You aren't listening."

"Yes I am –" (I made an effort of memory) "– You were talking about your spots."

"What can I do about them?"

"Honestly, Sun, I don't think they're important."

"Not important? *Not important?* Oh, it's easy for you to talk like that. You don't have to live with them."

I almost groaned aloud. Whenever someone makes me perfectly happy they go on to turn themselves into a problem. I gathered my energies to tackle the problem.

I said, "Your spots were first noted by Galileo in the sixteenth century, through his new improved telescope. Before that time you were regarded as the most perfect of all heavenly bodies –"

She gave a little wail: I said hastily, "But they aren't permanent! They come and go! They're associated with several good things, like growth. When you have a very spotty year the plants grow extra fast and thick."

She hid her face and said, "Why can't I have a perfect heavenly body like when I was younger? I haven't changed. I'm still the same as I was then."

I tried to console her. I said, "Nobody is perfect." She said nothing.

I said, "Apart from a few top-level physicists and astronomers, nobody gives a damn for your spots."

She said nothing.

I said, "The moon has spots all over her and nobody finds those unattractive."

The sun arose and prepared to leave. I gazed at her in horror, too feeble to move, almost too feeble to speak. I whispered, "What's wrong?"

"You've just admitted seeing other planets when my back is turned."
"Of course, but not deliberately. Everybody who goes out at night is bound to see the moon from time to time, but I don't see her regularly, like I see you."
She said, "Perhaps if I played hard to get you would find *my* spots interesting too. What a fool I've been to think that give give giving myself seven days a week, fifty-two weeks a year, a hundred years a century was the way to get myself liked and appreciated when all the time people prefer a flighty young bitch who borrows all her light from me! Her own mother! Well, I've learned my lesson. From now on I'll only come right out once a fortnight, then perhaps men will find my spots attractive too."
And she would have left without another word if I had not jumped up and begged and pleaded and told her a lot of lies. I said a great deal had been discovered about sunspots since Galileo's day, they were an electromagnetic phenomenon and probably curable. I said that next time we met I would have studied the matter and be able to recommend something. So she left me more in sorrow than anger and I will see her tomorrow.

But I can never hope to be perfectly happy with her
again. The sun is more interested in her spots
than in her beams and is ready
to blame me for them.

THE CRANK THAT MADE THE REVOLUTION

Nowadays Cessnock is a heavily built-upon part of industrial Glasgow, but two hundred and seventy-three years ago you would have seen something very different. You would have seen a swamp with a duck-pond in the middle and a few wretched hovels round the edge. The inmates of these hovels earned a living by knitting caps and mufflers for the inhabitants of Glasgow who, even then, wore almost nothing else. The money got from this back-breaking industry was pitifully inadequate. Old Cessnock was neither beautiful nor healthy. The only folk living there were too old or twisted by rheumatism to move out. Yet this dismal and uninteresting hamlet saw the beginning of that movement which historians call the Industrial Revolution; for here, in seventeen hundred and seven, was born Vague McMenamy, inventor of the crankshaft which made the Revolution possible.

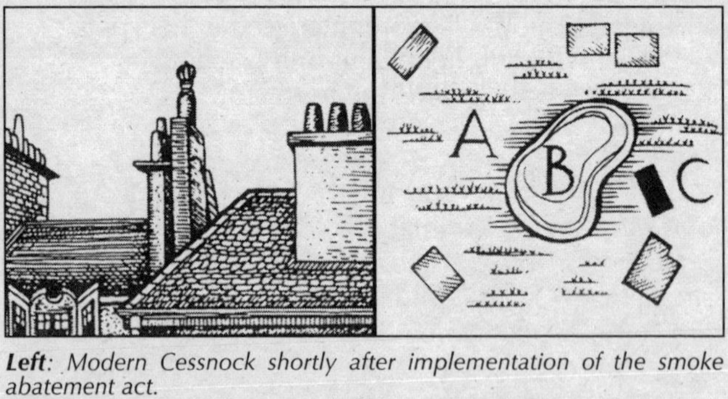

***Left**: Modern Cessnock shortly after implementation of the smoke abatement act.*
***Right**: Old Cessnock from General Roy's ordnance survey of 1739. Fig. A represents the swamp, B the duckpond, C the McMenamy hovel.*

There are no records to suggest that Vague McMenamy had parents. From his earliest days he seems to have lived with his Granny upon a diet of duck-eggs and the proceeds of the old lady's knitting. A German biographer has suggested that McMenamy's first name (Vague) was a nickname. The idea, of course, is laughable. No harder-headed, clearer-sighted individual than McMenamy ever existed, as his crankshaft proves. The learned Herr Professor is plainly ignorant of the fact that Vague is the Gaelic for Alexander. Yet it must be confessed that Vague was an introvert. While other boys were chasing the lassies or stoning each other he would stand for long hours on the edge of the duck-pond wondering how to improve his Granny's ducks.

Now, considered mechanically, a duck is not an efficient machine, for it has been designed to perform three wholly different and contradictory tasks, and consequently it does none of them outstandingly well. It flies, but not as expertly as the swallow, vulture or aeroplane. It swims, but not like a porpoise. It walks about, but not like you or me, for its legs are too short. Imagine a household appliance devised to shampoo carpets, mash potatoes and darn holes in socks whenever it feels like it. A duck is in a similar situation, and this made ducks offensive to McMenamy's dourly practical mind. He thought that since ducks spend most of their days in water they should be made to do it efficiently. With the aid of a friendly carpenter he made a boat-shaped container into which a duck was inserted. There was a hole at one end through which the head stuck out, allowing the animal to breathe, see and even eat; nonetheless it protested against the confinement by struggling to get out and in doing so its wings and legs drove the cranks which conveyed motion to a paddle-wheel on each side. On its maiden voyage the duck zig-zagged around the pond at a speed of thirty knots, which was three times faster than the maximum speed

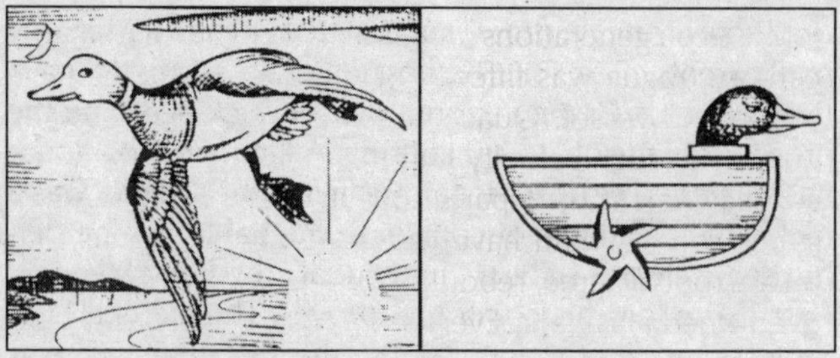

***Left**: Unimproved duck, after the watercolour by Peter Scott.*
***Right**: McMenamy's Improved Duck.*

which the boats and ducks of the day had yet attained. McMenamy had converted a havering all-rounder into an efficient specialist. He was not yet thirteen years of age.

He did not stop there. If this crankshaft allowed one duck to drive a vessel three times faster than normal, how much faster would two, three or ten ducks drive it? McMenamy decided to carry the experiment as far as he could take it. He constructed a craft to be driven by every one of his Granny's seventeen ducks. It differed from the first vessel in other ways. The first had been a conventional boat shape propelled by paddles and constructed from wood. The second was cigar-shaped with a screw propeller at the rear, and McMenamy did not order it from the carpenter, but from the blacksmith. It was made of sheet iron. Without the seventeen heads and necks sticking up through holes in the hull one would have mistaken it for a modern submarine. This is a fact worth pondering. A hundred years elapsed before The Charlotte Dundas, the world's first paddle steamer, clanked along the Forth and Clyde canal from Bowling. Fifty years after that the first ironclad screw-driven warship fired its first shot in the American Civil War. In two years the imagination of a humble cottage lad had covered ground which the world's foremost engineers took two generations to traverse in the following century. Vague was fifteen years old when he launched his second vessel. Quacking hysterically, it crossed the pond with such velocity that it struck the opposite bank at the moment of departure from the near one. Had it struck soil it would have embedded itself. Unluckily, it hit the root of a tree, rebounded to the centre of the pond, overturned and sank. Every single duck was drowned.

In terms of human achievement, McMenamy's duckboat ranks with Leonardo Da Vinci's helicopter which was designed four hundred years before the engine which could have made it fly. Economically it was disastrous. Deprived of her ducks, McMenamy's Granny was compelled to knit faster than ever. She sat in her rocking-chair, knitting and rocking and rocking and knitting and McMenamy sat opposite, brooding upon what he could do to help. He noticed that the muscular energy his Granny used to handle the needles was no greater than the energy she used to rock the chair. His Granny, in fact, was two sources of energy, one above

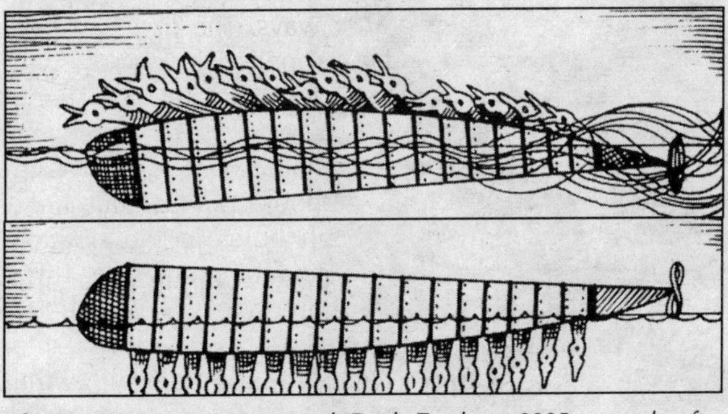

***Above**: McMenamy's Improved Duck Tandem .0005 seconds after launching.*
***Below**: McMenamy's Improved Duck Tandem .05 seconds after launching. (The ducks, though not yet drowned, have been killed by the shock.)*

the waist and one below, and only the upper source brought in money. If the power of her *legs and feet* could be channelled into the knitting she would work twice as fast, and his crankshaft made this possible. And so McMenamy built the world's first knitting frame, later nicknamed "McMenamy's Knitting Granny". Two needles, each a yard long, were slung from the kitchen ceiling so that the tips crossed at the correct angle. The motion was conveyed through crankshafts hinged to the rockers of a cast-iron rocking-chair mounted on rails below. McMenamy's Granny, furiously rocking it, had nothing to do with her hands but steer the woollen coils through the intricacies of purl and plain. When the McMenamys came to display their stock of caps and mufflers on a barrow in Glasgow's Barrowland that year, the strongest knitters in the West of Scotland, brawny big-muscled men of thirty and thirty-five, were astonished to see that old Mrs. McMenamy had manufactured twice as much as they had.

Engraving by Shanks in Glasgow People's Palace Local History Museum showing decadence of that art before Bewick's advent. Nobody knows if it portrays Provost Coats or McMenamy's Granny.

Vague, however, was modest enough to know that his appliance was improvable. The power generated by a rocking-chair is limited, for it swings through a very flattened arc. His second knitting frame was powered by a see-saw. His Granny was installed on one end with the needles mounted in front of her. Hitherto, Vague had avoided operating his inventions himself, but now he courageously vaulted onto the other end and set the mighty beam swinging up and down, up and down, with a velocity enabling his Granny to turn out no less than eight hundred and ninety caps and mufflers a week. At the next Glasgow Fair she brought to market as much produce as the other knitters put together, and was able to sell at half the normal price and still make a handsome profit. The other inhabitants of Cessnock were unable to sell their goods at all. With the desperation of starving men, they set fire to the McMenamy cottage and the machinery inside it. Vague and his Granny were forced to flee across the swamp, leaving their hard earned gold to melt among the flames. They fled to the Burgh of Paisley, and placed themselves under the protection of the Provost, and from that moment their troubles were at an end.

In 1727 Paisley was fortunate in having, as Provost, an unusually enlightened philanthropist, Sir Hector Coats. (No relation to the famous thread manufacturers of the following century.) He was moved by McMenamy's story and impressed by his dedication. He arranged for Vague to superintend the construction of a large knitting mill containing no less than twenty beam-balance knitting frames. Not only that, he employed Vague and his Granny to work one of them. For the next ten years Vague spent fourteen hours a day, six days a week, swinging up and down on the opposite end of the beam from the woman who had nourished and inspired him. It is unfortunate that he had no time to devote to scientific invention, but his only holidays were on a Sunday and Sir Hector was a good Christian who took stern measures against workmen who broke the Sabbath. At the age of thirty Vague McMenamy, overcome by vertigo, fell off the see-saw never to rise again. Strangely enough his Granny survived him by twenty-two years, toiling to the last at the machine which had been named after her. Her early days in the rocking-chair had no doubt prepared her for just such an end, but she must have been a remarkable old lady.

Thirty is not an advanced age and Vague's achievement was crowded into seven years between the ages of twelve and nineteen. In that time he invented the paddle boat and the ironclad, dealt a deathblow to the cottage knitting industry, and laid the foundations of the Scottish Textile Trade. When Arkwright, Cartwright, Wainright and Watt completed their own machines, McMenamy's crankshaft was in every one of them. Truly, he was the crank that made the Revolution possible.

McMenamy's tombstone, Paisley High Kirk, engraved for the 1861 edition of Samuel Smiles's "Self Help". (This corner of the graveyard was flattened to make way for a new road in 1911.)

THE GREAT BEAR CULT

In 1975 there came straight to Glasgow from a Berlin gig Pete Brown the poet, Pete Brown the friend of Horowitz, Pete Brown the songwriter and sometimes pop-song singer. And I dined with him at the home of Barbara and Lindley Nelson. As usual Pete was with a new girlfriend who received most of his conversation, but first he showed the Nelsons and myself a souvenir of Berlin, and that was what *we* discussed. It was a street photograph of Pete arm in arm with a bear. Berlin takes its name from a bear, so commercial cameramen prowl the streets with a suitably dressed partner. But though the bear in the picture was a disguised man he appeared so naturally calm, so benignly strong, that beside him Pete (who in isolation is as calm, benign and shaggy as a sapient man can be) looked comparatively shifty and agley. We were also intrigued to find the image in the photograph oddly familiar though Barbara, Lindley and myself had never seen another like it. Did it recall dim memories of our infancy in the thirties when the British bear cult was still a political force? As we discussed what we knew of the cult I realized that the time had come for a television programme on it, one which mingled public archive material (photographs, films and sound recordings) with dramatic re-enactments of what took place in

private. In 1975 the British Broadcasting Corporation was celebrating the fiftieth year of its charter, archive material was being daily broadcast and displayed, surely the BBC would be interested? It was not. I discovered that although Lord Reith's restrictions upon clothing, drink and sexual conduct had for years been matter for jest in the corridors of Broadcasting House and the Television Centre, his tabu upon all reference to the cult after Ramsay McDonald's famous broadcast to the nation was still in force. The BBC rejected my documentary drama. I offer it here, hoping readers will not be afraid to view it upon the television screen of their minds.

1 STUDIO INTRODUCTION

To a recording of *The Teddy Bears' Picnic* **the camera advances upon a commentator leaning casually against a table on which is displayed: a fancy-dress bear costume, a toy teddy bear, a Buckingham Palace sentry's bearskin helmet, a Daily Express Rupert Bear cartoon annual, and a copy of** *The House at Pooh Corner*.

RECORDING: *If you go down to the woods today*
you're sure of a big surprise!
If you go down to the woods today
you'd better go in disguise!
For every bear that ever there was
Has gathered there for certain
because
Today's the day the teddy bears have
their picnic!

COMMENTATOR: If you go down to the woods today, you'd better go in disguise. Yes. And if you were

clearing out an old cupboard recently it's very likely that you found one of these at the back of it.
(HE LIFTS THE BEAR COSTUME AND STANDS UP)
Perhaps curiosity prompted you to try it on. You can slip into them quite easily ...
(HE PUTS IT ON)
Once the zip is pulled up it's surprising how warm and comfortable you feel. And then, if you adjust the mask over your head, like this ... (HOLLOWLY) you are not only completely weather-proof, your voice has acquired a hollow, resounding note.
(HE REMOVES THE MASK)
The costume you found was almost certainly a relic of the great bear cult which swept Britain in the early thirties. Nobody who remembers those years likes talking about them, but most of you watching tonight were born rather later, so perhaps the time has come to give the origins of the cult, its wildfire spread and wholly unexpected collapse, some sort of dispassionate examination. So let me take you back to 1931, a year of world-wide trade-depression and economic crisis. There are nearly three million unemployed in Britain alone. A former socialist is prime minister of a National Coalition government with the conservative leader as his deputy. In Trafalgar Square the photographic business is in a bad way.

2 TELECINE: TRAFALGAR SQUARE, STUDIO, STREETS, LAWCOURT

Henry Busby, a licensed street photographer, squabbles with two others for the custom of a foreign visitor ("I saw him first!") who manages to escape all of them. Henry returns glumly to his studio and to George, his brother and partner. Ruin faces them. Must they also join the armies of the unemployed? Henry has a sudden idea – he has heard that in Berlin the street photographers have partners dressed like bears because there is a bear on the city coat of arms. Why not try that here? George objects that London has no bear on its

coat of arms and people come to Trafalgar Square to be photographed with pigeons. Henry shows a newspaper photograph of people queuing in hundreds to see a new bear acquired by London Zoo. Bears are popular – Rupert Bear in the Express, Winnie the Pooh etc. He rents a skin and persuades George to put it on. George finds it surprisingly comfortable. They go out into the streets arm-in-arm and reach the Square followed by a small crowd of laughing onlookers.

HENRY: Come on now, who'll be first to be photographed with this fine chap?

They do a brisk trade, drawing clients from their competitors, who complain bitterly that the bears are frightening the pigeons. But next day when they return to the Square they find the other photographers also accompanied by bears, a black bear, a polar, and a child dressed as a koala. They protest. A brawl develops. The bears are arrested, fined and bound over to keep the peace. However, the press and BBC are glad of some comic relief from a grim world situation, and the matter is widely publicized. The queues to see the new bear at London Zoo grow longer. *The Teddy Bears' Picnic* **becomes a popular hit. Furriers start marketing teddy bear suits for children.**

3 ARCHIVE MATERIAL: RECORDING OF BBC NEWS PROGRAMME *IN TOWN TONIGHT* **Dr. Karl Adler, discoverer of the inferiority complex, is visiting London for an international psychiatric conference. A BBC interviewer asks his opinion of the growing enthusiasm for bears. He replies that though the bear cult is (he believes) of German origin he feels it is destined to make great headway in Britain. He is asked the causes of the cult – why not an elephant or a tiger cult?**

ADLER: In the first place a bear is one of the few creatures that do not look ridiculous when walking about upon their hind legs. But there are more significant reasons for their popularity. They are not normally flesh-eaters

– their favourite food is honey and buns – so women and children feel safe with them. But they have claws and teeth which they can use if threatened, so men can identify with them without losing their self-respect. In my opinion a civilization such as ours has much to gain from this cult. The greatest part of a psychiatrist's work is with people who feel inadequate as human beings, and considered objectively most of them *are* physically and mentally inadequate; but dressed in a properly padded skin they make surprisingly adequate bears …

4 TELECINE: STUDIO, STREET AND LAWCOURT

The words of the interview emanate from a wireless-set in George and Henry's photographic studio. George, wearing the bearskin without the mask, sits reading a newspaper. Henry switches off the wireless, saying irritably:

HENRY: What blasted rot! … Take that thing off, George.

GEORGE: No. I'd feel cold.

HENRY: I feel cold, but do I complain?

GEORGE: Yes, all the time.

HENRY: Then you might have the common decency to give *me* a shot!

GEORGE (STANDING): I'm going for a walk.

HENRY: Like *that*?

GEORGE: Yes, why not? This is a free country. And I'm comfortable in it.

(HE FITS THE MASK OVER HIS HEAD)

HENRY: But you look utterly *ridiculous* … what's the use in talking? When you've your mask on you might as well be deaf.

George walks slouch-shouldered through Soho followed by a small jeering crowd, most of it children. He meets another bear followed by a similar crowd. Coming abreast they glance at each other's muzzles, suddenly stand erect, put their backs to the wall, roar and menace their persecutors with their paws. The children stop laughing and run away. The remaining

adults calls the bears "cowardly brutes" and one or two of the most belligerent accuse them of being "afraid to fight like men". The other bear hangs back but George flings himself on the critics and is badly beaten up in an affray which knocks over a costermonger's barrow. He is rescued by the police and accused of provoking a riot. He is brought before Lord Goddard, a highly punitive judge of the period. There is a man dressed like a bear in the public gallery and the judge begins by having him removed by the ushers. George's lawyer makes a dignified and convincing defence, pointing out that the accused has been the only person to physically suffer, that he was outnumbered and unjustly provoked etc. Nonetheless, the judge sees George as "one of these misguided individuals who seem determined to lead Britain backward to an age of primitive savagery" and condemns him to an unusually savage term of imprisonment, while regretting that the laws of the land make it impossible to have him publicly flogged into the bargain. George, asked if he has anything to say to this, responds with dignity and courage.

GEORGE: I do not blame the children who mocked me – I do blame the parents who failed to restrain them. I can't blame the roughs who attacked me – I do blame the society which deprives them of honest employment

and leaves them with nothing to do but roam the streets jeering at innocent animals. For I *am* innocent! Bears are strong, but bears are gentle! Lastly, I blame neither the police or the laws of Britain for bringing me here, but I will say this! I would rather wear a bearskin, and stand in the dock, than wear a wig, and sit on the bench, and pass such an inhumanly cruel sentence as *you*, my Lord, have passed upon me!
(A STORM OF APPLAUSE SWEEPS THE COURT. THE JUDGE ORDERS IT CLEARED.)

5 ARCHIVE MATERIAL: NEWSPAPER STILLS AND PATHE NEWSREEL CLIP
We see headlines denouncing unkindness to bears in popular and progressive newspapers, then photographs of bears at Hyde Park Corner demanding justice for their martyred brother, bears with collecting cans gathering money for an appeal fund; processions of bears with banners urging George's release; then the banner headlines annoucing that the appeal has been upheld. A newsreel clip shows George emerging from the wicket-gate of Wandsworth prison to be confronted by a cheering crowd, a third of it wearing bearskins. Two supporters assist him into one. He makes a speech before donning the mask.

GEORGE: Fair play has triumphed! For myself I am happy, but for my fellow Bruins I am jubilant. The British people have always admired us for our gentleness; they are now learning to like us for our strength, and believe me, we live in an age when strength was never more necessary. Sinister forces are abroad in the world, forces eager to tear the fur from our backs and the buns from the muzzles of our cubs. We must organize!
(HE PUTS ON THE MASK AND EMITS A HOLLOW ROAR)
A rapid montage of stills shows the growth of the cult, starting with trademarks for Bear-brand stockings, Polar-mints and the Metro-Goldwyn-Meyer panda growling through its celluloid arch. We see photographs of a bear-garden-party at Cliveden House which the German ambassador attends in the costume of a prehistoric grizzly. In Oxford Street shop windows expensively furred bears posture among the wax dummies. In poorer districts you can buy costumes made of rabbit-skin. In Piccadilly Circus furry prostitutes attract pin-striped businessmen by throatily roaring.

6 TELECINE: A SUBURBAN BUNGALOW
An insurance clerk, Mr. Osborne, returns excitedly from his work in the city carrying a big wrapped box.
MR. OSBORNE: I've bought you something, my dear.

MRS. OSBORNE: Ooh let me see, what is it?
(MR. OSBORNE TEARS OFF WRAPPING AND LID. HIS WIFE STARES INTO IT)
MRS. OSBORNE: Not one of those!
MR. OSBORNE: Why not? They're all the go you know.
MRS. OSBORNE: But I don't want to be a bear. I want to be a squirrel, a super squirrel with a great big bushy tail.
MR. OSBORNE (FIRMLY): No! You've got to be a bear.
(HE TAKES A PEAKED CAP FROM THE BOX AND CLAPS IT ON HIS HEAD)
I'm going to be the keeper.

6 ARCHIVE MATERIAL: NEWSPAPER STILLS AND PATHE NEWSREEL CLIPS.
We see photographs of main streets in Liverpool, Manchester and Glasgow with a high proportion of bears among the passers-by. At Brighton and Blackpool they are being photographed in family groups. Then, in newsreel, we see a guard in a sentry box outside Buckingham Palace. His conical steel helmet has a Prussian spike projecting from the top, a Norman nosepiece and Viking horns sticking out each side.
NEWSREEL COMMENTARY: For more than eleven hundred years – ever since the days of Ethelred the Unready – the Guards of the British Royal Family have worn the traditional horned helmet, popularly known as the Wanky.
(WE SEE THE HORNED HELMET BEING PLACED IN A GLASS CASE)
NEWSREEL COMMENTARY: Today the Wanky is consigned to a niche in the Imperial War Museum and the guards are on parade wearing a new kind of headgear! Bearskin helmets!
(WE SEE THE CHANGING OF THE GUARD) NEWSREEL COMMENTARY: Traditionalists may sneer, but throughout the Empire many will find reassurance in the thought that the British monarchy is able and willing to move with the times.

To the tune of *The Teddy Bears' Picnic,* **photographs and headlines show George Busby becoming eminent through the British Bear Cult. We see him attending rallies in public parks where bears hug each other and share buns and honey in perfect freedom.**

RECORDING: *Every teddy bear who's been good*
is sure of a treat today!
There's lots of wonderful things to
eat and marvellous games to play!
Beneath the trees where nobody sees
They hide and seek as much as they
please,
Today's the day the teddy bears
have their pic-nic!

(CUT TO NEWSREEL OF TORCHLIGHT RALLY WHERE GEORGE, IN WHITE POLAR SKIN, IS EXCHANGING CHANTS WITH A MASSED BEAR-HORDE)

GEORGE: Bears are gentle!
HORDE: Bears are strong!
GEORGE: Our fur is soft!
HORDE: Our claws are long!

NEWSREEL COMMENTARY: Many find this fervent emotionalism tasteless and unBritish, but one thing cannot be denied: bears know how to encourage one another, and in grim times like the present, who can blame them?

Headlines announce that George Busby will stand for parliament in an East Croydon by-election. Photographs show a junior branch of the Bear Cult, the Cubs, canvassing for him in the streets. Headlines announce his victory over the communist candidate by a narrow majority.

8 TELECINE: A CITY STREET, SUNDAY MORNING

To the sound of church bells a well-dressed spinster, approaching the corner of an avenue leading to a church, is passed by a furtive little brown bear going the opposite way. Turning the corner she stumbles on something, looks down and screams.

9 ARCHIVE MATERIAL: CUTTING

News headlines announce: **CHOIRMASTER CLAWED TO DEATH IN COVENTRY PAVEMENT CARNAGE!**

10 TELECINE: SUBURBAN BUNGALOW

We see a wooden 1930s wireless set on a sideboard and hear six pips from a quartz clock followed by:

BBC ANNOUNCER: Here is the six o'clock news. Just two hours ago the body of Kevin Streedle, former welterweight champion of the world, was discovered clawed to death in a shrubbery near Greenwich Observatory. This is the eighth murder of the type to take place in the past five days. George Busby, leader of the British Bear Cult and member of Parliament for Croydon East, has expressed grief at the incident and hopes the police will soon …

(A FURRY PAW SWITCHES THE SET OFF. IT BELONGS TO A BROWN BEAR IN A FLOWERY APRON. SHE CONTINUES SETTING TABLE FOR THE EVENING MEAL. THE DOOR OPENS AND A LARGER BROWN BEAR ENTERS CARRYING A BRIEFCASE AND A COPY OF THE TIMES)

LARGER BEAR (HOLLOWLY): Thank God I'm home again!

(HE FLINGS DOWN HIS LUGGAGE, WRENCHES OFF HIS MASK AND EMERGES AS MR. OSBORNE. HE STARES AT THE SMALLER BEAR)

MR. OSBORNE: I do wish you'd take that thing off.

MRS. OSBORNE (HOLLOWLY): It was you who bought it for me.

(SHE REMOVES THE MASK)

MR. OSBORNE (UNZIPPING): That was just for a lark – but it's serious now. Haven't you read the papers? The hidden claw has struck again. And there are more bears on the streets than ever. Even little old ladies are dressing like this.

MRS. OSBORNE (UNZIPPING): Well, the killers aren't likely to attack their own kind, are they now?

MR. OSBORNE: Fur isn't sexy any more, it's become a uniform. More than half the tube tonight was filled with bowlerhatted grizzlies. (HE STEPS OUT OF HIS COSTUME) Promise me something, dear!

MRS. OSBORNE (STEPPING OUT OF HER COSTUME): What?

MR. OSBORNE: Wear that thing in the street, but not at home with me. I'd rather you were a squirrel again. Or even a woman.

(THEY EMBRACE SHYLY IN THEIR UNDERWEAR)

MRS. OSBORNE: Can't the police do something?

MR. OSBORNE: Apparently not.

MRS. OSBORNE: Can't the government do something?

MR. OSBORNE: *The Times* says they've scheduled a debate.

11 TELECINE: THE HOUSE OF COMMONS

James Maxton, Leader of the Independent Labour Party, arises to ask what the government intends to do about the wave of killings which everyone in Britain associates with a certain political movement, a movement backed by the international fur trade, a movement whose leader occupies a bench in this very chamber.

David Lloyd George, leader of the Liberals, declares that

he does not find it in his heart *possible* **to blame these misguided people who have taken to wearing bearskins. Bearskins are ridiculous! They are ridiculous! But they are also warm, and comfortable, and cosy, and we live in chilling times. He** *does* **blame the** *government* **which in spite of all its promises has** *failed* **to give people the** *coal* **to keep them** *warm* **enough to** *dispense* **with bearskins. Ramsay MacDonald the prime minister rises to reply. He says that in a democracy like ours every section of the community must be represented. The Bear Cult is still a minority party but anyone who walks the streets of Britain can see that it already musters more support than (say) the Independent Labour Party. Moreover he is sure that the bear who did the killing is a minority of the minority, and no responsible government will condemn a broadly based popular movement for the action of a fanatical extremist whose activities have been mainly confined to the south London district. The killer must certainly be found and punished, but this is a matter for the police. And now George Busby stands up to speak for the British Bear Cult. He does not remove his mask.**

GEORGE (HOLLOWLY): Mr. Speaker, a new and terrible slur has been cast upon those I represent. Yes, in South London – the centre of the Great Bear Movement – yet another innocent victim has been clawed to death. The hearts of every true British Bruin must bleed for the relations of the bereaved, but that is not enough, not enough by a long chalk. We must not rest until the criminals are captured and who are the criminals? Not bears, at any rate!

(CRIES OF OH! OH! HE RAISES HIS VOICE) Bears are strong but bears are gentle! Bears do not kill choirmasters, welterweight boxers or innocent ratepayers! We too are innocent ratepayers! Bears have claws and know how to use them, but our claws are only used in self-defence! I have no hesitation in declaring that when the culprit is finally tracked down he will prove to be an enemy of our movement, a fanatical socialist or liberal, hell bent on bringing our party into disrepute! I declare the author of these crimes to be a bare-faced human being and I personally promise that the police will have the help of every true British Bruin in their sacred task of bringing these obnoxious beasts to book!

12 ARCHIVE MATERIAL: BBC NEWS ANNOUNCEMENTS, PRESS AND NEWSREEL EXTRACTS

In response to widespread criticism of their failure to arrest the Hidden Claw murderer, the London Metropolitan police make a special announcement. The bobby on the beat feels he commands too little respect among the population as a whole, so as an experiment it has been decided to try a new kind of uniform in certain districts. This is a black bearskin with extra large claws, and the mask, instead of covering the head, rests on top of it, the constable looking out of eyeholes in the chest. South London patrolled by eight-foot high Rocky Mountain grizzlies. With the help of Scotland Yard these manage to arrest a little man who admits to being the Hidden Claw murderer. His aunt is secretary of East Croydon Labour Party. At a rally in Trafalgar Square George cries out to the assembled Bearhorde: "The miserable Faustus responsible for these crimes is in the hands of the police, but where, I ask you, is the Mephistopheles?" Bearhordes attack local Labour Party headquarters throughout South London. The police remain aloof until the riots are nearly over and most of the people they arrest are left-wing and furless.

13 ARCHIVE MATERIAL

Collapse of the National Coalition Government. Ramsay MacDonald announces an election in three weeks time. George Busby announces that bears will be contesting at least 260 seats.

14 TELECINE: THE TRIAL OF THE HIDDEN CLAW

While the small man insists he is the criminal, and the police are sure he is, the only evidence against him is the word of the respectable spinster who saw a bear leave the scene of the first killing. She stands in the witness box and the prosecuting counsel ends his examination with the time-honoured words, "Look carefully around this courtroom. Do you recognize anywhere the individual in question?"

We see the Old Bailey with the eyes of the witness: the pathetic brown bear in the dock, the jury-box half full of bears, the public gallery crowded with them, a bear's muzzle sticking out of the judge's wig and coal-black eight-foot grizzlies towering behind everyone else. She screams and faints. The case has to be dismissed for lack of evidence. And before the prisoner is discharged word comes through that the Hidden Claw has struck again – in Hampstead. North London is no longer safe.

15 TELECINE: A ROOM IN SCOTLAND YARD

The detective responsible for the case is visited by a Scottish forensic expert with an international reputation.

EXPERT: No doubt about it, yon poor devils were killed by bears.

DETECTIVE: Of *course* they were killed by bears. But what kind? Brown bears? Polar? or Grizzly?

EXPERT: A grizzly, most likely. But it could be a bigger than average brown bear or a smaller than average polar. Koalas and pandas are out.

DETECTIVE: *That's* not much help! There are hundreds of thousands of these species in South London alone.

EXPERT: Havers. There can't be more than a couple of bears at large in the entire United Kingdom.

DETECTIVE: Do you mean a *real* bear is responsible?

EXPERT: That's what I'm telling you! The digits of the human hand are incapable of carving someone to death like that – even if they did have artificial claws on the ends.

The detective starts investigating circuses and zoos and

learns that a few weeks earlier a couple of bears escaped from the private zoo of the eccentric and senile Lord Pabham.

16 TELECINE: A SUBURBAN BUNGALOW

Mr. and Mrs. Osborne sit on either side of their fireplace listening to Sandy McPherson on the BBC cinema organ. She is patching his skin – a piece of fur was nipped off by a door in the underground. They are waiting for a special announcement to the nation by the prime minister. The music stops. Big Ben chimes. Reith, the governor of the BBC, personally introduces the Right Honourable Ramsay MacDonald.

MacDONALD: Good evening. Isn't modern science a wonderful thing? Here am I sitting comfortably in my Downing Street study talking to all of you seated beside your hearths throughout the length and breadth and depth of Britain. But I have something more important to tell you than just that, because, of course, you know that already. What I have to say is this. At a special emergency cabinet meeting this afternoon the government decided to make it illegal to dress up like bears in public places for the foreseeable future. I know this will come as a shock to many decent honest folk throughout the length and breadth and depth of Britain, but …

He explains the the police have no hope of catching the real bears while so many of the artificial kind roam the streets. The police themselves are abandoning that sort of uniform. He is sure the public will co-operate. Perhaps, after all, the cult of the bear has been based on a misunderstanding. Bears, though strong, are not always gentle, it now appears. The broadcast ends with a recording of Blake's *Jerusalem* **while Mr. Osborne jumps up, snatches the skin from his wife's knees and, despite her protests, stuffs it dramatically into the fireplace, causing a great deal of smoke.**

17 TELECINE: VARIOUS PLACES

Throughout the country people thrust bear-skins into dustbins and cupboards shouting, "I told you it was silly!" We see George at a desk, frantically telephoning in an effort to hold together his crumbling organization.

GEORGE: These murderers are not real bears – bears are strong but bears are gentle – these bears are only criminals because they have been soured by captivity! In next week's General Election bears will be fighting two hundred and sixty seats! Every furrier in Britain is behind us! We don't need skins, we'll wear badges instead!

The real bears are detected, netted and sent back to the zoo. Under exploding rockets we see a crowd in an East End street dancing the Hokey-Cokey round a bonfire with several stuffed bearskins burning on top.

18 ARCHIVE MATERIAL

Headlines announce the 1931 general election result: the National Coalition government is returned to power with a substantial majority. George Busby, Britain's only Bear Cult M.P., forfeits his deposit. All the other bears withdrew at the last moment.

19 THE TELEVISION STUDIO

The commentator, wearing his costume without the mask, sits before the table of cult objects with an expert beside him.

COMMENTATOR: And that, politically speaking, was the end of the bear cult. I have with me the renowned social anthropologist Professor Grotman. Professor, we are all aware that the beast in man lies only a little way under the surface so I will not ask you to refer to the psychological basis of the cult, I will ask how it came to disappear so utterly.

GROTMAN: In my opinion the psychological basis of the cult has been much exaggerated. It is now clear that the main cause of the movement lay in the coal shortages of the winter of 1931. It was actually warmer to dress as a bear in those days. What killed the movement politically was not disillusion with bears as a species. By 1932 it had become abundantly clear to the intelligent part of the population that a second World War, with its promise of full employment for everyone, lay just round the corner. What killed the movement, in fact, was hope for the future.

COMMENTATOR: But is the movement *really* dead? Remember, at its peak it had a following which numbered well over three million. Perhaps the person most qualified to answer that question is the Great Bear himself, the founder of the cult, George Busby: still remarkably fit and active for a man of 68 and living at present in a bed-sitting room on the Old Kent Road.

20 VIDEOTAPE RECORDING

George Busby, white-haired, spectacled, with the air of a vaguely dissolute grand old man, sits in a small room crowded with trophies of his former grandeur: stuffed

bearskins of the three main species, framed photographs of such moments of glory as the programme has revealed. He wears a yellow pullover, check trousers, a badge with a Rupert Bear head on, and is flanked by a shelf of every sort of beardoll from Winnie the Pooh to Paddington. Answering the questions of an invisible interviewer he speaks sadly of the collapse of his cult, of his present situation (he still receives cheques from the children of furriers who made their fortunes in the 1931 fur boom)

and his hopes for the future.

GEORGE: My movement was ahead of its time. So the adults decided to forget it. But the children remember. Children know without being taught, you see. So the bears *will* return one day soon, to save England in her hour of need. Though I may not be there to see it.

(HE TURNS AND CONTEMPLATES A FOUR FOOT HIGH PADDINGTON DOLL. THE CAMERA SLOWLY RECEDES FROM THIS FINAL IMAGE OF GEORGE AS AN OLD MAN ALONE WITH HIS DREAMS AND MEMORIES)

21 THE TELEVISION CENTRE

Freeze frame, then the camera zooms further back to show the image of George multiplied on the monitor screens of a television gallery. The control surface of a console occupies the foreground. A hairy paw appears and turns a switch. We see the whole gallery is staffed by bears: a large polar director stretching himself, a panda secretary scribbling on a clip-board, a grizzly technician with headphones. The director stands, stretches, yawns hollowly, then walks through into the studio where the commentator is in the act of fitting on his mask. Professor Grotman is zipping himself into a costume of his own.

DIRECTOR: That didn't go too badly.

COMMENTATOR: No hitches then?

DIRECTOR: None to speak of. Coming to the staff club for a drink, Professor?

GROTMAN: Certainly, certainly. Just wait till I adjust my dress. (HE PLACES THE MASK ON HIS HEAD. TOGETHER THE THREE BEARS, CHATTING AMIABLY, STROLL OFF DOWN CORRIDORS FULL OF VARIOUS BEARS GOING ABOUT THEIR VARIOUS BUSINESSES.)

THE START OF THE AXLETREE

I write for those who know my language. If you possess that divine knowledge do not die without teaching it to someone else. Make copies of this history, give one to anybody who can read it and read it aloud to whoever will listen. Do not be discouraged if they laugh and call you a liar. Perhaps they are dull herdsmen who think milk and wool more important than history. Their own history is a tangle of superstition and confused rumours. Those who lived inside the great wheel used to call them the perimeter tribes. "Were you born outside the rim?" we would ask someone who was acting stupidly or strangely and this question was a grave insult. The perimeter tribes lived so far from the hub that they only saw the axletree for a few months before it was completed and then only on unusually clear days. Even at sunrise its shadow never quite touched them, so now they say it was the last impiety of a

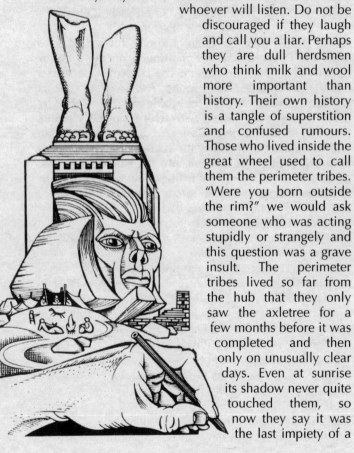

mad civilization, an attack upon heavenly god which provoked instant punishment and defeat. But the axletree was a necessary inevitable work, soberly designed and carefully erected by statesmen, bankers, priests and wise men whose professional names make no sense nowadays. And they completed the axletree as intended. For a moment the wheel of the civilized world was joined to the wheel of heaven. The disaster which fell a moment later was an accident nobody could have foreseen or prevented. I am the only living witness to this fact. I have been higher than anybody in the world. The hand which writes these words has stroked the ice-smooth, slightly-rippled, blue lucid ceiling which held up the moon.

I was born and educated at the hub of the last and greatest world empire. We had once been a republic of small farmers in a land between two lakes. Our only town in those days was a walled market with a temple in the middle where we stored the spare corn. Our land was fertile so we developed the military virtues, first to protect our crops from neighbours, then to protect our merchants when they traded with the grain surplus. We were also the first people to shoe horses with iron, so we soon conquered the lands round about.

Conquest is not a difficult thing – most countries have a spell of it – but an empire is only kept by careful organization and we were good at that. We taxed the defeated people with the help of their traditional rulers, who wielded more power with our support than they could without, but the empire was mainly held by our talent for large-scale building. Captains in the army were all practical architects, and private soldiers dug ditches and built walls as steadily as they attacked the enemy under a good commander. The garrisons on foreign soil were built with stores and markets where local merchants and craftsmen could ply their trade in safety, so they became centres of prosperous new cities. But our most important buildings were roads. All garrison towns and forts were connected by well-founded roads going straight across marsh and river by dyke and viaduct to the capital city. In two centuries these roads, radiating like spokes from a hub, were on the way to embracing the known world.

It was then we started calling our empire the great wheel. Surveyors noted that the roads tended to rise the further from the capital they got, which showed that our city was in the centre of a continent shaped like a dish. It became common for our politicians to start a speech by saying *This bowl of empire under this dome of heaven …* and end by saying *We have fought uphill all the way. We shall fight on till we reach the rim*. This rhetorical model of the universe became very popular, though educated people knew that the hollow continent was a large dent in the surface of a globe, a globe hanging in the centre of several hollow globes, mainly transparent, which supported the bodies of the moon, sun, planets and stars.

The republic was controlled by a few rich families who worked in the middle of an elected senate, but one day it became clear that whoever commanded the army did not need the support of anyone else. A successful general proclaimed himself emperor. He was an efficient man with good advisers. He constructed a civil service which worked so well that trade kept flowing and the empire expanding during the reign of his son, who seems to have been a criminal lunatic who did nothing but feed his worst appetites in the most expensive ways possible. It is hard to believe that records tell the truth about this man. He was despised by the puritan aristocracy who filled the civil service, but loved by common citizens. Perhaps his insane spending sprees and colossal sporting events were devised to entertain them. He also obtained remarkable tutors for his son, men of low and foreign birth but international fame. They had made a science out of history, which till then had been a branch of literature.

When their pupil became third emperor he knew why his land was heading for disaster.

Many nations before ours had swelled into empires. Nearly all had collapsed while trying to defeat a country, sometimes a small one, beyond the limit of their powers. The rest had enclosed the known world and then, with nothing else to conquer, had gone bad at the centre and cracked up through civil war. The emperor knew his own empire had reached a moment of ripeness. It filled the hollow continent to the rim. His roads touched the northern forests and mountains, the shores of the western sea, the baking southern desert and the wild eastern plains. The perimeter tribes lived in these places but we could not civilize them. They were nomads who could retreat forever before our army and return to their old pasture when it went away. Clearly the empire had reached its limit. The wealth of all civilization was flowing into a city with no more wars to fight. The military virtues began to look foolish. The governing classes were experimenting with unhealthy pleasures. Meanwhile the emperor enlarged the circus games begun by his father in which the unemployed poor of the capital were entertained by unemployable slaves killing each other in large quantities. He also ordered from the merchants huge supplies of stone, timber and iron. The hub of the great wheel (he said) would be completely rebuilt in a grander style than ever before.

But he knew these measures could only hold the state for a short time.

A few years earlier there had appeared in our markets some pottery and cloth of such smooth, delicate, transparent texture that nobody knew how they were made. They had been brought from the eastern plains by nomads who obtained them, at fourth or fifth hand, from other nomads as barbarous as themselves. Enquiries produced nothing but rumour, rumour of an empire beyond so great a tract of desert, forest and mountain that it was on the far side of the globe. If rumours were true this empire was vast, rich, peaceful, and had existed for thousands of years. When the third emperor came to power his first official act was to make ambassadors of his tutors and send them off with a strong expeditionary force to investigate the matter. Seven years passed before the embassy returned. It had shrunk to one old exhausted historian and a strange foreign servant without lids on his eyes – he shut them by making them too narrow to see through. The old man carried a letter to our emperor written in a very strange script, and he translated it.

> **THE EMPEROR OF THREE-RIVER KINGDOM GREETS THE EMPEROR OF THE GREAT WHEEL. I can talk to you as a friend because we are not neighbours. The distance between our lands is too great for me to fear your army.**
>
> **Your ambassadors have told me what you wish to know. Yes, my empire is very big, very rich, and also very old. This is mainly because we are a single race who talk the same language. We produce all we need inside our borders and do not trade with foreigners. Foreign trade leads to warfare. Two nations may start trading as equals but inevitably one grows rich at the expense of the other. Then the superior nation depends on its enemy and can only maintain its profits by war or threats of war. My kingdom has survived by rejecting foreign trade. The goods which appeared in your market were smuggled out by foreigners. We will try to stop that happening again.**
>
> **If your people want stability they must grow small again. Let them abandon empire and go back inside their old frontier. Let them keep an army just big enough for defence and**

cultivate their own land, especially the food supply. But this is useless advice. You and I are mere emperors. We both know that a strong class of merchants and generals cannot be commanded against their will. Wealthy nations and men will embrace disaster rather than lose riches.

I regret that I cannot show a way out of your difficulty. Perhaps the immortal gods can do that. Have you approached them? They are the last resort, but they work for the peasants, so people of our kind may find them useful.

The emperor was startled by the last words of this intelligent and powerful man. Several countries in the empire worshipped him as a god but he was not religious. The official religion of the state had been a few simple ceremonies to help it work as smoothly as possible. An old proverb *Religion is the wealth of the conquered* described our view of more exotic faiths. But the religions of conquered people had recently become fashionable at the hub, even with very wealthy citizens. These religions had wide differences but all believed that man had descended from someone in the sky and were being punished, tested or taught by having to toil in the world below. Some faiths believed that a leader would one day come down from heaven, destroy all who opposed him and build a kingdom on earth for his followers. Others bowed to prophets who said that after death the ghosts of their followers would enter a walled garden or city in the sky. These politically stable goals appealed to the emperor. He consulted priests in the hope that unreason would answer the question which reason could not.

He was disappointed. The priests explained that the eternal kingdom was achieved by sharing certain beliefs and ceremonies, following certain rules, and eating or avoiding certain food. Those who obeyed the priests often enjoyed intense feelings of satisfaction, but even if the whole empire adopted one of these faiths the emperor did not think it would be less liable to decay and civil war. Many priests agreed with him. "Only a few will enter the heavenly kingdom," they said. The emperor wanted a kingdom for the majority. He sent agents to consult prophets and oracles in more and more outlandish places. At last he heard of a saint who lived among the perimeter tribes in a wild place which no bribe could persuade him to leave. This saint's reputation was not based on anything he taught, even by example, for he was an unpleasant person. But he had cured impotence, helped someone find a lost legacy and shown a feeble governor how to master a difficult province. Most people who brought him problems were ordered rudely away but his successes were supernaturally startling. The emperor went to see him with a troop of cavalry.

The saint was small, paunchy and bow-legged. He squatted before a crack in a rocky cliff, grinning and blinking mirthlessly, like a toad. The emperor told the soldiers to wait, went forward, knelt before the saint and talked about the problem of empire. After a silence the saint said, "Are you strong?"

The emperor said, "My life has been easy but my health is excellent."

The saint felt the emperor's pulse, examined the insides of his eyelids then said gloomily, "You are strong enough, yes, I can help you. But I won't enjoy it. Give me some gold."

The emperor handed him a purse. The saint stood up and said, "Fetch wine and oil from your men and come into my house. Tell them they won't see you till tomorrow evening. Make that perfectly clear. If they interrupt us before then you won't learn a thing. Let them pass the time making a litter to carry you in, for when you reappear you will be in a sacred condition. The expression of your face will have completely changed."

Nobody had spoken to the emperor like that since he was a small boy and the words made him feel strangely secure. He did as he was told and then followed the saint into the crack in the rock. It led to a cave they had to stoop to enter. The saint struck a flint, lit a twisted rag in a bowl of fat, then picked up a wooden post. His dwarfish body was unusually powerful for he used the post to lever forward a great boulder till it blocked the entrance and shut out all daylight. Then he squatted with his back to the boulder and stared at the emperor across the foulsmelling lamp on the floor between them.

After a while he said, "Tell me your last dream."
The emperor said, "I never dream."
"How many tribes do you rule?"
"I rule nations, not tribes. I rule forty-three nations."
The saint said sternly, "Among the perimeter people a ruler who does not dream is impossible. And a ruler who dreams badly is stoned to death. Will you go away and dream well?"
The emperor stared and said, "Is that the best you can say to me?"
"Yes."
The emperor pointed to the boulder and said, "Roll that thing aside. Let me out."
"No. You have not answered my question. Will you go away and dream well?"
"I cannot command my dreams!"
"Then you cannot command yourself. And you dare to command other people?"
The saint took a cudgel from the shadows, sprang up and beat the emperor hard for a long time.

The emperor's early training had been stoical so he gasped and choked instead of screaming and yelling. Afterwards he lay against the cavern wall and gaped at the saint who had sat down to recover his breath. At last the emperor whispered, "May I leave now?"

"But will you go away and dream well?"
"Yes. Yes, I swear I will."
The saint groaned and said, "You are lying. You are saying that to avoid being beaten."
He beat the emperor again then dropped the cudgel and swigged from the wine-flask. The emperor lay with his mouth and goggling eyes wide open. He could hardly move or think but he could see that the saint was in great distress of mind. The saint knelt down, placed a tender arm behind the emperor's shoulders, gently raised his head and offered wine. After swallowing some the emperor slept and was assaulted by horrible nightmares. He was among slaves killing each other in the circus to the wild cheering of the citizens. He saw his empire up on edge and bowling like a loose chariot-wheel across a stony plain. Millions of tiny people clung to the hub and to the spokes and he was among them. The wheel turned faster and faster and the tiny people fell to the rim and were whirled up again or flung to the plain where the rim rolled over them. He sobbed aloud, for the only truth in the world seemed to be unending movement, unending pain. Through the pain he heard a terrible voice demand: *"Will you go away and dream well?"*
He screamed: "I *am* dreaming! I *am* dreaming!"
The voice said, *"But not well. You are dreaming the disease. Now you must dream the cure."*
And the emperor had a general impression of being beaten again.

Later he saw that the boulder had been rolled aside. Evening sunlight shone through the entrance. The saint, who had cleaned the bruises with oil, now made him drink the last of the wine. The emperor felt calm and empty. When the saint said, "Please, please, answer my question," the emperor shook with laughter and said, "If you let me go I will pray *all the gods* to give me a good dream."
The saint said, "That is not necessary. The dream is now

travelling towards you. Only one more thing is needed to make sure it arrives."
He beat the emperor again and the emperor did not notice, then he picked the emperor up and walked from the cave and laid him on the litter prepared by the soldiers. He said to the commanding officer, "Carry your master carefully, for he is in a very sacred condition. Write down everything he says because now his words are important. And if he recovers tell him not to apologize for what he bribed me to do. Giving men dreams is my only talent. I never have them myself."

The emperor was carried to the hub in slow stages for he was very ill and often delirious. At the first stopping-place he dreamed of the axletree. He saw the great wheel of empire lying flat and millions of people flowing down the roads to the hub. From the hub a great smooth shaft ascended to the sky and ended in the centre of the sun. And he saw this shaft was a tower, and that everyone who had lived and died on earth was climbing up by a winding stair to the white light at the top. Then he saw this light was not the sun but a flame or a flame-shaped opening in the sky, and all the people were passing through and dissolving in the dazzling white.

For a month after his return the emperor saw nobody but doctors and the architect of the city's building programme, then he called the leaders of the empire to his bedside. His appearance shocked them. Although he had reacted against a libertine father by tackling the worries of government he had been a robust, stout, stolid man. His body was now almost starved to a skeleton, the lines of care on his face were like deep cracks in an old wooden statue, his skin, against the bank of pillows supporting him, looked livid yellow; yet he regarded the visitors with an expression of peculiar levity. His voice was so strong and hollow that he had to rest between sentences, and at these moments he sucked in his lips and bit them as if to prevent laughter. He waited until everybody was comfortably seated before speaking.

"My political researches outside the rim have damaged my kidneys and I cannot live much longer. I have decided that for a few years most of the empire's revenue will be used to build me a tomb. I invite you to form a company responsible for this building. Your time is precious, I don't expect you to give it for nothing, and, if things go as I plan, work for this company will double your present incomes. If anyone dies before the great work is complete the salary will go to his successor."
He rested until expressions of regret, loyalty and gratitude died away then indicated some architectural drawings on the wall near the bed. He said, "Here are the plans of the tomb. The basic shape is a steep cone with a ramp winding up. It is designed so that it can be enlarged indefinitely. I have not indicated the size of the completed work. Yourselves or posterity can decide that. My body will lie in a vault cut into the rock below the foundation. It will be a large vault, for I expect my descendants will also lie there."

He smiled at the heir to the throne then nodded kindly at the others.
"Perhaps, gentlemen, you will make the tomb so big that you will be able to bury yourselves and your families in chambers adjacent to mine. Indeed, I would like even quite humble people who help the great effort to end under it, although their graves would naturally be narrower and less well furnished than ours. But you will decide these things. As to the site of the structure, it will be in the exact centre of the city, the exact centre of the empire. Has the high priest of war and thunder anything to say?"
The head of the state religion shrugged uneasily and said, "Sir, everyone knows that spot is the most sacred in the empire. My temple stands there. It was built by the hero who founded our nation. Will you knock it down?"

The emperor said, "I will rebuild it on a grander scale than ever before. The space above the burial chambers will be a pantheon to all the gods of our heaven and empire, for a great building must serve the living as well as the dead, or nobody will take it seriously for long. And my tomb will have room for more than a mere temple, even though that temple is the biggest in the world. Look again at the plans. The temple is the circular *core* of the building. Vast stone piers radiate from it, piers joined by arching vaults and pierced by arched doors. The spaces between the piers can be made wide enough to hold markets, factories and assembly rooms. These spaces are linked by curving avenues ascending at a slope gradual enough to race horses up. As you know, when I came to the throne I swore to rebuild our city on a grander scale than ever before. And what is a city but a great house shared by a community? The wealthy will have mansions in it, the poor can rent apartments. Parks and gardens will be planted along the outer terraces. And you, the construction company, will have your offices in the summit. As this rises higher the whole administration of the empire will move in beneath you ... But a dying man should not look so far ahead. What do our businessmen say? Can they supply the materials to build on an increasingly large scale for generations to come? Can they provide food for a steadily enlarging labour force? I ask the heads of the corn and stock exchanges to give an opinion. Don't consider the matter as salaried members of the construction company, but as managers of the empire's trade."

Toward the end of the emperor's speech the faces of the leading businessmen had acquired a dreamy, speculative look, but the head of the stock exchange roused himself and said, "We can tackle that, certainly, if the government pay us to do so."

Everyone looked at the civil service chief, who was also the imperial accountant.

He said slowly, "Ever since our armies reached the rim our provinces have been complaining about heavy taxation.

We could once justify that by attacking enemies outside the borders. We have no enemies now, but if we allow the provinces to grow rich they will break away from us. Yes, we can certainly finance this structure. And there will be no shortage of labour. We are already paying huge doles to the unemployed, merely to stop them revolting against us."
The commander of the armed forces said, "Will expenditure on this building require a reduction in the armed forces?"
The imperial accountant said, "Oh no! The army may even have to be enlarged, to keep the taxes coming in."
"Then I like the idea. The emperor has called the structure a great house. I call it a castle. At present the city has overflowed the old fortifications, our hub is a sprawling, indefensible mess. A high walled city will not only be easier to defend, it could be easier to police. Let the great doors between the different levels of the structure have heavy portcullises in them. Then with very little effort we can imprison and starve any part of the population which gets out of hand."
"But the outer walls must be faced with shining marble!" cried the head of the arts council. "If it looks beautiful from a distance I am sure foreign provinces will gladly let us continue taking their food, materials and men at the old cheap rate. Everyone wants to admire something wonderful, support something excellent, be part of something splendid which will not fail or die. Are you all right, sir?"
The emperor was shuddering with what seemed silent laughter but his teeth rattled and his brows sweated so it was probably fever. When he recovered he apologized then said, "Now I will tell you a dream I had."
He told them the dream of the axletree.

"Sir!" said the high priest in an inspired voice, "You have given the empire a new way to grow! You have offered a solution to the political problem of the age, and mentioned the dream which gave the idea as an afterthought. But all dreams are sacred, and the dreams of a ruler are most sacred of all. Perhaps the heavenly gods are growing lonely.

Perhaps mankind is becoming fit to join them. Let us tell the world this dream. You may be the prophet who will lead us all to the golden garden in the sky."
"I like that idea," said the emperor languidly. "And, certainly, let people know the dream occurred. But don't explain it, at this stage. You would antagonize religions whose prophet has already arrived. When the temple part of the building is complete dedicate it to god and his true prophet, but don't name them. Keep the official religion a kind of *cavity* which other religions can hope to fill if they grow big enough. But you mentioned gold. In spite of his mad spending my father left a fortune which I have been able to increase. I want it all converted into gold and placed beside my body in the vault. Let people know that the construction company can use it in emergencies. But never do so. The fact that it exists and you own it will give the company more power over men than mere spending could give. Lend on the security of this gold, borrow on the security of this gold, if creditors press you hard *cheat* upon the security of this gold. But never, never touch it."

The emperor closed his eyes and seemed to doze. The politicians whispered to each other. Suddenly he cried out in a great voice, "Do not call it a tower! Towers are notorious for falling down. Tell the fools you are building a connection between two absolutely dependable things. Call it an axletree." Then he giggled faintly and said, "I suppose one day the world will be governed by people whose feet never touch the ground. I wonder what will happen if there is a sky, and they reach it … I wonder what the child will look like."

The emperor died, and his tomb was built in the centre of the capital city, and enlarged to enclose everything he had wanted. For two thousand years this construction gave employment to mankind and a purpose to history. But there was a sky. We reached it. Everyone knows what happened after that.

FIVE LETTERS FROM AN EASTERN EMPIRE

DESCRIBING ETIQUETTE GOVERNMENT IRRIGATION EDUCATION CLOGS KITES RUMOUR POETRY JUSTICE MASSAGE TOWN-PLANNING SEX AND VENTRILOQUISM IN AN OBSOLETE NATION

FIRST LETTER

DEAR MOTHER, DEAR FATHER, I like the new palace. It is all squares like a chessboard. The red squares are buildings, the white squares are gardens. In the middle of each building is a courtyard, in the middle of each garden is a pavilion. Soldiers, nurses, postmen, janitors and other of the servant-class live and work in the buildings. Members of the honoured-guest-class have a pavilion. My pavilion is small but beautiful, in the garden of evergreens. I don't know how many squares make up the palace but certainly more than a chessboard has. You heard the rumour that some villages and a small famous city were demolished to clear space for the foundation. The rumour was authorized by the immortal emperor yet I thought it exaggerated. I now think it too timid. We were ten days sailing upstream from the old capital, where I hope you are still happy. The days were clear and cool, no dust, no mist. Sitting on deck we could see the watchtowers of villages five or six miles away and when we stood up at nightfall we saw, in the sunset, the sparkle of the heliograph above cities, on the far side of the horizon. But after six days there was no sign of any buildings at all, just ricefields with here and there the tent of a waterworks inspector. If all this empty land feeds the new palace then several cities have been cleared from it. Maybe the inhabitants are inside the walls with me, going out a few days each year to plant and harvest, and working between times as gardeners of the servant-class.

You would have admired the company I kept aboard the barge. We were all members of the honoured-guest-class: accountants, poets and headmasters, many many headmasters. We were very jolly together and said many things we would not be able to say in the new palace under the new etiquette. I asked the headmaster of literature, "Why are there so many headmasters and so few poets? Is it easier for you to train your own kind than ours?" He said, "No. The emperor needs all the headmasters he can get. If a quarter of his people were headmasters he would be perfectly happy. But more than two poets would tear his kingdom apart."

I led the loud laughter which rewarded this deeply witty remark and my poor, glum little enemy and colleague Tohu had to go away and sulk. His sullen glances amuse me all the time. Tohu has been educated to envy and fear everyone, especially me, while I have been educated to feel serenely superior to everyone, especially him. Nobody knows this better than the headmaster of literature who taught us both. This does not mean he wants me to write better than Tohu, it shows he wants me to write with high feelings and Tohu with low ones. Neither of us have written yet but I expect I will be the best. I hope the emperor soon orders me to celebrate something grand and that I provide exactly what is needed. Then you will both be able to love me as much as you would like to do.

This morning as we breakfasted in the hold of the barge Tohu came down into it with so white a face that we all stared. He screamed, "The emperor has tricked us! We have gone downstream instead of up! We are coming to the great wall round the edge of the kingdom, not to a palace in the middle! We are being sent into exile among the barbarians!" We went on deck. He was wrong of course. The great wall has towers with loopholes every half mile, and it bends in places. The wall which lay along the horizon before us was perfectly flat and windowless and on neither side could we see an end of it. Nor could we see anything behind it but the high tapering tops of two post-office towers, one to the east, one to the west, with the white flecks of messenger pigeons whirling toward them and away from them at every point of the compass. The sight made us all very silent. I raised a finger, summoned my entourage and went downstairs to dress for disembarking. They took a long time lacing me into the ceremonial cape and clogs and afterwards they found it hard lifting me back up to the deck again. Since I was now the tallest man aboard I had to disembark first. I advanced to the prow and stood there, arms rigid by my sides, hands gripping the topknot of the doctor, who supported my left thigh, and the thick hair of Adoda, my masseuse, who warmly clasped my right. Behind me the secretary and chef each held back a corner of the cape so that everyone could see, higher than a common man's head, the dark green kneebands of the emperor's tragic poet. Without turning I knew that behind my entourage the headmasters were ranged, the first of them a whole head shorter than me, then the accountants, then, last and least, the emperor's comic poet, poor Tohu. The soles of his ceremonial clogs are only ten inches thick and he has nearly no entourage at all. His doctor, masseuse, secretary and chef are all the same little nurse.

I had often pictured myself like this, tall upon the prow, the sublime tragedian arriving at the new palace. But I had imagined a huge wide-open gate or door, with policemen holding back crowds on each side, and maybe a balcony above with the emperor on it surrounded by the college of headmasters. But though the smooth wall was twice as high as most cliffs I could see no opening in it. Along the foot was a landing stage crowded with shipping. The river spread left and right along this in a wide moat, but the current of the stream seemed to come from under the stage. Among yelling dockers and heaped bales and barrels I saw a calm group of men with official gongs on their wrists, and the black clothes and scarlet kneebands of the janitors. They waited near an empty notch. The prow of our barge slid into this notch. Dockers bolted it there. I led the company ashore.

I recognized my janitor by the green shoes these people wear when guiding poets. He reminded us that the new etiquette was enforced within the palace walls and led us to a gate. The other passengers were led to other gates. I could now see hundreds of gates, all waist high and wide enough to roll a barrel through. My entourage helped me to my knees and I crawled in after the janitor. This was the worst part of the journey. We had to crawl a great distance, mostly uphill. Adoda and the doctor tried to help by alternately butting their heads against the soles of my clogs. The floor was carpeted with bristly stuff which pierced my kneebands and scratched the palms of my hands. After twenty minutes it was hard not to sob with pain and exhaustion, and when at last they helped me to my feet I sympathized with Tohu who swore aloud that he would never go through that wall again.

The new etiquette stops honoured guests from filling their heads with useless knowledge. We go nowhere without a janitor to lead us and look at nothing above the level of his kneebands. As I was ten feet tall I could only glimpse these slips of scarlet by leaning forward and pressing my chin into my chest. Sometimes in sunlight, sometimes in lamp-light, we crossed wooden floors, brick pavements, patterned rugs and hard-packed gravel. But I mainly noticed the pain in my neck and claves, and the continual whine of Tohu complaining to his nurse. At last I fell asleep. My legs moved onward because Adoda and the doctor lifted them. The chef and secretary stopped me bending forward in the middle by pulling backward on the cape. I was wakened by the janitor striking his gong and saying, "Sir. This is your home." I lifted my eyes and saw I was inside the sunlit, afternoon, evergreen garden. It was noisy with birdsongs.

We stood near the thick hedge of cypress, holly and yew trees which hide all but some tiled roofs of the surrounding buildings. Triangular pools, square lawns and the grassy paths of a zig-zag maze are symmetrically placed round the pavilion in the middle. In each corner is a small pinewood with cages of linnets, larks and nightingales in the branches. From one stout branch hangs a trapeze where a servant dressed like a cuckoo sits imitating the call of that bird, which does not sing well in captivity. Many gardeners were discreetly trimming things or mounting ladders to feed the birds. They wore black clothes without kneebands, so they were socially invisible, and this gave the garden a wonderful air of privacy. The janitor struck his gong softly and whispered, "The leaves which grow here never fade or die." I rewarded this delicate compliment with a slight smile then gestured to a patch of moss. They laid me flat there and I was tenderly undressed. The doctor cleaned me. Adoda caressed my aching body till it breathed all over in the sun-warmed air. Meanwhile Tohu had flopped down in his nurse's arms and was snoring horribly. I had the couple removed and placed behind a hollybush out of earshot. Then I asked for the birds to be silenced, starting with the linnets and ending with the cuckoo. As the gardeners covered the cages the silence grew louder, and when the notes of the cuckoo faded there was nothing at all to hear and I slept once more.

Adoda caressed me awake before sunset and dressed me in something comfortable. The chef prepared a snack with the stove and the food from his stachel. The janitor fidgeted impatiently. We ate and drank and the doctor put something in the tea which made me quick and happy. "Come!" I said, jumping up, "Let us go straight to the pavilion!" and instead of following the path through the maze I stepped over the privet hedge bordering it which was newly planted and a few inches high. "Sir!" called the janitor, much upset, "Please do not offend the gardeners! It is not their fault that the hedge is still too small."

I said, "The gardeners are socially invisible to me." He said, "But you are officially visible to them, and honoured guests do not offend the emperor's servants. That is not the etiquette!"

I said, "It is not a rule of the etiquette, it is convention of the etiquette, and the etiquette allows poets to be unconventional in their own home. Follow me Tohu."

But because he is trained to write popular comedy Tohu dreads offending members of the servant class, so I walked straight to the pavilion all by myself.

It stands on a low platform with steps all round and is five sided, with a blue wooden pillar supporting the broad eaves at each corner. An observatory rises from the centre of the sloping green porcelain roof and each wall has a door in the middle with a circular window above. The doors were locked but I did not mind that. The air was still warm. A gardener spread cushions on the platform edge and I lay and thought about the poem I would be ordered to write. This was against all rules of education and etiquette. A poet cannot know his theme until the emperor orders it. Until then he should think of nothing but the sublime classics of the past. But I knew I would be commanded to celebrate a great act and the greatest act of our age is the building of the new palace. How many millions lost their homes to clear the ground? How many orphans were prostituted to keep the surveyors cheerful? How many captives died miserably quarrying its stone? How many small sons and daughters were trampled to death in the act of wiping sweat from the eyes of desperate, bricklaying parents who had fallen behind schedule? Yet this building which barbarians think a long act of intricately planned cruelty has given the empire this calm and solemn heart where honoured guests and servants can command peace and prosperity till the end of time. There can be no greater theme for a work of tragic art. It is rumoured that the palace encloses the place where the rivers watering the empire divide. If a province looks like rebelling, the headmasters of waterworks can divert the flow elsewhere and reduce it to drought, quickly or slowly, just as he pleases. This rumour is authorized by the emperor and I believe it absolutely.

While I was pondering the janitor led the little party through the maze, which seemed designed to tantalize them. Sometimes they were a few yards from me, then they would disappear behind the pavilion and after a long time reappear far away in the distance. The stars came out. The cuckoo climbed down from his trapeze and was replaced by a nightwatchman dressed like an owl. A gardener went round hanging frail paper boxes of glow-worms under the eaves. When the party reached the platform by the conventional entrance all but Adoda were tired, cross and extremely envious of my unconventional character. I welcomed them with a good-humoured chuckle.

The janitor unlocked the rooms. Someone had lit lamps in them. We saw the kitchen where the chef sleeps, the stationery office where the secretary sleeps, the lavatory where the doctor sleeps, and Adoda's room, where I sleep. Tohu and his nurse also have a room. Each room has a door into the garden and another into the big central hall where I and Tohu will make poetry when the order-to-write comes. The walls here are very white and bare. There is a thick blue carpet and a couple of punt-shaped thrones lined with cushions and divided from each other by a screen. The only other furniture is the ladder to the observatory above. The janitor assembled us here, struck the gong and made this speech in the squeaky voice the emperor uses in public.

"The emperor is glad to see you safe inside his walls. The servants will now cover their ears.
"The emperor greets Bohu, his tragic poet, like a long-lost brother. Be patient, Bohu. Stay at home. Recite the classics. Use the observatory. It was built to satisfy your craving for grand scenery. Fill your eyes and mind with the slow, sublime, eternally returning architecture of the stars. Ignore trivial flashes which stupid peasants call *falling* stars. It has been proved that these are not heavenly bodies but white-hot cinders fired out of volcanoes. When you cannot stay serene without talking to someone, dictate a letter to your parents in the old capital. Say anything you like. Do not be afraid to utter unconventional thoughts, however peculiar. Your secretary will not be punished for writing these down, your parents not punished for reading them. Be serene at all times. Keep a calm empty mind and you will see me soon.

"And now, a word for Tohu. Don't grovel so much. Be less glum. You lack Bohu's courage and dignity and don't understand people well enough to love them, as he does, but you might still be my best poet. My new palace contains many markets. Visit them with your chef when she goes shopping. Mix with the crowds of low, bustling people you must one day amuse. Learn their quips and catch-phrases. Try not to notice they stink. Take a bath when you get home and you too will see me soon."

The janitor struck his gong then asked in his own voice if we had any polite requests. I looked round the hall. I stood alone, for at the sound of the emperor's voice all but the janitor and I had lain face down on the carpet and even the janitor had sunk to his knees. Tohu and the entourage sat up now and watched me expectantly. Adoda arose with her little spoon and bottle and carefully collected from my cheeks the sacred tears of joy which spring in the eyes of everyone the emperor addresses. Tohu's nurse was licking his tears off the carpet. I envied him, for he would see more of the palace than I would, and be more ready to write a poem about it when the order came. I did not want to visit the market but I ached to see the treasuries and reservoirs and grain-silos, the pantechnicons and pantheons and gardens of justice. I wondered how to learn about these and still stay at home. The new dictionary of etiquette says *All requests for knowledge will be expressed as requests for things*. So I said, "May the bare walls of this splendid hall be decorated with a map of the new palace? It will help my colleague's chef to lead him about."

Tohu shouted, "Do not speak for me, Bohu! The emperor will send janitors to lead the chef who leads me. I need nothing more and nothing less than the emperor has already decided to give."

The janitor ignored him and told me, "I hear and respect your request."

According to the new dictionary of etiquette this answer means *No* or *Maybe* or *Yes, after a very long time*.

The janitor left. I felt restless. The chef's best tea, the doctor's drugs, Adoda's caresses had no effect so I climbed into the observatory and tried to quieten myself by watching the stars as the emperor had commanded. But that did not work, as he foresaw, so I summoned my secretary and dictated this letter, as he advised. Don't be afraid to read it. You know what the emperor said. And the postman who rewrites letters before fixing them to the pigeons always leaves out dangerous bits. Perhaps he will improve my prose-style, for most of these sentences are too short and jerky. This is the first piece of prose I ever composed, and as you know, I am a poet.

Goodbye. I will write to you again,

From the evergreen garden,

Your son,

Bohu.

DICTATED ON THE 27th LAST DAY

OF THE OLD CALENDAR.

SECOND LETTER

DEAR MOTHER, DEAR FATHER, I discover that I still love you more than anything in the world. I like my entourage, but they are servants and cannot speak to me. I like the headmaster of literature, but he only speaks about poetry. I like poetry, but have written none. I like the emperor, but have never seen him. I dictated the last letter because he said talking to you would cure my loneliness. It did, for a while, but it also brought back memories of the time we lived together before I was five, wild days full of happiness and dread, horrid fights and ecstatic picnics. Each of you loved and hated a different bit of me.

You loved talking to me, mother, we were full of playful conversation while you embroidered shirts for the police and I toyed with the coloured silks and buttons. You were small and pretty yet told such daring stories that you sister, the courtesan, screamed and covered her ears, while we laughed till the tears came. Yet you hated me going outside and locked me for an hour in the sewing box because I wore my good clogs in the lane. These were the clogs father had carved with toads on the tips. You had given them many coats of yellow lacquer, polishing each one till a member of the honoured-guest-class thought my clogs were made of amber and denounced us to the police for extravagance. But the magistrate was just and all came right in the end.

Mother always wanted me to look pretty. You, father, didn't care how I looked and you hated talking, especially to me, but you taught me to swim before I was two and took me in the punt to the sewage ditch. I helped you sift out many dead dogs and cats to sell to the gardeners for dung. You wanted me to find a dead man, because corpse-handlers (you said) don't often die of infectious diseases. The corpse I found was not a man but a boy of my own age, and instead of selling him to the gardeners we buried him where nobody would notice. I wondered why, at the time, for we needed money for rent. One day we found the corpse of a woman with a belt and bracelet of coins. The old capital must have been a slightly mad place that year. Several corpses of the honoured-guest-class bobbed along the canals and the emperor set fire to the south-eastern slums. I had never seen you act so strangely. You dragged me to the nearest market (the smell of burning was everywhere) and rented the biggest possible kite and harness. You who hate talking carried that kite down the long avenue to the eastern gate, shouting all the time to the priest, your brother, who was helping us. You said all children should be allowed to fly before they were too heavy, not just children of the honoured-guest-class. On top of the hill I grew afraid and struggled as you tightened the straps, then uncle perched me on his shoulders under that huge sail, and you took the end of the rope, and you both ran downhill into the wind. I remember a tremendous jerk, but nothing else.

I woke on the sleeping-rug on the hearth of the firelit room. My body was sore all over but you knelt beside me caressing it, mother, and when you saw my eyes were open you sprang up, screamed and attacked father with your needles. He did not fight back. Then you loved each other in the firelight beside me. It comforted me to see that. And I liked watching the babies come, especially my favourite sister with the pale hair. But during the bad winter two years later she had to be sold to the merchants for money to buy firewood.

Perhaps you did not know you had given me exactly the education a poet needs, for when you led me to the civil service academy on my fifth birthday I carried the abacus and squared slate of an accountant under my arm and I thought I would be allowed to sleep at home. But the examiner knew his job and after answering his questions I was sent to the classics dormitory of the closed literature wing and you never saw me again. I saw you again, a week or perhaps a year later. The undergraduates were crossing the garden between the halls of the drummaster who taught us rhythms and the chess-master who taught us consequential logic. I lagged behind them then slipped into the space between the laurel bushes and the outside fence and looked through. On the far side of the freshwater canal I saw a tiny distant man and woman standing staring. Even at that distance I recognized the pink roses on the scarlet sleeves of mother's best petticoat. You could not see me, yet for a minute or perhaps a whole hour you stood staring at the tall academy fence as steadily as I stared at you. Then the monitors found me. But I knew I was not forgotten, and my face never acquired the haunted, accusing look which stamped the face of the other scholars and most of the teachers too. My face displays the pained but perfectly real smile of the eternally hopeful. That glimpse through the fence enabled me to believe in love while living without it, so the imagination lessons, which made some of my schoolmates go mad or kill themselves, did not frighten me.

The imagination lessons started on my eleventh birthday after I had memorized all the classical literature and could recite it perfectly. Before that day only my smile showed how remarkable I was. The teachers put me in a windowless room with a ceiling a few inches above my head when I sat on the floor. The furniture was a couple of big shallow earthenware pans, one empty and one full of water. I was told to stay there until I had passed the water through my body and filled the empty pan with it. I was told that when the door was shut I would be a long time in darkness and silence, but before the water was drunk I would hear voices and imagine the bodies of strange companions, some of them friendly and others not. I was told that if I welcomed everyone politely even the horrible visitors would teach me useful things. The door was shut and the darkness which drowned me was surprisingly warm and familiar. It was exactly the darkness inside my mother's sewing-box. For the first time since entering the academy I felt at home.

After a while I heard your voices talking quietly together and thought you had been allowed to visit me at last, but when I joined the conversation I found we were talking of things I must have heard discussed when I was a few months old. It was very interesting. I learned later that other students imagined the voices and company of ghouls and madmen and gulped down the water so fast that they became ill. I sipped mine as slowly as possible. The worst person I met was the corpse of the dead boy I had helped father take from the canal. I knew him by the smell. He lay a long time in the corner of the room before I thought of welcoming him and asking his name. He told me he was not an ill-treated orphan, as father had thought, but the son of a rich waterworks inspector who had seen a servant stealing food and been murdered to stop him telling people. He told me many things about life among the highest kinds of honoured-guest-class, things I could never have learned from my teachers at the academy who belonged to the lower kind. The imagination lessons became, for me, a way of escaping from the drum, chess and recitation masters and of meeting in darkness everyone I had lost with infancy. The characters of classical literature started visiting me too, from the celestial monkey who is our ancestor to emperor Hyun who burned all the unnecessary books and built the great wall to keep out unnecessary people. They taught me things about themselves which classical literature does not mention. Emperor Hyun, for instance, was in some ways a petty, garrulous old man much troubled with arthritis. The best part of him was exactly like my father patiently dredging for good things in the sewage mud of the north-west slums. And the imperious seductive white demon in the comic creation myth turned out to be very like my aunt, the courtesan, who also transformed herself into different characters to interest strangers, yet all the time was determinedly herself. My aunt visited me more than was proper and eventually I imagined something impossible with her and my academic gown was badly stained. This was noted by the school laundry. The next day the medical inspector made small wounds at the top of my things which never quite healed and are still treated twice a month. I have never since soiled cloth in that way. My fifth limb sometimes stiffens under Adoda's caresses but nothing comes from it.

Soon after the operation the headmaster of literature visited the academy. He was a heavy man, as heavy as I am now. He said, "You spend more days imagining than the other scholars, yet your health is good. What guests come to your dark room?"
I told him. He asked detailed questions. I took several days to describe everyone. When I stopped he was silent a while then said, "Do you understand why you have been trained like this?"
I said I did not.
He said, "A poet needs an adventurous, sensuous infancy to enlarge his appetites. But large appetites must be given a single direction or they will produce a mere healthy human being. So the rich infancy must be followed by a childhood of instruction which starves the senses, especially of love. The child is thus forced to struggle for love in the only place he can experience it, which is memory, and the only place he can practise it, which is imagination. This education, which I devised, destroys the minds it does not enlarge. You are my first success. Stand up."
I did, and he stooped, with difficulty, and tied the dark green ribbons round my knees. I said, "Am I a poet now?" He said, "Yes. You are now the emperor's honoured guest and tragic poet, the only modern author whose work will be added to the classics of world literature." I asked when I could start writing. He said, "Not for a long time. Only

the emperor can supply a theme equal to your talent and he is not ready to do so. But the waiting will be made easy. The days of the coarse robe, dull teachers and dark room are over. You will live in the palace."

I asked him if I could see my parents first. He said, "No. Honoured guests only speak to inferior classes when asking for useful knowledge and your parents are no use to you now. They have changed. Perhaps your small pretty mother has become a brazen harlot like her sister, your strong silent father an arthritic old bore like the emperor Hyun. After meeting them you would feel sad and wise and want to write ordinary poems about the passage of time and fallen petals drifting down the stream. Your talent must be preserved for a greater theme than that."

I asked if I would have friends at the palace. He said, "You will have two. My system has produced one other poet, not very good, who may perhaps be capable of some second-rate doggerel when the order-to-write comes. He will share your apartment. But your best friend knows you already. Here is his face."

He gave me a button as broad as my thumb with a small round hairless head enamelled on it. The eyes were black slits between complicated wrinkles; the sunk mouth seemed to have no teeth but was curved in a surprisingly sweet sly smile. I knew this must be the immortal emperor. I asked if he was blind.

"Necessarily so. This is the hundred-and-second year of his reign and all sights are useless knowledge to him now. But his hearing is remarkably acute."

So I and Tohu moved to the palace of the old capital and a highly trained entourage distracted my enlarged mind from the work it was waiting to do. We were happy but cramped. The palace staff kept increasing until many honoured guests had to be housed in the city outside, which took away homes from the citizens. No new houses could be built because all the skill and materials in the empire were employed on the new palace upriver, so all gardens and graveyards and even several streets were covered with tents, barrels and packing-cases where thousands of families were living. I never used the streets myself because honoured guests there were often looked at very rudely, with glances of concealed dislike. The emperor arranged for the soles of our ceremonial clogs to be thickened until even the lowest of his honoured guests could pass through a crowd of common citizens without meeting them face-to-face. But after that some from the palace were jostled by criminals too far beneath them to identify, so it was ordered that honoured guests should be led everywhere by a janitor and surrounded by their entourage. This made us perfectly safe, but movement through the densely packed streets became very difficult. At last the emperor barred common citizens from the streets during the main business hours and things improved.

Yet these same citizens who glared and jostled and grumbled at us were terrified of us going away! Their trades and professions depended on the court; without it most of them would become unnecessary people. The emperor received anonymous letters saying that if he tried to leave, his wharves and barges would catch fire and the sewage ditches would be diverted into the palace reservoir. You may wonder how your son, a secluded poet, came to know these things. Well, the headmaster of civil peace sometimes asked me to improve the wording of rumours authorized by the emperor, while Tohu improved the unauthorized ones that were broadcast by the beggars' association. We both put out a story that citizens who worked hard and did not grumble would be employed as servants in the new palace. This was true, but not as true as people hoped. The anonymous letters stopped and instead the emperor received signed petitions from the workingmen's clubs explaining how long and well they had served him and asking to go on doing it. Each signatory was sent a written reply with the emperor's seal saying that his request had been heard and respected. In the end the court departed upriver quietly, in small groups, accompanied by the workingmen's leaders. But the mass of new palace servants come from more docile cities than the old capital. It is nice to be in a safe home with nobody to frighten us.

I am stupid to mention these things. You know the old capital better than I do. Has it recovered the bright uncrowded streets and gardens I remember when we lived there together so many years ago?

This afternoon is very sunny and hot, so I am dictating my letter on the observatory tower. There is a fresh breeze at this height. When I climbed up here two hours ago I found a map of the palace on the table beside my map of the stars. It seems my requests are heard with unusual respect. Not much of the palace is marked on the map but enough to identify the tops of some big pavilions to the north. A shining black pagoda rises from the garden of irrevocable justice where disobedient people have things removed which cannot be returned, like eardrums, eyes, limbs and heads. Half-a-mile away a similar but milkwhite pagoda marks the garden of revocable justice where good people receive gifts which can afterwards be taken back, like homes, wives, salaries and pensions. Between these pagodas but further off, is the court of summons, a vast round tower with a forest of bannerpoles on the roof. On the highest pole the emperor's scarlet flag floats above the rainbow flag of the headmasters, so he is in there today conferring with the whole college.

Shortly before lunch Tohu came in with a wood-cut scroll which he said was being pinned up and sold all over the market, perhaps all over the empire. At the top is the peculiar withered-apple-face of the immortal emperor which fascinates me more each time I see it. I feel his blind eyes could eat me up and a few days later the sweet sly mouth would spit me out in a new, perhaps improved form. Below the portrait are these words:

Forgive me for ruling you but someone must. I am a small weak old man but have the strength of all my good people put together. I am blind, but your ears are my ears so I hear everything. As I grow older I try to be kinder. My guests in the new palace help me. Their names and pictures are underneath.

Then come the two tallest men in the empire. One of them is:

Field-marshal Ko who commands all imperial armies and police and defeats all imperial enemies. He has degrees in strategy from twenty-eight academies but leaves thinking to the emperor. He hates unnecessary people but says "Most of them are outside the great wall."

The other is:

Bohu, the great poet. His mind is the largest in the land. He knows the feelings of everyone from the poor peasant in the ditch to the old emperor on the throne. Soon his great poem will be painted above the door of every townhouse, school, barracks, post-office, law-court, theatre and prison in the land. Will it be about war? Peace? Love? Justice? Agriculture? Architecture? Time? Fallen apple-blossom in the stream? Bet about this with your friends.

I was pleased to learn there were only two tallest men in the empire. I had thought there were three of us. Tohu's face was at the end of the scroll in a row of twenty others. He looked very small and cross between a toe-surgeon and an inspector of chicken-feed. His footnote said:

Tohu hopes to write funny poems. Will he succeed?

I rolled up the scroll and returned it with a friendly nod but Tohu was uneasy and wanted conversation. He said, "The order-to-write is bound to come soon now."

"Yes."

"Are you frightened?"

"No."

"Your work may not please."
"That is unlikely."
"What will you do when your great poem is complete?"
"I shall ask the emperor for death."
Tohu leaned forward and whispered eagerly, "Why? There is a rumour that when our poem is written the wounds at the top of our thighs will heal up and we will be able to love our masseuse as if we were common men!"
I smiled and said, "That would be anticlimax."

I enjoy astonishing Tohu.

Dear parents, this is my last letter to you. I will write no more prose. But laugh aloud when you see my words painted above the doors of the public buildings. Perhaps you are poor, sick or dying. I hope not. But nothing can deprive you of the greatest happiness possible for a common man and woman. You have created an immortal,

Who lives in the evergreen garden,

Your son,

Bohu.

DICTATED ON THE 19th LAST DAY
OF THE OLD CALENDAR.

THIRD LETTER

DEAR MOTHER, DEAR FATHER, I am full of confused feelings. I saw the emperor two days ago. He is not what I thought. If I describe everything very carefully, especially to you, perhaps I won't go mad.

I wakened that morning as usual and lay peacefully in Adoda's arms. I did not know this was my last peaceful day. Our room faces north. Through the round window above the door I could see the banners above the court of summons. The scarlet and the rainbow flags still floated on the highest pole but beneath them flapped the dark green flag of poetry. There was a noise of hammering and when I looked outside some joiners were building a low wooden bridge which went straight across the maze from the platform edge. I called in the whole household. I said, "Today we visit the emperor."
They looked alarmed. I felt very gracious and friendly. I said, "Only I and Tohu will be allowed to look at him but everyone will hear his voice. The clothes I and Tohu wear are chosen by the etiquette, but I want the rest of you to dress as if you are visiting a rich famous friend you love very much." Adoda smiled but the others still looked alarmed. Tohu muttered, "The emperor is blind." I had forgotten that. I nodded and said, "His headmasters are not."

When the janitor arrived I was standing ten feet tall at the end of the bridge. Adoda on my right wore a dress of dark green silk and her thick hair was mingled with sprigs of yew. Even Tohu's nurse wore something special. The janitor bowed, turned, and paused to let me fix my eyes on his kneebands; then he struck his gong and we moved toward the court.

The journey lasted an hour but I would not have wearied had it lasted a day. I was as incapable of tiredness as a falling stone on its way to the ground. I felt excited, strong, yet peacefully determined at the same time. The surfaces we crossed became richer and larger: pavements of marquetry and mosaic, thresholds of bronze and copper, carpets of fine tapestry and exotic fur. We crossed more than one bridge for I heard the lip-lapping of a great river or lake. The janitor eventually struck the gong for delay and I sensed the wings of a door expanding before us. We moved through a shadow into greater light. The janitor struck the end-of-journey note and his legs left my field of vision. The immortal emperor's squeaky voice said, "Welcome, my poets. Consider yourselves at home."

I raised my eyes and first of all saw the college of headmasters. They sat on felt stools at the edge of a platform which curved round us like the shore of a bay. The platform was so high that their faces were level with my own, although I was standing erect. Though I had met only a few of them I knew all twenty-three by their regalia. The headmaster of waterworks wore a silver drainpipe round his leg, the headmaster of civil peace held a ceremonial bludgeon, the headmaster of history carried a stuffed parrot on his wrist. The headmaster of etiquette sat in the very centre holding the emperor, who was two feet high. The emperor's head and the hands dangling out of his sleeves were normal size, but the body in the scarlet silk robe seemed to be a short wooden staff. His skin was papier mâché with lacquer varnish, yet in conversation he was quick and sprightly. He ran from hand to hand along the row and did not speak again until he reached the headmaster of vaudeville on the extreme left. Then he said, "I shock you. Before we talk I must put you at ease, especially Tohu whose neck is sore craning up at me. Shall I tell a joke, Tohu?"
"Oh yes sir, hahaha! Oh yes sir, hahaha!" shouted Tohu, guffawing hysterically.

The emperor said, "You don't need a joke. You are laughing happily already!"
I realized that this was the emperor's joke and gave a brief appreciative chuckle. I had known the emperor was not human, but was so surprised to see he was not alive that my conventional tears did not flow at the sound of his voice. This was perhaps lucky as Adoda was too far below me to collect them.
The emperor moved to the headmaster of history and spoke on a personal note: "Ask me intimate questions, Bohu."
I said, "Sir, have you always been a puppet?"
He said, "I am not, even now, completely a puppet. My skull and the bones of my hands are perfectly real. The rest was boiled off by doctors fifteen years ago in the operation which made me immortal."
I said, "Was it sore becoming immortal?"
He said, "I did not notice. I had senile dementia at the time and for many years before that I was, in private life, vicious and insensitive. But the wisdom of an emperor has nothing to do with his character. It is the combined intelligence of everyone who obeys him."
The sublime truth of this entered me with such force that I gasped for breath. Yes. The wisdom of a government is the combined intelligence of those who obey it. I gazed at the simpering dummy with pity and awe. Tears poured thickly down my cheeks but I did not heed them.
"Sir!" I cried, "Order us to write for you. We love you. We are ready."

The emperor moved to the headmaster of civil peace and shook the tiny imperial frock into dignified folds before speaking. He said, "I order you to write a poem celebrating my irrevocable justice."
I said, "Will this poem commemorate a special act of justice?"
He said, "Yes. I have just destroyed the old capital, and everyone living there, for the crime of disobedience."

I smiled and nodded enthusiastically, thinking I had not heard properly. I said, "Very good sir, yes, that will do very well. But could you suggest a particular event, a historically important action, which might, in my case, form the basis of a meditative ode, or a popular ballad, in my colleague's case? The action or event should be one which demonstrates the emperor's justice. Irrevocably."
He said, "Certainly. The old capital was full of unnecessary people. They planned a rebellion. Field-marshal Ko besieged it, burned it flat and killed everyone who lived there. The empire is peaceful again. That is your theme. Your pavilion is now decorated with information on the subject. Return there and write."
"Sir!" I said, "I hear and respect your order, I hear and respect your order!"
I went on saying this, unable to stop. Tohu was screaming with laughter and shouting, "Oh my colleague is extremely unconventional, all great poets are, I will write for him, I will write for all of us hahahaha!"
The headmasters were uneasy. The emperor ran from end to end of them and back, never resting till the headmaster of moral philosophy forced him violently onto the headmaster of etiquette. Then the emperor raised his head and squeaked, "This is not etiquette, I adjourn the college!"
He then flopped upside down on a stool while the headmasters hurried out.

I could not move. Janitors swarmed confusedly round my entourage. My feet left the floor, I was jerked one way, then another, then carried quickly backward till my shoulder struck something, maybe a doorpost. And then I was falling, and I think I heard Adoda scream before I became unconscious.

I woke under a rug on my writing-throne in the hall of the pavilion. Paper screens had been placed round it painted with views of the old capital at different stages of the rebellion, siege and massacre. Behind one screen I heard Tohu dictating to his secretary. Instead of taking nine days to assimilate his material the fool was composing already.

Postal pigeons whirl like snow from the new palace, he chanted.

Trained hawks of the rebels strike them dead.
The emperor summons his troops by heliograph:
"Fieldmarshal Ko, besiege the ancient city."
Can hawks catch the sunbeam flashed from silver mirror?
No, hahahaha. No, hahahaha. Rebels are ridiculous.

I held my head. My main thought was that you, mother, you, father, do not exist now and all my childhood is flat cinders. This thought is such pain that I got up and stumbled round the screens to make sure of it.

I first beheld a beautiful view of the old capital, shown from above like a map, but with every building clear and distinct. Pink and green buds on the trees showed this was springtime. I looked down into a local garden of justice where a fat magistrate fanned by a singing-girl sat on a doorstep. A man, woman, and child lay flat on the ground before him and nearby a policeman held a dish with two yellow dots on it. I knew these were clogs with toads on the tips, and that the family was being accused of extravagance and would be released with a small fine. I looked again and saw a little house by the effluent of a sewage canal. Two little women sat sewing on the doorstep, it was you, mother, and your sister, my aunt. Outside the fence a man in a punt, helped by a child, dragged a body from the mud. The bodies of many members of the honoured-guest-class were bobbing along the sewage canals. The emperor's cavalry were setting fire to the south-eastern slums and sabering families who tried to escape. The strangest happening of all was on a hill outside the eastern gate. A man held the rope of a kite which floated out over the city, a kite shaped like an eagle with parrot-coloured feathers. A child hung from it. This part of the picture was on a larger scale than the rest. The father's face wore a look of great pride, but the child was staring down on the city below, not with terror or delight, but with a cool, stern, assessing stare. In the margin of this screen was written *The rebellion begins*.

I only glanced at the other screens. Houses flamed, whole crowds were falling from bridges into canals to avoid the hooves and sabres of the cavalry. If I had looked closely I would have recognized your figures in the crowds again and again. The last screen showed a cindery plain scored by canals so clogged with ruin that neither clear nor foul water appeared in them. The only life was a host of crows and ravens as thick on the ground as flies on raw and rotten meat.

I heard an apologetic cough and found the headmaster of literature beside me. He held a dish with a flask and two cups on it. He said, "Your doctor thinks wine will do you good."

I returned to the throne and lay down. He sat beside me and said, "The emperor has been greatly impressed by the gravity of your response to his order-to-write. He is sure your poem will be very great." I said nothing. He filled the cups with wine and tasted one. I did not. He said, "You once wanted to write about the building of the new palace. Was that a good theme for a poem?"

"Yes."

"But the building of the new palace and the destruction of the old capital are the same thing. All big new things must begin by destroying the old. Otherwise they are a mere continuation."

I said, "Do you mean that the emperor would have destroyed the old capital even without a rebellion?"

"Yes. The old capital was linked by roads and canals to every corner of the empire. For more than nine dynasties other towns looked to it for guidance. Now they must look to us."

I said, "Was there a rebellion?"

"We are so sure there was one that we did not enquire about the matter. The old capital was a market for the empire. When the court came here we brought the market with us. The citizens left behind had three choices. They could starve to death, or beg in the streets of other towns, or rebel. The brave and intelligent among them must have dreamed of rebellion. They probably talked about it. Which is conspiracy."

"Was it justice to kill them for that?"

"Yes. The justice which rules a nation must be more dreadful than the justice which rules a family. The emperor himself respects and pities his defeated rebels. Your poem might mention that."

I said, "You once said my parents were useless to me because time had changed them. You were wrong. As long as they lived I knew that though they might look old and different, though I might never see them again, I was still loved, still alive in ways you and your emperor can never know. And though I never saw the city after going to school I thought of it growing like an onion; each year there was a new skin of leaves and dung on the gardens, new traffic on the streets, new whitewash on old walls. While the old city and my old parents lived my childhood lived too. But the emperor's justice has destroyed my past, irrevocably. I am like a land without culture or history. I am now too shallow to write a poem."

The headmaster said, "It is true that the world is so packed with the present moment that the past, a far greater quantity, can only gain entrance through the narrow gate of a mind. But your mind is unusually big. I enlarged it myself, artificially. You are able to bring your father, mother and city to life and death again in a tragedy, a tragedy the whole nation will read. Remember that the world is one vast graveyard of defunct cities, all destroyed by the shifting of markets they could not control, and all compressed by literature into a handful of poems. The emperor only does what ordinary time does. He simply speeds things up. He wants your help."

I said, "A poet has to look at his theme steadily. A lot of people have no work because an emperor moves a market, so to avoid looking like a bad government he accuses them of rebelling and kills them. My stomach rejects that theme. The emperor is not very wise. If he had saved the lives of my parents perhaps I could have worked for him."

The headmaster said, "The emperor did consider saving your parents before sending in the troops, but I advised him not to. If they were still alive your poem would be an ordinary piece of political excuse-making. Anyone can see the good in disasters which leave their family and property intact. But a poet must feel the cracks in the nation splitting his individual heart. How else can he mend them?"

I said, "I refuse to mend this cracked nation. Please tell the emperor that I am useless to him, and that I ask his permission to die."

The headmaster put his cup down and said, after a while, "That is an important request. The emperor will not answer it quickly."

I said, "If he does not answer me in three days I will act without him."

The headmaster of literature stood up and said, "I think I can promise an answer at the end of three days."

He went away. I closed my eyes, covered my ears and stayed where I was. My entourage came in and wanted to wash, feed and soothe me but I let nobody within touching distance. I asked for water, sipped a little, freshened my face with the rest then commanded them to leave. They were unhappy, especially Adoda who wept silently all the time. This comforted me a little. I almost wished the etiquette would let me speak to Adoda. I was sure Tohu talked all the time to his nurse when nobody else could hear. But what good does talking do? Everything I could say would be as horrible to Adoda as it is to me. So I lay still and said nothing and tried not to hear the drone of Tohu dictating all through that night and the following morning. Toward the end, half his lines seemed to be stylized exclamations of laughter and even between them he giggled a lot. I thought perhaps he was drunk, but when he came to me in the evening he was unusually dignified. He knelt down carefully by my throne and whispered, "I finished my poem today. I sent it to the emperor but I don't think he likes it."

I shrugged. He whispered, "I have just received an invitation from him. He wants my company tomorrow in the garden of irrevocable justice."

I shrugged. He whispered, "Bohu, you know my entourage is very small. My nurse may need help. Please let your doctor accompany us."

I nodded. He whispered, "You are my only friend," and went away.

I did not see him next day till late evening. His nurse came and knelt at the steps of my throne. She looked smaller, older and uglier than usual and she handed me a scroll of the sort used for public announcements. At the top were portraits of myself and Tohu. Underneath it said:

> *The emperor asked his famous poets Bohu and Tohu to celebrate the destruction of the old capital. Bohu said no. He is still an honoured guest in the evergreen garden, happy and respected by all who know him. Tohu said yes and wrote a very bad poem. You may read the worst bits below. Tohu's tongue, right shoulder, arm and hand have now been replaced by wooden ones. The emperor prefers a frank confession of inability to the useless words of the flattering toad-eater.*

I stood up and said drearily, "I will visit your master."

He lay on a rug in her room with his face to the wall. He was breathing loudly. I could see almost none of him for he still wore the ceremonial cape which was badly stained in places. My doctor knelt beside him and answered my glance by spreading the palms of his hands. The secretary, chef and two masseuses knelt near the door. I sighed and said, "Yesterday you told me I was your only friend, Tohu. I can say now that you are mine. I am sorry our training has stopped us showing it."

I don't think he heard me for shortly after he stopped breathing. I then told my entourage that I had asked to die and expected a positive answer from the emperor on the following day. They were all very pale but my news made them paler still. When someone more than seven feet tall dies of unnatural causes the etiquette requires his entourage to die in the same way. This is unlucky, but I did not make this etiquette, this palace, this empire which I shall leave as soon as possible, with or without the emperor's assistance. The hand of my secretary trembles as he writes these words. I pity him.

To my dead parents in the ash of the old capital,

From the immortal emperor's supreme *<u>nothing</u>*, *Their son,*

Bohu.

DICTATED ON THE 10th LAST DAY OF THE OLD CALENDAR.

FOURTH LETTER

DEAR MOTHER, DEAR FATHER, I must always return to you, it seems. The love, the rage, the power which fills me now cannot rest until it has sent a stream of words in your direction. I have written my great poem but not the poem wanted. I will explain all this.

On the evening of the third day my entourage were sitting round me when a common janitor brought the emperor's reply in the unusual form of a letter. He gave it to the secretary, bowed and withdrew. The secretary is a good ventriloquist and read the emperor's words in the appropriate voice.

> *The emperor hears and respects his great poet's request for death. The emperor grants Bohu permission to do anything he likes, write anything he likes, and die however, wherever, and whenever he chooses.*

I said to my doctor, "Choose the death you want for yourself and give it to me first."
He said, "Sir, may I tell you what that death is?"
"Yes."
"It will take many words to do so. I cannot be brief on this matter."
"Speak. I will not interrupt."
He said, "Sir, my life has been a dreary and limited one, like your own. I speak for all your servants when I say this. We have all been, in a limited way, married to you, and our only happiness was being useful to a great poet. We understand why you cannot become one. Our own parents have died in the ancient capital, so death is the best thing for everyone, and I can make it painless. All I need is a closed room, the chef's portable stove and a handful of prepared herbs which are always with me.
"But sir, need we go rapidly to this death? The emperor's letter suggests not, and that letter has the force of a

passport. We can use it to visit any part of the palace we like. Give us permission to escort you to death by a flowery, roundabout path which touches on some commonplace experiences all men wish to enjoy. I ask this selfishly, for our own sakes, but also unselfishly, for yours. We love you sir."

Tears came to my eyes but I said firmly, "I cannot be seduced. My wish for death is an extension of my wish not to move, feel, think or see. I desire *nothing* with all my heart. But you are different. For a whole week you have my permission to glut yourself on anything the emperor's letter permits."

The doctor said, "But sir, that letter has no force without your company. Allow yourself to be carried with us. We shall not plunge you into riot and disorder. All will be calm and harmonious, you need not walk, or stand, or even think. We know your needs. We can read the subtlest flicker of your eyebrow. Do not even say *yes* to this proposal of mine. Simply close your eyes in the tolerant smile which is so typical of you."

I was weary, and did so, and allowed them to wash, feed and prepare me for sleep as in the old days. And they did something new. The doctor wiped the wounds at the top of my thighs with something astringent and Adoda explored them, first with her tongue and then with her teeth. I felt a pain almost too fine to be noticed and looking down I saw her draw from each wound a quivering silver thread. Then the doctor bathed me agian and Adoda embraced me and whispered, "May I share your throne?"

I nodded. Everyone else went away and I slept deeply for the first time in four days.

Next morning I dreamed my aunt was beside me, as young and lovely as in days when she looked like the white demon. I woke up clasping Adoda so insistently that we both cried aloud. The doors of the central hall were all wide open; so were the doors to the garden in the rooms beyond. Light flooded in on us from all sides. During breakfast I grew calm again but it was not my habitual calm. I felt adventurous under the waist. This feeling did not yet reach my head, which smiled cynically. But I was no longer exactly the same man.

The rest of the entourage came in wearing bright clothes and garlands. They stowed my punt-shaped throne with food, wine, drugs and instruments. It is a big throne and when they climbed in themselves there was no overcrowding even though Tohu's nurse was there too. Then a horde of janitors arrived with long poles which they fixed to the sides of the throne, and I and my entourage were lifted into the air and carried out to the garden. The secretary sat in the prow playing a mouth-organ while the chef and doctor accompanied him with zither and drum. The janitors almost danced as they trampled across the maze, and this was so surprising that I laughed aloud, staring freely up at the pigeon-flecked azure sky, the porcelain gables with their coloured flags, the crowded tops of markets, temples and manufactories. Perhaps when I was small I had gazed as greedily for the mere useless fun of it, but for years I had only used my eyes professionally, to collect poetical knowledge, or shielded them, as required by the etiquette. "Oh, Adoda!" I cried, warming my face in her hair, "All this new knowledge is useless and I love it."
She whispered, "The use of living is the taste it gives. The emperor has made you the only free man in the world. You can taste anything you like."

We entered a hall full of looms where thousands of women in coarse gowns were weaving rich tapestry. I was fascinated. The air was stifling, but not to me. Adoda and the chef plied their fans and the doctor refreshed me with a fine mist of cool water. I also had the benefit of janitors without kneebands, so our party was socially

invisible; I could stare at whom I liked and they could not see me at all. I noticed a girl with pale brown hair toiling on one side. Adoda halted the janitors and whispered, "That lovely girl is your sister who was sold to the merchants. She became a skilled weaver so they resold her here."
I said, "That is untrue. My sister would be over forty now and that girl, though robust, is not yet sixteen."
"Would you like her to join us?"
I closed my eyes in the tolerant smile and a janitor negotiated with an overseer. When we moved on, the girl was beside us. She was silent and frightened at first but we gave her garlands, food and wine and she soon became merry.

We came into a narrow street with a gallery along one side on the level of my throne. Tall elegant women in the robes of the court strolled and leaned there. A voice squeaked, "Hullo, Bohu" and looking up I saw the emperor smiling from the arms of the most slender and disdainful. I stared at him. He said, "Bohu hates me but I must suffer that. He is too great a man to be ordered by a poor old emperor. This lady, Bohu, is your aunt, a very wonderful courtesan. Say hullo!"
I laughed and said, "You are a liar, sir."
He said, "Nonetheless you mean to take her from me. Join the famous poet, my dear, he goes down to the floating world. Goodbye, Bohu. I do not just give people death. That is only half my job."
The emperor moved to a lady nearby, the slender one stepped among us and we all sailed on down the street.

We reached a wide river and the janitors waded in until the throne rested on the water. They withdrew the poles, laid them on the thwarts and we drifted out from shore. The doctor produced pipes and measured a careful dose into each bowl. We smoked and talked; the men played instruments, the women sang. The little weaver knew many popular songs, some sad, some funny. I suddenly wished Tohu was with us, and wept. They asked why. I told them and we all wept together. Twilight fell and a moon came out. The court lady stood up, lifted a pole and steered us expertly into a grove of willows growing in shallow water. Adoda hung lanterns in the branches. We ate, clasped each other, and slept.

I cannot count the following days. They may have been two, or three, or many. Opium plays tricks with time but I did not smoke enough to stop me loving. I loved in many ways, some tender, some harsh, some utterly absent-minded. More than once I said to Adoda, "Shall we die now? Nothing can be sweeter than this" but she said, "Wait a little longer. You haven't done all you want yet."
When at last my mind grew clear about the order of time the weaver and court lady had left us and we drifted down a tunnel to a bright arch at the end. We came into a lagoon on a lane of clear water between beds of rushes and lily-leaves. It led to an island covered with spires of marble and copper shining in the sun. My secretary said, "That is the poets' pantheon. Would you like to land, sir?"
I nodded.

We disembarked and I strolled barefoot on warm moss between the spires. Each had an open door in the base with steps down to the tomb where the body would lie. Above each door was a white tablet where the poet's great work would be painted. All the tombs and tablets were vacant, of course, for I am the first poet in the new palace and was meant to be the greatest, for the tallest spire in the centre was sheathed in gold with my name on the door. I entered. The room downstairs had space for us all with cushions for the entourage and a silver throne for me.

"To deserve to lie here I must write a poem," I thought, and looked into my mind. The poem was there, waiting to come out. I returned upstairs, went outside and told the secretary to fetch paint and brushes from his satchel and go to the tablet. I then dictated my poem in a slow firm voice.

THE EMPEROR'S INJUSTICE

Scattered buttons and silks, a broken kite in the mud,
A child's yellow clogs cracked by the horses' hooves.
A land weeps for the head city, lopped by sabre, cracked by hoove
The houses ash, the people meat for crows.

A week ago wind rustled dust in the empty market.
"Starve," said the moving dust, "Beg. Rebel. Starve. Beg. Rebel."
We do not do such things. We are peaceful people.
We have food for six more days, let us wait.
The emperor will accommodate us, underground.

It is sad to be unnecessary.
All the bright mothers, strong fathers, raffish aunts,
Lost sisters and brothers, all the rude servants
Are honoured guests of the emperor, underground.

We sit in the tomb now. The door is closed, the only light is the red glow from the chef's charcoal stove. My entourage dreamily puff their pipes, the doctor's fingers sift the dried herbs, the secretary is ending my last letter. We are tired and happy. The emperor said I could write what I liked. Will my poem be broadcast? No. If that happened the common people would rise and destroy that evil little puppet and all the cunning, straightfaced, pompous men who use him. Nobody will read my words but a passing gardener, perhaps, who will paint them out to stop them reaching the emperor's ear. But I have at last made the poem I was made to make. I lie down to sleep in perfect satisfaction. *Goodbye, I still love you. Your son,*

Bohu.

DICTATED ON THE OLD CALENDAR'S LAST DAY.

LAST LETTER

AN APPRECIATION OF THE POEM BY THE LATE TRAGEDIAN BOHU ENTITLED *THE EMPEROR'S INJUSTICE* DELIVERED TO THE IMPERIAL COLLEGE OF HEAD-MASTERS, NEW PALACE UNIVERSITY

My Dear Colleagues, This is exactly the poem we require. Our patience in waiting for it till the last possible moment has been rewarded. The work is shorter than we expected, but that makes distribution easier. It had a starkness unusual in government poetry, but this starkness satisfies the nation's need much more than the work we hoped for. With a single tiny change the poem can be used at once. I know some of my colleagues will raise objections, but I will answer these in the course of my appreciation.

A noble spirit of pity blows through this poem like a warm wind. The destroyed people are not mocked and calumniated, we identify with them, and the third line:

A land cries for the head city, lopped by sabre, cracked by hooves, invites the whole empire to mourn. But does this wind of pity fan the flames of political protest? No. It presses the mind of the reader inexorably toward *nothing*, toward death.

This is clearly shown in the poem's treatment of rebellion:

We do not do such things. We are peaceful people.
We have food for six more days, let us wait.

The poem assumes that a modern population will find

the prospect of destruction by their own government less alarming than action against it. The truth of this is shown in today's police report from the old capital. It describes crowds of people muttering at street corners and completely uncertain of what action to take. They have a little food left. They fear the worst, yet hope, if they stay docile, the emperor will not destroy them immediately. This state of things was described by Bohu yesterday in the belief that it had happened a fortnight ago! A poet's intuitive grasp of reality was never more clearly demonstrated.

At this point the headmaster of civil peace will remind me that the job of the poem is not to describe reality but to encourage our friends, frighten our enemies, and reconcile the middling people to the destruction of the old capital. The headmaster of moral philosophy will also remind me of our decision that people will most readily accept the destruction of the old capital if we accuse it of rebellion. That was certainly the main idea in the original order-to-write, but I would remind the college of what we had to do to the poet who obeyed that order. Tohu knew exactly what we wanted and gave it to us. His poem described the emperor as wise, witty, venerable, patient, loving and omnipotent. He described the citizens of the old capital as stupid, childish, greedy, absurd, yet inspired by a vast communal lunacy which endangered the empire. He obediently wrote a popular melodrama which could not convince a single intelligent man and would only over-excite stupid ones, who are fascinated by criminal lunatics who attack the established order.

The problem is this. If we describe the people we kill as dangerous rebels they look glamorous; if we describe them as weak and silly we seem unjust. Tohu could not solve that problem. Bohu has done with startling simplicity.

He presents the destruction as a simple, stunning, inevitable fact. The child, mother and common people in the poem exist passively, doing nothing but weep, gossip, and wait. The active agents of hoof, sabre, and (by extension) crow, belong to the emperor, who is named at the end of the middle verse:

The emperor will accommodate us, underground.

and at the end of the last:

Bright mothers, strong fathers ... all the rude servants
Are honoured guests of the emperor, underground.

Consider the *weight* this poem gives to our immortal emperor! He is not described or analysed, he is presented as a final, competent, all-embracing force, as unarguable as the weather, as inevitable as death. This is how all governments should appear to people who are not in them.

To sum up, *THE EMPEROR'S INJUSTICE* will delight our friends, depress our enemies, and fill middling people with nameless awe. The only change required is the elimination of the first syllable in the last word of the title. I advise that the poem be sent today to every village, town and city in the land. At the same time Field-marshal Ko should be ordered to destroy the old capital. When the poem appears over doors of public buildings the readers will read of an event which is occurring simultaneously. In this way the literary and military sides of the attack will reinforce each other with unusual throughness. Field-marshal Ko should take special care that the poet's parents do not escape the general massacre, as a rumour to that effect will lessen the poignancy of the official biography, which I will complete in the coming year.

I remain your affectionate colleague,

Gigadib,

Headmaster of modern and classical literature.

DICTATED ON DAY I
OF THE NEW CALENDAR

JUDGEMENT
LEARNING
WITT
INVENTION
SWEETNESS
STILE

LOGOPANDOCY

The
Secret and Apocryphal Diurnal
of
SIR THOMAS URQUHART
OF CROMARTIE
Knight

Recently Discovered and Published
Against the Author's Expressed Will & Command
for the
Instruction and Reformation
of the
Brittanic League of Commonwealths;

Wherein is recorded a dialogue with the late Protector Cromwell's Latin secretary, which neatly unfolds a scheme to repair the divided Nature of Man by rationally reintegering God's Gift of Tongues to Adam by a verboradical appliancing of Neper's logarythms to the grammar of an Asiatick people, thought to be the lost tribe of Israel, whose language predates the Babylonic Cataclysm;

With auxiliary matter vindicating the grandeur of SCOTLAND from the foul Infamy whereinto the Rigid Presbyterian party of that nation, out of their covetousness and their overweening ambition, hath most dissembledly involved it.

Oh thou'rt a Book in Truth with love to many
Done by and for the free'st spoke Scot of any.

THE EXACT VERNAL EQUINOX ANNO CHRISTUS 1645: IN THE TOWER OF CROMARTIE.

This diurnal to be maintained for my eyes and pleasure alone, I herein downsetting such honest self-estimates as throngers of kirks, courts and markets would castigate as vainglorious; and herein recording those embryonical conceits which quaversally disposed intellects too often neglect, abort and aberuncate for clamouring projects more fully formed; and herein deploying a style less orgulous, magnifical, and quodlibetically tolutiloquent than is proper to my public emittings.

2 It is six years since my just action to reclaim the armaments raped from here by the Lairds of Dalgetty and Tolly led to the first death (a ball thro' the occiput of my groom Frazer, an inept parasite but loyal) in that rascally rebellion which reptile parliaments of both nations attempt to dignify with the adjectival appellation *great*, as if grandeur were magnitude of multitude distinct from all noble and worthy intent.

3 It is five years since (for holding Aberdeen nearly a fortnight against the leagued forces of the Covenant) the Seventh Regally Annoynted High Steward of Scotland and Second to Overlord the intire Brittanic Island, did Knight me in the gallery of Whitehall three days before the publication of my *Epigrams: Divine and Moral*.

4 It is three years since my father, on deathbed in the chamber adjoyning, led my five brothers to swear, under pain of his everlasting curse and execration, to assist, concur with and serve me to the utmost of their power, industry and means, and to spare neither charge nor travel to release me from the undeserved bondage of the domineering Creditor, and extricate our crazed estate from the impestrements in which it hath been involved by his too good, too credulous, too hopeful nature; three years also since I voyaged beyond Byzantium, letting rents embank at home for the leniencing and clementizing of the Creditor.

5 It is one week since, homing it through London, I saw off the press my *Trissotetras*, wherein I lay the ground of an intirely new Science.

6 This day, having entered upon the family mansion, I discover that by false inept bailiffs and chamberlains, deputies and doers, my rents and receipts have been so embezzled, malingened, pauchled and mischarged that little or no moneys have accrued to me, while the creditors have sold their claims on the estate to usurers yet more fanged, pangastrical and Presbyterian than themselves. It is a well founded prevision of Jehovus that I am, since Neper of Marchiston, the foremost Apostle in Brittain of that Holy Minerva who inspired Moses, Aristotle, Julius Caesar and the mighty Rabelais, for were I not the wisest, therefor luckiest man I know, I would be the most miserably depressed and straightened. So I here cast an accompt of the great goods of my condition, balancing the bads against them to see which predominate.

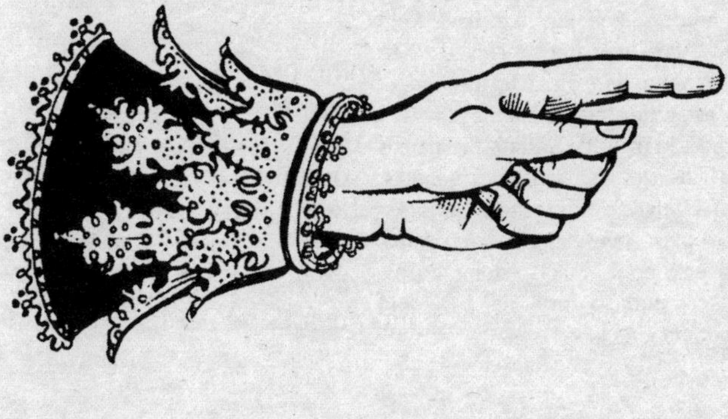

PRO ME	**CONTRA ME**
Ancestry: Toward the stock, stem, vine, clew, cable and navelstring of my pedigree Saturn's scythe hath been so blunted that I can iluct its labyrintheon through innumerable changes of monarchy and estate among the Regal Houses of Scotland, Ireland, Portugal, Gallicia, Murcia, Andaluzia, Granada, Carthage, Egypt, Amazonia, Greece and Israel, back to Adam surnamed the Protoplast, who was quintessence of that red earth created in time, of nothing, by the word of TRIUN JEHOVUS the ETERNAL FATHER, SON AND GHOSTLIE MINERVAAMEN.	**Ancestry**: Though verboradically demonstrable, the middle part of my geneology lacks inscriptory provenance, and will be doubted by pedant sciolasts and fidimplicatary gownsmen who can neither admit the eductions of informed inspiration, nor comprehend the congruency of the syllabic with the Sibylene.
Rank: I am Knight of Bray and Udol, Baron of Fichterie and Clohorby, Laird Baron Cromartie and Heritable High Sheriff thereof, having Admiralty of the seas betwixt Catness and Innernasse, and therefore Jehovus Depute (under the Steward Crown) in that part of Brittain autochthonously colonized by oriental polistactical patricians and their followers, which is why so many towns, castles, churches, fountains, rivers, nasses, bays, harbours, and the like, have from my family name received their denomination, and why the shire of Cromartie alone, of all the places of the Isle of Brittain, hath the names of its towns, villages, hamlets, dwellings, promontaries, hillocks, temples, dens, groves, fountains, rivers, pools, lakes, stone heaps, akers and so forth, of pure and perfect Greek.	**Rank**: Nothing.

PRO ME	CONTRA ME
Frame: In portliness of garb, comeliness of face, sweetness of countenance, majesty of very chevelure, with goodliness of frame, proportion of limbs and symmetry betwixt all the parts and joints of my body, I am heroical in the mould of, not Hercules, Ganimed.	**Frame**: Nothing.
Nature: Jovial, yet Saturnine, my venereal fervour (for the better ingendering of brain-babes) chastened by Diana, inharmonied by Apollo, promoted with Martial vigour, ripened through Minerval cogency and quickened by Mercurial urgency, though this last only in learning and combat, since I lack all lust to transmute baseness into coyn of any metal.	**Nature**: Nothing.
Home: This noble mansion-fort, the stance whereof is statelie, the tower of notable good fabrick and contrivance.	**Home**: The windows lack glass.
Library: Not three books therein but are of my own purchase, and all of them together (in the order wherein I will rank them) compiled like a compleat nosegay of flowers, which in my travels I gathered out of the gardens of sixteen several different kingdoms.	**Library**: Still unpacked.
Estate: Lands in the shires of Cromartie and Aberdeen yeelding a thousand pounds Sterling of rent, with many especial royalties, privileges and immunities, preserved from the days of Nomoster in the 389th epoch before Christ, untill the perfect age and majority of my father, who received it without any burthen of debt, or provision of brother or sister or other kindred alliance to affect it, whereunto was then added, by his father-in-law Lord Elphingstone, the then High Treasurer of Scot-	**Estate**: Twelve or thirteen thousand pounds Sterling of debt, five brethren all men and two marriageable sisters to support, and less to defray all this by six hundred pounds Sterling a year, in a time of frantic anticivilian warres and garboyles, than my father inherited for nothing, in a peaceful age, to maintain himself alone. Meantime the Church Commission maintain in my kirks three cutpurse Mammoniferous ministers of their own make who, loathing my loyaltie to the Episcopal liturge, demand

PRO ME

land, my mother, Lady Christian, with whom he received no inconsiderable fortune. Also the patronage of the parriches of Kirkmichel, Cromartie and Cullicuden.

Tenandrie: All are descended (as they themselves avouch) from pregenitors who accompanied my ancestors Alypos, Belistos, Nomostor, Astioremon and Lutork in their aborignarie acquest of the land, receiving from these such good yeoman leases for the digging and manuring of it that they very suddenly took deep root therein, and bequeathed to their children the hereditary obedience owed to their masters. Each hamlet by that means having its own Clan, as we call it, or name of kindred, none will from that portion of land bouge, any interflitting between conterminal parrishes being as mutually displeasing to them as an extrusive exile to the Barbadoes or to Malagask. I have farmers who dwell in the selfsame house inhabited by their ancestors from dad to brat, sire to suckling, above nine hundred years together and though none can read, they nevertheless exchange discourse with any concerning the heathenish deities of the Grecolatin Pantheon, whose temples, delubres and fanes, of a circularie, oval, triangulary or square figure, my own forefathers erected in groves and high places before the time of Christ, the stones whereof may still be ascribed to Jove, Juno,

CONTRA ME

for their tythes a fifth of the rent of the land, and combinate in synods and concils with creditors and neighbours to put upon me alone the charge of garrisoning troops in this district, thereby intending to inchaos the structure of ancient greatness into the very rubbish of a neophitic parity.

Tenandrie: These much plundered and rouped of goods, gear and rents by the soldiery without hope of redress; while their Kirkomanatickal presbyterian pastors vilipend, pester and flite them for tenaciously clinging to their frets of old, which often send them at set times to fountains, oak-trees, little round hillocks and stone-heaps where, with preconceived words and motions, they worship in accordance with the poetical liturgies of Hesiod, Theocritus and Ovid; And my ministers demand that I magisterially prohibit and persecute these practices as things of charm, fascination, inchantment or infernal assistance! There is a silly old wife who, for doing some pretty feats wherein she has been instructed by her mother, according to a prescript set down in some verses of Homer, whom neither had the skill to use, is accused of witchcraft by one who, being a professor of the Greek, whipt a boy for not getting these verses by heart: as if it were a duty for him to study what is felonie for others to enact. Being resolved to conduct myself by the light of reason, I openly acquit many of both sexes whom flagitory zealots accuse of incubation, succubation and peragration with fairies, and am forthwith

PRO ME

Palas, Apollo &cetera by the eye of the intelligible Mythologist.

CONTRA ME

reputed an obstinate assertor of erroneous doctrine. Even as a raw youth I would not without examination trust to aged men in matters contrary to commonsense and experience, for I caused brought to my father's house one of either sex that were supposed rivals in diabolical venerie, the male with the succub, the female with the incub. The young man was two-and-twenty years old, very bashfull, yet prone to lasciviousness, and a handsome youth; she was some five-and-twentie, nothing so pleasant as he, and had it not been for a little modesty that restrained her, a very sink of lust. All this I perceived at first view, and after I had spoken kindly with them in generals, I entreated them with all gentilnesse possible, to tell me freely whether it was so or not, as it was reported of them; and their answer was (for they were not suspicious of any harm from me) that it was true enough; whereat I straight conceived that they had a crack in their imagination. The better to try an experiment thereon, I commanded to be given unto each of them an insomniatorie and exoniretick potion, for stirring up a libidinous fancie; I also directed one of my footboys to attend the woman with all possible respect and outward shew of affection; the like I required of one of my mother's chambermaids to be done in behalf of the young man. Which injunctions of mine were by these two servants with such dexterity prosecuted, that the day after each of their night's repose with these two hypochondriacks, when I called for them, and, after I had fairly insinuated myself into their mind by a smooth discourse, asked whether that night they had in their bodies felt any carnal application of the fowl spirit, or if they did, in what likeness they received him? To this both made reply that of all the nights they had ever enjoyed, it was that night respectively wherein the spirit was most intirely communicative in feats of dalliance, and that he acted in the guise of the boy and chambermaid whom I had appointed to await on them as they went to bed. This confirmed me in my former opinion, which certainly increased when I heard a short time after, that the imagination of two had become a regular fornication of four; by which (though I caused to punish them all) the fantasists were totally cured, who afterwards becoming yoke mates in wedlock to the two servants of our house, were in all times coming sound enough in fancie, and never more disquieted by diabolical apprehensions.

PRO ME

Nation: Betwixt pole and tropicks there has been no great engagement wherein Scotsmen have not (by valiantly slaughtering each other on behalf of all the greatest Christian states in Europe) made their nation as renowned for its martialists as have its promovers of learning for their literatory endeavour. I here set down the greatest names on all sides since the jubilee of 1600, instellarating thus * such as creep in from an earlier age, since it is not my custom to maintain a rank by excluding an excellence.

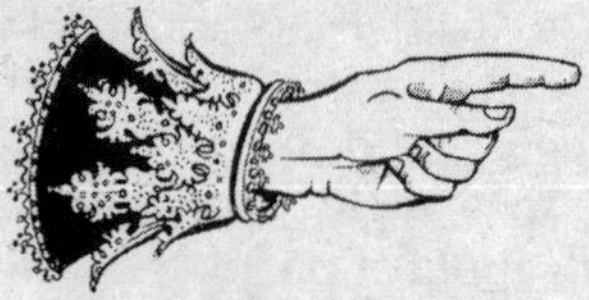

CONTRA ME

Nation: I will not enlist opposite the flaming sparks of their country's fame those coclimatory wasps of the Covenanting crue whose swarms eclipse it. I will discourse but generally, or by ensample, of those viper colonels who do not stick to gnaw the womb of the Mother who bears them, and of those ligger-headed Mammoniferous ministers, those pristinary lobcock hypocritick Presbyters (*press-biters* rather) who abuse learning in the name of God, as if distinct truths could oppose THE TRUTH.

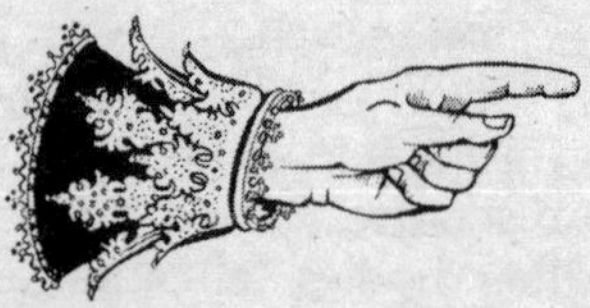

PRO SCOTIA

ARMS

FOR THE KING OF SWEDLAND GUSTAVUS CAESEROMASTIX AGAINST DANE, POLE, MUSCOVITE AND HOLY EMPEROR.

General James Spence (created Earl of Orcholm), Sir Alexander Leslie (governor of the cities of the Baltick coast), Marquis James Hamilton (General over 6,000 English in the Swedish Sevice) with these Scottish colonels:

Sir George Cunningham
Sir John Ruven
Sir John Hamilton
Sir John Meldrum
Sir Arthur Forbas
Sir Frederick Hamilton
Sir Francis Ruven
Sir William Ballantine

with (to be rapid) these colonels: Armstrong, Balfour, another Balfour, Bucliugh, Crichton, Cockburn, Culen, Edmistoun, Gun, Hamiltoun, Henderson, Johnston, another Johnston, Kinninmond, another Kinninmond, Leckie, Leslie, Liddel, Livistoun, Sandilands, Scot, Seaton, another Seaton, Sinclair, Spence, Stuart.

FOR THE KING OF POLE AGAINST SWEDE, MUSCOVITER AND TURK

Colonel Lermon
Colonel Wilson
Colonel Hunter
Colonel Robert
Colonel Scot
Colonel Gordon
Colonel Wood
Colonel Spang
Colonel Gun
Colonel Robertson
Colonel Rower

ARTS

LORD NEPER OF MARCHISTON. The artificial numbers by him first excogitated and perfected are of such incomparable use, that by them we may operate more in one day than without them in the space of a week; a secret that would have been so precious to antiquitie, that Pythagoras, Socrates, Plato, Aristotle, Archimedes and Euclid would have joyntly concurred in deifying the revealer of so great a mystery. My country is more glorious for producing so brave a spark, than if it had been the conquering kingdom of a hundred potent nations. Neper also had the skill (as is commonly reported) to frame an engine which, by virtue of some secret springs, implements and substances inclosed within the bowels thereof, could clear a field of four miles circumference or more (proportional to its bigness, for he could make it any size at all) of all living creatures exceeding a foot in hight, by which he was able to have killed thirty thousand turkes, without the hazard of one christian. Of this, upon a wager, he gave proof on a large plaine in Scotland, to the destruction of a great many herds of cattel and flocks of sheep, whereof some were distant from other half a mile, some a whole mile. When earnestly desired by an old acquaintance, at the time he contracted the disease whereof he died, not to take the invention of so ingenious a mystery with him to the tomb; he replied, That for the ruine and overthrow of man-

CONTRA SCOTIAM

ARMS

What have we here? A Scotland racked, retching and rampant with intestinal dissent. How may a politic body rampantly menace others while bloodily rending itself? Regard us and know. Four armies prowl this realm prepared to fight 1. For King and Covenant, 2. For King against Covenant, 3. For Covenant against King, 4. Against both Covenant and King. This rebelion, here begun on a point of liturgy by Scottish blatterers of extemporaneous prayer, spread hence to the English who took to it on a matter of taxation and, fighting a two-sided rectilinear war, soon concluded in a clear conquest for the Cromwel parliament last year on Marston Moor. But the Northern Realm, where the Royal Steward was first betrayed, still holds the last loyalists to fight for him victoriously under that lapsed Covenanter the Marquess Montross. This fills me with a confusion of pride and regret. When will our turmoyles cease to involve us in stultifying self dissent? May we only win glory by serving the foreigner? If so our best hope is to be integered into one united British Imperium, by imblending the Scottish Lords and Commons with the English as hath been done with the Welsh equivalent. But should that fail to grant us long prosperity of achievement, then our last hope is an enemy of the sort Cromwel is to the Irish, but less cunning; an enemy so crass, antagonistic and dully ignorant of Scotland's state that we must needs all con-

ARTS

At home our arts have come under the scourge of an uncontrolled Kirk whose hierarchical jurisdiction is neither monarchical, aristocratical or democratical, but a meer Plutarchy, Plutocracie or rather Plutomanie; so madly do they hale after money and the trash of this world, which I here ensample by but one instance. The great Doctor Liddel, astronomical disciple of Tycho Brahe and professor of the sciences of sensible immaterial objects in Heidelberg, bequeathed fourty pounds English money a year to Aberdeen university for the maintenance of a mathematical professor, with this *proviso*, that the nearest of his own kinsmen, *caeteris paribus* should be preferred before any other. The chair falling vacant when the Doctor's nephew, Master Duncan Liddel, was of sufficient age and skil to exercise that duty, did the good Senators of Aberdeen attend the honest doctor's will? No, forsooth, the oracle must first be consulted with; ministerian philoplutaries, my tongue forks it, I have mistaken it seems one word for another, I should have said philosophers, decide his uncle's testament must be made void; for, say they, Master Duncan Liddel hath committed the hainous sin of fornication, he hath got a young lass with childe! Which presbyterian doctrine, had it bin enforced in the daies of Socrates, would have pearched him up on a penitentiary pew for having two wives at once (neither whereof, either Xanthippe or Myrto, was as handsome as Master

PRO SCOTIA

ARMS

FOR THE GRAND DUKE OF MUSCOVY AGAINST THE SWEDE, TURK AND TARTAR
Sir Alexander Leslie generalissimo of all forces of the whole empire of Russia with
Colonel Crawford
Colonel Gordon
Colonel Keith
Colonel Mathuson
Colonel Kinninmond
Colonel Garne (agnamed the Sclavonian, who for the height and grossenes of his person, being greater in compass than any within six kingdoms of him, was elected King of Bucharia, and only refused the sovereign crown, sword and sceptre belonging to the supreme majesty of that nation, because he had no stomach to be circumsized).

FOR THE HOLY ROMAN EMPEROUR OF GERMANY AGAINST THE SWEDES, DUTCH AND VENETIAN
Colonel Henderson
Colonel Johnston
Colonel Lithco
Colonel Wedderburne
Colonel Bruce
Colonel Gordon (now high Chamberlain to the Emperour's Court)
Colonel Leslie (who is made hereditary marquess and colonel-general of the whole infantry of the imperial forces).

FOR THE DUTCH WILLIAM OF ORANGE AGAINST SPAIN AND FRANCE
These colonels:

ARTS

kind there were already too many divices framed, which, since the malice and rancor in the heart of man would not suffer these to diminish, by no conceit of his would their number be increased. Divinely spoken, truly.

CRICHTON * AGNAMED THROUGHOUT EUROPE ADMIRABILIS SCOTUS OR THE WONDERFUL SCOT:

who in one day at the Sorbonne in Paris, from nine in the morning to six at night, did argue in Hebrew, Syriack, Arabick, Greek, Latin, Italian, English, Flemish, Dutch, Spanish, French and Sclavonian, in prose and verse, at his disputants' discretion, thereby resolving the knurriest problems propounded to him by the choicest and most profound philosophers, mathematicians, naturalists, mediciners, surgeons, apothecaries, alchymists, civil law doctors, canon law doctors, grammarians, rhetoricians and logicians in that greatest of all cities which is truly called the Abridgement of the World; and ilucting the most umbraged obscurities, and prostrating the sublimest mysteries to the vulgar capacity, by the easie and accurate promptness of his speech. When the Rector of the University awarded him a purse of gold and a diamond ring, the nimblewitted Parisians raized such thundering plaudities that the rarified air over the echoing concavities of the colleges could not support the birds in flight, who fell from the sky in a feathered showr. And the

CONTRA SCOTIAM

ARMS

front it together or sink into total penury and nonfunction.

ARTS

Liddel's Concubine) and cast all the later ages of man kind under a cloud of ignorance by quenching the light of Plato, Aristotle and Euclid, who would have betaken themselves to some other profession than philosophy, if the presbytery of Athens had supplied the academical chair thereof with the bum of a more sanctified brother, whose zealous job-bernolism would have mudded and fowled at its source the world's first clear fountain of pure learning. Such a sort was that convenanting gentleman who burnt a great many historical and philosophical books thinking they had been books of popery, because of the red letters he saw on their titles and inscriptions. The nation of Scotland hath produced many excellent spirits whose abilities, by the presbyterian's persecutions, have been quite smothered, and excellent books have perished for want of able and skillful printers, the author happening to dy; whereupon the wife and children, to save a little money, make use of his papers, without any regard to the precious things in them, to fold perhaps their butter and cheese into. So unfortunate a thing is it that good spirit should be struck by presbytery into penury and have their writing fall into the hands of ignorants. That poverty is an enemy to the exercise of vertue, is not unknown to anyone acquainted with the sovereign power of money; and if the great men of the land would be pleased to salve that sore, which, possibly would not be expensive to them as either their hawks or hounds, then peradventure by such gallant incitements, through a vertuous emulation who should most excel other,

PRO SCOTIA

ARMS

Robert Munro of Fowls
Obstol Munro
Assen Munro
Hector Munro (who wrote a book in folio called Munroe's expedition)
George Leslie
Robert Leslie
John Leslie (agnamed the omnipotent)
Alexander Leslie
Alexander Hamilton (agnamed dear Sandy)
William Cunningham
Alexander Cunningham
Finess Forbas
Alexander Forbas (agnamed the Bauld)
Alexander Forbas (another)
Borg (who took a Spanish General in the field upon the head of his army)
Edmund (who took the valiant Count de Buccoy twice prisoner in the field)
Urchart (who is a valiant soldier, expert commander and learned scholar) and
Dowglas the ingenious engineer general, and many more who became colonels and general persons under Gustavus Adolphus.

FOR THAT TETRARARCH OF THE WORLD ON WHOSE SUBJECTS THE SUN NEVER SETS, THE GREAT DON PHILIP OF SPAIN, AGAINST THE DUTCH AND THE FRENCH
the thrice renowned
Earl of Bodwel
Colonel Sempill
Colonel Boyd

ARTS

very next day to refresh his brains, as he said, went to the Louvre in a buff-suit, more like a favourite of Mars than one of the Muses' minions; where in the presence of the Court and great ladies, he carryed away the ring fifteen times on end, and broke as many lances on the Saracen. The picture of Crichton, with a lance in one hand and a book in the other, is to be seen in the bedchambers and galleries of most of the great men of the Italian nation, where he was murdered in a fitte of jealous rage by the Prince of Mantua; and most of the young ladies likewise, that were anything handsome, had his effigies in a little oval tablet of gold hanging twixt their breasts, for many yeeres that intermammilionary ornament being held as necessary for the setting forth of their accoutrements, as either fan, watch or stomacher.

DOCTOR SEATON: made Professor of the Roman Colledge of Sapience by Pope Urbane the eighth, but falling at ods with the Jesuites, he retired to France where I have seen him circled about at the Louvre with a ring of French Lords and gentlemen, the greatest clerics and churchmen, the aldest barristers and advocates of the Parlement of Paris, all in perfect silence the better to congest the pearls of discernment falling from his lips into the treasuries of their judgements. Le Sieur de Balzac, who for eloquence was esteemed to surpass Cicero, presented to Seaton a golden pen, in token of his infinitely greater supereminency in

CONTRA SCOTIAM

Scotland would produce, for philosophy, astronomy, natural magick, poesie and other such like faculties, as able men as ever were:

Duns Scotus *
Sacroboscus *
Reginaldus Scotus *

and other compatriots of these three great Scots, whose name I do not insert in the roll of the rest, because they flourished before 1600. Only one Scot; of able intellectual parts, that I ever knew, had his sound mind unmobilated by money, and that through the corruptions of courtiership: Sir William Alexander, afterward Earl of Sterlin, who made an insertion to Sir Philip Sidney's *Arcadia*, and composed several tragedies. He was born a poet, and aimed to be a king; therefor would he have his royal title from King James, who was born a king and aimed to be a poet; so Jamie Steward bestows on him the sovereignty of that tract of polar ice and rock recently named Nova Scotia. Had they stopped there, it had been well; but like King Arthur, he must have his knights, though not limited to so small a number. Whosoever wished to be a gentleman and gave King Sterlin one hundred and fifty Sterling pounds, could at once flaunt the orange riban to testify he was Knight Baronet. The King nevertheless, not to stain his royal dignity by awarding honour to meer wealth, also gave them land for their money at six pence an acre, which could not be thought very dear, considering how pretilly in the respective legal parchments of disposition they were described as fruitful corne land, watered with pleasant rivers running alongst most excellent and spacious meadows; and if they lacked an abundance of oaken

PRO SCOTIA

ARMS

Colonel Lodowick Lindsay Earl Crauford, also a Scottish Colonel whose name is upon my tonge's end and yet I cannot hit at it; he was not a souldier bred yet for many years he bore charge in Flanders under Spinola. In his youthood he was so strong and stiff a Presbyterian, that he was the onely man Scotland made choice of, to be the archprop and main pillar of that government; but waining in his love of the Presbytery as he waxed in knowledge of the world, from a strict Puritan he became the most obstinate rigid Papist that ever there was on this earth. It is strange that I cannot remember his title; he was a lord I know, nay more, he was an earle, aye that he was, and one of the first of them. Ho now! Peascods on it, Crauford Lodi Lindsay puts me in mind of him; it was the old Earle of Argile, this present Marquis of Argile's father; that was he. That was the man.

FOR THE THIRTEENTH LEWIS OF FRANCE AGAINST THE DUTCH AND SPANISH
Lord Colvil
Lord James Douglas
Sir William Hepburn
Hepburn of Wachton
(Had these survived the days wherein they successively dyed the bed of honour, they had all of them been made Marischals of France)
Sir Andrew Gray
Sir John Seatoun
Sir John Fularton
Sir Patrick Moray

ARTS

that art. Many learned books were written by this Seaton in the Latin tongue, which, to speak ingenuously, I cannot hit upon.

HUGO DE GRIEVE: whose nativity in a dank border-town engirdled by many torrents so impressed his mind with the axiom *everything flows*, that he firmly fixed himself in those operations by which mind is changed, and made some 32 books of verses wherein antique and demotic tongues, political rhetoric and all the natural sciences are by violence yoked together to deny, prophetically simulataneously and retroactively, every conclusion he arrives at, excepting this: that the English are a race of Bastards. He thus engendered a manifold of grandly meaning sentences without system, for the which I did honour him, until compelled to bring against him a suit-at-law for his barefaced plagiarism of my LOGOPANDECTEISON, which suit requires but the enscrieving and publishment of the said LOGOPANDECTEISON to have this scheming and scurrilous succubus of other men's genius brought low, and costs awarded to pursuer.

CAMERON, AGNAMED THE WALKING LIBRARY: who being renowned through all the provinces of France for his universal reading, took occasion to set forth an excellent folio volume in Latin intituled Bibliotheca Movens.

CONTRA SCOTIAM

groves in the midst of very fertil plains, it was the scrivener or writer's fault; for his majestie ordered that, on the receipt of three thousand Scots marks, there should be no deficiency in quantity or quality, in measure or goodness of land, with here and there most delicious gardens and orchards and whatever else would be content their fancies, as if they were purchasing ground in the Elysian Fieldes, or Mahumet's Paradise. And if the clerk writing the charter, on receipt of some small coin to himself, slipped in a thousand more acres than was agreed at first, he cared not. At last, when some two or three hundred Knights had among them purchased several million Neo-Caledonian acres, confirmed to them and their for ever under the great seal (the affixing thereof cost each of them but thirty pence more) finding that the company was not like to become more numerous, he bethought of a course more profitable for himself, and, without the advice of his Knights (who represented both his houses of parliament, clergy and all) like an absolute King indeed disponed heritably to the French both the dominion and property of the whole continent of that kingdom of Nova Scotia for a matter of five or six thousand pounds English.

And this is a true example of that charm, fascination, inchantment and infernal assistance of men's imaginations by the gold of the Spanish conquerors, which makes many believe they may become magnates and grandees with no more labour than is needed to purchase a royal patent, fit a ship, navigate a passage, and plunder an astonished people by the power of artilleriendal assault. The followers of such adventurers may indeed reap good harvest

PRO SCOTIA

ARMS

Colonel Erskin
Colonel Lindsay
Colonel Morison
Colonel Hume
Colonel Mouatt
Colonel Liviston
Colonel Leslie
Colonel Forbes

FOR VENICE AGAINST THE GERMAN EMPEROR
Colonel Dowglas
Colonel Balantine
Colonel Lyon
Colonel Anderson

FOR VENICE AGAINST THE TURK
Captain William Scot,
vice-Admiral of the Venetian fleet, the onely renowned bane and terror of Mahometan navigators, for he did so tort and ferret them out of all the creeks of the Adriatic gulph that many of them, for fear of him, did turn land-souldiers or drovers of caravans.

****

From this list I have omitted all mention of gallant Scottish duelists such as Francis Sinclair, natural son to the late Earle of Catnes, who performed this notable ex-ploit in the city of Madrid: Eight Spanish noblemen being suspicious of Sinclair's too intimate familiarity with a kinswoman of theirs, did altogether set on him at one time, which unexpected assault moved him to say:
"Gentlemen, I doubt not but you are valiant men, therefor my entreaty is that you take it as becomes men of valour, by trying your fortune against mine, one at a time."

ARTS

MASTER ALEXANDER ROSSE: who hath written manyer books, both in good Latine and English, prose and verse, than he hath years, and whose Poeticus proveth, that the Pagan Gods are but names for the separated faculties of our TRIUN GOD, so that Christians need no longer lie under the reproach which the Oriental nations fixe upon us, of seeing with but one eye, for Master Rosse hath so vindicated in matter of knowledge our Western World, as to make the Chineses, by force of reason, of whose authority above them they are not ashamed, glad to confess that the Europaeans, as well as themselves, look out of both their eyes and have no blinkered minds.

MELVIL: who has six hundred ducats a year, for translating into Latine or Spanish, some hundred few books of these six hundred great volumes, taken by Don Juan de Austria at the battel of Lepanto from the Great Turk, which now lie in the great library of that magnifick palace the Escorial near Madrid.

DEMPSTER: who is chiefly recommended to posterity for his Latin index of five thousand illustrious Scots from the earliest ages to the last liver whereof dyed above fifty years since.

CHALMERS: bishop of Neems.

CHIZUM: bishop of Vezun.

CONTRA SCOTIAM

abroad, but only by digging and planting, (in fear of the natives they have dispossessed) what could be cultivated at home with better advantage to themselves and their country. It is the greater readiness of Scottishmen to adventure abroad, rather than develop what we have, that is our nation's ruin. By which I am reminded, that I have a certain harbour or bay, in goodness equal to the best in the world, adjacent to a place, which is the head town of the Shire; the shire and town being of one and the same name with the harbour or bay; whose promontaries on each side, vulgarly called Souters, from the Greek word σωτηρες, that is to say, Salvatores or Savers, from the safety that ships have when once they are entred within them, having had that name imposed on them by Nicobulus the Druyd, who came along with my predecessor Alypos in the dayes of Eborak, that founded York some 698 years before Ferguse the First; at which time that whole country, never before discovered by the Greeks, was named Olbion by the said Alypos.
This harbour, in all the Latine maps of Scotland, is called *Portus Salutis*; by reason that ten thousand ships together may within it ride in the greatest tempest that is as in a calm by vertue of which conveniency some exceeding rich men, of five or six several nations, masters of ships, and merchant adventurers, promised to bring their best vessels and stocks for trading along with them, and dwell in that my little town with me, who should have been a sharer with them in their hazard, and by subordinating factors to accompany them in their negotiations, admitted likewise for a partner in their profit and advantages.

PRO SCOTIA

ARMS

The Spaniards pretending to be men of honour, swore by an oath made on their crossed swords that they should not faile therein; in a word, conform to paction, they fell to it, and that most cleverly, though with such fatality on the Spanish side, that in less than the space of half an hour he killed seven of them apassyterotically, that is, one after another; gratifying the eighth, to testifie that he had done no wrong to the rest, with enjoyment of his life. As for pricking down here those other Scots renowned for valour and for literature, I hold it not expedient; for the sum of those named doth fall so far short of the number omitted, that apportioned to the aggregate of all who in that nation since the year 1600, have deserved praise in arms and arts, jointly or disjunctly, either at home or abroad, it would bear the analogy, to use a lesser definite for a greater indefinite, of *a subnovitri-partient* eights; that is to say, in plain English, the whole being the dividend, and my nomenclature the divisor, the quotient would be nine, with a fraction of three-eights; or yet more clearly, as the proportion of 72 to 625. But let me resume the account of my especial self by inditing:

ARTS

TYRY: assistant to the General of the Jesuites, and second person in that vast ecclesiastical republick, which reaches beyond the territories of all Christian kings to cover the continent of the World.

KING JAMES 6th AND 1st: History cannot afford us (Solomon and Alfonso of Aragon being laid aside) any monarch who was near as learned as he, as is apparent by that book in folio intituled, "King James His Works"; despite that peevish remark by the young king's old tutor, the republican pedagogue George Buchanan, that the king's faculty as a scholar, equalled his notorious deficiency as a souldier, since by skelping the arse of the Lord's annoynted the best he (Buchanan) had been able to make of poor Jamie was a pedant, as the Royal Steward lacked substance to shape anything better.

PRO ME

Deeds Armorial: In my early years, to ripen my brains for eminent undertakings, my heart gave me courage to adventure through foreign climes, wherein it thrice befell me to enter the lists against men of three several nations, to vindicate my native country

CONTRA ME

Deeds Armorial: Nothing, in that never was I in any fight defeated, though sometimes obliged to withdraw before overwhelming power, as hath befallen Scipio Africanus, Robert de Bruis and Adolphus Maleus Caesarorum.

CONTRA SCOTIAM

By which means, the foresaid town of Cromarty, for so it is called, in a very short space, would have easily become the richest of any within threescore miles thereof; in the prosecuting of which designe, I needed not to question the hearty concurrence of Aberdeen, which, for honesty, good fashions and learning, surpasseth as far all other cities and towns in Scotland, as London doth for greatness, wealth, and magnificence, the smallest hamlet or village in England.

Nor was I suspicious of any considerable opposition in that project from any town, save Invernasse alone, whose magistrates, to the great dishonour of our whole nation, did most foully evidence their own baseness in going about to rob my town of its liberties and privileges.

Yet was that plague of flagilators, wherewith my house was infected, so pernicious to that purpose of mine, that some of them lying in wait, as a thief in the night, both for my person and means, cannibal-like to swallow me up at a breakfast; they did, by impediting the safety of my travelling abroad, arresting whatever they imagined I had right unto, inhibiting others from bargaining, most barbarously and maliciously cut off all the directory preparatives I had orderly digested for the advantage of a business of such main concernment, and so conducible to the weal of the whole Island, to the great discouragement of those gallant forreners; of which that ever-renowned gentilman for wit and excellencie in many good parts, Sir Phillip Vernati by name, was one; who being of Italian parents, by birth a Dutchman, and by education expert in all the good languages of the Christian world, besides the

PRO SCOTIA

PRO ME

from the slanders wherewith they had aspersed it. God was pleased so to conduct my fortune that, after I had disarmed them, they in such sort acknowledged their error, and the obligation they did owe me for sparing their lives, that in lieu of three enemies that were I acquired three constant friends both to myself and my nation, which by several gallant testimonies they did later prove, in many occasions. Thus I outdid the Gasconad of France, Rodomontad of Spaine, Fanfaronad of Italy, and Bragadochio brags of all other countries, who could no more astonish my invincible young heart, than could the cheeping of a mouse a bear robbed of her whelps. Then in the May month of 1639, when 1200 Covenanters of the North assembled at Turrif, I with a loyal force of but 800, did altogether repel, route and disperse them, with no advantage on our side but complete surprize and four brass cannon. Thus was quelled the first armed mustering against the monarchy since Mary Steward fled Langside field. Thus issued the first battel in this most uncivil War. Would to Jehovus the loyalists had done so well since.

Deeds Minerval: (completed and potential) whereby my name will resound to the end day of alltime, by reason of, these shining books which will work huge reformation, transformation and revolution in every branch of human tecknics, politics and thought.

1. EPIGRAMS: DIVINE AND MORAL

The Muses never yet inspired

CONTRA ME

Deeds Minerval: Lacking Scots printers my texts amass till convoyed South.

CONTRA SCOTIAM

Arabick and Sclavonian tongues, wherein he surpassed, had a great ascendent in counsel over all the adventrous merchants of what nation soever; whereof, without the foresaid lets of those barbarous obstructors, some by all appearance had so concurred with me, that by their assistance I would ere now have banished all idleness from the commons, maintained several thousands of persons of both sexes, from the infant to the decrepit age, found employments proportionable to their abilities, bastant to afford them both entertainment and apparel in a competent measure; educing from various multitudes of squameary flocks of several sizes, colours and natures, netted out of the bowels of the ocean both far and neer, and current of fresh water streams, more abundance of wealth than that whole country had obtained by such a commodity these many yeers past; erecting ergastularies for keeping at work many hundreds of persons in divers kindes of manufactures; bringing from beyond sea the skillfull'st artificers could be hired for money, to instruct the natives in all manner of honest trades; perswaded the most ingenious hammermen to stay with me, assuring them of ready coin for whatever they should be able to put forth to sale; addicting the abjectest of the people to the servitritiary duty of digging for coals and metals, of both which in my ground there is great appearance, and of the hitting of which I doubt as little, as of the lime and freestone quarries hard at my house of late found out, which have not been these two hundred years remarked; induced masters of husbandry to reside amongst my tenants, for teaching them the most profitable way, both for the manner and the season, of tilling, dig-

PRO SCOTIA

PRO ME

sublimer conceptions in a more refined style, than is to be found in the accurate strains of these most ingenious Epigrams. Printed in London, 1641.

2. **THE TRISSOTETRAS**

Wherein I set forth, with all possible brevity and perspecuity, orthogonospherical and loxogonospherical tables which permit the easy application of Neper's logarythms to every dimension of space and any volume of bulk, and by resolving those cranklings, windings, turnings, involutions and amfractuosities belonging to the equisoleary system, I facilitate and reform the work of all artists in pleusiotechny, poliechryology, cosmography, geography, astronomy, geodesy, gnomonicks, catoptricks, dioptricks, fortification, navigation and chiaroscuro. Printed in London 1645, last week.

3. **TTANTOXPONOXANON**

A peculiar promptuary of time, wherein is recorded the exact lineal descent of the VRQUARTS since the beginning of motion. Unprinted.

4. **ISOPLASTFONIKON**

Demonstrating the cubification of the sphere through Pythagorean acousticks, whereby a well-tuned fiddle or taut kettledrum may be perswaded to yield the exact side of a squared solid equal in volume to any symmetrical rotundity whatsoever. Unprinted.

5. **FOINIXPANKROMATA**

or, the Rainbow-Phoenix, wherein is counter-blasted Signor Galileo's contention that colour is meer sensation, by proving that

CONTRA SCOTIAM

ging, ditching, hedging, dunging, sowing, harrowing, grubbing, reaping, threshing, killing, milling, baking, brewing batling of pasture ground, mowing, feeding of herds, flocks, horse and cattel; making good use of the excrescences of all these; improving their herbages, dayries, mellificiaries, fruitages; setting up the most expedient agricolary instruments of wains, carts, slades, with their several devices of wheels and axle-trees, plows and harrows of divers sorts, freezes, winders, pullies, and all other manner of engines fit for easing the toyl and furthering the work; whereby one weak man, with skill, may effectuate more than fourty strong ones without it; and leaving nothing undone that, by either sex of all ages, might tend to the benefit of the labourer in applying most industriously the outmost of their

PRO SCOTIA

PRO ME

the boundless prime matter of the universe is not the Water of Thales, Air of Anaximenes, Fire of Heraclitus, Atoms of Democritus or Quadressential Porridge of Trismegistus, but white light; that gold, green, azure, deep-sea blue, violet, purple, crimson and pink are light in decay; that self-interpenetrating circulation of colours through the Macrocosm creates, not just its appearance, but its tangible, fructible, frangible bodies; and that darkness is light travelling backward too fast to be catched by the eye. Unprinted.

6. **ALETHALEMBIKON**
or the True Alembick, demonstrating that a quincunxial chamber of reflecting plates, mathematically disposed, will enable to be wrought, at no cost, identical solid duplicates of any object laid therein, by the admission to it, at a point on the globe's equator, of a beam of midsummer noonday sun. Unprinted.

7. **THE HEROICK DEEDS AND SAYINGS OF THE GOOD GARGANTUA AND HIS SON PANTAGRUEL**
a translation from the French, which, since their lexicons hold but three quarter of the words we can use, will be one third longer than the original, as if Doctor Rabelais had

CONTRA SCOTIAM

vertue to all the emoluments of country farms or manual trades. I would likewise have encouraged men of literature, and exquisite spirits for invention, to converse with us for the better civilizing of the country, and accommoda-ting it with a variety of goods, whether honest, pleasant, or profitable; by vertue whereof, the profes-sors of all sciences, liberal disciplines, arts active and factive, mechanick trades, and whatever concerns either vertue or learning, practical or theoretick, had been cher-ished for fixing their abode in it. I had also procured the resi-dence of men of prime faculties for bodily exercises, such as riding, fencing, dancing, military feats of mustering, imbattleing, handling the pike and musket, the art of gunnery, fortification, or any-thing that in the wars belongeth either to defence or assault, volting, swimming, running, leaping, throwing the bar, playing at tennis, singing, and fingring of all manner of musical instruments, hawking, hunting, fowling, angling, shooting, and what else might writ in English, with my resources. Not begun yet. 8. I recall not what this is. C o c k s crow, sky pales, I m a y n o w sleep a little per-hap-s

any way conduce to the accomplishment of either body or minde, enriching of men in their fortunes, or promoving them to deserved honours.

All these things, and many more, for export of the commodities of this Island to the remotest regions of the earth, import from thence of other goods, or transport from one forraign nation to another, and all for the conveniency of our British inhabitants, I would undoubtedly have ere now provided to the full, in being a Maecenas to the sckolar, a protector of the trades-man, and up-holder of the yeoman, had not the impetuosity of the usurer overthrown my resolutions, and blasted my aims in the bud.

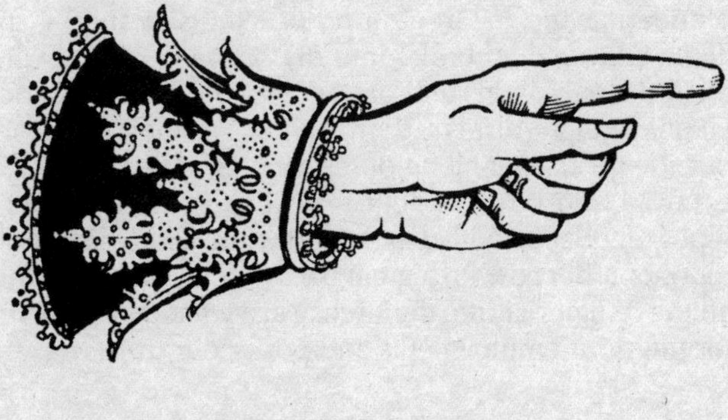

13 NOVEMBER 1651: IN CUSTODY OF CAPTAIN ALSOP, THE TOWER OF WINDSOR CASTLE.

Logopandecteison is the name of that great work which, in my weary state, I could not recall, it being too large and near for recognition, as a man counting the chief features of his lands omits the tower he surveys them from, though that the chiefest feature of all.

2 This diurnal or day-book returns to me by the magnanimity of Master Braughton, an officer of Colonel Pryde's regiment, who, perceiving it in the street-gutter of Worcester among a mixter-maxter of other papers, in a drizzling rain which had stuck the loose sheets fast to the ground, near by to a heap of seven and twenty dead men lying on one another, commanded that a servant of his take all up, cleanse off the mire and keep safe for his circumspection.

3 The separate sheets prove to be but a parcel of my preface to the Logopandecteison, over a thousand other manuscript pages of the grammar and lexicon, with mathematical, chronological, mythological, metaphysical and dialectical commentaries, all annotated for the printer, having been pillaged, pilfered, ravaged, robbed and rifled from seven large portmantles full of precious commodity, in the lodging I took at the house of Mr. Spilsbury, a very honest confectioner with a very good wife.

4 He learned that while the puritan souldiery were plundering the town, a string of exquisite sharks and clean shavers had broke into my baggage and, seizing the red cloaks, buff suits, armaments and other such rich chafer, straight dispersed my writings to their camerads outside for packeting up of raisins, figs, dates, almonds, caraway and other sweetmeat, while some did kindle pipes of tobacco with a great part while some did kindle pipes of tobacco with a great part thereof, and threw out all the remainder into the street, save what they reserved for inferiour employments and posteriour uses.

5 Of the dispersedly rejected bundles of paper most were gathered up by grocers, druggists, chandlers, pie-makers, or such as stood in need of any cartapaciatory utensil, to the utter undoing of the writing thereof, both in matter and order; so Master Braughton (who hath no cause to ly) doth inform me.

6 I lay for some hours in great dumps, though less sad than most of the Scots beaten, but not killed, in Worcester fight, for many thousands have been driven like cattel to London, and there inclosed in little room and treated with great rigour, many perishing for want of food, or dieing of all diseases, the survivors to be shipped to the American plantations and there sold as slaves. Is this not a new thing in warfare between Christian nations who talk with the same or similar tongues? But I am used with the clemency due to my rank, and talent, and the ransom they will get by me, though not called ransom, sequestration.

7 Since my last (and first) entry much has passed. The First Charles Steward has been uncapited to the middle bone in his neck. The rump of the Parliamentary party has proclaimed England a *public thing*, a *res publica*, a *republick*. For two years the Second Charles hath been King of Scotland only, and would be king there still, had not the Presbyterial part of his subjects decided to prove their faith in God by fighting the Cromwel army without their King's advice, without help from allies who worship God differently, without obedience to their own general; for against orders they deserted a superior for an inferior place and engaged an out-manoeuvred enemy on such bad ground that the Almighty (who will not tolerate for ever those who scorn his Angel, commonsense) let them be slaughtered in great numbers. From which they drew this lesson, that their faith was not sufficiently pure. At last the King had no other course, but to leave Sterling, his securest Capital, and march upon England, there to recruit the saner support of the English Royalists. But at Worcester these did not join us. The Royal party in

Brittain is utterly routed. The King escaped abroad. I did not. Perhaps Brittain will remain a *public thing* till the end of time.

8 It is growing clear to me that my future fame may be insured by this diurnal, if from now forward I each day indite in it a record of all public doings which reach my ear, or even eye, for my imprisonment is not strict. My parole allows me to wander some distance, and when I am moved to the Tower of London I will be within what is now, by grace of the army rather than God or parlement, the govourning Capital of the four ancient Kingdoms of England, Wales, Ireland and Scotland, with prospering colonies in Amerigo Vespucci-land and many embattled trade-forts in the Barbadoes, East India, Malagask, Africa and Europe.

9 Who, loving knowledge, would not give all the wealth they possess, yea, and pawn their family inheritance till the end of time, to recover from the shades and hold in their hand, a daily record of things done, seen and heard by a percipient citizen of Periclean Athens, Caesarial Rome or any other heroickal time? How much more wealth would we give for such a diurnal in the manuscript of a Euclid, Vergil or Roland of Roncevalles?

10 Let me start, therefor, by stating that this morning

MIDSUMMER EVE 1653: THE TOWER OF LONDON

This day concluded much. The Chief Secretary of State arrived soon after the board of this chamber had, by my command, been decked with wine, baked meats, pickles, fruit and other viands suited to a sckolastic colloquial symposiasmos, for his greek is not much inferiour to my own, though I exceed him utterly in power of invention, for like all politicians he is no philomathet, so cannot proconceive and concert well-measured symplasmical forms; in common english, his imagination is fanatick not poetick.

2 He entered to me peeringly, having the use of a single eye, and that a failing one, yet I saw it allowed him enough light to admire my figure, and this admiration I was able, in part, to return, for although neither of us very small men, we both lack that redundant height and girth which gross multitudes think commonplace: his manner also was pleasingly jocund and his voice familiar to my ear, for he pronounced his R, *littera cannina*, the latin dog-letter, extreme hard as we Scots do, a certain signe of a Satyricall Wit.

3 We furthered our amity by also discovering, beneath radically opposed views of church and state, an equal hatred of Presbyters (*press-biters*, he called them; I did not disclose that the like witticism had occurred to myself) I because of the malign difluence these coine-coursing collybists have cast upon my best endeavours, and because they have betrayed two kings, one of them unto death; he because they have ignored or saught to censor his proposals to replace universities by simple, sensible foundations, and to make divorce of marriages an easy thing entirely dependant on the husband's will, and also because (turning traitour to their own treason) they opposed the monarch's juridicial apokakefalization.

4 He had himself been offered (I gathered) the office of state licenser of all Brittish bookes, and might be obliged to accept that post to prevent it falling into worse hands; though he was determined to pass without question every book submitted to him, excepting such as would foster naked libidinal lewdness and atheism.

5 He then turned the talk neatly to my own published Introduction to the Universal Language, prologueing his remarks with a disclaim, that he spoke as a publick officer; whereat I girded my intellects for a cruxiferous encounter.

6 I began by asserting that all men originally shared the same language, since mankind had been made in one place at one time: he nodded agreement.

7 And before I could say more, recited verbatim the first nine verses of the eleventh chapter of Genesis, first in the Hebrew, then (because he said, it contained no very glaring innacuracie) in that translitteration authorized for the press by King Jamie in 1608, the year of my birth.

> *And the whole earth was of one language, and of one speech.*
>
> **2** *And it came to pass, as they journeyed from the east, that they found a plain in the land of Shinar; and they dwelt there.*
>
> **3** *And they said one to another, Go to, let us make brick, and burn them thoroughly. And they had brick for stone, and slime had they for mortar.*
>
> **4** *And they said, Go to, let us build us a city and a tower, whose top may reach unto heaven; and let us make a name, lest we be scattered abroad upon the face of all the earth.*
>
> **5** *And the Lord came down to see the city and the tower, which the children of men builded.*
>
> **6** *And the Lord said, Behold, the people is one, and they have all one language; and this they begin to do: and now nothing will be restrained from them, which they have imagined to do.*
>
> **7** *Go to, let us go down, and there confound their language, that they may not understand one another's speech.*
>
> **8** *So the Lord scattered them abroad from thence upon the face of all the earth: and they left off to build the city.*
>
> **9** *Therefor is the name of it called Babel; because the Lord did there confound the language of all the earth: and from thence did the Lord scatter them abroad upon the face of all the earth.*

8 I hid my surprize, by suavely thanking him for anticipating me, and asking, How God had worked to confound the first speech he had given men to use? Was the Latin Secretary of the British Republick one of those who believed Jehovah had miraculously and simultaneously infused, into the Babel-builders' brains, entirely differing sets of grammars and vocabularies?

9 He answered saying, No; he agreed with the Rabins, that the first confusion was of accent meerly, the foundation speech of these accents not deeply changing, until by dispersal around all the earth, the scattered nations of men were divided one from another by almost impassible distances of desert wilderness, mountain chains and nearly non-navigable seas: for each nation encountering different soyls, plants, creatures and climates, was compelled to devize new tools, arts and oeconomies to cultivate them, new sciences to understand them, new words to describe them, so that in time, lacking all written records, the old verbal tokens of our common oeconomy on Shinar's plain were by new speech utterly ousted and submerged, leaving one accurate account of the paleological confusion among a people living near the place where it happened, the rest retaining but foggy legends of a primitive catastrophe.

10 Then it behoves us to enquire (said I) how God, operating within one single city-state on Shinar's plain, came to stunt that great work by diversity of accent; for you and I are rational not supersititious men; we know God works His changes on earth by the agency of nature, his deputy magistrate, who in men is called human nature: what fact of human nature made men inarticulate to one another, who were united in a great project which, while certainly presumptuous, would otherwise have succeeded?

11 To this he replied, *The desire for supremacy over their own kind*.

12 I had intended, by a skilled deployment of Socratic questioning, to educt from his own lips conclusions which were precisely my own; his answer was so unexpected that I responded to it with open mouth and arched eyebrows, which he interpreted as an invitation to explicate.

13 We may only understand these nine verses rightly, said he, if we remember two things: firstly, that when Jehovah said, *Nothing will be restrained from men, which they have imagined to do,* He was speaking ironically to his Angels, for although the Almighty had not read the astronomy of Signor Galileo, He well knew the Grandeur of the Heavens He had Builded, and knew that they were far beyond the reach of any earthly construction; had the tower rizen one or two short miles above the surface of the plain it would have entered a region of air too rarified to support human nourishment; if this tremendous irony is forgot, then God's words sound like the peevish pronuncimentos of a meer absolute Monarch, who dreads that his people will usurp his privelege.

14 But the knowledge that the tower would never reach Heaven belonged to more than God, it belonged to the architect, Nimrod, that valiant warrior who (Moses tells us) was the first conqueror to substitute the monarchical yoke for the patriarchal independancy of the nomadic tribes; for had Nimrod believed Heaven could really be reached by a tower, he would have commenced to build, not on a flat plain, but on the summit of Ararat, or any other toplofty peak.

15 Like all overweening edifices, the tower was devized to raize a pack of lords and their followers above the heads of the commons; who were perswaded to support the superiour stance by the usual publick lie: that the overexaltation of some would in time lead to the benefit and happiness of all; but the building itself was the happiness at which the imaginations of the builders aimed, for as they gazed out across the heads of their fellows, they felt themselves to be gods; and this was the false heaven, this the bad eminence, which the True God of Heaven came down to confound, and did so most mercifully, out of the builders' mouths.

16 For men who overmaster their own kind cannot long continue to deceive and servilize them without the cloak of a different language, by the cause that knowing little about the handling and making of solid things, and their chiefest concern being management of those who do, their speech becomes a jargoning about bonds, monopolies, legal niceties, scholastick abstractions, ostentatious sophistry, flattery, backbiting, gossip about those positioned higher than themselves and contempt of those below.
17 At last they sound so different from the commoners as to be almost unintelligible to them, and vice-versa, and this provokes the just Nemesis of God.
18 For the less they understand the suffering cries from underneath, the harder they press, in their pursuit of wealth and eminence, upon the necks of those who feed, cloath and build for them; till in tame nations an utter civil collapse ensues, and in brave ones, a revolt.
19 The most notorious modern example of Babelonian enterprize (he said) was the newmade mosque of the Bishop of Rome, pretentiously lifted up to the Glory of God, but really to the glory of an immund impanative Papacy, the funds being raized by selling pardons for crimes not yet committed, to the rich and poor sinners of Germany; which act soon split all Christendom into four times as many Christian sects as there are Christian governments.
20 He also predicted, that if the rumour hath substance, that young Lewis the French Autocrat will wall off the discontents of his people by building, outside Paris, the biggest Regal dwelling since Nero's Golden House in Rome, then Lewis will one day perish in the same schismatick cataclysm that befel Nimrod, the Roman Caesars, and the Papal Catholicks.
21 I thank God, he concluded, that the British, at least, have proved they are not tame; and placing a finger on one side of his neck, he drew it rapidly across to the other.

22 I told him that, as a Royalist and a Scottish Knight-Baron, I could not concur in the levelling tendency of his remarks, but certainly, our habit of cultivating the recognition of our kind by a speech which makes us unintelligible to most of them, is a paradox as notorious as our habit of seeking peace by multiplying the instruments of warfare.

23 Every trade and profession fortifies its power in the state by turning its mastery into a mystery, and cultivating a jargon which is never fully disclosed to the uninitiated.

24 Even under the present Commonwealth the sckolars and grammarians, whose duty it is to increase the national stock of wisdom (that is to say, intelligible thought) so entrench and fortify themselves behind recondite polysyllabilification, that they hardly understand each other, and mean nothing to the soldier who defends them or the ploughman who grows their bread; and some such mystification must, indeed, have undermined Nimrod's Colloseum, and scattered the first nation abroad.

25 But, said I, since that first broadcasting of mankind some 3870 years ago, two events have transformed the faith and renewed the hope of every well-informed soul: Eternal Goodness, incarnate in Christ Jesus, hath promised Heaven to whoever loves Him, and England, by embracing the experimental sciences of Lord Verulam and Galileo, is now foremost navigating nation in the whole aquaterrestrial sphere. (I might also have mentioned the Dutch, but was arguing *ad hominem*.)

26 The first event teaches us, that it is no longer impiety, but our sacred duty, to set our imaginations upon Heaven, and work for it, aye, even here upon this earth, providing we toyl by the light of Christian common sense: the second event makes plain, that the dispersed nations of men are becoming known to one another again, and in one or two centuries will all know each other completely, if the schisms between our separated tongues be sufficiently healed.

27 This healing can only be worked, by a universal and artificial language capable, by the conciseness and abundance of its expression, of involving the excellencies of every other; for in the passage of more than three millenia each language hath received so distinct a character, from the national genius of the many excellent spirits who have spoken and written therein, that it is now not possible to transliterate a profound truth from one speech to another, without somewhat changing the originarie sense: thus the philosophy of the Greek, which is the clearest language for subtile thought, loses as much by being expressed in Latin, the best language for distinct curt commandments, as in modern Italian, which is best for mellifluent courtierlike urbanity.

28 Only a multiverbal logopandocy can express without distorting the Dialogues of Plato, Laws of Justinian, Romances of Ariosto, and what is still to be retrieved from the languages of East and West Indians, the Civil Aztecs, Toltecs, Japaneses and Chineses.

29 I have devized this new language.

30 If widely adopted it will speed the traffick of human thought as greatly as modern navigation hath speeded traffick in commodities; for like the mercantile fleet which brings the potato, coffee, pepper, ginger, sugar and tobacco from the Americas to Europe and the Orient, and Oriental silks, muslins, tea and opium to the Americas and Europe, and European clocks, printing presses and gun-powder to everywhere, my new speech will carry the Christian message of salvation with the new European learning into pagan and heathen nations, while instructing us in the arts and sciences whereby these nations have also reconciled themselves to the Loving Wisdom of God and His Mighty Depute, Nature.

31 And truly, it is a harmonious dictat of Jehovus (he bit his lip, God, I swiftly added) that an inhabiter of Brittain should divize this language, for these Islands, which to Greeks were the last land and Ultima Thule before the arctick Pole, and to Romans an unruly colony on the verge of intransitive Ocean, is now the amphitheatrickal centre and meridial point between the cradeling paradise of mankind in the East, and those new Atlantises, some not found or founded yet, which await us in the West.

32 He aroze and paced the chamber before saying, that he himself was too inchanted by exotick learning not to be sympathically stirred by my over-splendid esteem of it, but he must open his heart to me with the words of Ecclesiastes, the preacher: *For in much wisdom is much grief: and he that increaseth knowledge increaseth sorrow*. Which truth is also to be evinced trifold from the oldest book of Holy Writ, form the life of individual men, and from universal history.

33 Genesis shows the Satanic snake flattering our first mother with falsely gorgeous hopes until, by the filching of an apple and breaking of a law, sin, sadness and new knowledge all enter the world together, the fall of man being a fall into knowledge of his own wilful divisions from Goodness.

34 Individual men are condemned to repeat this tragedy, for when suckling at the breast they will never be so purely happy again, as is testified by their blissful faces and tiny erected penes.

35 Universal history repeats this tragedy: the most notorious modern instance (which he viewed less complacently than myself) being Don Conquistadore's disclosure that the world held two more continents than the ancients knew, which uncovery brought slaughter, slavery and the Spanish inquisition to several proud nations; and to Europe so much silver and gold that the common currency hath ever since lost value, thus placing more and more oeconomies in the hands of usurors, and bringing also to Europe that disease of the generative root which makes men rot and bleed at the centre of their most poignant desires and pleasures.

36 He ended by saying, I am no friend of ignorance, but concur with Christ and Socrates in condemning as vainglory all knowledge that does not encourage right conduct, and since a language is but an instrument conveying unto us things good to be known, should a great linguist pride himself to have all the tongues that Babel cleft the world into, yet if he have not studied the solid things in them, as well as the words and lexicons, he is less truly learned than a yeoman or tradesman competently wise in his mother dialect only.

37 To this I responded courteously, that what he said was correct: words are indeed the instruments by which men denote things, but in being so used they become also the instruments by which we discover, and shape, and share our passions.

38 It follows from this, that a bad man cannot describe his reasons in good language without betraying himself.

39 It is inexactness of signification which permits false rhetoric to confuse causes with effects, accidents with intentions, abstracts with particulars, thereby provoking (to the corrupt rhetorician's advantage) misled passions in the heart of the malinformed hearer, who may also pass these wrong passions to others by parroting the ear-catching phrase whereby he first received them.

40 My new speech cannot be abused in this way; liars, using it grammatically, will at once contradict themselves or place within the listener's head ample evidence for their own speedy undoing; the greedy and vicious may not disguise their passions in it, and will be compelled to dissemble their vices under cloud of unsocial dumbness.

41 As for the variedly virtuous, the vocabulary of each will fluctuate to exactly fill the altering bounds of their experiential knowledge, growing more colourful or more austere as their passions wax or wane, but each passion clearly correlated by a thought-word to the unique state and thing which is its cause and aim.

42 Even fools will talk wisely in my new language for they will lack the materials to do otherwise.

43 He stared at me then asked sharply how such a language was devized?

44 By grammatical logarithms, said I, for each letter in my alphabet of twenty-five consonants and ten vowels, hath the value of a number linking it to a class of things (in the case of the consonants) or class of actions (in the case of the vowels).

45 The student of my language is taught very few and simple words, and these as example only, for he is given (to be metaphorickal) the bricks wherewith any word he needs may be builded, besides a grammar by which these words may be swiftly presented to the understanding of an instructed fellow.

46 This allows an educated man to bestow upon anything he encounters in the universe a name entirely different from any other, yet so intelligible that a well taught child of ten years can, from that name alone, even if it signifies a thing of which the child hath had no previous knowledge, imagine at once the form, colour, material, weight, bigness, usefulness or danger of the signified thing, and conceive it so accurately that, if the thing be artificial, the child can at once construct an accurate replica, provided only that he hath possession and mastery of the requisite tools.

47 This significant nomenclature would hugely benefit the art of wars; for if (as is the French custom) a new recruit received a *nom de guerre*, and it were in my new diction, so short a name as Kohudlitex or Palipugisk, whispered to a commander at a review of troops, would let him know a soldier's rank, regiment, age, birthplace, ancestry and character, and inable him to address that man with that familiarity which inspireth true loyaltie and devotion, when manifested by the nobility toward

****
****
******* *HERE A GREAT PART* *******
******* *OF THE MANUSCRIPT* *******
******* *HAS BEEN ATE BY MICE* ******
****
****

uttered in such nonsounding things as silence, or tears.

83 I asked him for a particular example of what he meant; he said he would relate a peculiar domestic circumstance.

84 My wife's family were of the Royal faction (said he, sighing) which I did not know at first, for her father owed mine money he was unwilling to repay, and for fear of a lawsuit (my father was a scrivener and understood the courts) he conversed only upon such topicks as did not promote disunion.

85 Indeed, my good wise father, knowing that I yearned toward matrimony, and that his debtor had a marriageable daughter, proposed an alliance which would sink the debt in a marriage settlement, which proposal was not unwelcome; so I was taken to the girl, and finding her meek mannered, without apparent defects of face and form (indeed, she was beautiful) I gladly bestowed myself upon her.

86 I was thirty-five years of age at that time, and since early youth, when it first dawned upon my developing soul that God had endowed it with no ordinary qualities, I had prepared myself to write a book which the world would not willingly let die, partly by reading everything great which preceeded me: yes, but also by the cultivation of fortitude, sobriety and chastity, for no good thing may emanate from a bad man.

87 I had conceived an Epic on the story of King Arthur, and was now sure I needed nothing to begin it but that well of constant sensible solace which is owed by a wife to the husband of her body.

88 What my wife brought me was silence; meek she had seemed and meek her manner remained, as befitted one not much more than half my age, but that meekness enclosed a cold sullen obdurate resistance which granted to my mind, heart and soul *nothing*.

89 Our conjoyned society was therefor mutual torture, but my torture was greater, for whether beside her or apart from her I desired her continually and hopelessly, whereas she found a little happiness in my occasional absences.

90 After a very few weeks she got a pretext for visiting her family in Oxfordshire, and refused to return from thence, being supported in this rebellion by her Royalist father and brothers (the King had just inaugurated a greater Rebellion by making Oxford his capital city, where his followers gloried in their first slight early triumphs).

91 Did I not find her departure a great relief? Oh no I did not.

92 My publick self did not suffer, I infused new vigour into my service to the Commonwealth, authoring in a brief space no less than four treatises on divorce, and one upon a general reform of education, and one defending the right of all to print what they willed: for the Pressbiters were snarling at my heels – I did but prompt the age to quit their clogs by the known rules of ancient liberty, when straight a barbarous noise environed me of owls and cuckoos, asses, apes and dogs.

93 I also saw off the press a complete collection of my short earlier poems, but this was in some sort a farewell to poesy: for despairing of all lawful domestic solace (for my advocacy of divorce had not perswaded the rational part of parlement to change the laws) I must despair of all honest manhood: so my plan to write a great Protestant Christian Epic which would cleanse the matrix of Civil Liberty and Justice from the obfuscs put upon it by the too voluptuous pens of courtly Ariosto, Spencer and Tasso, had become dross rubbish to me.

94 And I am certain poetry would have remained dead to me, had not my wife's family opened negotiations to return her, for Cromwel was begining to take the helm of state, and clearly the King would not now last long in England; so in tears she returned to me and –

95 He paused, himself overcome by tears.

96 Seeing that his flagon was emptied I refilled it, remarking softly that I was glad the Royal defeat had brought unity to one family at least.

97 Whatever produced those tears, (he cried suddenly aloud) her repentance, her wish to be one with me was genuine and complete, and these appealing tears, melting my very marrow, made me see that I had erred as greatly as she, for feeling unloved by her, my love of God had become without true content or gratitude: to me the Grandeur of the Creation, the Incarnation, Christ's Loving Mercy, the Resurrection of the Flesh had been meer words, meer empty words without her tearful return.

98 I asked him if he had not placed upon the domestic bond a greater weight than it could bear: he seemed not to hear that question.

99 And now (said he) though I will soon be as stone blind as Homer was, my mind's eye commands so wide a firmament that beneath it the matter of England, great though it be, appears as small a thing as would appear the matter of Troy, Rome and Jerusalem envisioned from the glowing Zenith by the Enthroned First Mover.

100 When time is ripe for it, my verse will do far more than illuminate the best essence of Thomas Malory's text, it will translate, clarify and augment the greatest and most truly Original Book in the Universe.

101 Such (said I) is my aim also, and I am thunderstruck to discover in the Puritan camp one who admires the work of Rabelais as greatly as I do; but speaking as a printed poet myself, I greatly doubt if verse is the fittest craft to convoy into English all the varied and witty exellencies of that

****
****
****
****
************* *MORE EXCISIONS HERE* *************
************* *BY TOOTH OF* *************
************* *EDITORIAL RODENTS* *************
****
****
****
****

algebra, which cannot yield the longitude; but by travelling the line of latitude, I would inevitably hit it.

144 He agreed that such a discovery must not only utterly transform and glorify myself who made it (if I made it) but equally transform and glorify whoever conversed with me afterward, and whoever afterward conversed with them &cetera, until by meer conversation the whole world was made again in God's image, every man, woman and child becoming (he sank here to a meckanical metaphor) a sounding pipe in the Creator's organ.

145 However (he lowered his voice still further) he knew that the Cabinet Council would by no reason clear my estate of its encumbrances, or finance such an expedition, and he hoped this news did not utterly gravel me, for though he had called here from curiosity rather than kindness, he now knew I was more than a meer madman, and his heart went out to me.

146 I walked to the end of the chamber and looked through the window to hide my face; having mastered myself I then turned, adopted the true stance of the acomplished rhetorician, and answered him in the words of my best epigram.

147 *We weep to breathe, when we to being come,*
After which Agon, all we gain is gift:
Air, sunlight, ground to stand on, yeah, disease
Which turns the soul to all from it bereft

By Adam's greed, pain showing what was, left.
Delight *without* disease *would stand us still.*
Hell *herds us hence to* Heaven: *ill antidotes ill.*

148 He nodded and smiled with one side of his mouth as if I had uttered a negligible truth, and I realized that I was again confronted by the jealousy of a fellow poetizer; but after a pause he said that the Council of State did not think that I greatly menaced the Commonwealth, and would soon admit me to perfect freedom.

149 I answered that such freedom would be worse than the vilest slavery, for it would leave me free to do nothing but grappel till death with clusterfist creditors and esurient Kirkists; I now had a vision of a nobler sprout than my family tree; if meerly released I must live to tend the latter with pain, vexation and ingratitude: it would be better if I could escape abroad, for in that case I would be at least welcomed by friends of the Steward in exile, and be some degrees nearer my Goal.

150 After long silence he said, that shortly, if the parole which for more than two years has permitted me to wander wheresoever I list within the liberties of London, were withdrawn, and Lieutenant Apsley knew that any omission to lock me in would be set down to an underling's negligible oversight, then what thereafter befel would reflect dishonour upon nobody; but I must know his words were idle, random, unintended and unlinked to any outcome, whether speculative or eventual. And he took his leave absently, as though pondering something.

26 MAY 1660:
IN THE ERSTWHILE SCHISMATIC PAPAL PALAZZO OF AVIGNON.

Into all lugs is verbal gold poured! The glib tongue of informed rumour dinneth it abroad that, lacking their Lord Paramount Protector (his tumble-down son Dick having proved a dwaibly mainstay) and the Model Army of the General Monck concurring, (the synagogical sanhedrins of the regicidal regiments glowring but holding aloof) the

London Lords and Commons hath done no less a thing than invite from his den in the Nether Lands, the Eighth Royal Steward and Second Steward Charlemagnus, to become this very day Instaurated, Instellarated and Incoronated upon the throne of the whole Brittanic League of Kingdoms and Commonweals! At which bruit fell I into such ecstasy of mirth that I was like to have departed this life. But my greatest attempt recalled me.

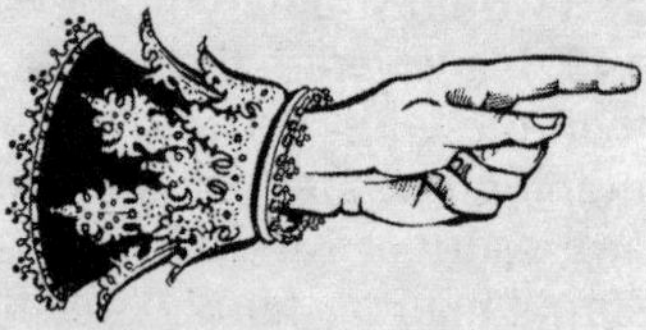

26 JUNE 1660:
IN THE STRADO CURTIZANO, VENICE.

The women of this republick leave a man as they discover him, but reduced.

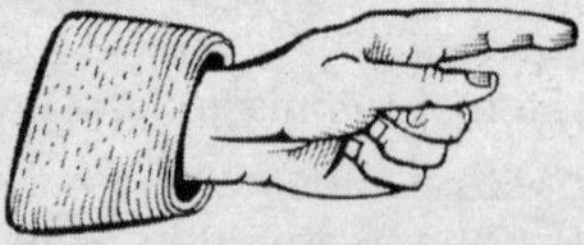

26 JULY 1660:
AT SEA BETWIXT BYZANTIUM
AND CRIM-T ART ARY.

A good wind, but misled by light. Cannot account for this phenomenon.

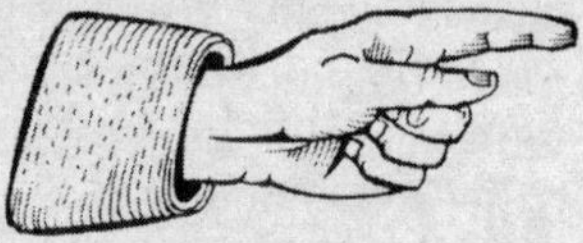

3 AY AE E OE 2 EOE E EIE EI I-AAY A AAA

ew ie i oo O ae i o oo ae a ie ae ea i e ei ie a aue e oe a eay a eei oe iaiaio ai uaio a aiio ee u ae a i e e I i ye aoui o a i eo ee I ae oui

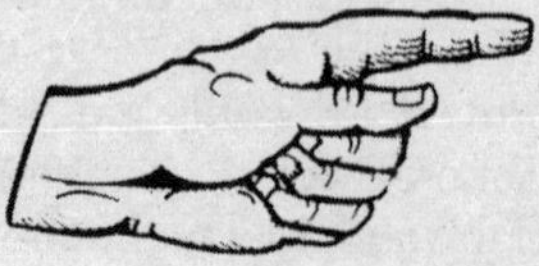

3 DS FTR TH CMT, 2 BFR TH CLPS: BTWXT CRM-TRTRY ND SMRKND. *179*

LOGO-PANDOCY

N wn s pr. ld wtr s nt gd. Wtr nd wn r qul n th vns. Whl hlf mtrs th thr hlf dcs. Wht flngs ls mgntn gns. Sbtrctn nd ddtn kp sch pc tht n th nd fnd mslf mntng t tht frst zr whr strtd cntng.

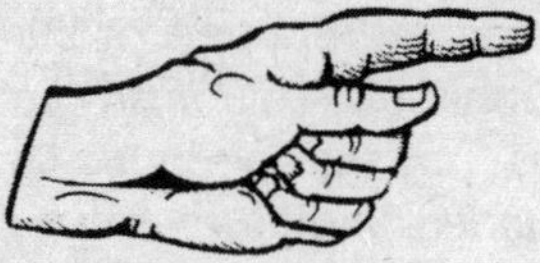

MORE THAN A YEAR AFTER THE FOREGOING: AMONG ROCKS.

My guide has absconded and I am at a loss to comprehend what the last four entries signify, in particular the previous two, which, were they not clearly indited in my own hand, would suggest the gibberish jottings of a dotard, drunkard or dizzard. Can I, in a moment of sublimity (which the Eternal Omniscience may wreak upon whom he listeth) have achieved that logopandocy whose Genesistical root Cromwell's latinist sectary agrees was split at Babelon, and I hold to be the concluding Revelation of the Holy Ghost operant through mankind generally, and myself especially? And have I since, like an overstrained athlete, lapsed so far below my best achievement as to find its memorials incomprehensible? Did I indeed, when fevered with ague on a foggy island in that wide marsh, write dialects of the tongues of the Cherubim and Seraphim? I doubt. I doubt. However cryptogrammed I am certain that a sentence of the archangelic tongue would twang my discernment with some resonance of pluterperfect Pythagorean jubilee, and these syllables, omnivowelant and omniconsonant, evoke a strangely familiar dulness. No water here, but I suck the dew which distillates between the fibrils of my cloak.

SOME YEARS AFTER THE FOREGOING: A NAMELESS TOWN.

I can describe this place but have no word for it. The speech of the people is so sing-song-sibilant that my ear cannot divide one syllable from another, nor detect the least root of any tongue, ancient or modern, within the recorded frontiers of Europe, Asia, Africa and those twin Columbias so unjustly cartographed and mappamundified as Amerigo Vespucciland. Their writing is no aid to understanding them, for it is hieroglyphical. The figure *man* I can easily distinguish, but always with some variant, viz. a hat, or the male member more protruberant, or the leggs a-jigging, or the posture prone, so that when I lay my finger on a figure and tilt my head and raize my eyebrows interrogatively, my host makes a sound which is each time completely novel. Maybe they do not use verb, adjective or adverb forms, but make a different noun for the same thing when it is differently engaged or favoured. We too use different noun-names for a man when he is of social rank, or tumescent, or gymnastickal, or dead. E.g. You are a presiding magistrate, you are a fornicator, you are a comedian, you are a corpse.

If the language of this people is indeed a linking of modified qualified nouns it is closer to my Logopandocy than any I have encountered. Do they speak the language used by Adam and Eve before Babel? No. Or if not no, they speak but a parcel of it, for the omnipotent Power who furnished us with these speech-tools of throat, tongue, roof of mouth, teeth and lips, must naturally have provided a language which, like a mighty choir, used these to the full; and though I could easier convey the jabber of these townsfolk by musical notation than by alphabet, their noise is all in the treble register.

The town covers a space of forty-four square miles, enclosed by a low earth embankment of no defensive value at all, but more of that anon. It is the rich metropolis of no nation, standing in a desert where three trade-routes meet, but industry and irrigation have given it an aspect that would keep me here, did pleasure and not a great enterprize drive me. In the early morning I climb up to the citadel, the only building with stone walls. It contains neither arsenal nor garrison, but is employed as a communal warehouse by the paper manufacturers. From here the town is a mass of trees and gardens with almost no houses to be seen, and I gaze across them at the distant but majestic mountains and wonder which divides me from my goal. As the heat of the day increases the dust of the plain beyond the rampart rizes up in a great cloud like a wall with nothing seen above it but the tips of a few snowy peaks. And then I descend to the town spread cool beneath the trees. But here again the names of things defeat me, for can they be called trees which lack bark, branches, twigs and leaves? The stems, though as tall as great elms, are pale, smooth and nearly translucid. A grove of five or six share the one root, but above ground slant and taper away from each other, each supporting a single great scrolled and ferny frond which casts a mild green shadow. Since it never rains here the groves are refreshed by melted mountain snow, brought hither through an aqueduct branching into slender canals floored with copper, furnished also with sluices which divert pure streams into every grove and garden. I have calculated there are no less than 2,000 places in the stone-paved streets and squares where iced water may be obtained free, sprouting freshly from fountains or served by ladles from earthenware reservoirs. These waterworks also contain bream, trout, eels, crayfish and prawns which are the best of their diet, adding savour to vegetables resembling oak, cedar and pine trees, but only a few inches high, and which must be softened by steaming in goblets of perforated bronze. The main manufactures of the place are saddles, swords, satin, silk, but paper most of all, every texture and thickness of paper from translucent tissue to waterproof-stout. Which brings me to their architecture.

Each building is founded on a well-paved stone platform containing a deep cellar. Above this, on a frame of poles, stands a pavilion with paper walls and roof. The visitor does not perceive their flimsiness at first as the women and children, especially in the poor districts, delight to paint these structures with the patterns of mosaic, and marquetry, and glazed tile inlay, so the town appears the richest in the world, though lacking that regularity and symmetry which exalts the architecture of Europe.

Soon after I arrived here a watcher on the citadel's single tower sounded a great gong which was repeated and re-echoed through every garden and grove. Quickly, but without panic, the squares and streets emptied as the citizens repaired to their homes, where they raized a stone in the foundation, descended to the cellar and sealed themselves in. My host pressed me to join him, but from curiosity I refused and went to my vantage point on the citadel where I sat crosslegged, the only man above ground. Presently, with a thunder of steady hooves, enters a band of tartar cavalry, ferociously visored, armoured and bannered, followed by a tribe of their women and children pushing great carts. The horsemen then ride in circles raizing a great yellyhoo, sounding horns and banging drums while their followers fill the carts with food from the market, goods from the workshops and such furniture and treasures as remain in the houses. The citadel was not attacked, though I was stared upon. My experience of men is, that the worst of them will seldom pester he who remains quiet, unafraid, keeps his weapons hid and offers no violence. When the carts were filled the cavalry set fire to the buildings and departed. The entire metropolis was burned to its foundations in a matter of minutes, after which the plundered citizens emerged and with great stoicism started sweeping away the cinders. I wondered at first why the invaders had not raided the cellars where the rich citizens store the best of their property; but realized this would delay the rebuilding of the city for a long time, giving the tartars less to plunder when they returned, which they do about twice a year. This style of warfare is therefor as civilized as ours. The only folk who lose everything by it are without riches stored below ground, and these folk, who belong to every country, are accustomed to losing. I have now seen the city raided three times, and always by the same tartar tribe. If these predators keep other plundering tribes from the place, then the whole region is more like a European state than the difference of language suggests.

Since the quantifying faculty of numbering and measuring is different from the naming faculty, I hoped that my skill as a geometer might make me useful and admired here, and so it proved. After witnessing the town's great conflagration I measured the platform for a house in my host's garden, which nobody was busy upon, and drew on a great scroll of good, smooth paper the plans and perspective elevations of a noble and symmetrical palace in the style of Whitehall, London, and which, using the local methods, could be erected in a few hours at the cost of a few shillings. I offered this to my host, who received it with expressions of pleasure which I could not doubt, and when I made designs for other buildings, drawing upon the memory of my extensive travels, and presented them to my host's colleagues and neighbours, they also laughed heartily and gave me gifts; so that I believed that in a week or two a nobler style of architecture would prevail, and the whole city have an aspect combining the best features of Aberdeen, Oxford, Paris, Florence, Venice and Imperial Rome. I found later, however, they had no conception of what my outline meant, for they filled between them with tincts of coloured water, very skilfully, producing patterns which they attached to standing screens, frequently upsidedown. I have been here too long, but have yet to find a suitable guide who can guess where I am going.

MANY DAYS LATER.

At last I am in the height of the mighty pass, and indite this hastily before descending to the plain, or valley, or ocean, which is hid below the bright mist. My seat is the fallen pillar of a Roman *terminus* or boundary stone, engrooved (if I misread it not) with the name and dignities of the Caesar Caligula; but it may be the prone stalk of a uniquely smooth tree whose bark hath been disfigured by accidentally runic crevices, for the mist is so dazzling-white that I can distinguish a very few inches past the coupled convergent apertures of my eliptical nose-thirls. The guide says we will arrive in an hour. She conveys her meaning by smiles and stroaks of the hand which I comprehend perfectly (there are waterfalls all round whose liquid cluckings, gurglings and yellings drown all words) and it occurs to me that the first pure language my ancestors shared before Babylon was not of voice but of exactly these smiles
and stroaks of the hand. I believe I am come
to the edge of the greatest
and happiest discovery
of my life.

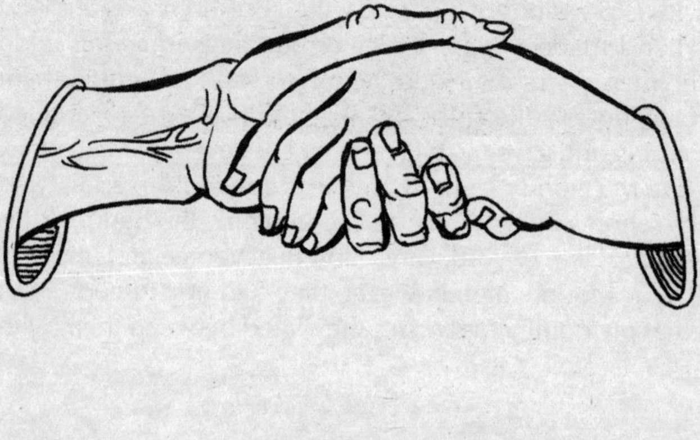

PROMETHEUS

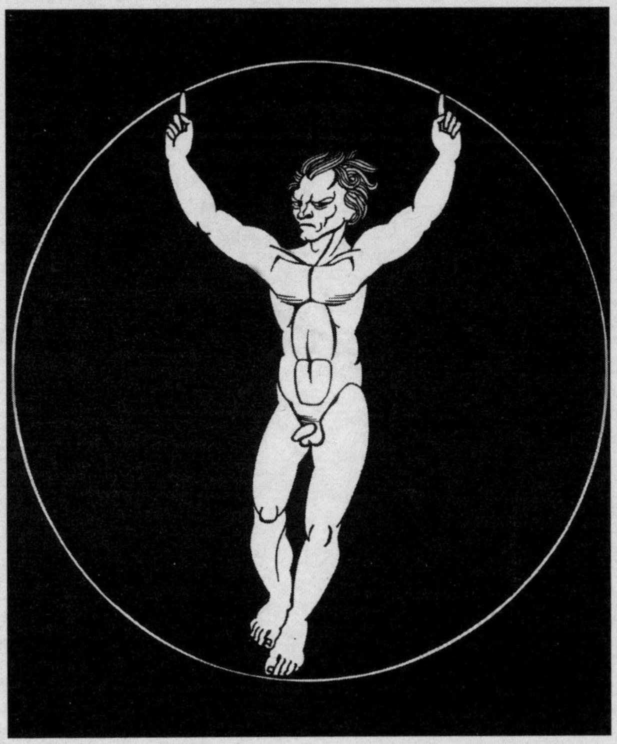

IT WAS UNKIND OF THE JEWS TO GIVE the job of building the world to one man for it made him very lonely. Earlier people saw the creator as a woman giving birth, which is sore, but not sore on the head, and fulfils body and soul until the empty feeling starts. But these wandering shepherds were so used to featureless plains under a vast sky (not even the sea is vaster than the sky) that they thrust a naked man into formless void and left him there forever with nothing to remember, not even the sweetness of a mother's breast.

Roman Catholics and the English parliamentary poet Milton evade the horror of this by placing the void below a mansion where God lives in luxury among angelic flunkeys. Satan, his sinister head waiter, provokes a palace rebellion resulting in a serious staff-shortage; so God, without leaving his throne, gives orders which create a breeding and testing ground (the earth) for a new race of servants (mankind). This notion is very reassuring to people with power and to those weaklings and parasites who admire them. Most citizens with a religion really do believe that heaven is a large private property, and that without a boss to command them they would be nobody. I reject this bourgeois image of God. If God is the first cause of things then he started in a vacuum with no support and no ideas except those arising from his passions. Some commentators present the void as a sort of watery egg on which God broods like a hen until it hatches. Oh yes, why not? This sweet notion is easily reconciled with the splitting of that grand primordial atom which scientists have made so popular. But I am better than a scientist. The Jewish Genesis intoxicates me by attributing all creation to a mind like mine, so to understand God I need only imagine myself in his situation.

First, then, black void, pure and unflawed by sensations. No heat, no cold, no pressure, no extent. What is there to do? Be. Being is all that can be done.

But gradually a sensation does occur, the sensation of duration. We perceive that we have been for a long time, that we will be forever in this darkness unless we do something. The more we endure of our dark self the less we can bear it. We move from boredom to unease and then to panic-horror of an eternity like this. We are in Hell. So the cry "Let there be light" is not an order but a desperate prayer to our own unknown powers. It is also a scream rejecting everything we know by committing us to an unimaginable opposite. And there is *light*. And oh, what appalling vertigo we feel when eternity becomes infinity also and we find ourselves floating beside above beneath that dazzling blank bright breadth, height, depth with no content but ourselves. The light is too much for us, we turn to darkness again. And the evening and the morning are the first day.

Genesis says God saw the light, that it was good, but I cannot imagine him standing happily upon that boundless floor of light before he has peopled it with creatures. His first creature is water, a body compatible with his agitation and as formless as his thinking at this stage. Its sparkling movement reflects and refracts the light into every possible tone and tint, there is a rainbow in each drop of it. With this water he makes the sliding architecture of the sea and the steady, starry flood of the firmament. Unscientific? Good. I would have it so. I will skip most of the other stages. By the sixth day God is almost wholly incarnate. We taste earth and dew through a million roots, our leaves and blossoms sense and scent the air, we graze on our herbs and strike beaks into our squealing flesh while our unutterable doubt of the whole enterprise sneaks searchingly through sunlit grass in the body of the serpent. Our largest intellectual powers are almost (but not quite) realized in Adam, who kneels to study, in a puzzled way, his reflection in a quiet stream. The reflection causes a stiffening in his ureter which has to do with the attached seedballs, but the stiffening is not sufficient to impregnate the image in the water or the moist gravel under it. What other body do we need? Eve, of course, our last and most intricate creature. So Adam knew Eve, his wife, and she conceived and bare Cain. And Cain knew *his* wife, who conceived and bare Enoch, who builded a city. And after more generations of knowing and conceiving, a Seventh-Day Adventist, Joseph Pollard, cleaved to his far more liberal wife Marie, who conceived and bare myself, the poet. If your education is adequate you already know I have been paraphrasing the start of my *Sacred Sociology*, printed privately at Dijon in 1934.

My infancy resembled that of God, my ancestor. I only dimly recall the dark time before I screamed into light, but I was in that dark, like all of us, and I screamed, and there was light. I may have found the light emptier than most. My mother once told me, in an amused voice, that as a baby I screamed continually until one day they sent for a doctor. He examined me minutely then said, "Madam, what you have here is a screaming baby." Clearly she had never wondered what I was screaming *for*. Herself, probably. But soon my vocal chaos acquired the rhythm and colours of articulate speech and I named and commanded a child's small universe. My command was not absolute. In my tenth year Marie Pollard eloped to Algiers with one of her husband's business acquaintances. I sympathized with at least half the feelings which compelled her. Illness had made Joseph Pollard hard to live with. His fits of blinding rage destroyed a great deal of furniture and did not always spare the human body. But I am grateful to him. Paul Cézanne once said, "My father was the real genius. He left me a million francs." Father Pollard was not such a genius as Father Cézanne, but in my eighteenth year he freed me from himself and the curse of earning my bread by succumbing to cancer of the spleen. The consequent income did not permit me to marry, or support a housekeeper, or to frequent respectable brothels; but I silenced the desperate hunger in my young heart by studying it, and the world containing it, and by learning to read all the great sacred books in their original tongues. And I depressed my professors at the Sorbonne by finally submitting no thesis. A poet need not truck with bureaucrats.

I am shy, fastidious and arrogant. I am unattractive, but do not need friends. I am a close reasoner, and love language. My poetic vision is deep, but lacks breadth. It is the drama of their infancy which makes men poets, but the writers of the greatest divine and human comedies are men of the world, they discover and represent that drama in commonplace streets, bedrooms and battlefields. I can only represent Gods, and lonely intelligences, and multitudes viewed from a very great distance. I will never be popular. To pay the printers of the *Sacred Sociology* and *Child's Dictionary of Abstractions** I went shabby and hungry for many days and these books made no great stir. An early act of folly cured me of seeking fame in the reviews. I sent Gide the *Sacred Sociology* with a letter indicating that his protestant education had made him capable of appreciating it. He returned the copy with a seven-word comment: "Literature cannot be founded on Larousse Encyclopedias." His rage, when his wife burned all his letters to her, still amuses me extremely. Bravo, Madame Gide! You hoarded these scribblings as long as you believed he had no other way of making love, but thrust them in the stove when you discovered he enjoyed that passion, physically, elsewhere. You refused to be a postbox through which the great man despatched himself to posterity, bravissimo. I am the opposite of Gide. I now address the public in order to be read by one woman I can reach in no other way. Love drives me to this. Gide was driven by vanity.

* M. Pollard clearly wishes to consign to oblivion his translation of Carlyle's *French Revolution* into heroic Alexandrines, published privately at Dijon in 1927.

I am as old as my century. In the late sixties the respectable working men who frequent the café where I dine began to be ousted by students and other members of the lower intellectual classes. This led to an increase of prices and one day I told the manageress that I could no longer afford to patronize her establishment. A shade of unease came to her face and was instantly quelled. After a moment she indicated that, to a customer of long standing, a reduction of five per cent was permissible. She was not being friendly. She had been friendly twenty years earlier, but I then made certain detailed proposals which she construed as insults. She is one of those strict atheists who determine themselves far more completely than a priest determines a good Catholic. Over the years her splendid body had come to depend on the corset for its shape but I still found the sight of it entertaining; she knew this and cordially detested me. I told her that a fifteen per cent reduction might ensure my continued custom and, after quelling a distinct flicker of wrath, she agreed. I left the café proud to be a Frenchman. The change in clientele was due to myself. Though unpopular I had clearly become famous, and where else in the world would intellectual eminence receive such tactful regard? I remembered also that my mail had recently become abundant, though I only open envelopes from publishers and from the bank which manages my estate. I decided to give myself a holiday. I usually study in a small useful library containing no publications after 1765. Today, in a spirit of sheer caprice, I visited the Bibliothèque Nationale and investigated the history of my reputation.

My books had suffered from an absence of agreement upon how to regard them. In the thirties, the only period when I associated with a political movement, my support of the National Front led the surrealists and left wing generally to regard the *Sacred Sociology* as a satire against religion in the fashion of Anatole France;

but Claudel called it a grand heresy revealing the truth through the agony of estrangement, Celine praised it as hilarious antisemitic comedy, and Saint-Exupéry noticed that it did not seek to deface or replace the scriptures, but to be bound in with them. In the forties the existentialists had just begun to bracket me with Kierkegaard when I printed *A Child's Plainchant Dictionary of Abstractions*. This was thought an inept satire against dictionaries and final proof that I was not a serious thinker. Twelve years later a disciple of Levi-Strauss discovered that, though printed as prose, each definition in my dictionary was a pattern of assonance, dissonance, half-rhyme and alliteration invoking the emotions upon which words like *truth, greed, government, distaste* and *freedom* depend for their meanings. My definition of *digestion*, for example, if spoken aloud, soothes stomachs suffering from indigestion. This realization brought me the reverence of the structuralists who now used my dictionary as a text in three universities. I was often quoted in controversies surrounding the American linguist, Chomsky. It seemed that among my unopened mail lay an invitation to join the French Academy and the offer of a Nobel prize for literature. There was widespread speculation about my current work. My first two books were of different kinds and I still pursued the habits of study which had produced them. It was noted that five years earlier I had begun subscribing to a journal devoted to classical Greek researches. All things considered, there was a chance that, before the century ended my name might be attached to a metro terminus.

I left the Bibliothèque Nationale knowing a new epoch was begun. I had become magnetic. In the café, when I raised a finger to order a Pernod, the manageress brought it then turned her haunches on me in a manner less suggestive of the slamming of a door. The glances of the other customers kept flickering toward my meagre person in a way which showed it reassured them. I was filled with social warmth which I did not need to express, dismissing importunate journalists and research students with a blank stare or aloof monosyllable. This procedure greatly entertained the respectable working men. I came to notice a nearby face, a well-exercised face of the sort I like. The fine lines between the brows and the corners of the mouth and eyes showed it was accustomed to smiling and scowling and was often near to tears; the main expression was eager and desperate. My own face is too big for my body and bland to the point of dullness. My only lines are some horizontal ones on the brow which show I am sometimes surprised, but not often and not much. I arranged my features to indicate that if I was approached I would not be repellent, and after hesitating a moment she left her table and sat down facing me, vastly disturbing in the circumambient field of attention. We were silent until it settled.

She was in the mid-thirties with long, rather dry, straw-coloured hair topped by a defiant red beret. Her other clothes (baggy sweater, trousers, clogs) had been chosen to muffle rather than display her not very tall figure, which was nonetheless good. My personality is modelled upon August Dupin. I eventually said, "There is a book in your handbag?"
She opened the bag and laid a thin pamphlet on the table between us. I could not read the author's name, but it was not by me, so must be her own, or by her lover, or perhaps child. I said, "Poems?"
She nodded. I said, "Why do you approach someone so famous for taciturnity as myself? Have you been rejected by the more accessible celebrities?"
She said, "In approaching you I have not been guided by reason. You are an almost complete reactionary. I ought to despise you. But when a young girl your dictionary gave me an ineradicable respect for the meaning, the colours, the whole *sense* of our language. If your talent is not dead from disuse, if you are not wholly the dotard

you impersonate, you may help me, perhaps. I so much want to be a good poet."

I am not accustomed to challenges, my usual habits prevent them. Her words released into my veins an utterly intoxicating flood of adrenalin. I gazed on her with awe and gratitude. She had turned her face sideways and tears slid down the curve of her cheek. I lifted the little book and said playfully, "If I dislike this you will think me a dead man; if I love it there is hope for me?"

She said coldly, "I am not a fool."

Her proud chin was at an angle as defiant as the beret, her small nose was as tip-tilted as a sparrow's beak. The bridge may have been broken. I, who have never touched a woman tenderly in my life, longed to lift and cradle her protectingly. So much sudden new experience could overstrain an old heart. I pocketed the book, climbed down to the floor and said, "Madam, my habits are invariable, you may find me here whenever you please. I will have read your book in two days."

For the second time in four years I allowed myself a holiday. On the sunlit pavement I was gripped by a walking frenzy. She had given me a precious part of herself (I stroked the book in my pocket) and defied me, and asked for help, and wept. I loved her, of course, and did not regret that this state, for me, would be painful and perhaps impossible. Romeo and Juliet, Anthony and Cleopatra found love painful and almost impossible. Phaedra and Medea found it quite impossible, but nobody doubts they were enhanced by it. I was enhanced by it. I am a wholly suburban Parisian who distrusts, as much as any provincial, that collection of stale imperial pie-crusts calling itself *Paris*. We require it to awe the foreigner who would otherwise menace our language and culture, but I refuse to be awed. So I was amused to find myself standing on one of the curving benches of the Pont-Neuf, my arms on the parapet, staring downstream at one of our ugliest* buildings with a strong sentiment of admiration and delight. Since I was physically unable to seduce her I must persuade her to seduce me. This required me to remain aloof, while feeding her with increasingly useful parts of my mind, cunningly sauced with flattery to induce addiction. Everything depended on her poems. If they were entirely bad I would lose interest and botch the whole business. I sat down and read.

I was lucky. The person of the book was intelligent, tough, and on the way to being a good writer. She was a feminist, vivisecting her mauled sexual organs to display the damage and making the surgery icily comic by indicating, in a quiet lip-licking way, "It's even more fun when I slice up him." Some poems showed her embracing and embraced by a lover and unable to tell him something essential, either because of his indifference or from her fear that big truths are too destructive to be shared by a society of two. It was entertaining to see a woman in these Byronic postures but she was potentially greater than Byron. Her best work showed respect for human pain at a profounder level than sexual combat. It was spoiled by too many ideas. A good poem is a tautology. It expands one word by adding a number which clarify it, thus making a new word which has never before been spoken. The seedword is always so ordinary that hardly anyone perceives it. Classical odes grow from *and* or *because*, romantic lyrics from *but* and *if*. Immature verses expand a personal pronoun ad nauseam, the greatest works bring glory to a common verb. Good poems, therefore, are always close to banality, above which, however, they tower like precipices. My woman avoided banality (which has, indeed, swallowed hordes of us) by turbulent conjunctions. Her book was filled with centaurs because she had not fully grasped the

* An insult to the home of the Academic Francaise.

complexity of actual people, actual horses. Her instinct to approach me had been sound. I could teach her a great deal.

I bought a note pad from a stationer in the Place Dauphin. It was Sunday. I entered the Louvre and fought my way through the polyglot mobs to the Maria de Medici salon where I always feel at home. The canvases adorning this temple to female government bubble with enough good-humoured breasts to suckle a universe. My favourite painting, which always gives me a wicked thrill, shows the Italian banker's fat daughter handing over the tiller of state to her son, a boy with the clothes, rigid stance and far too solemn face of a very small adult. The ship of state has a mast with Athene beside it pointing the way, her curves compressed by armour which recalls the corsets of my manageress. The motive power of the vessel is provided by lusty women representing Prudence, Fortitude, etc., who toil at heavy oars with pained, indignant expressions which suggest that work comes to them as a horrible surprise. Unluckily there is no sofa near this painting. I settled before the canvases which show Maria's coronation inaugurating a new golden age and there, in the severe language of literary criticism, wrote the first love-letter of my life. I was inspired. I filled twenty-four pages with minute writing before closing time, then walked home, corrected them in red ink, typed them, recorrected, retyped, then sealed them in a large manilla envelope of the sort used for preserving legal documents. My heart palpitated as I inscribed her name upon it.

I had said I would read her poems within two days. For a week I extended my lunch hour beyond the normal and on the eighth day her shadow fell across the print of the book I was reading. Without raising my eyes I placed the letter between us, saying, "You may wish to digest this in private."

I heard the envelope torn, then looked up. She was giving the letter an attention which excluded myself and everything else. She read slowly, and some passages more than once. An hour elapsed. She slid the pages into her handbag, gave me a full, sincere smile and said, "Thanks. You have misunderstood my work almost completely, but your warped picture of it conveys insights which I will one day find useful. Thanks."

She tapped the tabletop with her fingers, perhaps preparing to leave. I grew afraid. I said, "Will you now explain why, in our first encounter, you called me reactionary?"

"Your work explains that."

"The *Sacred Sociology?*"

"Yes, for the most part."

I sighed and said, "Madam, it is not my custom to justify myself or criticize others. Both practices indicate insufficiency. But to you I surrender. Your poems suggest you love freedom, and want a just communism to release human souls from the bank-vaults of the West, the labour camps of the East." "And from the hospitals and asylums!" she cried ardently. "And from the armies, churches and bad marriages!"

"Good. You desire a world-wide anarchic commonwealth where government may be safely left to a committee of retired housekeepers chosen by lot, like a jury."

She smiled and nodded. I said, "Madam, I wish that also. For centuries men have been misled by words like God, fate, nature, necessity, world, time, civilization and history: words which hide from us our cause and condition. The bourgeois say that because of these things our state can change very little, except for the worse. But these words are nothing but names for *people*. *We* are our God, fate, nature, necessity, world, time, civilization and history. Common people achieved these limbs, this brain, the emotions and the skills and the languages which share them. We have made every blessing we enjoy, including sunlight, for the sun would be a meaner thing without our eyes to reflect it. The fact that man is infinitely valuable – that man is essentially God – underlies every sacred code. And when I say *man is God* I refer least of all to God the landlord, God the director, God the ruler with power to crush a majority for the good of the rest. To hell with these overpaid demiurges! My gratitude is to God the migrant labourer, the collectivized peasant, the slave of Rio Tinto Zinc and the American Fruit Company. *He* is the heavenly host whose body is broken day after day to nourish smart people like you and me. The *Sacred Sociology* tried to make news of this ancient truth. Did it fail?"

"Yes!" she said. "It failed. The good wine of truth cannot be poured out of filthy old bottles. I will quote something. *Our largest intellectual powers are almost realized in Adam who kneels to study, in a puzzled way, his reflection in a quiet stream. It causes a stiffening in his ureter which has to do with the attached seedballs, but the stiffening is not sufficient to impregnate the image in the water or the moist gravel under it. What other body does he need? Eve, of course, our last and most intricate creation*. Ha! You have done nothing but reaffirm the old lie that a big man made the world, then created a small man to take charge of it, then begot a woman on him to mass-produce replicas of himself. What could be more perverse? You have been deceived, Mr. Pollard. There is a great garden in your brain which is in total darkness. You have been taken in by the status-quo of men and women and what sex is about, much as people were taken in by the Empire and the Church. You don't know *how* you have been oppressed because you have a penis."

I was silent for a while then said, "Correct. You have put your finger exactly upon my weakness, which is sexual. Speak of work which does not refer to the sexes. Speak of my dictionary."

She said, "It liberated me. My education was thoroughly religious in the worst sense but a cousin lent me de

Beauvoir's memoirs and your dictionary and they liberated me. At university you were my special study. Do you know how the professors use you? Not to free, but to bind. You are understood to support their systems. The students study commentaries on your book, not the book itself. I defended your assertion of the radical, sensual monosyllable. I was not allowed to complete the course."

I nodded sadly and said, "Yes. I support common sense with uncommon intelligence so the bourgeois have appropriated me, as they appropriate all splendid things. But my book is called *A Child's Plainchant Dictionary of Abstractions*. I wanted it set to music and sung in primary schools throughout France. Impossible, for I have no friends in high places. But if children sang my definitions with the voices of thrushes, larks and little owls they would get them by heart and easily detect fools and rascals who use words to bind and blind us. The revolution we require would be many days nearer."

"A dictator!" she cried scornfully. "You! A dwarf! Would dictate language to the children of a nation!" I laughed aloud. It is a rare relief when an interlocutor refers to my stature. She blushed at her audacity, then laughed also and said, "Intellectually you are a giant, of course, but you do not live like one. You live like the English authors who all believe the highest civic virtue is passivity under laws which money-owners can manipulate to their own advantage. The second Charlemagne* has made our country a near dictatorship. In Algeria, Hungary, Vietnam and Ireland governments are employing torturers to reinforce racial, social and sexual oppression. The intelligent young hate all this and are looking for allies. And you, whose words would be eagerly studied by every intelligence in Europe, say nothing."

* Charles de Gaulle, with no declared political programme, was ruler of France.

I said, "I have no wish to be the mundane conscience of my tribe. Our Sartre can do that for us." I was sublimely happy. She saw me as a position to be captured. I longed for captivity; and if I was mistaken, and she only saw me as a barricade to be crossed, might she not, in crossing, be physically astride me for a few moments? My reference to Sartre was making her regard me with complete disdain. I raised an imploring hand and said, "Pardon me! I have no talent for immediate events. My art is solving injustice through historical metaphor and even there I may be defeated."

"Explain that."

I looked directly into her eyes. I had expected sharp blue ones, but they were mild golden-brown and went well with the straw-coloured hair. I said, "You asked for my help to become a better poet. I need yours to finish my last and greatest work. I lack the knowledge to complete it myself."

She whispered, "What work?"

"*Prometheus Unbound.*"

I hoped this conversation would be the first of a series lasting the rest of my life. Her curt, impetuous words, together with a haunted look, as if she must shortly run away, had led me to speak of Prometheus at least a year before I intended, but it was now too late to speak of less important things. I asked her to be patient if I told her a story she perhaps knew already. She glanced at her wristwatch then nodded.

The early Greeks (I said) believed the earth was a woman who, heated by his lightningstrokes, fertilized by his rain, undulated beneath her first off-spring, the sky. She gave birth to herbs, trees, beasts and titans. The titans can be named but never clearly defined. There is Atlas the maker of space, and Cronos whom Aristotle identifies with time. There is also Prometheus, whose name means *foresight* and *torch*. He was a craftsman, and moulded men from the dust of his mother's body. The multiplying children of earth could not leave her. She tired of her husband's lust, needing room for her family, room to think. She persuaded Cronos to castrate his dad with a stone sickle. The sky recoiled from her and *time* became master of the universe. When people came to live in cities they looked back on the reign of Cronos as a golden age, for in those days we were mainly shepherds and food-gatherers and shared the goods of the earth equally, without much warfare. But we had cyclops too, great men who worked in metal. Cronos feared those and locked them in hell, a place as far below the earth as the sky is above her. And when Cronos mated with his sister Rhea he became a cruel husband. He knew how dangerous a man's children can be and swallowed his own as soon as they were born. The earth disliked that. She advised Rhea to give her man a stone when the next child came. Time, who has no organs of taste, swallowed this stone thinking it was yet another son. The boy's mother called him Zeus and had him privately educated. When he was old enough to fight his father for the government of the universe he tricked the old man into drinking emetic wine and vomiting up the other children he had swallowed. These were the gods, and Zeus became their leader. The gods were more cunning than the titans, but less strong, and only Prometheus saw that cunning would replace strength as master of the universe. He tried to reconcile the two sides. When this proved impossible he joined the rebels.

The war which followed lasted ten years. Prometheus advised Zeus to release the cyclops from hell and when this was done they equipped the gods with helmet, trident and thunderbolt. Zeus won, of course, being supported by his brothers, by the earthmother, by the cyclops, by Prometheus and by men. What followed? The new boss of the universe confirmed his power by threatening man-kind with death. Prometheus saved us by giving us hope (which allows us to despise death) and fire (which the gods wanted to keep to themselves). So Zeus punished Prometheus by crucifying him on a granite cliff. But Prometheus is Immortal. He writhes there to the present day.

"Madam," I asked my woman, "do these matters seem savage and remote from you? This oppressed mother always plotting with a son or daughter against a husband or father, yet breeding nothing but a new generation of oppressors? This new administration crushing a clumsy old one with the help of the skilled workers, common people and a radical intellectual, and then taking control with the old threats of prison and bloody punishment."

She nodded seriously and said, "It is savage, but not remote."

I said, "Exactly. Our political theatres keep changing but the management always present the tragedy of Prometheus or *foresight abused*. The ancient titans are the natural elements which shape and govern us when we live in small tribes. Foresight helps us build cities which give protection from the revolving seasons and erratic crops. Unluckily these states are also formed through warfare. They are managed by winners who enrich themselves at the expense of the rest and pretend their advantages are as natural as the seasons, their mismanagement as inevitable as bad weather. In these states the fate of Prometheus warns clear-sighted people not to help the commoners against their bosses. But wherever we notice that poverty is not natural, but created by some of us unfairly distributing what the rest have made, *democracy* is conceived. The iron wedges nailing Prometheus to his rock begin to loosen. This is why the poem which presents Prometheus as a hero was written for the world's first and greatest democratic state. I mean Athens, of course."

"Ancient Athens," said my woman firmly, "oppressed women, kept slaves, and fought unjust wars for gain."

"Yes!" I cried. "And in that it was like every other state in the history of mankind. But what made Athens different was the unusual freedom enjoyed by most men in it. When these men compared themselves with the inhabiters of the great surrounding empires (military Persia, priestridden Egypt, Carthage with its huge navy and stock-exchange) they were astonished by their freedom."

She said, "Define freedom."

I said, "It is the experience of active people who live by work they do best, are at ease with their neighbours, and responsible for their government."

She said, "You have just admitted that your free, active Athenians oppressed their neighbours and more than half their own people."

I said, "Yes, and to that extent they were not free, and knew it. Their popular drama, the first plays which the common memory of mankind has seen fit to preserve, shows that warfare and slavery – especially sexual slavery – are horrible things, and at last destroy the winners and the empires who use them."

"Which means," cried my woman, looking more like a tragic heroine with every utterance, "that the Athenians were like our educated bourgeois of Western Europe and North America, who draw unearned income from the poor of their own and other countries, yet feel superior to the equivalent class in Russia, because we applaud writers who tell us we are corrupt."

After a silence I said, "Correct, madam. But do not be offended if I draw a little comfort from just one Athenian achievement: the tragic poem *Prometheus Bound* which was written by Aeschylus and is the world's second oldest play. It shows Prometheus, creative foresight, being crucified and buried by the cunning lords of this world after they have seized power. But Prometheus prophesies that one day he will be released, and tyranny cast down, and men will see their future clear. Aeschylus wrote a sequel, *Prometheus Unbound*, describing that event. It was lost, and I can tell you why.

"The democracy of Athens, great as it was, flawed as it was, tried to become an empire, was defeated, and finally failed. All the great states which followed it were oligarchies. Some, like Florence and Holland, claimed to be republics, but all were oligarchies in which poets and dramatists were so attached to the prosperous classes that they came to despise, yes really despise, the commoners. They saw them as incurably inferior, deserving a tear and a charitable breadcrust in bad times, but potentially dangerous and at best merely comic, like the grave-diggers in *Hamlet*. No doubt the rulers of states thought *Prometheus Unbound* was seditious, but it must also have annoyed educated people by showing how slavish their best hopes had become. They could no longer imagine a good state where intelligence served everyone equally. In twenty-three centuries of human endurance and pain only one hero, Jesus of Nazareth, declared that a common man was the maker of all earthly good, and that by loving and sharing with him we would build the classless kingdom of heaven. And, madam," I told her, "you know what the churches have made of *that* message. How cunning the winners are! How horrible!"

And I, who had not wept since I was a baby, shed passionate tears. I felt her grip my hand across the tabletop and though I had never before felt such pure grief for abused humanity, I have never felt such happiness and peace. It was a while before I could continue.

"But one day France, madam, yes our own France declared that democracy must return; that liberty, equality, fraternity are indivisible; that what the Athenians started, we will achieve. We have not achieved it yet, but the world will never know peace until we have done so. The main task of poetry today is to show the modern state the way to liberty and peace by remaking the lost verse-drama, *Prometheus Unbound*. I have completed half of it."

She stared at me. I hoped she was fascinated. I described my play.

It starts with the supreme God (spelt with a capital G to separate him from lesser gods) standing on a mountaintop after the defeat of the titans. The sky behind him is a deep dark blue, his face and physique are as Michelangelo painted him, only younger – he looks about thirty. Round his feet flows a milky cloud and under the cloud, on a curving ridge, stands the committee of Olympus: Juno, Mars, Venus etcetera. These are the chorus. On two hills lower down sit Pan and Bacchus among the small agents of fertility and harvest: nymphs, fauns, satyrs and bacchantes with fiddles, drums, bagpipes and flutes. This orchestra makes music for the scene-changes. A dark vertical cleft divides the two hills. At the base of it is spread out a great tribe of common people who may as well be played by the audience. Their task is to enhance the play with their attention and applause until, at the end, the release of Prometheus releases them too. But at the start God's gravely jubilant voice addresses the universe while the sky grows light behind him.

He speaks like any politician who has just come to power after a struggle. Together (he tells us) we have destroyed chaos and oppression. Prosperity and peace are dawning under new rules which will make everybody happy. Even the wildest districts are now well-governed. My brother Neptune commands the sea, storms and earthquake. My brother Pluto rules the dead. Let us praise the cyclops! The powers of reason would have been defeated without the weapons they made. They have been sent back to hell, but to an improved, useful hell managed by my son Vulcan. He is employing them to make the thunderbolts I need to coerce law-breakers. For alas, lawbreakers exist, hot-heads who protest because my new state is not equally good to everyone. It is true that, just now, some must have very little so that, eventually, everyone has more; but those who rage at this are prolonging sufferings which I can only cure with the help of time ... God is interrupted here by a voice from the ridge below him. Minerva-Athene, his minister of education, or else Cupid his popular clown, point out that the recent war was fought to destroy old time yet now God says he needs time to let him do good. Yes! (cries God) for time is no longer your tyrant, he is my slave. Time will eventually show how kind I am, how good my laws are, how well I have made everything.

Throughout this speech God's nature is clearly changing. From sounding like the spokesman of a renewed people he has used the language of a lawmaker, dictator, and finally creator. At his last words the cloud under him divides and floats left and right uncovering the shining black face of the earth-mother. It is calm and unlined, with slanting eyes under arched brows like a Buddha, and flat negro lips like the Sphinx. The white cloud is her hair, the ridge where the gods stand is her collarbone, the orchestra sits on her breasts, the audience in her lap. God, erect on top of her head, with one foot slightly advanced and arms firmly folded, looks slightly ridiculous but perfectly at home. When she parts her lips a soft voice fills the air with melodious grumbling. She knows that God's claim to be a creator is false but she is endlessly tolerant and merely complains instead of shaking him off. Her grammar is difficult. She is twisting a huge statement into a question and does not divide what she knows into separate sentences and tenses.

EARTH
Who was before I am dark
without limbs, dancing, spinning
space without heat who
was before I am alight
without body, blazing, dividing
continents on rocking mud who
was before I am breathing
without eyes, floating, rooted
bloody with outcry who

was before I am a singing
ground, wormy-dark, alight
aloud with leaves, eyes and
gardeners, the last plants I grew who
uplifted you who
was before I am?

GOD
Who is before you now!
I grasp all ground, mother.
The gardeners you grew were common men, a brood
too silly and shapeless to be any good
outside my state, which has made them new.
They cannot remember being born by you.
They are my image now. I am who
they all want to obey, or if not obey, be.

EARTH
Not Prometheus.

GOD
Yes, Prometheus! Punishment is changing him into a cracked mirror of me.

There is a sudden terrible cry of pain. Two great birds with dripping beaks fly out of the cleft between the earth's breasts. Light enters it and shows the crucified Prometheus, a strong man of middle age with a bleeding wound in his side. Though smaller than his mother he is a giant to the God who stands high above him and declares that this is the end of the titan who made men, and made them hard to govern, by giving them hope of better life. The great mother, with a touch of passion, tells God that though he is supreme he is also very new, and his state will perish one day, like all states, and only Prometheus knows how. God does not deny this. He says he has a lot of work to do and will reconsider the case of Prometheus when he has more time. He turns and goes down behind the earth's head.

The cloud closes over her. Prometheus, twisting his face up, asks the gods on the ridge to tell him the present state of mankind. They sing a chorus describing the passage of over two thousand years. Men combine into rich empires by many submitting to a few. They discover the world is vaster than they thought, and add new realms to tyranny. Liberators are born who create new religions and states, and the rulers of the world take these over and continue to tighten their grip. At last human cunning grasps, not just the world but the moon and the adjacent planets, yet half mankind dies young from bad feeding, and young courage and talent is still warped and killed by warfare. The controllers of the world fear the people under them as much as each other, and are prepared to defend their position by destroying mankind and the earth which bore them. This is the final state to which we have been brought by cunning without foresight. Prometheus cries out, "This cannot last!" From the middle of her cloud this cry is repeated by the great mother, then by the chorus and orchestra, and then (the cloud clearing) by God himself, who stands on the height with his arms flung sideways in a gesture which resembles the crucified Prometheus. God is also now a middle-aged man. He walks down from the height, sits on the edge of the cleft and tries to engage Prometheus in friendly conversation. He is sorry he punished Prometheus so harshly and promises not to set vultures on him again. When he came to power he had to be harsh, to keep control. People needed strong government, in those days, to drag them out of the idiocy of rural life. But the whole world now belongs to the city states. He is sure Prometheus knows that neither of them is completely good or completely bad, and have a lot to give each other. If they cooperate they can save mankind. He asks Prometheus for the secret of the force which will destroy him. Prometheus asks to be released first. God is sorry, but he cannot release Prometheus. If he did Prometheus would seize power.

GOD

I am not the stark power who chained you here.
I am softened by what you endured, while my laws
have made you a hard reflection of the tyrant I once was.
It cannot be right to enthrone
a killing revenge the world should have outgrown,
or if right, then right will make greater wrong.

PROMETHEUS

It is right to give back what you stole – liberty.
You see me as I am. You cannot see
who I will become when I am free.
Why do you think I will kill?

GOD

Your every glance threatens me terrible ill.

PROMETHEUS

I am in pain! My illness, the illness you dread,
is yours, is you!

GOD

Then endure my terrible nature!
I must endure it too.

(God has lost his temper. Prometheus laughs bitterly.)

PROMETHEUS

At last you unmask, old man
and show what you are again:
the ruler of a kingdom kept by pain.
All history has added nothing to you
but a mad wish to be pitied for what you do.

I paused. My woman said, "What happens then?" I said, "I cannot imagine."
She started laughing. I said, "To end happily my play needs a new character, someone we have already seen, without much interest, in the chorus, or even audience. The action until now is between a man, a big woman, and another man. To strike a balance the fourth character must be a woman. She is a new wisdom who will unite our imprisoned intelligence with the productive earth, reducing government from a form of mastery to a form of service. She is sensuous, for both governments and rebels keep asking us to crush our senses in order to gain an ultimate victory which never arrives. But she is not disorderly, not a beatnik, not careless. She is living proof that when our senses are freed from fear our main desire is to make the world a good home for everyone. I cannot concive such a heroine. Can you conceive her? Could we conceive her together?" My woman looked thoughtful then said slowly, "I am qualified to assist you. I have been a daughter and a mother, a victim and a tyrant. I saw my father torment his wife into her grave. I have driven a man to suicide, or very nearly. I know how love heats and warps us, but I feel there is still hope for me, and the world."
I said, "That indicates a kind of balance."
"I have climbed mountains in Scotland and Germany. I have swum underground rivers in the Auvergne."
I said, "That also indicates balance, but a balance of extremes. The tension you feel must be nearly unbearable. We must connect the extremes where you squander so much energy with the centre where my knowledge lies chained and stagnant."
Her mouth and eyes opened wide, she raised her chin and gazed upward like the Pythoness on the tripod when Apollo enters her. For nearly a minute she became pure priestess. Then her gaze shrank, descended and focussed on the table where my great, droll, attentive head rested sideways on my folded arms. A look of incredulity came

upon her face. I had never before seemed to her so improbably grotesque. She pretended to glance at her wrist-watch, saying, "Excuse me, I must go."

"May I write to you, madam? A literary collaboration is perhaps best prosecuted by letter."

"Yes."

"Your address?"

"I don't know – I am moving elsewhere, I don't know where yet. I have many arrangements to make. Leave your letters with the management here. I will find a way to collect them."

I said, "Good," and achieved a smile. She arose, came to my side and hesitated. I signalled by a small headshake that condescension would be unwelcome. She turned and hurried out. I sat perfectly still, attending to the beaks of the vultures tearing at my liver. They had never felt so sharp. The manageress came over and asked if I felt well? I grinned at her and nodded repeatedly until she went away.

After that I waited. I could do almost nothing else. Study was impossible, sleep difficult. I addressed to her a parcel of worknotes for *Prometheus Unbound* and it lay on the zinc beside the till, but I was always sitting nearby for I wanted not to leave the only place where I might see her again. I waited a day, a week, three weeks. I was dozing over my book and glass one afternoon when I grew conscious of her talking to the manageress. She seemed to have been doing it for some time. They frowned, nodded, glanced towards me, shrugged and smiled. I was very confused and prayed God that when she sat facing me I would be calm and firm. She patted the manageress's arm and walked straight out through the door. I screamed her name, scrambled down from the chair, charged into the crowded street and ran screaming to the right, banging against knees, treading on feet and sometimes trodden on. Not seeing her I turned and ran to the left. As I passed the café door I was seized and lifted, yes, lifted up by one who held her face to mine so that our noses touched, and whispered, "Mister Pollard,

this conduct does you no good. I have a letter."
I became very icy and hissed, "Put me down, madam."
I should have asked to be taken home. I could suddenly hardly walk. I got to my table and opened the letter, noticing that my parcel lay uncollected beside the till.

My dear friend,

I no longer wish to be a poet. It requires an obsessional balancing of tiny phrases and meanings, an immersion in language which seems to me a kind of cowardice. As a man and poet I can respect you but only because you are also a dwarf. For people of ordinary health and height, with a clear view of the world and a wish to do well, it is a waste of time making signboards pointing to the good and bad things in life. If we do not personally struggle towards good and fight the bad, people will merely praise or denounce our signs and go on living as usual. I must make my own life the book where people read what I believe. I decided this years ago when I became a socialist, but I still grasped, like a cuddly toy, my wish to be a poet. That wish came from the dwarfish part of me, the frightened lonely child who hoped that a DECLARATION would bring the love of mother earth, the respect of daddy god, the admiration of the million sisters and brothers who normally do not care if I live or die. Your critical letter had an effect you did not intend. It showed me that my declarations are futile. It has taken a while for the message to sink in. I am grateful to you, but also very bitter. I cannot be completely logical.

My sweet, you are the cleverest, most deluded man I ever met. Rewriting PROMETHEUS UNBOUND is like rewriting GENESIS, it can be done but who needs it? It is just another effort to put good wine in a filthy old bottle. I was touched when you poured over me your adolescent enthusiasm for ancient Athens but I also wanted to laugh or vomit. I am educated. I have been to Greece. I have stood on the Acropolis facing the Erichtheon and can tell you that Greece represents:

men against women

war against peace
business " play
intellect " emotions
authority " anarchy
hierarchy " equality
discipline " sensuality
property-inheritance " sexuality
patriarchy " everything

Yet you see civilization as an unfinished story the Athenians started and which a few well-chosen words will help to a satisfactory finish! You are wrong. The best state in the world was that primitive matriarchy which the Athenians were foremost in dismantling. Men were happy and peaceful when women ruled them, but so naturally wicked that they turned our greatest strength (motherhood) into weakness by taking advantage of it and enslaving us. Men have made hell of the world ever since and are now prepared to destroy all life in it rather than admit they are wrong. Masculine foresight cannot help our civilization because it is travelling backward. Even our enemies realize this. In the last fifty years they have driven us to the brink of the dark age. The rational Greek foundation of things has been unbuilt, unlearned. And you did not notice! My poor dwarf, you are the last nineteenth-century romantic liberal. That is why a corrupt government wishes to make you a national institution.

Which brings me, beloved, to what you really *want from me: cunt. In your eyes it probably looks like an entrance to the human race. Believe me, you are human enough without. No good was ever done by those who thought sexual pleasure a goal in life. I speak from experience. I divorced a perfectly nice husband who could only give me that stultifying happiness, that delicious security which leads to nothing but more of itself. But if you require that delight you can have it by merely relaxing. As a national institution – a blend of tribal totempole and pampered baby – you are ringed by admirers you have so far had the sense and courage to ignore. Weaken, enjoy your fame and get all the breasts you want: except mine. When I first spoke to you I accused you of impersonating a dead man. That was jealousy speaking. I admired you then and I regret I unhinged you so easily. I did not want to do that. I love you, but in a way you cannot perceive and I cannot enjoy. So I also hate you.*

I am a monster. The cutting words I write cut my heart too. I am under unusual strain. I am about to do something difficult and big which, if discovered, will end my freedom forever. My friends will think me insane, an unstable element, a traitor if they learn I have told you this. But you love me and deserve to know what I am leaving you for, and I do trust you, my teacher, my liberator. Adieu.

Is printing the above letter for the world to read a betrayal of her trust? Is a secret police computer, as a result of this story, stamping the card of every female, blonde, brown-eyed, snub-nosed poet with a number which means *suspect political crime investigate*? No. This story is a poem, a wordgame. I am not a highly literate French dwarf, my lost woman is not a revolutionary writer manqué, my details are fictions, only my meaning is true and I must make that meaning clear by playing the wordgame to the bitter end.

Having read the letter I sat holding it, feeling paralysed, staring at the words until they seemed dark stains on a white surface like THIS one, like THIS one. I was broken. She had made me unable to bear loneliness. And though we had only met twice I had shown the world that women could approach me. I sat at the table, drinking, I suppose, and in the evening a girl sat opposite and asked what I thought of de Gaulle's latest speech? I asked her to inform me of it. Later we were joined by another girl and a young man, students, all of them. It seemed we were on the brink of revolution. I ordered wine. Said the young man, "Tomorrow we will not protest, we will occupy!"

"You must come with us, Mister Pollard!" cried the girls, who were very excited. I agreed and laughed and bought more wine, then grew enraged and changed my position. I quoted Marx to support de Gaulle and Lenin to condemn the students. The uselessness of discourse became so evident that at last I merely howled like a dog and grew unconscious. And awoke with a bad headache, in darkness, beside a great soft cleft cliff: the bum of my manageress. I had been conveyed into her bed. I was almost glad. In the morning she said, "Mister Pollard, you know I have been a widow for seven months."
I said nothing. She said, "Some years ago you made to me certain detailed proposals which, as a respectable, newly-married, very young woman I could not entertain. What you suggested then is now perfectly possible. Of course, we must first marry."

Lucie, you have made me need you, or if not you, someone. Lucie, if you do not return I must fall forever into her abyss. Lucie, she makes me completely happy, but only in the dark. Oh Lucie Lucie
Lucie save me from her. The one word this poem
exists to clarify is *lonely*. I am Prometheus.
I am lonely.

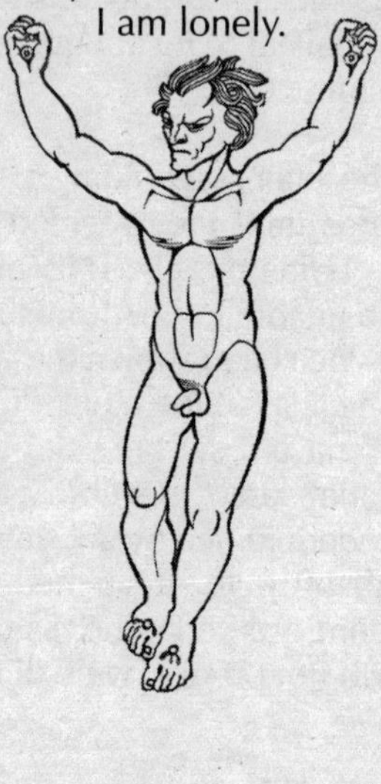

THE END OF THE AXLETREE

The emperor died, and his tomb was built in the centre of the capital city, then enlarged to enclose everything he had wanted. His suggestions for the name were also adopted. The inhabiters called it *the work*, outsiders called it *the axletree*. People travelling there saw it for a fortnight before arriving and I speak of the work itself, not the pillar of cloud overhead, creamy-gold on bright days, thunder-black on dull ones, and flickering with reflected orange light in the hours of darkness. As the traveller drew near, the huge solitary bulk so filled his mind that sometimes he grew frightened and turned back before seeing the canals and merchant navies entering the artificial sea around the foundation. The roads bridged this by viaducts sloping up to market-gallery-level, a full mile above sea-level, yet rising so easily that blind travellers thought they were flat. It was a safe structure in those days and foreign kings bought shares in it as a way of banking their wealth. The construction company became the government of the empire – our emperors dropped their ancient title and were known as company chairmen. The first of these was a man of simple tastes who had a farm near the top of the work where he grew his own vegetables. He liked to feel he did not need the earth below, but everyone else in the axletree was fed off that. People in the nearest provinces usually looked thin and glum. It must also have been very depressing to live where half the world bent up to shut you out. Dwellers in remoter provinces saw us as a steep-sided mountain on the horizon, but to insiders we were not one thing but many: our living rooms and the rooms of friends, some connecting galleries lined with shops and parkland, the offices where we calculated or the scaffolding where we laboured. The simplest thing we knew was the world spread below like a map. Merchants, soldiers and tax-collectors had to visit that. Most of us were luckier.

Not everyone inside the great work was happy there. When the structure was repaired the masons found odd cavernous spaces full of mummified bodies. These had been slaves who died while putting the building up. They were buried this way because it did not interrupt the labour, and because the founding emperor wanted everyone who worked on his tomb to end up inside. But the re-opened crypts held signs of life: rough tables with winestains and cheap candlesticks on them, and there were gaps in the surrounding stonework just big enough to admit people on their hands and knees. The police discovered that these crypts were used by a society of slaves, labourers and women who met there once a week to exchange subversive gossip. The society was co-operative. Members paid small sums to an agent who cooked them a communal meal and guarded their articles of association. These articles set out the wildest hopes of uneducated people in the language of company law. They said:

1. God had designed the axletree as a home for all who worked on it.
2. The construction company had stolen it and was building for private profit.
3. When the top touched heaven the divine architect would come down and lock up the directors and shareholders in their treasure vaults.
4. And give members of the co-operative society an eternally happy home.

Members sometimes disagreed about whether they would occupy the finished work as ghosts or bodies, or use it as a stair to enter heaven. Their disputes were settled by the works foreman, the society's chief agent. He was supposed to know far more about building than the company chairman, though he was elected for his ability as a caterer.

The company chairman thought this society would start a rebellion among his labour force. It was banned and the police killed many of its agents, including the first two foremen. Yet it gained members and grew, for it helped the worst-paid people believe that their enslavement to the axletree would eventually do them good.

One day the rim of the empire was penetrated by a fast-moving barbarian horde. They came so near the axletree that distant shareholders grew afraid of losing touch with their wealth and started drawing it from the company vaults. This had a bad effect on trade, and discontented provinces demanded independence. Building came to a halt. In the resulting unemployment it was clear that the co-operative society was giving ordinary folk courage and hope which cost the construction company nothing. The company chairman sought an interview with the works foreman and afterwards they announced that:

1. The entire work belonged to God now, and everyone in it was his servant.
2. The co-operative was now a legal building society. The company chairman had joined it, so had the major shareholders, and God would welcome them into heaven when the work was done.
3. The foreman of the work, in God's name, had taken over the summit of the work, and was now in charge of the building, which would be paid for out of co-operative funds.
4. The construction company would hold onto the treasure-vaults, the markets and government offices, in order to guard the foundation and maintain the fabric.

The news made many people happy. We thought rich and poor would unite to defend the empire and complete the building.

But the empire was being attacked on every side and there was no labour to spare for the building. The construction company kept an appearance of order by bribing enemies to stay away. Our market shrank, the canals silted up and the pillar of cloud, which was mainly produced by body-heat, gradually dissolved. Then an army of barbarians too large to bribe marched inside and plundered as they pleased. The scale of the work so daunted them that they could not plunder everything, but when they finally left we found that the last of the company chairmen had absconded with the last of the company's gold. The vaults of the work became the lair of bats and foxes. The population dwindled to a few farmers grazing their herds on the dry bed of the ancient sea. The only government left was the works foreman. Once a week he served meals to his followers on the great floor surrounding the founder's sarcophagus, and once a year he supervised the shifting of a stone from the foundation to the summit where it was cemented firmly into place. This was the end of the first big building-boom.

Meanwhile the separate provinces fought the invaders and lost touch with each other until the biggest unit of government was a war-lord with a troop of horsemen and a fort on a hill. Language dissolved into a babble of barbaric new dialects. But agents of the building society travelled around the continent opening branch-offices shaped like the work at the centre. Members used these offices as holiday homes, schools and hospitals. Since there was no currency they paid their contributions in gifts of food and labour, and the agents served everyone with regular meals as a foretaste of the day when all good people would live together in God's eternal house. Society business was conducted in the language of the old construction company, the only language which could be written and read, so the local rulers needed the help of an agent before they could send a letter or inscribe a law. When at last, under threat of new invasions from the rim, the warlords united into dukedoms and kingdoms, the building society provided them with a civil service. The new kingdoms did not exactly correspond to the ancient provinces. They fitted together like the wedges of a cut cake, the thin edges touching the axletree at the centre. Trade revived, gold flowed into the foreman's vaults, the work was gradually re-peopled and repaired. Then building resumed. The work arose in arching buttresses and glittering pinnacles until it vanished into the bright cloud which reappeared above it. The work now went ahead as in the days of the old construction company, but with a different aim. The old company had been making a safe home for shareholders and their servants in the present. The new building society offered a safe home to everybody in the future.

When the great work entered the cloud many of us thought heaven had been reached and our foreman was talking to the divine architect. Everyone with spare money travelled to see him and tried to eat a meal in the works canteen. This led to over-crowding, so a foreman was elected who promised to enlarge the canteen and decorate it more lavishly than before. But finding himself short of cash he raised it by issuing a block of shares and auctioning them round the continent. These promised the buyers priority over other members when God came to allocate comfortable apartments in the finished work. Unluckily, however, the building society was still nominally a co-operative, and its advertisements still promised the best apartments to the poorest members, partly to compensate them for the living conditions they endured while the work was being built, partly because their labour was more important to it than gold. An angry agent working at ground level in a northern kingdom nailed up a list of objections:

1. The great work belonged to God, so nobody could buy or sell a place in it, and the foreman's shares were useless paper.
2. The new canteen was a waste of money and labour. The first and best foremen had been rough labourers who served humble meals in dark cellars.
3. Corrupt agents inside the axletree had brought real building to a halt. In recent years the only work on the summit had turned it into a pleasure-park for the amusement of the foreman and his friends.

The foreman replied that:

1. The work certainly belonged to God, who had decided to sell some of it and had told the foreman to act as his broker.
2. The canteen was the most essential part of the axletree, for nobody would work on it without regular meals. The earliest foremen had indeed been poor cooks by

modern standards but only because the laws of the time stopped them using a decent kitchen.

3. Building had not come to a halt. More people laboured on the work than ever before. There was no amusement park on the summit, just a good hotel for important visitors.

The protesting agent responded by calling on kings and people everywhere to seize the axletree and restore it to co-operative management. So great armies assembled, some to defend the work and some to seize it, for many were jealous of the wealth it contained.

Before the fighting began one of the architects employed on the fabric made a surprising suggestion. He said the building had run into financial trouble because it was conical – every three feet on the height required an addition of two to the entire circumference. This ensured stability, but unless the workforce continually increased it also ensured that the growth of the building became imperceptible, as was the present case. Since steady growth was financially impossible the work was therefore condemned by its shape to a history of booms and slumps. The last slump had destroyed the old construction company. The next would break up the building society, unless it used a cheaper method of working. He suggested that if the axletree were built on a framework of iron beams and hoops it could rise from the present summit in a straight, safe, and surprisingly cheap shaft. Even if heaven were twice the height of the present structure he would undertake to reach it in fifty years. Our foreman and the protesting agent found the idea so ludicrous that they hardly even denounced it, for both thought the shape of the axletree was as much God's gift as its purpose, and to doubt one was to doubt the other. So armies marched inside and warfare spread along every gallery from base to summit.

At first the foreman's people held the high places and the attackers tried to starve them by intercepting food supplies from the base, but the base was vast, and when the attackers got onto higher platforms they lost control of it. Soon both sides held vertical sections converging at the top and separated by uncertain people in the middle. The contestants paused to gather more wealth and weapons from their supporters on the ground, and during this pause leaders on both sides started squabbling – each was a king in his own lands and disliked sharing his gains with the rest. So by mutual agreement, by force or by fraud the great work was split into as many sections as the surrounding nations, and this arrangement was also unstable. Many had fought for their king because he had promised to share out the profits locked in the axletree. They now found they had given him extra power to tax them and were not even getting the social benefits granted by the building society. Revolts broke out at ground level, kings fought their own people and did not always win. Many new sorts of government got into the axletree but all looked rather like the old construction company. We had monarchies ruled by a company chairman, and plutocracies with a strong board of directors, and republics with a parliament of shareholders; yet all got their food, fuel and raw material from poorly paid people on the ground outside. Half these companies acknowledged the works foreman and ate food cooked by his agents, but they did not pay him enough money to go on building. His hotel on the old summit was now ringed by a crown of separate summits, for each national company had begun building on the highest part of its own side, using the methods of the discredited architect. Iron frames were common but conservative companies built as much as possible with stone, so their summits tended to top-heaviness. Very competitive companies over-awed their rivals with grandiose summits of bravely painted plaster, for the highest had reached a level of calm air high above the cloud and winds which soaked and buffeted the building lower down. And all these summits were bright with flags and glittering weapons, though fear of warfare at that height prevented fighting from rising far above ground level. It was a long time before the strength of the super-structures was tested. The managers in them were much closer to each other than to their employees lower down, so the summits were linked by bridges which provided reinforcement, though each bridge had a section which could be pulled back when neighbours quarrelled. And the word *tower* was never spoken, because towers were still notorious for sometimes falling down.

Now that a dozen competing companies owned the axletree it grew so fast that the continent below could no longer supply enough material. Our merchants crossed oceans, deserts and mountains to tell remote people of God's great unfinished house in the middle of the world, and to persuade them to contribute to its enlargement. They were being honest when they spoke like this, for from a distance the axletree was clearly a single work. Some foreigners tried to resist us but they could not withstand the tools and weapons we had devised to elevate our axletree. The best produce of every sea and continent on the globe was brought by ship and carriage into our insatiable market. The food was eventually excreted in rivers of sewage which streamed for leagues across the surrounding country and fuel was turned into mountains of cinders which kept light from the inhabiters of the lowest galleries. Smoke poured down from vents in the national towers, staining the clouds and discolouring everything below them.

And then the national companies found the material of the whole world was not enough for them and began fighting for it in the biggest wars the world has ever seen. Armies fired on each other from ground level up to the axletree's highest platforms. Summits crumbled and toppled through clouds in avalanches of soldiers, flags and weapons which crushed whole populations on the lower levels, sweeping them down to the ashes and excrement of the land beneath. The axletree seemed to be reducing itself to a heap of ruin, but when the smoke cleared most of it was intact and only very old-fashioned parts were badly damaged. One superstructure was so top-heavy that all the directors and shareholders went down in the first shock of war, and the remaining managers were labour-leaders who tried to organize their people into a co-operative building society. Critics say they eventually failed in this, and the workers were as ill-treated as in the worst construction companies. Even so, the new co-operative worked until its summit was one of the biggest, and other summits were repaired just as quickly. The death of millions delayed the building by only a few years, for the strength of the work was not in armies and leaders, but in the central markets and bankvaults which companies shared while their employees murdered each other in the sunlight. Some historians suggested that great wars were the axletree's way of shedding obsolete structures and superfluous populations, and described the great work as a growing creature with its own intelligence. Others said that a growth which shed old branches by burning off its healthiest leaves and fruit did not show intelligence of a high kind.

An uneasy time began. The managers of the largest summits tried to keep their fights for material to remote lands producing it, while secretly preparing for a war vast enough to kill everyone in the world. Construction companies tried to raise their profits by pressing down the wages of the workforce, and labour leaders fought back by organizing strikes and threatening to turn their companies into co-operatives. Some of the worst-run companies did turn co-operative, and signed treaties with the first co-operative, which wanted allies. And whether they headed construction companies or co-operatives, very few directors in the high summits trusted their employees, but spent more and more money on spies and policemen. And the summits went on rising until one day, among rumours of revolt and corruption and increasing poverty and accumulating weapons, we came to the sky.

A college of investigators had been founded to protect summits from lightning, to study and stabilize the weather, and to maintain ventilation. This college employed clever people from most companies in the work, for no single company could control the climate alone, and although each company liked to keep knowledge to itself they noticed that knowledge grew faster among people who shared it. I was a secretary in that college, recording its achievements and reporting them to the directors of the highest summit of all, for I had been born there.

One evening I sat beside the professor of air, checking rockets at a table on the balcony of our office. This was in a low part of the work above a gate where the coalfleets sailed in, for one of our jobs was to superintend the nearby smoke station. We had found that smoke, enclosed in bags, could lift large weights, and had used this discovery to create a new transport system. My chief was testing the powder which made the rockets fly, I tested the fuses. Without raising my eyes I could see fat black ships wallowing up the shining creek from a distant ocean. They docked directly under us but it would be a week before they unloaded. This was mid-summer and a general holiday. All building had stopped, most fires were damped, the college had made a gale the night before and swept the sky clear and blue.

The cries of children and picnickers came tiny and shrill, like birdnotes, from the green hills and valleys beside the creek. These smooth slopes had been made by giving ashbings a coat of soil and turf, and the lowest people liked to holiday on them. Even I had happy memories of playing there as a child. But the companies had started turning the old ashes into brick, and already half the green park had been scraped flat. The diggers had uncovered a viaduct of arches built two thousand years before by the old imperial construction company. The sight might have given me a melancholy sense of the booms and slumps of history but I was too excited. I was going to visit the height of the axletree.

The chief packed his rockets in a slingbag. I shouldered a light launching tube. We walked through our offices in the thickness of the outer wall and down some steps to the smokestation.

A two-seater lift was locked to our platform. We climbed in and arranged cushions round us while the bag filled up. It was a light blue bag with the college sign on the side: a yellow silk flame with an eye in the centre. The chief unlocked us and we swung into the hot oblique updraught used by very important people. We crossed the docks, the retorts and crucibles of the furnacemen and a crowded circus cheering a ball-game. We passed through the grate of an ancient portcullis, ascended a canyon between sewage cylinders with cedar forests on top, then swooped through a ventilator in the first ceiling. Within an hour we had pierced ceilings which separated six national companies, the customs officers leaping up to salute us on the lip of the ventilators as soon as they recognized the college colours. In solemn music we crossed the great canteen, rising into the dome as the foreman of the work, like a bright white bee, served the sacred food to a swarm of faithful on the floor below. The ventilator in the dome opened into a windcave where an international orchestra was distilling rain with bright instruments into an aquarium that was the head water of three national rivers. We lost the hot updraught here but the chief steered us into a current flowing up a slide of rubble where an ancient summit had been shaken down by earthquakes during the first big slump. It was landscaped with heather, gorse and hunting lodges. Above that we entered the base of the tallest summit of all, ascending vertically through floors which were all familiar to me: hospitals, nurseries, schools, emporiums, casinos, banks, courts and boardrooms. Here we were stopped at a ventilator for the first time, since the highest inhabited parts of the tower belonged to the military. The chief spent a long time proving that his rockets were not weapons but tools for testing the upper air, and even so he was only allowed through when I showed the examining colonel, by a secret sign, that I was not only a member of the college but an agent of his company. So we were allowed to rise up the glass funnel to the scaffolding. On every side we saw officers in neat identical clothes tending the huge steel catapults and firing pans poised to pour down thunderbolts and lightning on the other parts of the work, especially toward towers with co-operative connections. We passed through a builders' village, deserted except for its watchmen, then nothing surrounded us but a frame of slender rods and the deep blue blue blue of the gloaming sky. The thin cold air began to hurt my lungs. We stopped when our bag touched the highest platform. The chief slung the rockets from his shoulder and climbed a ladder to the very top. I followed him.

I had never known such space. The pure dark blueness was unstained by the faintest wisp of cloud. I lay flat on the planks with my head over the platform edge, trying to see the sunset on the horizon, but the golden shine of it was cut small by the web of bridges linking the summits lower down. I felt like a fly clinging to the tip of an arrow, the first of a flight of them soaring through infinite air. Lights were blinking on the tips of summits below. These were the signals of college men who would observe our experiments with lens and theodolite. The chief signalled back at them with a handlamp. He even blinked at the spiky summit of the great co-operative, which was nearest. This was a joke, because the co-operative pretended to ignore the work of our college, while watching it very closely.

The chief set the tube to launch a rocket vertically for a quarter of a mile: the colour and length of the fiery tail would show the nature of the air it travelled through. All being ready, he told me to start the water clock, then lit the short fuse. My eyes, of course, were on the clock, which ticked off only four drops before I heard an explosion. Looking up I saw a great shower of sparks. Our rocket had broken at a height of sixty feet. "A dud," said the chief, and fired another, which also broke up too soon.

"Sir!" I said, staring at the clock. "It has exploded at exactly the same height."

"Coincidence!" grunted the chief, but checked the third rocket very carefully before firing, and that also broke at the same height. I trembled and the chief was sweating. With great precision he angled the tube and fired the fourth rocket upward along the diagonal of a square. It exploded six drops later. We fired the remaining rockets at the same angle in twenty different directions with the same result. Which showed there was a very wide obstruction sixty feet above our heads.

You cannot understand our feelings unless you realize that for several centuries men had stopped believing that the world hung like a yolk inside an eggshell of sky. Holy people still thought the sky was God's home, and in wartime the heads of most big companies declared their tower was closest to God's original plan and would reach heaven first. But clearly the various companies were not building to reach anywhere but to surpass each other for financial and military reasons. So educated men regarded the universe as an infinite space only measurable by the distance between the bodies it contained. We thought we could go on building for ever.

The chief and I stared upward. It was hard to believe that these starry globes we had studied from infancy (some shining with reflected light, some composed of it) were on the far side of a barrier. We were roused by a breath of breeze. Lights on the lower summits were blinking frantic questions at us. The chief took his lamp and signalled that he would confer on the matter soon, then led me down the ladder to the lift. He said, "I believe you spy for the directors of this tower. How can I obtain an immediate interview with its president?" I told him the president could be most quickly contacted through his generals. We descended to the military level where the officer in charge let the chief write this note, and took us into custody while it was delivered.

> Sir: Shortly before midnight I conducted tests which show there is a vast obstruction sixty feet above the top platform of your tower. This is either a zone of intense heat or the under-surface of that great transparent ceiling our ancestors called *the sky*. Please allow me to supervise the final stage of your building and test the nature of the barrier it will strike. As professor of air, director of international climate and inventor of the smokelift I am clearly qualified to do this.

We were taken to the president's office soon after dawn. He sat at the head of a long table with directors and generals down each side, and we stood at the foot of it, but were not greatly impressed. This was the most powerful committee in the world but it had the exhausted, unshaven look of men who had been arguing all night, and compared with his official portraits the president seemed small and furtive. Without raising his eyes from a paper on the table he read these words in a quick monotone.

> "By virtue of the powers invested in me by this great Company I grant your request to supervise the final stage of the work. You are allocated a director's salary, office, and apartments at the highest executive level of our summit, and your employment commences upon signing your agreement of the following conditions.
> FIRSTLY Your superior in this project is the commander of the armed forces. All requests for materials and assistance, all orders and all communications with the world below will pass through his office.
> SECONDLY You will create as soon as possible a thick cloud to hide our building operation from other summits, and will give scientific reasons for this which raise no political, financial or religious speculations in the management of other summits or in the general public.
> THIRDLY On reaching the sky you will conduct tests for the purpose of answering these questions:
> How thick is it?
> Can it be penetrated?
> Is the substance of it commercially useful?
> Does the upper surface support life?
> If so, is that life intelligent and/or belligerent and/or commercially useful?
> Can the upper surface support men?
> Is it strong enough to support big buildings?
> LASTLY All your activities, and the reasons for them, and any discoveries you make, are official secrets, and from the present moment in time any

failure to fulfil these conditions is a treasonable act punishable by life imprisonment or death without public trial as stipulated in the Company Laws Employees Protection Section paragraph 73 clause 19."

The president raised his eyes and we all looked at the chief, who nodded thoughtfully then said, "I am grateful for the trust you have placed in me, sir, and will try to deserve it. But secrecy is impossible. My tests last night were observed by experts on all the adjacent summits. Several hours have passed since then, and although this is a holiday I see that our neighbour in the east is already shifting large amounts of building material onto his upper platform."
One wall of the room was a single sheet of glass and the directors and generals sprang up and crowded to it. The co-operative summit had become very dark and distinct against the brightness of the ascending sun and there was spiderlike activity among the bristling cranes at the top. The commander of the armed forces punched one hand with the other and cried, "If they want to make a race of it they haven't a hope in hell! We've sixty feet to go, they've six hundred. Professor, I'll see you later." He strode from the room. After a variety of exclamations the rest of the company stared at the president who had sunk into his chair looking very tired and cross. At last he sighed and said, "Well, if other governments know the facts already we can show we have nothing to hide by announcing them publicly. But God knows how the stock exchange will react. On second thoughts, no public announcements. I bind everyone here to the strictest secrecy. I will pass the information to other heads of state in a private memorandum. I'm sure that even old –" (he named the chairman of the co-operative) "– will see the value of keeping his people ignorant. So sign the agreement, professor, and get on with the job."

Three days later I stood with the chief on top of a strong, prefabricated silver pylon, and the sky was a few inches above my upturned face. It was too transparent to be seen directly, but glanced at sideways the lucid blue was rippled by rainbow glimmerings like those golden lines cast by sunlight on sand under shallow water. The ripples came from the point in the sky where the sun's rays pierced most directly, and their speed and tints changed throughout the day. At dawn they were slow and tinted with saffron, quickening toward noon with glints of gold, green and crimson, then gradually toward purple-blue in the gloaming. It took a while to recognize this. The summit was swaying through a wide circle, so the ripples crossed our vision in a cataract of broken dazzlings until the pylon started travelling in the same direction, and then they only became clear for five minutes. At these times I did not feel I was looking up. The whole axletree seemed a long rope tied to my heels. I felt I was hanging above a heavenly floor from a world as remote as the moon. Yet I was not dizzy. I liked this immensity. I wanted the axletree to break and let me fall into it. As gently as possible I stretched out my hand and touched. The sky was cool and silken-smooth with an underlying softness and warmth. I felt it with my whole body. The feeling was not sexual, for it excited no part more than the rest, not even the fingertips touching the slender rippling rainbows. The sway of the tower began diverging from the flow of the ripples, which took on a broken look. Fearing that the loveliness was escaping, my hand pressed instinctively harder and a tide of blood flowed down from the fingertips, staining the arm to the elbow. I stared at it, still pressing hard and feeling no pain until the chief struck my arm down and I fainted.

I woke with a bandaged hand and four fingers shortened by the length of the nails. It was late afternoon and the chief was poking the sky with little rods. He stopped when he saw I was conscious, asked about my

exact sensations before fainting, wrote them down, then pointed east and said, "We are no longer alone."
Several towers had sprouted surprisingly in the last three days. One of them, by employing acrobats as construction workers, had gained a mile-high superstructure of bamboo canes. But the big co-operative summit, though still the second highest, had grown very little in spite of its early start. And now the vastest smokelift I have ever seen was tethered to the top of that summit by many cables. The bag was shaped like an upside-down pyramid. The top surface was level with our platform, and in the centre a crouching figure handled something which flared and sparkled. We heard a brief humming of almost painful intensity and above the lift appeared a white mark which sped across the sky and curved down into a cloud which hid the horizon. The chief said, "He's started testing it with fire. I'm leaving that till last."

Next day the company's directors came up to the platform and stared at the sky with all the expressions of men faced by a beautiful woman. The eyes and mouths of many gaped very wide and a few were moved to tears. The president kept sighing and nodding as if the sky was defeating him in a crucial argument. The commander of the armed forces frowned and fidgeted as if it was wasting his time; he was more interested in the co-operative lift, on which a group of men like our own had gathered. Only the chief looked eager and happy. He grinned determinedly upward as if saying, "Yes, sky, you dazzle and baffle other men, but not me. You won't be able to keep anything from me."
We went down to the president's office, sat round the table, and the chief read out this report.

> "Gentlemen, you have just seen a transparent surface which encloses the earthly globe at an altitude of 22 parasangs, or 572 stadia, or 62,920 fathoms. Although this surface is in rapid movement it feels

beguilingly smooth, soft and lukewarm if touched gently, but repels anything solid which presses hard, dissolving flesh, crumbling bone and wood to powder, and making stones, metal and crystals explode with a violence growing greater with the density of the mineral and the force driving it into contact. These explosions exert downward with no effect upon the heavenly surface, a fact with political consequences. Less advanced summits are building catapults at their tops with the clear intention of testing the sky from a distance by throwing things at it. This will cause blasts big enough to damage the advanced summits. We should make it plain that we will regard such tests as acts of war. When jets of water, ink, acid, mercury and molten metal strike the surface it absorbs them without stain or alteration, but a strong flame leaves a white scar which allows us to observe and measure the surface movement. Above our summit the heavenly continent is turning westward at 7¾ parasangs per hour. The play of prismatic colours across the surface is an effect of the sunlight, and quite unrelated to the real movement of the heavenly sphere, which is regular, continuous, and takes 27⅓ days to turn around the earthly sphere. In other words, it rotates with the moon.

"You have asked me questions about the heavenly continent: how thick, if pierceable etcetera. At least one more test is needed before I can answer accurately, but I can now tell you what is imaginable and what is likely.

"Classical astronomy would regard the heavenly firmament as the inner surface of a glassy shell carrying the moon. But a rigid shell would be shattered by the speed of its rotation and our air would not stop a liquid shell falling to the earth below. The classical model only holds good if the sky is made of transparent vapour, at once lighter than air and as dense as molten metal. Such a vapour is impossible.

"So let us imagine there is a dense, transparent fluid filling the entire universe. Our earth occupies a bubble of air in this fluid, a bubble at the centre of a whirlpool. The heavenly bodies are floating round us in different currents at different speeds, the nearest current carrying the moon. This idea is both attractive and convincing: until we remember that the light of the farthest and steadiest stars would be reaching us through fluid moving in different speeds and directions. This would give the highest heavens a warped and shifting aspect they do not possess.

"I offer you a third model. You perhaps know that all water has a skin protecting it from air. This skin is invisible to the human eye, impalpable to human touch, yet tough enough for small insects to hang from, walk across, and build upon. Imagine, then, that there is a light vapour which lies upon air as air lies upon water, and reacts with air to create a tense surface, perhaps only a few atoms thick. This surface has properties which human insects cannot understand before they have sampled the vapour on the far side, but it moves with the moon because the moon pulls it along as it pulls the oceans of the world below. The greater speed is explained by the absence of shores and a solid bottom.

"This is the likeliest model of the world we occupy, and I ask leave to test it by the following means.

"Only flame impresses the heavenly surface, so let us build in our summit a furnace with a ring of burners, and let us direct against the sky a circle of flame five feet in diameter. If this does not cut a hole into the upper universe let us keep the furnace burning for a lunar month of 28 days. This should engrave a fault-line round the inside of the cosmic egg-shell, perhaps splitting it open long enough for us to grab a sample of what lies beyond.

"This test should endanger nobody, unless, perhaps, those beside the burners, foremost of whom will be myself. The sky will suffer no great injury. Flames mark it, yes, but since the start of the world it has been pierced from above, every night, by jagged meteorites of white-hot stone and iron. The heavenly surface would be scarred all over if these had done lasting damage. You can authorize my test in the knowledge that the natural forces maintaining the sky will start repairing it as soon as we relax our efforts. Man can no more destroy the sky than he can destroy the ocean."

The chief laid his paper on the table. The president muttered, "You shouldn't have mentioned the ocean. The excrement from our factories and refineries has poisoned most of it."

The chief seemed not to hear. He folded his arms, leaned back in his chair and remarked conversationally, "Our utmost skill, of course, may fail to pierce this barrier. In which case your great summit will soon be equalled by all the others in the work."

There was a long silence. The eyes of nearly everyone round the table seemed to be staring inside themselves. Then a director spoke in a low voice which gradually grew very loud.

"I am a religious man. That sky we gazed upon less than an hour ago – that moving sea of heavenly blossom – was the loveliest work of God's hand I have ever beheld. I am certain that this sky, like everything else men have not corrupted, exists for a great good reason. Humanity has lived beneath this dome, been sheltered by this dome from the dawn of creation. And you, professor, ask us to rip it open tomorrow like a can of beans? You have given us three little toy pictures of the universe, and told us to believe in the safest one, and asked permission to test it. The fact that you need to test it shows your ignorance. Your test may destroy something essential and beautiful which you did not make and cannot replace. Mankind has taken the whole of human history to reach this height. Why should we not pause for a couple of years and consider the situation carefully?"

"Because of the co-ops!" cried the commander of the armed forces. "And because of our so-called allies. Believe me, that sky is going to be shafted by someone sooner or later, and whoever reaches the far side first will have a *colossal* military advantage. Just now the advantage is ours. The co-ops know everything we know, but they can't float a furnace on a smoke-filled envelope. Give them a month or two, though, and they'll carve their way through and claim the upper surface for themselves. We've got to get there first and claim it for free people everywhere. Then we can hold it against all comers."

"Gentlemen," said the president, "I do not wholly agree with my military adviser. The sky is not a territory we should defend against other summits – that would unite the whole world against us. But the sky *must* be pierced, not to give us advantages in a future war but to prevent war beginning here and now. Our entire structure is committed to growth. All wealth which does not go into building goes into weaponry. If we do not expand upward we must do it sideways, which means absorbing the bases of the neighbouring summits. In a quiet way our company is doing that already, but at least we have the excuse of needing the extra ground to build higher. Without that excuse our enlargement will be an obvious act of naked aggression. Professor, make this burner of yours as big as you can. Employ all the skill and manpower you can, use more than you need, build several damned furnaces in case one of them goes wrong. Blast a hole the entire axletree can use. And maybe we'll be able to maintain a stable state for another twenty years. By that time the world will have run out of building materials. But it won't be our problem."

There was a director who served on an international committee which attended to plumbing in the axletree's basement. He compensated for this squalid work by writing wildly hopeful poetry about the future of mankind. He said, "Mr. President, your description of our unhealthy state is accurate, but you suggest no cure. It is clear that for many years continuous expansion has done us great harm. The highest summits in the work contain the greatest extremes of wealth and poverty, the greatest expenditure on soldiers and policemen, and the greatest fears for the future, as your speech has demonstrated. The safest summits are a few low ones whose tops can still be seen by people on the ground outside, structures whose comforts and opportunities are shared by a whole community. I realize we cannot halt the whole great work by simply refusing to build, so let us announce, today, that we will leave the sky intact and build no higher if other companies and societies will stop building too. And let us call for the formation of an international parliament to rule the heavens, and let us give our highest platforms to that parliament. Then the sky can be tested, not rashly and rapidly, but carefully, over a period of years."

"You have not understood me," said the president. "If I even hint at halting our building programme the shareholders will withdraw their money from the constructive side of the work and invest it in the destructive side, the military side, which consumes nearly half our revenue already. Then allies and enemies will think we are about to make war, and will over-arm themselves too. In a matter of weeks this will lead to the catastrophic battle everyone dreads, the battle which destroys the whole axletree."

"But we are the most powerful company in the world!" said the poet. "Let us make our shareholders invest in things which do people good! Directly or indirectly we control the world's labour force, yet most labourers live very poorly. Mountains of grain rot in our warehouses while thousands of families die by famine in the lands outside."

"There is no profit in feeding poor people," said the financial secretary, "except on rare occasions when it will prevent a revolt. Believe me, I know people on the ground outside. They are lazy, ignorant, selfish and greedy. Give them a taste of wealth and security and they'll demand more of it. They'll refuse to obey us. They'll drag us down to their own sordid level. Not even the co-operatives are crazy enough to trust their surplus to the folk who produce it."
"But we are using our surplus to organize disasters!" said the poet. "If those who have grabbed more food and space and material than they need would share it, instead of bribing and threatening the rest with it, the world could become a splendid garden where *many* plants will grow beside this damned, prickly, many-headed, bloodstained cactus of a poisoned and poisoning TOWER."
"Strike that word from the minutes!" said the president swiftly.

Directors had jumped to their feet, one hid his face in his hands, the rest stared haggardly before them. The poet looked defiant. The chief seemed amused. The president said quietly, "Sit down, gentlemen. Our colleague is over-excited because his work at the lowest level of government has given him exaggerated notions of what can be done at the highest. We do as things do with us, and the biggest thing we know is the axletree."
The poet said, "It is not bigger than the earth below."
The president said, "But it has cut us off from the earth below. On the common earth men can save nothing, and their highest ambition is to die in one of our works hospitals. But the axletree is full of comfortable, well-meaning people who expect to rise to a higher position before they die and who mean to pass on their advantages to their children. They can only do this in a structure which keeps getting larger. They cannot see they are dealing out crime, famine and war to the earth below, because the axletree shelters them from these things. If

we oppose the unspoken wishes of the people in the axletree – unspoken because everybody shares them – we will be called levellers, and in two days our closest supporters will have replaced us."

There was silence, then the religious director said sadly, "I used to wish I lived in the age of faith when our great work was a shining structure with a single summit revered by the whole continent. I now suspect it only did good during the slump when it was a crumbling ruin whose servants fed hungry people upon ordinary ground. Until recently I still believed the axletree was planned by God to maintain art, knowledge and happiness. I now fear it is a gigantic dead end, that human history is an enormous joke."

"The fact remains," said the commander of the armed forces, "that we can only prevent an overall catastrophe by preparing what may become an overall catastrophe. People who can't face that fact have no place in politics."

"I disagree once more with my military adviser," said the president. "There is always a place for the idealist in politics. Our poet has given us a wonderful idea. He suggests we form an international parliament to rule the heavens. We certainly will! Our allies will like us for it, our competitors will think they can use it to delay us. Loud-mouthed statesmen everywhere will feel important because they are members of it, which will reduce the risk of war. I hope, sir" – he addressed the poet – "I hope you will represent us in this parliament. The whole conception is yours. You will be inaugurating a new era."

The poet blushed and looked pleased.

"Meanwhile," said the president, "since the formation of this parliament may take years, mankind will advance to its destiny in the sky. Science will open a gateway into a universal store-house of empty space, remote minerals, and unbreathable gas."

My chief and the army commander worked hard in the following days and all the people of the summit were drawn into money-making activity. Low-level fuel-bunkers and furnaces were built beneath crucibles from which pipes ran up the central lift-shaft. Lifts with clamps fixed to them now slid up cables attached to the axletree's outer wall. The top pylon sprouted three huge burners, each differently shaped, with spire-like drills in the centres and domes beneath to shield the operators. Meanwhile, foreign statesmen met the poet in a steering committee to draw up an agenda for an international legal committee which would write a constitution for an international parliament which would govern the heavens. The steering committee's first meetings were inconclusive. And then the first big test was held.

It lasted six seconds, made a mark on the sky like a twisted stocking, and produced a sound which paralysed the nearest operators and put observers on other summits into a coma lasting several hours. The sound was less concentrated at ground level, where the irritation it caused did not result in unconsciousness. And inside the axletree nobody heard it at all, or experienced it only as a pang of inexplicable unease: the outer shape of the building baffled the vibration. The chief announced to the directors that the test had been successful. He said, "We now know that our machines work perfectly. We now know, and can guard against, their effect on human beings. My technicians and all foreign observers are being issued with padded helmets which make the wearers deaf to exterior vibration. People on ground level can protect themselves by plugging their ears with twists of cloth or withered grass, though small lumps of rubber would be more suitable. We will start the main test in two days' time."
"You intend to deafen half the dwellers on the continent for a whole *month*?" said the president. "Listen, I don't like groundlings more than anybody else here. But I need their support. So does the axletree. So do you."
"We have enough resources to do without their support

for at least four weeks," said the director of food and fuel.
"But that din causes headaches and vomiting," said the president. "If twisted grass is not one hundred per cent effective the outsiders will swarm into the axletree and swamp us. The axletree will be the only place they can hear themselves think."

"All immigration into the axletree was banned the day before yesterday," said the director of public security. "The police are armed and alert."

"But here is a protest signed by many great scientists," said the president, waving a paper. "Most of them work for the professor's college. They say the tests have been planned on a too-ambitious scale, and the effect on world climate could be disastrous."

"Our new wave of prosperity will collapse if tests are curtailed," said the financial secretary. "Even outsiders get employment through that. They should be prepared to suffer some inconveniences."

"The scientists who signed that paper are cryptocooperators," said the army commander.

The president got up and walked round the room. He pointed to his chair and said, "Would anyone like to take my place? Whoever sits there will go down in history as a weakling or a coward, no matter what he decides to do."

Several directors eyed the chair thoughtfully, but nobody moved. "Right," said the president. "Let all outsiders on the earth below be supplied with earplugs and sleeping-pills. I authorize a test lasting one whole night, starting at sunset and ending at dawn. The public reaction will decide what we do after that. They may want us to hand over the whole works to our scribbler's heavenly parliament. The steering committee has agreed on an agenda now. I promoted that crazy scheme to distract attention from our activities, but I fear it will soon be my only hope of shedding *unbearable* responsibility. So now get out, all of you. Leave me alone."

Preparations for the big test were organized very quickly, and security precautions on our summit were so increased that movement there became very difficult. Machinery was being installed which only the army chief and the leading industrialists understood. The president seemed unwell and I was employed to guard and help him. He announced that he would pass the night of the test on the ground outside, using nothing but the protection supplied to ordinary people, and this was such good publicity that the other directors allowed it. So he and I travelled west to a mild brown land where low hills were clothed with vines and olives. We waited for sunset on the terrace of a villa. The president removed his shoes and walked barefoot on the warm soil. He said, "I like the feel of this. It's nourishing."

He lay down with his head in a bush of sweetsmelling herb. Bees walked across his face. "You can see they aren't afraid of me," he muttered through rigid lips. He sat up and pointed to the axletree, saying, "Everybody in there is crazy. I wonder what keeps it up?"

The sky overhead was clear and smooth but beyond a range of blue mountains lay a vaster range of turbulent clouds. These hid the axletree base so that the rest did, indeed, seem built on cloud.

The air grew cold, the sun set and the land was dark, but above the clouds the axletree was still sunlit. No separate summits were distinct, it looked like a golden tusk flushing to pinkness above the dark advancing up it form the base. Inside that dark the tiny lights of many windows defined the axletree against the large, accidental, irregular stars. My eye fixed on the top which flushed pink, then dimmed, and a white spark appeared where it had been, and the spark widened into a little white fan.

The noise hit us soon after that. We thrust rubber plugs into our ears, and that reduced it, but it was still unbearable. We would certainly have swallowed the sleeping-pills (which caused instant stupor) had I not produced helmets and clapped them on our heads. The relief was so profound that we both felt, I know, that absolute silence was the loveliest thing in the world. We were sitting on chairs now, and the moon was up, and the earth at our feet began gleaming moistly with worms. All creatures living in the earth or on solid bodies were struggling into the air. Ants, caterpillars and centipedes crawled up trees and clung in bunches to the extreme tips of twigs. Animals went to the tops of hills and crouched side by side, predators and victims, quite uninterested in feeding, but eventually clawing and biting to get on top of each other's backs. Birds tried to escape the air they usually felt at home in. Robins, partridges and finches packed themselves densely into the empty rabbit-holes. Winged insects fled to openings and clefts in animal bodies, which gave the best insulation from the sound. The president and I leapt to our feet, scratching and slapping ourselves in a cloud of midges, moths and mosquitoes. We ran to our cars, followed by the armed guards who came floundering out of the shrubberies.

The journey back was the most fearful in my life, far worse than what came after, because that was so unexpected that I had no time to fear it. On the moonlit road we passed pedestrians without pills who stumbled along retching with hands clapped to their ears. The air above was full of gulls, geese and migratory fowl who had sensed the zone of silence in the axletree. A parasang from the base I removed my helmet and found the noise had dwindled to the intensity of a toothache. The president huddled in the car corner muttering, "Oh no. Oh no. Oh no." He took off his helmet when he saw me without mine and said, "The sun rose two hours ago." I nodded. He said, "They're still burning the sky." From the summit a white scrolling line like an unbroken thread of smoke undulated toward the western horizon.

I told him that the pills eaten by the populace would keep them unconscious for another five or six hours. He said, "Can very small babies go so long without food?" His maudlin tone annoyed me and I answered briskly that babies were tougher than we knew.

The entrance was heavily barricaded and we would not have got in if the soldiers of our guard had not fired their weapons and roused comradely feelings among the soldiers inside. At the office of the weather-college the president was surrounded by officials who shouted and complained. An influx of rodents was making the lower dwellings unhabitable. The president kept whispering, "I'll try. Oh I'll try." We were lifted to the base of the great summit and found it as stoutly barricaded as the entrance. The guards were surprised to see us and took a long time to let us through. It was late evening when we reached the presidential office. The president said, "They're still doing it."
He uncorked a speaking tube which ran to the control room under the burners. A hideous droning came out. He screamed and corked it up and whispered, "How can I talk to them?"
I said I would carry a note for him.

Here is the text of notes which passed between the president and the control room in the next three days.
<u>President to control:</u> STOP. STOP. YOU ARE KILLING PEOPLE. WHEN WILL YOU STOP.
<u>Control to president:</u> WE EXPECT A MAJOR BREAK THROUGH IN THE NEAR FUTURE.
<u>President to control:</u> MASS SUICIDES ON GROUND BELOW. THOUGH SPRING, TREES, CROPS WITHER. RAT INVASION THREATENS AXLETREE BASE WITH BUBONIC PLAGUE. WHAT *GOOD* ARE YOU DOING?
<u>Control to president:</u> REGRET EXTREME MEASURES NECESSARY TO MAINTAIN STABLE ECONOMY.
<u>President to control:</u> CO-OPERATIVE ULTIMATUM

DECLARES TOTAL WAR IF YOU DON'T STOP IN TWENTY-FOUR HOURS.
Control to president: WE'RE READY FOR THEM.
President to control: RAPIDLY CONVENED HEAVENLY PARLIAMENT ORDERS YOU TO STOP. FOREMAN OF WORK DECLARES GOD WANTS YOU TO STOP. EVERYONE ON EARTH BEGS YOU TO STOP. PLEASE STOP. NOBODY SUPPORTS YOU EXCEPT SHAREHOLDERS, A CORRUPTED TRADE UNION, THE ARMY, AND MAD EXPERIMENTERS WITHOUT RESPECT FOR HUMAN LIFE.
Control to president: SUPPORT SUFFICIENT. THE SPIRIT OF MAN IS TOO GREAT TO BE CONFINED BY A PHYSICAL BOUNDARY.
The control room was always a comforting place after the hysteria below. In complete silence (everyone wore helmets) the chief, the army commander and the financial secretary sat round a triangular table controlling the industrial process which produced the flame. Their faces showed the stern jubilation of masterly men who understand exactly what they are doing. Dials and graphs indicated the current bank-rate, stock exchange index, food and fuel reserves, activity of stokers at furnaces, position of soldiers guarding them, flow of chemicals to the crucibles, flow of gas to the burners, and the heat and width of the flame. A needle would flicker, then a hand would change the angle of a lever, or write and despatch an order. Between these times the triumvirate played knockout whist.

I was taking the final note down in the lift when I sensed a silence. Shielding my eyes I leaned out, looked up and saw the blue heaven opening and coming down to us. A lovely white flower bloomed whose hundred petals and stamens reached down and embraced us all. I was suddenly in white mist beside a white wall. The cable holding the lift must have snapped. I was spinning (I now know) downward through drenching whiteness, but I thought I was going up. Until I glimpsed collapsing pinnacles with whiteness gushing round them, water of course. I spun in drenching whiteness down cataracts of drenching whiteness flecked with rubble, bodies or furniture. And then I was in sunshine a few yards above plunging water and, ah, great waves. I went beyond these waves. I saw an edge of foaming water racing across fields, islanding woods and villages. Tiny figures waded, gesticulating from doors, then a huge wave engulfed them. A few floated up, some clinging to each other, then a vaster wave smashed down on them and nothing floated after that. The wind which carried the lift took me skyward and then back toward that white pillar, that waterfall from the sky beneath which the work of two thousand years was melting like a sandcastle. I grinned as I flew toward that dazzling pillar but I did not strike it, the lift went down again and out with the waves again to that foamy edge racing across the ordinary green and brown earth. Later I lost sight of the pillar. Either the heavenly continent had healed up or dissolved completely into water. The sky has been a lighter shade of blue ever since.

I must have managed the lift intelligently for I came down in shallow water near a ridge of rocks, a shore of the new sea. I sat a long time on those rocks, sometimes howling, sometimes weeping, always staring at the waves which drowned everything I knew and will drown it forever. I tried to think of a reason for living and failed, but life is too strong to need reasons. Next day two quite new sensations, hunger and loneliness, made me walk until I met a tribe of nomads. They have strange notions of hygiene but are otherwise tolerant and generous. When I had learned their language they valued my ability to exactly weigh, measure and record their herds and produce. I now have sons who are keen to learn arithmetic but refuse to learn, and will certainly never read, the language of the axletree. The older tribesmen know something about the axletree but the knowledge confuses them. They prefer to forget it. Yet I am the man who touched the sky! And when I try explaining this to my boys, because sons should admire fathers, the younger nudges the elder who says, "Did you visit the sun too? Did you stand on it, Dad? Was it hot?"

A week ago we pitched tents below a rocky cliff. Broken columns stood before the entrance to a ravine, which I explored. It led to a marble block carved with these words in the language of the old empire:

OZYMANDIAS
3D EMPEROR OF THE GREAT WHEEL
RECEIVED
FROM
GOD
IN
THE CAVERN
BEHIND
THIS STONE
THE
PLAN
OF THE
AXLETREE
LOOK ON HIS WORK YE MIGHTY
AND DESPAIR

The block has a crack the width of my finger between the top edge and the granite rock above. Tests with a stick show that the sheepskin on which I write this account can be slid through to fall in the cave behind. The marble is too vast to be moved by any but administrative people commanding a large labour-force to satisfy idle curiosity, so unless there is a shattering earthquake my history will not be found till the next world empire is established. Many centuries will pass before that happens, because tribes dispersed round a central sea will take longer to unify. But mere love-making and house-keeping, mere increase of men will bring us all together again one day, though I suppose ruling castes will speed the business by organising invasion and plunder. So when unity is achieved the accumulation of capital which created the first great tower will lead to another, or to something very similar.

But men are not completely sheeplike. Their vanity ensures that they never exactly repeat the past, if they know what it is. So if you have understood this story you had better tell it to others.

A LIKELY STORY OUTSIDE A DOMESTIC SETTING

"Listen, you owe me an explanation. We've had such great times together – you're beautiful – you know I love you – and now you don't want to see me again. Why? Why?"

"Jings, you take everything very seriously."

A LIKELY STORY WITHIN A DOMESTIC SETTING

"Fuck who you like but the rent is overdue and the electricity is going to be cut off and we've no food and the baby is hungry."
"Our love once meant much more to me than money so I'm not giving you any."

Alasdair Gray

LEAN TALES

FOR AGNES OWENS
AND JAMES KELMAN

LONDON 1996

THE STORY OF A RECLUSE

MY FATHER WAS THE REV. JOHN KIRKWOOD OF EDINBURGH, a man very well known for the rigour of his life and the tenor of his pulpit ministrations. I might have sometimes been tempted to bless Providence for this honourable origin, had not I been forced so much more often to deplore the harshness of my nurture. I have no children of my own, or none that I saw fit to educate, so perhaps speak at random; yet it appears my father may have been too strict. In the matter of pocket-money, he gave me a pittance, insufficient for his son's position, and when, upon one occasion, I took the liberty to protest, he brought me up with this home thrust of inquiry: "Should I give you more, Jamie, will you promise me it shall be spent as I should wish?" I did not answer quickly, but when I did, it was truly: "No," said I. He gave an impatient jostle of his shoulders, and turned his face to the study fire, as though to hide his feelings from his son. Today, however, they are very clear to me; and I know how he was one part delighted with my candour, and three parts revolted by the cynicism of my confession. I went from the room ere he had answered in any form of speech; and I went, I must acknowledge, in despair. I was then two and twenty years of age, a medical student of the University, already somewhat involved with debt, and already more or less (although I can scarce tell how) used to costly dissipations. I had a few shillings in my pocket; in a billiard room in St Andrew's Street I had shortly quadrupled this amount at pyramids, and the billiard room being almost next door to a betting agency, I staked the amount on the hazard of a race. At about five in the afternoon of the next day, I was the possessor of some thirty pounds – six times as much as I had ever dreamed of spending. I was not a bad young man, although a little loose. I may have been merry and lazy; until that cursed night I had never known what it was to be overpowered with drink; so it is possible I was overpowered the more completely. I have never clearly been aware of where I went or what I did, or of how long a time elapsed till my wakening. The night was dry, dark, and cold; the lamps and the clean pavements and bright stars delighted me; I went before me with a baseless exultation in my soul, singing, dancing, wavering in my gait with the most airy inconsequence, and all at once at the corner of a street, which I can still dimly recall, the light of my reason went out and the thread of memory was broken.

I came to myself in bed, whether it was that night or the next I have never known, only the thirty pounds were gone! I had certainly slept some while, for I was sober; it was not yet day, for I was aware through my half-closed eyelids of the light of a gas jet; and I had undressed, for I lay in linen. Some little time, my mind hung upon the brink of consciousness; and then, with a start of recollection, recalling the beastly state to which I had reduced myself, and my father's straitlaced opinions and conspicuous position, I sat suddenly up in bed. As I did so, some sort of hamper tore apart about my waist; I looked down and saw, instead of my night-shirt, a woman's chemise copiously laced about the sleeves and bosom. I sprang to my feet, turned, and saw myself in a cheval glass. The thing fell but a little lower than my knees; it was of a smooth and soft fabric; the lace very fine, the sleeves half way to my elbow. The room was of a piece; the table well supplied with necessaries of the toilet; female dresses hanging upon nails; a wardrobe of some light varnished wood against the wall; a foot bath in the corner. It was not my night-shirt; it was not my room; and yet by its shape and the position of the window, I saw it exactly corresponded with mine; and that the house in which I found myself must be the counterpart of my father's. On the floor in a heap lay my clothes as I had taken them off; on the table my pass-key, which I perfectly recognized. The same architect, employing the same locksmith, had built two identical houses and had them fitted with identical locks; in some drunken aberration I had mistaken the door, stumbled into the wrong house, mounted to the wrong room and sottishly gone to sleep in the bed of some young lady. I hurried into my clothes, quaking, and opened the door.

So far it was as I supposed; the stair, the very paint was of the same design as at my father's, only instead of the cloistral quiet which was perennial at home, there rose up to my ears the sound of empty laughter and unsteady voices. I bent over the rail, and looking down and listening, when a door opened below, the voices reached me clearer. I heard more than one cry "good night"; and with a natural instinct, I whipped back into the room I had just left and closed the door behind me.

A light step drew rapidly nearer on the stair; fear took hold of me, lest I should be detected, and I had scarce slipped behind the door, when it opened and there entered a girl of about my own age, in evening dress, black of hair, her shoulders naked, a rose in her bosom. She paused as she came in, and sighed; with her back still turned to me, she closed the door, moved towards the glass, and looked for a while very seriously at her own image. Once more she sighed, and as if with a sudden impatience, unclasped her bodice.

Up to that moment, I had not so much as formed a thought; but then it seemed to me I was bound to interfere. "I beg your pardon –" I began, and paused. She turned and faced me without a word; bewilderment, growing surprise, a sudden anger, followed one another on her countenance.

"What on earth –" she said, and paused too.

"Madam," I said, "for the love of God, make no mistake. I am no thief, and I give you my word I am a gentleman. I do not know where I am; I have been vilely drunken – that is my paltry confession. It seems that your house is built like mine, that my pass-key opens your lock, and that your room is similarly situate to mine. How or when I came here, the Lord knows; but I awakened in your bed five minutes since – and here I am. It is ruin to me if I am found; if you can help me out, you will save a fellow from a dreadful mess; if you can't – or won't – God help me."

"I have never seen you before," she said. "You are none of Manton's friends."

"I never even heard of Manton," said I. "I tell you I don't know where I am. I thought I was in – Street, No. 15 – Rev. Dr Kirkwood's, that is my father."

"You are streets away from that," she said; "you are in the Grange, at Manton Jamieson's. You are not fooling me?"

I said I was not. "And I have torn your night-shirt," cried I. She picked it up, and suddenly laughed, her brow for the first time becoming cleared of suspicion. "Well," she said, "this is not like a thief. But how could you have got in such a state?"

"Oh!" replied I, "the great affair is not to get in such a state again."

"We must get you smuggled out," said she. "Can you get out of the window?"

I went over and looked; it was too high. "Not from this window," I replied, "it will have to be the door."

"The trouble is that Manton's friends –" she began, "they play roulette and sometimes stay late; and the sooner you are gone, the better. Manton must not see you."

"For God's sake not!" I cried.

"I was not thinking of you in the least," she said; "I was thinking of myself."

And then Robert Louis Stevenson laid down his pen

leaving a fragment of perfect prose which has tantalized me since the mid sixties when I read it in a little secondhand book bought for one shilling from Voltaire and Rousseau's shop at the corner of Park Road and Eldon Street. The cover is soft black leatherette with a copy of the author's signature stamped in gold on the front, a grove of three gold palmtrees on the spine, and on the titlepage, in red, the words *Weir of Hermiston: Some Unfinished Stories*.

Suetonius says that the Roman Emperor Tiberius enjoyed asking literary men awkward questions like, what songs the sirens sang? What name Achilles used when disguised as a girl? In the seventeenth century Doctor Browne of Norwich suggested these questions were not wholly unanswerable, so in our century the poet Graves tested his muse by making her answer them. Can I deduce how *The Story of a Recluse* would continue if Stevenson had finished it?

I must first get Jamie out of this house which is so miraculously like and unlike his own. By like and unlike I mean more than the coincidence of architecture and doorlocks, the difference of moral tone. In both the Rev. Dr Kirkwood's manse and Manton Jamieson's Grange a spirited youngster of twenty-two, one a boy, one a girl, lives with an older man they are inclined to dread. Stevenson had a habit of creating characters dialectically. Perhaps every author works in this way, but Stevenson's antagonistic or linked opposites are unusually definite. In *Kidnapped* the cautious lowland Whig, David Balfour, contains a pride and a courage which only become evident when he is coupled with the touchy highland Jacobite, Alan Breck Stewart, who displays his pride and courage in his garments. *The Master of Ballantrae* is about two brothers, one a dutiful, long-suffering toiler who hardly anyone likes, the other an adventurous, revengeful waster with charming social manners. In *Weir of Hermiston* each character is the antithesis of one or two others, with the Scottish State Prosecutor, Lord Weir, maintaining unity by being the antithesis of everybody. In *The Strange Case of Dr Jekyll and Mr Hyde* a respected healer and detested murderer alternate inside the same skin. Manton Jamieson can only be the counterpart of the Rev. Dr Kirkwood if he is a dominant antifather, a strong lord of misrule. Since men drink and gamble in his house this has been already indicated, but if he too gambles it must be with no fear of losing. He must be formidable. No more need be deduced just now about this character. Several pages will pass before Jamie meets him, because Stevenson had already written a story about a young man blundering at night into a strange house containing a young woman and being caught there by a formidable older man.

The Sire de Malétroit's Door is one of his poorer tales. His imagination works best when he deals with Scotland, and this tale is set in the blood-and-thunder France of *The Three Musketeers*. A young nobleman, fleeing from enemies, escapes through a mysteriously open door at the end of a cul-de-sac. He finds he has got out of one trap into another, a trap set by a rich old man for the lover of his niece. The old man refuses to believe that the nobleman and niece do not know each other, and gives them till dawn to choose between being murdered or married. Stevenson had a deliberate policy of putting heroes into exciting positions for which they are not responsible. He expounds it in his essay, *A Gossip About Romance*, where he declares that most human life is a matter of responding to circumstances we have not chosen, and that "the interest turns, not upon what a man shall choose to do, but on how he manages to do it; not on the passionate slips and hesitations of the conscience, but on the problems of the body and of the practical intelligence, in clean, open-air adventure, the shock of arms and the diplomacy of life. With such material as this it is impossible to build a play, for the serious theatre exists solely on moral grounds, and is a standing proof of the dissemination of the human conscience. But it is possible to build, upon this ground, the most joyous of verses, and the most lively, beautiful, and buoyant tales." The lively, beautiful and buoyant tales Stevenson wrote in accordance with this theory are *Treasure Island* and *Kidnapped*. The heroes of these are boys, but so obedient to ordinary, conventional promptings, and keen to be thought adult, and so trusting, and mistaken, and fearful, and capable of the rare brave act, that folk of any age or sex can feel they would be that sort of boy in those circumstances. And the circumstances are so interesting! *The Sire de Malétroit's Door* is a poor story because only the circumstances are of interest. The trap which closes on the young nobleman squeezes nothing out of him but a gallant speech about his readiness to die. This wins him the niece's affectionate respect and a marital conclusion which is meant to be triumphantly life-affirming but is actually servile. This hero is not believable.

But Jamie Kirkwood is believable; and at first sight, and to my mind, is a far more distinct person than Jim Hawkins and David Balfour. No wonder. These youngsters cheerfully leave home with a fortune in view, getting trapped for a few hours on the way to it by Long John Silver and Captain Hoseason. But Jamie Kirkwood, a man of twenty-two, eats and sleeps inside the trap where he was born. His jailer is no 18th century buccaneer but a 19th century, rigidly respectable, damnably ungiving Edinburgh clergyman who offers his son a choice of three courses: servility, hypocrisy, or rebellion. But Jamie will not turn hypocrite to get a little of the freedom he craves. By honestly answering his father's home thrust of enquiry he brands himself – in his father's eye and in his own – as a rebel and a cynic, the last of which he certainly is not. A cynic would have lied to get more money. This is a moral story about human conduct and the passionate slips and hesitations of the conscience. The circumstances which drive Jamie are the circumstances of a father's overbearing nature pressing to a division his son's appetites for freedom and for truth. Truth wins, and drives the son to despair. Despair drives him to gamble and drink the winnings. It is now highly likely that a young man of his class, and city, and century, will impose himself on a strange woman in a disreputable house. Jamie's blackout, the coincidence of doorlocks and bedrooms, lets Stevenson cut whole pages of transitional scenery and present this likely outcome as an achieved fact, while screwing our curiosity to a new, surprising level. What now?

To hold our curiosity, to give Jamie's feelings time to develop through the exercise of his own curiosity, he must leave this house without learning much more about it. Of course, he knows the architecture. The back door opens into a kitchen and cellar region where at least one servant is waiting for guests to depart and the master to go to bed. Jamie must leave by the front door, opening and closing it in stealthy silence. His pass-key allows this. The danger is that someone may unexpectedly leave the gaming room and catch him creeping through the hall. The girl, with another sigh, tells Jamie that she will return to the company downstairs, announce she has changed her mind about retiring, and hold their attention for four or five minutes. She seems in no doubt of her ability to do this. She fastens her bodice, ignoring Jamie's thanks and apologies with the look of someone about to lift a familiar, weary burden. She descends the stairs. He follows her halfway, then waits. He hears a door open, one boisterous shout of welcome, a door firmly closed. Shortly afterward a piano strikes out a tune by Offenbach. This is his signal to escape. He therefore uses it to do so.

But in the second paragraph of his story Jamie said, "I came to myself in bed, whether that night or the next I have never known." If this means that he never gets back to the daily calendar of events in his father's home then he *must* be caught by Manton and Manton's friends while attempting, with the girl's help, to leave the Grange. Her conduct shows that Manton is jealous and powerful. If he is also intelligent, and the young people tell him the truth, he will neither quite believe nor disbelieve them. If he is a kind of 19th century de Malétroit, a touchy megalomaniac, he could offer Jamie a choice between emigration or public disgrace. Let Jamie depart at once for America, without the girl, and Manton will pay him something more than the fare out; otherwise Manton will hand him to the police on a charge of unlawful entry. Stevenson certainly had the skill to make such an operatic twist seem plausible, but why should he? It would not bring the end of the story an inch nearer, that end which has been announced at the very start, indeed before the start. This is The Story of a Recluse. Jamie will divide himself from humanity and have no children of his own, or none he sees fit to educate. A high-spirited young man who may be merry and lazy, but is brave enough to be honest while in difficulty, will become a deliberately lonely, coldhearted rake who cares less for his children than his own harsh parent cared for him. If the splendid interview in the study, and the debauch, and the meeting with the girl, produce nothing but Jamie decamping abroad then they are trivialized, because many different stories could start like that. They are equally trivialized if Jamie is charged before a magistrate, reported in the press, expelled from university and disinherited by his father. If we are to feel more than some shoulder-shrugging pity for a very unlucky fellow we must see him develop before attracting the blows which warp him. He must whole-heartedly desire something, and fight hard for it, and be horribly defeated.

What stops him noticing the day of the week for a long time is a sudden, almost total lack of interest in his immediate circumstances. This begins a few moments after leaving the Grange. As Jamie strides along the pavement, each street lamp casting his shadow before him as he passes it and behind him as he approaches it, his feeling of delighted release is replaced by astonishment at his close dealings with an attractive, brave, interesting woman. Everything to do with her which embarrassed and frightened him is now a vivid, intimate memory. He has worn her night-dress, slept in her bed, seen her in a privacy allowed only to lovers and husbands. She has talked to him as an equal, conspired with him as a friend, and saved him from social ruin. He and she now share a secret unknown to anyone else in the world, yet he does not even know her name! He cannot believe that he will not meet her again.

He gets home, stealthily opens the door and closes it more stealthily behind him. He is perplexed to see that the hall, dimly lit through the fanlight window by a lamp in the street beyond, is exactly as it was when he last saw it – surely it should have changed as much as he has changed? And it is doubly familiar, for without the different arrangement of hats and coats on the hallstand he could be entering the house he left half an hour before. He tiptoes across the hall and upstairs, so exactly reversing his recent actions that he hesitates before his bedroom door, heart thudding in hope and in fear that when he opens it he will again see the girl's bedroom. However, this is no tale of the supernatural. He undresses, puts on his own night-gown, slips into bed and lies remembering what happened after he last found himself in this situation. He recalls especially the girl's sigh and her long, very serious look at herself in the mirror. He is sure he knows what she was thinking at the time: "Who am I, and why?" Although most young people ask themselves that question the thought makes him feel nearer her. And who is Manton Jamieson, this man she lives with but dare not trust with the truth about herself? Her husband? (The idea brings a touch of panic. He dismisses it.) Her brother? Uncle? Step-father? (Few women in Scotland, in those days, would call their own father by his first name.) Whoever Manton is, he gambles for money with his guests while providing them with strong drink; no wonder the girl is discontent. (And Jamie, who has so recently gambled and drunk, does not notice he is viewing Manton from his father's standpoint.) In the midst of these speculations he falls asleep.

And is roused as usual next morning by a housemaid tapping his door, and lies for a while staring blankly at the ceiling, knowing he is in love. I assume that Jamie's nurture has depended so exclusively on his father because his mother died young – perhaps in childbirth. Before what now seems a dreamlike encounter with the girl Jamie has met only two kinds of women: the mainly elderly and unco good who belong to his father's congregation, and those who drink in pubs and shebeens used by nearly penniless medical students. Jamie cannot *not* be in love with the girl. He feels no need, at this stage of his passion, to be more than gloriously astonished by it. He dresses, goes downstairs and breakfasts with his father. This meal is usually eaten in a taciturn silence broken only by his brief replies to infrequent paternal questions. These questions always take the form of remarks. His father never asks Jamie where he spent a day or evening, but says, "I am informed that you were seen last Thursday in Rose Street," or, "You did not come directly home from college last night." This morning his father makes several such remarks which Jamie hardly hears but responds to with a nod or a murmur of "Yes indeed." Near the end of the meal he notices that his father has risen and now stands with his back to the fireplace, declaring in firm tones that he fears Jamie is not attending properly to his studies; that man is born to earn his bread in the sweat of his brow; that a minister of religion is required to set an example to the community and that he, personally, has no intention of supporting a mere idler, wastrel and profligate. Instead of hearing these familiar words with an expression of sullen resentment Jamie nods a little, murmurs that he will give the matter thought, and absentmindedly leaves the room and the house.

Thirty minutes later, pass-key in hand, he discovers himself about to enter the drive of the Grange. With a quickened pace he continues along the road, almost amused. He has been too busy mixing hopes and speculations with memories of the night before to notice where he is going. He spends most of that day and the next two or three days in the same walking dream. The Grange is a fairly new building so I imagine it in a line of prosperous villa residences, part of the western suburbs along the Glasgow road near Corstorphine hill. Twice or thrice a day he strolls past the front of it from a great distance on one side to a great distance on the other. More frequently, and taking great care not to be seen by servants, he prowls the mews lane at the back, for there he can see her high bedroom window. Sometimes, like someone shaking off a lassitude, he hurries into the city and wanders the city streets near the kind of fashionable shop she must occasionally visit, or sits on a bench in Princes Street gardens, watching the strollers in the comforting but not yet urgent knowledge that if he could sit there for three or four weeks he would certainly see her passing. He believes that the chance which brought them together will certainly, if he stays ready and alert for it, bring them together in a perfectly ordinary, social way which he will manage to build upon. He fears she cannot be thinking about him as much as he thinks of her, but is certain she thinks of him sometimes, and if it is with even a fraction of his own emotion he believes he can persuade her to break free of twenty Mantons. Meanwhile the notion of a strong, jealous Manton strengthens him. If the girl was wholly free or only slightly confined he might feel compelled to hurry, but he is sure that Manton can keep her for him. He is also fascinated by the kind of person he is becoming under her influence: patient, determined and steady. He has nothing now to say to the friends he met in pubs and betting shops. None are fit to share the secret he is nursing. He is close to monomania. All the loving capacities of a soul starved of love are flowing, silently, in one direction. The nearly unbroken silence in which he breakfasts and dines with his father no longer seems a gloomy oppression to be avoided. His spirit is grateful for it. This is fortunate. Days must elapse before his next small allowance and he lacks the means to eat elsewhere.

But if Jamie's obsession is not fed by a new occurrence he will be driven to keep it alive by some rash initiative which I cannot imagine. I have read, and so has Jamie, of lovers who further their intrigues by bribing and plotting with a servant, but Jamie is too stiff-necked to make a social inferior his confidant. He also assumes that even servants are inclined to honesty, so any approach he makes will be reported to the master of the house. Also he has no money for bribes. His love is doomed to fade and dwindle unless providence – who in this story is me masquerading as Robert Louis Stevenson – provides another useful coincidence, and why should I not? Nowadays the wealthier folk of Edinburgh know each other very well; they were certainly not more ignorant a century back. After a few days Jamie, in mere restlessness of spirit, resumes attendance at the university. He tries to hammer down his memories of the girl (which are no longer pleasurable, but frustrating) by concentrating on the demonstrations of his lecturers. He tries to believe that everything which disturbs him is located in a circulatory, respiratory, digestive system animated by nervous shocks similar to those generated in the Galvanic pile or Wimshurst apparatus, but here generated in a cerebral cortex reacting to external stimuli. Later, feeling very dismal, he stands in the cold dusk on the range of steps overlooking the great, grey, classically pillared and pilastered, gaslit and cobbled quadrangle. Let there be a haze of fog in it, seafog from the Firth tinted brown and smelling of smoke from the Edinburgh lums, and making opal haloes around the lamps, and making ghostly the figures of the students hurrying singly and in groups toward the gate, and making their voices very distinct in the thickened air.

"Good night Charlie! Will I see you later at Manton's place?" cries someone.

"Not me. I'm clean out of funds," says another. Jamie leaps down the steps and overtakes the last speaker, who is known to him, under the high arch of the entrance. They turn side by side into Nicolson Street. Jamie asks, "Who is Manton Jamieson?"

In answering this question I must describe the person who does so, for Stevenson, like nature and like every good storyteller, creates nobody to inform and change someone else without giving them an equal fulness of life. Those who appear most briefly speak for whole professions or communities. See the doctor in *Macbeth*, the housepainters in *Crime and Punishment*, the itinerant barber at the start of *Kidnapped*. If they are a bigger part of the plot they often emphasize the main characters' obsession by lacking it while resembling them in other ways: thus Macduff is given the same rank, courage and royal prospects as Macbeth, but less ambition and a less ambitious wife; Raskolnikov's best friend is also a clever student in poor circumstances, one who works to get money by translating textbooks instead of murdering a pawnbroker. Stevenson frequently coupled young men in this contrasting way because (quite apart from his dialectical habit of mind) young men often do go in twos, and he was more fascinated by the beginnings of lives than by the middle and later periods. Since I have hinted that Charlie is a fellow student who has also lost money by gambling I will enlarge him by basing him partly on Alan in the novella *John Nicholson* and partly on Francie in *Weir of Hermiston*. He is more elegant and popular than Jamie and his guardian grants him a far larger allowance, but he has squandered it and will be poor for a while to come. Though in love with nobody but himself he greatly likes company. He has recently started avoiding his wealthy and fashionable friends because he owes money to some of them. He is shrewd enough to know that the casually superior manner which makes him acceptable to such people will make him obnoxious to those he considers their inferiors. Although Jamie is a very slight acquaintance, and not one he would normally want to cultivate, he is disposed to treat him, for the time being, as a kindred spirit. He assumes that Jamie's interest in Manton is the same as his own, and the most natural thing in the world: the interest of an outsider in a special sort of glamorous elite. It will soothe his hurt pride to instruct Jamie in the ways of Manton's world, and eventually lead him into it.

So what strong lord of misrule can preside in this douce, commercially respectable, late 19th century city where even religious fanaticism reinforces unadventurous mediocrity? Scotland had many wealthy landowners who were equally indifferent to gambling losses and bourgeois opinion but almost all these had shifted their town houses from Edinburgh to London a generation earlier, and the names of the few who remained would be known to the sons of the professional classes, especially if they had the same social habits as the Prince of Wales. Jamie has not heard of Manton Jamieson when the story starts. Despite Manton's Scottish surname he is a wealthy, recent incomer. Let him be the son of depressed gentry or educated tradespeople or a mixture of both. The death of his parents at an early age leaves him a little money, but not enough to buy an officer's commission or a professional education. He has no special talent but a deal of energy, courage and practical ability, so he takes these abroad to where they will best profit him. He is pleasant, tough, cautious, and whatever he does is done well, but for many years he keeps losing his gains by shifting to places where there are rumours of better opportunities. Let him eventually (though this is a cliché) make a pile of money in the Californian gold fields, not by prospecting but by selling necessities to prospectors. Let him take it to San Francisco where he manages to increase it on the stock exchange. He resides with, perhaps even marries (this is vague) the widow or mistress of a dead rich friend. She also dies, leaving him her money and making him guardian of either her daughter or her much younger sister – this also is vague. And now he tires of San Francisco. One reason for his many restless shiftings has been a secret desire for social eminence. He knows he can never shine among the millionaires of Nob Hill because their lavish expenditure would bankrupt him; it also strikes him as childish and hysterical. He is almost fifty, and because he has formed no strong attachment to any other place the memories of his native city are increasingly dear to him. He decides to return there. This is a mistake.

Since the days of Dick Whittington, the exile who returns transformed by foreign adventure is as common in popular fiction as in history books, and a lot more distinct. His earliest struggles are described in *Robinson Crusoe* and parodied in *Gulliver's Travels*. He arrives unexpectedly in Gaskell's *Cranford* to save his genteel old aunt from working in a sweetie shop, and in Galt's *The Member* he cheerfully uses a fortune made in India to make another in the corruption of British politics. Suddenly, in Dickens' day, his cheerful bloom quite vanishes. *Little Dorrit* has him sent to China by an unloving mother and returning, after years of clerical toil, to confront a land run by greedy rentiers, callous civil servants, venal aristocrats and shady capitalists. *Great Expectations* has him transported to Australia by an oppressive government and returning, after years of manual toil, to a land where he is a hunted criminal and an embarrassment to those he enriched. In Stevenson's day stories about prosperous, rather stuffy citizens suddenly shocked by intrusions from a dangerously unBritish past had become commonplace. They were plausible because although middle-class conventions had become more rigidly confining, the middle class was full of monied adventurers who adopted these conventions. Manton cannot adopt them because he never learned them. Like all returned exiles his memory of the homeland is out of date. The Edinburgh of his youth was dominated by free-thinking, hard-drinking lawyers and the remnant of a gentry who could still entertain themselves by using that demotic lowland speech which had been the language of the Scottish kings. Manton was sure that only poverty excluded him from this society. His notion of good living is to dine, drink and converse where his wide knowledge of life will receive attention, followed by some gentlemanly gambling where his superior skill will bring a profit. He knows this last amenity is enjoyed by many thousands in Paris, the German spas and Saint Petersburg. He finds it is now illegal in Britain and thought wicked and foolish in an Edinburgh whose social leaders belong to rival kinds of Presbyterian church. Manton is no churchgoer and his social chances are further reduced by the young woman he introduces as "My ward, Miss Juliette O'Sullivan, the daughter of a very dear friend". He jealously oversees all her actions but is silent (so is she) about her marriage prospects. In such a man, in an age when marriage is a respectable girl's only prospect, this suggests she is his mistress or his bastard. Only rakish bachelors, itinerant members of the acting profession and defiant youths of Jamie's age visit the Grange. Manton must feed his sense of eminence by teaching college students his own slightly vulgar notion of gentlemanly conduct.

The superficial part of all this is told by Charlie to Jamie as they stroll south along Nicolson Street, their breath adding puffs of whiter density to the haze of the fog. Jamie learns little more than he suspected already, but Charlie's suspicions of the girl's status in that household fill him with a queer sick excitement. He stands still and says, "Can you take me there?"

"Nothing easier," says Charlie. "You're a sort Manton would take to. The deuce of it is, I'm clean out of funds just now. Not that gaming is compulsory at the Grange, but it's the done thing. We'll be given all the champagne we want, so it's common decency that at least one of us hazards something on a game. How much have you got?"

"Nothing!" cries Jamie, staring at him.

"Not even a watch?"

Jamie hesitates, then detaches a watch from within his overcoat and hands it over. Charlie snaps open the silver case and brings it near his eye with something like the professional regard of a pawnbroker. He says, "This is a good watch – we can raise quite a bit on it. Shall I show you where?"

An hour later, with coin in their pockets, they are received by Manton at the Grange.

He is a calm, bulky man with a quietly attentive manner. His heavy lidded, rather narrow eyes, and bushy, welltrimmed whiskers, and mouth half-hidden by a neatly brushed moustache, all convey amusement without definitely smiling. I am modelling him slightly on Edward, Prince of Wales, whom Stevenson found interesting enough to parody in two quite different ways, as the hapless hero of *John Nicholson* and as Prince Florizel of Bohemia in *The New Arabian Nights*. For this reason I will also have him playing baccarat when the young men call – roulette is kept for later in the evening. But first he introduces Jamie to, "My ward, Miss Juliette O'Sullivan, the daughter of a very dear friend."

The girl regards Jamie with a face as impassive as his own. Does she wear the black velvet gown he remembers? He is too full of whirling emotions to notice. It is her face he wants to gaze and gaze into so he tries not to see her at all, bowing deeply and turning again to Manton. He hears her murmur "Good evening" and on a louder, welcoming note greet Charlie with a "How nice to see you, Mr Gemmel." He is glad she knows how to dissemble. She is the only woman present and plays hostess to those not engaged by the cardplay. Jamie stands watching it, ensuring, by slight turns of the head, that she is always in the corner of his eye, never the centre of it. This is easy, for he can now see that the gown she wears is white satin. He is not jealous of those who chat with her, for they cannot know her as intimately as he does, and he is sure she is now as conscious of him as he of her. Meanwhile he watches the baccarat, a game unknown to him. It is a form of the games known nowadays as pontoon and Black Jack. Manton, being host and the richest person present, is of course the banker. Charlie joins the game and wins a little, then loses a little, then wins more, then much more, then loses everything. Charlie suggests that Jamie takes his place at the table. Jamie refuses but gives Charlie money to play for him. In a pause for refreshment Juliette goes to the piano and accompanies herself in a song. Her voice is slight but sounds sweet and brave for she is clever enough not to force it beyond its range. If Jamie attended closely it would bring him to tears, so he stands beside the fire with his host, for it is from Manton that the girl must be won. Manton's conversation is entertaining, anecdotal, and polished by years of use. A bawdy element in it is not too heavily emphasized. He presents himself as onlooker or victim rather than cause of strange events, and seems as ready to listen as to speak. By occasional questions and an unmoving, attentive expression he usually draws from raw young men news of their families, college experience, hopes and opinions; but he draws very little from Jamie. Jamie sees that Manton is condescending to him, and dislikes it, but he still attends as closely to Manton as he did to the cardplay, and for the same reason – he wants to defeat him. So he notices what few others notice on their first visit to the Grange. Whether gaming or conversing, Manton's mind is only half occupied with his immediate company. As he and Jamie stand side by side with their back to the fire, both are keeping half an eye on the white figure at the opposite end of the room. Manton is less sure of her than Jamie is! The thought fills Jamie with a giddy foretaste of supremacy. Gaming is resumed. Again Jamie watches, but with greater understanding, and all at once his close-contained, highly stimulated, busily searching mind conceives a plan, a plot which will bring together himself, the girl, the Grange, Manton, cardplay, his father's tiny allowance and even Charlie in a single scheme of conquest. Throughout the evening Jamie (like Manton) has drunk almost nothing. The slightly tipsy Charlie is about to stake the last of the money on a new game. Jamie lays a firm hand on his shoulder and says, "We must go now."

He approaches his hostess, says "Good night Miss O'Sullivan," and is now bold enough to give her one steady glance. She turns to him the bright smile she has been bestowing on someone else, bids him good night and turns away leaving him disconcerted by her powers as an actress. Manton, perhaps flattered by the close attention of this taciturn guest, escorts both young men to the door, cheerfully commiserating with Charlie's misfortune and inviting both young men back with a particular nod to Jamie.

The cold night air slightly sobers Charlie. He says glumly, "I shan't be back there in a hurry. It's nearly a month till my next allowance and my brute of a governor won't allow me another advance on it. You are walking beside a desperate man, Kirkwood. You were wise to drag me away when you did. I usually hang on to the bitter end, because of Juliette, you know – the beautiful Miss Juliette O'Sullivan. But I've no hopes there. What do you think of her, Kirkwood? Isn't she a woman to die for?"

Jamie finds these remarks impertinent. He holds out his hand, palm upward, and with a sigh Charlie places the last sovereign on it saying, "Sorry I didn't do better for you, but luck was against me."

"Luck does not exist," says Jamie firmly. "Luck is superstitious nonsense. You lost to Manton like everybody else did, because he is skilful and you are idiots."

Charlie is inclined to be angry but is daunted by the small tight smile Jamie gives him. He says, "Could you have done better?"

"Of course not, so I did not play. When I go back there, Charlie – when we go back there, Charlie – we will play and win because we will have made ourselves better than Manton."

"How?"

"By study and practice. By practice and study. There are books about cardgames are there not? Books by dependable authorities?"

"Well, Cavendish is considered pretty good, and two or three French fellows."

"We'll work on them. A month just might be sufficient if we apply ourselves hard. After all, you have nothing better to do with your time."

And at breakfast next morning Jamie says to his father, "I have a favour to ask you, sir. I believe I will do better in my studies if I share them with a college friend, Charlie Gemmel. Since this house is a quieter place than his lodgings I want us to work most evenings in the privacy of my bedroom. Would you object to him sharing our evening meal beforehand?"

The Rev. Dr Kirkwood looks at his son for a while. Jamie's

face flushes a hot red. The father says quietly, "I can have no objection to that."

So each evening and for most of the weekends Jamie shuts himself up with Charlie in that room which is so like yet unlike *her* room. On the doorward side of a small table they make a barricade of medical books high enough to hide a card-pack and Cavendish's book on games of chance. (This is mainly a guilty ritual, for the Rev. Dr Kirkwood is not one who would enter his son's room unannounced.) They play game after game, and catechize each other on the details of the Cavendish strategy, and sometimes probe a foreign work which gives other strategy and teaches the techniques of foul play under the guise of warning against them. But at this stage Jamie neither intends to cheat nor suspects Manton of doing so. He is striving for purely conventional mastery. His obsessions with the girl and with the game are now identical. Each card dealt or lifted seems to put him in touch with her, with every petty victory he feels she is closer. Since Charlie does not share this erotic drive he is frequently exhausted, less by the games than by the intricate post-mortems which follow. He scratches his head woefully and cries, "We would soon be qualified doctors if we gave our medical studies this degree of attention."

Jamie smiles and shuffles the pack and says, "You're tired, Gemmel. Be banker this time."

So Charlie also becomes an obsessive player. The manse is a good place to evade his creditors and responsibilities. The meals there are well cooked, well served, and cost nothing. His only social life now is cardplay with Jamie. We can become addicts of almost any activity prolonged past the healthy limit. People have drunk themselves to death on water, the anorexic finds hunger intoxicating, some of the worst treated learn to welcome pain. The freedom of pushing faster toward death than our body or society requires is the essence of every perverse satisfaction, gambling included. Charlie, in the circumstances, is bound to get hooked on this cardgame, though not as absolutely as Jamie. When outside his room Jamie now plays imaginary games in his head. He no longer seems obstinately silent or fretful in his father's company, just thoughtful and deliberate. His step is firm, his manner composed, and though he eats as much as ever he has grown thinner. He never visits public houses, billiard rooms or betting shops. All pocket money is hoarded for the decisive game with Manton.

And one day, on the corner of the study table where a certain number of florins are usually placed for him, he finds as many guineas. He stares at his father with open mouth. The elder Kirkwood says, "I am giving you more, Jamie, because you deserve more. A while ago you asked for an allowance worthy of a gentleman's son while declaring that you would not spend it as a gentleman ought. You have changed since then, Jamie! When I look at you I no longer see an ordinary, thankless young drifter, I see a man determined to make his way in the world, a man I can trust."

Jamie continues to stare. His father is smiling at him with a futile expression of pride and approval and Jamie has a desolate feeling of loss. This is the first proof he ever received that his father loves him. He remembers once being a person who longed for such proof and would have been changed by it. That person no longer exists. Jamie would like to weep for him as for a dead brother, and also yell with laughter at the good money he has earned, yes, earned, by his love of a woman and devotion to a game his father would abhor. He sighs, whispers "Thank you sir," picks up the guineas and leaves the room.

For me that is the climax of the story. The catastrophe may be sketched rapidly and lightly.

That evening or the next Jamie suddenly grasps the

nature of this baccarat which Cavendish so clearly explains. It is only partly a game of skill – anyone following the Cavendish system will play it as well as it can be played but, as in roulette, the main chances will always favour the banker: the banker has most money and therefore most staying power. Manton's superior skill merely maintains his lead in a game which is already on his side. Banks, of course, can be broken by *runs of luck*, but very seldom. Jamie knows that the chance which introduced him to Juliette will not wed him to her. With rage, then horror, then resignation, he sees that to win by skill he must win by cheating. He has now complete ascendancy over Charlie. They devise and practise signals which strike them as impenetrable, but are not. They decide to hazard all they can on a game: Charlie's quarterly allowance, Jamie's hoarded pocket-money, and money borrowed at exorbitant interest from a professional lender, I imagine an evening at the Grange when the whole company gradually gather round the table to watch the play between Jamie and an increasingly grim-faced Manton. Just before or just after Jamie breaks the bank his fraud is exposed by the girl, who is Manton's accomplice and supporter in every possible way. We have no reason to think she ever found Jamie interesting. He was not, perhaps, an attractive young man.

LACK OF MONEY

IN BRITAIN ONLY SNOBS, perverts and the wholly despairing want friendship with richer or poorer folk. Maybe in Iceland or Holland or Canada factory-owners and labourers, lumber-jacks and high court judges eat in each other's houses and go holidays together. If so they must have equally good food, clothes and schools for their children. That kind of classlessness is impossible here. Mackay disagrees. He says the Scots have democratic traditions which let them forget social differences. He says his father was gardener to a big house in the north and the owner was his dad's best friend. On rainy days they sat in the gardener's shed and drank a bottle of whisky together. But equal incomes allow steadier friendships than equal drunkenness. I did not want to borrow money from Mackay because it proved I was poorer than him. He insisted on lending, which ruined more than our friendship.

I needed a thousand pounds cash to complete a piece of business and phoned my bank to arrange a loan. They said I could have it at an interest of eleven per cent plus a forty-pound arrangement fee. I told them I would repay in five days but they said that made no difference – for £1000 now I must repay £1150, even if I did so tomorrow. I groaned, said I would call for the money in half an hour, put down the phone and saw Mackay. He had strolled in from his office next door. We did the same sort of work but were not competitors. When I got more business than I could handle I passed it to him, and vice versa.

He said, "What have you to groan about?"
I told him and added, "I can easily pay eleven per cent et cetera but I hate it. I belong to the financial past. I agree with Maynard Keynes – all interest above five per cent strikes me as extortion."
"I'll lend you a thousand, interest free," said Mackay pulling out his cheque book. While I explained why I never borrow money from friends he filled in a cheque, tore it off and held it out saying, "Stop raving about equality and take this to my bank. I'll phone them and they'll cash it at once. We're still equals – in an emergency you would do the same for me."
I blushed because he was almost certainly wrong. Then I shrugged, took the cheque and said, "If this is what you want, Mackay, all right. Fine. I'll return it within five days, or within a fortnight at most."
"Harry, I know that. Don't worry," said Mackay soothingly and started talking about something else. I felt grateful but angry because I hate feeling grateful. I also hated his easy assumption that his money was perfectly safe. Had I lent *him* a thousand pounds I would have worried myself sick until I got it back. If being aristocratic means preferring good manners to money then Mackay was definitely posher than me. Did he think his dad's boozing sessions with Lord Glenbannock had *ennobled* the Mackays? The loan was already spoiling our friendship.

Five days later my business was triumphantly concluded and I added a cheque for over ten thousand pounds to my bank account. I was strongly tempted *not* to repay Mackay at once just to show him I was something more dangerous than decent, honest, dependable old Harry. I stayed honest longer by remembering that if I repaid promptly I would be able to borrow from him again on the same convenient terms. Since handing him a cheque would have been as embarrassing as taking one I decided to put the cash straight back into his bank. Despite computerization my bank would have taken two or three days to transfer the money, which would have meant Mackay getting it back the following week. I collected ten crisp new hundred-pound notes in a smooth envelope, placed envelope in inner jacket pocket and walked the half mile to Mackay's bank. The morning air was mild but fresh, the sky one sheet of high grey cloud which threatened rain but might hold off till nightfall.

Mackay's bank is reached by a road where I lived when I was married. I seldom go there now. On one side buildings have been demolished and replaced by a cutting holding a six-lane motorway. Tenements and shops on the other side no longer have a thriving look. I was walking carefully along the cracked and pitted pavement when I heard a woman say, "Harry! What are *you* doing here?"
She was thin, sprightly, short-haired and (like most attractive women nowadays) struck me as any age between sixteen and forty. I said I was going to a bank to repay money I owed and ended by asking, "How are your folk up at Ardnamurchan, Liz?"
She laughed and said, "I'm *Mish* you idiot! Come inside – Wee Dougie and Davenport and Roy and Roberta are there and we haven't seen you for ages."
I remembered none of these names but never say no to women who want me. I followed her into the Whangie, though it was not a pub I liked. The Whangie's customers may not have been prone to violence but its drab appearance had always made me think they were, so the pleasure I felt at the sight of the dusty brown interior was wholly unexpected. It was exactly as it had been twenty or thirty years before, exactly like most Scottish pubs before the big breweries used extravagant tax reliefs to buy them up and decorate them like Old English taverns or Spanish bistros. The only wall decorations were still solidly framed mirrors frosted with the names and emblems of defunct whisky blends. This was still a

dour Scottish drinking-den which kept the prices down by spending nothing on appearance, and it was nearly empty, being soon after opening-time. Crying, "Look who's here!" Mish led me to people round a corner table, one of whom I knew. He said, "Let me get you a drink Harry," starting to stand, but, "No no no sit down sit down," I said and hurried to the bar. Apart from the envelope in my inner jacket pocket I had just enough cash to buy a half pint of lager. I carried this back to the people in the corner. They made room for me.

A fashion note. None of us looked smart. The others wore jeans with shapeless denim or leather jackets, I wore my old tweed jacket and crumpled corduroys. Only my age marked me off from the rest, I thought, and not much. The man I knew, a musician called Roy, was almost my age. The one oddity among us was the not-Mish woman, Roberta. Her hair was the colour of dry straw and stood straight upright on top of her skull, being clipped or shaved to thin stubble at the back and sides. The wing of her right nostril was pierced by several fine little silver rings. Her lipstick was dull purple. She affected me like someone with a facial deformity so to avoid staring hard I completely ignored her. This was easy as she never said a word the whole time I was in the Whangie. She seemed depressed about something. When others spoke to her she answered by sighing or grunting or shrugging her shoulders.

First they asked how I was getting on and I answered, "Not bad – not good." The truth was that like many professional folk nowadays I am doing extremely well even though I sometimes have to borrow money. It would have been unkind to tell them how much better off I was because they were obviously unemployed. Why else did they drink, and drink very slowly, at half past eleven on Thursday morning? I avoided distressing topics by talking to Roy, the musician. We had met at a party where he sang and played the fiddle really well. Since then I had seen him busking in the shopping precincts and had passed quickly on the other side of the street to avoid embarrassing him, for he was too good a musician to be living that way. I asked him about the people who had held the party, not having seen them since. Neither had Roy so we discussed the party. Ten minutes later we had nothing more to say about it and I had drunk my half pint. I stood up and said, "Have to go now folks."

They fell silent and looked at me. I felt that they expected something, and blushed, and spoke carefully to avoid stammering: "You see, I would like to buy a round before I go but I've no cash on me. I mean, I've plenty of money in my bank – and I have my cheque book here – could one of you cash a cheque for five pounds? – I promise it won't stot."
Nobody answered. I realized nobody there had five pounds on them or the means of turning my cheque into cash if they had.
"Cash it at the bar Harry," said Mish.
"I would like to – but do you think the barman will do it without a cheque card?"
"No cheque card?" said Mish on a shrill note.
"None! I've never had a cheque card. If I had I would lose it. I'm always losing things. But the barmen in Tennent's cash my cheques without one ..."
Davenport, who had a black beard and a firm manner, waved to the barman and said, "Jimmy, this pal of ours wants to cash a cheque. He's Harry Haines, a well-known character in the west end with a good going business –"
"In fact he's loaded," said Mish –
"– and you would oblige us by cashing a cheque for him. He's left his cheque card at home."
"Sorry," said the barman, "there's nothing I can do about that."
He turned his back on us.
"I'm sorry too," I told them helplessly.

"You," Mish told me, "are a mean old fart. You are not only mean, you are a bore. You are totally uninteresting." At these my words my embarrassment vanished and I cheered up. I no longer minded my social superiority. I felt boosted by it. With an air of mock sadness I said, "True! So I must leave you. Goodbye folks."
I think the three men were also amused by the turn things had taken. They said cheerio to me quite pleasantly.

I left the Whangie and went toward Mackay's bank, carefully remembering the previous ten minutes to see if I might have done better with them. I did not regret entering the Whangie with Mish. She had pleasantly excited me and I had not then known she only saw me as a source of free drink. True, I had talked boringly – had bored myself as well as them – but interesting topics would have emphasized the social gulf between us. I might have amused them with queer stories about celebrities whose private lives are more open to me than to popular journalism (that was probably how the duke entertained Mackay's father between drams in the tool shed) but it strikes me as an unpleasant way to cadge favour with underlings. I was pleased to think I had been no worse than a ten-minute bore. I had made a fool of myself by wanting credit for a round of drinks I did not buy, but that kind of foolery hurts nobody. If Mish and her pals despised me for it good luck to them. I did not despise myself for it, or only slightly. In the unexpected circumstances I was sure I could not have behaved better.

The idea of taking a hundred-pound note from Mackay's money and buying a round of drinks only came to me later. So did the idea of handing the note to Mish, saying, "Share this with the others," and leaving fast before she could reply. So did the best idea of all: I could have laid five hundred-pound notes on the table, said, "Conscience money, a hundred each," and hurried off to put the rest in Mackay's account. Later I could have told him, "I paid back half what I owe today. You'll have to wait till next week for the rest – I've done something stupid with it." As he heard the details his mouth would open wider and wider or his frown grow sterner and sterner. At last he would say, "That's the last interest-free loan you get from me" – or something else. But he would have been as astonished as the five in the pub. I would have proved I was not predictable. Behaving like that would have changed me for the better. But I could not imagine doing such things then. I can only imagine them since I changed for the worse.

I walked from the Whangie toward Mackay's bank brooding on my recent adventure. No doubt there was a smug little smile on my lips. Then I noticed someone walking beside me and a low voice saying, "Wait a minute."

I stopped. My companion was Roberta who stood staring at me. She was breathing hard, perhaps with the effort of overtaking me, and her mouth was set in something like a sneer. I could not help looking straight at her now. Everything I saw – weird hair and sneering face, shapeless leather jacket with hands thrust into flaps below her breasts, baggy grey jeans turned up at the bottoms to show clumsy thick-soled boots laced high up the ankles – all these insulted my notion of how a woman ought to look. But her alert stillness as her breathing quietened made me feel very strange, as if I had seen her years ago, and often. To break the strangeness I said sharply, "Well?"

Awkwardly and huskily she said, "I don't think you're mean or uninteresting. I like older men."

Her eyes were so wide open that I saw the whole circle of the pupils, one brown, one blue. There was a kind of buzzing in my blood and the nearby traffic sounded fainter. I felt stronger and more alive than I had felt for years – alive in a way I had never expected to feel again after my marriage went wrong. Her sneer was now less definite, perhaps because I felt it on my own lips. Yes, I was leering at her like a gangster confronting his moll in a 1940 cinema poster and she was staring back as if terrified to look anywhere else. I was fascinated by the thin stubble at the sides of her head above the ears. It must feel exactly like my chin before I shaved in the morning. I wanted to rub it hard with the palms of my hands. I heard myself say, "You want money. How?"

She murmured that I could visit my bank before we went to her place – or afterward, if I preferred. My leer became a wide grin. I patted my inner pocket and said, "No need for a bank, honey. I got everything you want right here. And we'll take a taxi to my place, not yours." I spoke with an American accent, and the day turned into one of the worst in my life.

MISTER GOODCHILD

NOBODY OVER FIFTY can tell where or how they'll live a few months hence Mrs … Mrs?"

"Dewhurst."

"Look at me, for instance. A year ago I was headmaster of a very good comprehensive school in Huddersfield. My wife made me take early retirement for the good of *her* health – not mine. She thought the warmer climate in the south would suit her so down to Berkshire we came. Fat lot of good *that* did. A fortnight after settling into the new house she died of a stroke. Since I do not intend to follow her example I will pause here for a few seconds Mrs … Mrs?"

"Dewhurst. Let me carry that," she said, pausing at a bend in the staircase.

"No no!" he said putting a cumbersome suitcase down on a higher step without releasing the handle. "I was talking about losing my wife. Well my son has a garage with five men working under him in Bracknell. 'Come and live with us, Dad,' says he, 'we've tons of room.' Yes, they have. New house with half an acre of garden. Huge open-plan living-room with dining alcove. *Five* bedrooms no less, one for marital couple, one each for my two grandchildren, one for guests and one for poor old grandad. But poor old grandad's bedroom is on the small side, hardly bigger than a cupboard and although I have retired from education I have not retired from public life. I am now ready to proceed – to *continue* proceeding – upward Mrs … Dewhurst."

They continued proceeding upward.

"I edit the You See Monthly Bulletin, the newsletter of the Urban Conservation Fellowship and that requires both space and privacy. 'Use the living-room!' says my son, 'it's big enough. The kids are at school all day and if you work at the sun patio end Myra won't disturb you.' Myra did. How could I get a steady day's work done in a house where lunch arrived any time between twelve and one? I didn't complain but when I asked for a shelf in the fridge where I could keep my own food to make my own lunch she took it for a slight on her housekeeping. So *this*!" said Mr Goodchild putting the suitcase down, "is my fourth home since last September. I'm glad my things arrived."

He stood beside Mrs Dewhurst in a high-ceilinged room that had been the master bedroom eighty years earlier when the mansion housed a family and six servants. An ostentatiously solid bed, wardrobe, dressingtable and set of chairs survived from that time. The gas heater in the hearth of a white marble fireplace was recent, also a Formica-topped table, Laura Ashley window curtains, wall-to-wall fitted carpet with jagged green and black pattern. The carpet was mostly covered by twenty-three full cardboard boxes, a heap of metal struts and shelving, a heavy old typewriter, heavier Grundig tape player, a massive black slide and picture projector called an epidiascope which looked as clumsy as its name.

"I am monarch of all I survey, my right there is none to dispute," said Mr Goodchild. "Forgive me for stating the obvious Mrs Dewhurst, but you are NOT the pleasant young man who showed me this room two days ago and asked for – and received! – what struck me as an unnecessarily huge advance on the rent."

He smiled at her to show this was a question. Without smiling back she told him the young man was an employee of the letting agency and she did not know his name because that sort come and go; she, however, lived in the basement with her husband who cleaned the hall and stairs and shared bathroom. He also looked after the garden. It was her job to collect the rent, change sheets, pillowcases and towels once a fortnight and also handle complaints.

"You will hear no complaints from me or about me, Mrs Dewhurst. A quiet, sensible, sober man I am, not given to throwing wild parties but tolerant of neighbours who may be younger and less settled. Who, exactly, are my neighbours on this floor?"

"A couple of young women share the room next door. They do something secretarial in the office of the biscuit factory."

"Boyfriends?"

"I haven't bothered to ask, Mr Goodchild."

"Admirable! Who's above and who's below?"

"The Wilsons are above and the Jhas are below: both married couples."

"My age or yours Mrs Dewhurst? For I take you to be a youthful thirty-five or so."

A very slight softening in Mrs Dewhurst's manner confirmed Mr Goodchild's guess that she was nearly his own age. She told him that the Wilsons were young doctors and would soon be leaving for a bigger place because Mrs Wilson was pregnant; that Mr Jha had a grocery in a poorer part of town, his wife was much younger than him with a baby, a very quiet little thing, Mr Goodchild would hardly notice it.

"Jha," said Mr Goodchild thoughtfully. "Indian? Pakistani? African? *West* Indian?"

"I don't know, Mr Goodchild."

"Since I have no prejudice against any people or creed on God's earth their origin is immaterial. And now I will erect my possessions into some kind of order. Cheerio and off you go Mrs Dewhurst."

Off she went and Mr Goodchild's air of mischievous good humour became one of gloomy determination.

He hung his coat and jacket in the wardrobe. He unpacked from his suitcase a clock and radio which he put on the mantelpiece, underwear he laid in dressing-table drawers, pyjamas he placed under the pillow of the bed. Carrying the still heavy suitcase into a kitchenette he took out bottles, packets, tins and placed them in a refrigerator and on shelves. This tiny windowless space had once been the master's dressing-room and had two doors, one locked with a putty-filled keyhole. This useless door had once opened into the bedroom of the mistress, a room now rented by the secretaries. Mr Goodchild laid an ear to it, heard nothing and sighed. He had never lived alone before and sounds of occupancy would have soothed him.

In the main room he rolled up shirtsleeves, produced a Swiss army knife, opened the screwdriver attachment and by twenty minutes to six had efficiently erected four standing shelf units. Returning to the kitchenette he washed hands and put a chop under the grill. Faint voices from the next room showed it was occupied though the tone suggested a television play. He opened tins of soup, peas and baby potatoes and heated them in saucepans which he clattered slightly to let the secretaries know they too were no longer alone. Ten minutes later he ate a three-course dinner: first course, soup; second, meat with two vegetables; third, cold apple tart followed by three cups of tea. Meanwhile he listened to the six o'clock news on the BBC Home Service. Having washed, dried and put away the kitchenware he brooded long and hard over the positions of the rented furniture.

The Formica-topped table would be his main work surface so had better stand against the wall where the wardrobe now was with his shelf units on each side of it. He would shift the small bedside table to the hearthrug and dine on that. The dressing-table would go beside the bed and support the bedside lamp and his bedtime cup of cocoa. The wardrobe could then stand where the dressing-table had been. The boxes on the floor would make these shifts difficult so he piled as many as possible

onto and under the bed. The hardest task was moving the wardrobe. It was eight feet high, four wide and a yard deep. MrGoodchild, though less than average height, was proud of his ability to make heavy furniture walk across a room by pivoting it on alternate corners. The top part of the wardrobe rested on a base with a deep drawer inside. He discovered these were separate when, pivoting the base, the top section began sliding off. He dropped the base with a floor-shuddering thump. The upper part teetered with a jangling of wire coathangers but did not topple. Mr Goodchild sat down to recover from the shock. There came a tap upon the door and a voice with a not quite English accent said, "Are you all right in there?"
"Yes yes. Yes yes."
"That was one heck of a wallop."
"Yes I'm … shifting things about a bit Mr … Jha?"
"Yes?"
"I've just moved in and I'm shifting things about. I'll be at it for another hour or two."
"Exercise care please."
Mr Goodchild returned to the wardrobe and wrestled with it more carefully.

Two hours and several heavy thumps later the furniture was where he wanted it and he unpacked his possessions, starting with a collection of taped music. After putting it on a shelf beside the Grundig he played Beethoven symphonies in order of composition while unpacking and arranging books and box files. Handling familiar things to familiar music made him feel so completely at home that he was surprised by rapping on his door and the hands of his clock pointing to midnight. He switched off the third movement of the *Pastoral* and opened the door saying quietly but emphatically, "I am very very very very –"
"Some people need sleep!" said a glaring young woman in dressing-gown and slippers.
"– very very sorry. I was so busy putting my things in order that I quite forgot the time and how sound can propagate

through walls. Perhaps tomorrow – or some other day when you have a free moment – we can discover experimentally the greatest volume of sound I can produce without disturbing you, Miss ... Miss?" "Shutting your kitchen door will halve the din where we're concerned!" hissed the girl. "I'm surprised you haven't heard from the Jhas. He's up here complaining if we drop as much as a book on the floor." She hurried away.

With a rueful grimace Mr Goodchild closed the door, crossed the room, closed the kitchen door and pondered a moment. He was not sleepy. The encounter with the young woman had pleasantly excited him. Sitting at his newly arranged work table he wound paper into what he thought of as "my trusty Remington" and, starting with the boarding-house address and date in the top right-hand corner, typed this.

My Very Dear Son,

You receive this communication at your work-place because I am no stranger to married life. If it arrived with other personal mail on your breakfast table Myra might feel hurt if you did not let her read it and equally hurt if you did. I must not offend either partner in a successful marital arrangement. My fortnight in Foxdene was a worthwhile but unsuccessful experiment. It has proved me too selfishly set in my ways to live without a room where I can work and eat according to my own timetable, a timetable which others cannot

He was interrupted by hesitant but insistent tapping and went to the door full of lively curiosity.

The young dressing-gowned woman outside was different from the previous one. He smiled kindly and asked, "How can I help you Miss ... ?"
"Thomson. Gwinny Thomson. My friend can't sleep

because of the clattering your machine makes. Neither can I."

"To tell the truth Gwinny, when typing I get so engrossed in words that it's years since I noticed my machine made any noise at all. Your room-mate must be flaming mad with me."

Gwinny nodded once, hard.

"What's her name, Gwinny?"

"Karen Milton."

"Tell Karen that from now on my name is not George Goodchild but Mouse Goodchild. She won't hear a squeak from the kitchen tonight for I will go to bed with a small malt whisky instead of my usual cocoa and toasted cheese. But she must first endure the uproar of a flushing toilet if that sound also pierces your walls. Does it? And YOU must remember to call me George."

"We're used to the flushing so it doesn't bother us, Mr … George."

"Then Karen may now rest in peace. Good night, sleep tight Gwinny."

Gwinny retired. Mr Goodchild changed into slippers and pyjamas, took towel and toilet bag to bathroom, brushed teeth, washed, shat and smiled approvingly into the lavatory pan before flushing it. Sleek fat droppings showed that his inside still harmonized with the universe.

Next morning he arose, shaved, washed, dressed, breakfasted and waited until he heard the girls leave for work. Then he switched on the end of the *Pastoral* symphony, read the last six lines of his interrupted letter and completed it.

`My fortnight in Foxdene was a worthwhile but unsuccessful experiment. It has proved me too selfishly set in my ways to live without a room where I can work and eat according to my own timetable, a timetable which others cannot be expected to tolerate.`

This is my second day of boarding-house life and I am settling in nicely. My closest connections so far have been with Mrs Dewhurst our saturnine house-keeper, Mr Jha an excitable Asiatic shopkeeper, and two young secretaries in the room next door. Karen Milton is sexy and sure of herself and thinks I'm a boring old creep. No wonder! Gwinny Thomson is a sort teachers recognize at a glance: less attractive than her friend because less confident and needing someone she feels is stronger to hide behind. I'm afraid Karen bullies her sometimes. Gwinny ought to "shack up" (as the Americans say) with an experienced man who thoroughly appreciates her, then she might blossom. But I'm far too old for that little job.

So have no fear, son o' mine. When I kick the bucket all I have will be yours, apart from £2500 for the UCF who will probably spend half of it renovating a Victorian drinking fountain on Ilkley Moor and waste the rest attaching a bronze plaque inscribed to my memory. I should put a clause in my will forbidding such wicked waste but there are uglier ways to be remembered.

The Fellowship is forwarding my mail here. A big stack arrived by first post this morning so my editorial work with the newsletter has not been interrupted. The only upsetting thing here is the pattern of the carpet. It looks fierce enough to bite off any foot standing on it. Give my love to Myra and the kids. I will visit Foxdene for a couple of days when she feels fit enough for a short dose of me. Ask her to suggest a weekend when I can babysit while you take her out for "a night on the town". Take care of yourself, son.

Mr Goodchild lifted his fountain pen from a small glass tray of stamps and paperclips, pulled the letter from the drum and wrote *Love from Dad* neatly at the foot of it. A week later he typed this.

Dear, Dear Harry,

I have solved the problem of the carpet by turning it upside down. Through the weave of the brown backing the jagged pattern looks faded, antique and restful. When Mrs Dewhurst called for the rent yesterday she stared at the carpet, then at me. I smiled sweetly back. She must think I'm daft.

I would have liked a reply to my last letter because I've been feeling a bit lonely and dreaming a lot about your mother. She comes to me quite unlike her usual self and accuses me of all sorts of improbable crimes – dismantling the British rail system was the worst. A family man suddenly deprived of family must feel low until new friendships fill the gap and last night I had a surprising social triumph.

Gwinny Thomson, probably acting under orders from Karen, had come to me the night before and said she and her friend were going to have a party – not a rowdy do, but there might be music and chat till after midnight if I had no objection. I said I had no objection to anything which happened at their party as long as I was invited. She was horrified but tried to hide it by saying "of course" I was invited. But I let the girls down gently by joining the party late after it had plenty of time to warm up. But it hadn't warmed up. The guests were all office workers in their twenties and early thirties, female colleagues of the girls and male colleagues of their boyfriends. They stood huddled in groups of three or four, talking in low voices and obviously waiting for the earliest possible moment to leave without seeming rude, while Karen served them drinks and tried without success to get them chatting and mingling. The source of embarrassment was Gwinny and her boyfriend, Tom. Gwinny was on the verge of tears. Tom kept turning his back and talking to other women whenever she came near.

Enter Mr Goodchild looking exactly like his name – small, stout, cheery and too innocent to notice anything wrong. This act of mine is not a phony one. Humanity would have become extinct centuries ago if what holds folk together were not stronger than what pulls us apart. My act worked. Folk clustered round me. The UCF also came in handy. Karen's boyfriend is an architect and thanks to the Fellowship urban conservation is a source of more profitable commissions than it was ten years ago. Karen's bloke asked such detailed questions about our projects that I took him back to my room to show him photographs. Karen was not pleased about that and came too, so I sweetened her by offering both of them a tot of The Macallan. Then everyone but Gwinny and Tom came here too so I set up the epidiascope and gave my introductory lecture on the renovation of Britain's industrial heritage. You've never attended my lectures, Harry, so don't know that this one, though devised for schoolchildren, draws bigger laughs from adults. I got a round of applause which brought the Dewhursts up from their basement. Them too I sweetened with nips of The Macallan. Lastly Tom and Gwinny entered hand in hand, him grinning as smugly as an office boy who had just seduced a company director's daughter, her as bashful as a bride on her honeymoon. They had obviously been reconciled by a bout of what the Scotch call "hockmagandy" and the nasty lad liked flaunting the fact more than poor Gwinny did. I sent everyone away by saying it was my bedtime.

I understand your silence, Harry. Perhaps my stay at Foxdene would have ended more kindly – or not ended at all – if I had discussed my domestic problem with you instead of Myra. We might have found a solution she would have accepted – like me buying a modern Portakabin with all mod cons, one you could have set up behind the big hedge hiding the kitchen garden from the lawn. Myra need never have seen me during the day and I could have shared the regular evening meals and Sunday lunch, and helped the kids with their homework. You and I could have enjoyed an occasional game of chess like in the old days and my music would have irritated nobody. But you and I never discuss things. It's my fault. When you were little I always told you everything I knew in such detail that you recoiled into reticence like your mother and, unlike your mother, never told me to shut up. No wonder you won't answer letters. But I will burble on to you since I have nobody else.

I enclose bulldozer, roadroller and pickup truck for Nigel's Dinky Toy collection, and a set of Flower Fairy books for Tracy.

Love from

Dad.

Exactly a week later Mr Goodchild started typing his last letter in that boarding house.

Dear Harry,

When I came here a fortnight back I told the housekeeper that nobody over fifty can foretell how they'll be living a few months hence. I was wrong. A few days, a few hours hence would be more accurate. I'll explain this.

On the evening of the day after the party I accidentally passed Karen, then Gwinny on our landing. The quick angry manner of one and the glum look of the other suggested a quarrel, though their replies to my greeting showed it was not with me. Later I heard a slamming of doors then silence. Thinking both had gone out I started playing Mendelssohn's "Italian" symphony louder than I've dared play anything since my first night here. The rhythm was helping me rattle through my report for our annual general meeting when someone tapped the door. Was this Mr Jha? Had my long-lost son motored over from Bracknell? It was Gwinny. I said, "Sorry, I thought you were out, I'll turn down the noise."

"I like that music – it's cheerful," said she.

"Come in and listen," said I, "if you can stand the noise of my typewriter too."

She sat by the fire while I finished the report, then I put on Vivaldi's "Seasons" and made us a little snack. We consumed it seated on opposite sides of the table like a married couple. Suddenly she said, "Karen's not the bad one. It's me who's bad. I'm jealous of her lovely boyfriend so I make scenes when she borrows my hairbrush or leaves a crumby plate on the mantelpiece."

I hate heartfelt confessions. I told her I enjoyed the company of quiet folk and sometimes liked the company of talkative ones but complainers bored me, especially if they complained about themselves. She pulled a sour face at that then suddenly cheered up and told me horrible stories about her boyfriend Tom, playing them for laughs. She's a good little comedian so I laughed quite a lot though I said not one word for or against him. I told her I wanted to do some reading now and if she decided to stay she could play any of my tapes she liked. That's how the rest of the evening went. At half past ten I noticed her listening for the return of Karen so got rid of her by saying it was my bedtime and we parted with expressions of mutual esteem – I said she'd been as good as a pussy cat. I tell you all this, Harry, to show that I did not invite what follows.

Last night noises from next door suggested that once again the residents were not in perfect harmony. At my usual hour I went to bed with a mug of sweet hot chocolate and J B Priestley's history of the old northern music halls. Around midnight the door softly opens and Gwinny creeps in, dressed for outdoors and with a finger to her lips. In a low voice she explains that horrible Tom had invited her to spend the night at his place, but when she got there he was so horrible that they'd quarrelled and split up, probably for good. Returning to her own room she found Karen in bed with her bloke who was obviously expecting to spend the night there. Gwinny, in no mood to explain her change of plan, pretended she'd come back for a toothbrush or something, grabbed it, went downstairs then realized she hadn't money for a hotel and a respectable bed-and-breakfast place would not want a girl without luggage. So here she was!

Without a word I got up, put two armchairs together and made them up as a bed using cushions, a quilt, a bedcover I do not need, and two overcoats. I told her that I would not be gentlemanly and give her my bed, because if I lay on the chairs my old bones would stop me from sleeping and force me to crawl in beside her. I offered to make her a cup of cocoa. She refused. I returned to bed and lay with my back to her while she undressed and lay down, then I put the light out.

But I was quite unable to sleep and restless movements from her part of the room showed neither could she. Sounds from the room next door were to blame. After an hour or two she heaved a great sigh and began talking about her family and Karen and Tom. I think most of it was complaints but her low monotonous voice worked like a lullaby. I kept muttering "I see" and "that's a pity" between moments of dozing off. At last she said something complicated which I asked her to repeat: "I'm afraid I'm developing a father-fixation on you." I said she shouldn't use Freud's vocabulary when she'd never read him. She said, "You're right. Why must you always be right? You're giving me an inferiority complex."

I told her that now she was quoting Adler and that before Adler described the inferiority complex folk just said they felt shy. For a while we lay listening to the faint sounds of Karen gasping and her architect grunting in unison. I had forgotten to shut the kitchen door. I was about to ask Gwinny to shut it because she was nearer when she asked in a tiny voice if I'd like her to join me in bed. I said I would. Nothing much came of it but enough for us to fall comfortably asleep together afterwards. We slept sound till nearly ten in the morning.

Over the breakfast table (usual English breakfast) she apologized for being bad at lovemaking. I asked why she thought she was. She said Tom had said so. I asked how often they had made love. After a lot of hesitation she said once, on the night of the party. I chuckled at that and said all she needed was some more lovemaking with someone she did not think horrible. She stared at me then said, "Are you asking me to . .?" and went on staring without another word. I said cheerily, "Nay! At my age I can ask nothing from lovely young women but I can't stop hoping. I'm a great hoper."

I felt young, Harry. Twenty years younger at least. I still do. Is that stupid of me?

Suddenly she laughed and jumped up saying, "I don't care if those two next door ARE still in bed, it's my room as much as Karen's and I'm going in, see you later George."

She grabbed her things and rushed out. That was forty minutes ago. Now just suppose, Harry,

Mr Goodchild stopped typing and thought hard, then went to the kitchen and made a cup of camomile tea. From the next room came sounds of two women and a man exchanging casual, friendly words. Once Gwinny said something and the others laughed. Mr Goodchild sat before his typewriter again and stared at the unfinished letter until someone forcefully knocked on his door. Mrs Dewhurst stood outside. She said, "A visitor for you," and went away. Her place was taken by a big man wearing a business suit.

"So the mountain has come to Mahomet! Come in," said Mr Goodchild pleasantly. "Would you like a cup of tea? Have a seat."

The big man entered but did not sit. His mouth and eyes resembled Mr Goodchild's but their expression was careworn. Glancing round the room he asked, "How are you, Dad?"

"Never better. How's the garage?"

"Listen, Dad, I've talked to Myra about your Portakabin notion. She agrees to it."

"That's interesting but there's no need for haste, Harry. Let her think it over for a month or two. How's Nigel and Tracy?"

"They keep asking for you. Come back to us. Do it today."

"Don't be daft, Harry! It'll take months for you to get planning department permission for a cabin in your vegetable patch, no matter how many palms you grease. I asked how the garage is doing."

"It needs me there as much as it always does!" said his son impatiently. "A small businessman can't afford days off and I'm not going to stand here gassing. Myra says you shall have your shelf in the fridge and make your own lunches till the Portakabin comes."

"Anything else?" said Mr Goodchild, staring hard at him.
"You can also use our guest room as a work room."
"Where will your guests sleep, Harry?"
"On the bed settee in the living-room," said Harry, sighing.
"At last, my son, you are talking sense. Shake!" said Mr Goodchild holding out his hand. His son shook it a little wearily but with obvious relief, then left after another minute of conversation.

Mr Goodchild walked to his typewriter and stared at the single sheet of paper typed closely on both sides. After a moment he pulled it out, tore it carefully into small bits and dropped them in a waste basket. He then entered the kitchen, put four glasses on a tray, poured a small measure of The Macallan into each and placed the tray on his work table. Then he left the room, opened the door of the room next door and stuck his head round it without knocking. Karen, Karen's architect and Gwinny sat with mugs in their hands, staring at him.
"Boo!" he said. "You must all come into my place – now – this instant. I have something to celebrate and can't do it alone. Leave those mugs! Drink will be provided."
He returned to his room. They filed in after him, Gwinny looking as curious and willing to be pleased as the others but slightly apprehensive. He gave her a reassuring nod as he handed round the whisky glasses. Glass in hand he then faced the three of them, proposed a toast to family affection, clinked his glass with theirs and took off the contents of his own in one swallow. As they sipped theirs he told them of Harry's visit and what he had said.
"... which brings my stay here to a satisfying conclusion. Of course I knew before I came he would want me back. I just didn't know when. Now YOU! –" (he told Karen's architect) "– have a car. Right?"
The architect nodded.
"Half an hour from now you must drive us to the best restaurant you know where I will order and pay for a slap-up celebration champagne lunch. Of course the driver

won't be allowed more than a couple of glasses. But this is not an unselfish proposal. Afterwards you must help me pack my things, because a van will arrive this evening to take me and them back to Bracknell."
Gwinny said, "I'm not coming. I'm expecting a phone call from Tom."
She put down her glass and left the room so abruptly that she left a silence.

Mr Goodchild looked enquiringly at his two remaining guests. After a moment Karen said apologetically, "She used to be quite a sensible girl – I would never have shared a room with her if she'd always been so moody. I thought it was Tom who upset her but an hour ago she came home from a night with him so cheerful and relaxed I thought he'd done her some good for a change. She was chatting quite happily before we came in here. I'll never understand her now. Maybe it's my fault."
The kitchen door was open and from the room next door they heard faint sounds of sobbing. Mr Goodchild drowned them by talking in a more Yorkshire accent than he normally used.
"Nay lass, you aren't the world's conscience! You can help some people sometimes but nobody all the time – that's my philosophy. Let's go for that lunch I promised you."

THE GRUMBLER

THERE IS A SOUR TASTE in my mouth no matter how hard I brush my teeth, and though I change my underwear every morning and take a bath every night I am haunted by a faint, stale odour. Maybe the sourness and staleness is the taste and smell of myself. Is something rotting inside me? I have very little energy nowadays and often sweat for no apparent reason. My urine is the colour of very strong tea – I'm sure it used to be the colour of very weak tea – and I keep running to the lavatory and shitting almost nothing but wind and water. Last week, while shopping, the top half of my body suddenly felt too heavy for the bottom half and I got this pain round my middle, especially in the small of the back, a pain which made it hard to sleep at night. I saw two doctors: my General Practitioner who thumped me all over, said the pain was purely muscular and gave me a bottle of pills to reduce inflammation; and a chiropractor who said I had a slightly displaced vertebra then wrenched my thigh and shoulder before working on the inflammation with heat rays, massage and acupuncture. The backache remained. I went to bed and lay reading dull books I had read before and not enjoyed much, even then. I lacked the strength to read anything enjoyable.

It occurred to me that I was dying. I had a friend who once started dying. I saw him limping and asked why. He said there had been a pain in his knee the day before but it was much better now. For four years his leg was a bit worse every time we met but always much better than the day before, so he refused to see a doctor until he was unable to stand. Then, of course, he was taken to hospital where they diagnosed a heart condition and arthritis and psoriasis, and gave him treatment, and let him out a bit better than he went in, but not much. He hirpled around for another year getting worse and worse again, but always feeling better than the day before, till at last he was dead.

Well, as soon as I thought I was dying I felt a lot happier. I greeted visitors with a smile of patient tolerance. My voice became soft, slow and monotonous. When asked how I felt I replied that I was experiencing no pain, really – just a slight, continuous discomfort. Which was true. I felt magnanimous toward the world. "In a short year or two," I told it, silently, of course, "you and I will cease to trouble each other." However, I gave medical science one last chance. I went to the two doctors and told them there was no improvement. My G.P., with a touch of impatience, said again that my condition was muscular and I should keep taking the pills. The chiropractor frowned in a puzzled way and gave me more acupuncture. I still felt magnanimous. "There are some conditions medical science will never understand," I thought, "before it is too late," and I was about to put off all arrangements and appointments for the foreseeable future when the backache vanished! It suddenly did not exist. This hurled me into my former depression. I went out and got drunk and woke in bed next morning with no clear memory of where I had been the night before and with a huge bruise on my right shoulder which still hurts when I move my arm.

Why must I complain all the time? I have nothing nowadays to worry about except the state of the world as a whole. Especially the part where I live. It is a comparatively prosperous district but even here there is an increase of cracked pavements, rusty lamp-posts and litter in the streets, and women and children with aggressively ugly clothes and hair, and many more haggard, ill-dressed and mad-looking people. Britain grows fouler and fouler as it retreats from the full employment and social welfare it enjoyed when I was a student in the fifties. But I must admit that in the fifties, sixties and even seventies I spent a lot of time feeling like a lonely outcast. I had many friends, and saw them often, but they too felt like lonely outcasts. We grumbled a lot. We decided that our city was completely cultureless because it refused to blend imagination with political commitment. We hired halls and organized meetings to agitate and change things, but we were too poor and useless to do much good. When I say "poor and useless" I do not mean that I, personally, was ever penniless or unemployed, but I felt poor and useless because I had hardly any sex life and was getting older all the time.

When my marriage stopped a certain pub became the centre of my social life. Twice or thrice a week I drank with people I met nowhere else, university people, and Linda who was a dental receptionist, and her boyfriend who worked in a travel agency. One evening, when slightly drunk, Linda asked me, in a perfectly friendly way, why I hung about with people so much younger than me? Honestly, till that moment I had not noticed they were younger than me, but they were, by at least ten years. I sat with them because I enjoyed their company and supposed they liked mine, but when I thought about it I realized that their conversation bored me. What I enjoyed was exactly their youth, especially the youth of the women, though I had no hope of going to bed with one. I had become a harmless middle-aged lecher.

Several years after I had stopped visiting that pub I passed some other young people in the street, and an attractive girl left them and said, "Excuse me sir, may I kiss you on the mouth?"
"Of course!" I said, and embraced her, but she got

embarrassed and broke away and ran back to her friends, who were laughing heartily. They must have dared her to say that because I appeared to be a very respectable, easily shocked old chap. It was a great relief when something similar happened which looked like ending differently. Around closing time one night a girl ran out of a pub door, slipped her arm through mine and said, "You look sexy. Will you take me for an Indian meal?"

I am sure she was not a prostitute. She looked dull, ordinary and overweight, but so do I, so I did not mind. I said, "Of course I'll buy you a meal," and led her to a place I know. I swear to God I did not expect us to make love that night. She was not a prostitute and I was not a fool. The most I hoped for was a flirtatious conversation with some double entendre and innuendo etcetera, and later we would separate with perhaps a slight squeeze and a kiss. I would also give her my telephone number, which might lead to something later if she learned to trust me. When we came to the eating place she halted and said, "This isn't an Indian restaurant."

It was not. It was dearer than an Indian restaurant, but I was friendly with the management, who allowed me credit, and as I had very little money on me there was nowhere else where I could get her a meal that night. I persuaded her to enter and we sat in a glass-roofed courtyard beside a waterlily pond and were served by some very friendly waitresses. She hated it. She ate fast with her face low over the plate. I kept filling her wineglass and she kept emptying it but she spoke not one other word till we were out on the street again, when she asked me to lend her money for the bus fare home. I gave it to her and she hurried off. That was typical of my sex-life in those days.

Why remember such miserable things? I lived for my work in those days and I was good at it, though a lot of folk said my methods were unsound. I suppose that is why the marriage stopped – I earned very little at first.

My wife thought me a poor provider, so when she took a job of her own she didn't want to share anything at all with me, not even the children. But I knew I was right. I plodded straight on as if nothing had happened, and eventually some big men started referring to me in the trade journals. At the age of forty-five my bank manager allowed me to open a new account with a really gigantic loan. I left that bank feeling like a child of eight released from school by the summer holidays. Safety, power and freedom! At last all were mine again. Something tight and hard in me uncoiled, or maybe lay down and died. I was finished with love, sex, women. They had never wanted me, I no longer wanted them.

Shortly after, within the space of a week, I had an enjoyable time in bed with four different women, two of whom I had known for years and who had never shown the slightest interest in me. I don't know why this suddenly happened. I had not become a local celebrity. My reputation in the trade meant nothing to these women, and as for money, nobody ever got money out of me. Recently I read an article about Hollywood which said that if a woman there takes a lover, "all her best friends go through him like an express train". But these women were not acquaintances, so I was definitely not being passed around. There was a royal wedding that week, perhaps it inflamed some irrational passions, I can think of no other explanation. However, I found that I disliked casual sex. I started visiting regularly the only two who regularly want me. They are quite unlike each other, apart from being highly independent and not at all aggressive or malicious. They do not know each other but they know of each other, so I am not deceiving them. I am astonished by myself. I had thought this sort of luck was enjoyed only by aristocrats in improbable romances. I now have all I ever wanted or ever dreamed of wanting: professional respect, prosperity, independence and as much love as I need.

At first it was very nice but I've got used to it and it's driving me mad. It feels like a happy ending. There seems nowhere to go but downhill. I've started drinking too much. Friends ask me what's wrong, but when I tell them I have everything I want they are unable to sympathize. My education is to blame. Two important things I learned at school were worry and boredom. My teachers, who were themselves usually worried and bored, seemed to think we would only become decent human beings if we were like that. Perhaps they taught me too well. I now turn everything I enjoy into worry and boredom in order to feel like a decent human being. This must stop. I refuse to be the creature of my education, a creature of habit. I will change myself tomorrow.

Yes, tomorrow. Tomorrow.

FICTIONAL EXITS

BECAUSE OF A MISTAKE (though I do not know whose) someone was shut in a windowless room with nothing to look at but a door which could only be opened from outside, a lavatory pan and a wall poster showing the face of the nation's ruler. After imagining a great many dealings with this official the prisoner tried to find pleasure in a landscape behind the face. This first soothed by its suggestion of spaciousness, then annoyed by its completely tame nature. On one side wellcultivated farms receded to a distant line of blue hills, on the other was a seat of government, a cathedral, university, and very clean factory and workers' residential block. There were no clumps of forest or winding rivers to explore; the bland distant hills clearly contained no ravines, torrents, cliffs, caverns or mountain passes, they were a mere frontier, shutting off the horizon. Though designed to advertise a sunnier world than the electrically lit cell, the poster showed the inside of a larger jail.

On the brink of melancholy madness the prisoner found a pencil on the floor behind the lavatory pan. When this had been carefully nibbled to a sharp point it might have been used to draw anything on the whitewashed walls: faces of friends, bodies of lovers, the scenery of great adventures. Not able to draw these convincingly the prisoner carefully drew a full-size copy of the room's unopenable door, with one difference. The drawn door had a key in the lock, and it could be turned. Then the prisoner turned the lock, opened the door and walked out. Though describing how fantasy works this is a realistic story. Free will being the essence of mind, everyone who feels trapped must imagine escapes, and some of them work. New arts and sciences, new religions and nations are created this way. But the story of the door can be told with a less happy ending.

A blind man living alone in a municipal housing scheme heard people breaking through his front door, so phoned the local police station. While he was asking for help the housebreakers got to him and knocked him down. They were policemen who had mistaken his door for the door of someone they suspected of selling dangerous drugs without a licence. The mistake was discovered when one of the housebreakers lifted the telephone receiver and found he was talking to a colleague. He told the colleague in the police station not to worry, because the blind householder would be *stitched up*. So the blind man was summoned to a court of law and charged with assaulting the police while they were trying to do their duty.

In Britain all emergency phonecalls to police stations are recorded twice: once by the police stations for the use of the police: once by the British telecommunication company for the use of the caller. The blind man's defence lawyer played the Telecom recording to prove that his client was innocent, pointing out that *stitched up* was slang for arrested on false evidence. The police witness agreed that stitched up meant that in criminal slang, but explained that in police slang it meant *properly arrested with no hint of falsehood or perjury in the procedure*. The sheriff on the bench (magistrates are called sheriffs in Scotland) believed the police witness, since our nation will sink into anarchy if magistrates distrust the police. So the blind man was fined, but not imprisoned, as would almost certainly have happened in an old-fashioned fascist or communist nation.

Like the sheriff on the bench my sympathy is mainly with the police. Opening a door with *the big key* (which is police slang for sledgehammer) is a desperate deed, even if you think someone behind the door is wicked, and that if you grab them fast enough you may find proof of this. Nearly all our experience and education, besides the natural law of do-as-you-would-be-done-by, teaches us to handle doors gently. They are usually quiet, unthreatening, protective creatures. Some of our dearest joys and most regular functions have been made easier by them, so smashing one MUST feel like punching a face, or bombing pedestrians from an aeroplane in broad daylight. We may earn a wage by doing it, we may believe we are defending decency and justice by it, but we cannot help feeling abnormally excited, so mistakes are inevitable. I also sympathize slightly with the blind man, for I am not one of those who think everyone in a municipal housing scheme deserves what is done to them. The man's blindness may not have been his own fault, and may have stopped him seeing he ought to live in a better part of the city. But he should certainly have used his imagination, which would have let him see in the dark.

The big key unlocked the blind man's door in 1990 when Glasgow was the official Culture Capital of Europe. The story was not reported by the press. I give it here because the police, like the prisoner in my first story, found themselves in a terrible situation but imagined a way out. They created a fictional exit which worked.

INCHES IN A COLUMN

I READ THIS STORY many years ago in a newspaper. It had no big headline and filled very few inches but I cannot forget it.

A London lawcourt sentenced a man to several years' imprisonment because, not for the first time, he had been found guilty of getting money by false pretences. Handcuffed to a policeman he was driven to the yard of a London gaol; there the cuff round the policeman's wrist was unlocked before being attached to a warder's. At that moment our man broke free and ran through the yard gateway which was still open. In the road outside a taxi stood at traffic lights which were about to change. Our man leapt in giving the name of an expensive hotel. The cab accelerated. He was free.

Though the paper did not say so I suspect this sequence took less than a minute and he entered the taxi with pursuers close behind. If they saw the taxi drive off the story is certainly from days before taxis had radios. Not till later that afternoon had the driver reason to think anything was wrong.

Our man's position was this: he was penniless with the police in pursuit of him and a right hand he must keep in his pocket to hide the handcuffs locked to its wrist. He was being driven without luggage to the Ritz or Dorchester or Royal Hilton by someone who would expect payment. If he jumped out at lights before reaching the hotel the driver also would start chasing him. His only advantage was a voice and manner which persuaded folk he was rich.

On the way to the hotel he asked if the driver had other business that day. The driver said no. Our man said, good, in that case he would hire the cab for the afternoon, but first they must have lunch. They entered the hotel where our man told the cabby (who probably wore the peaked cap worn by most London cabbies and chauffeurs in those days) to sit down in the foyer lounge. He then went to the reception counter, gave a false but impressive name, booked a room for the week and explained that his luggage would arrive from abroad later that afternoon. He was very particular in ordering a room facing the quiet side of the hotel and in arranging that a hot-water bottle be put in his bed at 11.30 exactly, since he would soon be going out and might return late. Meanwhile he ordered for himself and his driver a snack lunch of sandwiches and champagne to be served in the foyer lounge, also a racing newspaper. The waiter who served the champagne would also naturally pour the first glass so our man was able to eat and drink with his left hand only. He asked the cabby to look through the paper and tell him what races were on that afternoon. The fact that he asked others to do everything for him must have made him a more convincing member of the British officer class. He decided to be driven to Epsom or Ascot or Goodwood – I cannot remember the racecourse, perhaps the report I read failed to mention it. On the journey there he borrowed money from the driver, saying he would cash a cheque later, and in the crowd at the races he managed to lose the driver in a way that seemed accidental.

But the police knew his methods of work and had phoned hotels until they found the one where he had booked a room. His order of a racing paper gave a clue to his destination. When two plain-clothes policemen suddenly grabbed him in the crowd he played his last trick. Pulling his right hand from his pocket he waved the cuff locked to his wrist in the air by its chain and in commanding tones shouted to everyone around, "I am a police officer! Help! Help me arrest these criminals!" The trick did not work. Our man was again brought to court where a judge added more time to his first jail sentence. The taxi driver, appearing as witness, said his day with the swindler had been one of the pleasantest in his life.

Were I writing this story as fiction I might imagine the driver saying that but would leave it out. Such details are too sentimental for convincing fiction.

The whole incident tells a lot about the British class system but hints at something greater. Sooner or later most of us find life a desperate effort to postpone meeting the foe who will one day catch and shut us up forever. I prefer the reckless and witty hero of this short story to more famous confidence men who are sometimes praised, sometimes blamed but always celebrated in longer newspaper articles, and official biographies, and history books.

I hope he thoroughly enjoyed his last taste of champagne.

I OWE NOTHING, I OWN NOTHING

THE MOUNTAIN HAD TWO SUMMITS. One of them had been excavated to uncover ridges of rock around the main contours, ridges with flat upper surfaces and sheer cliff-like sides. I noticed that some ridges were not natural rock but reinforced with concrete.

The site manager and head ganger stood beside the workmen's huts staring hard at the second summit, a dome-shaped mass with granite outcrops. The site manager wanted to know if it could be concreted over by the following night? The head ganger was uncertain. The site manager said, "Let's take a closer look."
He turned and called to me, "Like to come?"
I followed them to a small vehicle used for inspection purposes. The driver was already seated, for there was one place available for me at the back. When I stepped in and sat down the tops of my thighs were as high as the vehicle's side.

From a state of rest we started straight up the mountain so fast that I was terrified of being jerked out backward by my inertia. I desperately wanted something to cling to but the only sure grip was on the edge of the vehicle's underside a few inches above boulder-strewn soil against which it continually banged and scraped without once reducing speed. I passed the journey in a state of fear while also feeling the amazement and exhilaration of flying over ground where folk normally only plod or crawl. We swooped up a curving path between the two summits. I expected us to turn a corner and crash into a rocky rampart, but when we reached one it was red earth

and pierced by an arch. We ran through this into a huge quarry or amphitheatre enclosed by walls of scree curving up all round on to cliffs of vertical rock. The vehicle, powered by a strong four-wheel drive, ran part way up a slope of rubble, reversed faster down it, then sped up it even faster, the driver clearly building up momentum to take him on to the vertical. I shouted, "This can't be done!" but the vehicle rushed up an angle of the quarry wall and at the moment of reaching vertical twisted sideways on to the lowest point of a sloping cornice and we ran safe on to a rounded part of the second summit. The manager indicated it with a Napoleonic wave of the arm. "Tomorrow night?" he asked the ganger.
"We can try, anyway," said the ganger.
The site manager pointed at me, said, "This can't be done!" and chuckled. I saw he had asked me along so that my terror of the ride would emphasize his understanding and control, and make it easier for him to persuade the head ganger to attempt the impossible.

Later I was in a big crowded shed among the workmen's huts. Men were queuing in long lines before little booths fixed to the walls, booths containing oxygen masks. They were preparing to work in the thin air of the second summit by breathing deeply from these. Signs above the booths said that more than six minutes' oxygenation was bad for the health. I suspected that the whole business was bad for the health, a mere management trick to make the men believe their needs were being attended to. Having no intention of working on the second summit I went next door into a bleaker, emptier shed which was the restaurant. The only food was sandwiches in white polystyrene trays covered with transparent plastic. I knew the white bread of the sandwiches was as flavourless and un-nourishing as the polystyrene, but being hungry I chose an egg sandwich and a ham sandwich, and my mouth watered, anticipating with some glee the taste of the fillings. Since we had no better food we got great satisfaction from whatever flavour it contained.

As I lifted my sandwiches I was greeted by an old workman wearing spectacles and a dirty raincoat. He also was not going to work on the second summit. He said, "I'm getting a bit old for these impossible jobs. Mind you, I've nothing to complain about."
He pointed to a plastic table-top on which someone had scratched the words: *I own nothing, I owe nothing*. He said, "That's me too, yes. I can only manage the odd day's work now and then but I like to hang around the site and listen to the lads when they come back in the evenings. You hear a lot of different views of life if you keep your ears open. I hope I'm not boring you?"

THE DOMINO GAME

TWO BIG MEN CALLED A AND B are discussing how to cut up a territory which is in contest between them. Their organization, their cunning, their success are about equal. The contest, if continued, will so weaken them that both will fall prey to X, a much bigger man who has hitherto held aloof. This is partly because he is doing very well in a distant territory where he has destroyed or absorbed every other competitor, and partly because he knows A and B will unite against him if he tries to destroy or absorb either. Their problem is that the disputed territory cannot usefully be cut in two. For geographical, religious and linguistic reasons, splitting it will more than wipe out the profit to be got by taking it over. Yet they cannot leave it alone. The disputed ground is occupied by small independent people who mostly want to stay small and independent, but some of the richer among them also want, with foreign help, to grow bigger at the expense of their neighbours. If A or B do not offer this help X will regard it as a sign of weakness and move into the territory himself. Of course, if A and B combined forces they could easily run the whole territory for the profit of both, but when B suggests this A says, "Combine under who?"
And the subject is dropped

The discussion is a long one. They exhaust themselves trying to find a solution to the problem. At last A sighs and says, '"Why can't we decide it by playing a game of dominoes? Winner take all." B laughs and says, "Why not? The winner will be a hell of a lot richer, the loser won't be one penny the poorer."

They relax by discussing the idea.

Neither has played dominoes since childhood and they suspect it is mainly a game of chance. A suggests that if there is any skill in it they had better play snakes-and-ladders, to equalize their chances. B disagrees. Snakes-and-ladders in played with dice, and dice, like card games, are associated with nervous tension, cheating, social ruin, knife fights and suicide. Dominoes is a game with friendly, jocular associations which harmonize better with the whole idea. They should play it in the dining-car of a train running through splendid scenery. They will invite X along as a guest and witness. It is essential that he sees they are good friends who trust each other before the game, and also during it, but especially after it. Yes, after it especially, X must see that although the game ends in a great acquisition by the winner, the loser is not sullen, humiliated, and keen for an ally who will assist him in a counter-attack. X must also see that the winner will not be made so greedy by his gains that he will do a deal with X to cut up the loser between them. And of course, the loser must see this too.

"What a surprise for old X if we settled it that way!" says B, chuckling. "He might even learn something from us."

"Yes!" says A, "if we did it that way we would be starting a new era in civilization. However –" and he shrugs. "– while I trust you, B, I certainly can't trust C, D and E." These are members of A's organization. One of them, though nobody can yet say which, will replace him when he falls sick or retires.

"I know exactly what you mean," says B, who also has ambitious men under him, "We'll just have to combine forces."

"Combine under who?" asks A. "Will you agree to settle *that* by a domino game?"

And they both laugh heartily. Each knows now the other will not serve under him. They also know that an organization cannot work with two heads.

So their contest continues to spread frustration and anxiety among their employees, poverty and fear among small independent people. It will continue until one of them is so weak that he accepts X as his ally, thereby winning a victory which will leave him, too, in the power of X. This future, which they see very clearly, pleases neither of them, but they have four consolations.

1 They are not young, the years seem to flash past them faster and faster, they will soon have to leave what they sense is an increasingly dangerous world.
2 Though not young, their conspicuous place in a well-reported contest makes them feel young.
3 They have private fortunes which the contest increases.
4 A contest which profits them is only natural.

EDISON'S *TRACTATUS*

PERHAPS YOU KNOW that musclemen – hard men who want to be extra strong – have a habit of eating big feeds of steak and chips, and the minute the last mouthful is swallowed they heave big weights, or run great distances, or work machines that let them do both at the same time. This converts all the food in their guts into muscle without an ounce of additional fat. When a dedicated muscleman overeats, sheer strength is the only outcome.

There was once a man who trained that way to strengthen his brain. Not only after but *during* big feeds he would read very deep books – trigonometry, accountancy, divinity, that class of subject – and think about them fiercely and continually till he felt hungry again. He grew so brainy that before you said a word to him he guessed the sort of thing you meant to say and quoted Jesus or Euclid or Shakespeare who had said it better. This destroyed his social life but at first he didn't care.

One day he was sitting in a restaurant reading Edison's *Tractatus* and beasting into his third plate of steak and chips when he noticed a young woman across the table from him eating the same stuff. She had cut it into small bits and was forking them steadily into her mouth with one hand while writing just as steadily with the other. She wrote in red ink on a block of the squared paper scientists use for charts and diagrams, but she was writing words as clear as print, words so neat and regular that he could not stop staring at them although they were illegible from where he sat being upside down. He noticed that the woman, though not a small woman, was neat and regular in a way that suggested a school mistress. He could not imagine what she would say if she spoke to him and the strangeness of this put him in a confusion through which at last he heard his voice ask if she would please pass the salt cellar, which was as close to him as to her.

The woman glanced at the salt cellar – at him – smiled – put her fork down and said, "What will I most dislike about you if I let that request lead to intimate friendship?"

He hesitated then said frankly, "My breadth of knowledge. I talk better about more things than anyone else. Nobody likes me for it."
She nodded and said, "What do you know about the interface between pre-Columbian Aztec pottery, Chinese obstetrics during the Ming dynasty and the redrawing of constituency boundaries in the Lothian Region subsequent to the last general election?"
He said, "They are perfect examples of inter-disciplinary cross-sterilization. When William Blake said that *The dog starved at his master's gate predicts the ruin of the state* he was stating a political fact. The writer who traced a North American hurricane back to a butterfly stamping on a leaf in a tropical rain forest was reasoning mathematically. The absurd interface you posit is (like most post-modernist and post-constructionalist concepts) a sort of mental afterbirth. Are you writing about it?"
"No but you can reach for the salt cellar yourself," she said and went on writing. The man felt a pang of unintelligent grief. He tried to quench it with manly anger.
"Tell me just one thing!" he said sternly. "If we had conversed intimately what would I have most disliked about you?"
"My depth of sympathy," she answered with a patient sigh. "No matter how loud-mouthed, boastful and dismissive you grew I would realize you could never be different."
"O thank *God* you never passed me that salt cellar!" he cried.

And continued reading Edison's *Tractatus*
but could no longer concentrate.

EPILOGUE TO EDISON'S ***TRACTATUS***

In 1960 I went on holiday to Ireland with Andrew Sykes, a tough small stocky man with a thick thatch of white hair and a face like a boxer's. Like myself he dressed comfortably rather than smartly. We had met when he was a mature student at Glasgow University and I a very callow one just out of Glasgow Art School. We were from the working class who had benefited when two post-war governments (Labour and Tory) agreed that all who qualified for professional educations might have them whether or not they or their parents could pay. Andrew, who had been a sergeant with the British army in India, eventually won a doctorate through a paper on trade unions in the building industry, getting his knowledge by the unacademic ploy of working as a navvy. His army experience and a course in economics had also given him insights into the workings of our officer and financial class. He took malicious glee in gossiping to me about the insider trading by which this minority manipulate the rest. My notion of Britain had been formed at the end of the Second World War when our government announced the coming of a fairer society and the creation of social welfare for all. I had thought Britain was now mainly managed by folk who had mastered difficult processes through training and experience. Andrew explained that, as often today as in the past, most British civil service and business chiefs had stepped into senior positions because they had been to three or four expensive boarding schools and a couple of universities in the English east midlands: institutions where exams mattered less than their parents' wealth and friends they had made. He persuaded me that

Britain was not (as most of our politicians and publicity networks claimed) a democracy, but an aristocracy.

I thought Andrew disliked this unfair system since he was entering a profession through a socialist act of parliament. On our Irish holiday (we were guests of his friends Greta and David Hodgins at Nenagh in Tipperary) I was surprised to find he hated almost any group who wanted to change the dominant system. He even hated the Campaign for Nuclear Disarmament. He forgave me for being a member but we could not discuss it. The only political hope we shared was a wish for a Scottish self-government. I enjoyed what I saw of Ireland but enjoyed his company less than I had expected. His hobbies were wrestling and judo. He told me that body builders convert steak into muscle by a course of weight-lifting immediately after a meal. I will say more about him because he gave me more than the first sentence of "Edison's *Tractatus*".

He became Strathclyde University's first Professor of Sociology in 1967, retired in 1989, died in 1991. His closest relatives were aunts with whom he lodged in a Glasgow tenement until they died long before he did. His job gave him prestige and colleagues. His holidays with the Hodgins in Tipperary gave him a family whose children regarded him as an uncle, a community which treated him as an equal. From a Labour Party member he became a xenophobic Tory. In the university staff club he once aimed a judo kick at a black visitor who was quietly minding his own business. Since his special study was trade unions in the 1980s he became a salaried advisor of the British government, telling Margaret Thatcher how to weaken them. He took self-conscious glee in the bowler hat, tailor-made striped trousers, black jacket and waistcoat he acquired for visits to Downing Street. I fear he did a lot of harm but not to me. From 1961 to 1974 he was my only steady patron. He bought paintings and lent money when I was in need, usually taking a drawing as repayment. He lent me money as if it was an ordinary, unimportant action, leaving my self-respect undamaged. I cannot type so he got his secretaries to type my poems, plays and first novel onto wax stencils from which (in days when photocopying was hugely expensive) they printed all the copies I needed without charge. In 1974 he arranged for the Collins Gallery of Strathclyde University to give the largest retrospective show my pictures have ever had, getting a Glasgow Lord Provost to open it.

Yet in his last fifteen years I hardly saw him at all, maybe because I no longer supported a family so had less need to borrow. After his retirement he became a recluse and solitary drinker, his only human contacts being a cleaning lady and a weekly phone call from Greta Hodgins in Ireland. I felt sad and guilty when he died. He had given me much more than I had ever given him.

I will now list other ingredients which went into "Edison's *Tractatus*".

1 In the 1960s I heard that Wittgenstein's *Tractatus* was a very brainy book. I thought it might not be too brainy for me but never got hold of a copy.

2 I am too shy and pessimistic to start conversations with strangers but when public transport or an eating house places me beside an attractive one I sometimes fantasize about talking to them. This habit led to my first television play and a novel which is still in print. In 1982 I worked with Liz Lochead, Jim Kelman and Tom Leonard on a review called *The Pie of Damocles*. I scribbled a sketch in which a young woman at a café asks a depressed young man to pass her the sugar bowl and he insists on discussing what this might lead to before refusing. My friends did not think it funny. I discarded it.

3 I started hearing the word *interface* in the 1970s.

It seemed to be used by people erecting a barrier round their work practice while talking across it. The barrier made the job they had mastered feel safer but conversation across it sometimes made new work, as forensic medicine had developed from the interface between policing and doctoring. My facetious attitude to new words led me to link activities between which no interface was possible – the gap between Aztec pottery and Chinese obstetrics, for instance, seemed unbridgeable. Around the same time I heard a lecturer amuse a university audience by referring to something as "an example of interdisciplinary cross-sterilization".

4 For several years I have been perplexed by the adjective *post-modern*, especially when applied to my own writing, but have now decided it is an academic substitute for *contemporary* or *fashionable*. Its prefix honestly announces it as a specimen of intellectual afterbirth, a fact I only noticed when I reread my brainy character saying so.

5 A few years ago I heard that a scientist had shown how a butterfly stamping on a leaf in a tropical rain forest might precipitate a hurricane in North America. This may or may not be true.

6 In the first months of 1994 I conducted a creative writing class at St Andrews University. Going home by train to Glasgow I sat opposite a young woman who was writing in red ink on a block of graph paper. I could not read her words but they were shaped with unusual clearness and regularity. She was slightly bigger than average, neatly dressed and with no apparent make-up or anything to catch the eye. I felt a strong prejudice in her favour, believing, perhaps wrongly, that she was unusually intelligent. I suddenly wanted to put her in a story exactly as she appeared. She sometimes exchanged words with a young man but their conversation did not interest me.

I broke my journey home at Markinch to visit Malcolm Hood in Glenrothes Hospital. Two years earlier he had been paralysed by a cerebral stroke: his brain was in full working order but his body could give no sign of it. He was now able to speak and move a little. On this visit I read him a story from Somerville and Ross's *Experiences of an Irish R.M.* and occasional comments and snorts of laughter showed his enjoyment. When students at Glasgow Art School forty years before we had often read aloud to each other from amusing authors. My favourites were Max Beerbohm and Rabelais, Malcolm's were Dickens and Patrick Campbell. Campbell – an Anglo-Irish humorist not much read now – probably gave us our first taste of Blarney, which I define as *the employment of an Irish idiom to make an unlikely story more convincing*. The Somerville and Ross tale was full of it.

When I boarded a homeward-bound train at Markinch "Edison's *Tractatus*" was germinating. I scribbled most of it in a notebook before reaching Glasgow, and as I did so imagined an Irish voice saying it, an Irish voice deliberately constructing an improbable tale. That is why I gave it an improbable title. Were I to read it aloud I would do so in my Scottish voice, but when writing "Edison's *Tractatus*" the sentences moved to a second-hand Irish lilt.

7 This lilt must come from more than a fortnight in Tipperary thirty-five years ago and from renewed pleasure in the Blarney of Somerville and Ross. Flann O'Brien's writings are an ingredient because, though Joyce, Synge and O'Casey use Blarney on occasions, O'Brien is the only Irish genius whose work is Blarney throughout. In the previous six months I had also read with pleasure "This Fella I Knew", a short story by my friend Bernard MacLaverty who never talks Blarney and hardly ever writes it. This one story is an exception. It appears in his anthology, *Walking the Dog*, published in 1994.

8 A week after scribbling the first version of "Edison's *Tractatus*" a student in my St Andrews class asked how I got ideas for stories. I gave a long confused answer because each novel, short story or play seemed to form differently. What set it going might be a story I had read which I wanted to tell differently, or a day dream, or dream remembered on waking, or a fantasy I had evolved during conversation, or an incident which had befallen someone else but it was unforgettable because of its oddity, humour or injustice. Ideas have sometimes come from commissions to write on a particular subject. Thereafter the idea grew through alternation of writing and deliberate day-dreaming. If a narrative drew in many memories, ideas and phrases which had lain unused in my brain it sometimes expanded to a novella, novel or play. All but my first novel came that way. The first came from childhood faith in a long printed story as my surest way of getting attention. I daydreamed and scribbled it for years before accumulating enough ideas and experiences to finish it. I have also developed stories by telling or reading parts to friends before completion. Most authors I know avoid this because displaying unfinished work reduces their enthusiasm for it, but some listeners' suggestions have expanded my tales in ways I might not have discovered myself.

The student's question produced this account of what went into "Edison's *Tractatus*". There is probably more than I am conscious of, but I believe the brainy hero is mainly a caricature of traits which Andrew Sykes and I had in common. We were both inclined to turn sexual urges into clever, sometimes boring monologues. The urge to deliver an uninterrupted monologue is the energy driving most teachers, storytellers and politicians. "Edison's *Tractatus*" is obviously a portrait of someone too wordy for his own good, which also explains the addition of this bit of intellectual afterbirth.

HUFF HARRINGTON: A Tale Due to Kipling

OUR COLONEL WAS EVERYTHING such a British officer should be, though not always as clever as he believed. He enjoyed playing chess and had never lost a game before Harrington joined us. Before then his only steady chess partner was near retirement age and kept having to be reminded how the pieces moved. After one game with the Colonel everyone else refused his challenges saying, "No point in playing you Sir! We know the result beforehand."

He took that as a compliment. On Harrington's first night in the mess he was pleased when the young man admitted to enjoying an occasional chess game, while declaring he was a very poor player. The Colonel may not have known that every player who is not a grand master says that before playing a new opponent, because he replied cheerfully, "Then you will probably learn something by playing me."

Those of us who understood chess gathered to watch this game with unusual interest.

It began as usual with the Colonel recklessly swapping pieces to maintain a very slight advantage, while leaving gaps in his defence that showed he was either a very cunning or very stupid player. Harrington soon decided which. After securing his king behind a small barrier of pawns he gave a polite show of futile resistance while letting his rooks, castles and a bishop be taken. Twice he left openings that would have given an alert opponent immediate victory, but the Colonel was enjoying the game too much to notice these. At last he removed Harrington's queen and asked pleasantly, "Had enough, Harrington?"

With a slight sigh Harrington brought his remaining bishop

across the board from a far corner and placed it murmuring, "Checkmate."
The Colonel stared at the new position, at first in bewilderment, then with gradual understanding. His face reddened. His eyebrows concentrated in a scowl. His underlip protruded further and further beyond his moustache. Harrington said quietly, "Sorry Sir. I should not have done that, especially as I am new here."
In the monotonous, distinct growl only used when he was extremely angry the Colonel said, "Are you suggesting that it is etiquette for my junior officers to let me win?"
After a pause Harrington said, "Surely Sir, a soldier of your standing is entitled to a few privileges in private life, and my victory was probably beginner's luck."
For nearly two minutes the Colonel thought hard about this, then suddenly grinned and clapped Harrington on the shoulder saying, "Right on both counts, my boy! I can see you will go far."
From then on he treated Harrington with great affability, but never again challenged him to a chess game.

That is how Harrington came to be called Had Enough, which was shortened to Huff in case the Colonel overheard us use the longer form and remembered why. Huff did go far because in tricky situations he usually won through at the last minute. When he became a general his men called him Old Huffy, though by then perhaps even he had forgotten why.

THE WORST TALE

THIS HAPPENED IN 1971 OR 72 when public education and health were better funded, when British manual workers were better paid, when the middle classes were almost as prosperous but less in debt than today, when the richest classes were (by their own obviously high standards) much poorer. Other tales in this book have sour endings but none as bad as this because the others are fiction. I heard it from Angel Mullane, once a colleague of the teacher who is the story's most active yet least interesting character.

A school in the east of Glasgow taught children who could barely read, or found it hard to sit still and concentrate, or had other traits which unsuited them for normal schooling. In times of full employment (and this was in a time of full employment) such children can be prepared for ordinary jobs by teaching them to read, count and talk with greater confidence, but they cannot be taught really well in classes of more than ten. The average class size was twenty-five so the teachers often had to teach badly. Before 1986 this meant threatening and sometimes inflicting physical pain. Deliberately inflicted pain was in those days used by teachers in schools for normally healthy and even wealthy children – why should the damaged children of poor folk suffer less?

The pupils mostly came from a council housing scheme built for the very poor in the early 1930s. People there felt that the police were more of a threat than a protection, so small weak people believed that a strong male member of their own family was their likeliest defender. In many Scottish schools the most effective-sounding threat a pupil could hurl at a punitive teacher was, "I'll get my dad to you!" This threat was almost a ritual. Teachers had a stock of equally ritualized replies to it. But many children in the school I speak of had no father or uncle or big brother in their family, and knew that their teachers knew it. A few had mothers with dogs, perhaps for protection. These were able to say, "I'll get my dug to you."

One day at this school a small boy faced a teacher wielding a leather belt designed to strike palms of hands. The boy was either trying to stop himself being beaten or had been beaten already and wished to show he was not completely crushed. Either in fear of pain or in a painful effort to keep some dignity he cried out, "I'll get my –" and hesitated, then cried, "I'll get my *Alstation* to you!" He lived with a granny who could not afford to keep a big dog. The way he pronounced Alsatian proved that his dog was nothing but a badly learned word – a word without power – a word which got the whole class laughing at him.

THE MARRIAGE FEAST

I MET JESUS CHRIST only once, in Cana, at some sort of marriage feast. I say "feast" because that word was distinctly printed on the invitation card, though it aroused expectations which were not fulfilled, for the parents of the bride had either pretensions beyond their incomes or were downright stingy. The waiters' tardiness in refilling our glasses suggested the booze was in short supply, and long before we finished the unappetizing main course there was none to be had. The person most obviously upset about this was a little old Jewish lady who had already (I seem to remember) consumed more than her fair share of the available alcohol.

"They have no wine!" she hissed in a stage whisper which was heard throughout the room and embarrassed everyone except (apparently) our hosts. I was compelled to admire their equanimity in the face of so audible a hint. The little lady was addressing a man who looked like – and actually was – both her son and a carpenter wearing his best suit. Like many mothers she was blaming her offspring for other people's faults, but his reaction surprised me.

"Woman!" he declared, "My time is not yet come!"

This struck us all as a meaningless remark, though I later realized it was advance publicity for his brief, disastrous career as a faith healer. However, a moment afterwards he beckoned the head of the catering staff, and whispered something which resulted in more wine being served.

At the time I assumed Christ had himself paid for extra booze so was almost inclined to feel grateful, but Freddie Tattersal (who is also Jewish) told me, "Remember that

Christ belonged to the self-employed tradesman class, and that sort don't lash out money in acts of reckless generosity. There must still have been a lot of wine at that feast, but the waiters were saving it for themselves and the guests at the main table. Christ put the fear of God into the caterers by threatening to make a stink if they did not serve everyone equally, especially him – and he would have done it! They probably watered the plonk to make it go round." I still find this hard to believe. The plonk they served later was nothing to boast of but it was genuine plonk. I now believe I met Christ in one of his better moods. He was an unpleasant person who went about persuading very ordinary fishmongers and petty civil servants to abandon their jobs and wives and children and go about imitating him! There were a great many such self-appointed gurus in the sixties. Who cares about them nowadays?

MORAL PHILOSOPHY EXAM

A BIG TELEVISION COMPANY regularly broadcast a news programme informing the viewers of bad deeds: not the bad deeds of corporations who might withdraw advertising revenues, or the bad deeds of big businessmen and government officials who could afford to bring strong libel actions, but the exploitive practices of private tradesmen. This did some social good and entertained viewers, who were also encouraged to help the programme by supplying it with evidence of scandalous instances. The broadcasters heard of a man who liked horses but had become so poor that the few he owned were badly fed and stabled. The broadcasters tried to contact the man but he hid from them. A camera crew besieged his house until he emerged and was filmed fleeing from an interviewer who ran after him shouting unanswered questions. This was broadcast along with distant views of the horses, the faces and voices of concerned neighbours, the comments of a qualified animal doctor. The owner was subsequently charged with cruelty to animals by the Royal Society for Prevention of Cruelty to Animals, was found guilty and jailed for several months as he could not afford to pay a fine. The horses were humanely killed because nobody else wanted them.

Which of the following cared most for the horses?

1 Their owner.
2 The RSPCA.
3 The broadcasters.

Who gained most by these events?

1 Lawyers conducting the trial.
2 The broadcasters.
3 Other horses with incompetent owners.

Who lost most by these events?

1 The owner.
2 The horses.

DECISION

I WAS IGNORANT when I was young. I didnae know that sex and children were connected – they seemed to belong to different worlds. My Mammy and her pals talked about sex in a queer oblique kind of way but they were quite open and direct when they spoke about children: "She's decided not to have a child yet," they said about a girl who had just married. I was sixteen when I married and I decided not to have a child either. I talked it over with my husband – he was a year older than me – and he entirely agreed. "Time enough for us to have children when we've a home of our own," he said, "and that won't be for a few years yet."

My Mammy thought it was a wise decision too. We were living with her.

Imagine my astonishment when my stomach swole up and the doctor told me I was pregnant. I said, "I can't be! I've decided not to have a child."

He said, "What precautions did you take?"

I didnae answer him. I don't take precautions when I decide not to have a cigarette, why take precautions when I decide not to have a baby? A woman in the bed beside me at the maternity hospital told me about birth control,

but a week after I came out

I was pregnant again.

A REALITY SHOW

NOWADAYS THE DANISH CROWN PRINCE is a keen amateur actor who only talks to friends, members of his family, civil servants and journalists in Copenhagen's Theatre Royal, on a stage set for the last act of *Hamlet*. Admission is free. On Tuesday and Thursday afternoons the front stalls are full of children brought by teachers from primary schools all over Scandinavia, as part of their social science education. At other times the audience is seldom more than eight or nine adults, mainly American tourists. Broadcasters agree that the prince's performances are lifelike and convincing but too dull to be recorded or televised. The prince believes that as standards of living and decency deteriorate throughout the world, many will start to enjoy watching what he calls "the banality of virtue".

AUTHORITY

I DID NOT STRUGGLE FOR IT. By accident alone five older brothers died before I took the crown of a thousand-mile-long kingdom, founded by our grandfather, when the T'ang dynasty could not hold China together. My handwriting was excellent. I was not blatantly unfaithful to my wife. Like a true philosopher I eschewed ambition and let landlords and merchants run the country. The Sung empire swallowed us whole. When ordered, I killed myself. Never mind. I once wrote my name on a famous painting. I am remembered, though my people are not.

TRANSLATION

THE ELDER GRANDMOTHER, or stipendiary magistrate, or rich farmer's prodigal son scratches, or ignores, or perhaps greedily enjoys the young slave-girls of the harem, or the petitioners from an unimportant suburb, or the white feathered-longnecked-furiously-hissing denizens of the poultry yard: while in another continent and century and civilization I turn a vertical row of pictograms into a horizontal sentence of phonetic type, without spilling a nuance.

HUMANITY

And one mild midsummer day, high among the rocky and heathery summits of Ben Venue, we found a small hollow brimful of perfectly smooth untrodden snow, and shouting "See the lovely white snow!" jumped into the middle of it with our great big boots.

ENOUGH MONEY

MY CEILING ADMITS NO RAIN. I admire the movement of clouds over the city. Every weather, every season has its unique beauty.

GLASWEGIANS

FOR
FLO ALLAN

LONDON 1990

ONE FOR THE ALBUM

JUNE is intelligent, and honest, and very lonely. She is also strikingly good looking, which does not help much. She likes admiration but most men's admiration becomes resentment when she refuses to let them bring it to a very ordinary sexual conclusion. She thinks slightly plainer women have an easier time. She was married once and that also ended for ordinary reasons. Her husband could not forgive her for earning more than he earned yet did not want her to stop work and have a child. At the time she was sorry. Now she is glad. Too many women, she thinks, use children to distract them from unsatisfying lives. Her salary from the civil service is now too big for her to risk losing the job, the job too unsatisfying to let her rest in it. She often dreams of taking a long break and finding work that pleases her, but perhaps (says her honesty) no such work exists. People who know what they want in life are guided to it by an obsession. June's only obsession is commonplace – she likes dressing well. When buying a garment which suits her rare kind of handsomeness she feels that life, after all, might become an exciting adventure. She has a large wardrobe of clothes to remind her of that wonderful, shortlived feeling. It does not stop her usually feeling like a Mercedes Benz forced to work as a taxi.

Her job has an advantage apart from the wage. By working overtime she can make Friday a holiday and walk about assessing fashions in shop windows and on the bodies of passers-by. Her favourite styles are those of the thirties and forties which flirt elegantly or luxuriously with the human outline. On this clear summer afternoon nearly everything she sees annoys her, the prevailing styles shout aloud that times are tough. Young men with money wear floppy suits and stubble on their chins. Jackets, waistcoats, woollens, shirts and skirts are worn in eccentric layers as if put on fast in an emergency. The commonest fabric is denim; the commonest garment a shapeless jacket with huge pockets suggesting a labour camp. This has been popular for years and makers have given it a new lease of life by dyeing it to appear dirtied by rough usage. Jeans and skirts are also made from this denim. Some young people (June is no longer young) wear jeans they have deliberately ripped; why? The only elegant garment she glimpsed is made of the toughest fabric of all. Someone slim and neat passes in a suit of gleaming black leather with silver zips. June has never worn leather but some shops sell nothing else. She experiences a faint, familiar thrill: she will hunt down an exciting new thing to wear. The leather shop welcomes her with a scent she finds comforting yet exotic – she has forgotten how good leather smells. But the skirts and jackets don't appeal to her and she does not even look at the trousers – trousers are not her style. An assistant asks what she is looking for.

"None of this, exactly," says June glancing discontentedly along a rack, "I want something more ... something less ..."
She is going to say "conventional" but blushes instead.
She does not exactly know what she wants.
"Perhaps you should have it made to order," says the assistant, briskly.
"Where?"
"The Hideout is quite near here – number 3798."
June wanders meekly into the sunlight again but her meekness is on the surface. *Hideout* adds a spice of Wild

West adventure to this hunt for something she cannot yet imagine.

The place is further than the assistant suggested. Beyond a crossroads June finds she has left the fashionable district. A poorer lot of people crowd along the cracked pavement but they look cheerful in sunlight. June is no snob, all that worries her is the absence of any place called The Hideout or numbered 3798. Between 2988 (a loan office) and 4040 (a betting shop) is a long row of boarded-up fronts. She walks up and down before these, excitement cooling to a familiar disappointment till she notices a car at the kerb: a cheap little Citroën with two wavy blue lines on the side. To the canvas roof, with great ingenuity, an arrow-shaped sign is fixed. A leather belt is stapled to the sign in a loop surrounding the words HIDEOUT LEATHERWEAR. The arrow points across the pavement at a dark little entry smelling of cat-piss and leading to steps worn to such a slant that June feels insecure on them. They bring her to a landing with a plank floor and three low doors, two faced with rusty metal and padlocked, one coloured vivid orange with a handwritten label saying *press hard* above a bell-button. June presses it, hard.

She has gone through the shadowy entry and up these stairs with the uneasy excitement of a huntress following game into a dangerous thicket, but when the door opens her uneasiness vanishes. A bright ordinary little woman in a print dress opens it and says, "I'm sorry, come in, I can't attend to you right now because I'm finishing something for someone but if you can wait a minute I'll be with you in a minute. What sort of thing are you looking for?"

She leads June down a short corridor to a long, low-ceilinged bare-looking room with six dusty windows above the shop fronts on the street. A sewing machine, a rack of hangers empty of garments, a table with tools and

samples on it are almost the only furniture. In a corner of the carpetless plank floor is an electric kettle plugged to a wall socket, two mugs, a jar of coffee powder, a bag of sugar, and a radio playing pop music. Beside the sewing machine sits a woman who scowls at June as if she was intruding. She is very like the woman who opened the door, though plumper and with thick black hair cut straight across the brow and shoulders like the wig of a sphinx. "I think," says June hesitantly, "I want a ... a skirt."
"Sit down and look at some patterns," says the woman pointing to a fat album on the table, "I'll be with you in five minutes," and she sits at the machine and resumes putting something through it while the other woman talks to her in a low penetrating voice which sounds conversational yet complaining.

The album has cuttings from catalogues and fashion-magazines mounted on big pages under transparent film. As June turns these pages she grows more and more frustrated. They show all sorts of leather garments, some conventional, some bizarre, but nothing June would wear in the street. She is too old to enjoy dressing before a mirror. Why did she come here? She finds she is straining to hear phrases which penetrate the stuttering bursts of sewing-machine sound and the din of pop music.
"... had her eye on me but I had my eye on her ..."
"... I said you don't buy what you don't like ..."
"... hotpants isn't just her middle name it's her first and last ..."
June shakes her head impatiently, turning the pages faster and faster until she reaches blank ones at the end. She is going to slam the book shut and leave when she sees the corner of a loose photograph protruding from those last pages. Pulling it out she discovers she is holding two black and white photographs, but for a long time the one on top has her whole attention.

A black leather skirt, calf-length and with a rear

fastening of silver studs from waist to hem, is worn by a woman who is photographed from behind. It would be too tight if most of the studs were not unfastened but a few top ones are fastened to hide an arse made proud by her high-heeled shoes. The shoes and skirt are all she wears as she presses against the wallbars of a gymnasium, stretching one arm up to grasp a bar just beyond the reach of her fingertips. Then June sees her wrist is handcuffed to that bar. Her free hand grips a bar at shoulder height, her legs are braced as far apart as possible to take all the weight she can off the steel bracelet round that wrist. Her head is flung backward. All that appears of it is a white line of brow and much unbound thick black hair cut straight across the shoulders in a way which reminds June of someone near her, but the reminder is not strong enough to break the dreamy enchantment cast by the photograph. If the woman gossiping by the sewing machine (… "and I said to her, I said, I said …") is the woman in the photograph she is more interesting, more enticingly beautiful in the photograph. Then June notices she is alone in that room, the voices are gossiping beside the front door, which slams. She hears someone approaching her and asking cheerily, "Well? Have you found what you want?"

"Not … exactly," says June after a pause, and as she still cannot draw her eyes from the photograph or bear to lay it down she starts talking as if the skirt, nothing but the skirt is the thing she stares at, is all that interests her.
"A front fastening, I think, and …"
She hesitates, having no other ideas.
"Pockets?" asks the woman.
"Well … yes."
"Big ones?"
"Perhaps …"
"Like hers?"
The woman takes the photograph uncovering the one beneath. It shows a tall lean woman in her early thirties,

her scalp shaved quite bald, standing arrogantly astride. She wears big baggy suede overalls with the the legs rolled above the knee. Saddlebag pockets on the thighs make them bulge out like jodhpurs but more noticeable is her smile of greedy pleasure, the thin cane she flexes in her hands.

"That's Miss Cain, our schoolteacher. Her real name is Harry – she's an artist. Lots of goodies in her pockets!" says the woman encouragingly. June stares, then nods, blushing.

"I know exactly what you want!" cries the woman enthusiastically. She lays both photographs on the table, grabs a pad and sketches on it saying, "Like this? ... and loops for the belt here ... Why not a front *and* back fastening ...?"

June finds herself agreeing to a skirt she has no intention of wearing.

Then the woman slides the photos back into the album and says confidingly "I nearly died when I saw you with those."

"Why?"

"They shouldn't be in that album – they're from an album my wicked clients use."

"Wicked?" says June, pretending not to understand.

"Not *horribly* wicked. But they enjoy games not everyone enjoys, so they like to be careful. I don't blame them! I'm a bit wicked myself – that's why they trust me. Now I'm going to measure you."

The woman kneels and as her light fingers put a tape round June's waist, hips, lower hip etcetera June looks absent-mindedly round the room. She sees no sign of another album.

"It's in a wee safe under the table," says the woman, who is making notes in her pad, "You see these photos don't just show available dress designs, they show available ... people, so they're rather tempting. Would you like a peep?"

She smiles at June who is too confused by having her mind read to say a word, but perhaps she nods because the woman shuts the pad briskly saying, "I'll maybe allow you a peep when you come for the fitting. When will suit you?"
"Friday?"
"Sure! Anytime next Friday will do. Give me your phone number in case something happens and there's a delay. But there shouldn't be."
June gives her phone number, asks the price of the skirt (which is reasonable) and offers a down payment.
"No need," says the woman, smiling, "I know you'll be back."

"You seem even more remote from us than usual," says June's boss to her in the office next Tuesday.
"I feel a bit peculiar," June admits.
"You look flushed. Take a day off."
"Maybe I will," says June, but she knows what her disease is. She is haunted by daydreams of a picturebook showing temptingly available victims and tyrants. Her heart beats faster at the memory. She feels – while knowing this irrational – close to a gladness and freedom she has not enjoyed since she was eleven and sex was a thrilling secret shared with a few special friends, not an anxious negotiation with a potentially dangerous adult. But that was long ago. To play truant from work and visit The Hideout before Friday and ask to see *the wicked album* will be admitting a sexual need. June has never in her life admitted a sexual need to another adult. She waits till Friday before returning to The Hideout, and forces herself to wait till mid-afternoon, instead of arriving like an eager little girl as soon as it opens.

And she stands on the cracked pavement between the loan office and the betting shop and stares at a space of reddish, brick-strewn gravel with a railway viaduct behind it. For a while she cannot believe the whole

building has vanished. She fights the desolate frustration she feels by examining the rows of buildings on each side of the space, and going into a pub across the road from it, though it is the sort of pub where lonely women are stared at. She orders a gin and tonic and asks the barman, "What happened to the tailoring business across the road?"
"Those shops were pulled down weeks ago."
"Oh no – they were there last Friday."
"Could be. But nobody's been in them for years."
"But there was a … a leathercraft shop upstairs in one. Called The Hideout. A small woman ran it. She advertised with a sign on a parked car."
"She couldn't have. Parking's illegal on that side."
June finishes her drink then goes to the fashionable leatherwear shop which gave her the address. The only information the assistant has is a card a stranger handed in with The Hideout name and address on it.
She says, "These small firms come and go very quickly. Will I give you the address of another?"
June goes home to her room and kitchen flat, buying a bottle of sherry on the way.

She has a very hot bath, washes her hair, then sits in her dressing gown on the hearthrug, sipping sherry and listening to a record. This does not cheer her. She feels empty and old, with nothing much to expect from life. A second glass leaves her gloomier and fuddled. The telephone rings. She lifts the receiver.
"This is Donalda Ingles," says an unfamiliar, anxious little voice, "I've got your skirt."
"*Who* are you?"
"Donalda. We met in The Hideout last week. Your skirt's ready!"
"I went there today and …"
"Yes, you saw what they did to us. Listen, can I bring it round?"
"Bring it here?"

"Yes. You aren't busy are you? I mean, nobody's with you, are they?"
"No, but ..."
"Give me your address and I'll bring it over right away, I'm sure you'll like it!"
There is an odd, pleading note in the little voice through the receiver. After a pause June gives her address and the voice says "I'll be there in twenty minutes."
June goes thoughtfully to her wardrobe. She is about to choose a dress when she changes her mind and puts on pants, bra and white cotton blouse with the dressing gown on top. She will wear the skirt for the maker of it, if for nobody else. This decision makes her feel young again.
The entryphone rings. June presses the admission switch and goes to the door. A woman in a long waterproof coat and carrying a suitcase comes up the stairs to June's landing and stands before her saying "Hello! Don't you remember me?"
It is the small plump woman with black hair like the sphinx's wig.
"Yes, but I didn't expect you, I expected –"
"Oh Senga couldn't come, she's very busy from having to shift, you see, and she thought you'd rather see me anyway."
"Why?" says June, letting the woman in and closing the door.
"Senga gets these notions. I never argue with her. This is a very nice room, do you mind if I take off my coat?" She asks this as if expecting to be refused. In The Hideout she seemed sullen and plaintive. Now she is an intriguing mixture of boldness and shyness, as if shoving herself forward against her will. When June says "Of course take it off!" she hesitates before quickly unbuttoning and dropping it on the sofa beside the suitcase, then she stands gazing at June in a helpless, pleading way. With a white silk blouse she is wearing exactly the high-heeled shoes and leather skirt she wore in the photograph, and to prove it she lifts both hands to shoulder-height and turns round

till she faces June again, having shown the rear fastening more than half undone. And June knows she is being seduced and has partly wanted it. Her heart beats hard and fast, yet she is able to smile with perfect confidence at the plump, sexy-looking, nervous little woman. Though June has never been seduced by a woman before, the situation is a familiar one.

"What about *my* skirt?" she asks. Donalda nods, opens the case, takes the skirt out. June slips off her dressing gown and stands with folded arms before the wardrobe mirror. Donalda kneels and fastens it round her, buckling the belt, patting and smoothing the leather over waist, stomach, arse and tops of the thighs and all the time murmuring, "There, isn't it nice? Aren't you lovely?"

June looks down on her with some of the loneliness, some of the contemptuous superiority she always feels with people who greatly desire her, though looking at the mirror she notices wryly that her own skirt is far more challengingly whorish than the one Donalda wears.

She also sees, as well as feeling, Donalda's arms embrace her waist, Donalda's face press into the angle of her neck and shoulder, Donalda's lips brush her ear and whisper, "There's a present for you in the right pocket."

June slides her hand under the pocket flap and pulls out the photographs which enchanted her in The Hideout. She stares at them as Donalda leads her to the soft rug before the fire, stares at them as she responds to the little beseeching murmurs and handpats by which Donalda brings her to lie down and open to her. She even stares at them while absentmindedly, with her free hand, returning some of Donalda's caresses. Donalda sobs, "Oh you devil! You lovely devil! You don't care for me at all, do you? It's *her* you wanted Senga to send!"

"I'm not sure," murmurs June, looking from the photo of the tempting victim to that of the exciting tyrant. Which does she like best? Which would she like to be? She really does not know.

Much later June lies with closed eyes, half satisfied and half dissatisfied as she always feels after lovemaking. She is conscious of Donalda's body against her back, Donalda's hand resting on her thigh, Donalda's small voice explaining or complaining about something. "You haven't once asked who I am or how I feel or what I want in life – I think you care for nobody but yourself but I must tell you about me. I come from a really big family, three older brothers and three younger sisters and I had to help my Mum look after the lot of them. I really loved my Mum, she was a really good woman who never thought of herself, she made herself old before her time slaving from morning till night for all those men and young lassies who never gave a damn for her. Well, when I turned fifteen I couldn't take any more – I was sick of helping her so I left home, I suppose because I'm wicked. We all have wicked dreams, don't we? And unless we bring one of our wicked dreams just a wee bit to life we live like zombies – the living dead – slaves like my Mammy, right? Right? Answer me! *Please!*"

"Right," says June, who feels too tired to disagree or think much and has begun to find Donalda Ingles a bore.

"I want to ask you another thing. Have you any arrangements this weekend? Are you going to see someone or are they coming here to see you?"

"I've made no arrangements," says June, and to stop Donalda suggesting one adds, "I like weekends to myself."

"Anyway," says Donalda, after a pause, "When I left my Mammy I got into big trouble. I won't go into details, they would only sicken you – I had a baby and all that. It was Senga who saved me. She's not much older than me, we were pals at school, but she's as sure of what to do as my Mammy is, though my Mammy is a slave and Senga is definitely a boss. When I help Senga I'm helping myself because … don't laugh … Senga is a fairy godmother who makes dreams come true. She's so good at it she earns her living that way. She told me to do this with you, please let me, it won't hurt," says Donalda, "Just turn over a bit."

June turns obediently over. She hears nothing now but the

unfastened skirt and the belt, which has several straps and buckles. June lets Donalda draw her wrists behind her back, cross them above the belt and loop a strap round them. The pressure of the strap suddenly becomes almost painful and June finds her wrists fastened there.

"And now?" she placidly asks. Donalda stands, goes to the kitchen and returns with three clean glasses. These she lays on the table and fills from the sherry bottle.

"What's happening?" asks June, puzzled. Donalda dips into the suitcase and brings out a radio telephone and a wide strip of adhesive bandage. She says, "A couple in a car downstairs have been waiting to see you so I'm asking them up. If you start screaming I'll gag you with this bandage."

June is too astonished to scream. She tries to stand which is hard without hands and impossible when Donalda sits on her legs and puts an arm round her neck.

"Listen!" says Donalda, and her voice is not hard or cruel, "Please believe this, Senga and I make other peoples' dreams come true but we haven't *begun* to help you yet – you're so locked up in yourself you don't know what your dreams are. You're under a spell and we won't let you go till we've broken that spell, because you're the loveliest thing we've ever met. But first, before Senga brings the teacher here ..."

She fastens her mouth on June's mouth in a kiss which is almost a bite, and for a moment June enjoys a melting delicious weakness like nothing she has known.

We will return to her later.

A DISTANT COUSIN OF A QUEEN

HARRY is a foetus before the sexual scanning of them is practical. She is pulled from her mother's body through a caesarian section because the mother believes a surgical delivery will ensure her husband's presence. Just before the operation she is told that a local, not a general, anaesthetic must be used.

"I felt every bloody thing they did to me down thea," she tells friends, "It didn't hurt, but it was loathsome."

When Harry is held up in the air her mother says, "Oh God a fucking little gel! For a boy I might have whipped up some maternal instinct but a gel is *not on*."

She weeps passionately and the husband and father pays no attention to Harry, who is also weeping passionately. He pats his wife's hand and says, "Don't worry, dia, it isn't important."

Harry's mother compensates for disliking her daughter by wanting more from Harry's nurses than they can give. For nearly two years all those who do the job resign or get dismissed before a month passes, often before a week. At last a woman from Greenock is employed. Her voice strikes Harry's parents as comically coarse and ill-bred but her quietly servile manner is just right, and she can produce Harry anytime looking as clean, pretty and passive as an expensive doll. Harry's mother wants Harry for coffee mornings, where she introduces her as, "My daughta, of course."

Harry sits with a straight back, hands folded in lap, looking hard at whoever is talking. This is usually her mother,

but other visitors find the small girl's close attention disconcerting. When someone asks her genially, "What have *you* to say for yawself?" Harry looks straight at her mother who tells the visitor, "Let ha off the small talk. Amusing topics are still beyond ha grasp."
A week or two later when a handsome military man asks Judy, "What a small people like you being taught nowadays?" she replies in a direct, clear little voice, "Please let me off the small talk. Amusing topics a still beyond my grasp."
This reply appears to delight all but Judy's mother who pretends not to hear, but that day, before giving her back to the nurse she kisses Harry more emphatically.

The nurse produces this perfect Harry by smacking and nipping her when they are alone together, not because Harry is bad but to stop her from becoming bad.
"If I hear *one word* of complaint about you from your mother," says the nurse, "I'll do *this* to you," and she systematically bruises parts of Harry's body which are usually hidden by a nappy and rubber knickers. (Harry needs these long after babyhood). Sometimes the nurse says, "If you breathe one word about me to another soul I'll do *this* to you," so Harry learns to choose words carefully and avoid them when possible. By the age of four Harry's face wears an intense frown as if she is trying to remember the exact shape of something stolen from her. This expression, with slight variations, stays to the end of her life and though she is not aware of it this makes strangers think she despises them. She grows tall, thin and wiry for her age. One day she unthinkingly answers a stinging slap from her nurse with a backhand blow of equal force, the first wicked act of her life. She and the nurse are equally astonished. The nurse has a cane she has often wielded as a threat but never used for a beating. In a mood of great excitement she goes to Harry's parents and asks for permission to use it. She has never brought them a problem before. They dismiss her and put Harry in a boarding school.

But a week or two pass before a suitable school is found. Harry is tended by another of her mother's servants who changes Harry's nappies and nearly faints when she sees what they hide. She shows it to Harry's mother who is less moved because she is pitiless.

"I'm quite pitiless because no-one eva pitied me," she tells her friends, but she agrees that the blue, black and red mosaic of bruises is an ugly sight.

"Paw kid," she tells Harry who is sobbing bitterly at losing the one person in the world she was allowed to depend on, "I *knew* that woman was too good to be true. Don't worry. We'll straighten you out."

The boarding school is an elegant little Georgian mansion with large garden, shrubbery and paddock near the city of Bath.

"Beware of me!" the headmistress tells Harry's mother happily, "I am a very dangerous liberal, and an atheist to boot. But if one of my little gels shows religious yearnings she is allowed to attend services in the church of ha choice and layta, if she stays firm, may receive instruction. The Ricardos a Jewish, though not awthodox of course. Their daughta is now a nun in Stanbrook Abbey."

"Harry might go that way. One of my in-laws is potty that way," says Harry's mother carelessly, "Though he is a Buddhist of course. Yaw fees …"

"No school has higha fees," says the headmistress swiftly, "Not in Britain anyway. Everything the gels see, use and a taught is of the best quality. I have neva befoa taken moa than twelve pupils but of course Harriet is exceptional. She will *not* be an unlucky thirteenth. My small numba of gels lets me enshaw nobody suffas or is bullied during what can be a very difficult and highly formative few yias." "I think most kids a improved by hard knocks in the early yias," says Harry's mother, "It toughens them. They learn to look to themselves, not to othas fo what they need, so in layta yias they make othas do tha bidding. That's my experience."

"Many books expound yaw theory at much greata length," says the headmistress, nodding and smiling as if she approves of brevity, "But I attended –" the headmistress mentions a more famous boarding school than her own – "It was and is a wondaful place with a wise and dedicated staff, but so big! We all made lots of valuable friends but I know for a fact that some gels had experiences which marked them fo life."

"And you emerged unscathed?" says Harry's mother softly, looking hard at the headmistress. Harry's mother believes all teachers are pæderasts: why else would they enter so loathsome a calling? She believes everyone but some people she knows belong to the servant class, so finds it hard to be polite to professional women who talk as if they are her equal. But the headmistress has agreed to take Harry so politeness is not now needed. After a pause the headmistress says in a slightly louder voice, "Yes. From what you tell me it is clia Harriet has suffad enough in ha short life. This is the first time I have agreed to take moa than twelve pupils and will certainly be the last, but I'm glad to help a child in Harriet's difficult position. She cannot help being exceptional." Still staring hard at the headmistress Harry's mother's face settles into the brooding frown which is always on Harry's face. She has mentioned that Harry still needs nappies, but the bruises are healing so there was no need to tell more. She believes this teacher is only admitting Harry to her school because Harry is related through her father to a European royal family. Harry's mother finds the connection useful because, as she tells her friends, "It opens doas," but she hates being reminded of it as she envies and dislikes her husband's family. She says at last, "I'm glad you think my daughta exceptional. Yaw old school wouldn't touch ha with a bargepole so hia she is! But I hia the guardians have given you Amanda's kid so yaw establishment probably instils the main decencies. I'm only sorry you've seen fit to admit new money."

Amanda's kid is a millionairess orphan, *new money* is

the daughter of a popular singer. Speaking clearly and carefully the headmistress says Harry's mother ought to meet the popular singer one day – he is kind, courteous and highly intelligent. Moreover, she enjoys having one pupil with a Bohemian background because it teaches the others to mingle without lowering themselves. While the last remark is emerging from the headmistress's mouth she notices with horror that it is meaningless snobbery, that she is groggy with insults from a duchess she believes she is helping.

"I've not been to Bohemia so that sounds nonsense to me," says Harry's mother, smiling pleasantly for the first time today and rising slowly to her feet. Not many do this without seeming decrepit. Harry's mother unfolds her body in a graceful upward flow which seems to leave her taller than before she sat down.

"Goodbye!" she says, extending a high hand which the headmistress automatically reaches up to touch, "No doubt you do yau useful job betta than most. If my daughta is spoiled by ha *very* expensive schooling nobody can blame me."

The headmistress was once a professional actress but finds she has been manoeuvred into talking and feeling like a caretaker with delusions of grandeur.

The headmistress was once nearly famous as a juvenile lead in a 1938 production of *Dear Octopus*. Her love of acting was not strong enough to survive the war so after it three things combine to make her a teacher. She likes small girls, finding it easier to behave like an adult with them than with anyone else. She has rich friends who want someone they know to manage their children. Her parents have left her a family home which she can only maintain by claiming the rates and cost of upkeep as expenses against taxation. Most of the servants live out; she and a housekeeper and a friend she met at drama school are the resident staff. They teach girls between the ages of four and fifteen how to keep clean, to eat, dress, walk and talk nicely, to read, write and count. Visiting tutors introduce them easily and without strain to singing, music, dancing, art, history, the French language, tennis, swimming and ponies – there is an adjacent riding school. None of these pursuits is compulsory but every girl develops a good appetite for two or three of them. No class has more than four pupils and on bright days it is easy for everyone to move outside and continue their lessons on the lawn, in the rose arbour, in the summer house or sunken garden. A few ordinary things are not taught. Each pupil learns to keep her room tidy but it is cleaned by the servants. To the end of her life Harry panics if expected to make a cup of tea or sign a cheque and pass it over a counter in a public building. The school teaches one great falsehood: that the pupils are finer than pupils of all other schools and much finer than people who could never pay fees their own people pay. Apart from that it does more good than harm to children whose parents, for various reasons, hardly exist for them.

There is a games room, a music room, a library and a lounge with a television set. On light evenings and at weekends the girls usually put on overalls or their oldest frocks and play in the shrubbery, which is really a wood thin in trees but thick in undergrowth. Here, playing mostly in couples, the girls make little nests and dens which they call houses, usually inside elder bushes because these have thickly overlapping outer leaves and a mainly hollow centre. Amanda's kid, nearly thirteen, has a gang of two or three smaller girls who have built for her a complicated wigwam called The Fortress. It is made of branches, turf, poles, tarpaulin and corrugated iron with a very low tiny door. The shrubbery is out of bounds to the teaching staff because, "It is important that children have freedom to invent private worlds of thea own," but the headmistress comes to know nearly all that happens in the shrubbery. At least once a fortnight each pupil is invited to a beautifully served dinner for two or a cosy afternoon tea for two. At these the headmistress chats about her problems and asks for advice.

"I'm worried about little Harriet. I call ha little, you see, to remind myself that she's only five even though she's much talla than you, who a a whole yia olda. She seems to have no friends. What does she do in the shrubbery? She's very fond of it."

"Climbs the tree, Efel."

"Try to call me *Ethel*. Which tree?"

"The conker beoind the ollies," says Linda, who was called *new money* by Harry's mother.

"The sweet chestnut. Not a bad tree fo a small wiry girl to climb," says the headmistress thoughtfully, "The boughs and branches a mainly horizontal. Is ha balance good? Does she take risks? Eat a strawberry tart while you recollect what you have seen. Chew it slowly so that you enjoy every crumb befoa replying."

Soon after these instructions Linda says, "She climbs very slow and careful. She goes very igh up, crawls out along a branch as far as she can get then just sits. If you wive to er she pretends she can't see. If you shout er name loud enough she goes back to the middle of the tree and gets onto a branch on the uver side."

After a while the headmistress says, "The tree is to Harriet what the piano is to Clara." Clara is an eleven-year-old who spends all her free time in the music room.

"Clara and Harriet a both very lonely gels," says the headmistress, "But it is now too late to help paw Clara. How can we help paw Harriet, Linda? The other gels avoid ha because she does nothing but frown when they speak to ha. The tyootas a lucky if she ansas them with moa than a monosyllable and so am I. The only thing she does in the gym is stretch haself for ouas on the wallbaas. Thank goodness she likes clay modelling, but it is a solitary art. How can we help ha, Linda?"

"The troof is, Efel, I'm too miserable to elp anyone," says

Linda, weeping, "I'll allwise allwise be an applicant."
The headmistress cuddles her, strokes her kindly then softly asks, "Is Hjordis still beastly to you?"
"I run errands for er, bring er all sorts of fings to add to The Fortress and she still won't let me in. Every week the ole gang examines me but Yordis says I'm still too young and must apply again next week. And the exams get arder and arder! Oh I'll never never see wot's inside!"
"Yaw in daynja of choking," says the headmistress, "Go to the lavatory and wash yaw face in *warm* wata, ending with a splash of cold. Then come back and eat this slice of excellent cheesecake. I will then tell you exactly what The Fortress contains, though I have neva entad it in my life."

When Linda is calm the headmistress tells her, "The Fortress contains a quite valuable Persian rug, a mirra framed in coppa, a large glazed photograph of Hjordis's motha with a very handsome man who was ha fatha for a while and some antique knick-knacks. All these vanished from Hjordis's bedroom soon after the central chamba of The Fortress was built. That was a yia before you came but they must be thea, apart from a few knick-knacks. She pawned these on a visit to Bath to raise money to purchase Turkish cigarettes. I will not interfia until she turns to marijuana. But the main thing you would discova in The Fortress is Hjordis in a bossia mood than you have eva seen befoa. I know you love Hjordis very much and no wonda! She is lovely, cleva, and very charming when it will get ha something. But when she was very small – much smalla than you, Linda – some terribly sad things happened to ha, things so sad I refuse to talk about them and Hjordis refuses to rememba them. The result of these sad happenings is that beautiful charming Hjordis hates and fias everybody who is not unda ha thumb. She can neva have a friend of ha own age. That is why she needs a gang and why nobody wants to be in it but the twins and you. The gang is a good thing fo the twins. It teaches them to work with a slightly larga group than themselves.

And how very important you make them all feel, Linda, meekly following them about, running errands fo them and continually failing the exams they set! Without you the gang would fall apart."

Linda understands some but not all of this. She says, "If I stop trying to get in I'll ave nobody to talk to. The uvers giggle whenever I opens me mouf."

"I can hardly blame them for that, Linda. I really think you *ought* to give me yaw fatha's record for a while."

Linda's mouth opens wide, her face whitens and she starts to choke. Her voice is like her father's, who talks and sings in the main dialect of Greater London. His new money has enabled him to buy a new wife and pension off the old one. Linda has been sent to this school to have the main dialect of Greater London rubbed out of her voice, the main dialect of the British rich stamped there instead. This has not yet happened because Linda cannot sleep unless she first plays one of her father's records, turning the sound low, putting her ear near the speaker and dreaming he sings just to her; dreaming also that he, she and her mother still live in a brick terrace house with two cosy rooms downstairs and two up, a house with a small park near by where she can run and tumble with children whose friendly voices sound like her own. If someone suggests to Linda that she part with the record she starts to suffocate.

"I apologize!" says the headmistress, flinging her arms up in a gesture of surrender, "I promise not to suggest that again. I will eventually destroy your father's record because you beg me to and then you can begin to speak the language of Shakespia and Docta Johnson. But Harriet is a lot lonelia than you, Linda, and *she* neva giggles at how you speak. *She* neva giggles at anything. If you made friends with ha you would be helping ha, and yawself, and (I confess it) me! I am a selfish businesswoman, Linda. Mine is not a good school, it is a bad school if the cousin of a queen and the daughta of a famous singa are both lonely little gels hia."

Linda thinks hard about this, sighs and says wistfully, "I would like that a lot, Efel, but I wouldn't dare. The troof is, Yordis would do somefing orrible to me if I joined the enemy."

"Is Harriet the enemy? I thought I was that," says the headmistress cheerfully.

"You are, but there's two of you since Harry came."

"Let us have a glass of lemonade, Linda! I have not had so interesting a conversation fo yias."

The headmistress is not as surprised as she pretends by what Linda now tells her; it adds details to a picture she knows in its main outlines. Hjordis, like all leaders, uses frequent broadcasts to entertain her followers and impress the surrounding universe. On warm weekends, when the girls have collected well-filled lunch baskets from the kitchen and taken them to the shrubbery, Hjordis walks up and down in front of The Fortress, sandwich in hand, delivering between bites loud speeches which sometimes provoke a muffled giggle or derisive shout from the depths of an elder bush. The twins sprawl and munch and listen on a blanket on the grass near by, nudging each other whenever Hjordis uses a word they think rude. Linda, hands clasped on top of head, stands under a tree in the only spot where applicants are allowed to stand. She has paid for this privilege with her lunch, which Hjordis (who often declares she prefers birds to people) has crumbled and scattered for the tits and robins. "Oua enemy boasts she is a Liberal!" cries Hjordis, "What does that mean? Mr Pargetta fo history says it's to do with gun-boats and free trade – with freedom. What freedom does the enemy allow us? The freedom to choose a bush in ha rotten shrubbery!"

"You have a fortress!" sings a distant voice.

"I have a rubbish heap!" shouts Hjordis, "A sawdid rubbish heap when I should have a geodesic play-dome with a trampoline floa and walls of opaque or transparent panels in the pattern of my choice! One of my uncle's

factories makes nothing else! The enemy soon shot his offa down! *In the shrubbery I prefer all my little gels to start as equals*. Lies! Foul lies! She doesn't give a damn for equality! In this world equality means just one thing: equal rights fo the equally rich. Do we have that? Do we hell! Oua people a a bloody sight richa than she is, she wouldn't let us in ha school if they weren't. But wha does that jumped up bourgeois bitch sleep and wha do we? She sleeps in ha motha and fatha's beautiful old bedroom on the second floa while we sleep in the attics! The servants' quartas! Each in a paw little room with a sloping ceiling that once belonged to a skivvy or housemaid or valet! And wha do we usually eat? In a cella off the kitchen, a cella that was once the servants' dining room. Don't be fooled by the Laura Ashley curtains and the windows above ground level, we eat in a putrid basement! And oua splendid modern classrooms and sculptcha studio and record lab, wha a they located? In the old stables and kennels, the outhouses wha a lot of animals and thea stinking grooms once lived! None of you object to that, do you? No, yaw all perfectly happy because now and then Lady Muck invites you upstairs to see how nicely she can handle the family silver and tinkle the teacups in The Land That Time Forgot – the breakfast room and dining room and drawing room which a *still* ha private property because of the *money* she gets from OUA people! OUA people! OUA people!"
"You'll bust a gut, Hjordis," warns an American voice. It belongs to a millionairess from Texas, the only pupil Hjordis fears apart from a tall gangling untidy girl who reads the *New Statesman*. One of the twins approaches and holds out a dish with a chocolate éclair on it and a thermos mug of sweet milky coffee. Hjordis lifts these and walks slowly round The Fortress, eating and sipping in an effort to calm herself. Her brain is teeming with the sort of notions which always come to her when she talks loudly.

"This rotten system has got to stop and I mean to stop it!" she announces, returning, "The enemy has told you the cousin of a queen is coming hia. She has *not* told you that my motha and Harry Shetland's motha were very very very close friends, so Harry is going to be *my* special friend, a closa friend than any two of you a! I am going to take ha unda my wing – my gang will protect ha."

"What from?" sings the distant voice.

"From exploitation!" screams Hjordis, "The British public don't give a tuppenny fuck fo how awdinry rich people like us get exploited by the middle classes, but they've a soft spot for royalty! Imagine the headlines! QUEEN'S COUSIN IN LIBERAL POVERTY TRAP! My uncle owns all the British newspapas. He and I will make the govament investigate this school aw fawce it to resign."

"Bosh!" says a weary voice from nearby, probably the voice of the *New Statesman* reader, and elsewhere someone giggles. "Alright!" says Hjordis querulously, "My uncle only owns nialy half the British newspapas, but half is enough!"

She flings the empty mug toward The Fortress entrance and faces her gang.

"At ease!" she tells Linda. Linda thankfully lowers her hands, sits on the grass and rubs her legs. Hjordis strolls about muttering in a discontented tone only heard by those in the clearing: "We aren't a propa gang, we haven't an ally. We have everything else … strong leada … powaful enemy … a Fortress … an army …" (she stares at the twins until they salute her) "… a hopeless horde of frantic applicants …" (she grins sarcastically at Linda, who blushes guiltily) "… but no ally. Don't worry. The ally will soon be hia."

But Harry disappoints Hjordis. Harry answers the intensely whispered message, "*My motha was yaw motha's best friend!*" with the same gloomy stare then turned-away face she gives everyone. Nor can Hjordis get her alone to explain things more fully. Harry is not given a bedroom in the attics, but one beside the headmistress's bedroom on the second floor. In the shrubbery she at once climbs to a high branch of the tallest tree, shifting to the opposite side when Hjordis tries talking to her from underneath. For two weeks Hjordis, like Hitler after the loss of Stalingrad, is too ashamed to make a public announcement, but she is braver than Hitler. One Sunday she declares to the world, "I was wrong, I admit it! The daughta of my motha's best friend has joined the enemy! The descendant of Teutonic warlords is now spying fo the liberals! I don't know what you get up to in these bushes of yaws and I don't care – it's none of my business. But Big Sista Is Watching You! These beady little eyes in the sky don't miss a thing that happens unda the leaves! Thank God my Fortress has a solid roof! And there's room in it for everyone! Why not join me in it? I've a big tin of lovely biscuits."

"Pipe down you silly sow!" says someone wearily.

"Dismiss!" Hjordis whispers quickly to the twins, then runs to The Fortress and shuts herself deep inside. She cannot weep when others see or hear her.

Linda is too young to hide grief. A week later, tear-stained and furious from yet another failed examination, she charges to the foot of the chestnut tree and yells up into it, "Come down, Harry Shetland! Come down ere to me you bloody bitch! You gotta be my friend! You gotta ply wiv me now now *now*! Efel says you gotta and I'm so lonely I want to kill meself oh!"

She bangs her brow seriously against the trunk until half-stunned and dizzy she falls to the ground. Reviving after a moment she bangs the back of her head on the ground in a half-hearted way, then sighs and dozes off for a while. When she at last opens her eyes she sees the face of Harry frowning gloomily down at her from very near. Most of Harry's weight hangs from a hand grasping a branch among the leaves overhead, one leg kneels on a low bough, the other dangles, she sucks the thumb of her free hand. The pose suggests she is wondering whether to climb lower or higher and has been wondering for a long time.

"*Will* you play wiv me?" asks Linda, sitting up. After a watchful moment Harry puts both knees on the bough and creeps swiftly to where it dips near the ground before curving up into broad-leaved branches. She sits in the dip with her back very straight, ankles crossed and hands folded neatly on lap. Linda approaches and stands before her, hopeful and awed.

"Let us consida the case!" says Harry suddenly and clearly, "Of a certain paw very dirty little gel. She has been wawned repeatedly against dirt and against opening ha mouth about you and me, dearie. She has been shown what will happen to ha if she ignores these wawnings. Yet she she ignoas these wawnings. She gets dirty. She talks. Quick! What must be done to ha?"

"The troof is," explains Linda, "I want to play kings and queens, though I don't know much about them. You must know a lot, so you can tell me what to do. You're taller than I am so *you'd* better be king. I don't mind if you boss me a bit."

"No royals please!" says Harry sharply, "Royals a just *not on*. We have no time for interlopas be they German, Greek, black, brown on Irish. We do not speak for the lost cause of racial purity. We speak against boredom. Please direct yaw attention to this paw little horried gel who does not deserve ha great advantage. How will we punish ha? Smacking and nipping a the usual thing."

"Alright," says Linda in a resigned voice, "You be queen and I'll be king. But I must sit beside you like we're on a frone togever. Will you elp me up?"

"We said *no royals!*" Harry reminds her, "We said *smacking and nipping a the usual thing*. We a prepared to hia anything else you propose, but ponda well befoa you speak! Just now you a the dirtiest and smallest of us. Yaw voice is comically coarse and ill-bred, it brands you as an interlopa from the start. Perhaps you a the paw paw paw

dirty dirty *dirty* little girl of whom we speak!"
"No I'm not!"
"Then it must be me," says Harry, twisting round and hanging over the bough with her legs on the near side, arms and head on the other, the seat of her blue corduroy overalls level with Linda's face.
"Begin!" she commands in a muffled voice. But Linda's mind has not been shaped by dread of punishment. The idea of hurting someone puzzles and repels her.
"I can't!" she complains, and "Wy should I?"
"This very horrid little gel has been expecting it fo weeks and weeks and weeks," Harry explains, "And it gets worse the longa she waits. She'll be so glad and grateful when you stop. And then you may kiss ha and say *You and me ur still pals dearie ur we no? Ur we no*?"
"That's stupid!" says Linda.
Harry twists round and up then creeps swiftly along the bough toward the tree trunk.
"Oh don't go awy!" cries Linda in alarm, trotting beside her, "Honest, I meant no arm!"
"Thank you fo a lovely aftanoon," says Harry coldly, gripping a higher branch, giving a little leap and disappearing quick as a cat into the upper foliage. Linda is left crying, "Come back, please come back! I didn't mean to annoy you!"

Linda's cries are not answered. She stands thinking for a while, then abruptly turns and trots quickly through the bushes to the clearing. The ramshackle conical tower of The Fortress vibrates with a muffled voice declaring that A Hard Rain's Going To Fall. The only other life is some small birds pecking the remains of Linda's lunch from the grass. She goes to the tree where applicants are allowed to stand, lifts up a half brick and bangs it on a sheet of rusty iron hung by a rope from a branch. The noise is loud. She drops the brick and waits. At last a twin emerges. She is wearing jeans and a bush shirt and smoking a slender brown cigarette. She strolls around

the clearing until, seemingly by accident, she stops in front of Linda. After looking at her thoughtfully from the shoes up to the bruise on her brow the twin blows a cloud of smoke over Linda's head and says, "Well?"
"I got infomytion," says Linda in a small voice.
"About?
"Enemy."
"Which?"
"One in tree."
"Don't move," says the twin, and returns quickly to The Fortress. The noise of the record stops, then both twins emerge followed by Hjordis.

Pupils who show interest in make-up are given lessons in it by the headmistress and usually learn to subtly accentuate their most pleasing features. Hjordis deliberately uses white face powder, scarlet lipstick, dark eye-shadow and eyebrow pencil to model herself on the Wicked Queen in Walt Disney's *Snow White*. She wears a black dress and black opera cloak lined with scarlet silk which flutters behind her as she goes straight to Linda and says, "What have you discovad?"
Linda tells her. Hjordis gets her to repeat it slowly, then questions her closely about tones of voice and exact positions, then says, "You a moa cleva than I thought, Linda. The time is nia when I believe you may be fit to join us."
"Oh!" whispers Linda.
"Don't get happy too quickly!" Hjordis warns her, "I have one moa test fo you. Pass that and you could be inside The Fortress befoa teatime with me yaw friend fo life. If you fail I don't want to see you again. Eva. You will be *entie-aly* friendless hia."
"Wot's the test Yordis?"
She is told and trembles with fear and anxiety. It is a terrible test, but the reward for passing, the punishment for failing, is overwhelming.

She returns apparently alone to the chestnut tree and

shouts up forlornly, "Arry I'm very sorry I didn't do wot you said! Please come down! Please ply wiv me please! I'll do exactly wot you tell me to do!"
She shouts this at intervals for a very long time, standing near the dip in the long low bough. After five minutes she would gladly stop but is now aware of Hjordis behind a nearby holly bush. Linda becomes so conscious of Hjordis that she is suddenly surprised to see Harry sitting upright on the bough before her, ankles crossed and hands folded as if she had never left it.
"What is wrong with this little gel?" asks Harry almost kindly, frowning at Linda in a puzzled way. Linda's mouth is opening and shutting, trying to tell Harry noiselessly to go back up the tree. Hjordis walks over to them saying pleasantly, "Hello Harry Shetland! I hia my friend Linda failed to oblige you. May I help?"
Harry wriggles up to kneel on the bough, but a twin is sitting astride it between her and the trunk, and another twin approaching from behind. Linda gives a little wail and runs away.

Linda's terror does not stupefy but makes her sensible. She pushes as fast and straight as possible through a rhododendron clump, nearly tumbles down a steep slope to the sunken garden, charges across three flowerbeds, up a flight of stone steps, through the rose arbour and across the lawn. As she passes two older girls in bikinis and dark glasses sunbathing on a blanket, she gasps, "Efel! Where's Efel?"
"Boozing in her private apartment I guess," says the Texan millionairess. Linda toils up a slope to the terrace, runs across it to an open french window, charges through the music room (where Clara, a fine pianist were she not tone deaf, struggles with Rachmaninov) and into the hall. Only then does she start shouting.

The headmistress is enjoying a glass of sherry and a glance through *Encounter* when she notices the shouts.

They make no sense until she goes to the head of the stairs, hears "Efelefelefel!" and sees a small sturdy figure striving up toward her.
"Well Linda?" she asks. Linda halts and gasps, "Yordis Arry conker *stop* em Efel! *Stop* em!"
"Speak moa slowly."
"Arry asked I smack er I wouldn't Yordis is!"
The headmistress cannot move without dignity but can walk faster than many people run. She walks straight to the chestnut tree by the exact route Linda took from it, even striding over the flowerbeds. She is slowed by her height when pushing through the rhododendrons, so Linda catches up. They hear a wild wailing with several words in it but at first only *please* is distinct, *please* repeated very often. Arriving beside the tree they do not see exactly what they expect, though nearby the twins cling together as if afraid of something.

Harry lies flat on her front on the ground, head pillowed on arm and turned sideways so they can see her calm, absentminded, no longer frowning face. Hjordis squats beside her, whacking at her bottom with wild windmill flailing of the arms and crying frantically, *"Please* beg fo mercy! *Please* beg fo mercy! Aw just ask! Oh *please, please, please* ask me to stop doing this!"
"I ask you to stop doing it Hjordis," says the headmistress firmly, "Stand up. Stand up and take my hand quick quick quick! You too Harriet. Help Harriet up, Linda. Good. Take my hand, Harriet. Linda, take Harriet's otha hand and don't let go. Twin one, hold Hjordis's otha hand. Twin two, hold Linda's other hand. Now we must all hold tight to each otha and not let go fo I am taking you all to a wondaful place you have neva seen befoa. Follow me!"
The headmistress is perfectly happy. Such moments (she knows) bring out the best in her. Childish souls have ground each other into chaos and now she will strike a nobler order into them. Hjordis, mewing at intervals, (that is how she sobs) clutches her hand almost gratefully.

Harry is relaxed, blank-faced and docile, Linda and the twins awed and excited. Looking like a goose at the head of a flight formation the headmistress leads them from the shrubbery by the easiest way, making a slight detour to pass the sunbathers on the lawn. She likes to feel she can still astonish older pupils. As they approach the terrace Linda says, "I'm sorry I told Yordis wot you said to me, Harry."

"No need for sorrow!" says Harry, absentmindedly quoting her mother's words to a guest who dropped a delicate porcelain cup he had been asked to admire, "You have taught me a lesson I will rememba till my dying day. I am almost grateful to you."

Linda gasps. The headmistress squeezes Harry's hand and says, "That is the longest speech I have eva heard you make, Harriet, and a very good speech it is. Though a bit hard on paw old Linda. You and Linda don't know it yet but yaw going to be great friends one day."

Judy looks down at Linda with curiosity, Linda looks apprehensively up at Harry.

The headmistress leads them into the hall, up the broad stairs to the landing of her own apartments, round the stairwell past the drawing room and dining room, then stops beside a door they have not seen open before. She says, "Let go hands everyone and listen carefully, especially you, Hjordis. The Fortress is a thing of the past. Tomorrow Hjordis will take ha possessions from it and bring them hia, and in the evening we will set fia to it, perhaps letting off a few squibs and rockets at the same time. Yaw new gang headquartas, Hjordis (I speak as one leada to anotha), lie behind this daw. It is a very special place. No child has been in it since I was a child, no grown-up but myself and a cleaning-woman has seen it since my parents died. Am I correct, Hjordis, in thinking Linda and Harriet are membas of yaw gang?" She stares hard at Hjordis who at last realizes she is dealing with an intellect greater than her own and murmurs, "Yes Ethel."

"Then open the daw and lead us in, Hjordis."

The door opens on a staircase much steeper than that which rises to the attics, and unlike the attic stair it is windowless. It ends in a loft under the central shed of the roof, and lit by big skylights through which nothing can be seen but the summits of surrounding chimneystacks and a small white cloud in the blue. Huge crossbeams and struts under the skylights cast bars of shadow on a floor whose centre is covered by six edge-to-edge carpets, they do not reach the loft's dark edges and corners. They are well-worn carpets; this loft has clearly been used as a lumber-room, box room and games room for generations. It contains so many things to play with, look into, climb over and hide behind that merely staring around from the same spot gives a minute of pure pleasure. Suddenly Harry walks to a rocking horse of the unsafe Victorian kind, its hooves fixed to wooden crescents. Sedately she mounts and starts rocking. Linda squeals and runs to a half-open wardrobe with a cracked mirror on the door, 1920s coats and dresses hung inside above a decade of footwear. The twins join her as she rummages.

"I will show you something special," says the headmistress, leading Hjordis apart from the others, "In one of yaw public addresses you called me *bourgeois*. You wa quite correct. My family did not build this house. It was purchased in 1827 by my great-great-grandfatha, who made money by providing the betta part of London with splendid drains. This loft was the favourite haunt of his son, his son's son, his son's son's son (who was my fatha) and *his* son, who was my brotha."

They approach an eight-legged billiard table with a network of wee railway-tracks on the faded green cloth. The headmistress lifts and winds with a key the clockwork of a Hornby locomotive, couples it to a goods train with tiny cows, sheep and milk cans in the open trucks, and releases it. With small pistons churning it pulls out of a perfect tin model of Crewe station in the 1930s, snakes away between bright cardboard bungalows and factories of that period, then climbs an easy gradient through a cardboard pine forest on to a Meccano replica of the Forth railway bridge. This spans a looking glass laid flat and grey with dust, but made oceanic by a fleet of battleships on it, beside a Spanish galleon in full sail, three pleasure yachts, two china swans, a shore of real seashells where a stuffed seagull stands. The sizes of these, in reverse scale to the possible, seem a miracle of perspective. The train slows as it leaves the bridge and comes to halt half in and half out of a tunnel through the base of a rock with Edinburgh castle on top exquisitely modelled in papier mâché. A battalion of bright little Gordon Highlanders is formed on the esplanade; knights in mediaeval armour stand on the higher battlements and turrets.

"This used to be *my* secret kingdom," says the headmistress, sighing, "My brotha built it. I helped him. He was the only man in my life. Most little gels worship tha olda brothas, I am told. I may have worshipped mine too much. He fell at the retreat from Dunkirk. Perhaps I am the only British woman living who remembas a British soldia who died at Dunkirk. The British public wa told the retreat was a sawt of triumph, to stop them seeing it was an avoidable fiasco caused by addlepated senia officas telling a dud government that the Germans would neva try to fight us *seriously*. Do you like this place, Hjordis?"

"I do, Ethel. Yes."

"Then it is all yaws – on condition that you take nothing out. I will not set foot hia again befoa you leave this school. What you tried to do to Harriet in the shrubbery was pretty awful, but if she and Linda play happily hia unda yaw supavision I will forget that. It is very thrilling to deliberately rob a smalla person of all dignity, but

from now on you will resist that temptation. You despise my brand of liberalism of cawse, but did you know that on the island of Sark is a boarding school even more private and expensive than this one? It is run by two enthusiastic fascists with an insane, unscientific and highly fashionable faith in shock treatment: also aversion therapy. In my school, as you know, I learn everything that happens. If I eva again discovad you had made Harriet or Linda miserable *fo any reason at all* I would expel you. I would also give yaw guardians such a report, and such advice, that they would send you to that school on Sark, wha yaw very soul would be painfully twisted into a vile and unnatural shape to prove a shameful theory. The staff would be careful not to make a vegetable of you, but you would often beg them to do so – in vain. Look hard at my face. Hjordis. Do you think I am joking?"
Hjordis looks. The headmistress is smiling – all her large perfect teeth are visible. Hjordis shudders.
"*Am* I joking, Hjordis?"
Trembling violently, Hjordis shakes her head in urgent denial.
"Good! Now run away and enjoy yawself. I will go below and have a snack sent up from the kitchen. And you had betta wash yaw face, Hjordis. Those who use a lot of thick make-up should avoid strong sensations."

The headmistress skips downstairs, thankful for her drama-school training and relieved that the school on Sark does not exist – for half a minute she thought it did. Her brother died a month before the Dunkirk retreat of a haemorrhage unconnected with military stress. She never knew or liked him much and still thinks his obsession with miniature worlds was unhealthy – why manipulate toys when there are so many *real* people to play with and rearrange? Several children have enjoyed the loft since the school started, for twice before she has used it to seduce or bribe a troublesome clique. And now her four youngest and most difficult pupils play in a secure place near by with her one bothersome teenager, and are grateful for the privilege.

Linda is so grateful that a fortnight later she brings the headmistress her father's record and says, "Brike it if you want to."

"No!" says the headmistress, "He is a fine singa and these songs delight millions. I will keep it fo a yia, and you will like it even moa when you get it back. It will no longa obsess you because yaw own voice will sound quite different then."

A year later Linda speaks in the main dialect of the British inheriting and investing class. She condescends to her father in an amused ironical drawl which makes him feel his money has been well spent, but it destroys her friendship with Harry. This develops slowly for a few months, giving both of them a new experience of confidence and hope, then for no obvious reason the friendship dies. Both feel sad, lonely and betrayed. Harry cannot be friendly with someone whose voice does not strike her as comically coarse and ill bred. Twenty seven years pass before she meets Senga.

THE PROPOSAL

SENGA is still a schoolgirl before contraceptive pills are cheap and widely used. In these years many girls under eighteen have no steady boyfriend, those with one are usually virgins, a popular girl can be friendly with several boys who do not necessarily dislike each other or distrust her. Senga at fifteen has a reckless gaiety which many find attractive. Instinctive caution usually inclines her to Tom who is not very amusing or good looking. He is tall but walks as if ashamed of that. He dresses well, but moves and sits as though to stop his clothes getting creased. He is two years older than Senga and her other friends find him dull. They belong to a small group who attend the same school and meet most evenings in a local café. Tom has more pocket money or is more generous than the others. He buys drinks for the group which it would not consume if expenses were shared equally. Senga's other friends think this is Tom's way of buying the pleasure of their company and the pleasure of sometimes walking home with Senga, though she never invites him inside. But Senga is not mercenary. What she likes in Tom is her power over him.

She feels it one evening on the stairway of a tower block owned by the district council. They come by lift to the fourteenth floor and instead of going to the door of her home she lets him persuade her onto the stairs, which can be used to compensate for the difference in their height. It is too late for children to be playing there and far too early for dossers or thieves. She lets him embrace her, and slip his hands under her jacket, then under her sweater. He lacks courage to pluck her blouse out of her jeans waistband and grope under that, but the most intimate sensation in his life is the warm soft feel of her back through thin nylon, also the softness of her neck beneath his lips, for he lacks courage to rise to her mouth. She is amused and intrigued by the changes in his breathing, by the fifth limb growing suddenly out from between his legs and poking at her thigh. Keeking down sideways at his closed eyes and mindless expression she feels slightly jealous of how overwhelmed he is. It seems an ecstatic state. Senga cannot imagine herself overwhelmed by any boy or by anyone not superior to her. The only superior people she knows are a few film stars (mostly women) and her mother, a widow who has endured several emotional adventures without losing her composure, her efficiency, her very observant daughter's friendship.

But Tom's hands, though still fearful of entering her blouse, are pressing her down toward the cold hard steps. She lightly slaps his cheek saying, "Time up lover boy." He sighs and releases her, staring into her face with such wide-open tragic eyes that she chuckles and quickly kisses his mouth as a consolation prize.

"Do you *like* me, Senga?" he pleads.

"Of course! I'm crazy about boys. But it's time you were hame with your mammy and daddy."

He continues staring, astonished by so much pain flowing from who a moment ago was his greatest source of delight. He once gloomily told the group that his parents influenced him too much. He now knows he is mocked for that. Senga decides to console him again. Slipping an arm round his arm she leads him briskly along the corridor to the door where he will get a last quick goodnight kiss, but tonight he refuses to be easily dismissed. He says

awkwardly, "Senga, I got my prelim exam results today. I've failed my English. I won't be able to see so much of you for a while. I'll have to do more homework."
"Is that right?" she asks coolly.
"I'll see you twice a week," he assures her.
"I'll like that fine ... if I'm free."
This worries him. He says, "Senga, you won't get fonder of someone else, will you, when I'm not around?"
"How do I know? It depends on who turns up."
"It's only three or four months to the exam, Senga! I can see you all the time after that."
"Aren't you going to the university?"
"Well?"
"Don't you have exams at the university? Won't you have to study when you're there?"
Tom gapes at her. He cannot understand how he has missed seeing this obvious fact.
"I like you Tom," says Senga, "But I won't spend five nights a week at home because you're trying to be a doctor or something."
"I don't want to be a doctor."
"Well, whatever it is. What's wrong with you?"

An idea has occurred to Tom, an idea so enormous that he is ecstatic with his eyes open. He grasps her hands and says, "Listen, will you marry me?"
"What?"
"Marry me! I love you, haven't you noticed?"
She stares hard at him. He plainly means it. She cries, "Oh Tom, you're wonderful! You're daft but you're wonderful!"
He lets her hands go and says with a touch of anger, "Yes or no?"
"How can we get married?"
"We need a room to ourselves," he says, his mind working fast, "A rented room of course, a rented *furnished* room so first I need a job. And I've got qualifications! I've failed English but I'm fine in chemistry, maths and technical drawing. I'll see the careers teacher tomorrow. It won't be

easy at first but at least we'll be together with no damned parents putting pressure on us."

"But what will they say, your mum and dad?" asks Senga, whose mother puts no pressure on her, or none she has noticed.

"It doesn't matter what they say! If you lo ... lo ... (ach I hate that word, it sounds stupid) if you love me, Senga, I can do anything! So yes or no?"

She is awestruck by her power over him and a bit awestruck by him too. She says, "Come here a minute."

She takes his head between her hands and gives him a kiss she learned a month ago from a boy who walked her home from a dancehall, a boy she won't see again. It is a prolonged yet delicate kiss done with lips slightly apart and pouted forward as if talking French. Tom is pleased by it but more interested in what she will say when it ends. When it ends she has been most influenced by it.

"How *can* I say yes?" she asks in a voice so full of longing and of approaching tears that he suddenly feels very strong and cries, "Don't say yes. Don't say a word yet. Give me a day to work out how to do it. And I'll meet you tomorrow in the usual place at half-past six before the others arrive and I'll tell you how we're going to do it and *then* you'll say yes – I know you will."

She weeps at this, laughing and shaking her head at the same time. He embraces and kisses her, feeling stronger than ever, and for a moment she is almost overwhelmed.

Senga takes a long time preparing to enter her home after Sam leaves. Even so her mother, sitting before the television set, looks at her closely and says,

"What's the matter with you?"

"Nothing."

"Who was tonight's lucky lad?"

"Tom."

"Tom again?" says her mother with a smile of friendly amusement. "Are you two getting entangled?"

"It's not as bad as that, Ma," says Senga, and goes to her bedroom.

Tom, elated, strides homeward through lamplit streets but grows depressed when halfway there. He used to like home more than most children like it. His parents were elderly, and treated him as one of themselves, and gave him all he wanted. He remembers happy evenings in the living-room, fitting together, sometimes with his father's help, increasingly expensive and elaborate models of aeroplanes, painting each one afterward with great exactness. But since the age of ten he has discovered wants and emotions which have no room in his parents' house. It, too, is in a building owned by the district council, but called a villa because it holds only four apartments, each with its own piece of a small surrounding garden. Most dwellers in villas feel more important than those in the tower-blocks and tenements. Tom's parents feel this. His determined stride does not slacken as he nears the garden gate but (though he despises himself for it) he walks more softly on the tips of his toes. He knows that behind the orange-curtained living-room window his mother and father are quietly pretending to do different things while listening for sounds in the street, hoping every approaching footstep is his. Tom, like Senga, has had a door-key from an early age. He enters quietly and moves quietly toward his bedroom. Passing the living-room he hears his father say, "Come in here, Tom."
He sighs and enters.

His father, a sturdy but not large man, sits with rolled-up shirt sleeves at the dining table, carefully copying receipts and invoices into an account book. Tom gets his height (not breadth) from his mother. She sits on the sofa knitting with quick nervous jerks which stop when her son enters. In this house nobody looks straight at each other. She says, "Where have you been, Tom?"
"Seeing friends."
"That Senga, was it?"
"What if it was?"

"That is no way to speak to your mother, Tom," says his father, still writing.
"She's not good enough for you, Tom," says his mother plaintively, "And she's far too young. People must be laughing at you."
"Well," says Tom turning back to the door, "Goodnight."
"How are your studies going?" asks his father.
"Not bad."
"Your English teacher thinks otherwise," says his father, "He was in the shop this morning. He told me you've failed preliminary English."
"Since you know about it why ask me?"
"Tom!" says his mother, shocked, "That is no way to speak to your father."
"Well I'd better go and study, eh? Goodnight," says Tom, and turns to the door.
"I'll bring some cocoa and a biscuit in half an hour, Tom," says his mother cajolingly.
"Thanks a lot, Ma, but don't bother," says Tom quietly but distinctly, "I'm not hungry and not thirsty but thanks very much all the same."
He leaves the room with the bitter satisfaction of knowing his mother now feels what the mother of a noisier family would feel if her son seized her offerings of cocoa and biscuit and smashed them to the floor.

Tom's room would be a bleak one without the model aeroplanes which hang by threads from the ceiling. He shuts the door and sits on his bed, breathing deep because he wants to howl with rage. Instead he pulls a wallet from his pocket, removes a strip of small photographs taken in a coin-operated booth and stares at them. The first shows Senga's naturally smiling face, the rest are more or less comic distortions of it. He gazes at these until he sighs with relief, relaxes and smiles back. A minute later he lays the photos on a table beside school books and walks up and down muttering, "The trouble with you two is you cannae *enjoy* life. You do nothing for fun, nothing for fun at all but watch

TV or go to a show. You've no friends and you're so damned snobbish you won't even ask your relations in for a drink in case the neighbours think we're low class or something. Well I've got friends, I've got a girl who likes me, I like her and . . ."

His door is tapped and opened by his father who peers in grinning and says, "Talking to yourself again?"

Tom looks back without speaking.

Tom's father is more relaxed with his son when his wife is not near. He enters, closes the door, sits on the bed and says, "I know what you're thinking."

"Do you?"

"Of course! You work all day at school and probably hard. No wonder you want some freedom in the evenings. Do I give you enough pocket money?"

"Yes Dad. Thanks."

"I'm not asking for thanks! Like half the folk around here my own dad was unemployed between the wars. I left school at fourteen to work as an errand boy and every penny I earned went to my mother. Son, I *want* ye to have money. I also want you to do more with your life than I've done with mine."

"You havnae done badly, Dad."

"All right, I keep a paper shop and make adequate money by it. But with a decent education I could have been a, a, a lawyer, a doctor, a teacher even! One of the people who give something important to the world and who never lose their jobs when a depression comes. Because the professional classes know how to protect themselves. And that's the chance I'm giving you!"

"I don't want to be these things."

"When you get to university you can choose to be anything you want! Even a shopkeeper if you think that's fun. But it isn't."

Tom suppresses a sigh. They have discussed this many times, usually in the same words, so he is surprised when his father adds, "And don't get entangled, Tom."

"What do you mean?"
His father, pointing to the strip of photos on the table says, "Why are you keen on this wee dolly bird?"
"She likes me," says Tom defiantly.
"Wait till you're at university, Tom. You'll meet girls of your own sort there."
"What sort is that?"
"Dependable?" suggests his father.
"I am NOT dependable!"
"Then you're well suited to Senga!" says his father, grinning, "I hear a lot of things in the shop, you know, and I can tell you –"
"I don't want to know anything you have heard about Senga!"
His father stands up to face him and says just as fiercely, "Then don't get entangled!"
They stare at each other. The father is first to look away. He says, "If she's keen on you she wants you to make something of your life. If you're keen on her you want to provide her with a decent home. Does that make sense?" "Oh yes it makes sense!" says Tom bitterly. His father frowns at his shoes and mutters, "Your mother is worried sick about you."
Tom says uncomfortably, "Tell her not to worry, Dad."
"Then you'll work at your English?" his father pleads, "You'll start tomorrow night and really grind at it? It's only four months till the Highers but four months at your age can make or break you for life – I only want what's best for you."
"I want what's best for me too!" says Tom desperately. "I've only done badly in one subject! Won't you trust me to do what *I* think right?"
He too is pleading. He has never before pled with his father, who first stares astonished, then smiles thankfully, pats Tom's shoulder and says, "Thanks for setting my mind at rest, son. I'm sorry if I'm hard on you at times – I can't help it. My dad was like that with me. But I'll tell your mother not to worry. I know you won't disappoint us."
He leaves. Tom wants to howl again, but instead thinks

very hard about what he must do tomorrow. He sleeps very little that night.

Neither does Senga. She has never before been given the chance of completely changing her life. She cannot help loving Tom for giving her this enormous chance, though at the moment he gave it she saw he is not a man she can live with, not even a man who attracts her: hence her hysteria. In bed she fantasizes about what might happen if Tom were more interesting. In sleep the fantasies become delicious nightmares which shock her awake. Tom Dracula's horde of lovely victims pursue her, begging her to join them. Next morning at breakfast her mother asks, "Is it your time of the month again?"

"Nearly, I suppose."

"Take a day off school, I'll write you a note."

"It's not as bad as that, Ma," says Senga crossly. She cannot yet reject the gift of Tom's proposal. Her mother's sensible mirth at the idea would destroy it at once, so she tells nobody but a friend whose credulity prolongs it, one she meets in the girls' lavatory during the morning interval and swears to secrecy. But the secret is too exciting to be kept. No other girl of her age has had marriage proposed to her in that school, and proposed by a tall, well-dressed older boy who has never before surprised anyone. At lunch break in the playground a crowd forms around Senga, a quarter of it composed of very little girls who ask to see her engagement ring.

"I'm not engaged!" says Senga with angry annoyance which is only half pretence, "He proposed to me, I haven't said yes yet, Dona shouldnae have told anybody, she promised not to."

"But you will say yes?" ask girls who have admired Tom from a distance and a number who have not.

"I havnae made up my mind yet. I might and I might not. I mean, I don't *need* to marry him, I'm not *pregnant,* for God's sake."

This causes a silence. Most of the girls find *marriage* an excitingly romantic word and *pregnant* not. Several of the small girls do not know there are sometimes connections between marriage and pregnancy, and most older ones now suspect she must be pregnant since she mentioned the possibility. Senga's reputation for boldness comes mainly from a speech-style learned from her mother. Tom never uses words boldly, another contrast which makes their affair interesting to the general public.

The school has three playgrounds: one for boys, one for girls, and a playing field with entrances from the other grounds where both sexes can mingle. By the afternoon interval Tom's proposal is general knowledge among all the girls and most of the older boys, also the fact that Tom, after an early morning visit to the school careers adviser, left the building and has not returned. Only two girls and a boy in Senga's group know the café where he has arranged to meet her at six-thirty. They tactfully offer to stay away. She says, "No, don't. I'll need all the support I can get."

She is now frightened by the publicity she has gained. She enjoys being the star of a small group but now an audience of three or four hundred expects her to perform. This audience will be satisfied by an engagement or elopement, otherwise it will boo or applaud Tom's humiliation by a girl who has made his honestly loving proposal public before refusing him. She fears that if Tom comes to the café with a practical marriage plan she will not have the courage to refuse him. She is glad to have her ordinary pals beside her in the café, especially the group humorist who treats the whole business as a joke. Senga smiles at his jokes but is unusually quiet. Her two girl friends watch her closely.

At seven o'clock the joker says, "Mr Romeo seems to have run out on you, Juliet. He's probably at Scotch Corner on the M1, hitching a lift to London."

"I don't think so," says Senga firmly.
At quarter to eight the joker suggests that Tom has been locked in his bedroom by his mother and offers to lead an expedition to free him. Senga laughs until she cries real tears. Tom's arrival and non-arrival are now equally dreadful to her. Between eight-thirty and nine it dawns on them that Tom will not come tonight and at once all of them grow happier, especially Senga. She feels she has wakened from a colourful but embarrassing nightmare which can now be treated as a joke.
"'*Yes or no?*' he demands and I go really tragic, real tears pouring out of me, '*How can I say yes?*' I cry and he really rises to the occasion. Tom can easily do the dramatic Hollywood thing when he wants. '*Don't say yes! Leave it all to me! I will save us from our evil parents,*' no he didnae really say that but –"
They are all laughing but eventually quieten. At quarter past nine, shortly before the café shuts and when the group are the only customers, Tom enters. He walks taller than usual but looks worn and tired and so, untypically, do his clothes. He says "Hullo" to the group and to Senga, "Sorry I'm late. Can I have a word with you?"
He goes to an empty table. Senga's limbs tremble. For a moment she feels too weak to stand. The feeling passes. She gets up, gives a little smile and shoulder-shrug to her observant companions and follows Tom to the nearby table. She is relieved by his subdued manner but also saddened. She assumes he too has realized they must not marry.

She sits facing him. He says, "Sorry I'm late, I had trouble with the room. But it's all right, the deposit is paid. It isn't a very nice room but we can shift to another if you find a better one at the same rent. That's your problem, however. At eight tomorrow morning I start as a window cleaner."
"What are you talking about?"
"Tomorrow I start work as a window cleaner," says

Tom patiently, "Twelve pounds five shillings a week or seventeen with overtime. It won't be for ever. Five months from now I can start as an apprentice technician with Colville's or Scottish Electricity, or Dexter Delvers, or Shedden Maguire. It will mean, at first, a drop in our weekly wage, but after four years I will be earning a far bigger wage than my dad earns so I'll be able to support you. Until then you'd better think of getting a job too. I mean, what I earn will feed us and pay the rent, but you may want a few luxuries on top of that like clothes and a fancy cooker. Anyway, you can collect the marriage form from Martha Street registry office as soon as you like."

"I can collect the marriage lines?" says Senga, faintly.

"Senga," says Tom more patiently than ever, "I apologize. I am very sorry that just now I am unromantic, and practical, and very very tired, but I have had an exhausting day. I have visited three government offices: the Youth Employment, the Labour Exchange and the Ministry of Pensions. I had to queue for more than an hour in every one of them and they were no help at all. The only good news I got was from the school's careers teacher who told me about my apprentice technician prospects. But he would not believe I needed to start earning money *now*. I couldn't tell him that I'm going to marry you and you are not the waiting kind. If I'd done that the news would have been all over the school in a couple of hours. He would also have told my mum and dad. So I looked for a job in the newspaper adverts and I got one, didn't I? Didn't I? Yes I did, a job where they don't even want to know my National Insurance number or anything else if I start first thing tomorrow at eight. But of course I couldn't wait for my first week's wages before I got us a room. I went to the only man who might lend me money, my uncle the bookie who's never asked to our house. I told him everything and asked for twenty quid. He gave me sixty straight away as a wedding present. He probably did it to annoy Mum and Dad who'll disown me when they hear about it. And then it was half-past seven and I still had to find the room. Well, I've found one. It's wee, you'll hate the wallpaper, I wish we could have looked for it *together*, Senga, but of course I can't expect you to go to a bother like that. So now you know what I've done for us today and I honestly think I deserve some thanks, even if you are incapable of gratitude."

The possibility of a completely new life now opens its jaws in front of Senga like an enormous trap. The sight makes her shudder. She says, "I don't think I like you, Tom. You're trying to bully me and we're not even married."

"Am I a bully just because I expect you to go to Martha Street to collect our marriage lines?" asks Tom querulously, and she suddenly sees that though he has worked amazingly hard to make the new life possible, he too now feels it a trap. She says, "I don't want to marry you, Tom, and you don't want to marry me – not if you've to work as a window cleaner and live in a poky wee room."

This is more truth than Tom can at once swallow. A great rage enters him which would drive a noisy man to shout and a violent man to smash things. Tom gasps, nods and says grimly, "That's what you think, is it?"

She says, "Yes. That's what I think."

Tom puts his elbows on the table and rests his brow on his fists.

Then looks up and sees the three at the other table craning their heads to listen. He sees by their faces that they know all about his proposal. He leans across the table and whispers to Senga, who now looks like and is a frightened little girl, "You've made a right fool of me, Senga McGuffie. You must be right proud of yourself." She stares at him dumbly. He stands and says aloud, "You and I are finished now. Done. Totally and completely and absolutely and … and totally finished."

"You said that before," says a voice from the other table.

"Said what before?" demands Tom.

"Totally. You said it twice."

"Shut your face or I will shut your face," says Tom

ominously, "And here, Miss McGuffie, is a wee present for you."
He takes the strip of photographs from his inner breast pocket intending to rip it and fling the bits at her, but he likes her too much to do that. He hesitates, lays it gently on the table and hurries out. Senga has another fit of hysterics. Her girl friends rush to her, cuddle her, stroke her, wipe her tears with handkerchiefs and make soothing noises.
"He's daft! He's daft! He's utterly daft!" she raves between fits of weeping and laughter, and "I never *wanted* him to ask me to marry him!"
"Then why get upset about it?"
"Because he isnae really daft."

Tom enters his home with no attempts at quietness. "Tom! Come here!" calls his father. Tom enters the familiar living-room where his father stands glaring and pointing and shouting, "Tom, last night you asked me to trust you, asked me to tell your mother you would resume your studies! And you have not even come home for your tea!"
"Good news!" cries Tom, flatly and bitterly. "Senga and I are finished with each other."
After a moment his parents' faces, struck suddenly blank, brighten a little though they are too polite to smile. His father strokes his chin. "Finished, eh?"
His mother says quietly, "Tom, do you know what I'm going to tell you?"
"Yes," says Tom, "You are going to tell me yet again that she isn't good enough for me, by which you mean that her mother works in Woolworths and my dad owns a paper shop."
"You're completely wrong," says his mother firmly, "I was going to say she's a *flirt*."
"Why should she not be?" cries Tom passionately. "She's full of life, she wants to enjoy it, a lot of men are keen on her, why shouldn't she flirt? She was the best thing that

ever happened to me, and she liked me a lot better than the others."
"Then why have you finished with her?" asks his father.
"Because she's refused to marry me!" screams Tom through clenched teeth.
His parents look to each other for support and see nothing in each other's faces but bewilderment. Tom masters his emotions and speaks more calmly. "Another thing," he says, "I'm starting work in May as an apprentice technician, probably with Colville's. I've spoken to them at school about it and the careers teacher says it will be the best thing for me. So the university notion is out, done with, totally scrubbed and I must say it's a relief."
His father stares at him in such a stricken way that Tom in tenderness and pity goes to the smaller man and places a fatherly hand on his shoulder. "Ach don't worry, Dad! My job will be as good as anything folk are taught to do in university and just as well paid. And it will be work I can do with no bother, so there's no use worrying about it. Life's too short. I'm also very hungry just now."
He goes to the kitchen door, pauses and asks them wistfully, "I'm going to make some sandwiches. Would anyone else like one? And a cup of cocoa maybe?"
But his father stares at his shoes, his mother at the wool on her lap, as if searching for something in these. He sighs and leaves them.

After a while his father mutters, "I've got to speak to him but I don't know what to say."
His mother, who is trying to knit, flings the needles down and cries, "How dare that Senga refuse our Tom! The CHEEK of her! The CHEEK! The CHEEK!"

During Tom's last months at school he finds his proposal to Senga has done him good. Girls of his own age now look at him with interest. He stops wearing his suits as if afraid of creasing them, stops feeling ashamed of his height and starts finding it an advantage. He and

Senga never become close friends again though he never quite manages to stop loving her. Even after they have left school he keeps informed of her doings. Five years later he learns that Senga is engaged to a cranedriver in a shipyard. Tom is now an expert in precision grinding. His abilities are useful to several companies. He invites her to a meal in a good restaurant, expecting her to look older and more working-class than he remembers her, but he can see no difference, she is as attractive as ever, so he proposes again. He explains that he wants to start a family because a family is the only thing he lacks. His bullying nature is now obvious. Senga finds this second proposal purely comic and cannot hide the fact. She marries the cranedriver, a man with many friends who talks a lot about politics. Two months later Tom marries a woman who looks like Senga but was bred in a wealthier home and wants to be kept in another one.

THE MAN WHO KNEW ABOUT ELECTRICITY

DONALDA is usually met through other people. Today this is an old man who trots up and down a busy pavement, showing a light bulb to passers-by and asking them if they know about electricity. Most pretend not to see or hear him. A few pause for a second with pained smiles then shake their heads and hurry on. The old man is not discouraged. He is a peculiar little man with the bent back and knobbly joints of somebody who was once big. He wears black canvas gym shoes, a shirt printed with orange and purple silhouettes of palm trees, a fine tweed suit so large that the trouserlegs are turned up three inches at the ankles, the sleeves turned back as much at the wrists. Apart from these folds his clothes are neatly pressed and very clean. Maybe people are repelled by his voice. He has the accent of a city in north-east England and the pavement is in a city of the Scottish west.

At last the old man says, "Dost thee knoo aboot electricity John?" to a boy with a new leather briefcase full of books and with the badge of a new university on his blazer pocket. The boy knows a lot about electricity. He asks the old man to repeat his question and answers, "Yes".

"Good John! Good!" says the old man approvingly. "So thee can change a light boolb?"

As if offering a gift he holds up the bulb in its rectangular cardboard wrapper, new from the shop. The student sees

the old man's hand has a thick bandage round it secured by a safety pin over the palm, but the fingers sticking out look sufficiently flexible.
"Anybody can change a light bulb," says the student.
"Good John! Then thee'll step roond the cooarner and change me boolb? I'll pay thee, John! Nowt for nowt, I know the rooal, I've got a bob or two. Thee can spare a minute shooaly?"
The student ponders. He is going to the railway station an hour earlier than usual because a lecture has been unexpectedly cancelled. Trains which can take him home leave every half hour. Also, his parents have taught him to tell the truth and give help when folk ask for it. But he lives where everyone, even shopkeepers, are equally prosperous, or pretend to be, so by telling the truth and helping people he has made good friends without being inconvenienced. He is sure his parents would think it unwise to help beggars of the old man's sort, though the old man is not, apparently, begging. The old man's face staring hopefully up is brown and deeply lined by rough experiences, but the expression is the opposite of sinister.
"Change the bulb yourself," suggests the student.
"Nooah, John, I knoo nothing aboot electricity. Shooaly thee can spare me a minute?"
The student admits he can and is led round a corner into a street between soot-blackened stone warehouses.

The old man's home is more than a minute's walk away though the student walks so fast that the old man only manages to keep a fraction ahead of him with quick wee skipping steps that are more like a dance than a walk. They turn a second corner into a street which seems part of a city bombed by powerful enemies. The ground on each side is mostly torn earth, weeds, rubble and rags. Some remaining tenements have windows broken, or boarded up, or blind with dirt. The student did not know there was such a street near his university.

Behind the warehouse roofs he sees the summit of a glass and concrete tower. A window on the second floor from the top has a white rectangle in it, a poster facing inward which he fixed there a week ago. It advertises a students' Christian society he belongs to and he tries to recall what he saw through the window when putting the poster up. He remembers a wide view of various buildings which did not interest him, he had preferred to look at the surrounding hills.

"Here it is John," says the old man leading him into a tenement close, and he sees one upper window is unbroken and raised a little. Through the opening a hand is using a teapot to water marigolds in a window box, so the building is not wholly derelict, and when the old man leads him downstairs to the basement he sees it is not wholly abandoned by the local government. A gas lamp glows and hisses in a dirty passage with no other light. The student is fascinated. Before now he thought gas light belonged to the nineteenth century when Robert Louis Stevenson wrote about it. He sees too a dingy door with five or six keyholes. The old man stealthily turns a single Yale key in a hole he stoops to reach. Before pressing the door open he places a finger to his lips and whispers, "Be very quiet John! Me landlady is a woman and gets queeah ideas."
The door opens on what seems a dusty cupboard. The old man steps in and with another key opens a door in the far wall. The student, amused and curious, goes through.

He enters a room with a window onto a sunken area between the tenement and street. A thick blind covers the window and at first the dark brown light through it lets the student see nothing but egg-boxes, the sort that hold half a dozen each. Piles of them cover a sideboard, add height to a wardrobe, form a pyramid on the corner of a table in the middle of the floor. Growing used to the

poor light the student notices he stands under a web of wires radiating from a black mass in the centre of the ceiling. Wires go to a television set among the boxes on the sideboard, to an electric radiator on the floor, to a radio on the chair beside a bed, to something under a mound of coats on the bed which must be an electric blanket, to an electric hot-plate and an electric kettle on the table. After the old man has cautiously and quietly closed the the doors behind them the student says, "Have you no wall socket?" "Of coorse John, of coorse! Boot it gives off sparks and shocks and flames and things. Doant thee worry, I'm no fooal."
"That light fixture is overloaded – a fire hazard. Your landlady could be prosecuted for it."
"It would only oopset her John. Women are like that."

The student decides to put in the bulb and leave quickly. He lays down his briefcase, climbs onto the tabletop and peers at the cluster of adaptor sockets hitched to the light wire. A low wattage bulb sticks sideways from it. He says, "I'll see better if you raise the blind."
"Oo nooo John! Lots of valuable stoof in heeah John, lots of bad people aboot. They'd brack in and steal me stoof if they could see in heeah!"
"Is the light switch on or off?"
"Not working, is it John?"
The student points to the wireless set and says, "Switch on that."
The old man does. A loud blast of rock music happens.
The old man jigs about to it. The student points to the light switch beside the door and yells, "NOW SWITCH THAT OFF."
The old man hurries to do it. The music dies. The student unscrews the spent bulbs saying, "Give me the new one." He hands down the old one, tears the cardboard wrap from the new, clicsks the new into the socket. The old man presses down the light switch and several

things happen quickly. The light and music go on very bright and loud then die out at once. A door bangs then the door of their room is slammed open by someone dumpy, furious and female who shouts, "What the hell is going on here?" Near by a baby has started screaming.

"I'm changing a light bulb," says the student calmly. His stance on the table gives him a feeling of power. The woman is smaller than her anger at first makes her seem. Her hips and breasts are matronly but her face childish, thin and desperate. She wears a nightgown, dressing-gown and slippers, every lock of her hair is twisted into a tight helmet of pink plastic rollers. She turns to the old man shouting, "I telt ye! I warned ye not to bring folk here! Remember what happened last time! I think you're trying to kill me!"

In an embarrassed way the old man grins, shaking the light bulb beside his head as if listening to it. She turns back to the student saying, "Clear out. Clear out of here this instant and mend the bloody lights first. You've fused everything in this place."

"Relax," suggests the student.

"How *can* I relax? I've a yelling wean next door that cannae sleep with the light off Listen to it!"

"Where's your fuse-box?"

"Behind the front door."

"Any spare wire in it?"

"Aye. Mibby. I mean, I think so."

"Then attend to your kid and I'll attend to the fuses."

She heaves a huge sigh and hurries out.

"Good John! Good!" whispers the old man, smiling and nodding encouragingly. The student says sternly, "Before I get down from here tell me which you want: light, heat or entertainment. You can't have all three till your wallsocket is fixed."

The old man looks astonished. After a while he mutters miserably, "Wouldna mind soon light, John."

The student unplugs the wires from the adaptors, the

adaptors from the light socket, clicks the light bulb into the socket, jumps to the floor and lifts his briefcase.

Though the doors are now open into the cupboard-like lobby it is very dark. Working mostly by touch the student opens the fuse box, discovers and pulls down the main switch, removes the fuses, also a small card wrapped round with wire. Laying them on the briefcase he carries it like a tray into the brightest room. This belongs to the woman. The window here is hidden by thin print curtains pinned together in the middle. There is an old wooden sink with one brass water tap below the window, a rusty heavy iron gas cooker beside it, an iron fire range, a recess holding a double bed beside the door, a rope slanting up from a wall-hook to the wheels of a pulley on the ceiling, wheels with spars between them on which hang some stained triangles of yellowish brown linen. There is a faint smell of lavatory. The woman sits near a table pushing backward and forward a carry-cot pram with a baby in it. To the student this baby looks indecently small, red and wrinkled. Its wails have sunk to a fretful mewing which the woman soothes by saying softly, "Cool it Theresa, you're fine. Shut up. Pipe down. Pull yourself together."

The student lays his briefcase on the table and asks, "Have you a screwdriver?"

"I had but I lost it."

"Have you a nailfile?"

"Naw."

"Have you a tea-knife?"

"There's knives in that drawer and hurry up. This one needs her sleep."

There is a drawer at the end of the table. The student opens it and rummages through a mess of cutlery, saying, "Why can't the kid sleep with the light off?"

"Nobody likes the dark."

"Open the curtains, there's sunlight outside."

"This is a basement and I've had trouble enough with

nosy parkers. Whenever anyone looks in here some rotten thing happens."
"Like what, for instance? ... I've found your screwdriver, by the way."
He sits on the table edge and deftly loosens screws on the fuses. After a moment he says again, "Like what, for instance?"
"Well," says the woman, almost unwillingly, "When the old boy in there burnt his hand the SS came to see him and ..."
"SS?" says the student, puzzled.
"Social Security. Anyway they looked in here too and they cut my allowance right out. Just like that."
"Why?"
"Nothing to do with you," says the woman in a very low voice. He works away quietly. He notices that in the lengthening intervals betwen the baby's cries she has begun glancing at him furtively. At last she says, "Where are you from?"
"Helensburgh."
"One of the snobs, eh?"
"Not really."
"A student?"
"First year physics. Not all of us are practical men with our hands. But I think ... this is just about ... right."
He is on the way to the lobby with the fuses but stops and looks back at the briefcase.
"Ach leave it!" she says impatiently, "I'll no' steal your books."
He wishes she had not read his mind but nods and enters the lobby.

The lights go on and the baby closes its eyes and mouth. The student returns for the case saying, "That will hold for a week or two but not much longer. Your wiring is no use at all, a real fire hazard. Get it seen to."
"You really know about electricity!" she cries.
"A bit."

"Could you sort my iron? It conked out three weeks ago and I really need it for drying the wean's nappies. I mean, she's got a rash."
He glances at his wristwatch and is astonished to see that less than fifteen minutes have passed since he met the old man. He shrugs and nods. She says, "You're a pal," and lays the iron on the table. He pulls a chair up to it, sits down and begins unscrewing the plug. She goes to a mirror and starts removing her curlers. She says, "Sorry I yelled at ye in there."
"It didn't worry me."
"You see I've had trouble with that auld bastard – excuse the language."
"I've heard worse."
"I suppose you think I'm … I suppose you think I'm a bad lot."
"No. Why?"
"Living here. Like this."
He glances around. The room strikes him as messier than it need be. The bed is unmade. Dirty plates, crumpled clothes lie on and partly under a dusty sideboard and two sagging armchairs. He says, "Maybe you can't help it."
"I can't. That's right."
She lays down the last of her curlers, shakes her head and wanders nervously across the room. She shuts the door to the lobby, saying, "Do you believe in God?"
"Of course."
"So do I but he hasnae helped much."
The student senses something queer in her manner but thinks the best way to handle queerness is not to attend to it. There is nothing wrong with the plug so he starts unscrewing the iron. She says, "Life can be hell sometimes, can't it?"
"We have our ups and downs."
She stands so near that her dressing-gown touches his cheek. He bends over the work, sure she is going to ask for money and determined to refuse it. She says in a small quick voice, "Have you the time for a short time?"

He is relieved by this simple question, glances at his wristwatch and says, "Ten to four."
She moves away and sits in an armchair. He looks at her. She sucks her underlip like a small girl trying not to weep. Her mop of curly black hair reminds him of a girl he knew at school. She hugs her body tightly below her maternal breasts. This makes them more prominent. For the first time his voice has an uncertain note. He asks, "Did you … I mean, you *did* ask me for the time?"
"Right!" she says in a hard voice with a hard little smile and nod. He cannot stop looking at her breasts. She asks bitterly, "Is something wrong with me?"
"No but … but I need a … thing with a thin end. Like a needle."
She stands and plucks thoughtfully at her lower lip. "Will a kirby do?"
"Eh?"
"A hairgrip."
She takes one from the pocket of her gown, holds it out and walks toward him, her mouth and eyes wide open in a vacant frightened way. He stands to face her, reaching out his hand but not to take the grip. He does not exactly know what he wants to take for he is more sexually stupefied than sexually excited. A voice in his brain is asking, "What should I do first? What should I do first?"

At that moment the door of the room bangs open and a huge man steps in. He stands then announces in a hoarse Irish voice, "I'm interruptin yous."
"No you're not," says the student, taking the kirby grip.
"He's mending my iron," says the woman disgustedly, "And you've wakened the wean."
She pulls the pram to the armchair, sits down and pushes it back and forward.
"I say I'm interruptin yous!" declares the Irishman. He shuts the door behind him, goes to the table and sits slowly down in a chair facing the student. The lavatory smell increases.

"Don't mind me young fella!" he says, "Carry on with what you were doin."
The student sits. His heart still beats fast from recent surprises but he sees the Irishman is not dangerous. The hugeness is all in his height. His face and hands are so thin and white that his weight seems mainly a matter of clothes. Four outer garments are almost buttonless and the student sees a plastic raincoat, black overcoat, corduroy jacket, tweed waistcoat, knitted cardigan and striped pyjama jacket. There are probably some shirts and vests under these for his chest looks far too broad for his very long narrow neck, which has a clean silk scarf wound round it. Nothing else he wears is clean, not even the woollen balaclava helmet with a flat cap on top, the rimless spectacles which give his gaunt face a clerical look. Despite these clothes he often shivers as if terribly cold. He removes the spectacles and wipes them on the end of the scarf muttering, "Don't mind me, don't mind me."
"I don't mind you," says the student, busy with the iron, "The old boy next door got me in to change a light bulb then she asked me to sort this."
"He knows about electricity," says the woman offhandedly.
"Yes, there's big futures in electricity," says the Irishman. He takes a flat-sided bottle from the overcoat pocket, is about to swig from it but pauses, to say in an apologetic note, "You'll not be offended if I offer you none? This stuff is right for the likes of me, in fact it's indispensable. But it wouldn't do for a young fella who still had his health … Make the man a cup of tea, Dona!" he shouts at the woman, who obediently stands and fills a kettle at the sink.

The student now wants to leave as soon as possible. He concentrates on mending the connection while the Irishman drinks, coughs then says, "I trust I amn't upsettin you? I'm a disgustin spectacle, that's true. Well, I'll leave in a minute."

"You don't disgust me," says the student easily.

"Still, judgin by your clothes you don't often sit in a room with a coupla cases like us."

"It might interest you to know," says the student after a pause, "That my grandfather was a riveter with Harland and Wolff."

"Indeed! So you feel a degree of solidarity with the workin classes?"

The student thinks about this. People who speak for the working classes are supposed to be socialists and the student distrusts left-wing organizations. But his father once told him that most of the British working classes vote Conservative. At last he says, "I think I can say that."

"Good for you!" says the Irishman, raising a triumphant forefinger, "But you see, we are NOT workin class, we are ... how can I put it ... casualty class."

"There's no such thing," says the student crisply.

"No?" says the Irishman, holding his bottle to the light. It is nearly empty. With a sigh he puts it down and says, "This used to be a workin classes district. Casualties lived here too, but the majority were decent labourers and tradesmen. Not people I always see eye to eye with, though the best of them were Irish like meself. One day the area is scheduled for redevelopment, somethin to do with a ring road or a college, I don't rightly recall which. So the landlords stop repairing the properties and the workin classes shift to expensive homes in posh new housin schemes like Easterhouse, Castlemilk, Drumchapel. And now the entire area – the part not knocked down – is full of the unemployed and elderly, and moral casualties like me, and sentimental casualties like her."

He points at the woman beside the cooker who stands holding the handle of the kettle, waiting for it to boil.

"Leave me out of this!" she tells him.

"It's her own fault, of course. Before she had the child she was earnin seven pounds ten a week in a Bridgeton lemonade factory."

"But can she not –" begins the student. The Irishman interrupts.
"Exactly! Of course! I tell her that myself. 'If you loved Theresa,' I say, 'Give her to the social workers. Have her adopted. Get rid of her and do both of yous a favour.' She refuses to listen. She is one mass of utterly disreputable primitive instincts."
"For Christ's sake hold your bloody tongue!" shouts the woman, and adds for the student's benefit, "Excuse the language."
"We'd be lonely people if it wasn't for my tongue, Dona," says the Irishman quietly. The student, resting an elbow on the table and chin in the palm of a hand, finds the conversation interesting. He says "What sort of casualty is the old boy next door?"
"Temporary. He is a trusted nightwatchman of many years standin and will be back on the job when the hand heals. Of course he's nearly seventy and won't last for ever. Besides, this buildin's condemned, they'll knock it down soon and we'll all be hard put to it findin a place to stay. Why, I hear that even quite *prosperous* people have trouble gettin new houses."
"Well, my parents aren't exactly prosperous, but when we moved to a new house last year we had to pay *twice* what it would have cost ten years ago."
"Exactly!" says the Irishman with a pleased air, "So you will understand that things are *equally* difficult for the like of us. Strange isn't it, the vast improvements we've seen in recent years, new towns, more cars, more roadways, bigger buildins. Yet all the time the casualty class grows bigger too. Is there a connection, do you think?"
"Couldn't say."

The woman puts the mugs of milky sweetened tea on the table saying, "Sorry there's no biscuits."
"You're a lovely girl, Dona," says the Irishman. The woman goes to the pram and bends over it.
"Just look at the way she moves! Isn't she a lovely girl?"

"She's not bad," says the student, glancing and sipping the tea.
"Do you hear that, Dona?" cries the Irishman, "The gentleman thinks you're *not bad*. When a laconic fellow like him says that about a woman it's better than a whole cargo of compliments from the like of me."
The woman turns and shouts, "You're a pimp! You're a pimp!"
"Well if I am," he says strongly, "I'm the worst paid pimp in Glasgow."
They glare at each other. The student, afraid to hear more, devotes himself to the iron. The woman sits down in the armchair with arms folded and legs crossed. The Irishman again examines his bottle, sighs and sips tea instead.

A moment later he addresses the student on a confiding note. "She doesn't really think I'm that. I'm not a pimp. Pimpin is a middle-class occupation. A pimp is a sort of employer and I haven't the dynamism, the qualities of get-up-and-go to employ a whole woman like Dona. My feelin is mainly fatherly, and she thinks she's safer with a man around, an undemandin fella who doesn't lose his temper and can be trusted with the baby when she needs out for a breath of air. I am alcoholic, you see, but am not, and have never been, a drunkard. Liver, lights, stomach, genitals, circulation, they're crumblin, slow and sure. But the brain is in control. The brain will stay in one piece for another year at the least ... What am I talkin about?"
"Why you live with her."
"We need company, you see, and I'm the best she can find in the circumstances. But she deserves better and despite what she called me a moment ago there is no financial bond between us, none at all. And would you believe it, her social security money was cut off a week ago because someone decided she was *cohabitin* with me. Whatever that means."
The student has almost put the iron together again. He

feels the Irishman stare at him as if expecting a response. He says crisply, "Bad luck."

"That's it in a nutshell!" cries the Irishman enthusiastically, "Bad luck! That is what a Frenchman would call *le mot juste*. Education has certainly given you a way with words young fella."

The student smiles slightly. He is too wise to be upset by the mockery of unimportant people. The Irishman says, "I am in danger of borin you. Tell me this, have you a girlfriend?"

"Yes."

"Goin steady?"

"Nearly a year."

"But you live with your parents?"

"Yes."

"Who does the girl live with?"

"Let's not talk about her, eh?"

"You are a gentleman sir, and I apologize for my intrusion. It's just I have a theory, you see, that a lotta nonsense is talked nowadays about what they call permissiveness. If you read the papers, sir, you'd think those in their teens are indulgin in all sorts of startlin practices. Now I believe that most young people are just as respectable, and cautious, and unadventurous, and miserable as we were in my own young day. Here a minute!"

He leans toward the student and beckons. The student cocks an ear toward him. He murmurs into it, "Dona there – hardly seventeen – been to bed with a young fella nearly twice in her life and *that* was almost a year ago. *And* little good it did her. So when I came in and saw the pair of you – well, I misunderstood the position entirely and for a moment I felt … hopeful, you might say. I like her. I like her. And she needs a bit of healthy appreciation from someone in her own age group. She's a fine strong girl you see. She needs …"

His voice has grown louder.

"Money!" shouts the woman, "Money for food and rent!"

"Oh Dona, you need an awful lot more than that!" says

the Irishman reproachfully, "Don't be put off by her rough tongue, sir. That is a temporary consequence of superficial economic tensions – she's afraid of bein chucked out into the street. Solve these tensions and you'll find her the most docile creature imaginable. *You'll be able*," he whispers,
"Well," says the student rising to his feet, "I think I've fixed it. Where's your wall socket?" he asks the woman. She points to one beside the fire-range.

He carries the iron to it but pauses before plugging in. "Does this give off shocks and sparks and flames and things?" he asks with a slight smile. She shakes her head.
"Just testing," he says, and plugs it in, and stands for a while without looking at her.
"How much do you need?" he asks suddenly.
"Six pounds," she says in a low voice, not looking at him.
"That's not a lot," says the student, "Can the old boy next door not help? I mean, if you lose this place so will he."
"He's already paid me three weeks in advance. And I still need six pounds."
"Not a bad owld fella," mutters the Irishman, and drinks the last of his bottle.
"Well," says the student, bringing out his wallet, removing two pounds, showing them and laying them on the mantelpiece, "At the moment this is all I can spare. Sorry."
"Thanks," says the woman stonily, "I'll get the rest somehow."
"Good," says the student. He touches the iron lightly, says "It's working," switches it off and unplugs it. The woman sighs and says, "Thanks mister."
Then she smiles as if putting worry behind her and suddenly she looks like any young woman thanking a friend for a bit of help. The student is glad things are ending well. He picks up his case.
"You're surely not leavin?" cries the Irishman, shivering.
"Goodbye," says the student to the woman.
"But you'll be back? It's a lonely life for her here by herself all day – she'll be glad to see you anytime –"

"Will you shut up?" says the student. The Irishman does.
"Cheerio. You've been a pal," says the woman in an ordinary friendly way, and looking at her now without embarrassment the student is startled by her likeness to the schoolgirl he once knew, and by how attractive she is. He hesitates, nods and steps into the lobby.

And is confronted by the old man smiling and nodding and whispering, "Good John you did it! Catch this John! Catch this!"
He thrusts two tenpenny pieces toward the student's face.
"What's that for?" asks the student staring.
"Thee mooney John! Thee changed me boolb. Nowt for nowt, that's the rooal ye ken!"
The old man drops the coins into the student's blazer pocket and skips back into his room, slamming the door. The student makes to open it but hears the lock snibbed. He starts knocking and shouting, "Open up! This won't do! It's silly! I don't need ..."
He hesitates, then speaks in a voice which is even louder. "Listen, I'll come back tomorrow and look at your wall socket! In the afternoon, say about two-thirty! Don't forget, two-thirty I'll be here. Remember that."
He looks back to make sure the kitchen door is still open. He opens the front door, stares amazed at the gas lamp (it seems years since he last saw it) then runs upstairs. He also runs along the streets to the station, not because he is late for a train (the whole episode took less than forty minutes) but to use some of the great power he feels inside him. He also feels the world is a more exciting place than he realized, and will allow him delicious experiences he secretly dreams of but had never expected to make realities.

In the kitchen the woman and the Irishman, who have heard him of course, sit for a long time as still as if they had heard nothing. The woman is Donalda Ingles twenty-two years before she meets June.

MR LANG AND MS TAIN

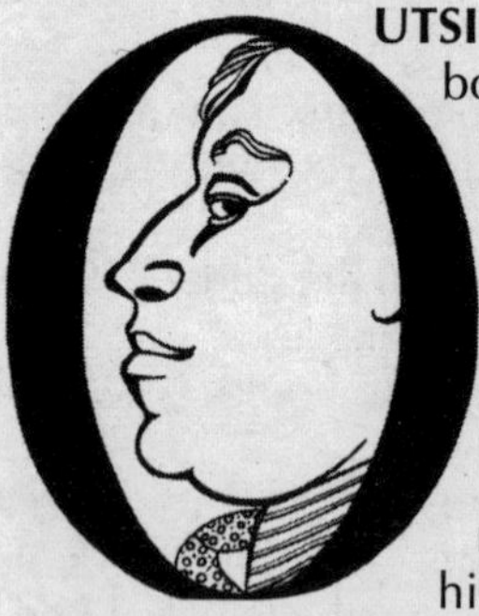

OUTSIDE the film industry most modern bosses distrust entourages. They like to see their underlings one at a time, or round a table where they sit at the top holding agendas to control proceedings. When Tom gets his own business he enjoys having people nearby who depend on his wishes and must not intrude on him. With his heels on his desktop, his heavy muscular body tilted back in a solidly crafted swivel chair, he talks loudly over the phone in the presence of one actual and one potential employee. "We dispatched exactly what you asked for, Mr Cockport," he says. "Our correspondence shows it. The only item missing is your original order form which I will have to hand when the last of our filing cabinets arrive. But why not consult your own records? You'll see the problem is not mine but yours. Good day."

He puts the phone down, yawns, stretches and asks "Anything else, Ted?"

"The storage racks in the loading bay," says his undermanager, "The head joiner wants overtime."

"The hell he does! Send him in." The under-manager leaves. Tom tells a young woman standing near the door, "Not long now Miss er ..."

The head joiner enters and Tom puts his feet on the floor. The two men talk truculently. Tom is aggressive, the joiner obstinate. A verbal bargain is struck and the joiner leaves. Tom phones his under-manager and says, "I've sorted out the joiner, Ted. He'll finish the job at the agreed price and he'll finish it this week. He thinks that

next week he'll be putting up shelves in the basement, but find another firm for that job will you? We can't trust this lot."
Tom puts the receiver down and says, "I've been a bad lad leaving you standing here all this time though I must say you stand well Miss er ...?"
"Tain," says the woman.
"June Tain," agrees Tom, nodding at a letter on his desk. "The agency has told me all about you. You've had experience as a receptionist, I see, but in a receptionist experience counts a lot less than appearance so let's have a look at you."
He looks at her.

Ms Tain has subdued her appearance in a charcoal grey suit and sweater, low-heeled shoes, no jewellery. Her dark brown copious hair is fixed in a bun on the nape of her neck. She wears just enough cosmetic to make her pale skin look ordinary. She cannot subdue her finely shaped figure and face which strike some people as romantically Spanish, some as classically Greek. Her expression is gloomy and patient.
"You look well and you stand well," says Tom cheerily, "How do you walk?"
She stares at him, not understanding.
"*Walk* for me, June!" he explains. After a moment she strolls across to the window and looks out at a street with the high wall and cranes of a dockyard on the other side.
"Top marks for walking," says Tom cheerfully, "Now it says here you've done some book-keeping."
"Not much and only for my last employer," says Ms Tain, turning round and looking worried, "He was a dentist."
"Well that might be useful to us. You see receptionists always have time on their hands," says Tom and summons in a neat middle-aged woman in black.
"Tell me about Marian, Mrs Campbell. Why does she always seem to be polishing her nails? Is she lazy?"
Mrs Campbell says that her assistant book-keeper is not

lazy but has only enough work to occupy her two or three hours a day. The work is a simple record of invoices and receipts, nothing needing concentration. A receptionist in a business like theirs should easily manage it between dealing with phone calls and the occasional visitor. Ms Tain agrees to try.

"Wonderful!" says Tom, "I need coffee. This is *not* the coffee break but coffees all round, Mrs Campbell. How do you take yours, June?"

Ms Tain takes hers black with one spoonful of sugar and asks if she can sit down.

"You were free to sit where you liked the moment you came through that door," says Tom magnanimously.

Mrs Campbell enters a small adjacent kitchen and Ms Tain, looking gloomier, sits on a low easy chair beside a low table. Tom lights a cigarette and says, "Cheer up June, I've only one more hurdle to put you across and that's a matter of overtime. We pay twice the usual rate for it, there isn't a lot of it but it's erratic."

After a moment Ms Tain says, "If you could give me a day's notice ..."

"Sometimes. Usually not."

"If I had *some* warning ..."

"Can't guarantee it. How do you like the decor?"

He flaps his hand toward the walls. Each is occupied by a green dragon on a scarlet ground or scarlet dragon on a green ground. Doorways to the kitchen and a cloakroom-washroom have curtains of coloured glass beads. The lights are disguised as Chinese lanterns. A corner of Ms Tain's mouth twists in a small smile. She says, "Very colourful."

Tom grins and says, "You think it's ghastly. Admit it."

She smiles symmetrically and admits it.

"It's like me!" says Tom happily, "Rich-looking, loud, vulgar and you can't ignore it, right?"

Ms Tain smiles and agrees.

"I always wanted an office like this," says Tom, "You

should have seen our last premises. A dirty little shop with two back rooms and a basement you couldnae swing a cat in. Now, suddenly, boom, we've arrived, we're expanding, even big firms buy equipment through me. Know how that happened?"
"A Scottish Industries Development grant?" suggests Ms Tain. For a moment Tom is taken aback.
"Well, yes, we got *help* from them," he admits, "but the real reason is that firms can order from me at short notice and I deliver on the dot. They can phone me at twenty-five past five on Friday, ask for thirty gross two-point-two tungtanium needle bits and the consignment will be on their doorstep on Monday morning."
He looks at an ebony statuette beside his telephone. It represents an ancient man with flowing robes, very long whiskers and a sly grin which from some angles makes him look like a buffoon. Tom places an affectionate hand on the bald bulbous head saying, "This old chap is the Chinese god of wealth. I sometimes burn a joss stick in front of him."
"Mr Lang, it will be difficult for me to work overtime without *some* notice," says Ms Tain in a distressed voice.
"You got a kid?" asks Tom, looking at her hard.
"You have nothing at all to do with my private life!" she tells him sharply. He grins approvingly and says, "Quite right! Quite right! But ten minutes warning is all I can promise you – enough time to make a few phone calls."
Ms Tain stares at the floor, sighs and murmurs, "Alright."

Mrs Campbell returns with coffee.
"Meet June Tain, our new receptionist," says Tom, receiving a mug from her.
"Glad you're joining us," says Mrs Campbell, setting the two other mugs on a low table by Ms Tain, who thanks her. Mrs Campbell also sits on a low chair facing the desk.
"So when can you start?" asks Tom.
"Tomorrow?"

"That's the spirit!" says Tom, and sips coffee, and leans comfortably back, "Better make it Monday though. Mrs Campbell, put the bullet into Marian for Monday will you? I personally will see to Alice. Alice, our leetle receptionist. It wasnae her refusal to do overtime that decided me to get rid of her. I can forgive a girl a lot if she's decorative. But Alice is *fat*. I came in yesterday, looked at her and said to myself, "No! No, that is not the image I want to greet the customers of *Lang Precision Ltd*."

Suddenly Mrs Campbell and Ms Tain start speaking at the same time. Both stop, glance at each other, Ms Tain nods, meaning *you first*. Mrs Campbell says, "Mr Lang, just now Marian takes over from the receptionist during lunch and coffee breaks. Who will take over from Miss Tain? There's only me or the typist."

"Don't worry about it," says Ms Tain quickly swallowing some coffee then standing up. "I'm not taking this job."

Both women look at Tom who frowns slightly, pondering a response consistent with dignity. At last he asks on a note of vague curiosity, "Why?"

Ms Tain, giving him a sudden lovely smile, says "Personal reasons," and walks out of the room.

A moment later he strides after her down the corridor calling, "June! Wait a minute June!"

She keeps walking.

He says, "Please Miss Tain! Please stop and hear me a moment!"

She keeps walking. He walks beside her and says quietly, "Listen! I need a receptionist and you need a job."

"That's no reason why I should eat dirt!"

He sighs, slips in front of her and blocks the way, hands clasped as if in prayer. He says, "Please Miss Tain! I want to explain something. All I ask is five more minutes of your time – they won't be wasted – I can promise that." He ushers her back along the corridor knowing she is partly moved by curiosity and partly by the coercion of his bulk.

In the office Mrs Campbell is gathering the mugs onto a tray.
"Leave them, don't wash them Mrs Campbell!" says Tom. "Just check our orders from Newcastle. We should have heard from Newcastle by now."
He sits upright, not sprawling behind his desk. Mrs Campbell leaves, exchanging with June a perfectly neutral glance which means *that man!* It would be a smile if he were not watching them closely. He says, "Sit down, June."
"We're not on first-name terms Mr Lang," she reminds him, not sitting. He nods and says, "You think I'm a bastard."
"You invited me to your office," she says in a thoughtful voice, "you kept me watching you for minutes while you acted the great big boss, then you made me parade like a mannequin. You were going to sack another woman because you thought you'd talked me into doing two jobs instead of the one you advertised, then you leaned back chuckling and gloating and expecting to be admired!" She looks at him with an astonishment she seems keen for him to share. He nods seriously and says, "I recognize the picture, Miss Tain. Yes. A dirty pressurizing bastard. That's how I get the world to work for me. All bosses are like me, you see, though some of them fool folk into thinking otherwise. I think foolery's a waste of time – that's my trouble."
"All bosses are not like you."
"No? Perhaps you're right. Of course you're right. I read in the papers that the Duke of Westminster is the most charming man in Britain, besides owning most of it. All his servants love him, it seems. The charm was probably inherited along with the servants, *and* his first hundred million, *and* central London, *and* half of Scotland. Or is it Wales? I can't remember. I know this though, I'm a small businessman struggling to get bigger. If I acted like the Duke of Westminster I'd be done for. Folk would laugh at me. So I act like a businessman in an American

movie: not the golden-hearted kind nobody believes in, but the pressurizing bastards everybody believes in."
"I don't like working for bastards. May I leave?"
"Wait a minute! I'm a *clever* bastard. I won't try to pressurize you again because you've shown you won't stand it. You'd be a great receptionist. I need one and you need a job. Try me for a week or two, I improve on acquaintance. While you ponder that proposal I will make us another cup of coffee with my own fair hands – please don't tell Mrs Campbell, she's a very jealous lady."

Tom busies himself in the kitchen. Ms Tain yawns, slumps back in a chair and closes her eyes until he returns. He puts a mug on the table near her but sits on the far side saying, "So what do you think?"
She says, "I'll be your receptionist if you don't fire anybody."
"Right, Marian stays. But you'll do overtime for me? You won't go back on that?"
"What work can a receptionist do outside normal office hours?"
"Help load a van," says Tom chuckling, "We all muck in sometimes – even me. It speeds delivery and means we all get home earlier. *And* everyone's paid double rates for the full hour, even if we finish the job in ten minutes – which is frequent in the circumstances. It's also healthy exercise after sitting at a desk all day."
She smiles and says, "Then I'll put up with it."
He gives her a quick, almost shy glance and says, "Why aren't you a secretary? You're clever enough."
"I can't type and don't know shorthand."
"Take lessons."
"If I ever go back to studying I'll learn something interesting – law, perhaps. And while we're being honest I'd better tell you – I may stay here as long as a year, but six months is all I can promise."
"You little bitch!" says Tom, greatly amused.

"Please don't swear … You understand me, don't you?"
"Can't say I do."
"There aren't many interesting office jobs for women, you see, and after a few weeks you're either harassed for sexual favours or taken for granted like a piece of the furniture. Those who get bored with a job usually change it."
Tom points a finger and prophesies: "You will work here longer than you think!"
She looks at him sceptically.

A great certainty moves his heavy big body to rise and stroll lightly round the room, happy with an audience who deserves him: an attractive woman with an independent mind. He says, "Lang Precision bores nobody who works for it – we're changing too fast for that. Six months ago I had a staff of eight. Now I've twice that. What'll we be like in another six months? A lot bigger, I say. You'll work bloody hard Miss Tain but I promise you won't be bored. And I'm sorry, you'll have to get used to my swearing."
He stops by the window, hands in pockets, and looks kindly at the dockyards. She says, "Yes, it's a dangerous time for you."
He turns and stares.
"Most successful small firms go bankrupt when they try to expand," she reminds him, adding, "I worked with one. A boss easily manages a small staff personally, but a big one is different. Unless you learn to delegate you go under. You can't be everywhere."
"Can't I?" asks Tom in an odd voice, then grins, chuckles and announces, "I must be mad, but you're such a bloody little know-all I want to tell you everything. Can I trust you? With a secret, I mean?"
The question worries her. He says, "Alright, don't answer, I do trust you. Come and see this. When you said I can't be everywhere you forgot the miracle of modern science."

He goes behind his desk. She rises and follows puzzled and curious. He pulls open a very deep drawer, but the inside seems only deep enough to hold two pairs of light earphones. He lifts these out and points to dials and switches on the surface underneath.
"Where to?" he asks. "Reception? Accountancy? Loading bay? There was trouble in the loading bay, we'll go there."
He puts on the earphones and presses switches. Beginning to understand but still curious she too slips on the earphones. A hissing reaches her, some tweets and hiccups then a vast roaring which settles into the noise of wood being sawed. A distant voice bellows, "I hate that big bastard."
Someone sounding close behind her shouts "Nae wunner."
"Know what the accountants call him?"
"Naw."
"The Great I Am. The Great I Am."
"Good, they're on the job," says Tom cheerily, removing his headphones and switching the sound off.
"What a cheap, nasty trick!" says Ms Tain, handing back hers. Her voice conveys distress more than rage.
"Not cheap! The wiring alone cost more than five hundred. Say it, though – I'm a bugger!"
He grins. She is distressed and says, "I feel like walking out of here and not coming back."
"But you will come back," he tells her gravely, "because you're interested, and need the money, and I trust you."
She does not deny this but walks away murmuring, "Sickening. Sickening."

And hears a sigh and turns. He sits behind the desk, elbow on top, chin propped on the thumbs of interlocking fingers. He says, "You're right of course. This is a difficult time. I've been bankrupt already for exactly the reasons you mentioned. I hate delegating. I don't trust people and why should I? Most of them are a gang of lazy, lying cowards without an ounce of imagination. If I didn't

boss them they would do nothing – nothing at all. So I pile loads on them, loads *I* can easily carry, but they havenae the sense or guts to tell me when it's too much for them. Then suddenly without warning they walk out. It's infuriating."
"I'll give you at least a fortnight's warning before I walk out on you."
"Don't plan too far ahead. You'll be more than a receptionist before you leave Lang Precision Ltd."

Ms Tain starts work the following Monday at five to nine. At ten to eleven Marian takes her place at the reception desk and she has coffee in the accountant's office with Mrs Campbell and young Teddy, the undermanager. Her conversation with these two does not flow smoothly. There are strange pauses when there should be explanations, and Ted conveys so many states of feeling by facial and bodily gestures that at last she stares openly at him and starts to laugh. Mrs Campbell hands her a note with *We are being taped* scribbled on it, and says, "Where are you lunching today, June? I usually eat in The Tempting Tattie on Argyle Street. It's quite near and not expensive."
"Then I'll go there too, today," says Ms Tain, and adds, "Where does our noble employer usually eat?"
"On days like this, when the firm needs him at his desk," says Mrs Campbell primly, "Mr Lang orders his luncheon by phone from the kitchen of the Central Station Hotel. A taxi brings it."
"Only the best is good enough for TL!" says Ted, laughing every way except audibly.

In The Tempting Tattie Mrs Campbell says, "This is our third week in the new premises and we've already lost two new members of staff. The last receptionist, Alice, had to go. She was useless on the phone, and lost us an order. And Tom had a secretary all to himself for two whole days. She walked out at the start of the third."

"The usual reason?"
Mrs Campbell nods and says, "It was partly her fault. She was young and silly, just out of typing college, and dressed and wriggled in an 'I'm all yours, sir' way though she wasn't that type at all. He wouldn't have pestered a sensible girl. It's a pity his wife isn't sensible. She's a disaster – a doormat."
"Will the firm last?"
"It may if he keeps away from the office. In a firm that's just starting a lot of office work is intelligent waiting, but Tom can't bear that. He tries new arrangements to keep us working all the time, so we interfere with each other and will be in a real mess if a lot of work suddenly arrives."
"But he isn't a fool."
"I know! Such a gassy big windbag ought to be a fool, but he knows everything about precision tools, he's good with buyers and suppliers, he'll go anywhere to chase up business."

Tom's business trips sometimes take him to south Britain. On one of these Ms Tain gets a call from a voice which sounds like Tom pretending to be a Yorkshireman. The speaker says he has a complaint and blabs of it in a rambling way, ignoring her patient efforts to learn if he is an unpaid supplier who should speak to Mrs Campbell, or a displeased buyer who should talk to Teddy. The voice suddenly becomes distinctly Tom saying, "You handled that well June, I mean Miss Tain. I wasn't joking, just testing. I'll explain tomorrow."
Next day he tells her he needs a personal secretary, one the receptionist puts clients on to at once, whether he's in the building or not. He says, "Believe me a lot of important people are going to be phoning this place and I want them to be impressed by a clear firm voice which seems to know its business. You've got that."
"But I can't –"
"Shorthand isn't needed now. You dictate letters to a

machine and give it to the typist. The job won't be a sinecure – that's why you'll get a twenty per cent wage rise. When I'm away you'll be handling the business from my angle."

"But surely Teddy –"

"Teddy has enough work with the deliveries. Besides, I'm always going for more customers than I'll ever get. The ones I get make us richer. Why need anyone but you and me know about the others?"

"Where will my office be?"

"Here. There's no room for another office in the building, and that desk was intended for my personal secretary." He points to a desk across the room from his own. Ms Tain does not look at it, but looks questioningly at him. He blushes slightly, and says, "You'll have heard in The Tempting Tattie that my last secretary and I had a misunderstanding. There's no danger of me misunderstanding you. Try the job for a week or two and see how you feel."

The employment agency sends a new receptionist and Ms Tain moves into Tom's office. The job and Tom are more interesting than she expected. Normally, or when things go badly, Tom is brisk, friendly and cheerful. Successes bring out the worst in him, making him almost comically pompous. Since Ms Tain does not always hide her amusement he learns to watch her warily at such times. He inclines to forget the morning and afternoon breaks. The best way to remind him is to make coffee in the small kitchen and put a mug of it on his desk while carrying one to her own. This greatly pleases him though he tries not to show it. He sometimes breaks off a phone call saying, "I must leave you now – my secretary has just brought the coffee in and she's a very jealous lady." Then he stretches his arms, takes the mug and talks about his problems or ideas for improving business efficiency. She offers suggestions which lead to some ideas being modified and the rest forgotten. He says, "I see things

more clearly when I bounce them off you."
As he expected, she has an excellent way of talking to clients. The firm also works more smoothly when his orders to the staff are passed through her. This he did not expect, but soon assumes he did.

Her only relief from Tom during working hours is when he is away on a business trip. The first time it happens she sends for Teddy, meets him at the office door and hands him a note saying *Find if this room is taped too.* She shows him the drawer with earphones. He puts them on, fingers switches, opens a panel in the side. Suddenly he announces indignantly, "We're not being taped at all – this is nothing but a bugging device! We could have said what we liked whenever he was out of the building!"
"I still want you and Mrs Campbell to have coffee here today," says Ms Tain consolingly.
They do, and Ms Tain now finds them boring. As they can now discuss Tom openly they discuss nothing else – not even Tom talks as much about Tom Lang as they do. On a later occasion when he is away for nearly a week she gets so furiously bored that she calls in an electrical firm to remove the bugging system.
"He must have discovered we knew," says Teddy, staring at Ms Tain, "How did he find that out?"
"Not from me," says Ms Tain quietly.
"But I bet you got him to do it," says Mrs Campbell, "You're the only one he listens to around here. Fancy him having all those expensive hidden microphones ripped out of the walls before the van men's very eyes! I'll never understand that man."
Teddy stops a chocolate biscuit halfway to his mouth and says, "I hear footsteps."
"When the cat's away the mice will play," says Tom gloomily entering and dropping his briefcase on Ms Tain's desk. He trudges toward his own with the tragic gait of a statesman exhausted by preserving the prosperity of an

ungrateful nation. The others nod to each other. The trip has been successful.
Ms Tain asks crisply, "Coffee? Tea, Mr Lang?"
He slumps into his chair, tilts it back, heaves heels onto desk-top, folds hands on stomach, yawns and says, "No coffee. No tea. I have not slept six hours in the last forty-eight. I have driven over seven hundred miles, seen a dozen firms and am shagged out. Finished. Done for. Go on eating your biscuits. Nibble biscuits all day if you like. In ten minutes I'll be off home to my kip and that's the last you'll see of me till nine. Sharp. Tomorrow."
He closes his eyes. Teddy and Mrs Campbell get up and leave. They know he dislikes them having coffee in his room and are intrigued that Ms Tain can pretend not to know.

She starts putting utensils on a tray. Without opening his eyes Tom says drowsily, "June!"
It is the first time in three months he has used her first name without correcting himself. She says, "Yes?"
"Pour me a whisky. Please!"
From a cocktail cabinet she takes bottle and glass, pours a measure from first into second, places both on desk before him. He sits up, sips, sighs, looks at her and asks, "Well?"
She stands with arms folded and back to her desk, half leaning, half sitting on it. She says, "No special correspondence. The orders from Colville's Clugston Shanks went through as planned. A late order from Lairds caused a strike among our one available van driver. Teddy ironed that out."
"A good lad, Teddy."
"You don't pay him enough."
"I know. He stands for it."
"Unless you pay him more he'll leave you. He's talking about it."
"Then I'll raise his wages. Thanks for the tip. I've missed you, June."

He is watching her, solemnly. She smiles back and says lightly, "Have you, Tom?"

"I've missed you very much."

"All the same, you're probably going to fire me."

"Why?"

"I've had your bugging system removed. The firm which unwired it took it away as part payment for doing the job quickly."

Tom opens his desk drawer, looks inside then slams it and looks hard at Ms Tain, his face and hands growing very red. He whispers, "Why?"

She is suddenly frightened. She says, "It's wicked to spy on people," her voice quivering a little.

"*Wicked*!" he shouts, jumping up, "*Wicked*! What a childish thing to say! Every government in the world does it!"

"They don't."

"They do!"

"Well if they do they're wicked and rotten and it made you ridiculous, Tom. Everybody knew about it. They were all laughing at you."

"How could they know? Who told them? You?"

"The electricians who installed it drank at a local pub and told a barman who told our drivers. Things like that can never be hidden, Tom. You were being laughed at!"

She still leans against her desk. He walks up and down shouting, "Let them laugh at me all they like! I don't care if they're doing what I tell them! That system worked for me even if they did know about it, in fact it worked better, yes of course it did! They had to keep their mouths shut about me or talk in sign language so they felt I was always beside them, always listening! It kept me in their thoughts – like God!"

His glaring face is an inch from hers, his fists hammer the space on each side of her body.

She whispers, "God?"

He has never been so menacing or she so subdued. He clasps, kisses her and is embraced. Her mouth yields

to his, which is hard at first then softens as he starts to tremble, feeling he is losing all control of things. Still holding her tight he withdraws his face, gasps for breath and demands, "Who did you tell them ordered that unwiring?"
"You, Tommy! I told them you ordered it! They were tremendously astonished and impressed!"
Her voice and face are eager, submissive and amused. He groans and they kiss again. Full of wonder he says, "I know nothing about you! Nothing at all."
"I'm very ordinary, Tommy."
"Do you like me, June?"
"You're a very impressive man, Mr Lang."
"But do you like me?"
"I ... I'm not sure. I like this, though."

A few minutes later they separate. He pulls his crumpled clothes straight and says soberly, "I want you down on the carpet with me."
"A bad idea," she says, going into their washroom.
"Listen!" he calls through to her, "I'm going to phone my wife and tell her I'm still on the M1. that I've had a breakdown and I'll be back tomorrow, right? She's used to that happening. Then I'll drive to Renfrew airport and book a room for us in the hotel. You finish here at five thirty as usual, look up and go to Central Station where you take a taxi straight out to me, right?"
"I don't think we should be hasty," she says, emerging, "My mother expects me for tea and I've arranged to meet a friend afterward."
"Does that mean we discuss it tomorrow?"
"Yes, at nine. Tomorrow. Sharp."
"You've a sense of humour," he tells her, sighing. They kiss and cling again for a moment, then he tells her to photocopy the orders in his briefcase and pass them to Teddy. They look at each other for a moment. He leaves.

Three days later they stay overnight in the airport hotel. Next day a kiss before lunch break leads to a coupling, interrupted by a phone call, on the carpet. Ten days later they spend another night in a hotel. Ms Tain finds he has just one short way of pleasing a woman intimately, and likes doing it three or four times a night. This makes him perfectly happy ("Oh I needed that!" he exclaims, almost every time) but she feels hardly any intimacy at all. For over a month Ms Tain gives her mother's poor health as a reason for not meeting Tom privately, and there are no more carpet fucks. Then one weekend he takes her for a two-day holiday to Paris.

The season is not spring but the weather is spring-like and fresh. They do not sit together on the plane in case someone recognizes him, but the flight, taxi-ride and arrival at a fine little hotel on a narrow street near the Arc de Triomphe make her happy and hopeful; their first fuck in the bedroom ten minutes later even enhances that mood. She would now like to drift about gazing at things, exploring without urgency the quais and parks beside the Seine, chatting about what they see, reminiscing about childhood and getting to know each other better. But Tom cannot enjoy looking at things. Drifting makes him uneasy. He assumes every stroll needs a destination and a schedule for reaching it. He takes her to Versailles and examines it with an offended frown, sometimes muttering, "Oh very nice, if you could afford it."
He is jealous of the monarchs who once lived here, not at all consoled by it now being public property. He talks a lot about his unhappy marriage. He is paying for this holiday so she murmurs sympathetically, feeling guilty that she can hardly stand his company now, guilty that the first thing she will do when they return to work will be hand in her notice, but beside the guilt, she also feels hopeful. She is dressed beautifully, her hair hangs freely down her back, she draws several admiring glances.

These gradually make Tom feel enviable and secure. At dinner that night he is amazed by the splendid woman across the table from him and says solemnly, "This is the happiest moment of my life."
She manages to smile. He drinks nearly two bottles of wine and three large brandies without apparent effect, but when they go to bed he falls asleep at once. She is glad, although she does not sleep for a long time. She feels her first holiday in Paris, like Tom Lang in private, should be better than this.

Next morning he wakens her by satisfying himself. He would do it again but she says she has a headache. He becomes gentle, apologetic, says, "I know I'm too much sometimes. Will I get you a cup of tea? Or coffee, maybe?"
She realizes Tom does not know there is more to love than he learned in his teens. Given time, a tactful and experienced woman could make a very satisfying lover out of Tom, but he will never give a woman enough time and luckily he is not the only man in her life.

They return by an afternoon flight. It is Sunday. On Wednesday she hands in her notice. He is appalled, offers to double her wages, declares the firm needs her, proposes marriage, announces he will buy a house for both of them anywhere she likes while the divorce is going through. She leaves and six months later marries someone who is rather like Tom Lang, but fonder of home and less obviously selfish. The marriage does not last. She has a habit of getting entangled with the same sort of man and only discovering it later.

Lang Precision Ltd does not last either, though it receives a Scottish Industries Award for being the most successfully competitive small firm of 1975. It supplies tools to factories in a province where heavy industries are being closed or shifted south, where light industries are sending their labour to factories in Taiwan and Thailand. Tom, with the assistance of an expert accountant, goes profitably bankrupt. He moves to London where his ability to deal with buyers and suppliers is found useful by a subsidiary of a gigantic company whose directors will never know his name or face.

IN THE BOILER ROOM

THE boiler room is entered from a dirty little yard behind an old hotel with a grand big front. The room has a concrete floor and walls of unplastered, unpainted brick. It is windowless and lit by a bare bulb hung from the ceiling at the end of the room not occupied by the boiler – the end with the door. The boiler is like the engine of an old steam locomotive without wheels and cabin. It has the same circular front of riveted steel plates, the same large dials indicating water level and pressures, the same small grim furnace underneath. It eats the same sort of fuel. Near by is a heap of small coal and a heap of coke. A long-handled and short-handled shovel lie on these, an iron-handled rake and a stout sweeping-brush with very coarse bristles. In a corner a heap of tumbled-together chairs slopes up to the ceiling, chairs too old or damaged for the hotel and sent down here for use as kindling. There is a stack of expensive but out-of-date fashion magazines sent down for the same purpose. These heaps are all close together because the boiler fills most of the room.

It may not seem a comfortable room but some find comfort here. The boiler pipes are old and leak a bit, so the hot air is neither too moist nor too dry and on this late January afternoon the heat is welcome after the freezing slush of the yard and the streets beyond. Even the thin sharp fume of burning coke smells pleasant by association, and after a while has a slightly narcotic effect. Three gold-lacquered basket chairs, chipped and soiled but with

wicker frames too difficult to break up for kindling, stand in a small space before the boiler for the convenience of visitors. The boilerman prefers a plain wooden chair on which he sits by the furnace door, smoking his pipe and reading a library book. He is tall, lean, craggy and old; he wears a black boilersuit, big boots and flat cap, also spectacles with a fractured earpiece bandaged by electrical insulating tape. He does not hear a faint distant sound of dance music until it swells louder as the door opens and a small determined woman walks in, followed by a worried little boy. She wears a plastic headscarf and plastic raincoat and carries a heavy suitcase in each hand. The boy wears a thick duffel coat with the hood up and clutches a doll wearing the clothes and equipment of an American soldier in Vietnam. The boilerman looks at them blankly then says, "Hullo Senga."
She says firmly, "Yes, hullo Granda. I'm finished. I'm through. I've had all I can take."
She puts down her cases and tells the boy, "Shut that door." He does.

The boilerman, nodding thoughtfully, stands and points to a chair near his own. He says gently to the boy, "Sit down son."
He does not ask the woman to sit. She is clearly in no mood for that. She takes a packet from her pocket, removes a cigarette, asks for a light. The boilerman hands her matches. She lights the cigarette and returns the matches saying, "Thanks. Yes I've had it, had it up to here" – she makes a slicing gesture across her throat – "I'm leaving him and this time it's final ... Take your coat off and sit down like your granda says," she tells the boy, who has been staring at her uncertainly. He obeys her. The boilerman looks thoughtfully at the bowl of his pipe then pockets it with an air of decision. He says, "I'll get you a snack from the kitchen, we've a wedding reception tonight ..."
"Huh! *Wedding* reception! Save your trouble, I don't need a snack."

"Did he lay hands on you?" askes the boilerman quietly. The wife, smoking in quick little angry puffs, grins grimly and says, "Hit me? I'd like to see him try. I'd have him in the Marine Police Station before he could blink. His feet wouldnae touch the pavement."

The boilerman glances at the boy who seems not to be listening and murmurs, "A woman, maybe?"

"Oh I wish it was! I wish he'd do something I could take him to court over, but no. No it's because of something ordinary. He went out for a drink last night, as usual, and said he'd be back in forty minutes. As usual. And as usual he comes rolling in at half-past eleven. Met a pal and went up to his house for a chat about the future of socialism while muggins here is left alone in the house with the kid and the telly. As usual."

"Does he never let you out by yourself?"

"Oh aye! All for sweet human reason is that man of mine. 'When you want a night out just tell me,' says he, 'I'll sit in with the wee chap, no problem.' Where can I go for a night out? I've no pals to talk politics with. The only folk I know are a lot of silly women with nothing in their heads but babies and food prices and bingo. I married that man for his *company* and the bastard won't stay in the room with me for more than an hour at a time if we're no in bed with the light off. That's the only time we're together and it isnae enough."

She is close to weeping, so he takes a deep breath and says, "I shouldnae call him a bastard, Granda, because he's your son. You know what I mean, but."

"I think so Senga."

"Funny. I can say anything I like to you and you never take me wrong."

"That's because I'm neutral, Senga."

"Aye, you keep saying that, but I know you're on my side. Listen, I'm leaving the kid here for half an hour while I see about a room. I met a friend last week who needs a lodger. I havnae seen her for years, she's not very bright but she's got a good heart and she lives three streets from here."

"Would you like a cup of tea first?"
"Definitely not."
She goes to the boy and makes small adjustments to the collar of his shirt, the sleeves of his pullover. She tells him quietly, "I won't be long, Hughie," and leaves. The boilerman strokes his chin and studies the boy for a moment. The boy, hunched over the doll on his lap, seems to be studying the furnace door. The boilerman quietly coughs. The boy looks at him. The boilerman raises a forefinger, says, "Hughie, I'm going to get you something," and walks out. The boy turns back to the furnace door and frowns thoughtfully, sometimes moving his lips as if talking to it.

The boilerman returns with a plate containing triangular sandwiches, vivid pastries and a glass of green liquid under a layer of white froth. He lifts a crate from the floor, stands it short-end-up beside the boy's chair and lays the plate on top. He says, "That's for you."
"Not hungry."
"Then we'll let it rest there."
The boilerman sits down, lights his pipe and resumes the library book. After a while the boy says, "Granda, what's the worst trap you were in?"
The boilerman looks at him closely.
"I mean in the war," explains the boy, "The first war."
"Passchendaele, I suppose."
"Did you kill many Germans?"
"You're keen on war, eh?"
"I've got three action men," says the boy earnestly, "An infantryman, a paratrooper and a frogman. Of course they're just toys but you can learn things from them, can't you? I mean the wee weapons are all to scale. Look at this! Look at the wee grenades."
He holds up his doll. The boilerman glances at it briefly then blows a smoke ring.
"Tell me about the first war!" pleads the boy.
"Yes," says the boilerman and lays his book down, "Well.

You know the big greenhouse with the palm trees in it behind the museum on the Green?"

"Aye."

"That was where I slept on the night of the day war was declared."

"Why?"

"When I read about the war on the placards, you see, I joined at once. I was seventeen, you see, and I'd been working as a clerk on a weighbridge at the docks. Oh yes, my parents had great hopes for me, but it was not a job I liked. As a hobby I had joined the volunteer reserve, which was a free kind of night classes in soldiering. So when war was declared, I was prepared. I signed on like a shot and bought my first tin of pipe-tobacco with the shillings they gave me. So many of us signed on they had to billet us in all kinds of queer places. So there was I, lying on my palliasse on the walkway of the People's Palace conservatory, under a tree with a label on it saying *Phoenix dactilifera*. That was the very first night I ever slept outside a house with my parents in it, and every hour I wakened to a queer dank jungle smell and saw that label with the words *Phoenix dactilifera*."

"Yes," says the boy, "but –"

"Next day!" says his grandfather, lifting a forefinger, "We were sent up to Dunfermline and billeted in a whisky bonding warehouse. Three months later twelve of us marched down Queensferry Road to the railway station and marched onto the Glasgow train, just as if we were a picket. Now what do you think of that?"

"What's a picket?"

"A small group of soldiers with a special warrant to travel on a train without tickets. But we had no warrant."

"Why?"

"We had been three months without leave, you see, and felt justified in taking what was called *French* leave, which is without permission. Well, just before the train came into Queen Street station, it halted in the shunting yards of Saint Rollox. The money in our pockets added up

to just less than five shillings, which was judged too little to bribe the ticket collector at the barrier. So we jumped out of the carriage, ran across the lines, climbed the fence and … walked back to our proper homes. Now listen!"
The boilerman points a finger. "The next evening, at ten to nine, two polis-men knocked at the door to ask if Private MacLeod was at home. He was. A laggard among us had been caught skipping over the fence and had clyped on us. I was taken down to Old Dalmarnock Road polisstation –"
"Someone maligning the police again?" asks a policeman who has quietly entered.
"Aye, there you are Fergus," says the boilerman but pays the policeman no other attention, so the boy ignores him too. The policeman enters a dark space between the coke heap and the boiler-room wall. He does something with his arms inside a tea-chest while the boilerman says, "They took me to Old Dalmarnock Road polis-station, where it was discovered they had no food, and that I was hungry, for they'd arrested me before supper-time. So a polis-man went back to my mother's house and she gave him food for me, and to spare. I was put in a cell with a stone bed and stone pillow, both painted red. There was also a fine fire blazing in the hearth –"
"There is not, and has never been, a Scottish police-station cell with a fireplace in it," says the policeman firmly, returning to the space before the boiler. He carries a paper cup of clear liquid, sits down and sips from it. After a pause the boilerman tells the boy mildly, "As I was saying, a fire in the hearth. I sat there with a couple of friendly inspectors, eating my mother's scones and … just talking. Just talking. I slept that night wrapped in a blanket on that stone bed and the next day I was marched to Tobago Street where I met the others, all twelve of us. Two unarmed polis-men walked us to Maryhill Barracks where a small company of fixed bayonets marched us to the train back to Dunfermline."
"What did they do to you? The officers, I mean."

"Sixty days confined to barracks," says the boilerman promptly.
"That's not a *real* war experience," mutters the boy.
"It could have happened at no other time."
"You should ask about my war experiences," says the policeman.

The policeman is not a young man but has an unlined, indefinite face which at first sight seems boyish.
"Were you – ?" the boy asks hopefully.
"Yes indeed son. You see before you one of the original desert rats. North Africa nineteen-forty. And so on."
"You fought for General Montgomery?"
"Monty?" says the policeman, "A big balloon! There was only one general the British soldier respected in that concise area of conflict. Will I tell you his name?"
The boy nods vigorously.
"Rommel."
"Did you *see* Rommel?"
"I had not that honour. My own North African campaign was passed in a supply depot: a fuel-tank of the military apparatus. All kinds of armaments and food and drink passed through our hands, and furnishings, you know, for the top brass."
The policeman sighs nostalgically.
"Our tents had wall-to-wall carpets in them with dressing-tables and three-piece suites. Crazy paving was laid up to the front flap of each, and every morning my barber wakened me sharp at eleven with a bottle of champagne."
"Fergus," says the boilerman, "I am aware that strange things happen in supply depots but I find your crazy paving hard to take."
"It was a fact!"
"Were you a … a major or something?" the boy asks, awed.
"A humble lance-corporal."
"But how did *you* have a barber?"
"We were in a very poor part of the world, you see, and

there were always a lot of homeless children hanging around to do anything you liked for a coin or a half-bar of chocolate. One of them attached himself to me – two or three years younger than you he was, an orphan, but intelligent. I trained him to shave me in bed in the mornings. I would waken to the warm lather going on to my cheeks and I would be shaved and dried without my head once leaving the pillow."

"But did you never *fight?*"

"Indeed!" said the policeman, nodding, "Yes, each day after lunch we swept the horizon with our binoculars and if we saw anything unusual we reported it to the commanding officer. 'Beg to report sir, a duck has appeared beside the palm tree at half-past three o'clock.' 'Right! That duck is our enemy! Open fire!' Whizzbang, whizzbang. Ten thousand pounds of explosive missile waste their sweetness on the desert air."

"But *why*?" asks the boy, exasperated by this waste of explosives.

"There was a *war* on son! If we hadn't exploded a certain number of shells per week the brass at headquarters would have thought we weren't doing our bit. Of course it wasn't a typical situation – not everyone did well in that war. In fact I've heard that in the thirty-nine-forty-five affair it was the civilians who suffered most."

"There you are *wrong*, Fergus!" cries the boilerman forcefully, "I know the blitz was gey hard on the Londoners and Clydebankers, but life here in Britain during the war was far kinder and more decent than before or since. We had a working government then, controlling the industries and regulating the prices. Full employment for all! And food rationed, and clothes rationed, so the rich got no more than they needed and the poor no less. Even the king was eating spam off his gold plate in Buckingham Palace. No petrol for private cars then – we *all* used the trains and trams and buses. People with big houses had to give rooms to bombed-out kids from the slums, and the miracle is, hardly anyone grumbled! Even the advertisements had a democratic look. WORK OR WANT, they said. MAKE DO AND MEND, COUGHS AND SNEEZES SPREAD DISEASES, DIG FOR VICTORY. People with gardens were encouraged to plant vegetables in them. Now listen to this!"

From the stack of fashion magazines he seizes one, leafs through, then reads aloud:

"*The young admire it for its reckless good looks. Their parents like it for its thrifty fuel consumption. Not everyone can afford the life-style indicated by a Blenheim table cigarette lighter, but those who can usually own one*. What is that but a sneer and a gibe at working people who could pay three months *rent* with the price of their fancy cigarette lighter? Here's another advert for a holiday in the Bahamas. It is aimed at young working women and is a straightforward invitation to them to prostitute themselves! *Rich boys know how to enjoy life, it says. They have the money and time. Meet them in their favourite playgrounds for …*"

The policeman, who has been smiling and shaking his head at the boilerman's vehemence, laughs aloud and raises his hand.

"Cool it Mr McLeod, cool it!" he says. "Less of the communist manifesto and a bit more judicial calm." The boilerman becomes calm instantly. He puts the magazine back on the stack and says quietly, "Quite right."

Another man has entered and sat down with them, a no-longer-young man wearing neat but not expensive clothing. The boilerman and the boy pay him no special attention though he is the son of the first and father of the second. But perhaps his arrival stimulates the boy who says with sudden vehemence, "Granda, did you never, you know, stand waiting with your bayonets fixed till the order came to go over the top and then you charged across no man's land and jumped into shell-holes to miss the shells and then came to the German trenches and jumped down into them and you know what I mean? You *did* do that didn't you?"

"I did as little of that as I possibly could!" says the boilerman firmly.

"Nobody will tell me about fighting," mourns the boy.

"Why do *you* want to hear about fighting?" asks his father.

"Because I might pick up useful tips – useful for school, I mean. I don't always know what to do, you see. I mean, what can you do when they chase you into the lavatory, and you're holding the door shut, and two of them are shoving it to try to get in, and one is reaching his hands under the door to grab at your legs, and another starts climbing in over the side wall? What can you do?"

The men glance at each other, thoroughly disconcerted. They do not want to tell the boy he is in a world which cannot be improved, but only the boilerman has a suggestion for improving it. He says softly, "Take a cake, Hughie."

The boy looks at the plate and selects a tight spiral of yellow crumbs and scarlet jam. He bites it and talks mainly to himself.

"James Bond is full of tricks: guns and explosives inside fountain pens and the heel of his shoes. I don't want to *kill* anybody, but it would be great if I could give them an electric shock whenever they touch me. Or what if I flashed a light that blinded them – not for ever, but for an hour or two. That would be all right, wouldn't it?"

The last question is another appeal to the adults. The policeman is the least embarrassed by it. He says, "Wait till you're a bit older, son, then you can send for *me* if thugs get on to you. Oh yes, we know how to handle thugs. When you first arrest these big tough guys they're very sure of themselves, calling you all kinds of names. But the nearer they get to the station the quieter they become. And by the time they're inside – if they've sense – they're as mild as wee lambs."

He imitates a cringing whine: *"Don't give me the stick! Not the stick!"*

He chuckles as if it is a cheerful memory.

"What bothers me," grumbles the boy, "Is that you've all been in the army and none of you talk about the killing you've done."

"*You* were in the army?" the policeman asks the father, surprised.

"Yes. National Service. Cyprus."

"Kill any terrorists?" says the policeman, interested.

"No, but I broke an old woman's china teapot."

They stare at him. He sighs and says gloomily, "We were stationed on this village for a while – nice enough folk, they seemed, and they liked football, so we got up a team to play them. It was a good game. They beat us two-nil but there were no hard feelings. Afterwards one of our boys went to a well for a drink. It was booby-trapped. His head, legs and other bits travelled a long way in different directions, a sight to sicken you. Then one of us remembered that during the game a young kid had gone to the well for a drink and a woman – an ordinary housewife – had called it away. We saw that the whole village had known about the booby-trap! Well, we had to search the place then and of course we made a right meal of it. There were quite a few breakages, and lots of pillows, mattresses and cushions got ripped. Oh, they didnae sleep soft *that* night I can tell you! I didnae enjoy doing that. It was a relief to be doing *something* of course but I felt bad afterwards. I mean, they werenae all bad people, but when the soldier went for a drink at the well could the woman not have warned him away too?"

"If she had, the terrorists might have … done something to her," says the boilerman quietly.

"I know!" says the father with a hopeless shrug.

"You have no cause for self-recrimination!" says the policeman loudly, "In certain circumstances the forces of law and order cannot afford to be mealy-mouthed. You were defending your country, defending an artery of trade that was essential to Britain's survival as a nation."

The two other men look at him. The boilerman says, "What artery is that, Fergus?"

"Gibraltar. Cyprus. Suez. Aden. India."
"Fergus, the Suez Canal was blocked for three years before my boy was sent to Cyprus, and for about six after he came back."
"Is that right?" the policeman asks the father, who nods. The policeman frowns then remembers something which cheers him up again: "Without the British presence the Greeks and Turks would have torn each other apart, like the Irish in Ulster," he explains, "If they now live in peace it is because we taught them to. If they're still carving each other up it shows they needed us."
"Everybody talks about *politics*," grumbles the boy. After a silence his father says, "I loved Cyprus."
Nobody asks for an explanation so after more silence he says, "If you take a walk in the country side here, what do you see? Cows and sheep looking over fences. But in Cyprus ... I remember being on sentry go at the edge of a camp up in the hills. Stony bare hills they were, hardly any green, but lots of gnarled kinds of bushes with big leaves. I was the only one awake when the dawn came up. You never see colours like that in dawns nowadays – I mean not here. No sound but a few birds cheeping and some sheep-bells or goat-bells clanking down in the valley. And this slight feeling of danger keeping you alert to it all. Because the Eeky-Oakies might be somewhere near."
"We all had moments like that," says the boilerman thoughtfully. The policeman nods.

The door bangs open and the wife enters. Her lips are pressed very tight together. The boilerman stands up and says, "Senga."
She says, "Give me a light, Granda."
She lights a cigarette with his matches and returns them.
"Any ... luck?" he asks delicately.
"Luck? For me? You must be crazy. Donalda Ingles used to be a decent wee girl but she's turned into a slut. Her sink's full of dirty old bean tins, the place stinks like

a lavatory, she's living with a tinker and smells like a midden. She needs help, poor soul, but I cannae give it. I cannae stay in a place like thon."
The husband rises and walks to the suitcases his wife brought in earlier. He says crisply, "So you are coming home?"
"Oh!" she jeers, "You want me *home* do you?"
"I didn't say that," says the husband, "When you have a place to live in, go there and good luck to you. Meanwhile, are you coming home? I'll carry the cases."
He bends to lift them. She cries, "Don't you touch my things! I'll mibby spend the night here. It's a hotel, isn't it?"
"Senga," says the boilerman gently, "The cheapest room here will cost you ten pounds a night."
"Senga," says the husband, "If you're leaving me you cannae afford that sort of money. You're far too impetuous – you'll never get away from me by charging out the house like a madwoman. You must plan things calmly. If you do I'll *help* you for godsake. It will mean less damage, especially to ... to ..." With a small gesture he indicates the boy, then stoops to the cases again, saying, "Do I take these home?"
She says coolly, "Take them where you bloody like."
He lifts them and says to the boy, "Come on, Hughie."
The boy stands up looking worried. He says, "Do I go with him, Ma?"
"Up to you, intit?" says his mother, blowing out smoke.
"I'll stay with you, Ma, if ... if you want me."
"Hm! And who do you want?"
The boy stares at her looking terribly lost. Her husband says in a low voice, "Senga, that isnae fair."
"Oh go with your dad!" she cries impatiently. "I'm coming soon enough. Just clear off both of you and let me finish a fag in peace."
The father with suitcases, the boy with his doll, go to the door. Before leaving the man turns and says, "One thing, Senga! Don't think I've apologized to you. I've done

nothing I'm ashamed of, nothing I'm sorry for, nothing I won't do tomorrow night. Come on son."
They leave.

The wife walks up and down, puffing angrily.
"You heard them, didn't you?" she asks the two others.
"He wasn't exactly brutal to you, Mrs MacLeod," says the policeman.
"And would he be with two witnesses here? And one of them a policeman?"
The drink is giving the policeman a pleasant sense of extended intellectual powers.
"Well you know," he says, "A husband is entitled to beat his wife to the point of correction. That statute is graven on the foundation stones of the British Legal Constitution."
"You're blethering, Fergus," says the boilerman, "There is no such thing as a British Legal Constitution."
"The Scottish legal system is the finest in the world," the policeman announces to nobody in particular, "And I am fifty-five per cent *certain* that it permits a man to beat his wife *up to*, but not *beyond*, the point of correction. But where do we locate that point? Aha! That is the point!"
He chuckles at his wit. The wife throws the cigarette down and stands on it, saying, "I'm getting out of here."
The boilerman goes to her saying, "Fergus is drivelling, Senga, at least stay for something to eat."
"No thanks, Granda. I'll see you when you've more ... privacy."

She leaves. The boilerman wanders back to his seat murmuring, "Poor souls."
"I'm sure you were wrong about the Suez Canal," says the policeman. Britain did not fight in that war for nothing. I shall look into it."
He throws the empty paper cup onto the coke heap, stands and pulls his tunic straight. He says, "Aye aye. Everyone goes about saying how much they want war, and they're right to want it, because war is a very fine thing. But in my

humble opinion war keeps manufacturing tensions which can only be resolved by a thorough-going peace."
The policeman notices the boilerman watching him and stroking his chin. A sudden doubt occurs to him. He asks, "Did I say that the wrong way round, Mr MacLeod?"
"I honestly don't know, Fergus."
"Neither do I. Well, duty calls."
He leaves. The boilerman looks at the dials, opens the furnace door and flings three shovelfuls of coke along a red-hot gullet of flames. Then he shuts the door, puts the shovel away, sits down, lights his pipe, and continues reading.

QUIET PEOPLE

DOORBELL rings. Mrs Liddel opens to Mrs Mathieson who says, "I took my pain to the doctor – I've just got back from him."

"Would you like a cup of tea?" asks Mrs Liddel. Mrs Mathieson enters the sitting-room. Mrs Liddel enters the kitchen where Mr Liddel reads a library book, a kettle of water steams gently over a low flame.

"Mrs Mathieson!" explains Mrs Liddel preparing tea and biscuits. Her husband says, "Mhm."

In the sitting-room Mrs Liddel pours two cups of tea as Mrs Mathieson draws a deep breath and announces, "The very first thing he did was tell me to strip myself naked all over."

"Oh dear!" whispers Mrs Liddel. As the story continues her kind, alert face expresses wonder, sympathy, dismay and dread. These expressions are genuine. Mrs Liddel, her husband and two grown-up daughters have never been painfully ill, drunk or quarrelsome, or accidentally involved with criminal or indecent or eccentric behaviour, so most people's lives strike them as surprising. They have no television set because the things shown on it strike them as too surprising for comfort. When a visitor has no more to say Mrs Liddel can only shake her head and say, "Fancy that!" or "That should not be allowed."

When the visitor leaves Mrs Liddel takes the tea things back to the kitchen saying, "Mrs Mathieson took her pain to the doctor this morning. The first thing he made her do

was strip herself naked all over."
While talking she washes and dries tea things and restores them to exact places in cupboard, sideboard and drawer, sometimes pausing when the gravity of the news makes movement impossible. Mr Liddel is slightly ashamed of being the only one who knows his wife gossips. A casual observer might think he was ignoring her – he has raised his eyes only a fraction above the book held open before him. When the recital ends he says, "Well well!" and resumes reading, or else, "I see. So that's the way of it. I'd better take a wee walk. Come on Tippy."
Their old dog follows him to the park where he strolls up to the flagpole in dry weather or through the museum when wet. He broods deeply on what his wife has told him. It usually confirms what he deduces from newspapers and wireless broadcasts: Britain is getting worse.

Mrs Liddel is small and pretty, Mr Liddel massive and handsome. He is asthmatic. This shows if he moves quickly so he never moves quickly. A tram-driver from 1928 to 1961, he fails the army medical exam and is promoted to ticket inspector a year before trams are replaced by buses. He never learns to love the buses as he loved the trams and his world-view is shaped by this. He remembers when Glasgow tram lines reached to Loch Lomondside and most of industrial Lanarkshire; when the head of Glasgow Public Transport was invited to cities in North and South America to advise them on the running of municipal light railway systems. The scrapping of Glasgow tramcars is mingled in his mind with the Labour Party's retreat from socialist intentions. His favourite reading is biography and novels which present a rich social variety in a strong moralizing sauce. Dickens and Victor Hugo are his favourites, and only the confusing Russian names stop him enjoying Dostoevsky. He has read Upton Sinclair, J.B. Priestley, A.J. Cronin and Grassic Gibbon, but compared with Dickens and Hugo most twentieth-century writing strikes him as feeble. His detailed knowledge of modern existence now depends mainly on his wife, who is too busy to read.

Since marriage the Liddels have lived in a ground-floor flat in Minard Road, a street of tenements which offers better-paid workers most of the domestic amenities of the wealthy, apart from spaciousness. An entrance porch as large as a doormat has a double outer storm-door and an inner door which is two-thirds frosted glass. This opens into a tiny lobby which the Liddel daughters (shortly before they married and left) insisted in calling The Hall. Here are doors to a cupboard with a coalbunker in it, to a lavatory two feet wider and four feet longer than the bath, to a back kitchen with a bed recess facing the window and sink, to a front bedroom one and a half feet wider and five feet longer than the bed, to a front sitting-room with enough room to walk comfortably round a heavy three-piece suite which boxes in the fire-place. The sitting-room also has a bed recess facing the window: a bay window divided from the street by a garden filled by a privet hedge round it and two small rhododendrons. The gardens and bay windows give Minard Road its prosperous look, but Mr and Mrs Liddel would feel well housed without them. They are glad that each of their daughters has a whole bed of her own: indeed, the eldest has a whole bedroom. When the eldest marries and leaves, the youngest inherits the bedroom and the kitchen bed recess is converted to a dining alcove. When the youngest leaves the older people move to the bedroom, returning after a week to the bed in the sitting-room recess because they sleep uneasily without a wall on three sides of them. They are slightly ashamed of this lack of sophistication, but Mr Liddel says, "We must accept ourselves as we are."

The furnishings of the house are got when the Liddels marry and carefully kept, cleaned and polished ever

since. In the mid thirties they purchase an electrically powered vacuum cleaner, and nearly thirty years later a refrigerator and washing machine. By the seventies it is evident that the sitting room needs a new carpet – they can no longer turn it round so that the worn parts are hidden by furniture.
"I am loth to dip into our savings," says Mr Liddel, "since the cost of living is increasing at a rate faster than our pensions, and despite what Harold Wilson says this trend will continue, since the blighter will not tackle the problem at the root. But a new carpet is essential. Shall we consider letting the bedroom? If I hunted the barrows for a wee secondhand fridge and hot-plate and electric kettle we could turn it into a bed-sitting room."
"Oh dear! Would they not need to come into the kitchen?"
"That would be subject to negotiation. And remember, we need take in nobody who strikes us as unsuitable."

So Mr Liddel, who once did unpaid secretarial work for his branch of the Transport and General Workers Union, writes on a plain postcard that a small bed-sitting room with homely atmosphere is available for £5 per week c/o Liddel, 51 Minard Road, use of shared bathroom and kitchen between stated hours subject to negotiation, and two minutes' walk to nearest launderette. On payment of half a crown this is displayed in the nearest newsagent's window. The first to respond is a smartly dressed man who calls late next evening when the Liddels are about to have supper.
"Well now!" he asks briskly, "What can you show me?"
Mrs Liddel ushers him into the bedroom with a meekness which is half pretence, for she is very proud of how neatly they have fitted everything in. The stranger glances round and says, "A lot smaller than I expected for the price. Never mind, this is a good district, I'll take the room. I'll only want it for a fortnight – you don't mind?"
"Oh no!" says Mrs Liddel thankfully, for there is

something about the man she does not like. He steps to the door, closes it, opens it and rattles the knob saying, "Where's the key?"

"I'm afraid it hasn't got one – the tenants before us must have lost it and we never felt the want of it – all the other doors have keys."

"Hm! That isn't exactly satisfactory now, is it? Five pounds a week for a room without a key! I'll tell you what I'll do. I'm starting work with a firm of locksmiths. Tomorrow or the day after I'll put on a really good mortise lock. Don't worry about the labour – I won't charge you for that. You won't even need to pay the full price of the lock, I'll give you a trade discount of thirty-three and a third per cent. The cheapest you'll pay for a good quality mortise lock is seven pounds ten shillings, two-thirds of which is a fiver – exactly my first week's rent. How about that?"

Mrs Liddel is appalled to hear herself murmuring, "Thank you."

"Don't mention it. Well, I've had a hard day and feel like an early night," says the man, removing his coat and jacket in one piece and casting them over the bed foot, "Don't wake me tomorrow. I'll probably be up and out before anyone else has opened their eyes."

"But your luggage!"

"I travel light. I'll get what I need tomorrow," says the man, removing his necktie.

"I'd better introduce you to my husband – he's in the kitchen."

"No introductions tonight!" says the stranger firmly, unbuttoning his shirt and walking toward Mrs Liddel until she retreats before him into the lobby. "Tomorrow will be time enough!" and he closes the door on her.

Mrs Liddel enters the kitchen and tells her husband of this. He says, "Was that wise?"

"I'm *sure* it wasn't wise!" she says, almost tearfully. "I don't want a lodger who goes to bed without even brushing his teeth."

"Did he tell you the name of the locksmiths he'll be working for?"
"No. I wanted to ask who they were but it didn't seem polite."
"I'll have a word tomorrow with that lad!" says Mr Liddel darkly, "Thank goodness you didn't give him the key to the front door."
They eat Welsh rarebit on toast with a cup of warm milk, then Mrs Liddel cleans up and sets the table for breakfast while her husband uses the bathroom, then she uses the bathroom and follows him to bed. She lies as still as possible beside him till three in the morning then says, "I can't sleep for worrying."
He says, "Nor can I."
She rises and makes two cups of cocoa. They drink them with an aspirin pill which they think good for nervous states, then they sleep soundly till half-past ten. They have never wakened so late since their youngest daughter was teething.
"Perhaps he's left for work?" says Mrs Liddel hopefully.
"We'll soon see!" says her husband. He washes, shaves and dresses with even more care than usual, then knocks firmly but quietly on the bedroom door. No answer. He opens it. The door opens inward but not far, because the bed is behind it. Peering round the edge Mr Liddel's eyes meet those of the stranger who lies on the quilt in his trousers, vest and stockings, looking straight across the top of a paperback book in his hand which has an indecent picture of a woman on the cover.
"Now you know why paying guests prefer doors with keys," says the stranger, smiling unpleasantly. Mr Liddel is too embarrassed to reply.

He closes the door, returns to the kitchen and after an hour of closely reasoned thought returns to the bedroom, knocks once loudly and enters with a firm tread. He says, "It is customary for paying guests to give rent in advance."

"But your wife and I agreed that ..."
"My wife agreed to nothing – it was you who did all the talking. If you are not prepared to observe customary procedures I will not tolerate your presence here."
"Are you suggesting I am a cheat?" cries the stranger indignantly.
"I suggest nothing because I know nothing!" says Mr Liddel steadily, "I know neither your name, nor occupation, nor antecedents, nor destination. You may be a cheat. You may be an honest man. The burden of proof lies with you."
The stranger sighs then says frankly, "Mr Liddel, it is clear that you and I have kicked off on the wrong foot. I feel it will be better if I seek accommodation elsewhere."
"I agree."
"However, I don't see why I should be penalized for a lack of communication between you and your wife. It may take several days for me to find a room as convenient as this at such unexpectedly short notice."
"You may stay here rent-free for one more night but no longer!" declares Mr Liddel, and next morning the stranger vanishes taking nothing with him but a bathroom towel, leaving nothing but some stains on the bed-sheets and the pornographic book.

Mr Liddel spends an hour tearing the book into small pieces and flushing them down the lavatory pan – if he put it in the midden a cleansing worker might find it and think a tenant of the close had been reading it.
"Shall we take the postcard out of the shop window?" asks Mrs Liddel after airing the bedroom and changing the sheets.
"Goodness me, I forgot it was still there!" says Mr Liddel, astonished. The doorbell rings.

Outside a whimpering little girl is held up with difficulty by a woman who seems not much bigger, and who says, "Is this the place that has the room?"

Mrs Liddel is so full of a wish to take the child into her bathroom and wash it that she does not answer until the question is repeated.

"Yes!" she says, glad to feel her husband looming behind her, "But it's too small for more than one lodger. Look!" She opens the bedroom door to prove she is telling the truth. The small woman not only looks but edges inside and gives a cry of delight: "But this is a great wee room! I've no seen a room as nice as this for years – it's got everything! Look at the wee fridge! And that picture of a horse! And that lovely quilt on the bed! My man will like this fine."

"We are not prepared to let so small a room to a family of three," says Mr Liddel heavily, "It would be fair to neither the family nor ourselves."

"We're very *quiet* people," explains Mrs Liddel anxiously.

"Oh we're quiet people too!" cries the small woman, "And we're in a basement in Cessnock just now and it's damp, dead damp and Theresa has this cough which won't go away and a lovely clean room like this is just what we need and MacFee my man is a real hard grafter out all day and half the night you'll hardly ever see him *please* can we *please* can we stay I mean oh Mister what if Theresa died I don't think she'll ever get better in that place and nobody wants a couple with a wee wean och Mister be a sport!"

Mr Liddel is alarmed to find three female faces looking up to him, his wife anxiously, the small woman eagerly, the small girl (who has fallen silent) with open-mouthed astonishment. He clears his throat but it brings no ideas. At last he says, "You may stay here for a week – or a fortnight at most – while you search for alternative accommodation of a more suitable nature. But the rent, the rent will *not* be five pounds, it will be … it will be six! In advance!"

"Oh thanks Mister that's great I'll just run off now and we'll come in an hour or two it's a great relief getting a room in a nice quiet clean place for a change I don't think

we'll ever find a more suitable place than this cheerio see you later!"
She leaves. The Liddels stare at each other.
"The arrangement I proposed was a purely temporary one," says Mr Liddel, "Did I not make that plain?"
"Oh yes!" says his wife, nodding, "But I'm not sure she took it like that."

After dark that evening the mother and child return with a small man who shakes Mr Liddel's hand and a bigger man who stands behind the small man, watching. "Thanks a million, you won't lose by this," says the small man, "My pal here is helping with the flitting. Mum's the word – you won't hear a thing."
Mr Liddel watches from the kitchen doorway with Mrs Liddel keeking round his arm as the men deftly, swiftly, almost furtively carry into the bedroom old suitcases tied with rope and a variety of bulging sacks, some hessian and some plastic. When the bedroom door is finally closed with all the luggage and visitors inside, the Liddels shut themselves into their kitchen. Mrs Liddel prepares supper. Mr Liddel sits at the table, drums his fingers on it then says ruminatively, "I wish our paying guests would tell us their names and occupation, discuss procedures for sharing the bathroom, and pay their rent in advance. Shall I go and talk to them about it?"
"Perhaps not tonight – let them settle in first," suggests Mrs Liddel, spreading mashed sardines on buttered slices of hot toast. While eating these they gradually hear a faint slithering rustle. It comes from the bottom edge of the kitchen door. In little jerks the point of something brown and triangular is creeping across the linoleum, growing larger as it advances. Mrs Liddel shudders with dread. Her husband slowly rises, goes to the door, stoops, grips the point of the thing between thumb and forefinger, pulls the whole of it out and lifts it up. It is a cheap envelope with six crumpled pound notes inside.

"Goodness!" sighs Mrs Liddel thankfully, "It just goes to show."
"Show what?"
"That if you leave people alone they usually do the right thing."
"Mibby. Time will tell."

Before dawn next day the Liddels are wakened by their front door stealthily opening and closing. Seconds later departing footsteps sound from the street.
"That'll be him going to work," says Mrs Liddel, "He must be on an early shift."
She suspects she hears two pairs of departing men's feet but is not sure of this and has no wish to alarm her husband. "Mhm!" says Mr Liddel who suspects the same thing and has no wish to alarm his wife.

That morning the only sign that the Liddels have guests are three visits from enquiring neighbours. At one o'clock a strong smell of frying spreads through the house from the bedroom. At two Mr Liddel goes a thoughtful walk with the dog and ten minutes later Mrs Liddel taps the bedroom door. After a while it is opened wide enough to show an inch-wide vertical slice of face with an eye and corner of mouth in it.
"Is something wrong?" asks the mouth. Mrs Liddel had meant to ask that. Instead she says, "When would you like to use the bathroom? For a bath, I mean."
The small woman is so astonished she opens the door wide enough to show her whole face saying, "I thought you didnae want us outside this room."
Mrs Liddel blushes because this is almost true. She says, "Will I put the immersion heater on? You can have a bath in forty minutes."
"Aye. Sure. Thanks a lot."
"And would you mind raising the blinds and opening the curtains?" asks Mrs Liddel, noticing the woman is fully clothed, "Three neighbours noticed they were shut this

morning and called to ask if Mr Liddel or me was ill. You needn't be afraid of people looking in from the street when the blinds and curtains are open – the lace half-curtain and rhododendron make that impossible."
"Sorry, I didnae know. I'll open them now."
While the woman does this Mrs Liddel peers in and sees the wee girl sitting on the bed staring at her with an astonishment she shows to everyone but her mother. She wears a frilly nylon party frock much too big for her, and most surfaces in the room are covered with a huge variety of cheap colourful children's clothing. Mrs Liddel wonders if the mother has spent the day dressing and undressing her daughter like a doll. She says carefully, "Mr Liddel has gone for a walk in the park – would you like a cup of tea?"
"Oh yes!"
"On Thursdays Mr Liddel changes his library book. He won't be home till five. Would your wee girl like to play on the kitchen floor? I keep it very clean."

Under the influence of strongly sweetened tea and Mrs Liddel's talent as a listener the small woman explains that her name is Donalda, that MacFee her man is a scrap merchant, that he is not Theresa's father.
"Oh?" says Mrs Liddel.
"No," says Donalda, "Definitely not. Do you like sex?"
"It is not something I'm able to talk about," says Mrs Liddel gently.
"I'm not surprised – it's not a nice thing. In fact it's nasty. I hate it most of the time. MacFee's different – he's very keen on it. He'd thump me if I didnae give it to him once a week. I wonder if he does it the right way. I mean, if that's all there is to it why is there all this fuss about it?"
"I've sometimes wondered that," admits Mrs Liddel.
"Still, give sex its due – I wouldnae have met MacFee if it hadnae been for sex."
"Oh?"
"No. You see I was once a very bad girl – a real hard case.

I went on the streets – know what I mean?"
"I think so."
"The SS had cut my money and were after Theresa so I parked her with my mammy who's a very decent spud if you don't try her too often, then I went to Bath Street and sort of stood about. Some other lassies were doing it too but they were bigger than me so I kept well away from them. Then a guy comes up and says 'Hiya honey how's tricks? Where we gonna go?' He wasnae a Yank, he just talked that way. I says 'I don't know where to go. Do you know a place?' He says 'Deed a do' and takes me round a corner into a lane, then he pushes me into a doorway and starts acting like a lunatic. He slaps me real hard and says 'Don't scream or I'll murder you! Who are you and what do you mean? What do you mean?' Then he slaps me again and says 'Who's your man?'"
"Oh no!" cries Mrs Liddel, who has heard nothing so appalling. Donalda is pleased by this reaction. She says, "Well of course I was bubbling and greeting but I was too feart to scream so I says 'I'm nobody! I'm nothing! I don't mean anything at all! I don't have a man!' That made him madder than ever. He says 'How can you be nobody when you're taking bread out of decent people's mouths? My woman's a professional and you're nothing but a stupid cheap wee amateur, I hate you!' and he slaps me a lot more. And I girn and greet and say I'm sorry and promise if he lets me go away I'll never come back and never do it again. He says 'Life is not so simple as that hen. The polis are pals of mine. If I call the cops and charge you with soliciting they'll put you in jail.' So I beg and plead till he says he'll give me another chance, then he takes me to Mrs Mitchel."
"Who was she?"
"She lived near the start of Parliamentary Road," says Donalda, "I was to bring guys to her place and she'd lend me a bedroom and handle the money. She helped me tart myself up a bit, then he took me back to Bath Street.
"Well, the next guy who comes along says 'How about

it, dearie, are you game?' I say 'Yes Mister Sandilands,' because he was my old history teacher. He says 'Oh God, Donalda *you* aren't doing this are you? Go home to your mother, girl!' I says 'I'd like to Mr Sandilands but it's no possible and I really need the money.' He looks from side to side then slips me four quid and says 'You shouldnae be here and neither should I but I'd like to see Lorraine. Do you know if Lorraine's around?' I says 'No I just started tonight,' so he groans and rushes away. Next second the man who slapped me is beside me taking the four pounds off me. He says 'Four pounds for two minutes chat is nice work, doll. Maybe you've talent. Try leaning against the wall with your legs crossed.'

"Well, the next guy who comes along is MacFee who says 'Have you a place?' I say 'Yes, near the start of Parliamentary Road.' He says 'I know that place. I have wheels. Let's go.' He takes me round the corner to his van. I get inside and he drives to a place near Parkhead Cross. 'Oh God!' I think, 'another lunatic!' He takes me up to a room and does it to me, then says it was very nice and did I like it too? 'Oh yes!' says I, 'Lovely. But can I please have some money now?' 'Before we discuss that I think we should eat something because I feel distinctly peckish,' he says, 'There's the cooker, there's the sausages, there's the eggs. Do your best.' Well I was starving, really starving, so I made a really big fry-up. I fried nearly everything I could see because I'm thinking 'If I get nothing else out of him at least I'll get a decent feed.' I use half a pound of margarine and most of a white pan loaf. When we've scoffed it he says 'You are a first-class cook. You fry like a duck takes to water.' I ask him for money again and he says 'I will not deceive you. I *have* money – a lot of money – but I need it for petrol because in my business I must keep on the move. But there are more important things in life than money. Why do *you* want money?' he says. I tell him about Theresa and he says 'The man's back is broad.

Let's pick her up.' So he drives us to my Mammy's house, we pick up Theresa and that's that. I've kept well away from Bath Street ever since. MacFee is not a bad soul. He never gives me money but if I need something he always manages to get it, eventually."

Mrs Liddel rests her head on her hand for it feels heavy with the news inside. She is so stupefied by this news that she lets slip a sentence which sounds like a judgement:

"You're not married."

"Oh I'm married!" says Donalda glumly. "Married for three years, though I havenae signed anything. I wouldnae mind a real wedding with a white dress and organ and cake and confetti – it would be a day to remember but who would pay for it? *The man's back is broad*. I wonder who he was talking about? There was nobody in the room but him and me."

"I think he was referring to himself," says Mrs Liddel cautiously.

"But MacFee's back isnae broad – or no very."

"I think he meant he was able to carry burdens."

"So MacFee thinks me and Theresa are … That's not fair! I don't like that! MacFee is a decent enough provider but it's me who always finds us places to stay, especially nowadays when he's in trouble *Oh!*"

Donalda claps a hand over her mouth, removes it and says, "I shouldnae have said that."

After a long pause Mrs Liddel says faintly, "You'd better tell me about it."

"I will. MacFee would thump me if he knew but you are definitely not a clype – you're a decent spud, like my Mammy. Anyway, MacFee is very good at stripping lead and copper and zinc and iron from old factories and houses that are going to be demolished – folk pay him to do that, and when work is short he never goes on the burroo. 'If I registered with them I'd be done for,' he says, so he sometimes takes stuff out of places whose owners arenae easy to contact and mibby don't want it taken away. I'll give you an example. Like, he sees this old tractor in the corner of a field he keeps passing – it's been there for years so he goes there one night with his brother-in-law (no my brother – his sister's husband's brother) and they take it to bits and go off with it. But someone sees the number of the van, so there are enquiries. Personally, I think the brother-in-law shopped him, but never mind. Everywhere we stay for a while the police come sniffing around and we have to move on. I'll hate having to leave this place. As soon as I saw you and your man in the lobby out there I felt *safe*. I havenae felt safe for years. But maybe they'll no find him here, or not for a long time. Anyway, thanks for the tea and chat, it's fairly cheered me up. Do you think the bath-water's ready?"

Mrs Liddel is so overwhelmed by this story that when her husband returns she cannot repeat a word of it and alarms him by sighing and shaking her head. She tells him when they are both safe in bed that night and then she falls asleep. He cannot sleep for he cannot now doubt that Britain is getting worse. He remembers the thirties and the prostitutes he saw when on the tramcars, especially nightshifts. Some were hard and aggressive, some gloomy and passive. None seemed happy with their work, but who ever is apart from removal men? For a while Mr Liddel ponders why men shifting furniture seem cheerier than other manual workers, with the possible exception of housepainters. He comes to no conclusion, but is sure that in the forties and fifties he saw very few prostitutes and hardly any brawls between poorly dressed youths. In those years the country was mobilized to fight Hitler or repair the damage of having done so. There was full employment, working-class leaders in the Labour Party, Tory leaders who had promised that Britain after the war would be better for everyone. But in the sixties unemployment climbed past the million mark again and has been growing with inflation ever since. Inflation, of course, has benefited those whose annual incomes increase without them having to strike: lawyers, doctors, most managements and directors, brokers, bankers, higher civil servants, the police, members of parliament, the monarchy: also electricians. For a while Mr Liddel ponders why the electrical workers are better off than miners, dockers, seamen, railwaymen, postmen. He sighs, recalling a time in the fifties when he was a loyal member of the local Labour Party. An election was approaching and the branch secretary suggested that if Mr Liddel put himself forward he might be chosen and elected. He did not put himself forward. A gas board official was elected who is now in the House of Lords. "Perhaps if I had stood I could have tipped the balance," thinks Mr Liddel, and starts imagining the Britain he would have helped to create. It would have a decent minimum wage for everyone, a sensible maximum one too. Unemployment would be abolished by forbidding all overtime work and introducing the Australian system of giving a whole year of fully paid holidays to those who have worked for seven years. Such thoughts have almost soothed Mr Liddel to sleep when he is roused by a nearby clicking.

Someone outside the bay window and very close to it is tapping discreetly on glass, the glass of the bedroom window. Mr Liddel remembers the new lodgers have no house key, so this is MacFee returning. The time is half-past one in the morning. Mr Liddel hears Donalda stealthily open the bedroom and front doors. They click shut again after what sounds like several people have crept softly through them, but he may be wrong about this. Mr Liddel knows that people who spy on others are likely to exaggerate what they hear. However, Britain is getting worse again. Mr Liddel fears he may see again before he dies the hateful things he took for granted in childhood: undernourished children in the streets;

nurses with tins begging passers-by for money to keep their hospitals running; well-fed voices explaining that the poor have caused their own poverty by being too lazy, greedy or selfish to work longer hours for less pay; unemployed youngsters fighting, even killing, because of religious differences which should not matter a damn. He is glad he belongs to the middle class, the kind who will not grow much richer or poorer through the mismanagement of the nation.

Meanwhile, what should he do? He cannot enter a police station and say, "My wife tells me our lodger tells her that her lodger's man sometimes steals scrap metal – a tractor, for example." To knowingly shelter a criminal is a criminal act, but nobody should be suspected of crime on the basis of gossip and hearsay. And if the police did investigate and arrest MacFee what would happen to the mother and child he supports? The mother would probably lose her daughter or return to prostitution or both. A queer question strikes Mr Liddel: is the bedroom next door being used just now as a brothel? Yes, that seems possible, but he has no evidence, and he has always been sorry for people who snoop after such evidence. He has not forbidden his lodgers to invite guests to their room – a landlord who made such a rule would be a tyrant. All a good landlord should expect of his tenants is quiet and orderly conduct, especially at night, and his lodgers have been as quiet as possible, in the circumstances. Tomorrow he will give them a door-key.

Having decided this a relaxation which is almost happiness pervades Mr Liddel. Cautiously he moves his large pyjamad body backwards until it touches Mrs Liddel without waking her. Instinctively she nestles close against him, placing an arm as light as a ribbon

across his waist. They both sleep.

THE BUM GARDEN

HARRY is an odd but elegant girl, strikingly tall, thin, supple and strong. This comes from solitary acrobatics in the school gymnasium where she often hangs upside-down on the wall-bars for many minutes. She normally walks on tiptoe with rapid little steps and knees close together, body and neck and head so erect that viewed from the hips upward she seems to stand still while the world slips past her. She has no conversation. Her few brief remarks are in a clear little voice which seems to arrive from a great distance. Any question which cannot be answered by yes or no she answers with a slow gloomy nod. She reads every book the tutors give her very fast, with the brooding concentration she brings to comic papers and film magazines. When asked to write essays on her reading she quickly covers many pages with lines which look like different lengths of knotted string. If told to write slowly so that her words can be read she takes half an hour to form a sentence, often stopping to consult a dictionary and ponder, so her occasional eccentric spelling reads like subversive criticism.

PRIDE AND PREJUICE IS A STUPID BOOK UNLESS YOU LICK MR DANCY.

All her readable sentences are a simple statement with one reservation, laboriously written in minute, widely-spaced capitals.

MOBY DICK IS A GREAT BOOK UNLESS YOU LACK WHALES.

HUCKLEBERRY FUN IS GREAT FUN UNLESS YOU LOCK CIVILIZED PUPIL.

"I spy intellect hia. I hope it is conscious intellect," says the headmistress. "I feel on the verge of knowing what she means."

In another child Harry's mannerisms would be thought signs of a damaged mind, but they are fascinating in a cousin of a queen. Even older girls would gladly be her friend but she treats everyone with an equal aloofness they think truly regal.

Harry is happiest when modelling clay. Her character has been shaped by two people: a mother who wanted a passive bit of female cleanness on which to exhibit some astonishingly expensive and fashionable little frocks, a nurse who worked to make her exactly that. She overcomes it all when she puts on denim overalls and grapples with a wad of cold, grey, tough but yielding muck. In her first year at school she likes the clay as wet as possible, splashing as she moulds until her surface is like the surface of the sloppy mound on the stand. One day in her second year she achieves a smooth dome, cuts a groove across it and works on each half, pinching it rough and stroking it smooth until the art tutor, delighted to see a distinct form, cries, "That is the best thing you've done! Let's pop it in the kiln."

Two days later the work has been fired and cooled. Harry takes it to the play-loft, returns to the sculpture studio and starts again.

"Are you making anotha of these?" asks the tutor. When modelling clay Harry's voice sometimes loses its distant bell-like tone and sounds almost drowsy.

"I am besotted by a dream of total privacy," she murmurs. "You cannot imagine how much a paw woman sometimes craves fo absolute, uninterrupted privacy."

Later that day she asks the headmistress if she can do her modelling in the play loft. This is the first time she has asked anyone for anything since she asked Linda to smack

her. The headmistress says, "Why not? I'm shoa Hjordis won't mind."
Hjordis is no longer a hysterical dictator who thrives by rejecting people. She allows a modelling stand and bin of clay to be brought to the loft and placed near the space where the others play. Harry starts work at once. Hjordis watches her for a while then asks, "Is that a bum?"
Harry pauses and looks at the cleft dome on the stand as if expecting it to reply for her.
"It could be fatta," says Hjordis, and goes to play with the others.

Harry makes many cleft domes, eventually using cement fondu as that dries solid without needing to be fired. She also shapes energetic waves which bend into loops or twist together like snakes, but she always returns to the serenity of domes, partly because Hjordis also likes them. "I wish you would make me five really big ones," says Hjordis, "Bums big enough to sit on. And a lot of small supporting bums, as many as you can."
"Material," says Harry.
"I'll arrange that. And I'll organize extra help too, if you want it."
Very few young artists are given such an opportunity. Harry is inspired. The five big ones she makes by herself, but shows the twins how to build up rough globes and slice them in two with a wire. With a trowel she swiftly gashes each hemisphere, and Harry smooths the surfaces of the result. Meanwhile Hjordis strides around a space cleared for the first British bum garden, sometimes stooping to mark the floor with chalk. The small domes are placed to mark the edges of a lane spiralling inward through nine revolutions and ending at a small arena protected by the five big ones.
"And now I want a HUGE bum fo the very middle!" shouts Hjordis. "A bum as big as me!"
"No," says Harry, and refuses to be persuaded. Hjordis falls back on another idea.

"Every Wednesday afta dinna the gang will come up hia, march to the middle with me in front, sit on a bum and talk about very rude things. I want you all to think very hard and come up with a very rude thing to talk about next Wednesday. Make it as sawdid as you can."

On Wednesday they march to the middle as arranged but find the central bums far too hard to sit upon. Only Hjordis insists on doing so. The rest squat on the floor and lean against theirs.

"Right! Who starts?" demands Hjordis.

Twin one, after nudging from twin two, says Ethel should be covered all over with her own poo-poo then made to lick it off.

"Very good!" says Hjordis approvingly, "Yes, that's a highly satisfactory rude idea. Next!"

Twin two's rude idea involves the assistant headmistress and is otherwise the same as twin one's. Linda says suddenly, "Wouldn't it be great if we all –" then goes white and can't be persuaded to say another word. Nobody expects Harry to speak.

"What a dull lot of wets you all a!" says Hjordis bitterly, "I have some wondaful dirty things I meant to tell you, all about Christine Keela and boy scouts and Lawd Mota Museum and the queen and Harold Wilson and President Kennedy and Marilyn Monroe, but I won't tell you a thing if that's all I'm getting from you. Anyway, yaw too young to undastand me. You don't know a thing about biology."

But the bum garden has social consequences. Older girls hear of it, make discreet enquiries, and are one at a time invited up to look. Near the door Hjordis introduces the visitor to her artist and workers, then escorts the guest round the lane to the bum centre. Both sit on cushions, nibble liqueur chocolates, smoke Turkish cigarettes and sip very strong black sweet coffee. These refreshments are served by Linda, who wears a turban and beaded Edwardian ball-gown pinned up round her to look

oriental. When she withdraws Hjordis says, "I'm afraid Linda is a bit of an eye-soa."
"Don't apologize!" says the *New Statesman* reader, "You've worked wondas. Last yia you wa an obnoxious little prat, Hjordis, and now yaw an intelligent woman who can get things done. You *a* a woman, an't you? Biologically, I mean."
Hjordis nods, willing herself not to blush.
"Then you should start seeing less of these little gels and mingle moa with yaw own age group. You won't find that easy at first. Yaw so filthy rich the othas can't help envying you a bit, but I am a socialist," says the guest, whose father is a Labour cabinet minister, "I loathe class prejudice in all its forms. You can no moa help being a millionaire than the pawest slum-child can help being a paw-pa. I am willing to be yaw friend."
If Hjordis could weep openly she would shed tears of relief, joy and gratitude. Instead she gulps and nods.

Then takes her things from the loft and never returns. Linda and the twins find it an unglamorous place without her and go back to playing in the shrubbery where they can glimpse the exciting older girls. Surveying the solitude of the loft Harry's slight sensation of abandonment is gradually replaced by a lovely feeling of power over space. She shifts all her favourite objects into the centre of the bum garden: the modelling stand, clay and cement bin, rocking horse, stuffed seagull and a bust of Garibaldi. To replace the gang she models fat, tadpole-like figures with features which resemble them. Linda's head is mostly mouth. The twins are a single body with two heads. Hjordis is biggest, with distinct breasts and a sting in her tail. The headmistress enters, watches the progress of the work for a while then says, "Since Violet Stringham and the Sickert-Newtons left I have three vacant bedrooms wha the otha gels sleep, Harriet. Shall we go and see if tha is one you would like to occupy?"
"Oh no."

"I do not wish to deprive you of a bedroom wha you have slept fo nialy faw yias, Harriet, but by sleeping so close to me you exclude yawself from many pleasant romps and pyjama parties. Is tha nobody you would like to be nia? Nobody you would like to tap to through the wall if you felt lonely at night? Most of the gels would gladly be yaw chum if you allowed them an opening. Linda and you wa once so fond of each otha."

"Oh no."

"But if you neva communicate with othas how will you learn to communicate with *yawself* Harriet? I realize that yaw art is a way of doing that, but the highest art is made through intacoss with all humanity, Harriet. At least study yaw contemporaries in the relevant publications, Harriet." Harry nods thoughtfully and the headmistress sighs. She knows that if she orders Harry to sleep in a room beside the others Harry will do so without complaint and revert to bed-wetting and peeing her knickers. The headmistress says, "I cannot let you stay lonely fo eva, Harriet. In a few weeks I will enrol three new little gels. On wet weekends they will play hia. If you awganize some games fo them, well and good. If you cannot do that, please stop them bullying each otha. If I learn that you fail to do even that I will lock this place up and you will return to pigging along with the otha gels in the sculpcha studio."

Harry prepares for the invasion by surrounding the bum garden with a wall of furniture, but also takes the headmistress's advice and studies the work of her contemporaries in international art magazines. She finds that most of her work has so far been well within the modern Euro-American art tradition and that her recent tadpole figurines are distinctly avant-garde. The magazines also stimulate new ideas. When the little girls arrive she has a use for them. On rainy days they put on waterproof boots, coats and hoods and follow her on exciting expeditions to derelict farm and factories, disused railway sidings and old overgrown quarries. Harry strides in front wearing a knapsack holding sandwiches, thermos flask, a kit of spanners, hammer, hacksaw and electric torch. She carries a spade over her shoulder. One of her followers is allowed to carry a coil of rope, the other two a crowbar. They are in search of anything Harry regards as queer and interesting. They discover, dig up or dismantle into handleable sections boulders, knotted roots and branches, balks of timber, rusted implements and machinery. In shifting these to the loft Harry provides most of the physical leverage but the united ant-like force of the smaller girls has nearly equal traction power. Hjordis in her Fortress days ruled her people through bribes and terrorism. Harry is no democrat either but rules by example. She drives her people hard but herself hardest. They have no time to bully each other. They help Harry accumulate heaps of things which give her ideas for new sculpture.

One evening after a strenuous excursion Harry is soaking in a warm bath when the headmistress enters. This she can easily do because the bathroom is between their bedrooms and has a door into each, a useful arrangement in years when Harry still needed prompting in the everyday uses of a lavatory. Ethel's manner reminds Harry of these years so she has no sense of intrusion. A more intimate intrusion follows, but Harry's formative experiences were all intrusions. When this one begins she feels she has waited a long time for it.

The headmistress says, "I am going to teach you something enjoyable. I had hoped you would learn it from one of the otha gels, because it is most fun if learned from a chum of yaw own age or slightly olda. Still, a stale old loaf is betta than malnutrition. Half the madhouses in Britain are full of people who neva learned to do this propaly. Lie comfatably back while I pop this rubba cushion unda this bit of you. Part yaw legs a little. I am now very gently poking about fo a little spot which feels

enjoyably tickly when gently stroked … Have I found it?"
After a while Harry says, "Mm."
"Does mm mean yes?"
"Mm," says Harry dreamily. She would not complain if the headmistress were much rougher,
"In a few minutes I will stop doing this and you can continue doing it for yawself. You have a very nice body, Harriet, it is beginning to bloom. Yaw body will not only look nice, it will feel nice if you stroke it in otha places. Hia … and hia … hia also … Do you eva think of things which make you tingle?"
Harry frowns more deeply than usual.
"Everybody, Harriet, has ideas which make them tingle, ideas which make stroking themselves and even stroking otha people moa fun. These ideas a to be found in litritcha, art, films, advertisements and the games we play. Some of these ideas would be harmful if taken seriously, but only stupid people take ideas seriously. The French – Germans – Russians – Irish sometimes take ideas seriously, but in England we a all liberals at heart, as wise as serpents and harmless as doves. We know that the wildest ideas a just ways of adding funny tingly feelings to a world managed by old-fashioned business methods, methods no serious person questions. Is this kind of talk boring you, Harriet?"
"A bit."
"Then concentrate on yaw own tingly little dream world and let this talkative old lady stroke you a little longa fo I too am lonely sometimes. Sex is the root of it. Miss Harmenbeck has told you in biology how babies a made, but babies a expensive! Unless you want one the wisest sort of sex is little tingly stroking games with yawself or anotha gel. Do you eva think about boys – about men, Harriet?"
"No."
"I neitha, but we should not despise, we should pity them. Naytcha created them to help women have babies, but they do that in less than a minute. By tha late teens they

have passed tha sexual peak and it is downhill all the way fo them. They cannot enjoy sex as much as women, eitha. They stay fertile longa, but it does not console them. They turn jealous and destructive, hence wife-battering, wawfare and most of what is taught as history. Some truly great men try to refawm themselves but usually make a hash of it. Paw Tolstoy. But Leonard Woolf was all right. Leonard was a good old stick."

The daydreams which make Harry tingle are about Hjordis spanking people, but are unlike what happened in the shrubbery. That event was so unexpected and so quickly over that she hardly noticed it at the time. Gradually her imagination has falsified it into something splendid with Hjordis an enthroned witch-queen ordering the twins to spank Harry in terrible ways; sometimes ordering her to spank them back. These daydreams are not satisfactory. The voices sound wrong.

Harry's mother visits the school for the second time on the day her daughter finally leaves it. She asks, "So what has my daughta learned hia, apart from keeping clean and getting out of a sports car without showing ha knickas?"
"She has learned what she wants to do with ha life. She will be a sculptress. She will achieve fame."
"Everybody's daughtas a into art, or drama, or fashion nowadays," says Harry's mother carelessly, "I rather hoped you would make a nun of ha, as you almost promised me the last time we met. Will art be the only love of ha life? Will she be capable of a husband, kids, etcetera?"
"No," says the headmistress serenely, "She will neva be a family woman. She had no propa home life befoa you brought ha hia so I had nothing to build upon. The best I could do was help ha to self-respecting self-sufficiency. She will always be eccentric and lonely, but will not turn to drink, drugs or shoplifting."
"I'm glad you've straightened ha out a bit but I cannot feel grateful," says Harry's mother, "You've extracted a

small fortune from ha fatha – thank God I manage my own money. Did she *need* ha own welding equipment? Ha own pneumatic drill and rivet gun? What *use* to ha wa lessons in glass blowing?"

"Ha genius requiad them. True genius grasps in its teens the implements which mia talent acquias in its twenties. James Watt and Mozart a cases in point. Harriet will soon be very famous."

"Yes indeed!" says Harry's mother bitterly, "Ha happy and glorious in-laws will ensure that. The prospect of a sale to a national collection is bound to bring dealas flocking."

The headmistress and Harry's mother are both correct. In her first year at a great London art school the staff find they can teach Harry nothing. In the second an international art dealer says, "Let me take you unda my wing."

Harry can build austere, grotesque or threatening forms out of fibreglass, cement, metal, wood, bricks, plastic and combinations of these. She can mould a five-foot-high tooth or big toe in clay and have it carved in granite or cast in brass or stainless steel. She can cover a floor with a lattice of rusty iron rods mysteriously reminiscent of fallen branches, or with a lattice of fallen branches mysteriously reminiscent of themselves. She can fill a room with suspended tubes and aluminium sheets which tinkle and thunder at the faintest human vibration. There is no shape or assembly of shapes she cannot create or represent, apart from a life-like head or torso. The only human forms she creates are sexless, featureless dummies hanging from real pieces of gymnasium equipment. The Tate Gallery buys one of these. She sells well in the USA too, though her entries in the Venice Biennale, her retrospective in the Pompidou Centre are ignored or disdained by Italian and French art critics. Her dealer says this is because the European mainland is so bloody insular. Harry shrugs. She really does not care what people think of her work. The excitement of imagining and making it, the satisfaction of setting it up somewhere are what she lives for. She likes it to be sold, because then she need not see it again. Anything returned to her is eventually broken up to make something else, so her dealer stores everything he thinks saleable and leaves the rest in her studio until it coheres in a marketable form. Harry's indifference to her completed work, indifference to criticism, refusal to attend the openings of fashionable art shows including her own, make many intelligent folk think she too is intelligent. Only her old headmistress knows she cannot write more than her name without a lot of concentrated thought and a severe headache; that ordering a meal in a restaurant or making a snack in her studio are equally beyond her powers, though she handles dangerous industrial equipment with ease and safety. The married couple who feed her and buy for her, the secretary, accountant and dealer who handle her correspondence, money and work often tell each other, "The woman's an idiot!" yet do not mean she is foolish. They are mocking, but also acknowledging, an intelligence they think greater than their own because it is alien.

Since Harry is splendidly gaunt, related to royalty and makes weirdly fashionable objects she is photographed for glossy publications financed by art and property manipulators. Writers hired to embellish the photographs with amusing comments find the job difficult. It is hard to be entertaining about someone with no apparent sex life, social life or conversation. Judy's publicity falls into four divisions –

1 Her family connections.
2 Her studios. (In London and San Francisco she has a vast skylit loft in a converted dockland warehouse, where she lives among her constructions and equipment. Next door to each is a small luxury flat for the married couple who look after her.)
3 Her range of techniques. (This is best conveyed by camera. Harry welding, sand-blasting or casting

something has been described as Wagnerian by Bernard Levin.)

4 Theoretical twaddle about her place in the history of British art.

"Aren't you sick of being a Post-Modernist?" asks a man from the colour supplement of a Sunday newspaper. He is famous for his articles on artistic topics because he refers knowingly to famous foreigners in a way suggesting that no intelligent Briton need bother with them. He wants to annoy Harry into saying something interesting for an article to be called THE SHETLAND ENIGMA. Harry replies with a vague nod. He says, "Listen! The last truly great modern artists had reached maturity when you wa still a kid. They wa trained in a tradition which started with the Greeks, was revived by the Italians, was passed by Michelangelo to Rodin and brought to a conclusion by Moore, Hepworth, Frink, Brancusi etcetera. Do you neva envy these *truly* creative artists?"

"No."

"But to most people nowadays the new things in the galleries look like doodling! They add very little beauty or intelligence to the places wha they appia, none at all to those who see them. Does it occur to you that yaw art may be a game played for nobody's plesha but yaw own? Like doodling. Or mastabation."

"Yes."

"Does it occur to you often, or only when yaw depressed?"

Harry says slowly, "It occurred to me when you asked me about it."

"But it still strikes you as true?"

"I don't know. Ask Harvey about that."

Harvey is her dealer. He arranges all her interviews and censors the resulting articles. The journalist sighs and glances down at a list of questions unlikely to produce exciting answers, but better than nothing.

"What was yaw first major commission?"

"The bum garden."

"Eh?"

Harry explains about the bum garden.
"What became of it?"
"It's probly in the loft wha we left it."
"And could I ... could you ... could we go down with a photographa and have a look? This is impawtant! Really exciting! You say you wa seven when you made it?"
He stares hard at a space inside his head where THE SHETLAND ENIGMA has been replaced by HARRY'S BUM GARDEN.

The Georgian mansion near Bath is no longer a school, but on this warm mild May afternoon the former headmistress is delighted to take tea on the terrace with a photographer, a journalist and the most famous of her former pupils.
"Who would have thought that a staunch old liberal like me would turn Tory in her declining yias?" she asks, gazing contentedly across the pupil-less lawn, "What strange alterations I have seen! When I was a little gel England ruled a quarta of the globe, Harriet. Only a bit of Eye-a-land had got away. The Em-pie-a now has all gone, all gone, except fo a little bit of Eye-a-land, yet the golden days of my childhood in the twenties and thirties have at last returned. I neva expected that. When I made a school of the dia old place in the forties I thought I would eventually have to grapple with daughtas of coal minas and powa loom weavas befoa hobbling down at last to the village post office to collect my old age pension. What a pessimist I was! Not that I resent my yias of service to the young. I think I did you a lot of good, Harriet. I wish I had taught Hjordis the same self-sufficiency, but I dared not attempt it. She would have blabbed."
"How is Hjordis?"
"Dead. Dia me, how shocked you look! I thought everyone knew that, she hit the headlines fo six and no mistake. She was addicted to *men*, and popula ones – the most dangerous kind of man. She married a popula young brutalist stock-broka, then a student politician with

terrorist connections, then popula singas who excited themselves by eating dangerous chemicals. Hjordis ate them too and died in 1978. The twins also came to a sad end. They returned to tha people in New Zealand, one got married and the otha tried to kill ha. Fortunately they a friends again, but confined to an institution. They send me Christmas cards. And Linda writes to me. Afta two bad marriages and a publicity job and an arts degree she now lives in *Glasgow*. She and a few otha heroic souls a toiling to make the place suitable fo ... something. She and ha ilk, most of them English, work fo ... money of course, but also fo the good of the community. Linda is a very, very special sort of social worka: an exhibition offica, or fine arts advie-za, or arts administrata, or all three. And she has two lovely little gels in Dartington Hall, which is not quite as liberal a school as mine was but a lot cheapa. I'm surprised Linda has not contacted you, Harriet. She must still hold you in awe."

"Could we er –?" asks the journalist, looking at his wristwatch.

"Off you go. Harriet will escawt you to ha old haunt. You will see a difference Harriet. No jumble now to distract the eye from the starkness of yaw formations! In the seventies I perceived that the family lumba was steadily gaining value, Harriet, so I waited till I retie-ad and had it auctioned by Sotheby's. The Victoria and Albert Museum wanted the old clothes, three museums of childhood was afta the toys, but I had written to forma pupils in the States asking if they knew American collectas who might be interested. Indeed they did! A Yank took the lot, even the furnitcha and knick-knacks. I laughed and laughed and laughed. And a terribly dull pictcha I had loathed since childhood turned out to be by Corot. I do not owe my present affluence *wholly* to Mrs Thatcha's tax reliefs."

The photographer takes one look at the loft and quickly makes a phone call. Two hours later a big van arrives bringing a theatre electrician and lighting equipment. Another hour is needed to position the lights accurately; then the photographer scrambles about on the rafter beams until he achieves a wide-angle downward shot of Harry squatting cross-legged and pensive in the midst of two hundred and thirty-four bums. Each bum casts a distinct shadow on the bare planks of the floor. So does Harry, but her upturned face, hopelessly resigned to an ancient and terrible wrong, is the small tragic centre of the composition. This picture is given a double page spread in the centre of the supplement. Part appears on the cover with the title HARRY'S BUM GARDEN.

Two days later someone at the far end of a telephone wire says, "Guess who this is."

"Linda," says Harry.

"Yaw amazing Harry! Fancy you remembering my voice straight off like that afta nialy twenty yias! Listen, tha's so *much* I want to say to you and ask of you … I'm so afraid of getting emotional and being a dreadful boa … Can you put up with me fo foa or five minutes maybe?"

"Yes."

"Well first, congrats on the splendid coverage the *Sunday Times* gave you. I nialy fainted when I saw the dia old bum garden all ova the supplement. I'm in *Scotland*, Harry. I know yaw too unworldly to have television or read the newspapas but shoe-aly you've heard that Glasgow will be the European cultcha capital for 1990?"

"No."

"Well it is! So a lot of us have come hia to make the thing possible and take the curse off the place. Many intelligent people still think Glasgow is a bolshie slum full of drunks who slash each otha with ray-zas because nobody wants the ships they used to build. Well we *a* taking the curse off the place. Wia employing Saatchi and Saatchi! Yes, the firm that handles public relations fo Margaret Thatcha and the Conservative Party! How can we fail? We've also discovad a magnificent old neglected Victorian art gallery in the middle of Sauchiehall Street. The town council have owned it fo a century so nothing has apiad in it but local stuff, so now it's being splendidly renovated and wia arranging a programme of shows with a truly intanational appeal. This morning thea was a big committee meeting, and yaw name came up, and because of the *Times* thing even our pet councilla knew you wa Britain's most famous sculpta and a distant cousin of the thingmis. I was very cunning – I said not a word until they started to discuss *Can we get ha?* and at last one of them turned and asked (as they all have to eventually) *What do you think?* and I said very quietly, *She and I a quite good friends. We wa at school togetha. In fact I put the finishing touches to most of these smalla bums.* My dia, you should have seen tha faces! My standing soared like a fast lift up the Telecom towa! So they've asked me to beg and imploa you to *let them bring the bums to Glasgow.* We want to give you a whacking great retrospective hia, much bigga than the one in that ghastly Pompidou Centa (the French a so insula). Imagine this lovely curving white marble staircase, a double staircase with black marble balustas. It brings you to a vestibule whose floa is checkad marble with the bum garden spread all ova it! What otha artist has had a retrospective which starts with an installation of nialy three hundred pieces she conceived when she was seven?"

"Hjordis conceived it," says Harry and notices tears on her cheeks. Perhaps her breathing betrays this because Linda begins talking in a voice both vibrant and solemn.

"I loved Hjordis too, Harry. I loved ha as passionately as you did, though she despised me fo it. The bum garden is ha monument, Harry! You must not keep it from the world. You and I a the last of the gang, Harry, the twins don't matta now. It can't be mia coincidence that you and I a coming togetha on this thing. If I was religious I would say God wants us to do it. I'm not, so I say *fate* wants us to do it. You and I was once very good friends, Harry. Oh what went wrong?"

"Don't know," whispers Harry, surprised by how wet her

face is getting. "What does Harvey say?"
All phone calls to Harry pass through her agent's office to stop her being pestered by unprofitable business.
"He says he's enthusiastic about it if you a, Harry! The Scottish Museum of Modern Art in Edinburgh has nothing of yaws, Harry, which is ridiculous! Neitha has Glasgow or Abadeen. If you do this fo Scotland yaw bound to sell at least one may-ja-piece. We provide the venue and will pay fo transpawt and publicity, and aftawad the show can return to London and appia in a really important gallery like the Warwick or the Serpentine. Please say yes!"
"Yes excuse me headache," whispers Judy putting the phone down.

Since the separation from her nursemaid nothing shocks Harry as much as news that Hjordis is dead. Hjordis is the centre of Harry's love life. Basking drowsily in a deep bath of warm water after a hard day's work, Harry imagines erotic adventures with Hjordis in a shrubbery as big as a jungle at first, but in later years it enlarges to a planet. Harry is queen of this world, the most adored and desired person on it and also the weakest. Hjordis is the strongest and most feared. Hjordis is a wicked prime minister who has organized all the men into a cruel army and used it to seize power; but among wild scenery dwell bands of outlaws – cow girls and swamp women and pirate whores who rescue Harry from Hjordis or capture her for reasons of their own. The politics of this world appears in *Four Sisters*, the smallest but most popular of Harry's works.* Four women's shoes stand toe to heel in a square, each one cast or cut in a different almost colourless material: glass, maplewood, stainless steel and white leather. The leather shoe is real, the others modelled on it. Each stiletto heel

---

* The title was chosen by her dealer, who names all Judy's work. Most illustrated histories of modern British art show a photograph of *Four Sisters*, ascribing it to the Pop or Surrealist school. Ms Paulina Cameron, topiary adviser to the National Trust, is supervising the cultivation of a hedge shaped like *Four Sisters* for the Melcombe Priory National Heritage Museum. Visitors will be able to walk under the arches of the insteps.

pierces the toecap of the shoe behind it. Every work of art Harry made shows part of her imaginary world's enigmatic furniture, scenery or architecture. It is a world where imaginary pains produce some real ecstasy. Everyone recovers immediately from injuries, everyone is ravishingly beautiful, nobody grows old or sick or dies, and certainly not Hjordis. Always glorious and cruel, always plotting to satisfy herself but forever incapable of satisfaction, Hjordis keeps this dream world working. Harry has not seen or heard of Hjordis for over twenty years. There is no obvious reason for imaginary Hjordis to vanish because the real one dies, but it happens. The dream world becomes a reminder of death and of absence, then vanishes also. Harry cannot now imagine anyone who adores or desires her, cannot imagine anything at all.

She locks the studio door and squats on a small stool, hugging her body and rocking it to and fro. Sometimes she masturbates, but it is joyless exercise. She listens to a clear childish voice chanting *Give me somebody. Give me somebody*. It is her own voice. It is not praying to anyone, but is certainly praying. She feels nothing in the world can be done but rock and pray till she dies of exhaustion. Sleep is impossible. After several hours she hears voices mingling with her own. A muffled man's voice says her art is a childish game, like doodling or masturbation. Another slightly louder voice argues that the bum garden is a monument to Hjordis which must not be kept from the world.

Shortly after midnight she hears a voice calling faintly from a great distance. She stops praying to hear better. It falls silent, but sounds slightly nearer when she prays more quietly. Eventually she can make out the words *Harry Shetland* followed by a burst of hectic pleading. As the sun starts to rise her prayer has sunk to a whisper and the pleading is distinct, though as if shouted upward from a ground far below her:

Harry Shetland come down to me please yaw motha and

my motha wa friends! Wia the only two in this stinking hell-hole who need each otha! Oh please come down and visit me in my fortress! We'll shut everybody else out – even the twins! I've a lovely tin of delicious biscuits and all sorts of gorgeous things fo you! Chocolate and scent and a silk scarf and a little hampster in a cage shaped like a doll's house who's called Limpy Dan because one of his feet doesn't work but you can call him anything you like please come down! Please I'm so lonely!

Harry remembers a time when this pleading made her feel aloof, smug and powerful, but now the pain in it is a pain she feels through her whole body. She groans, sways dizzily and nearly faints, but is roused by a loud, commanding voice which sounds right beside her: *I want a huge bum to go in the middle, a bum as big as me!*

"Yes, I can give you that now," says Harry, suddenly knowing what to do. "Thank you Hjordis."

She yawns hugely, unlocks her door, phones an order for sandwiches and a glass of milk. She eats, drinks, then sleeps soundly. A day later, before phoning to arrange a meeting with her dealer and Linda, she stares hard into a mirror. Her appearance does not interest her, usually, but today she wants to appear as well as feel like a different woman. Her hair is cut like the fur of a sleek animal, for she hates brushing and combing. Abruptly she summons her hairdresser and tells him to shave her completely bald.

A FREE MAN WITH A PIPE

PHONE rings. Ella patiently lifts the receiver. Most of the calls she answers are for a friend who is seldom in. She says quickly, "Hello."

"Hello Jean!" says a loud eager voice, "I'm a free man."

"I'm sorry, Jean is out. She won't be back till quite late. Can I give her a message?"

She hears a sigh, then silence, then a sad little voice asks hesitantly, "Is that you, Elaine?"

"I'm Ella Warner, Jean's flatmate."

"Of course you are!" says the voice loudly, "You are Ella Warner, Jean's flatmate. We met at Jean's housewarming party and had an interesting chat. You think modern mothers allow their daughters too much freedom –"

"I don't think I said that."

"You wore a blue trousersuit –"

"A blue dress."

"I got the colour right. I'm Leo Brown and you don't remember a single thing about me."

The voice is triumphant and accusing. She says defensively, "I remember hardly anyone from that party. Why should I? It wasn't my party."

"You'll remember me when you see me, Ella. I'm coming round."

"Don't be stupid."

"I'm taking you out for a meal."

"I've just eaten."

"I'm taking you out for a drink."

"I don't like drinking, usually, and just now I'm studying. I've an exam on Monday. I don't know you and I don't think you know me."
The voice turns hard and ugly.
"All work and no play makes Jill a very dull girl indeed, Ella! What you need is a break from your routines, Ella! It will help your studies so I'll knock your door half an hour from now, right."
"I won't open it if you do."
Ella is firm about this but does not put the receiver down. She hears another sigh, and silence, and once again the sad little hesitant voice.
"Do you … know the lounge bar of The Lorne?"
"Well?"
"In half an hour I'll be having a drink there. I'll be smoking a rather unusual pipe. The bowl is carved to look like the head of a bull –"
"Oh!"
"*Now* you remember me?"
"No, but I remember your pipe."
After four seconds the voice says dully, "If you want a drink you know where to come," and the line goes dead.

Ella returns to her books but cannot concentrate on them. Why should the voice of a lonely, foolish man who wants company upset her so much? She too is lonely but likes loneliness, usually. Most people, she thinks, pay too high a price for company, married people especially. That is why she admires Jean, who for two or three years has avoided matrimony by something like promiscuity, and now talks of having a single-parent family. But Ella, who likes children, knows they are usually happier with a couple of married parents. These thoughts interfere with her studies. It is a warm evening, she needs a breath of open air, maybe a walk will freshen her. The way to the park passes the Lorne Hotel. Curiosity leads her into the lounge bar, which at that hour is almost empty. She buys a half-pint glass of cider and looks cautiously round.

The only single man sits in a corner, seemingly lost in thought. Ella is long-sighted. Removing her spectacles she sees on the table before him the unusual pipe beside an untouched half-pint glass of light ale. Though not young he is not elderly. His well-cut tweed suit is neither shabby nor ostentatiously fashionable. None of his features is notably strong or weak, but they and the whole slump of his body suggest a sad perplexity she finds attractive. His lips move slightly as if repeating past conversations.

She replaces the spectacles, takes her glass to his table and sits quietly opposite. He stares at her in a confused way, then says without enthusiasm, "Oh hullo. You made it," and adds reproachfully, "You should not have bought that drink. The treat must be on me. Waiter!" With a sweep of the arm he summons one of the bar staff and orders two whisky liqueurs. "But –" says Ella, who dislikes whisky in any form.

"No buts tonight! This calls for a celebration. You must be wondering why I asked you here."

"No."

"Surely almost total strangers don't ask you out every night of the week?"

"On the phone you sounded as if you needed to talk to someone. I thought you were lonely."

"Ella! How can you think so little of yourself? Ella, we hardly exchanged two words at that party but you have qualities men – some men – find unforgettable."

"What qualities?" asks Ella, interested but not overwhelmed. She knows most men see her as a nice young aunt.

"Oh your hair, your voice, your … the bits matter less than the way they fit together."

The waiter brings two glasses of liqueur. Leo pays him, lifts one then frowns into it as though it is far too deep. After a moment he puts it down and drinks the beer instead. It occurs to Ella that he too dislikes whisky liqueur. She says, "Is something wrong?"

"What do you mean?"
"One moment you're excited, the next you're flat and dull."
"I keep remembering a dream I had last night."
Ella, highly excited, cries, "I had a dream last night! Can I tell you about it?"
"Go ahead."
As Ella talks her mild face grows vivacious. He watches it closely, without pleasure.
"I was walking along a road in the country, it was a dull ordinary day and I was worrying about my exams when I suddenly felt this warm golden light shining down on me from behind. I didn't dare turn and look but I knew, I *knew* that a huge golden aeroplane was sweeping after me in the sky and the warm happy feeling came from that. I knew the aeroplane was the Concorde."
Leo drinks the last of his beer and says, "Well?"
"That's all but it left me feeling happy all day. What did you dream?"
"There was a stone head on my sitting-room floor, about six feet high, a piece of a statue of an Egyptian king. It should have been hollow but it was stuffed full of dirty rags and I was trying to pull them out through the mouth with my hands and then I realized there was … the corpse of some animal in the middle. I couldn't go on. I tried to cram the rest of the dirt back in but it wouldn't go in."
He pauses then says with vast indignation, "The whole room was an *utter mess!*"
She shudders and says, "No wonder you're depressed."

There is a change of feeling between them. Her sympathy has cheered him and she, seeing this, relaxes and murmurs, "I wonder if it means I'll pass the exams."
"What are you talking about?"
"My dream."
"Your dream means sex."
"Oh no!"
"Wait a bit!" he says, raising a forefinger. "You're walking along a dismal ordinary road worrying about exams.

That's ordinary life, right? Then you feel something warm and beautiful coming after you, something you're afraid to face. It's called the Concorde and you know what Concorde is French for, don't you?"

"Concorde is a place in America," says Ella, seeing a way out, but he smiles and talks over her like a firm but patient teacher: "Concorde is the French for *togetherness*, Ella. That dream is prophetic, Ella. It tells what the future holds if you have the courage to face it. I think that coming here tonight shows you *have* the courage to face it."

She is unwilling to be impressed by this and says, "What does your dream mean? Is it about sex too?"

"Let's change the subject," he suggests briskly. "What do you do? Are you a student?"

"A nurse. But I'm studying to be a physiotherapist."

"I know about that. Deep breathing. Physical jerks."

"The main thing is relaxation," says Ella, and adds dreamily, "Deep, controlled relaxation … I think I may be good at it."

"Why?"

"Well, we have a little boy with really bad asthma. It's so bad he's afraid to sleep at night. The doctors put him on steroids, but of course they couldn't keep him on these for ever – they destroy certain glands if you do – and now he's as bad as he was before. Do you know, even in his worst panics I can almost get him to breathe perfectly easily? I make him lie down flat – it's almost impossible to get asthmatics to do that – and with a little light massage I get him breathing slowly and evenly and deeply, and in ten minutes he's in a perfectly normal sleep. I've tried to teach the boy's mother to do this for him but she can't. She loves him, she'd do anything to make him well, but when she talks to him or touches him his muscles tighten. He doesn't trust her – doesn't trust her physically."

After a moment Leo says defensively, "I'm quite good at my job too."

"Yes?"

"Sales representative for Quality Fabrics. I realize that means nothing to you. I suppose you think travelling salesmen are a dying breed."

"No! Why should they be?"

"Because of chainstores, supermarkets, new shopping centres. Well let me tell you, we are NOT a dying breed. That sort of competition has done nothing but weed out weaklings. Survivors like me are travelling further and earning more than ever. When I took on this job Quality Fabrics gave me the central lowlands. Now all Scotland is my province."

He stares at her challengingly. She responds with a small smile which becomes bright when she thinks of something to say.

"You must pass through some lovely scenery."

"So I am told."

"But surely –"

"Ella, I am the best driver I know. In ten years I have not once had an accident that could be traced to my negligence. While driving I keep my eyes on the road and my mind on – not just the car ahead of me – but the car *in front* of the car ahead of me. I travel north to Thurso, east to St Andrews, south to Berwick, and for all the scenery I see I might be driving backwards and forwards through the Clyde Tunnel."

"That's terrible!"

"It never struck you that driving should be enjoyed for its own sake?"

"Never."

"Well, I enjoy driving for its own sake. That's why I'm good at it. Using a highly sophisticated implement which every year slaughters thousands, I am constantly achieving and reconciling two different things, maximum safety and maximum speed. This achievement absorbs my whole personality, I am glad to say. Too many folk nowadays do nothing with their personalities but flaunt them."

After a pause she says, "I agree."

Again they notice he has impressed her and again he grows more cheerful, clinking his glass against hers and saying *"Skol!"*

She smiles and sips as little as possible to avoid grimacing. He gulps his fast, perhaps for the same reason, and she feels inside her a definite tickle of amusement. She finds him entertaining, though perhaps not in the way he wants to be.

"You see," he says, with an air of reckless expansion, "I'm a free man. I choose my own hours and my own itineries, nobody sets me a routine. A routine job must be hell on earth. You must know that, working where you do."

"But I like my work. Hospitals are the best places in the world."

"They're terrible places!"

"They are not!" says Ella, angered into boldness, "If anyone throws paper on a hospital floor a cleaner picks it up. If an old man wets his bed there's somebody to wash him and change the sheets. If somebody is in pain and dying we have drugs to make them comfortable. Outside hospitals the only safe people are the rich people, but in hospitals nobody is neglected or starved or made to do work they're not fit for. There's always someone on duty, someone responsible in charge."

"How old do you think I am?"

"… Forty?"

"Thirty-five," says Leo in an injured voice, "And I have never once set foot in a hospital or visited a doctor. Yes, I'm fit."

"But not relaxed."

"Of course I'm relaxed."

"Why do you breathe like that?"

"Like what?"

"Quick and shallow instead of deep and slow."

He looks at her in a haunted way and does not reply. She says conversationally, "You've gone dull and flat again."

"Do you talk like this to everybody?" he asks in his ugliest voice.
"I'm afraid so."
"You must find it hard to keep a boyfriend."
"I do. Yes."
"I'm trying to help you, Ella, but my God you're making it hard for me ... My divorce came through today."

After a moment she pushes her glass towards him saying gently, "Would you mind finishing this drink?"
"Don't you like it?"
"I'm sorry. I've tried to. I'm sure it will do you more good."
He looks at it, drains it like medicine, coughs a little then says, "Ask me anything you like."
"But –"
"Don't worry, you won't be probing a wound. We've been separated for years."
"I see. Did you –"
"If you want to know if I was unfaithful to her or she to me the answer is no. In both cases. As far as I am aware. But we were incompatible. She kept telling me I got on her nerves and after a while this got on my nerves."
"How did you get on her nerves?"
"Well, when I got home from work in the evening I was exhausted. I've told you why. I was holding down more and more of Scotland for Quality Fabrics. I drove an average of 350 miles per day. Her office job must have left her with plenty energy for as soon as she saw me she started to *talk*. Telling me things. Asking questions. And she insisted on being answered. A simple 'yes' or 'no' or 'that's nice' wasn't good enough. She wanted detailed discussions when all I wanted was a quiet meal then an hour by the fire with the newspaper followed by a spot of television. What did I know about hats, shoes and the neighbour's dog? Why should I care about whether new wallpaper should be pink to harmonize with the carpet or green to contrast with it? Life is too short."
"She sounds as if she loved you. Or wanted to."

"If she'd shut her mouth for a couple of hours I could have loved her back, or sounded as if I did. But she kept driving me out of the house. To pubs like this, as a matter of fact, though I am definitely not a drinking man. A half-pint of lager is *my* normal limit."

"Did you talk to people in the pubs you visited?"

"Yes of course. Talk is easy in a pub, it happens without thinking. Before I married I talked to the wife all the time in pubs. But home should be different, it should let a couple enjoy silence for a change. I once read an article on how to make a success of your marriage, and one thing it said was *never let your wife feel you take her for granted*. That made me laugh. If you can't take your wife for granted who can you take for granted? Everybody else you meet – especially the women – you've got to be polite and entertaining, you've got to show yourself and sell yourself to them like I show fabrics to a potential buyer. Like I'm showing myself to you just now. But surely a wife should grow out of needing that treatment."

Ella frowns, purses her lips like a doctor considering a case then says, "No children?"

"None."

"You should have adopted one."

"Ella, I notice you are keen in the mercy and kindness approach to existence which makes you hard and insensitive at times. I know there are many helpless, unloved children in the world but would it be fair to get one in like a paperweight to stop an unlucky marriage blowing away?"

Ella says stubbornly, "Children are dying from lack of love and your wife had more of it than you could take."

"You're a hard woman, Ella," he says sadly, "A hard, hard woman."

"I'm sorry, Leo," she says with real regret, "I don't mean to be."

"That is the first time you've spoken my name."

"Oh?"

Her hand rests on the table. He places his own on it, saying softly, "Come home with me, Ella. We're on the

verge of saying important things to each other. A hotel is no place for genuine ... concord."
"Oh. Well ... all right, just for an hour, but it mustn't be any longer, Leo."
Her voice has the comradely sound of a private soldier in the great sex war talking to another. Unluckily Leo, being a man, thinks he belongs to the officer class.

He stands, waves to the bar and shouts, "Waiter! Two more whisky liqueurs!"
She stares at him. He snarls, "You pity me, don't you? That's why you're ready to come back with me. I'm one of your orphans."
She whispers fiercely, "Sit down! People are looking at us and I don't want a whisky liqueur."
"Then give it to me out of the kindness of your heart like you gave the last one.
"Why do you sneer at kindness?"
"It is insulting to man's essential nature."
"What is man's essential nature?"
"I don't know."
"You want me to be nice to you as if you were doing me a favour."
"I want to be admired!" cries Leo wildly, "Is that too much to ask?"
"Admired for what?"
"If you see nothing else in me you might at least notice I am made in the image of God!"
After this outcry he slumps into gloom again, adding lamely, "If you had a religion you might."
"Have you a religion?" asks Ella, who now has no idea of what they are discussing.
"No."
"Excuse me, sir, you have to leave," says the waiter. Leo is astonished.
"Why?"
"You're making too much noise. And swearing upsets the ladies."

"I didn't swear! We were discussing religion."
"That can lead to trouble sir. You'd better leave."
With quiet dignity Leo takes his pipe from the ashtray and rises saying, "Goodnight. You are not losing a regular customer, but you *may* be losing someone who might have *become* a regular customer."
Ella, beside him, has a fit of the giggles which her strongest efforts cannot quell before they stand on the pavement outside. He says, "You thought that funny."
"I'm sorry."
"Goodnight."
"Don't you want me to come with you?" she asks. He stares amazed into her calm friendly face, then smiles gratefully and seizes her hand.

He leads her to a terrace overlooking the park, a terrace built for the rich of the previous century. Wealth still resides there. They come to a building like a church with broad steps to a high door. The door is glass. Ella sees through it a refreshingly antiseptic floor of big black and white chequered tiles, a brown clay urn with huge spiky leaves sprouting from it, the door of a lift. Leo takes her in to the lift. Leo's apartment is a large sitting room with a glossy lavatory and small, well-equipped kitchen. The furnishings are the sort found in expensive modern hotels and fill Ella with a sense of desolation almost greater than poverty would. She thinks a huge stone head on the floor could only improve the place. However, she says, "How clean and tidy everything is."
"I can't stand mess," says Leo compacently and busies himself in the kitchen. Ella looks round in a puzzled way, seeking (though she may not be aware of this) a clue to his childhood or to a previous loving connection. A bookstand holds nothing but car manuals and trade journals. The only wall decoration is a large map of Scotland mounted on a board and stuck full of red-headed pins, so she studies that.
"My territory!" he calls from the kitchen. There are hardly

any pins inside the boundaries of the four great cities. Most are stuck in obscure little towns a few miles from these, towns which in recent years have been occupied by prosperous commuters and retired people. In the highlands some pins pierce the main tourist resorts, and there is a denser sprinkling through townships near the English border. One yellow-headed pin occupies a southern patch of brown moorland. She peers closely to discover the reason for its uniqueness.

"That marks the spot where mother nature once seduced me," says Leo, bringing in a tray of tea things and placing it on a low table, "I suppose you want to hear all about that."

"Oh yes please!" says Ella. For her own amusement as much as his she acts like an eager little girl, sitting on a chair with legs tucked under her, chin on fist and mouth and eyes expectantly open. Leo switches the table light on and the ceiling light off to give the room an intimate atmosphere. He sits on the sofa, pours two cups of tea, hands her one and says, "You see –"

He finds he cannot talk without referring to the map so rises and goes to it, switching on the ceiling light again. "I was driving along the coast from Stranraer one Saturday, just about here. In those days I got bonuses for weekend work. The day was hot, the road busy, I'd had an exceptionally hard week so instead of driving up to Ayr I turned inland north of Ballantrae. This line marks a thirdclass road. You can see why I thought it might be a short cut. Anyway, I ran up this twisting valley, and passed some old farms and came up onto these moors. There was a gate across the road (it's not marked) – I suppose to keep sheep from wandering. So I had to leave the car to open it. Otherwise nothing would have happened because the air was not just warm, it had little fresh breezes blowing through it and I could hear two or three of those birds going poo-ee poo-ee in the distance ... What do you call them?"

"Lapwings," says Ella.

"No. Curlews," says Leo, "That's the name. Curlews. Anyway, I shut the gate behind me and drove on for a mile or two and reached a second gate, where the yellow pin is. But instead of just opening it and driving through I lay back on a bank of heather for a puff at the old pipe. There was not a human being, or a telegraph pole, or another car than my own in sight, only heather and ferns and this hill opposite, with an old house among some trees at the foot of it. Everything was warm and … brilliant, and calm. I could hear a cricket near by, in the grass. Do you know what I did?"

He stares at her accusingly. She shakes her head. He speaks on a note of astonished indignation.

"I fell asleep! I fell asleep and woke up ninety minutes later with a splitting headache and a fit of the shivers! I was totally behind schedule. I got to Dalmellington all right but I was too late for Kilmarnock and Strathaven. That little nap of mine cost Quality Fabrics two hundred pounds' worth of business. It was a lesson to me."

"Were they angry?" asks Ella softly.

"Who?"

"Quality Fabrics."

"Certainly not! That loss is my estimate, not theirs. And it would need more than one accident of that kind to damage a man with a record like mine. But it showed I was human, like the rest. If I hadn't pulled myself together I could have gone to pieces entirely. Men do, in my business. Usually through drink. This yellow pin is a warning to me."

He sits beside her and sips tea. She murmurs sympathetically, "No wonder you can't relax."

He puts down the cup with a touch of exasperation.

"Ella, you haven't understood a word of what I've told you. I *can* relax, but I've chosen not to. You like routine but I'm an individualist, a *free man,* Ella. The price of freedom is eternal vigilance. June never understood this. In our three-and-a-half years of married life she never once sympathized with what I was doing for her."

"Were you doing it for her?"
He sighs and does not answer.

After a while, mainly to fill the silence, she says, "I'm surprised you haven't an ulcer."
"Perhaps I have. I get stomach pains after meals nowadays and … there's a swelling."
He puts a hand to his stomach. She sits up and says seriously, "You must see a doctor."
"I told you. I don't go to doctors."
"Let me look."
"There's nothing to see, but you can feel it I suppose." He unfastens the waistband of his trousers and leans back. She sits beside him, slips her hand in and palpates his stomach, frowning thoughtfully. She says, "I can't feel a thing."
"Lower down, in the middle."
Her fingers touch the swelling and rest on it. He murmurs, "What soft smooth fingers you have, Ella."
She murmurs, "Aren't you cunning?"
He draws her to him. She takes her hand from his trousers and removes her spectacles. They clasp and kiss. He is surprised by how easy this is. He says, "You aren't tense."
"Why should I be?"
"That talk about the suffering masses made me think you were more … rigid."
She smiles. Men are always surprised to find she isn't rigid. They undress and move to the bed. There is a lack of urgency and embarassment which amazes him. He says, "You're special."
"I'm not."
They clasp and kiss again. He murmurs, "Woman … is the downfall of the weak man but the relaxation of the warrior."
"What a silly thing to say."
"Napoleon said it."
"Then he was silly."
"Can I see you tomorrow?"
"Yes. I might wake up here."

"But tomorrow night?" he pleads.
"I think ... maybe."
"And the day after?"
"I've examinations then."
A little later he is so delighted that he cries, "June you're beautiful. You're so beautiful June."
She hits him hard on the side of the head.

She gets up and starts dressing. He crouches on the bedside, sucking the knuckles of a clenched hand. Her indignation lessens when she has fastened her skirt because what moves her most in this world is pity. She says, "I'm sorry I hit you Leo but you've been thinking about another woman all evening."
He does not move. She looks at him and says, "I'd better go now, hadn't I? It's quite late."
He does not move. She finishes dressing and says, "I really am sorry I hit you Leo but I'd better get back to my studies."
He does not move. She goes to the door, opens it and hesitates, trying to think of a more encouraging farewell. At last she says, "I admire you Leo. Really I do ..."
He does not move. Truth and the silence compel her to add, "... in some ways, just a little. Goodnight."
She leaves.

He huddles a long time on the bedside then starts glancing toward the telephone in a furtive way, as if it is an enticing drug with vile after-effects. He stands, pulls his trousers on, sits beside the phone and dials. A little later he hears a woman say, "Hello?"
He answers in his small, hesitant voice.
"Hullo June ... I wondered if ... I thought that after the legal business this afternoon perhaps you felt a bit ... lonely?"
"I can't help you any more Leo," says the woman sensibly, "It's too late. I'm sorry you feel lonely but it's too late to talk to me about it. Goodnight Leo."

She does not at once put the receiver down. Several seconds pass before he hears the deadening click. He keeps his own receiver pressed to his ear for another minute, slowly replaces it, lifts tobacco tin from mantelpiece, opens it and slowly fills from it the bowl of his rather unusual pipe.

CULTURE CAPITALISM

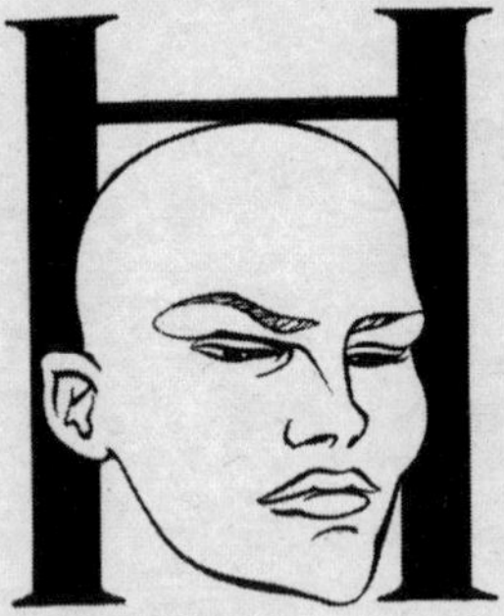

HARRY meets her dealer and Linda, who has come south to discuss Harry's 1990 exhibition in Glasgow.

"First tell me about the European Cultcha Capital thing," says the dealer. "Why Glasgow? How has a notoriously filthy hole become a shining light? Is it an advatising stunt?"

"Certainly, but we have something to advertise!" says Linda. "It all began when John Betjeman discovad Glasgow in the sixties and found what nobody had eva suspected. The city centa is a mastapiece of Victorian and Edwardian architectcha. But in those days it was unda such a thick coating of soot and grime that only the eye of a masta could penetrate it. Even moa off-putting wa the people. In those days most Scottish impoats and expoats passed through Glasgow, and the good middle bit was squashed up tight against docks and warehouses and the tenements of those who worked in them. What would visitas think of London if Trafalga Squaya was on the Isle of Dogs? If every day hordes of horny-handed men in filthy overalls percolated up and down Regent Street and half filled the Fleet Street pubs? But London is vast, so the classes segregate themselves easily and naturally. They couldn't do that in Glasgow so respectable Londonas passed through it in fia of thea lives. It is perhaps not logical fo well dressed British people to dread the working classes, but when they flagrantly outnumba us the recoil is instinctive.

"Anyway, nothing could improve Glasgow befoa all its old industries got taken out, but they have been. And befoa that happened all the people who worked in them got decanted into big housing schemes on the verge of things. So the middle of Glasgow is clean now and will neva be filthy again! The old warehouses and markets and tenements and churches are being turned into luxury flats and shopping malls and a surprising variety of very decent foreign restaurants. Which is wha we come in – I mean the English.

"You see Glasgow is in Scotland and from oua point of view Scotland is slightly like Rhodesia in the early yias of the century. Most British industry and money is in the south of England now, so it's crowded! But we English detest crowds. At heart each of us wants to be a country squia, with wide-open spaces nia oua house and grounds, and if possible a village atmosphia wha we can relax with a few like-minded friends. But a place like that costs a fawtune in England and the neara London you go the moa astronomical the fawtune gets. All the nice English villages have been bought. But by selling quite a small propaty in London you can get enough to buy –"

"Yes yes yes!" says the dealer impatiently, "I know about propaty development in the north, I own a small tax-avoidance forest near Invaness, but wha does the *cultcha* come from?"

"From the Thatcha govament," says Linda promptly, "and from Glasgow District Council. Glasgow once had the strongest local govament tha was, outside London. It owned a huge public transport system, housing schemes, docklands and lots of otha things Thatcha is allowing it to sell. Like local govaments everywha it is being steadily abolished, but since the people's elected representatives usually draw salaries until they die and get all sawts of perks *they* don't complain. Maybe they don't notice! Howeva, they want to show they can do moa than just sell public propaty to private speculatas, so they have gone in fo Cultcha with a capital C – and tourism. Commercially speaking cultcha and tourism a the same thing.

"The European Cultcha Capital notion was started by Melina Mercouri, the Greek minista fo aats. Athens had been stone-cleaned, she wanted tourists to know it, she suggested to Brussels that Athens be the first cultcha capital, then otha countries could have a shot. Nobody objected. Italy chose Florence; the Nethalands, Amstadam; Germany, Berlin; France predictably chose Paris. But being Cultcha Capital is expensive. You must advatise yawself. Put on extra shows and consats. Invite foreign guests. Stage boring receptions. Margaret Thatcha isn't keen on all that crap; anyway London has enough of it. Like a sensible monetarist she put the job up fo grabs and offad it to the lowest bidda. Bath and Edinburgh put in fo it, Cardiff, Birmingham and Glasgow: but only Glasgow gave a quiet little promise that if it got the job it would *not* ask the central govament fo cash. So Glasgow, which the Lay-ba Party has ruled fo ova half a century, was given the job by the Tory arts minista who announced that Glasgow had set an example of independent action which should be followed by every local authority in the United Kingdom. Wia funding the entaprize out of the rates and public propaty sales and sponsaship from banks, oil companies, building societies and whateva we can screw out of Europe.

"And Glasgow deserves the job! It's the headquartas of Scottish Opera, Scottish Ballet, Scottish National Orchestra, the Burrell Collection, the Citizen's Theata, the Third Eye Centa and an intanational drama festival: all of them directed and mostly administaed by the English, of course. Sometimes the natives get a bit bolshie about that but I'm very firm with them. I say very quietly, 'Listen! You Scots have been expoating yaw own people to England and everywha else fo centuries, and nobody has complained much about you! Why start howling just because wia giving you a taste of yaw own medicine?' They can't think of an ansa to that one."

"But shooali the natives have some local cultcha of tha own?" says the dealer, "What about these young paintas who've emerged? Campbell and Currie etcetera."
"The ones who did well in New Yawk? Yes, we'll put them on a show."
"Has Glasgow nothing else apart from Billy Connolly?"
"Some novels by Glasgow writas have had rave reviews in the *Times Lit. Sup.*, but I'm afraid they leave me cold. Half seem to be written in phonetic Scotch about people with names like *Auld Shug*. Every second word seems to be fuck, though hardly any fucking happens. The otha half have complicated plots like SM obstacle races in which I entie-aly lose my way and give up. As a matta of fact, Harry, I have one of these books hia to give to you! Some of it reminded me of games we once played with Hjordis."
"I'm sorry, what did you say?"

Harry, though scrupulously clean when not working, still finds dirt interesting. She stopped listening when she heard Glasgow is now a clean place; she retired mentally into the old play-loft, making occasional trips to the shrubbery. The name of Hjordis restores her wholly to the present. Linda repeats her last sentence and hands Harry a book entitled *Another Part of the Forest*. Harry stares longer at the cover design than Linda and dealer think it deserves. It shows what first seems a moonlit tropical jungle where eyes glow in the dark between vast blue-green leaves. Then Harry sees the leaves are not tropical but are hawthorn and elder and bramble leaves painted big. Deep among these leaves Harry hears her dealer ask if she wants her next retrospective to open in Glasgow?
She looks up and says, "No I'm done with retrospectives. Apart from the bum garden everything I've eva made has been shit – a waste of time – a silly game I played with myself. I don't know why others liked it, apart from you. You live by selling that sort of shit."

She is looking at her dealer and her clear distant voice

suggests neither blame nor regret. Aghast Linda is going to shout "But!" so the dealer says "Sh!"

Harry seldom talks at length and if interrupted stays silent for days. Harry says, "The bum garden was good because someone else wanted it. It was wanted by the only person who eva wanted me, too, once."

Tears stream from Harry's eyes though her face and voice stay calm and unmoved. Linda weeps in sympathy.

"But technically the old bum garden is kids' stuff. I will make it betta and bigga in polished steel and white glazed ceramic spreading through several spaces – large ones. How spacious is yaw Sauchiehall Street venue Linda?"

"Huge. Hia's a plan of it. This immense gallery opens into three equally big ones. We have two awdinri big galleries and two small ones in the cornas. Hia is the vestibule: a landing approached by the magnificent double staircase. Skylighting throughout in ceilings ova twenty feet high."

"It'll do. I'll put the shrubbery into the cornas. I've just seen how to tackle the leaves. Enamelled tin. The big middle gallery will be shrubbery too with birds everywha, birds of glass and polished wood among leaves, birds pecking broken ceramic cake from the green matting floa. Little gels stand in odd places nobody sees at first, little terracotta gels wearing real frocks of the period. One of them in overalls sits high up on a leafy trapeze. The olda gels will be glazed ceramic, the clothes ceramic too, all bright white except fo some culla whea they feel proud of it, red on lips, pink on cheeks, polka dots on a dress, candy stripes on a blouse. Anotha breed from us, the olda gels. We squawk, they murma and coo. I will record and play these sounds along with birdsong and the song from The Fortress, *I met an old woman* no *I met a young woman who gave me a rainbow*. But the huge dark bum-shaped Fortress is the middle of everything. Barbed wya brambles stop the adults getting nia but the light and music leak from chinks in the black walls made of tarry black wooden railway sleepas and tarpaulin, how they flamed when Ethel drenched them in paraffin and applied that match. What happened to Limpy Dan the

hampsta Linda? Did you see him inside The Fortress?"
"Thigh neva let me in!" sobs Linda, "I was nuffin but a applicant – allwise allwise allwise!"
"I feel excluded from something," says the dealer brightly, "Would you two ladies tell me what it is?"

They explain. He becomes furiously thoughtful. Nostalgia and grotesque infantilism are booming in many places, but especially Britain. From Christmas pantomimes and revivals of *Peter Pan* he has seen it expand through books, films, computer games, fashion design, interior decoration and architecture. Harry's work has so far been no more infantile than most contemporary work, but more noticed because of the surprising range of materials she uses, and because of her royal relations. These royals have no interest in her, have never said a word to promote her career, but important members of some purchasing committees do not know this, and one who wants a knighthood has boosted the sales-price of Harry's work to a height which knowing heads of the London art market think cannot last. Harry's dealer is one of these heads. He sees that if Harry now makes a lavish indoor sculpture park representing her eerily horrid schooldays (and with right help Harry can make anything) then Harry's work will be profitably sold by the London art market to the end of the century. So much can be said about it! – this tragically feminist remake of Pooh Corner, Never Never Land, the Secret Garden; this shrine to a dead millionairess who was loved by Marc Bolan, Jimi Hendrix and Sid Vicious, if only for a few minutes. Get the show an explanatory catalogue written by a brainier than usual popular writer (William Golding too old and grand perhaps but try him and Muriel Spark Iris Murdoch Fay Weldon Germaine Greer George Melly Angela Carter David Lodge or whoever wrote *The History Man* Adam Mars-Jones or whoever wrote *The Cement Garden* Roald Dahl Martin Amis *Tom Stoppard? Harold Pinter?* Whoever springs to mind seems suitable) it could be a small bestseller, a cult book if televised why not a feature film? Bill Forsyth directing? But first, the exhibition.

Dealer's flattened hand whacks arm of chair. "Funding!" he announces. "Funding! Harry I'm glad yaw think all yaw previous work is shit. Yaw wrong, but it means yaw going to astonish us with wildly exciting new things. But rooms full of steel, ceramic, polished wood etcetera need heavy funding. So do assistants. We need at least six: three high-tech boys and three gophas.* Linda! Let's see if you and I can crack the sponsaship problem from the Scottish end. Has Scotland a steel industry?"

"Yes, the remains of one. It limps from crisis to crisis, begging money from the govament and getting smalla all the time. It might welcome a bit of publicity."

Money talk bores Harry. She open *Another Part of the Forest* at random and enters a room where a white American woman is questioning a young black American woman sent by an agency that supplies rich folk with domestic servants. Harry, reading, begins to tingle. The questioning shows the older woman is selfish, bossy, cares for nothing but the comfort and appearance of her body, spends most of her life having it pampered and groomed for frivolous social appointments. She is fascinated by her potential servant and seeks to hide this under condescending insolence. The young black woman's answers show she is intelligent, can provide the sort of body care the other wants, but is not at all servile. She too is insolent, but her insolence is put in words which could be interpreted as compliance, and this is partly what fascinates her potential employer. All has been discussed, when suddenly, after a long silence, the white woman says in a low rapid voice, "Can you take shit?"

---

* A *gophor* is a fetcher and carrier in the film and other entertainment industries. It is unconnected with gopher, a burrowing pouched rodent or ground squirrel of the spermophil genus: unconnected with gopher, a miner who digs without hope of lasting achievement. (See Shorter O.E.D.)

"What does that mean?"

The white woman licks her upper lip, sucks her lower one then says, "Well. I'll tell you this. My momma once married a man who was a real gentleman, the finest gent you ever did see. She truly loved him, and so did I, except when he came home drunk and said things so filthy you couldn't believe. But we put up with it. Had to. He left after a while. I never knew my real daddy so this guy was … influential, I guess. And when I get low, which feels like half the month, I've a mouth like Satan's ass-hole. This shitty language pours out of me over anybody near, especially if they're – you know – subordinate. That's why I lost two husbands and why my maids keep checking out. So?"

The two women watch each other then the black woman says, "What kinda shit do you give? I need a sample."

"Well like … nigger bitch?"

"Oh that! I heard that one before. I slapped the face of the last white bitch who called me that."

"But she wasn't paying you twice what you earn in a high class hair salon."

The black woman lights a cigarette, inhales and after a while says, "For shit like that I want four times what they pay me in the salon."

"You mean it?" asks the white woman, staring.

"Yeah. I mean it."

"O.K."

"You mean it?" asks the black woman, staring. The white woman lights a cigarette, inhales and says "Yeah."

"You're rich!"

"Rich but no fool! I get value for money. I'll be mean as hell if I'm paying you that much."

"Just words?"

"What else could it be?" asks the white woman, smiling, "Tell me! I'm truly interested."

"It could be nothing but words," says the black woman firmly.

"Alright, that's the deal. Start tomorrow."

"The hair salon needs a week's notice – I promised that."

"For my money you start tomorrow."
After a pause the black woman says, "Give me my first pay cheque here and now – a month's pay in advance. I'll start when my bank clears it."
"Why you – !" cries the white woman and chokes back a word. Her face whitens but she calms herself and says,
"What guarantee have I you won't walk out of here and not come back?"
"None at all, but you're rich enough to risk it. And would I lose the chance of another cheque like that just because you shit through your mouth?"
"I don't think you will!" says the white woman quietly after a pause. "But I'm sure you won't mind signing a receipt just to put my mind at rest."
She writes a cheque and a receipt, signs the first as the black woman signs the second, then the bits of paper are exchanged. As the white woman hands over the cheque she says, "Take it! Nigger bitch."
"Why *thank* you Ma'am!" says the black woman with a sarcastic drawl, grinning triumphantly at the white woman who grins triumphantly back. End of chapter.

End of chapter, so Harry turns a page and encounters two wholly different women talking in a completely different land and century. Harry hunts forward and backward through the book but the two who made her tingle appear nowhere else. Each chapter contains a dialogue between women trying to trap each other but seem otherwise self-contained, with no male characters, no plot, no climaxes: nothing but furtive movements toward something sexy and sinister which never happens. *Is this supposed to be funny?* thinks Harry, exasperated.

"Stop filleting that book, Harry!" says her dealer. "We want to ask you something. You know how we got you that place in San Francisco so you could work and sell in America without a lot of dreary hassle over customs and impoat licences. Well there are equally good financial reasons fo you working in Glasgow while preparing the exhibition thea. I won't boa you with the details – they involve development grants, youth opportunity schemes, local govament politics and publicity of the dreariest kind. They also involve screwing a lot of money out of Scotland and some out of Europe. Linda says we can rent studio space beside a decent apartment wha the Hopcrafts can live and look afta you."

"Right in the heart of Glasgow!" cries Linda, "Not five minutes' walk from my office. I'll love being yaw Scottish business manayja! I'll help you higha and figha all the local assistance you need. I'll handle yaw publicity, and show you around. I'll even introduce you to the native chiefs, which is not essential, but ratha fun."

Harry hates restaurants, cannot face parties of more than four people, so on her first evening in Glasgow Linda takes her to dine at the home of a native chief. He is a former Lord Provost who now runs his own housing association consultancy and Harry is enchanted by him, listens open-mouthed to every word he says, brings to his occasional silences a hungrily expectant attention that compels him to say much more. Linda and the man's wife are astonished. He is three inches shorter than Harry, has the appearance, manners and conversation of many other British businessmen, and a voice with the tones and accents of Harry's long-lost, best-beloved nursemaid. It fills her with warm feelings of perfect safety and helpless anticipation. If he told her to climb on to the dining table and undress she would unthinkingly obey. He notices his effect on her and thinks it natural. When Linda and his wife leave the room for a moment he suggests a meeting two days later in a private lounge of the Central Station hotel. Harry nods and would faithfully keep that appointment but next day something happens which makes her forget him forever.

Harry spends the night where she will live for at least another year, in a block of converted offices and warehouses filling the north-west angle of Glasgow Cross. Next morning Linda calls to escort her to her new studio in a converted warehouse on the other side of the High Street. While waiting for the traffic lights to signal a crossing they are passed by many clusters of people talking with the tones and accents of Harry's long lost nursemaid.

"I'm afraid this always happens at weekends," says Linda apologetically, "Crowds of people from the housing schemes – employed ones who can afford to take a bus – use Argyle Street as a shopping senta. Also the barrows."

"Barrows?"

"A district nia hia full of little stalls, the sort you see in street markets all ova London. Glasgow has most of them in one place ... Do you want to wanda a bit?" asks Linda, seeing that Harry inclines to go with the crowd.

"Please."

They wander along the Gallowgate, through barrowland and across a corner of Glasgow Green. In London and San Francisco Harry knows very few places, and travels through the connecting streets in a car driven by one of the Hopcrafts. She has never before wandered through crowds where shabby and smart folk mix. Turning west along Clydeside they pass the old court house and are about to go under a castellated Victorian railway bridge when Harry stops at the entrance to a narrow but busy lane.

"Don't go in tha," says Linda, "It's too squalid."

"Dangerous?"

"Oh no! It's just a miserably poa market – a losers' market. You won't find bargains in it. Do come away."

"Mm," says Harry, and walks in.

Most of the market is in arched vaults under a disused railway viaduct, each vault lined with trestle tables spread with what seems the salvage of rubbish dumps. Everything still usable or wearable was of the worst quality when new and has since passed through several owners; everything once good-looking is hideously damaged. Yet a stream of people seem interested in buying. The queerest sights, however, are not in the vaults but on the cobbles of the lane outside. A woman with a twisted smile on her newly bruised face squats over a spreading pool of urine. Is she really trying to sell the last year's calendar, rusty forks and baby's plastic rattle on the stones before her? Is that barefoot man with the head of a broken-nosed, slack-lipped Einstein really trying to sell the cracked shoes in his hands?

"Hawf deid flooers tenpence!" screams someone, blocking Harry's vision with a huge bunch of half dead flowers, "Split the stalks, pit them in waater wi an asprin an thull revive! Thull revive!"

Harry giggles and walks on. Linda at Harry's elbow mutters vehemently, "I hate this. Hate it. I am not a socialist, but these people should not be allowed to flaunt themselves in this way. They should be put somewha wha we can't see them. The city plannas will pull this place down eventually, oh *God* make it soon!"

"I like it," murmurs Harry drowsily, "I think these people have as much right to exist as you or me. I will come hia often."

The lane ends in a small doorway. They go through it towards a car park and the glass and aluminium ziggurat of a vast shopping mall.

"It's easy fo you to be cold-blooded: yaw an aristocrat," says Linda sharply, "My daddy topped the hit parade in 1963, so I'm working class by breeding and bourgeois by education. Some sights I just cannot stomach."

"Has Glasgow an agency which will supply domestic servants?" asks Harry, still speaking drowsily.

"Probably. Why do you ask? Do you find the faithful Hopcrafts inadequate?"

"No, but I may need a lady's maid."

"A lady's maid?"

Linda stares at Harry who is dressed, as usual, in crumpled army combat trousers, shirt, tunic and boots. Several women of Harry's class sometimes wear neatly laundered forms of such clothes nowadays, but Harry has always dressed this way because it suits her work. With the addition of a machine-gun and facial hair she would look like a mercenary soldier in a tropical campaign.

"My motha had a lady's maid," murmurs Harry absentmindedly, "Throughout the Second World Waw, when everybody else's lady's maids went to work in munition factories, my motha somehow contrived to keep her lady's maid."

Harry finds an employment agency and pays it to send her applicants for the post of lady's maid. Each evening after work she waits for them in her flat, tingling with a hopefulness which dies when Mr or Mrs Hopcraft admits the applicant to her sitting room. Most are so alarmed by her appearance that they can only look at her sideways. She murmurs, "What can you do fo me?" and after they've told her says, "Well, I may be in touch."

That means *no*. Those who act more suitably have the wrong sort of voice because they are English (she forgot to tell the agency she didn't want that sort) or because they are Scots whose accents have an English sound. After a fortnight a small full-bodied woman is shown in who looks at Harry with a curiosity which is neither challenging or amused. Harry says, "I need a maid. What can you do fo me?"

"I honestly don't know," says Senga, "What do you want me to do? I'm good at hair – I'm a trained hairdresser – but you don't have any hair. So what do you want?" Harry sighs with relief because this woman is exactly right. "I want anything you want," Harry starts to say, but changes it to, "I want can I give you a drink?"

"Aye. Yes. Sure. I'll take anything but kicks and slaps. I've had too many of those."

Harry opens a well-stocked drinks cabinet: one installed by Linda and the Hopcrafts for the entertainment of her dealer and his associates. Harry last tasted alcohol when she was seventeen, hated it and has since drunk nothing but

lemonade and orange juice – even coffee and tea disgust her. She stares at the bafflingly labelled bottles and at last says, "I hate to be awkward but will you poa it for yawself? I'm hopeless at most things."
Senga, frowning thoughtfully, nods quickly several times, pours herself a large bacardi and soda and asks, "What will you have?"
"The same," says Harry automatically. Senga hands her a nearly full cut-glass tumbler and says, "Since we're drinking together could we mibby sit down?"
They sit primly at opposite ends of a long sofa. Senga says, "Cheers."
Harry sips her drink like an obedient child taking medicine. It tastes less poisonous than she expects. *I am growing up!* she thinks. Happy tinglings in her body make her so passively content that when Senga says cheerily, "Now then, out with it! What do you want me for?" Harry cannot answer.

So Senga asks once more. Speaking at first with difficulty but growing more fluent Harry says, "When I was tiny I was always dressed by somebody else. They got very cross if I did not sit very still in my nice frocks and be very good all the time. But you see I wanted to be wicked. And now I cannot CAN NOT buy nice beautiful clothes or care a damn how I look. I order hard-wearing useful clothes from illustrated catalogues and fling them on anyhow so I look like something the cat dragged in, usually. A fright. A tramp. But I had this very nia friend once," says Harry, laying down her glass and rocking her body forward and back, "I had this close friend who sometimes got very strange lovely clothes made fo me. I didn't always want to put them on because she enjoyed how I looked moa than I did, but when I submitted (and I always submitted, nobody was ever strong enough to disobey Hjordis) when I submitted and dressed up and did as she wanted – not how I wanted – I was entie-ally happy. Entie-ally happy, in those days, sometimes. But she died long ago and now I've

nobody. Nobody. Nobody. Please. Help. Me."
Forgetting that the Hjordis she has lost is imaginary Harry clasps her hands behind her head, drags it down between her knees and in that position wails as loudly as she can, which is not very loud. Senga puts her own glass down, goes behind the sofa and gently and firmly massages Harry's neck and shoulders, saying, "Don't worry. Calm down. Everything's going to be fine. You've found your wee Scotch auntie so your troubles are at an end."

After a while Harry comes to feel so safe and calm that they are able to talk about arrangements, though Senga suggests most of them.

"You don't need a living-in maid," she points out, "You work most of the day and don't wear special togs for that. I'm just a pal you want to relax with sometimes, a pal who'll overhaul your wardrobe and dress you up special for special occasions, or just for fun. I don't think the people who feed and clean up for you need know very much about us two. Now, I've a small business which doesnae pay very well. I make clothes for people, working from the house. What I need is a wee workshop, a room where you can see me when you need something or just want to relax a bit. The initial financial outlay need be nothing great, and well worth it in the long run. I'm full of ideas."

DAD'S STORY

I**F** a man is middle-aged between thirty-five years and fifty-five I have been old for several years. When I stopped being young I did not expect life to go so quickly but I have no other complaint. I will likely take twenty or thirty more years to die and it will be the smooth comfortable dying of someone protected by money. My ceiling admits no rain so I enjoy the movement of clouds over the rooftops. Every weather, every season has its unique beauty and this large window allows a good view of it. My flat is at the top of a building on a hill so I see right across the roofs of the other tenements and terraces. A tree-filled groove zigzagging among their roofs shows the course of a small river. This flows into a fine park in the middle distance, a park between two hills. One is crowned by the pinnacles of our mock-gothic university, one by the towers of an old theological college converted into luxury flats where my friend Leo lives. I see all this distinctly, and much of the city beyond, and on a clear day many fields and tree clumps on the hills beyond that. I am in the west end where most of the prosperous residential districts are in cities where the wind usually blows from the west. Even so, smoke from the east and other industrial districts so stained our finest buildings that a few years ago they made a very poor impression on visitors. Since the industries closed the richest districts have been extensively cleaned, partly with public money and partly through tax concessions to property owners. We now advertise our city as a splendid one and a lot of foreigners are buying places in the posh parts. I am lucky to have moved here from the east (where I was born and educated) before the prices went up. Like all poor parts of Britain the east end has got poorer in the last twenty years and will be poorer still when the poll tax is in full working order.

My job is making folk laugh, but I started my working life in that great ancient profession which never escapes from its education. My school qualified me for a university which qualified me for a college which qualified me for a school, but as a teacher. Many teachers marry each other. I was never sexually attracted by my kind, but used to like their company. My social life after four o'clock on weekdays was going to Brown's tearooms in Sauchiehall Street and sitting round a table with colleagues of the same age. For the first half hour we never spoke. Our voices were hoarse, our brains wasted by seven hours of deliberately depressing children of the ignorant working-class. (Our school served a poor district. Had it served a prosperous one we would have been equally shattered by seven hours of pushing middle-class children up to the level of their happy parents. Irony.) Slowly our brains would recover and *words* start to enter these silent conversations, then light badinage, gossip and facetious social and political commentary, all excellent training for me. I listened more than I talked. Professional humorists are never at the centre of happy groups, talking briskly and keeping everyone cheerful. We stay on the edge, listening carefully and trying to think of something better to say. And when we think of it we say it too late, or in the wrong tone of voice, so others don't hear it, or ask us to repeat it, and when we do there is a definite pause. The others may smile, but it can take them as much as a minute to start the conversation going again.

One or two who sat with us in the tearoom had gone into the Scottish BBC instead of the ordinary education system. One day the talk turned to religious prejudice and someone remarked that, despite the fact that our city had a very large Catholic population – certainly as many practising Catholics as there were church-going Presbyterians – there were many anti-Catholic slogans scribbled in the lavatories and on walls, but nobody could remember an anti-Protestant one. I suggested it was easier to write *Fuck the Pope* than *Fuck the Moderator of the General Assembly of the Church of Scotland*. Someone chuckled and the conversation turned to other things. But a fortnight after I heard my joke on a Scottish Home Service comedy show. *Fuck* had been replaced by *To hell with*, because it was illegal to say fuck on the wireless then but the joke was essentially mine. One of our BBC friends had passed it on to a professional mouthpiece. After that I stopped saying witticisms aloud. I saved them up, wrote them down and posted them to Jimmy Logan, Stanley Baxter, Rikki Fulton, Lex Maclean and Johnny Victory. Yes, all these immortals have owed the laughs they pulled to me. Not to me only. I know four other humorists in this city whose jokes are far more brilliant than anything I've written. I don't envy them. Though brilliant they are erratic, and professional comics need predictable streams of second-rate jokes more than brilliant gags that stop the show. Which is why I earn enough by my jokes to have left the teaching profession, and these brilliant boys have not; but I am too intelligent to feel smug.

For I am not a satisfactory man. I drink when not thirsty and hardly ever climb to the top of a high hill, though I used to enjoy reaching the top of hills and felt better, slept better when I came down. No wonder I am flabby in body and mind. My jokes are not radical criticism, they confirm what most of us feel: that black, brown, yellow people, the Irish and all foreigners, drunk men, the working classes, very fashionable folk, highly educated folk, all clergymen, homosexuals, wives and attractive women are essentially daft. Which may seem fair enough, but I never make fun of royalty, financial institutions, the police, higher clergy and politicians. Most professional comics won't buy jokes against these people. I do nothing about how my city and nation is governed, except occasionally vote for a party too small to change them. In the Athenian sense of the word I am an *idiot*. The old Athenians invented that word for people who take no effective hand in making the laws which control them. Let's drop the topic, it embarrasses me. I will describe exactly what happened last night with enough fanciful changes and additions to make the description interesting and believable. I met a woman who calls me Dad (though I am nobody's dad) and it felt like a turning point.

But that was not the first thing to happen. The first thing was feeling happy all day because Donalda was happy at breakfast-time. We had made love a few hours earlier, so, "I don't need you tonight," she said on a note of cheerful self-mockery. "Tonight you can do what you like."

I was careful not to look pleased as that would alarm her, but I was very pleased, though I said "I'll probably play chess with Q. And maybe I'll call on you afterwards, but of course I'll phone first."

This was a dangerous thing to say. If I failed to phone she might tell me later that she'd been unable to sleep for half the night. It would be no defence for me to say, "I did not promise to phone you, I said I *might* phone you. I said it to make you feel safer, and out of gratitude. I was grateful to you for saying I could do what I liked."

Why does Donalda seem like my jailor sometimes? Donalda is not a jailor, not a harsh schoolteacher. She is gentle. When busy and happy she has a shining quality, that quality of bright directness most people lose with childhood. Her lips do not shut in the firm line of those who want to control people. When working with her hands (she is a dressmaker) her lips stay slightly apart in a small, expectant smile. She has an emotional age of twelve or thirteen. This does not annoy me because my own emotional age is about that. Donalda shouts when angry, weeps when miserable, tells people when she is happy. But the longer I know her the less she turns her shining qualities on me, or perhaps the less I notice them. Nowadays most of her words seem to say now nasty and unsuitable I am. Certainly I drink too much. Why does she not get rid of me like other women who once loved me? I am good at being rejected. I don't rave, plead or quarrel, I stay polite and friendly. I am hurt enough for the rejecters to know they have shut me out of something wonderful and precious, not so hurt they need feel guilty about it. Why is Donalda FAITHFUL to me? I never expected faithfulness, or asked for it, or promised it. When we first dined together she told me she wasn't that sort at all. Which reminds me of the dream I had the first time we slept together. My book had just been published.

My book was published and I got very depressed. A few years earlier *Punch* had published a funny wee story of mine. That had made me ambitious. I wanted to be as famous as Q, so I started writing a whole book of funny stories. Unluckily I have only one basic joke. Conan Doyle, O'Henry and Thurber were like that, but my joke is about sex which makes it painfully obvious. I carefully set each story in a different time and place with characters whose voices, faces and jobs were different too. I hoped this would fool readers into thinking the joke was also different, and that readers who weren't fooled would read on to see how I disguised it next time.

Well, I sent the book to a London publishing firm and six months later it was returned with a letter saying they regretted not returning it sooner, since publication of it would reflect no credit whatsoever on themselves or on me.

That shattered me. Nine months passed before I was strong enough to post it to another London publishing firm, nine more before I had the courage to phone and ask if they liked it. A man said to me, "Haven't you heard yet? Yes, we're doing your book. I'm no judge of humour myself but two of our readers think you hit a contemporary nerve."

I lived in dread and anxiety another six months because I feared that when my book appeared nobody would laugh at it. I needn't have worried. The *Times Literary Supplement* called me "a major name in British humour" and only the *Sunday Post* complained about the sex. For a whole fortnight reviews appeared in periodicals which notice such things. For a fortnight every critic in Britain seemed to find my book as funny as I did, and then, suddenly, silence! They stopped laughing at it and went on reviewing books by other authors as calmly and approvingly as if I had never published a word. I realized that before they noticed me again I would have to get ANOTHER book written and published, and I am not a demonically industrious writer of the Enid Blyton, Iris Murdoch and Dickens sort. I enjoy writing, I forget myself when doing it as much as Leo forgot himself when driving a fast car, but unlike Leo I am easily distracted.

Anyway, I felt like a husband whose wife, after a deliriously happy honeymoon, elopes with a lot of other men. I got drunk and dimly remember a big gallery with paintings on whitewashed brick walls, a crowd which chattered and sipped wine with its backs to the paintings, a small, plump attractive girl with very black hair who seemed amused when I picked her up and whirled her about a bit. I don't often act so daft. A month later I met her at a party when I was sober and saw lines on her face which showed she was nearly forty. She still looked girlish. That deep anxiety all adults feel was half-hidden in her by unusual willingness to be pleased. When I asked her out for a meal she said, "Aye. Sure. Great, but don't tell anybody. If Senga finds out she'll murder me. Senga hates men."

She explained that Senga was her lover and occasional employer. I did not ask for details. My parents taught me it is wrong to ask for details of people's private lives. Had Senga been a man I would have called the affair off because I'm afraid of men. However, I met Donalda in a restaurant and was about to pour wine into her glass when she said sadly, "Better not. After a glass or two I'll go to bed with almost anyone."
I said, "Hooray!" and filled her glass to the brim, and after the meal she came home with me.

Of course I hoped we would make love, but in sexual play no man is more dependent than me on the will of the woman, so I was pleasantly surprised to find we could and did make love. Then I fell asleep and dreamed I was Baron Frankenstein. The monster, looking just like Boris Karloff, lay on the bed-like operating table they show in the films. My hand was on the switch which would pour in the life-giving current, but I had not pulled it yet, for I realized the monster's life would be a sad one and I would be to blame for it. But I did pull the switch, the monster opened its eyes and stared at me, I woke up and so did Donalda. When I told her my dream she burst out laughing. "That was me," she said happily, "that was me! You'll never get away from me now." I found this amusing. I felt safe because she had Senga and I too had another lover, though Donalda said firmly, "I don't want to know about her. Don't tell me *anything* about her. And never, please, never tell me when you visit her or she visits you."
I promised not to, feeling glad to know such a sensible woman.

How lucky I was then! Donalda usually visited me at lunchtime. I kept the curtains shut and, as the weather was cold, had my mattress on the carpet near the gas fire. I loaded that mattress with pillows, coloured cushions, a tray of fruit, cold meat, savoury cheese, pickles and wine. The lights came from five or six candles on the floor around us. I propped mirrors behind these so they seemed twice as many. The other woman sometimes came in the evening. She and I never fucked together (she had a satisfying husband) but we kissed, roly-polied around, ate, drank and talked a lot. A few days later Donalda made two discoveries, one that pleased, one that angered her. I forget which came first. The pleasant one was that Senga was having an affair with someone called Harry.

"As soon as I heard about it I ran round to the shop," Donalda told me gleefully, "and I said, 'Sit down Senga. I have something to tell you.' And do you know her face went as white as a sheet!"

Donalda then told Senga that she (Donalda) knew Senga was having it off with Harry, but she (Donalda) did not mind, as she (Donalda) was having it off with me, and from now on each couple should stick with their recentest lover and be nothing but good friends to the old one. Senga gloomily agreed this was probably the best arrangement, but said Donalda was a fool to get entangled with a man.

"But she wasnae cross with me or anything daft like that," said Donalda cheerfully, "So me and her are still doing business together."

The discovery that angered her was: when and how often the other woman visited me. She learned this from an observant neighbour of mine and behaved as if I had done what I promised not to do and told her myself. Her anger did not frighten me because I knew I had not been wicked, but the grief which accompanied her anger was terrible. The thought of me cuddling that other woman was a pain as real to her as raging toothache. I must not give pain like that to people and certainly not to a woman who is fond of me because I seduced her. I promised she would never again discover that I had loved someone else. I made that promise without guilt or remorse. I made it gently but firmly, like a doctor binding up a child's broken leg and explaining why the leg would heal and not get broken again. This treatment worked. At the time I did not know my promise was a declaration of marriage.

Yes, I am a married man. Donalda and me live so near together, she is so observant and inquisitive that I can never make love to someone else without her discovering, so I don't do it. This is no great deprivation but it makes me an unsatisfying lover. Lampedusa said once, "Marriage is a year of flames and thirty years of ashes." He was Sicilian. I doubt if Donalda and I flamed together for more than a fortnight. We sleep together four or five nights a week nowadays but lovemaking happens once a month, if I'm lucky. Nobody is to blame. In bed two nights ago she said, "When I first knew you I felt I couldnae have enough of you. Why are we different nowadays? Is it because we're older?"

I said, "Partly. And I think you are the last woman I will ever love, that after you comes nobody but death. The thought does not chill me but it makes excitement difficult."

"What a horrible thing to say! That I remind you of death!" cried Donalda, who is terrified of death. I hate deaths made by governments, business corporations and self-employed criminals, but when in good health the inevitability of death soothes or braces me. Donalda is different, so I tried to put the matter more tactfully. I said, "When we made love in the old days I was livelier because then I felt you were just one in a whole crowd of possible lovers."

"Do you mean that when we made love you were imagining other women too?"

It was worse than that. When we made love I imagined other women *instead* of Donalda, and other men instead of me. I could not ejaculate without imagining my prick belonging to someone more powerful and cruel than I am: a tyrant with a harem of captured brides, a cowboy sheriff with a jail full of deliciously sluttish prostitutes. My book is full of these fancies. I once read it aloud to Donalda, she laughed wildly at bits the *Sunday Post* called facetious chauvinistic pornography, and now she is upset by a reference to notions which make me randy! But we all know facts with part of our brain while using another part to think, talk and act as if facts don't exist. Donalda prefers to forget my sexual fancies and has never told me hers, yet she must think of more than me when we make love. I am an interesting fellow but too fat, wheezy and self-obsessed to fully occupy a woman's mind at these times. If she is not thinking of tomorrow's shopping list she *must* be glamorizing the occasion with something fanciful. I once knew someone who enjoyed hearing my fancies while we made love, but Donalda and me are shy at these times and say nothing aloud but our names. I sighed and turned my back to her feeling lonely and gloomy, though I had no reason to be. I am lucky to sleep beside her so often. Fucking is less important than the publicity for it suggests, but in the old days when Donalda and I did not fuck she at least slept in my arms. Nowadays we sleep back-to-back, and when I press as much of my back against her as possible she moves further away. Sometimes I wake in the morning and find I'm alone. My snoring has driven her into the spare bedroom. Yet she loves me and I like nobody better than her. We will almost certainly stay together until death interferes.

But the night before last, without warning, Donalda turned and embraced me and brought me alive and awake all over. She only does this nowadays when I least expect it, never after a quarrel but always when love seems impossible. At first I cooperate in a half-hearted way, then it feels perfectly possible and we swim together with me on top, because she prefers that. My body enjoys the exercise, my mind is nothing but a sad pleased blankness. But when Donalda murmurs that she wants me to ejaculate I can only do it by imagining wicked things. On this night I imagined a beautiful discontented customer walking into a shop like the one where Donalda works, a shop I have never visited. For some reason I cannot imagine wicked glamorous men nowadays or any sort of penis, but only women who seduce each other in sly cruel ways which have no base in my experience – the lesbians I know are rational folk who never seem to humiliate each other. The lesbians I imagine, however, did many things to this lovely discontented woman which made her completely content and helped Donalda and me to a satisfying conclusion. The next morning, which was yesterday, Donalda said, "I don't need you tonight. Tonight you can do what you like."

We got up, washed, had breakfast. She phoned for a taxi, swiftly painted her face, kissed my cheek making a distinct mouth-print on it ("To warn off others," she said) and left for the shop. When we first met she went to work by bus, so the shop must be doing well. The great thing is, I was left feeling happy and guiltless in my own place of work, which is home, thank goodness.

I never pitied my father when he left home for the factory each morning but I knew he drilled bolt holes through engine casings from necessity, not choice, and I had no wish to follow his example. Yesterday Donalda left me in charge of this quiet factory where I am the designer, craftsman, struggling apprentice, unskilled labourer, canteen staff and supplier of raw materials. All of us are equally important and are paid exactly the same. Our machinery is old-fashioned but my friends O and P and Q, who work with word processors, do not think my product inferior to theirs. I siphoned good black ink into the slender rubber well of my steel pen and laid reference books on a convenient table. I clipped sheets of lined paper to a board, sat down in the very comfortable chair I never use when I have visitors, and wrote the Darien Scheme section of my *CALEDONIAN*

ENCYCLOPAEDIA OF SCANDALOUS INSTANCES. The *ENCYCLOPAEDIA* is factual, and normally I cannot write the truth as fast as I write short funny things like this. Yesterday I mastered my material so quickly that whole sentences were conceived before the sentences leading to them. The scurrying this caused was all that disturbed the flow of work, apart from two visits to the kitchen to make and eat instant pizza. (Cover a slice of buttered bread with chopped onion and tomato, cover the whole thing with cheese and toast it.) I worked so well that the sun set and it was ten o'clock before I remembered I had been allowed to do exactly what I wanted that evening. It was too late to play chess, not too late for the pub. I phoned Donalda to tell her I would not visit her that night (she dislikes me when I've been drinking) but there was no reply. She must have been working late. The shop has no telephone so I had done all I could, and I went out with a guiltless conscience. As I entered a pub which cashes my cheques a woman leaving it stopped and said, "Hullo Dad, I'm reading your book again."

She was in her early thirties, very tall and gaunt but not anorexic. Her neck-tendons were distinct but muscular, her head completely bald. Bald women usually appal me but this one seemed a handsome specimen of a new race: not white, not black, not Semitic, not Asiatic. Her neck and smiling head were the colour of a light brown biscuit. Her chin was strong and sharp, her nose wee and snub, her small delicate pointed ears were pierced through the gristle (not the lobes) by the hoops of huge silver ear-rings. She wore an ankle-length leather coat with very wide lapels and her hoarse little voice seemed to come from a great distance. I did not know her name or profession but had seen her in a pub near Glasgow Cross frequented by the Print Studio crowd and other arty people. She said, "You have an astonishingly dirty mind. You made me feel quite ... mm mm."

I assumed mm mm meant sexy so I said, "Good."
We continued looking at each other. She did not stare at my face but closely watched it with this gloomy intense smile, her mouth turning down, not up at the corners. I was fascinated but did not know what else to say. Could she possibly desire me? If we became lovers what would Donalda do? She suddenly chuckled, touched my arm and went to the car park. I climbed some stairs to a crowded room where I joined O and P and the famous Q who saluted me smartly and said, "Good evening Major Name."
We discussed books, human freedom, the uselessness of Scotland's fifty Labour MPs, the culture capital of Europe in 1990 and its coincidence with the three-hundredth anniversary of the battle of Boyne Water. A happy heat was spreading through my veins while we spoke: adrenalin, of course. The woman who called me Dad had stimulated my heart.

She stimulated my heart and gave me the freedom of the universe last night. I felt able to swim over, under, inside every woman in the world, able to love and own the whole as completely as well-loved babies own it after a good meal. Outside babyhood hardly anyone feels healthy for long, but viewed in health and without prejudice the universe is an orchard of strange lovely bodies: fruit, stars and people freely grown for us by God (if we're religious) or by the universe itself, if we ain't. Most bodies cannot be visited or grasped without expense, danger or embarrassment – the moon, for example, and the woman who calls me Dad – but through mediums of light and air thousands of bodies harmlessly visit and touch every one of us. Donalda should not fear the nourishment I get from these light and airy contacts. All such nourishment makes me more fluid – more able to love her. I must tell her so. When I see her tonight (or on Monday night if she has to work the whole weekend) I will say, "Sit down Donalda, I have something to tell

you." No, that would alarm her. I will take her out for a very posh meal, maybe in that new restaurant boat which chuffs up and down the river. She will think I am compensating her for some pleasure I enjoyed without her, but she will not accuse me of it at once. She will ask what I did on Friday, Saturday, Sunday. When I left my house. Who I met. Where I ate and drank. What happened after that. I will give short accurate answers which will make her more suspicious than ever. She will try to annoy me into telling more by saying:
"So you had a real wild night."
"Of course I know you did more than just talk."
"Whose house did you fall asleep in?"
I will not be annoyed. I will say calmly, "It was an ordinary, enjoyable night."
"I talked and drank, that was all."
"I went home to my bed and nobody came with me."
At last Donalda will accuse me of hiding something so I'll tell her about my short talk with the bald woman. She will be furious. I will smile tolerantly and say, "You have nothing to fear. That talk led to a revelation which some folk would call religious. I realized ..."

I realized something which words will hardly explain, so why try? Like most middle-aged people I have had many revelations which felt like turning points and maybe were. If I am a different man from yesterday my actions, not my words, will show it. I will continue to act as usual but with more courage and firmness, perhaps. If Donalda notices a difference she may even like it.
She sometimes says she regrets
how bossy I let her be.

CLASS PARTY

DONALDA fastens her mouth on June's mouth in a kiss which is almost a bite and June enjoys a melting delicious weakness like nothing she has known. Her astonishment at this feeling is so great that she does not move when Donalda releases her, stands, touches buttons on the radio phone and says, "Senga? Senga, she's all ready for you, and she's got no arrangments this weekend, nobody's coming, or expects her ... Yes bring up the teacher."

Donalda, a little nervously (June thinks) straightens her skirt and tucks her blouse into the waistband without refastening anything. A buzz from entryphone. Donalda presses street-door switch, opens door to landing then stands beside it, listening to the coming of her friends. June has several seconds to think about screaming, a few seconds to do it. She doesn't do it because she is almost certain that most of her neighbours are out on Friday nights, and if some are at home, and come when she screams, and the visitors run away, what will the neighbours find? June nearly naked in an embarrassing skirt with her arms bound behind her. All her life June has dreaded embarrassment more than pain, which she has hardly ever experienced and even now does not expect. She feels part of a surprising play or dream which cannot hurt much – if it does she will walk out of it or wake up. The obvious reason for not screaming – that as soon as she starts Donalda will jump on her and gag her – does not enter her head.

Senga walks into the room like a woman glad to be home after a long holiday. She carries two red nylon hold-all bags and dumps them on the floor. She wears a long waterproof coat and casts it off onto the sofa before waltzing round the room with outspread arms.

"Notice!" she announces to the world in general, "That I am wearing our school uniform, the same sexy skirt and blouse my pal Dona wears, and which so fascinated one of my customers that she ordered it before she knew she was joining the school. She seems to have messed it up a bit but that always happens at playtime."

She stands still and looks hard at June who now sits up on the hearthrug, alert and puzzled but not frightened.

"How was she, Dona?" asks Senga

"Very nice," says Donalda, "Lovely at first. She lay down and opened up to me as easy as a wee pet lamb, just like what you said she would. But she soon got bored with me."

Senga puts her hands on her hips and tells June severely, "You are ignorant! I bet you've never made love for more than ten minutes at a time. You're too good looking to be so ignorant. Plain Janes like Dona and me had to learn to enjoy ourselves late in life because nobody else was keen on us, but hundreds must have wanted to teach you. How did you miss them? I bet the only people who taught you to be a woman were a frigid mother and some stupid men. You are very lucky that we caught you before you got too old … She's not too old for you, is she Miss Cane?"

Senga asks this of a woman who has entered the room behind her, also wearing a long coat which she has cast off onto the sofa. This is the lean bald lady of the second photograph, she wears the same big overalls with the bulging sidepockets, she now stands with her back to the door, legs astride. But despite her challenging stance and clothes she looks shy and downcast. She keeks at June sideways, her chin pressing hard into her naked shoulder as if trying to submerge in it. She mutters so softly the words are inaudible.

"I must explain about our school," Senga tells June cheerily, "Our headmistress needs discipline because nothing good can be learned without it, but she is an ideas person, not an enforcer, usually. She leaves discipline to the head girl, who is me. Please turn round, Miss Cane." Obediently the tall woman turns to the door and at once looks perfect. The shyly brooding evasive face is the only thing wrong with her. Senga, Donalda and even June stare entranced at her athletic figure, the broadshouldered naked back tapering to a slim waist under a couple of crossed straps, the fine legs with outstanding calf muscles below the trousers rolled up to her knees. Senga shakes her head, becomes businesslike again and points to a slender pocket between the tall woman's hip and knee. What seems a hook sticks from the top. Senga puts a finger under the hook and raises it far enough to show it is the handle of a flexible cane.

"I'm not showing you this to prepare you for a cruel orgy," Senga tells June, "We'll have a wee bit of one, of course, but our headmistress is too good a teacher to rely mainly on punishment. Usually she relies on me. Turn round again Miss Cane please."

The woman faces them and again looks peculiar.

"And now," says Senga, folding her arms and looking like a schoolteacher too, "I must once again ask you, Miss Cane, if you want to take the new girl? Do you like the look of her? Please speak up because we all need to know."

The woman whispers yes she's beautiful in a voice so soft and hoarse that June hardly hears it.

"Then money must change hands," says Senga firmly, "Among many useful items which I packed into your great big pockets, Miss Cane, is a pen and cheque book. Unbutton the pocket on your left leg and produce them."

For the first time the tall woman stares hard at June and seems unable to stop looking. Her hands, as if of their own accord, go to the pocket and take out what Senga ordered. Meanwhile June without conscious effort has risen to her feet. She stares back into the woman's face because it fascinates her. June also tugs at the strap which ties her wrists behind her, it does not yield but this does not distress her. Her body moves without consulting her mind. She hardly notices that Donalda and Senga now stand on each side of her.

"Write down the seventeenth of October nineteen eighty-nine," says Senga, "And Hideout Leathercraft and your name. I will then mention an exact sum of money. Have you written all that? Are you ready? Three thousand pounds."

The woman stares from June to Senga and whispers you're joking.

"Oh no," says Senga firmly, "You are buying the best weekend of your life and don't pretend you can't afford it. If you sell your holiday home in Greece you can buy a hundred weekends like this. But I'll give you thirty minutes to think about it, thirty minutes to see what you'll get for the price. I need a clock ... is this the bedroom?" Senga bustles towards the other room in June's flat and suddenly June awakens from something.

Suddenly June decides this is not a fascinating dream but an embarrassing and silly situation.

"Listen!" she cries, "I'm tired of this! The three of you are posturing all over my room as if I'm nothing but a ... a ... an audience and I don't like it. Untie my hands and clear out. At once. Now!"

"Hold her," says Senga firmly, fumbling in the pocket of her skirt. Donalda steps behind and puts an arm round June's waist, a hand over her mouth. The hand stays there by pinching June's nose between forefinger and thumb while June wrenches her head and tries stamping on Donalda's feet but plump wee Donalda is tough and heavy and inexorable. She does not move.

"Mouth," says Senga. June finds her mouth uncovered and draws a breath to scream but something hard enters, crushing her tongue. Across cheeks, ears and nape of neck she feels a strap tighten which no amount of head-wrenching shifts, though her hair is shaken over her face. It blinds her.

"Sit," says Senga. June is dragged backward and down till she sits on Donalda's lap, tied tight to Donalda's body by an arm round her waist and neck. June can do nothing but kick her legs about. Senga steps between them, parts the hair over June's face and says kindly, "The gag you are tasting will turn all your yells to moans and mumbles, but when you get used to it you will be able to say *please* and *thank you*."

She kisses June's brow then walks to the bedroom, goes in and reappears with a small stool and says, "I need some more nice things from your pockets, Miss Cane."

Senga steps up onto the stool and the bald woman hands her a bradawl, a gimlet with a long thick shank, a ring screw of the sort children's swings are hung from, then a pair of handcuffs. Senga bores an efficient hole in the underside of the lintel, screws the ring into it using the gimlet as a lever, and locks one of the handcuffs into the ring. As these preparations start making sense to June she grunts and kicks more wildly and uselessly than ever.

"Lift her," says Senga.

The lean woman embraces June's legs around the knees, Donalda stands and they carry her to the doorway.

"Higher!" says Senga. June is hoisted to shoulder-height with her face to the floor and stops struggling for fear of being dropped.

"Sensible!" says Senga, doing something to June's arms which frees them.

Senga grips a wrist, drags it up, clips the steel cuff round it. Then Senga steps off the stool and says "Stand."

June's feet are dropped onto the stool and she totters there trying not to fall off, flinging her free arm about to keep balance while the other arm wags above her head with the cold steel round the wrist.

"Steady!" says Senga from behind, putting her hands on June's hips on each side under the waist. This steadies her.

Not blinded by her hair now but by tears of rage and frustration, June only sees that she faces into her bedroom when Donalda, with a tissue, delicately dries her eyes and cheeks and says softly, "You've nothing to worry about – I wish I was you. Being a new girl is the best fun of all and you'll feel great afterward – a new woman!"

June's free hand hits the side of Donalda's face with a sharp crack like a gunshot. Donalda jumps back, her face whitening with shock. She fingers her right cheek on which a bright blush shaped like a palm with five dim fingers starts to develop.

"That hurt!" she complains sadly, "And I was only trying to be nice."

The lean lady chuckles, goes to Donalda, embraces her, smiles down at her mournful face then abruptly kisses her mouth. It is a long kiss. When Donalda is released she looks cheerful again and smirks at June as if saying: somebody likes me even if you don't. Senga, chuckling also, has grabbed June's free forearm and twisted it behind her back, hard enough to easily hold it there but not hard enough to hurt.

"Oo you wildcat!" coos Senga admiringly, "Oo you spitfire! Does she look wild and glaring and insulted and beautiful, Miss Cane? I can't see from here."

The lean woman sits down on the edge of June's bed with her knees wide apart and hands gripping them. She gazes at June's face, smiling and nodding.

"Good!" says Senga, "But our heroine has studied a photograph from my wicked album hard enough to know that she must stand a lot straighter than this and wear her highest heels. Look in the wardrobe, Donalda, and get me some of those magazines in case the heels aren't high enough."

June chokes with little sobs of fury while Donalda rummages eagerly in her wardrobe until she finds a pair of black open-toed shoes with four-inch stiletto heels and a slingback fastening. She then collects five or six *Vogue* magazines from a pile on the bedside table. June

is whimpering now. Senga kneels behind her, embraces June's legs, lifts her off the stool and knees it aside. June clutches with free hand the cuff round her wrist, clings tight to stop herself swinging by one arm. Donalda kneels humbly before her and fits and fastens each foot into its shoe, then Senga lets her legs go. For a sore second both of June's arms are stretched by the weight of her whole body, then her downward-yearning toes touch the pile of magazines slid under them, her heels touch it too, her weight is shared equally by every stretched muscle between her fingers and toes. Senga tests this tautness by rippling her fingers over her hips and bum, lightly caressing June's waist, stomach, breasts; lightly stroking her spine, shoulderblades, arms. Senga is breathing hard from recent efforts and another excitement. When June tries to spit at her she smiles and murmurs, "You wanted this, oh you wanted it!"
Beads of sweat now glisten on the naked parts of June's body. With a small moan Senga embraces her and explores her left armpit with nose, lips, tongue.
stop says the woman on the bed.
"I will not!" cries Senga turning fiercely to that woman, "She belongs to Donalda and me, you havenae bought her yet! Thanks for reminding me."

Senga goes to the bedside table, lifts the clock from it, changes the alarm switch and puts it on the mantelpiece where June can see the dial. "It will ring in thirty minutes," she tells June, "Then we'll give you a rest."
"You're being unkind," Donalda tells Senga, "Half an hour is a long time to stand like that."
"You stood like that for forty minutes," says Senga.
"Yes but I'm tough. I've had a hard life. She hasnae."
"She needs the exercise and I need a drink," says Senga, sitting down beside the bald woman.
"I poured drinks for us before I asked you up," says Donalda, "But of course nobody notices what I do."
"What was it?"

"Sherry. *Her* sherry. Harvey's Bristol Cream."

"Ugh," says Senga and the bald woman says bubbly.

"You heard her," Senga tells Donalda, "Bring the bags in."

"We may have a new girl now but I still seem to be the skivvy around here," grumbles Donalda, and squeezes sideways past June into the other room muttering, "Excuse me."

i'm signing that cheque says the lean woman, doing so.

"I won't take it till the alarm goes off," says Senga, staring at June. Senga's expression is not gloating or triumphant, she has the lost look of a child watching something wonderful which she is too poor to possess. Suffering makes most folk uglier but though June's face and breasts are glazed with a mingling of tears and sweat her distress makes her more beautiful than ever. She moves her head slowly from side to side, trying not to think, not to feel the strain in every part of her body. It is not a very great pain – she would faint if it was. It seems bad because it is continual, she cannot escape it, it is bound to grow greater. The clockface tells her that one and three-quarter minutes have passed, that she must stay for twenty-eight minutes twenty-five seconds. She knows that willing a clock to go faster is the worst way to pass the time, but cannot stop straining to see movement in the hour and minute hands while seeing nothing but torture in the slowly sweeping second hand. She tries to blind herself by shaking her hair over her face but her position prevents that. With the free hand she rakes some hair over her face but the steel ring bites so deep into the other hand that it is a relief to cling to it again and stand exactly as she was before with only one eye partly covered. She hears Senga say wistfully, "Wildcat has lovely hair."

yes

"Longer and thicker than Dona's."

yes

"Are you jealous of it, Miss Cane?"

very

"Excuse me again," says Donalda, squeezing sideways

past June and carrying a bag in each hand.

From one bag a bottle of good champagne is produced, also a small leather case of crystal goblets with stems. "Only the best for Miss Cane," says Senga, releasing the cork and pouring.

her health murmurs the bald woman, raising her glass.

"Here's to Wildcat," says Senga and drinks.

"That's you!" Donalda tells June.

As the trio stand sipping and contemplating her it strikes June again that they are the performers, she the audience of this show and she starts feeling a dazed acceptance of her position. This vanishes when Senga puts down her glass, removes a smart camera from a bag and says, "Will you take a few for the album, Miss Cane?" As the lean woman squats low and flashes the dazzling box at June, prowls closer and does it again, slips past the side of her and flashes her from behind, returns and directs Senga and Donalda to pose on each side of her, gets Senga to embrace June and kiss her armpit again, then finally flashes four dazzling closeups of her face, June twists her head and body about with many little choking outcries. Every bit of her body and soul hates, fights against being *taken, caught, kept* in prints which many others may see and enjoy. Shock and exhaustion at last leave her hanging in a daze of pain she accepts. Dimly and without protest she sees the lean woman recline full-length on her bed, sipping from a crystal glass and glancing from June to Donalda and Senga and back. Donalda and Senga are emptying June's wardrobe of all her clothes, holding them up, trying them on, whirling about in them with little squeals of excitement.

"Wildcat knows what to wear – she really understands glamour – she doesnae give a damn for ordinary fashions!" cries Donalda wrapping a silver sari round herself, "I'm too wee for this, you should wear it, Miss Cane."

The bald lady smiles.

"Notice something?" asks Senga, holding a scarlet flamenco dress to her body, "No trousers! No jeans, tight or baggy; no shorts, slacks, harem pants, not even a divided skirt. She definitely hates trousers. She'll look gorgeous in them."

"Yes, you've brought her the right present," says Donalda.

Senga says, "Tidying up time."

She and Donalda pack June's dresses, suits, skirts, jackets, coats, hats and shoes into black plastic sacks taken from one of the bags. They then empty all the drawers in the room onto the floor and pack the contents into more sacks: underwear, letters, photographs, jewellery and everything except the cosmetic articles. These are piled on the dressing-table. For a moment Senga pauses with a pair of dolls in her hands which June has never discarded, a teddy bear and a cloth Dutch girl so dilapidated that only a very poor child would play with them now. Before stuffing them into a sack Senga looks thoughtfully from one to another then tells June, "If you and I get to be pals – real pals – I might give you them back one day."

June nearly laughs aloud but aborts the laugh in a gasp and headshake. Laughter would destroy the stupor, the exact balance of pain and acceptance she now clings to as tightly as her free hand clings to the handcuff.

Donalda and Senga tie the mouths of the sacks with tape and pile them against the wall. The clock starts twittering. Senga silences it with the press of a fingertip and says, "All right Miss Cane. Give me that cheque."

She is given the cheque, reads it and pockets it. She says submissively, "Thank you very much Miss Cane. Can we give her a rest now?"

no says the lean lady, laying down her glass and standing up. She faces June and smiles slightly, then draws the thin cane from her hip-pocket, flexes it then suddenly slices the air with it in a swish which is almost a tweet. June starts wakening from her stupor. Senga takes another set of handcuffs from her skirt pocket, steps up onto the stool, cuffs Jane's free wrist to the ring also then steps down saying, "More comfortable?"

It is more comfortable. June's fingers are freed from the strain of clinging and the strain in her arms is now equal, though she stands rigid with dread.
"I don't like this," says Donalda loudly. She sits on the bed with her back to the others, "I don't think she needs it."
"She needs it," says Senga soberly, "Go to the bathroom and run the water. Don't make it too hot – test it with your elbow – and remember the salts."
Donalda gets up and takes a jar of coloured crystals from one of the bags. She does not look at June but mutters "Sorry" while slipping past her. The bald woman, with a beseeching look, puts her free arm round June's neck and tries to kiss her mouth, but despite her dread June twists her head from side to side and prevents this. tell her the lean woman whispers sadly to Senga, then slips past June to stand behind her. June is confronted now by Senga standing with legs wide apart and arms folded, looking angry.
"Our headmistress wants you to know," says Senga in a hard sarcastic voice, "That she is about to make you feel that her and you are the only two in the universe – the only ones alive. But before she makes you feel that, and after she makes you feel that, remember that no matter how much she hurts and loves you – no matter how much you get hurt and love her back – you are wearing the skirt you ordered from me, so she can't draw blood and you can't faint. Start when you like Miss Cane."

The pain which follows is so astonishing that June does not try to scream but jerks her body at each hard regular stroke with a small indrawn cry of "ah". After the second stroke she feels nothing exists but her body and Miss Cane. After the twentieth she feels only the strokes exist, nothing else, not even her body, and when only the strokes exist each one evokes, as a kind of echo, a sensation of luxury. The luxury grows until she chokes with laughter and is about to faint. Someone shouts "Stop!"

****
****
****
****
****
****
****
****
****
****
****
****
****
****
******** ********
******** ********
******** THIS REPLACES EIGHT PAGES ********
******** OF SADO-MASOCHISTIC MALE ********
******** FANTASY WHICH NOBODY ********
******** ********
******** SHOULD ENJOY. ********
******** ********
****
****
****
****
****
****
****
****
****
****
****
****
****
****
****
****

7 WAKENING

A mug of liquid black warmness is held to her lips by a motherly stranger who has raised her head by an arm behind her shoulders. The liquid smells of coffee and something peculiar, tastes sweet; she always hated sugar but drinks eagerly. Another full mug is offered. She takes it in her hands and drinks more slowly, feeling she has wakened into another dream. She can see nothing familiar. The pair of legs stretched along the bed before her move when she moves them but cannot be hers as she never wears pants. The room is like a display bedroom of a sort seen in big furniture shops. It holds no objects of personal use or ornament except a clutter of things not hers on a dressing table. In a corner is a sinister heap of fat black plastic sacks. There are three strangers. One beside her on the bed supports her shoulders. One sits sideways on the bed-foot looking glum. These are big-bummed, big-breasted little women with hectically messy hair, naked but for black aprons which June eventually sees are short leather skirts fastened carelessly at the waistband. The third stranger stands on tiptoe in the open doorway with arms stretching straight up. Seen from behind the figure is that of an amazingly thin tall bald beautiful gymnast with hips perhaps a little too broad to be male. But what makes this room unlike all others past or possible is the strong tones, clear colours, distinct edges of everything, everyone in it; also an ache of sexual longing. June feels this ache like the solid presence of a fifth person who knows them all intimately, has brought them all together, who stands invisible among them but cannot be handled.

8 A REVENGE ANGEL

Senga says cajolingly, "Stand up and look at our Revenge Angel."

She helps June stand (there is a moment of difficulty: June has never worn such high heels before) and helps her advance to meet the fifth person in the room who is not invisible at all: has the face of a fury and a figure so suavely, proudly female in elegant gleaming black that June instinctively bends to worship and the figure bows. At which June recognizes herself, memory returns, the room and things and people lose intensity. She knows who they are, how they happened. Stepping close to the mirror she studies the face which is obviouslycopied from the star of *The Rocky Horror Show*. The features present no problem. Her mouth can in minutes be given back its modest colour within natural boundaries. The menacing scroll-work of the thin eyebrows can be wiped off and replaced by the dark feathers of her old ones, carefully redrawn where they will grow again. With rings removed the pierced nostril and ear will have no conspicuous scar. A turban can cover her scalp until hair returns, though not fashionable it will not look bizarre. But what can she do with the wasps? Not the ones above the hairline, the ones at the outer corners of each eye? June groans with despair and exhaustion.

9 DEATH OF AN ANGEL

begin says a small clear voice from the doorway.
"She's to blame!" cries Senga eagerly pointing to the figure in the doorway and putting a cane in June's hand, "Remember what she did to you! Hit her anywhere you like! She deserves it! She wants it!"
begin says the voice.
"She's not to blame. You are, but I don't care," says June wearily dropping the cane. The thought of beating someone has never excited her much and certainly doesn't excite her now. She yawns, sits down and says, "I'm tired. Please unpack my things and go away."
"It hasnae worked," Donalda tells Senga flatly.
begin says the implacable little voice.

10 FINISHING THE JOB

Senga frowns and walks about the room, thinking hard, sighing and casting mournful looks at June who stonily ignores her. At last Senga tells June, "Listen, I know you're sick of us but we'll havetae be here a bit longer. We've a job to finish. But we'll be as quick as we can."

begin

Senga picks up the cane, offers it to Donalda and says, "You do it."

"Oh no. If Wildcat won't do it why should I?"

"Donalda, is this a strike situation?"

"Definitely!" says Donalda, folding her arms and pouting obstinately.

begin

"Alright I'll begin you bloody-fucking-upper-class-dyke-bitch-bully!" shouts Senga, "As usual at the end all the dirty work is left to me so here it comes! And I won't stop till you ask to go home, right?"

begin

So Senga beats Miss Cane hard and methodically all over, eventually doing it with leather thongs, and Miss Cane weeps, sobs and in her small voice begs Senga to stop but does not ask to go home till long after dawn has broken. Senga and Donalda release Miss Cane and help her into the bathroom. June kicks off her shoes, unties the neck of a plastic sack, tips it onto the floor and picks from the spillage a shirt she can use as a nightgown. She takes the rings from her face, wincing slightly. She unbuckles, unzips, removes the leather clothes, pulls on the shirt, slips between her bed-sheets. Bewildered exhaustion is what she mainly feels, but feels also that she will not sleep until alone in her own home.

11 AN APPOINTMENT

Senga enters the bedroom, glances at June, stoops and refills the emptied sack.

"Leave those things, they're mine," says June without force.

"I'm going to take them all away," says Senga sadly but firmly, "I know you're sick of me because you didnae enjoy these games much. Still, I showed you a bit of life, eh? I gave you some views of the potential. Tomorrow you'll likely hate my guts and the day after too, but in a few days you'll mibby want to see me again. Anyway, I want to see you again. I'm removing all this stuff to make sure that happens. I'll phone you near the end of the week." June is too weary to argue and dozes while Senga drags the sacks into the lobby.

12 CHEERIO

June is wakened by someone kissing her brow, Senga of course who says, "I've left a few things on the dressing table you may find handy. We're off now. See you later." "Cheerio!" says Donalda from the doorway, "I'm sorry if we did anything to upset you, but some of it was fun, right? No hard feelings, right?"

thank you fo a very agreeable night says a tall person behind Donalda, though three thousand is ratha steep I must have been mad to sign that cheque

"It's bought you credit with the firm for weeks to come. All out everyone," says Senga briskly and switches off the light as she leaves. June hears the front door slam. And sleeps.

NEW JUNE

JUNE wakes in dark, feeling robbed of something essential to life and dignity. Aching muscles in arm, leg and shoulder, various throbs and ticklings in the skin recall what happened. She rises, puts on light, telephones speaking clock, is told by rich and manly English voice that on the third stroke the time sponsored by Accurist will be 2 hours, 27 minutes and 30 seconds. She has slept dreamlessly for over nineteen hours. She now sees the theft of her clothes, personal ornaments, souvenirs, hair, the piercing and tattooing of her skin are not the worst that happened, though they constantly recall it. Her body has been deliberately toyed with and teased into a sexual hunger she only now fully feels, gnawing and dreadful hunger. Her one hope of satisfying it is someone who said "I'll phone you at the end of the week." The time is half-past two on dark Monday morning. If she had hope of finding where Senga lived she would hunt her up, break in on her, DEMAND satisfaction, spank her till she yielded it. Is there nobody else she can break in on? A man is not what June wants but would be better than nothing. However, for three years she has tried to give men up, and succeeded. The only man she knows who can be reached by taxi and would love to be invaded is her ex-husband. She shudders at the thought of him – better use her fingers. Which she does, but not at once.

First she wanders through the flat with a sheet twisted round her. She gazes at wardrobe mirror where she watched Donalda seduce her, the rug where they made love. She now knows it was opportunity missed, wonders why she was so passive. Like lonely old woman recalling childhood game she stands on tiptoe, reaches up toward two holes in lintel of bedroom door then goes to bathroom, wipes make-up off, has warm bath which fails to soothe as last one did. She goes back to bed and caresses herself as Donalda caressed her before Miss Cane said stop. June tries caressing herself more than that, but the extra caresses don't feel right. She goes to dressing table, sits naked before it, legs wide open as if still manacled there. With half-closed eyes she imagines the hand caressing her is Miss Cane's, that the face in the mirror is Senga's loving face before she (June) turned revengeful and pretended rapture she did not feel, rapture she now tries to create. She gets pleasure from this but too little. A sandwich would be more satisfying. The rapists did not steal her food. She gets up to visit kitchen; halts at sight of shoes, garments strewn by bed, the only clothes left her. Sitting crosslegged on carpet she examines them closely.

Pants, jacket have been made with love: all stitching in double rows, thread black as the leather but done as neat as if white: pure silk milk-white linings, exquisitely quilted, unstained by sweat from when she wore them last night. Embroidered on lining between jacket shoulders two small scarlet hearts both pierced by gold arrow, *TO J LOVE FROM S* underneath. June smiles, kisses embroidery, slips on jacket, zips up the long sleeves, fastens studs of front. A lot of her chest is bare, yet padded shoulders give warm protected feel. The pants have big outlined heart embroidered on lining of seat with *IT ALL STARTS HERE* and exclamation mark inside. Putting on pants takes many minutes. Seams down the legs are joined by small buckles and straps. She takes great care to exactly tighten each. The tightness comforts. She stands turning about before wardrobe mirror admiring side of each leg: from waist to mid-calf an inch-wide lane of her naked self shows under the buckles and straps. Between belt and jacket most of her stomach appears, two brave little wasps crawling left and right from her navel. At last she faces her head, staring hard at what she feared to see clearly before: bald weather-beaten head of plastic doll once seen on rubbish heap beside roofless cottage when she was wee and wept at the sight with pity and dread but now she knows what to do.

Go to dressing table. Sit. Choose cosmetics but not Miss Cane's. Draw on eyebrows like her usual eyebrows, only darker. Ignore wasps. Paint lips, tint cheeks, shadow eyes just as usual. Unframed by dark hair this face is now definite as Rocky Horror film face and more boney, subtle, alluring. Baldness and wasps still give this head discarded doll look but look of *expensive* doll discarded because it is a *dangerous plaything able to act for itself.* June once took nightschool ballet lessons, stopped after third. She leaps up, pirouettes wildly round room, wonders why she feels free, happy. It comes from *no hair*: hair was half of her once, why women envied her, why men looked twice. It framed her head, curtained and cloaked her, a soft warming house she could move with. Hair was religion learned from devout mother who taught her to love it, worship it, serve and suffer for it handfuls grabbed and twisted before she was twelve by boys, also girls. A new life is starting without it, one she cannot imagine nor can anyone else – not even Senga. Yes, this is freedom. She strides to telephone, again dials one two three. On the third stroke the time sponsored by Accurist will be 10 hours, 40 minutes and 30 seconds. She is over an hour late for work. She is about to dial her office when the phone rings.

Phone rings. She lifts receiver. Clear little voice says hello?
June knows that voice. Her heart starts beating differently,

a fact which astounds her more than the voice does.
hello a you tha can you hia me?
"Yes."
I'm phoning to thank you fo a truly lovely evening
A silence.
I say can you hia me a you still tha?
"Yes."
good you see I feel I owe you a lot so in yaw case I feel bad about stopping that cheque I say a you still listening?
"Yes."
I stopped the cheque first thing this mawning because three thousand pounds is much too much fo one night and the good bits wa just you and me we don't need these otha little people don't you agree?
June nods. Her heart changed rhythm when Miss Cane's voice reawoke this bodily hunger for love.
I say a you tha?
"Yes."
I'm besotted I need to see you I've money if money mattas I suppose it does can we meet to discuss it but three thousand was too steep
Silence.
when can we meet?
June's body wants to shout NOW but the eager woman pressing her had better be treated with the same caution as an eager man. June draws a deep breath and asks, "What do you suggest?"
I'd love to buy you a meal in the ubiquitous chip or pumphouse or rotunda or anywha
"I've never eaten in the Rotunda."
not great but good fun will I collect you by taxi say about seven?
"If you like."
Silence.
my name is harriet shetland I love you
Click of receiver put down.

"It is important not to go mad!" thinks June. What she most needs is going to be provided, but she is still a working woman, not a kept woman, and had better keep her job. She phones the senior executive of her department. He is delighted to hear June must stay at home today, maybe for several days. June has not said she is sick but, "I've overworked you, no wonder you're sick!" he says happily, "I hear it in your voice. Yes, you're tired, listless, completely worn out. Am I right?"

"Yes," says June.

"Good. I mean, it's good that you recognize your sickness, because sickness is the body's way of telling the mind, *leave me alone for a bit*. You've been far too conscientious, June. When we started this thing together you had only me to advise. Now you have Bleloch, Tannahill and the new publicity officer. You need an assistant, June. It's ridiculous that our office has only one trained legal mind to depend upon. Now promise me you'll take all the time you need to recover. I suggest a trip to one of those places which are at their most charming out of season: Italy, the Canary Islands, Miami. Relax. Sunbathe. A bit of romance will do no harm! You're, haha, a very attractive legal adviser, June, if a friendly male chauvinist swine may say so, and… and … yes, you'll be a new woman when you come back to us. These are not doctor's orders, they are boss's orders."

This boss is worried and reticent when facing people but can sound like another sort of man along a wire. June quiets the gibbering receiver by saying, "Thanks Mr Geikie," and putting it down. Very hungry now she makes pile of sandwiches, sits on rug before fire, wolfs food down with teacup of sherry (she never did that before), stretches out. Dozes off.

Is wakened by buzzing entryphone, leaps to it at once. "It's only me!" says Donalda. "I just want to tell you I've –"

"Wait there!" commands June and races barefoot down stairs, pulls open front door. No Donalda. June leaps out and down stone steps to pavement, glares fiercely round. Mild autumn cloudy noon: nothing moving on terrace but old lady with shopping bag recoiling in terror, a distant departing Citroën canvas-topped car with two blue wavy lines on the side.

"Sorry!" June tells old lady, goes angrily back up steps, through doorway, slams door. On floor under letter slot, padded envelope, her name on it. She takes it upstairs, squats on rug, rips it open. Inside a letter folded round thin clean wad of new banknotes: Clydesdale Bank fifty-pound notes, each engraved with a bewigged Adam Smith raising a reproving forefinger. June counts fourteen such notes. The letter is written in childishly clear, backward-sloping little words.

Dear Dear Dear Dear Dear Dear I can't seem to stop writing Dear Dear Dear June, I have been a cruel bitch but I am not a financial exploiter, hence the enclosed. You may wonder why it is not more, as a three way split between Dona, me and you would be £1000 each. The truth is, I cannot give anyone that much, will not have that much myself until Harry's cheque comes through tomorrow or the day after. £700 is all I have except a bit in my purse to tide me over. I have not the kind of bank account which allows me an overdraft. This is deliberate. I belong to the sort of people who never get out of debt once they are in it. My mother was respectable, never in debt in her life. Dona's dad had his legs broken because he owed money he could not pay back. I would steal (food from shops) rather than owe money. Which is why I am paying what I owe you right away though I know you will not break my legs! (A joke.) I want you to know as soon as possible that I am honest with money and not an exploiter. Dona won't mind waiting a day or two longer for hers as she and me have been pals for years. Anyway, she has a very decent sugar daddy.

Dear Dear Dear Dear (here I go again) Dear Dear Dear Dear June, I will not be paying you £300 when Harry's cheque comes through because the firm has had to meet certain expenses. Good handcuffs cost more than you would think possible and my customers are given only the best. Plastic cuffs hold well enough but would have been an insult. You looked so lovely in real steel I'm excited just remembering it, more excited than I was at the time. As a professional I must keep a cool head when on the job or everyone else is disappointed. You stay amateur! Maybe you and me could be amateurs together one day soon? (Like Friday?) Do you like the suit? It too is of the best, I spent hours on it. I know you did not order it but it will fit nobody but you. Please wear it for me.

Dear Dear Dear Dear I'm afraid you still hate my guts so I dare not phone you till Friday when maybe you will be calmer and ready for more. (Love.) Yours Truly, Truly Yours, Yours Truly, Truly Yours, Yours Truly, Truly Yours, ...

These words are repeated to the foot of the page and end with *Senga PTO* in the bottom right hand corner. June turns over and reads on the other side
PS Harry is Miss Cane's real name. She is a very famous artist.
PPS All your things are safe with me.

This letter astonishes June. On first meeting Senga she thought her an astute small businesswoman. In the past few hours she has thought her a sexual predator, a perverse psychologist, a social liberator. The letter shows she is still a small businesswoman, a sentimental and naive one who handles money stupidly. And money in crisp clean valuable notes is lovely stuff to handle. June lives carefully but comfortably within her income while buying her flat and adding to a fund that will let her retire at fifty-six with the same standard-of-living-index-linked income. She has nearly seven thousand pounds in two bank accounts and some British Petroleum and British Gas shares. She is careful to pay for everything which costs over a few pounds by cheque, and to note all the payments down. Like Senga she never accumulates an overdraft. She has never held so much money in her hands before: unexpected money, tax-free, free in every way. Like most who start their working life with very little June will never feel rich through her earnings, but this money makes her feel rich. She will not insult this love offering by turning it into numbers in a deposit account. She will buy magic, not security with it. She cannot imagine what will happen when she meets Harry tonight, but if she gets money (£1000? £1200?) she'll make sure the cheque is cleared (may tie the bitch up to ensure it) and give some money to Senga, perhaps.

She divides the wad in two, puts £350 in each breast pocket thinking smugly, "A chap should always have money in his pockets."

Senga left a pair of dark glasses on the dressing table. June puts these on, smiles at the result in the mirror. Her mother, sisters, best friends and ex-husband would not recognize her now if they stared in her face. She slips on the high-heeled shoes, remembers her ballet lessons and steps about in them. They are sore on the calf muscles, but the extra height is worth it. She phones for a taxi and is driven to the House of Fraser in Buchanan Street.

To the assistant in the millinery department she says, "I want to make my head less surprising."

She buys hats which cover her head from hairline to nape of neck: a black silk turban and one of black velvet, a black felt helmet with a small posy of black felt pansies on the side, and a Russian Cossack hat in black fur. In the lingerie department she buys black body stockings in fishnet and more elaborate open meshes, black silk slips and black lacy brassières. For old times' sake she now strolls to the first leather shop she visited. She carries all her new purchases in bags for she does not yet want to look less surprising. When dressed ordinarily she drew an amount of attention that mainly embarrassed her. She now draws five times as much attention and it amuses her mightily. She is surprised to notice that the cries of building workers on a construction site she passes sound as loud and harsh as usual, though the words are more aggressive. The tone of men signalling that they want to fuck her, and that they wouldn't fuck her with a ten-foot pole if they were paid a pension, sound much the same. In the leather shop she buys a black belted coat with big lapels and a military-looking hat with glossy skip. She contrives to be served by the assistant who introduced her to the Hideout, and at one point removes her glasses and says, "Do you remember me?"

After a wondering stare the assistant says, "Yes! ... Did you find that place you were looking for?"

"Oh yes."

"So you're happy now?" asks the assistant, smiling.

"Yes," says June, smiling.

POSTSCRIPT

June has usually been lonely, having cultivated reticence because her beauty has mostly attracted men she has found boring or predatory. She has therefore evaded or retreated from what she dislikes, never opposing or trying to change it. The discovery that her mere appearance now disturbs conventional, timid people feels like release. Stepping jauntily through the streets in her defiantly sexual suit she enjoys a freedom which is more than sexual. Next day, instead of brooding over Senga and what will happen when they meet at the end of the week, June returns to work as if nothing had happened. Her office job prevents loneliness and earns money, but today she approaches it with a mischievous interest in how her workmates will cope with her.

She is legal adviser in a government office created to help poorly paid folk who have been badly treated by other government offices. Efficiently run it would trouble several high-ranking public servants. If run by a clever ambitious Senior Executive Officer it would trouble them often. They have given the post to Mr Geikie who never expected to rise so high. Toward colleagues and superiors he feels sensations of inferiority mingled with adoration. If they smile and call him by his first name he feels perfectly safe. He is sure he can best serve the public by giving such people no trouble at all. When June joined his office he told her in a worried, preoccupied voice, "Our main job is to defuse potentially painful confrontations by arranging alternative procedures. This is not easy. It cannot always be done quickly." She discovers he deals with troublesome cases by postponing decisions until the applicant's legal aid fees expire, after which most of them have lost hope and accept a very small sum in compensation. If applicants have a generous lawyer who sticks by them and complains more vigorously Mr Geikie frankly admits that the fault is his, says the delay has been intolerable but cannot be helped: his office is under-staffed. When June started there she worked with Mr Geikie and three clerical assistants. The clerical staff are now twice as many, their typewriters have been replaced by word processors and their title changed to Administrative Assistants. The office has also been joined by two Higher Executive Officers who have nearly learned Mr Geikie's methods, but if one looks like bringing a troublesome case to a conclusion it is given to the other with instructions to tackle it differently. The office hums with activity and Mr Geikie can still complain he is understaffed. His superiors have now such confidence in him that his office will soon become a Department with himself the Principal of it. He will also have a greatly enlarged staff and one of his underlings promoted to Senior Officer and Deputy Assistant. He will obviously promote the most anxious and servile of his underlings, the one most like himself. June has never seemed servile, never said what she does not believe. She has avoided giving offence by being silent. Before returning to the office this morning she is trusted but not much liked by her workmates. She deliberately arrives ten minutes late, takes off coat and hat in the lift going up, carries them across the large room where the Administrative Assistants are working. She conveys who she is by saying "Good morning!" in the bright curt voice she always uses. They usually reply, but not today. She enters her room and shuts the silent starers out.

This room feels as good and friendly as a workplace ought to feel after a strenuous holiday. Here are things she can tackle, routines to help her do it efficiently. She settles at the desk to which Mr Geikie sends all cases too small to worry him, cases of official tyranny she can correct or compensate for. Through the intercom she first tells the other Executive Officers that she has returned and is now perfectly well, then she studies her desk diary and the contents of the in-tray, then dictates letters into her recorder. An hour later she calls in her Personal Administrative Assistant (or secretary) and explains how she wants the letters handled. She ignores the girl's fascinated stare by sitting sideways to it, until Jack Bleloch bursts in and says, "Excuse me for bursting in June but could you tell me if –" He then gapes, mouths silently for four seconds, mutters an apology and leaves without closing the door. As the secretary shuts it June asks in a thoughtful voice, "Do you think he prefers me in the charcoal grey skirt and sweater?"

The secretary sits down, giggling heartily. June joins her in this. The secretary, who is last to stop, says, "Did you meet someone?"

This is a daring question. June has never spoken about her private life before, though all the office know she is divorced. After a thoughtful silence June says slowly, "I did, yes. But it may not be important."

"*Not important?*" whispers the secretary, staring.

"Don't judge by appearances," says June, then they both laugh loud and long, the secretary so uncontrollably that June eventually gestures her to leave.

Shortly after this Tannahill jauntily enters, stares hard at her and at last says slowly, "My god! No wonder Bleloch is shitting himself. I really like this new style of yours – I've got a hard-on just looking at you. When are you and me going to have our weekend together?"

June gets up, opens the door and says in a voice almost loud enough to be heard by the clerical staff outside, "Jim Tannahill, you must feel very witty and manly and daring when you say things like that or you wouldn't keep calling in and saying them so often, but I find them boring and disgusting. I should have told you that years ago. I know you haven't enough work to fill your day but I'm luckier in that respect. Clear out of here and come back when you've something useful to say, but not before next week or better still, the week after."

He goes out past her like a sleep-walker. For the rest of the morning the Administrative Assistants (all women) seem larger and noisier than usual, often erupting in untypical laughter. The other Executive Officers (all men) seem comparatively rodent-like and furtive.

Ten minutes before lunchtime the Senior Executive Officer says over the intercom, "May I see you for a moment em June please?"

She goes to his room. He sits staring hard at a sheaf of typed pages on the desk before him. June sits opposite, takes a cigarette packet from her breast pocket, asks, "May I smoke?"

"Oh yes oh yes," he murmurs, pushes an ashtray toward her, stares out of the window for a while and then stares back at the sheaf. These shifts let him see June briefly from left to right and later from right to left. He blushes at the first glance, starts sweating at the second, eventually says to the sheaf of papers, "I'm em very *glad* you've recovered from your trouble Miss em June I mean."

"Thank you Mr Geikie."

"Are you *sure* you have recovered? I overwork you shamefully and em you are perhaps too em em con con conscientious."

"Quite sure Mr Geikie."

"But! –" he looks up for a second "– There is a *change* in your appearance Miss em em June I mean."

"I have been shaved bald for medical reasons but that will not affect my work," says June briskly and without forethought. This is the first lie she has deliberately told. She is surprised how easily it comes.

"Alopecia?" murmurs Mr Geikie, taking another peep.

"I refuse to discuss it," says June serenely.

"But there are *other* changes in your appearance Miss em June I mean."

She realizes he keeps calling her Miss because she is giving him the sensations of a very small boy with a mature schoolmistress. She draws thoughtfully on her cigarette, tips ash into the tray and says, "If I dressed as usual with a head like this Mr Geikie I would look pathetic – pitiable. This way every bit of me looks deliberate. You don't think I look pitiable, do you Mr Geikie?"

'No but surely ... a wig, perhaps?"

"I hate wigs. I hate all kinds of falsehood," declares June, so amused by how easily she lies that to prevent a wide grin she compresses the corners of her mouth, producing a smile which probably seems scornful. He cringes before it. Then rallies, straightens his back, places clasped hands on sheaf of paper, clears throat, gazes half an inch to the right of June's head and says, "However! The image our *office* (which will soon be a Department), the image our *office* presents to the general public is not consistent with our em ... new and em ... disturbing aspect."

"Our office presents *no* image to the general public, Mr Geikie," says June firmly, "Our clothes and hairstyles are as unknown to the people we deal with as our faces and personal characters. The public contacts us through lawyers who contact us by letter and occasional phone calls. And since we work in a commercial office block forty-five miles from Saint Andrew's House not even our civil service colleagues know or give a damn for my appearance."

"True Miss em June I mean but! Suppose!" says Geikie so eagerly that he now looks straight at her face, "Just suppose! As might one day happen! I fall ill and you have to represent our office before an arbitration tribunal! Or at an interdepartmental function! It might even be a *Royal* Function! Holyrood Palace!"

"I never knew you were considering *me* for promotion Mr Geikie!" says June, opening her eyes wide.

The idea is new to him also. He gets up, walks to the window, looks out, turns and says mildly, "Nothing definite has been decided, M ... June. Many things are still possible, I trust?"

His face shows unusual vitality – his imagination has started working. June feels inclined to pat him on the head but shakes her own head, smiles and says, "You're a wicked man Mr Geikie. You're toying with me. How can you think of promoting me when you have Bleloch and Tannahill to depend on?"

"I am *not* toying with you! I never *toy*. Surely you've noticed, June, that you do all the work which justifies the existence of this place? I and Bleloch and Tannahill do nothing but defuse potentially explosive confrontations. The fact is that Her Majesty's Government is cutting back the social services so vigorously that it is *detaching itself* from a big class of people it is supposed to govern. All I and Bleloch and Tannahill do is erect façades to the fact. Don't think I'm proud of myself."

June stares at him in wonder. She knows the truth of what he says but did not know he knew it.

He sits down behind his desk again looking as ordinary and dejected as he usually does but watching her wistfully sideways. She knows he has always thought her dazzling. He sometimes starts conversations aimed at asking her out for a meal, managing them so circumspectly that she easily changes the subject before he reaches it. He is the kind of married man who jokes about how much his wife dominates him. June decides she can do him good without granting sexual favours. She says carefully, "You are a stronger man in a stronger position than you've noticed, Mr Geikie. May I call you David?"

"You know that option has always been open to you em June."

"An office is not the best place to discuss office politics. Can we meet for a meal tomorrow night in the Grosvenor Steakhouse? Nobody we know will see us there. I'll wear a turban, David, and dress so conventionally nobody will notice me at all."

He pays her a predictable compliment.

So when June returns home from work she has more to think about than Senga. (Remember there is no Harry in this development of the story.) On the following night she starts persuading Mr Geikie that he will be in no social or financial danger if he prefers the public good to the comfort of his colleagues and superiors. When they bid each other goodbye with a handshake she knows the post of Deputy Principal will be hers.

On Friday Senga phones June and asks, "Do you still hate me?"
"No."
"And you'll meet me? Not just to get your things back?"
"Oh yes."
Senga tells June to go that evening to a street where a car will collect her. June says firmly, "No, I want to meet you without your little friend."
She tells Senga to meet her instead in the lounge of a hotel, then goes to the hotel with a suitcase and books a room. She spends an hour or two in it making herself as beautiful as possible. She puts on a little black dress she perhaps bought that afternoon. It distresses Senga, who comes to her in the lounge saying sadly, "Why aren't you wearing it?"
"Do you mean the suit? My work suit? I felt like wearing something romantic tonight."
"Work suit?"
"Yes. I wear it to the office to frighten the men."
"You've changed!"
"Yes, you changed me and I'm glad – I'm grateful. Why are you looking so worried?"
"Mibby I've changed you too much. I was always scared of you, June, you were so lovely. And now I'm terrified."
Senga is trembling. June says kindly, "I've booked a room upstairs – let's go there."
They go to the room, kiss, undress and make love nervously at first, then relax into gently exploring caresses which they prolong with variations for three or four hours.

"We don't need to be cruel to each other, do we?" asks June at one point and Senga says, "Not when it's just you and me now, like this. We're just starting together so we're fresh and equal. But sooner or later one of us will be up and the other down because nobody in love ever stays equal, and I'm the one who will be down this time because all my days I've managed to keep up and I'm so tired. I'll be forty next week. Oh I love you."
She weeps and June, who has never been happier, cuddles and comforts her, says they will love each other always and equally no matter what happens, and while she says so truly believes it.

And that was all I could imagine happening between June and Senga, but I easily imagined June and Mr Geikie three months later.

They are in Edinburgh, attending sessions of a tribunal arbitrating on the first case brought before it by Mr Geikie's new department. It concerns an honest, hard-working woman who loses her ability to earn money. Her hands get scalded in a restaurant whose owner has not provided the protective gloves required by health regulations. Her schooling has told her nothing about health regulations or employers' responsibilities so years pass before she is told she should have claimed compensation; meanwhile she loses her home, her four young children and most of her sanity with the assistance of officials paid to help her keep them. June has drawn up a detailed history of the case, given a precis of it to the judges and would gladly give further details if asked, but the tribunal finds her Principal's statement of the case satisfactory.
"Cutbacks in social welfare funding are no excuse for incompetence!' he concludes, "The main cause of this tragedy is a sinister absence of contact between the five offices dealing with the case, contact which could have been made at any time by the simple expedient of lifting a telephone. These offices – and the officials staffing

them – work hard and long at the grass roots level of their departmental em em em remit. It would be invidious to single out for blame the name of particular individuals. But my esteemed colleagues the departmental chiefs – and some of our more highly esteemed superiors – cannot hold themselves aloof from some measure of responsibility. My department can only work by drawing such facts to their attention. May they attend to them!"

"Well done," says June as they leave the building, although she wishes he had mentioned some individuals by name.

"Yes!" says Geikie. "I was astonished to hear myself lashing out so vigorously in every direction. Yet in the men's washroom only five minutes later Macgregor of Industrial Injuries smiled and nodded to me as if I had left him quite unscathed! What a remarkable man he is. I say, June, can I buy you a meal tonight to celebrate? I'll take you to my club. I'm a member of a very posh Edinburgh club. I was *astonished* that they let me join."

They are staying at the Sheraton Hotel and arrange to meet beforehand in the foyer. Since June's promotion she has not worn the leather suit but keeps it near her as a talisman. Feeling mischievous tonight she puts it on, and as her hair is again a conventional length has it shaved off by the hotel barber. On meeting her in the foyer Geikie says, "Oh dear I doubt if they'll let us into my club with you looking like that."

She takes his arm saying, "Nonsense, Dave. Women can look how they like and you're respectable enough for both of us."

The club is five minutes' walk away on Princes Street. Fewer passers-by stare and pass comments than would happen in Glasgow, but enough do it to stimulate Geikie's adrenal glands. His spine straightens. His face takes on a look of stoical endurance. His noble bearing and her careless one carry them past the doorman, the cloakroom attendants and up a stair to the dining room. Through large windows they see the lit mansions and battlements of the castle standing high in the air between black sky and black rock. At a corner table sit two businessmen with a lawyer who attended the tribunal that day and a Scottish politician who was once a cabinet minister and famous for interesting but unwise press announcements. The first three exchange nods with Geikie. The fourth turns completely round and gazes at June who deliberately sits with her back to him. She and Geikie consult menus.

Then Geikie murmurs, "Oh here comes Lucy."
"Lucy?"
"Short for Lucifer – that's what he likes to be called."
"Excuse me for butting in unasked and unannounced," says the politician pulling a chair to their table, aiming to sit on it and almost missing.
"Oopsadaisy David! David you MUST introduce me to your charming companion, even though she is staring at me as if I'm a kind of insect. And she should, because I AM a kind of insect. Looper T. Firefly, exiled President of Freedonia at your service Ma'am."
He blows her a kiss.
"June Tain my Deputy Principal," says Geikie coldly.
"God's boots Geikie! You are kicking out in EVERY direction these days. I hear you've actually brought a case to arbitration! Remarkable. BUT! The name of Geikie will enter the history of our race through your courage in promoting to senior rank a lady who has destroyed the STUPID old fuddy-duddy notion that our civil service is staffed by desiccated spinsters of BOTH sexes who dress to *show* they are dedicated, desiccated spinsters. Too few people have realized that a dozen years ago a new age dawned for Britain, HEIL MARGARET. She has given Britain back its testicles by turning government offices and free enterprises into businesses run by the same people. Highly profitable. And now every man with money and initiative can enjoy his woman and his bottle and his

woman and his tax-avoidance scam and his woman and his special boyfriend (aids permitting) without having his fun spoiled by hypocritical spoil-sport neighbours and a ghastly spook called PUBLIC OPINION. Because at last at last *at last* Public Opinion recognizes what poor Fred Sneeze told us a century ago, God is dead. So now we can all do what we like. By the way, when I say God is dead I don't mean every God is dead – that would be Blasphemy and I am a Believer. I refer only to Mister Nice-Guy in the sky, the wet-eyed, bleeding-heart bastard who told us to love our neighbours and enemies because the scum of the earth are going to inherit it. *That* God, thank God, is AS DEAD AS SOCIALISM and even the Labour Party is delighted, though it can't openly admit it yet. You are still looking at me as though I am an insect, my dear. Quite right, quite right. A glow-worm. My little tail is indeed aglow. Your fault, my dear."

"Lucy," says Geikie, "we want to eat."

"Not yet, Geikie!" says Lucy firmly, "Because I have something important to say. Fin de siècle! End of age, start of other and what rough beast, June Tain, shambles toward Bethlehem to be born? I'll tell you at the end of my next paragraph. I talk in paragraphs. Please remember all I say because tomorrow I won't recall a word.

"Now a lot of idiots think the British spy system sorry BRITISH INTELLIGENCE system is full of Russian double-agents. Nonsense. We've had a lot of these but our relationship with the Yanks ensures that it's the CIA who know most of our secrets and we have learned quite a few of theirs. Do you remember the Scottish Referendum, June Tain? When it looked like London might let us off the hook, haha? Well, a friend of mine – a fine fellow and a brave soldier – showed me the CIA plans for Scotland if it won some independence for itself, and the astonishing thing was –"

Mr Geikie, who has become restless, mutters, "Better not tell us these things Lucy."

"Pipe down Geikie you are not in the same LEAGUE as your charming assistant and me, she is a Hells Angel and I am a DRAGONFLY, a bright spark spawned by the burning breath of the Beast of the Bottomless Pit. A fine statesman, Pitt. Do you know, June Tain, that the Yanks were going to be quite kind to independent Scotland? A lot kinder than to Guatemala, Nicaragua etcetera. They were NOT afraid of us becoming a socialist republic because they felt we'd be even easier to manipulate than England – *fewer chiefs to bribe* was how my friend put it – and no trouble at all compared with Ireland, especially the north bit. And what I want to tell you is this."

Lucy leans across the table and tells June in a hissing whisper, *"The CIA. Scenario for an independent Scotland has not been scrapped and you are filling me with mysterious insights."*

He stands and speaks in a solemn and quiet voice which grows steadily louder.

"I am a Douglas on my mother's side, a descendant of that Black Douglas who was Stabbed to The Death by The Hand of A Kind. And if you tell me it was some other Douglas who was stabbed to death by Jamie the First or Second or Third or Fourth or Fifth I DON'T CARE! I STILL FEEL PROPHETIC! I PROPHESY THAT JUNE TAIN –"

He points a finger at June and says more intimately, "I prophesy that you, June Tain," then notices his friends are beckoning him and more people are entering the restaurant. He murmurs, "Forgive me – I'm boring you," and returns to his friends.

Dear reader, I – your author – cannot imagine how to continue this story. It has contained a strong hint that having been liberated by the work of Senga and Donalda, June the professional career woman, and Harry the inherited wealth person, will cut themselves off from their poorer employees and have fun together. You need not believe that ending but it is how things are normally arranged in Britain, and how they were arranged in 1990's Glasgow.

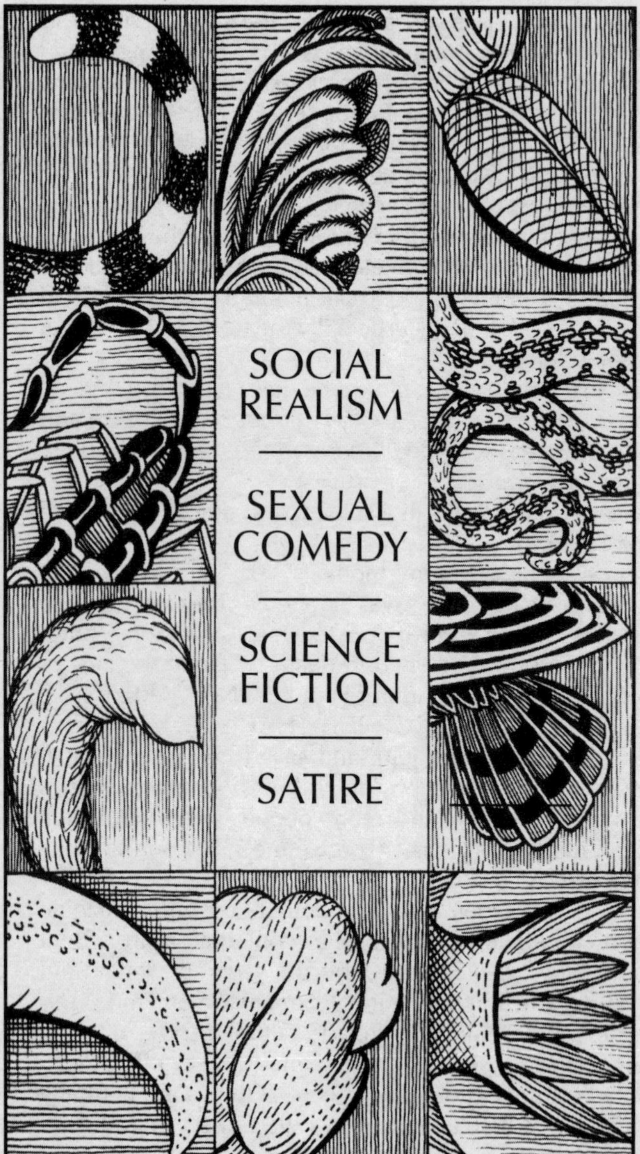
SOCIAL REALISM
SEXUAL COMEDY
SCIENCE FICTION
SATIRE

TEN TALES TALL AND TRUE

FOR
MORAG McALPINE
TOM MASCHLER
XANDRA HARDIE

LONDON 1993

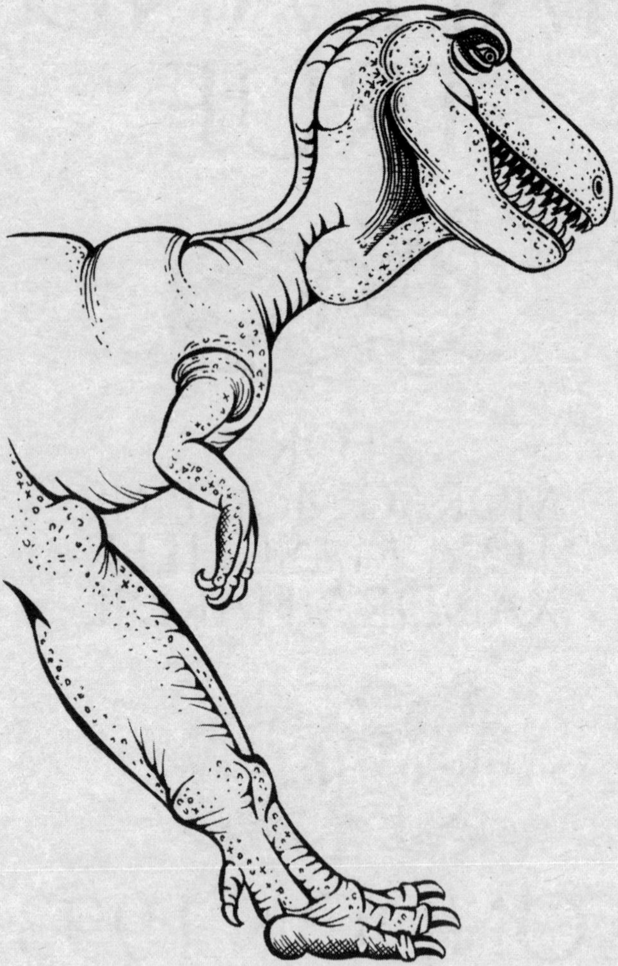

GETTING STARTED – A PROLOGUE

I AM THE DESCENDANT of a race whose stolid unimaginative decency has, at all times, rendered them the dependable tools of others; yet from my earliest infancy I grew self-willed, addicted to the wildest caprices, a prey to the most ungovernable passions until bound and weary I thought best to sulk upon my mother's breast. Too romantic.

Call Me Ishmael. Jesus wept. Reader, I married him. Pithiness prevents flow.

I remember the whole beginning as a succession of flights and drops, a little see-saw of the right throbs and the wrong. Far too vague.

A man stood upon a railway bridge in Northern Alabama, looking down into the swift waters twenty feet below. The man's hands were behind his back, the wrists bound with a cord.

That's the style for me.

HOUSES AND SMALL LABOUR PARTIES

EIGHT MEN DUG a trench beside a muddy crossroads, and the mud made two remember Italy where they had fought in a recent war. These two had not known each other in Italy, but both had seen a dead German who lay at a crossroads near Naples, though one thought it was perhaps nearer Pisa. They discussed the matter when the gang paused for a smoke.

"Not Pisa, no, Pisa was miles away," said one, "Naples was the place. He was a handsome big fella. We called him Siegfried."

"Our lot called him Adolf, because of the fuckin moustache," said the other, "He wasnae handsome for fuckin long."

"I don't remember a moustache, but you're right, he wasnae handsome for long. He went all white and puffy and swole up like a balloon – I think only his uniform stopped him bursting. The heavy traffic must have kept the rats away. Every time we went that road I hoped to God someone had shifted him but no, there he always was, more horrible than ever. Because eventually a truck ran over him and burst him up properly. Do you mind that?"

"I mind it fuckin fine."

"Every time we went that road we would say, 'I wonder how old Siegfried's doing,' and look out for him, and there was always something to see, though at last it was only the bones of a foot or a bit of rag with a button on it."

There was a silence. The older navvies thought about death and the youngest about a motorcycle he wanted to buy. He was known for being the youngest of them and fond of motorcycles. Everybody in the gang was known for something. Mick the ganger was known for being Irish and saying queer things in a solemn voice. One navvy was known for being a Highlander, one for having a hangover every morning, one for being newly married. One of the ex-army men was known for his war stories, the other for his fucking adjectives. One of them was a communist who thought *The Ragged Trousered Philanthropists* a better book than the Bible and kept trying to lend it; but schooling had given most of them a disgust of books. Only Old Joe borrowed it and he said it was a bit out of date. The communist wanted to argue the point but Old Joe was known for being silent as well as old. The youngest navvy liked working with these folk though he hardly ever listened to what they said. Too many of them wanted his attention. They remembered, or thought they remembered, when they too had been just out of school, sixteen and good-looking, happy because their developing muscles could still enjoy the strain of working overtime, happy because it was great to earn a wage as big as their fathers earned. The worst paid workers reach the peak of their earning power early in life.

"The Signoras!" announced the story teller suddenly, "The Signorinas! They were something else. Am I right? Am I wrong?"

"Aye, the fuckin Signoras were somethin fuckin else,"

said the other ex-army man. With both hands he shaped a huge bosom on the air before his chest.
"I'll give you a bit of advice Ian," the story-teller told the youngest navvy, "If you ever go to Italy take a few tins of bully beef in your suitcase. There is nothing, I'm telling you nothing you won't get from the Italian Signorinas in return for a can of bully beef."
"That advice may be slightly out of date," said Mick the ganger.
"You're sticking up for the Tally women because they're Papes and so are you, ye fuckin Fenian Irish Papal prick ye," said one of the ex-army men pleasantly.
"He's right, of course," the ganger told the youngest navvy, "I am a Papal Fenian. But if these warriors ever return to Italy they may find the ladies less welcoming now the babies have stopped starving."
He nipped his cigarette, stuck it under his cap brim above the right ear and lifted his pick. The gang began digging again.

Though their work was defined as unskilled by the Department of Labour they worked skilfully in couples, one breaking the ground with a pick, the other shovelling loose earth and stones from under his partner's feet and flinging it clear. At the front end Mick the ganger set a steady pace for all of them. The youngest navvy was inclined to go too fast, so Mick had paired him with Old Joe who was nearly sixty, but still worked well by pacing himself carefully. The two ex-army men were liable to slow down if paired together, so Mick always paired one of them with himself. The gang belonged to a workforce of labourers, brickies, joiners, plumbers, slaters, electricians, painters, drivers, foremen and site clerks who were enlarging a city by turning a hillside into a housing estate. During the recent war (which had ended seven years before but still seemed recent to all who remembered it) the government had promised there would be no return to unemployment afterward, and every family would eventually have a house with a lavatory and bath inside. The nation's taxes were now being spent on houses as well as armed forces, motorways, public health et cetera, so public housing was now profitable. Bankers and brokers put money into firms making homes for the class of folk who laboured to build them. To make these fast and cheaply standards of spaciousness and craftsmanship were lowered, makeshifts were used which had been developed during the war. Concrete replaced stonework. Doors were light wooden frames with a hardboard sheet nailed to each side. Inner walls were frames surfaced with plasterboard that dented if a door-knob swung hard against it. A tall man could press his fingers to the ceilings without standing on tiptoe. But every house had a hot water system, a bath and flush lavatory, and nearly everyone was employed. There was so much work that firms advertised for workers overseas and natives of the kingdom were paid extra to work at week-ends and during public holidays. In the building industry the lowest paid were proudest of what they earned by overtime work so most of this gang worked a six-day week. A labourer who refused overtime was not exactly scorned as a weakling, but thought a poor specimen of his calling. Recently married men were notoriously poor specimens, but seldom for more than a fortnight.

A heavily built man called McIvor approached the trench and stood for a while watching the gang with a dour, slightly menacing stare which was a tool of his trade. When his presence was noticed by the ganger, McIvor beckoned him by jerking his head a fraction to the side. Mick laid his pick carefully down, dried his sweating face with a handkerchief, muttered, "No slacking, men, while I confabulate with our commanding officer," and climbed out of the trench. He did not confabulate. He listened to McIvor, stroked his chin then shouted, "Ian! Over here a minute!"

The youngest navvy, surprised, dropped his spade, leapt from the trench and hurried to them. McIvor said to him, "Do you want some overtime? Sunday afternoons, one to five."

"Sure."

"It's gardening work but not skilled weeding, cutting grass, that sort of thing. It's at the house of Mr Stoddart, the boss. He'll give the orders. The rate is the usual double time. You get the money in your weekly pay packet."

"I thought Old Joe did that job."

"He does, but the boss says Joe needs help now. What do you say? Yes or no?"

"Aye. Sure," said the youngest navvy.

"Then I'll give you a word of advice. Mick here has pointed you out as a good worker so you'd better be, because the boss has a sharp eye for slackers – comes down on them like a ton of bricks. He also has a long memory, and a long arm. If you don't do right by Mr Stoddart you won't just get yourself in the shit, you'll make trouble for Mick here who recommended you. Right, Mick?"

"Don't put the fear of death into the boy," said the ganger, "Ian will do fine."

In the bothy where the navvies had their lunch an ex-army man said loudly and cheerfully, "I see the fuckin Catholics are stickin to-fuckin-gether as per fuckin usual."

"Could that be a hostile remark?" the ganger asked Ian, "Do you think the foul-mouthed warrior is talking about us?"

"Fuckin right I'm talking about yous! You could have gave the fuckin job to a fuckin family man like me with fuckin weans to feed but no, you give it to a fuckin co-religionist who's a fuckin wean himself."

"I'm not a Catholic!" said the youngest navvy, astonished.

"Well how do you come to be so fuckin thick with Mick the Papal prick here?"

"I recommended the infant of the gang for three reasons," said the ganger, "One, he is a bloody hard worker who gets on well with Old Joe. Two, some family men enjoy Sunday at home. Three, if one of us starts working around the boss's house he'll get the name of being a boss's man, which is good for nobody's social life, but Ian is too young to be thought that, just as Joe is too old."
"Blethers!" said the communist, "You are the boss's man here, like every ganger. You're no as bad as bastarding McIvor, but he comes to you for advice."
"Jesus Mary and Joseph!" cried Mick to the youngest navvy, "For the love of God get out of this and apprentice yourself to a decent trade! Go up to the joiners' bothy and talk to Cameron – they're wanting apprentice joiners."
"I'm not a Catholic, I've never been a Catholic," said the youngest navvy, looking around the others in the bothy with a hurt, alarmed and pleading expression. The Highlander (who was also suspected of being Catholic because he came from Barra, and someone had said everyone from that island were Catholics) said, "You are absolved – go in peace," which caused general amusement.
"Did you hear me, Ian?" said the ganger sharply, "I told you to get out of this into a decent trade."
"I might, when I've bought my Honda," said the youngest navvy thoughtfully. He saw the sense in the ganger's advice. A time-served tradesman was better paid and had more choices of work than a labourer, but during the apprentice years the wage would be a lot less.
"Why did a clever fella like you never serve your time as a tradesman, Mick?" asked the communist.
"Because at sixteen I was a fool, like every one of us here, especially that silly infant. I never wanted a motorbike, I wanted a woman. So here I am, ten years later, at the peak of my profession. I've a wife and five children and a job paying me a bit more than the rest of you in return for taking a lot of lip from a foul-mouthed warrior and from a worshipper of Holy Joe Stalin."

"You havenae reached the peak yet Mick," said the communist, "In a year or three they'll give you McIvor's job."

"No, I'll never be a foreman," said the ganger sombrely, "The wages would be welcome, but not the loneliness. Our dirty tongued Orange friend will get that job – he enjoys being socially obnoxious."

The foreman had given the youngest navvy a slip of paper on which was written *89 Balmoral Road, Pollokshields*, and the route of a bus that would take him past there, and the heavily underlined words *1 a.m. on the dot*. The boy's ignorance of the district got him to the boss's house seven minutes late and gasping for breath. He lived with his parents on a busy thoroughfare between tenements whose numbers ran into thousands. When the bus entered Balmoral Road he saw number 3 on a pillar by a gate and leapt off at the next stop, sure that 89 must be nearby. He was wrong. After walking fast for what seemed ten minutes he passed another bus stop opposite a gate pillar numbered 43, and broke into a jog-trot. The sidewalk was a gravel path with stone kerb instead of a pavement, the road was as wide and straight as the one where he lived, but seemed wider because of the great gardens on each side. Some had lawns with flower-beds behind hedges, some shrubberies and trees behind high walls, both sorts had driveways leading up to houses which seemed as big as castles. All of well-cut stone, several imitated castles by having turrets, towers and oriel windows crowned with battlements. Signboards at two or three entrances indicated nursing homes, but names carved on gate pillars (Beech Grove, Trafalgar, Victoria Lodge) suggested most houses were private, and so did curtains and ornaments in the windows. Yet all had several rooms big enough to hold the complete two-room flat where he lived with his parents, or one of the three-room-and-kitchen flats being built on the site where he laboured. But the queerest thing about this district was the absence of people. After the back of the bus dwindled to an orange speck in the distance, then vanished, the only moving things he saw were a few birds in the sky and what must have been a cat crossing the road a quarter mile ahead. His brain was baffled by no sight or sign of buildings he thought always went with houses: shops, a post-office, school or church. Down the long length of the road he could not even see a parked car or telephone box. The place was a desert. How could people live here? Where did they buy their food and meet each other? Seeing number 75 on another gate pillar he broke into an almost panic-stricken run.

Number 89 was not the biggest house he had seen but still impressive. On rising ground at a corner, it was called The Gables and had a lot of them. The front garden was terraced with bright beds of rose bushes which must have been recently tended by a professional gardener. A low, new brick wall in front hid none of this. The young navvy hurried up a drive of clean granite chips which scrunched so loudly underfoot that he wanted to walk on the trim grass verge, but feared his boots would dent it. Fearful of the wide white steps up to the large front door he went crunching round the side to find a more inviting entrance, and discovered Old Joe building a rockery in the angle of two gables.

"Hullo Joe. Am I late? Is he angry?"

"I'm your gaffer today so don't worry. Fetch ower yon barrow and follow me."

Behind the house was a kitchen garden, a rhododendron shrubbery and a muddy entry from a back lane. Near the entry lay a pile of small boulders and a mound of earth with a spade in it. Joe said, "Bring me a load of the rocks then a load of the earth and keep going till I tell ye different. And while we're away from the house I don't mind telling you ye're on probation."

"What's that supposed to mean?"

"He watches us. He's seen you already."

"How? Why do ye think that?"
"You'll know why when he talks to ye later."

As they worked on the rockery the young navvy looked cautiously about and gradually grew sure they were the only folk in the garden. The walls of the house where they worked were blank, apart from a wee high-up window that probably ventilated a lavatory. When he wheeled the barrow to the back entry he was in view of larger windows. He kept bringing boulders and earth to Joe who worked kneeling and sometimes said, "Put that there, son," or "Give a shovelful here." Nearly an hour passed then Joe sighed, stood slowly up, straightened his shoulders and said, "Five minutes."
"I'll just get another load," said the young navvy, lifting the shafts of the barrow. He was uneasily aware of the black little lavatory window above and behind him.
"We're entitled to five minute spells," said Old Joe quietly, "We need them."
"I don't need them. And I was late, you werenae." He went off with the barrow, loaded it and found Joe working when he returned. An hour later a gaunt, smartly dressed lady looked round a corner, called, "Your tea is in the tool-shed," then vanished behind the corner.
"Was that his wife?" asked the young navvy.
"His housekeeper. Are you working through the tea-break too?"
The young navvy blushed.

The tool-shed, like the garage, was part of a big newly built outhouse, and windowless, and had a roller shutter door facing the back entry. It smelt of cement, timber and petrol; had shelves and racks of every modern gardening and construction tool, all shiningly new; also a workbench with two mugs of tea and a plate of chocolate biscuits on it; also a motorcycle leaning negligently against a wall, though there were blocks for standing it upright.
"A Honda!" whispered the young navvy, going straight to

it and hunkering down so that his eyes were less than a foot from the surface of the thing he worshipped, "Whose is this?"
"The boss's son's."
"But he hasnae been using it," said the young navvy indignantly, noting flat tyres, dust on seat and metal, dust on a footpump and kit of keys and spanners strewn near the front wheel. What should be shining chromium was dull, with rust spots.
"He's got better things to think of," said Joe after swallowing a mouthful of tea, "He's a student at the Uni."
"Why does he no sell it?"
"Sentimental reasons. His da gave it him as a present, and he doesnae need the money."
The young navvy puffed out his cheeks and blew to convey astonishment, then went over to the bench. Since they were not in sight or earshot of anyone he said, "What's the boss like?"
"Bossy."
"Come on Joe! There's good and bad bosses. What sort is he?"
"Middling to average. You'll soon see."

Ten minutes later they returned to the garden and worked for over an hour before Joe said, "Five minutes," and straightened his back, and surveyed his work with a critical eye. The young navvy paused and looked too. He could see the rocks were well-balanced and not likely to sink under heavy rains, but the impending presence of the unseen Stoddart (maybe the biggest and bossiest boss he would ever meet) made him restless. After a minute he said, "I'll just get us another load," and went off with the barrow.

Half an hour later the rockery was complete. As they stood looking at it the young navvy suddenly noticed there were three of them and for a moment felt he had met the third man before. He was a massive man with a watchful, impassive face, clean white open-necked shirt, finely creased flannel slacks and white canvas sports shoes. At last the stranger, still looking at the rockery, said, "Seven minutes late. Why?"

"I got off at the wrong stop – I didnae know the street was so long."

"Makes sense. What's your name youngster?"

"Ian Maxwell."

"Apart from the lateness (which will not be docked from your wages) you've done well today, Ian. You too Joe. A very decent rockery. The gardener can start planting tomorrow. But the day's work is not yet done as Joe knows, but perhaps as you do not know, Ian. Because now the barrow, spade, fork, trowel go back to the tool-shed and are cleaned – cleaned thoroughly. There's a drain in the floor and a wall-tap with a house attached. Use them! I don't want to find any wee crumbs of dirt between the tyre and the hub of that barrow. A neglected tool is a wasted tool. What you'd better know from the start Ian (if you and me are going to get on together) is that I am not gentry. I'm from the same folk you are from, so I know what you are liable to do and not do. But do right by me and I'll do right by you. Understood?"

The young navvy stared, hypnotized by the dour impassive face now turned to him. Suddenly it changed. The eyes stayed watchful but the mouth widened into what the young navvy supposed was a smile, so he nodded. The big man patted him on the shoulder and walked away.

The navvies went to the tool-shed and cleaned the tools in silence. The youngest was depressed, though he did not know why. When they had returned the tools to their places (which were easy to see, because there were three of everything so a gap in the ranks was as obvious as a missing tooth) the young navvy said, "Do we just leave now?"

"No. We wait for the inspection."

They did not wait long. There was a rattling of at least two locks then an inner door opened and Stoddart came

through carrying a tray with two glasses, a whisky bottle and a jug of water. His inspection was a quick sideways glance toward the tool-racks before he said, "How old are you, Ian?"
"Nearly seventeen."
"Too young for whisky. I'm not going to teach you bad habits. But Joe and me haven't had our ne'erday yet. A bad thing, me forgetting old customs. A large one, Joe? Macallan's Glenlivet Malt?"
"Thanks, aye."
"Water?"
"No thanks."
"Quite right, better without ... Good stuff Joe?"
"Aye."
"How's the old back, the old lumbago, Joe?"
"No bad, considering."
"Aye, but age gets us all in the end – even me. I'm not as young as I was. We have to learn to take things easy, Joe."
"Aye," said Joe, and emptied the glass straight down his throat.
"God, that went fast!" said Stoddart, "Another one, Joe?"
"Goodnight," said Joe, and walked out. "Goodnight Joe, and goodnight to you Ian. See you next week on the dot of one youngster. Joe will be taking a bit of a rest. Right?"
"Thanks," said the young navvy, and hurried after Joe wondering why he had said thanks instead of goodnight when he had been given nothing, had not even been paid yet for his labour.

The young navvy overtook Joe walking into the back lane and said, "Are you no going for a bus, Joe?"
"No. This is a shortcut."
"Can I come with you?" asked the young navvy, wondering why he was asking. Joe said nothing. They walked beside each other in a lane with a brick wall on one side, a railway embankment on the other. It could have been in the depths of the country. Grass, daisies and clover grew between two parallel paths made by

car wheels and the verges were thick with dandelions, dockens, thistles, burdock. Branches from trees in the gardens behind the wall hung overhead. From the embankment hawthorns and brambles stuck thorny, leafy shoots between the sagging wires of a fence. The old and young navvy walked side by side in silence, each on one of the parallel tracks. The young one felt Joe was angry, feared it had to do with him, tried to think of something to say.

And at last said, "When the boss turned up beside us there I thought he was McIvor at first."

Joe said nothing.

"Don't you think he's a bit like McIvor, Joe?"

"Of course he's like McIvor. McIvor is a foreman. Stoddart is the foreman's foreman – the gaffer's gaffer. Of course he's like McIvor."

"But he's cheerier than McIvor – he calls ye by your first name. Have you had drinks with him before, Joe?"

"That was the first and last."

"The last? Why the last?"

"Because you've done for me."

"What do you mean?" asked the young navvy, suddenly seeing exactly what the old one meant but confused by two amazements: amazement that the boss preferred him to Joe, amazement at the unfairness and speed of the result. Together these amazements stopped him feeling very happy or very angry. But he liked Joe so the unfairness puzzled him.

"Are you sure he doesnae ever want ye back Joe? I never heard him say so."

"Then you need your ears washed."

"But that cannae be right, Joe! I've got more muscle than you but I havenae the head yet – the skill. That's why Mick keeps pairing us. If I'm working just by myself I won't do so much because I'll need to keep stopping to think."

"Too true!" said Joe, "Stoddart is stupider than he knows,

but he's a boss so nobody can put him right. In a week or two when he sees you arenae doing as well as you did today he'll think you've started slacking so give you the heave and get in someone else. Or maybe no! If ye arrive ten minutes early every day, and work your guts out till he tells ye to stop, and if you take a five minutes tea-break or none at all when the housekeeper forgets ye – well, if ye sweat enough at showing you're a boss's man he'll maybe keep ye."

Joe climbed over the fence and went up the embankment by a path slanting through willow herb and the young navvy followed, his confused feelings tinged by distress. Joe led him across three sets of railway lines to a gap in a fence of upright railway sleepers. They were now in a broad, unpeopled street between old warehouses. "What should I do Joe?" asked the youngest navvy. He was not answered, so said it again. After a long silence Joe suddenly said, "Get out of this into civil engineering, son. No bastard can own you in civil engineering because ye travel all over. Highland power stations, motorways in the Midlands, reservoirs in Wales – if ye tire of one job ye just collect your jotters and wages, clear out the same day and go to another. Naebody minds. No questions asked. And the money, the overtime is phenomenal. Once at Loch Sloy I worked a forty-eight hour stint – forty-eight hours with the usual breaks of course, but I was on the job the whole time without one wink of sleep. Someone bet me I couldnae but I could and I did. Civil engineering is the life, son, for folk like you and me. Of course most of the money goes on booze and betting, there's nothing much else to do with it. Some keep a wife and weans on the money but why bother? Ye only get to see them one week in six maybe. Family life is a con, a bloody imposition. Not that I'm advocating prostitutes! Keep clear of all women, son, is my advice to you: if they don't give you weans they'll give you some other disease. Chuck Stoddart and go into civil engineering. It's the only life for a man while he has his strength. That's what I did and I've never regretted it."

Joe seldom said more than one sentence at a time so the young navvy brooded over this speech. Booze, betting and prostitutes did not attract him. He wanted to hurl himself through the air toward any target he chose, going faster than a mile a minute with maybe a girl clinging on a pillion behind. But a good bike cost nearly £400. After paying his people two thirds of his weekly earnings in return for the home and services he had enjoyed since infancy, about £4 remained which (despite his intentions of saving £3 a week) seemed always to get eaten up by tram, café, cinema, dancehall, football, haircut and clothes expenses – he had begun to like dressing well on his few nights out. But if he worked on a big civil engineering job in the Highlands, and did all the twelve or sixteen hour shifts his strength allowed, and slept and ate cheaply in a workers' hostel, and paid his people a few shillings a week till he felt like returning, he might earn enough to buy a good bike in less than a year. Then the neglected Honda in the boss's tool-shed came to mind, and Stoddart's words A neglected tool is a wasted tool. He decided that next Sunday, perhaps during the tea-break, he would set the Honda in its blocks, clean it and tidy away the tools. Stoddart would certainly notice this and say something during the five o'clock inspection, and the young navvy had a feeling this might lead to something useful. He did not know what, but found the prospect oddly exciting, though he still felt sorry for Joe.

While he pondered these things they crossed a bridge over a railway cutting and came to Kilmarnock Road. It was a busy road with the railway on one side and on the other wee shops and pubs on the ground floors of ordinary tenements. The young navvy knew this road well. He travelled it by tramcar six days a week from his home to the building site and back. He was perplexed to find it so near the foreign, almost secret city of huge rich houses. A few blocks away he noticed a sign of a station where a subway train would take him home in time for the usual family tea. His distress vanished. He said, "I don't think my ma or da would like me going off to civil engineering just yet, Joe, but I'll take a crack at it one day. Thanks for the tip. See you the morrow."

Joe nodded and they separated.

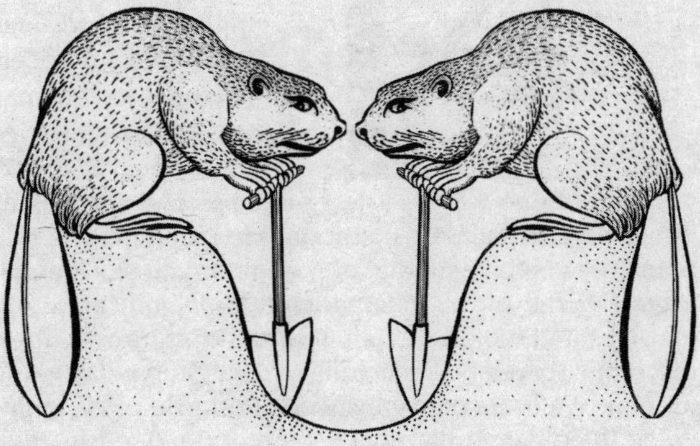

HOMEWARD BOUND

THIS thirty-year-old college lecturer is big, stout, handsome, with the innocent baby face of a man used to being served by women, the sulky underlip of one who has never been served as much as he wants. It is Sunday afternoon. He compares the dial of his wristwatch with that of a small ornate clock under a glass dome on his mantelpiece. Both indicate 2.49. He sighs and looks critically round the apartment like a mechanic surveying a machine that has stopped working for him. Walls are pale grey, woodwork white, the moss-green fitted carpet harmonizes (not too obviously) with his immaculate dark-green sweater. A large low bed lacks foot and headboard, has big blue cushions strewn on it, and derives an air of invitation from a nearby coffee table on which lie a board supporting cold roast chicken, oatcakes, pat of butter, knife, salt-cellar; a salver of apples, peaches, grapes; a dish of small bright cakes and sweets. A few stones in the marble fireplace look nothing like coal, but bright flames among them give the air warmth which would make undressing easy, without

making clothed people sweat. Through an oriel window a view of sunlit treetops can be blotted out (when wished) by smoothly running floor-length curtains, curtains with the light tone of his finely creased flannel trousers. Yet he sighs again, not feeling truly at home. Maybe an apple will help. He goes determinedly to the table but hesitates to disturb his arrangement of the fruit. A bell chimes softly. Smiling with relief he leaves the room, crosses a small lobby, opens the front door and says, "Vlasta."
A bitterly sobbing woman runs in past him. He looks out into the corridor, sees nobody else, closes the door.

Returning to the main room he stands watching the woman and thoughtfully rubbing his chin. She crouches on an easy chair, handbag on lap, sobbing into handkerchief. She is bony and fortyish with wild black hair flowing over the shoulders of her fur coat, a long black skirt and histrionic earrings. The sobs lessen. He tiptoes to the coffee table, lifts and places it softly near her right elbow, selects an apple and sits on a chaise-longue facing her. Cautiously he bites the apple. Her sobbing stops. She removes mirror from handbag and blots off tears, taking care not to damage make-up. He says softly, "I'm glad you came. Eat something. It sometimes helps."
She says hoarsely, "You are always so sweet to me, Alan."
She restores mirror and hanky to handbag, tears a wing from the chicken, bites, swallows and says, "Half an hour ago I threw out Arnold. He did not want to go. I had to call the police. He was drunk and violent. He cracked my tortoise, Alan."
"You were right to call the police."
"He was sweet to begin with – just like you. And then he went bad on me. Eventually they all go bad on me – except you."
She bites and swallows more chicken.

Then looks around and says, "Are you expecting someone?"

He smiles sadly, says, "Expecting someone? I only wish I was."

"But this food! ... And the room. You did not always keep it so spick and span."

"I do nowadays. I've become a real old woman since you left me, Vlasta, hoovering the carpet, dusting the clock – I've even grown cranky about food. I don't eat regular meals any longer. I keep plates of fruit and cold chicken beside me and have a nibble whenever I feel like it."

"How odd! But have you no little girlfriend? No mistress?"

With a harsh laugh Alan throws the apple core into a brass coal-scuttle he uses as a waste basket and says, "None! None! I know plenty of women. I've invited some of them up here, and they've come. A few stayed the night. But (I don't know why) they all bored me. After you they were all so insipid."

"I knew it!" cries Vlasta exultantly, "Yes I knew it! When I left you I told myself, You are destroying this man. You have taught him all he knows and now that you leave him his confidence will vanish also. In fact you are castrating him! But I had to do it. You were sweet but ... oh so deadly dull. No imagination. And so I had to leave."

"It was agony," he assures her.

"I knew. I was sorry for you but I needed excitement. I will take my coat off, this room is far too warm, how can you bear it?"

She stands and flings her chicken bone into the scuttle. But Alan has risen first. Slipping behind her he helps remove the coat murmuring, "Perhaps you'll remove more before you leave."

"What a fool you are Alan – you still know nothing about women. It was four years ago, not last week we ceased to be lovers. I came here for peace, not erotic excitement. In the last three hours I have had more excitement than many of the bourgeoisie experience in a lifetime."

"Sorry!" murmurs Alan, and carries coat to bed. He lays it there then sits on bedfoot, right elbow on knee, right hand supporting chin like Rodin's Thinker.

"I am a dreadful woman, I destroy men!" says Vlasta, yawning and stretching her arms, "Arnold kept shouting that while the policemen dragged him away."
"Please sit beside me. I'm very lonely."
She sits beside him saying, "Think of Mick McTeague, old before his time and drinking like a fish."
"He was a sixty-year-old alcoholic when you first met him."
"He's worse now. Last week I saw Angus pushing his baby in a pram in the park, a slave to a woman too foolish to understand him."
"He seems perfectly happy to me," says Alan, looking at her, "We play snooker sometimes."
She laughs aloud at his naivety.
"Oh Alan have you forgotten everything I taught you? Beneath the calmest of lives all sorts of dreadful things are happening: spiritual rapes, murders, incests, tortures, suicides. And the calmer the surface the worse what is hidden beneath."
Her perfume fills his nostrils, her body is an inch away, with real excitement he declares, "I love the way you turn life into an adventure, an exciting, idiotic adventure."
"IDIOTIC?" she cries, glaring.
"No no no no!" he explains hastily, "That was a slip of the tongue, a device by which my conventional bourgeois hypocrisy attempted to defend itself."
"Hm!" she says, only slightly placated, "I see you remember some of the things I taught you."
She sits beside him again, yawns and says, "Ahoo I am very tired. It is exhausting work, explaining life to thick policemen."
She lies back on the bed with her face upward and eyes closed.

A minute passes in silence. He stealthily pulls off his shoes, lies beside her and unfastens the top button of her blouse. Without opening her eyes she says in a small voice, "I told you I was in no mood."
"Sorry."

He sighs and resumes the Rodin's Thinker pose. After a while she says lazily, "I love you for being so easily discouraged." He looks hopefully round. Her eyes are open, she is smiling, then laughing and sitting up and embracing him. "Oh Alan, I can refuse you nothing! You are like an ugly old comfortable sofa I must always fall back upon."

"Always at your service!" he assures her. They stand, he pulls off his sweater, she starts removing her blouse and a bell chimes.

The doorbell chimes. He stands as if paralysed and whispers, "Fuck."

She cries, "You WERE expecting someone!"

"No. Nonsense. Ignore it. Please speak more quietly Vlasta!"

The bell chimes.

"Do you tell me you do not know who is there?"

"I swear it."

"Then go to the door and send them away," cries Vlasta, rapidly fastening her blouse, "Or I will!" The bell chimes. She strides to the lobby, he dodges before her and stands with his back to the front door hissing, "Be sensible Vlasta."

"Open that door or I will scream!"

Through clenched teeth he mutters, "Listen! This might be, just might be, a young woman I greatly admire and respect. She must not be upset, you hear? She must not be upset!"

The bell chimes. Vlasta smiles coolly, folds her arms, says, "So open the door."

He does. A stout man wearing a raincoat and trilby hat stands outside. He says, "Scottish Power. Can I read your meter sir?"

"Yes," says Alan. He opens a cupboard (Vlasta has strolled back to the main room) and the man directs a torch beam on the dials of a squat black box.

"Sorry I'm late Alan," says a small pretty girl of perhaps eighteen who strolls in.

"Hullo," says Alan. She goes into the big room and Alan hears her say brightly, "Hullo – my name is Lillian Piper." He hears Vlasta say, "You are one of his students of course."
"Yes!"
"What a coward he is."
"In Australia," says the stout man writing figures on a pad, "All meters have dials which can be read from outside the main door. I wish we had that system here sir."
"Yes. Goodbye," says Alan shutting the stout man out. Then he sighs and joins the ladies.

Vlasta (grim faced, arms folded, legs astride) stands in the middle of the room. Lillian stands near the fire looking thoughtfully at the rumpled bed-cover and his sweater on the floor beside it.
"Lillian," says Alan, "This is Vlasta – Vlasta Tchernik, old friend I haven't seen for years. She called unexpectedly ten or twenty minutes ago."
"He was seducing me when the meter man called," explains Vlasta, "He had my blouse off."
"Is that true?" Lillian asks him.
"Yes."
"Oh Alan."
Lillian sits down on a chaise-longue, Alan on the easy chair. They seem equally depressed. Vlasta, glaring from one to the other, feels excluded, awaits an opening.

At last Alan tells Lillian, "I wish you had come when you said you would. I'd given you up."
"I was only forty minutes late! I've been very punctual till now."
"I know. So I thought … since you didn't even phone … that you'd suddenly tired of me."
"Why did you think that? We got on so well the last time we met … Didn't we?"
"Oh I enjoyed myself. But did you?"
"Of course! I told you so."
"Maybe you were just being polite. A lot of women are

polite at those times. After I'd waited fifteen minutes I thought, She was being polite when she said she enjoyed herself last time. And after twenty minutes I thought, She's not coming. She's met someone more interesting."

Lillian stares at him.

"He has NO self-confidence!" cries Vlasta triumphantly, "He is a weakling, a coward, a liar, a cheat, and DULL! Oh so deadly dull."

"Nonsense," says Lillian, but without much force, "He says very clever things sometimes."

"Can you give me an example?"

Lillian thinks hard and eventually says, "We went a walk last Sunday and he said, The countryside looks very green today but I suppose that's what it's there for."

"He was quoting me," says Vlasta with satisfaction, "And I got it from a book."

"Were you quoting her?" Lillian asks Alan. He nods. She sighs then tells Vlasta that cleverness isn't important – that Alan says very sweet sincere things which matter a lot more.

"Oho!" cries Vlasta, inhaling deeply like a war-horse scenting blood, "This really interests me – tell me about these sweet sincere things."

She strides to the chaise-longue and sits beside Lillian.

"Would either of you like a glass of sherry?" asks Alan loudly. He has gone to the fireplace, unstoppered a heavy cut-glass decanter and now tilts it enquiringly above a row of frail glasses on the mantelpiece. The ladies ignore him. He fills a glass, swigs it, then fills and swigs a second.

Vlasta says, "Tell me just one of his sweet tender remarks."

"I'd rather not," says Lillian shortly.

"Then I will tell one to you. Let me think ... yes. When you get in bed together, does he stretch himself and say in a tone of oh such heartfelt gratitude Thank God I'm home again?"

Lillian is too depressed to speak but nods once or twice.

Vlasta notices Alan swallow a third sherry and says, "You are trying to give yourself Dutch courage."

"I'm trying to anaesthetize myself," he tells her sulkily.
Lillian goes to him saying, "Give me the sherry Alan."
She reaches for the decanter. He gives it to her.
She drops it to smash on the hearth tiles and says, "You don't deserve anaesthetic," and wanders away from him, clenching her hands and trying not to weep. He stares aghast saying, "Lillian! Lillian!" then sighs, kneels, takes a brass-handled shovel and broom from a stand of fire-irons and starts sweeping up the mess.

But Vlasta is more impressed than he is. She cries, "That was magnificent! You are wonderful, little Lillian! People think I am very fierce and violent because I always tell the truth, but believe me I am too timid to smash furniture."
Lillian asks harshly, "What other sweet things did he say to you?"
"Stop!" cries Alan. He pitches broom, shovel, broken glass into the scuttle and says firmly, "Leave us, Vlasta, we're as miserable as you could want us to be."
He is head and neck taller than Lillian, half a head taller than Vlasta, and for the first time today his bulk suggests dignity. But Vlasta says, "I enjoy myself! I shall not leave," and answers his stare with a hard bright smile, so he says quietly to Lillian, "Lillian I have been stupid, very stupid. Maybe in a week or two you'll be able to forgive me, or even sooner, I hope so. I hope so. But this is an indecent situation. Please clear out before she hurts you any more."
"She didn't hurt me," says Lillian, "You did. And I have no intention of being hurt any more. Vlasta! Thank God I'm home again. What other things did he say?"
"I get no pleasure from this conversation!" says Alan loudly, "You two may, I do not. Vivisect me all you like – behind my back. I'm going to my *mother's* house. Feel free to use the kitchen if you want a cup of tea. The front door will lock itself when you leave. Have a nice day."
By now he is in the lobby taking a coat from the cupboard.

He hears Lillian say, "He's very house-proud, isn't he? How much do you think this cost?"
"Oh a great deal of money," says Vlasta. "Will you smash it too?"
Through the doorway he sees Lillian standing with her hand on the glass dome over his clock. He drops the coat and goes to her with arms outstretched like a fast sleepwalker saying, "Lillian, no! That has a Mudge pirouette triple escapement oh please please don't jar the movement!"
Lillian retreats from the clock but grabs a slender clay ornament from the top of a book-case. She holds it straight above her head like a flagstaff saying, "What about this?"
"That is a terracotta by Shanks!" cries Alan in an agony of dread, "By Archibald Shanks, for God's sake be careful Lillian!"
"Strange how much he cares about things being hurt and how little about feelings being hurt," says Vlasta. Alan tries to master the situation with college lecturer's logic. "In the first place I haven't tried to hurt people's feelings, I've simply tried to, to, to enjoy myself. In the second place of course things are more important than feelings. Everybody recovers from hurt feelings, if they aren't children, but damage a well-made clock or ceramic and a certain piece of human labour and skill and talent leaves the world for ever. Please Lillian – put that figurine down."
"Smash it!" hisses Vlasta.

Lillian has never before had two adult people so interested in what she will do next. It makes her playful. She has also been slightly impressed by the last part of Alan's speech. The figurine, though too simplified to suggest a personality, is obviously female. Lillian cradles it in her arms, pats the head and says, "Don't worry little statue, I won't hurt you if your owner acts like a sensible boy and doesn't run away to his mummy whenever life

gets tough for him. Sit down Alan. What were you going to say about him Vlasta?"
She sits beside Vlasta on the sofa. Alan, after a pause, slumps down in the easy chair, notices the chicken, wrenches off a leg and tries to comfort himself by chewing it.
"Have you noticed," says Vlasta, "How he always plans his seductions with food nearby? Obviously sex and eating are very mixed up inside his brain. I have not worked out what that means yet, but something nasty anyway."
Alan stares haggardly at the bone in his hand then lays it down.
"Then again," says Vlasta, "He is not a very passionate lover physically."
"Isn't he?" asks Lillian, surprised.
"Oh I do not say that he gives us no pleasure but he depends upon words too much. He keeps whispering these little monologues, erotic fantasies, you know what I mean?" – Lillian nods; Alan sticks his fingers in his ears – "He can get you very excited by mixing this into his foreplay but when he nears the climax he just lies back and leaves all the work to the woman. Eventually this becomes dull. How long have you known him?"
"A fortnight."
Vlasta looks at Alan and shouts, "Take your fingers out of your ears!"
Lillian holds out the figurine by its feet at the angle of a Nazi salute. Vlasta shouts, "Remember the talent and skill which made this statue! Will you see them leave the world forever because you are ashamed of hearing a few simple facts?"
Alan withdraws fingers from ears and covers his face with them. The women contemplate him for a minute, then Vlasta says, "What monologues has he used on you?"
"The king and queen one."
"That is new to me."
"He pretends we are a king and queen making love on

top of a tower in the sunlight. There is a little city below with red roofs and a harbour with sailing ships going in and out. The sailors on the sea and farmers on the hills round about can see us from miles away. They're very glad we're doing that."

"Very poetic! Yet the scene is strangely familiar – Ah, I remember now! It is a picture in a book I lent him, Jung's *Psychology and Alchemy*. But have you never had to be Miss Blandish?"

Alan stands up looking dazed and walks, snapping fingers, to the bed, on which he flings himself flat with face pressed deep into coverlet. The women arise and follow him, Lillian with the figurine still cradled in her arms. They sit primly on the foot of the bed with Alan's heels between them.

"No," says Lillian, "I have never had to be Miss Blandish."

"He would have made you that eventually. *No Orchids for Miss Blandish* was a sadistic American thriller which made a great impression on him when he was ten or eleven. It is a pity Britain has no respectable state-inspected brothels, male adolescents here get initiated into sex through books and films which leave them with very strange ideas. Alan is such a milksop that I expected his intimate fantasies to be masochistic – no such luck! I had to be Miss Blandish while he raved like a madman in a phoney Chicago accent. Does that connect with his feelings for food? Yes of course! Too little breast feeding in infancy has made him an oral sadist. At the same time his clinging attitude to objects is a transference from the oral to the anal retention syndrome."

Alan, without moving, emits a small but sincere scream.

"End of round two," says Vlasta happily, "Enemy flat on canvas."

But Lillian is not happy. She lays the figurine carefully on the floor and says sadly, "You know, when he spoke to me at these times I used to feel so special ..."

"And now you know you have been to bed with a second-hand record player."

Speaking with difficulty Alan turns his head sideways and says, "If I – sometimes – said the same thing to both of you – it was only because you both – sometimes – made me feel the same way."
"How many women have made you feel the same way?" demands Vlasta, then sees Lillian is sobbing. Vlasta places a hand on her shoulder and says hoarsely, "Yes weep, weep little Lillian. I wept when I came here. YOU have not wept yet!" she tells Alan accusingly.
"And I'm not going to," he declares, sitting up and wriggling down to the bed-foot on Lillian's side. He hesitates then says awkwardly, "Lillian, I haven't had time to tell you this before but I love you. I love you."
He looks at Vlasta and says, "I don't love you at all. Not one bit. But since you don't love me either I don't know why you're so keen to crush me."
"You deserve to be crushed, Alan," says Lillian in a sad remote voice. He wriggles close to her pleading: "I honestly don't think so! I've been selfish, greedy, stupid and I told Vlasta a lot of lies but I never tried to hurt anyone – not even for fun. My main fault was trying to please too many people at the same time, and believe me it would never have happened if only you had been punctual Lillian …"
In order to see her face he stands up and shatters the figurine under foot. The women also stand and look down at the fragments.

Slowly he kneels, lifts the two biggest fragments and holds them unbelievingly at eye-level. He places them carefully on the floor again, his mouth turning down sharply at the corners, then lies flat again on the bed. Lillian sits beside him, supporting herself with an arm across his body. She says sadly, "I'm sorry that happened, Alan."
"Are you sympathizing?" cries Vlasta scornfully.
"I'm afraid so. He's crying, you see."
"You do not think these tears are real?"
Lillian touches his cheek with a fingertip, licks the tip,

touches the cheek again and holds out her finger to Vlasta saying, "Yes, they are. Taste one." Vlasta sits down too, presses Lillian's hand to her lips, keeps it there. Vlasta says, "What beautiful fingers you have – soft and small and shapely."

"Oh?"

"Yes. I'm more than a little butch, you know. How else could I have given myself to a thing like THAT?"

But Lillian is tired of this game and pulls her fingers away.

And leans closer to Alan, lays her hand gently on his neck and murmurs, "I'm sure Archibald Shanks has made hundreds of little statues. You can always get another."

In a muffled voice he says, "'Snot just that. I've ruined everything between you and me, you and me."

Lillian says, "I don't hate you, Alan," and snuggles closer.

Vlasta, watching them, feels excluded again, but knows anger and denunciation will exclude her even more. She also feels a softening toward Alan. Is it pity? No, it is certainly not pity, she has no pity for men and enjoys destroying them, especially smart manipulators like Alan. But when you have knocked such a man down, and don't want to go away and be lonely, what can you do but help set him up again, like a skittle?

"I too cannot exactly hate you Alan," she says, snuggling close to his other side. And he, with heartfelt gratitude, thanks God he is home again.

LOSS OF THE GOLDEN SILENCE

IN HER MID-TWENTIES she does not move or dress attractively so only looks handsome when still, like now. She sprawls on floor, arms folded on seat of the easy chair she uses as desk. Pencil in hand, notepad under it, she studies open book propped against chairback: the one book in a room whose furnishings show only that the users are neither poor nor rich. This a room to lodge, not live in, unless your thoughts are often elsewhere. She frowns, writes a sentence, scores it out, frowns and writes another. A vertical crease between dark eyebrows is the only line on her face.

A door opens so she puts cushion over book and notepad then sits back on heels, watching a man enter. Ten years older than she he wears good tweed overcoat and looks about in worried way muttering, "Keys. Forgot keys."

"There!" she says, pointing. He takes keys from top of sound-deck, returns toward door but pauses near her asking, "What did you hide under the cushion?"

"Nothing."
"Don't be silly."
"Why not look and see?"
"Thanks. I will."
He grasps cushion, hesitates, pleads: "Do you mind if I look?"
"Oh look look look!" she cries, standing up, "I can't stop you. It's your cushion. It's your room." He moves cushion, lifts book and turns to the title page: *The Pursuit of the Millennium, a Study of Revolutionary Anarchism in the Middle Ages*.
"Very clever," he murmurs, and puts the book where he found it and settles on a sofa, hands clasped between knees. This depressed attitude angers her. Looking down on him she speaks with insulting distinctness. "Shall I tell you what's in the battered green suitcase under our bed? Sidney's *Arcadia*. Milton's *Paradise Lost*. Wordsworth's *Prelude*. And a heap of notes for a thesis on the British epic."
He sighs. She walks up and down then says, "You'd better hurry, you'll be late for the office."
"What office?" he asks, astonished.
"Wherever you work between nine and five."
"You know nothing about my life," he tells her sharply, "Or have you been reading my letters?"
"Nobody writes to you."
"Good! When I go through that door each morning I become a mystery. Maybe I don't need to work. Maybe each morning I go to see my mistress. My other mistress!"
"Then you'd better hurry or you'll be late for your other mistress."
But he does not move.

She sits, tries to read her book, fails and puts it down. "Listen," she says in a softer voice, "I know men hate clever women. I've known it since I was twelve. But

we've got on well together. Forget I'm clever. I won't remind you."
"I'm not depressed because you're clever. I saw you were deep from the moment we met. I'm depressed because now I know what happens in your head. Next time you frown I'll think, 'Damn! She's worrying about her thesis.'"
"Why damn? Why will it upset you?"
"Because I'll feel obliged to say something cheerful and reassuring."
"Do you really resent making ordinary, friendly little remarks?"
"Yes."
"What a selfish attitude! Anyway, you couldn't reassure me on my thesis. You're too ignorant."
He stares at her. She blushes and says, "Sorry. You've no books and I take books too seriously. You're probably as clever in your own way as I am, what do you do for a living?"
"I won't tell you."
"Why?"
"If you get to know me well you'll despise me."
"Why? Are you in advertising?"
"Certainly not. But familiarity breeds contempt."
"Not always."
"Yes always!"
She rises and walks about saying, "Our friendship has taken a steep turn for the worse in the last five minutes and it's not my fault."
He sighs then asks, "Were you ever married? Or (because it comes to the same thing) did you ever live long with someone?"
"No. But men have lived with me."
"Long?"

She thinks for a moment. Her last lover was an exciting young man whose work and opinions, good looks and quick speech sometimes got him asked onto television shows. He needed a lot of admiration and support. She had easily supplied these until she found he was also the lover of her close friend and flat-mate, then she noticed he was an emotional leech who had stopped her investigating Chaucer's debt to Langland for over a month. She says grimly, "Far too long."

"Then you know about lack of privacy. We start sharing a bed and some rooms and meals which is fun at first, even convenient. Then we start sharing our thoughts and feelings and end in the shit. Have you noticed how cheerful I am in the morning?"

"I hear you singing in the lavatory."

"Does it annoy you?"

"A bit, but I can ignore it."

"You couldn't ignore it if you knew me well. My wife couldn't ignore it. If I sang or whistled or hummed she said I gave her a headache, so I crushed the melody in my bosom and became as miserable as she was. She was always very quiet in the morning. She got brighter in the evening, but not the early evening. I would come home from work and find her brooding. It was very strange. I knew that if I left her alone she would brighten eventually, but I couldn't. I found her black moods as much a pain as she found my cheerful ones. I would try nagging her into happiness: ask what was wrong then explain it was unimportant. Whenever we weren't equally bright or equally dull we nagged each other till we were equally miserable. All our conversations became wrestling bouts, like this one."

"This one?"

"This is our first real conversation and you've already called me selfish and ignorant. That nearly floored me."

"You started it."

"Yes guilty! Guilty! I'm like an alcoholic who can keep off his poison for weeks but after one sip can't stop till he's flat on his back. I've moaned to you about my

marriage, I've started telling you about my bad habits, if you don't shut me up you'll soon know about my childhood, schooling, how I make my money ..."
"Are you a hit-man for the Mafia?"
"Don't be silly. When I've cut myself into small pieces and handed them to you on a tray I'll get you to start talking."
She says shortly, "I don't like talking about myself."
"I know, but talk is the most infectious disease in the world. In a week or month or year we'll know each other thoroughly. You'll no longer be the lovely stranger who approached me in the singles bar, the mysterious she who shares my bed and breakfast. I'll have turned you into what we all are, basically – a pain in the arse with a case history behind it."
She laughs at that. Despite his words he is excited, almost cheerful, and watches her closely.

She sits down beside him, elbow on knee, chin on clenched fist. He lays an arm carefully round her shoulder but a slight shrug tells him she doesn't want that so he withdraws the arm. She is thinking that the trouble with his wife was probably sexual. In bed he leaves most of the initiatives to her. She does not mind this because though her last lover was more exciting he wanted applause for his performances and she found this exhausting. Does the man beside her think the last fortnight (the most restful and productive fortnight of her life) has been romantic adventure? Someone who can say I crushed the melody in my bosom without irony is almost certainly romantic. In a low voice she asks, "Do you really think me what you said? Lovely – mysterious?"
"I've managed it so far. You've been the greatest thing in my life since wee Moody."
"Wee Moody?"
"She visited me when I'd done too many things in too short a time. The doctor ordered a week of complete

rest so I sent the wife and kids away for a holiday, unplugged the phone and stayed in bed doing nothing but doze, watch the box and eat food out of tins. The privacy was wonderful. On the second day a cat ran in when I opened the door for the milk. She was a neat little thing with a smooth black coat but hungry, so I fed her. When I returned to bed she came and curled in the hollow behind my knees. I liked to stroke and pat her, she was so graceful and ... suave. When she wanted out she patted the door with her paw and I let her out, but she came in again next morning with the milk. We kept company for nearly a week without nagging or bullying each other. That was the happiest time of my life, before I met you."

"Thank you. What became of her?"

"When the kids came home they adopted her – they saw more of her than I did when I returned to work. When the family left me they took her with them."

"A pity. You wouldn't need me if she had stayed."

"Nonsense! You're a woman with arms, legs et cetera, the whole female works. You're much nicer to me than wee Moody ever was."

She gets up and walks away. Strong feelings stop her speaking: amusement, pity, despair and anger. Anger is uppermost. She forces it down, hearing him say, "Our friendship is entering a new phase, isn't it?"

"No!" she tells him, turning, "It had better not. I agree with you about talk. Words do more harm than good if they aren't in a poem or play, and even plays have caused riots. Let's switch on the silence again. We came together because like most mammals we can't bear sleeping alone. You find me fascinating because you don't know me. I like living here because you're clean, gentle, undemanding, and don't interest me at all. Have I floored you?"

He nods, his mouth open and face paler than usual. She

laughs and says, "Don't worry! I'll pick you up. I'm your mistress, not your cat. I've got arms." She lifts keys off the top of the sound-deck where he has dropped them again, puts them in his coat pocket, grasps his hands and pulls. He sighs and stands.

"Kiss me!" she says. He doesn't so she kisses him hard until his lips yield.

"Now go off to wherever you always go," she says, taking his arm and leading him to door, which she opens.

"But ..." he says, pausing.

"Sh!" she whispers, pressing a finger to his lips,
"I'll be here when you come back. Off you go."

He sighs, leaves. She shuts door,
goes back to work.

YOU

GO TO WEDDING and reception afterward where, as usual, the bride's people and groom's people are strangers to each other. Tension. The groom's family are English, new here trying not to show they are richer, feel superior to the bride's people, the Scots, the natives. Are in a small gang of bride's friends who know their best dresses will look cheap beside groom's sisters' and women friends' dresses, so deliberately dress down, making a uniform of jeans spectacularly ripped, tiny denim jackets showing midriffs and that we don't care how much money you lot like wasting on clothes. Bride's people are mortified. Feel sorry for them. Groom's people act amused, are perhaps not very, so to hell with them. This tall quite old man, nearly thirty – the well-dressed kind who knows he is suave – keeps looking, not openly staring but giving quiet little humble yet slightly amused glances meaning hullo, I'm turned on, do you think we could? He is careful nobody else sees him giving the eye, but stays with his own posh English sort but only with the men until wonder (disappointed) is he gay? and (indignantly) does he think this get-up just comic? Forget him.

While putting food on a plate at the buffet find him close beside saying, "Can I help you to some of this?" Thank him. Stand eating with back to the wall. So does he, saying thoughtfully, "Odd to be at my cousin's friend's wedding on the day my divorce comes through."

Look at him, surprised. He says, "I feel there's a lot of aggro going on under our jolly surfaces here. Do you?"
Agree.
"I don't think the tension is as Scottish-English as it looks. It's just bloody British. Whenever two British families come together one lot feel up, the other lot under. Guilt and resentment ensue and much silly jockeying. Even the Royals do it. I find these tensions boring. Do you?"
Agree.
"A woman of few words! I will shortly say good-bye to the chiefs of my lot and the chiefs of your lot, then I will drive to the Albany and enjoy one of the best things your country makes: a Macallan Glenlivet malt. Have you been to the Albany?"
Have not.
"It's nice. I never stay there but I can always find a quiet comfortable bar there. I would like you to have a drink with me because (to be honest) this wedding on top of the divorce is making me feel lonely, and you look a nice person to talk to. And I promise not to say a word about my ex-wife and her wicked ways. I'd rather talk about something more pleasant and different. I'd love to talk about you if you can stand being probed a little by a disgusting Sassenach. Please don't say a word because I am now about to leave. In fifteen minutes I will be at the carpark, sitting hopefully inside a puce Reliant Scimitar. It's a silly car with a silly colour but perhaps it suits me. I can't tell you how I got it."
Ask if they let girls dressed like this into the Albany.
"Don't be so boringly British. But of course you're teasing me a little."

He leaves. He has done this before. Be careful.

The Albany has lounges upstairs for residents and their guests. He is neither, but the waiter serves him without question. Can people with his kind of voice and clothes go anywhere? But he does not try to make drunk.

"Do you prefer sweet or dry drinks?"
Prefer sweet.
"Good. I will buy you a very special cocktail which I'm sure you will enjoy if you sip it as slowly as I sip my Macallan, then we can have a coffee and I'll drive you home. Do you stay with your people?"
Live in a bedsit.
"Shared?"
Not shared.
"Good! Bad idea, sharing. It has destroyed many a friendship. Tell me about your people. Having no family of my own now I like hearing about other families."
Tell him about Dad, Mum, relations. He says thoughtfully, "It's nice to know there are still pockets of affection in the world."
Ask about his mum and dad.
"Aha! A touchy subject. I hardly ever see them, not even at Christmas. My father is nothing – nothing at all. He made a big killing in property and retired like a shot. My mother is merely supportive. They live in Minorca now. They were never very close."
Frown, puzzled. His words suggest bodiless people separating or propping each other after a ghostly massacre. Sigh. Silence. Here come the drinks. Sip. Enjoy this. Tell him so.
"Thought you'd like it. May I ask what you do for a living?"
Tell him.
"What's the firm like, the boss like?"
Tell him.
"What – if it's not an indelicate question – do they pay you?"
Tell him.
"How very mean! Can you live on a wage as low as that? We ought to do something about that. You would earn a lot more if you came to London. I know, because I'm in Systems Analysis which deals with your kind of firm, among others."
Don't be fooled by that one. Tell him everything costs

more in London, especially the bedsits.
"Perfectly true, which is why London wages are higher too. But not everywhere. If you decide to come to London contact me first. And now I'll drive you home."

He does not try to touch on his way to the car or inside it, and stays in his seat on arriving. Not inviting himself in, he sits with hand on wheel smiling sideways. Think of saying thank you, good night, but instead ask him in. The loving is surprisingly good. He seems shy at first, not embarrassingly shy but charmingly shy, responds vigorously to hints, pleasuring first a long time with fingers and then with tongue, murmuring, "With this instrument I also make my money."
He pulls a condom on later saying, "I'm thinking of your health. You don't know where I've been." Feel safe with him. Have known nobody make love as long as he does. Say so. He says, "We share a talent for this. Let's do it again soon."
Yes do it again soon.

Of course his money smooths things. The second night starts with a meal in the Shandon Buttery costing more than a (not his) weekly wage, on the third night another ditto at One Devonshire Gardens, fourth night ditto in Central Hotel after the disco. Dislike these meals, excepting the starters and sweets. The main course is always too fancy, too sauced, too spiced. Never say so. And all the time he is kind, polite, funny, telling stories about people whose faces are seen, names and voices are heard on the news. His stories could never be told on the news, make giggle they are so stupid, blush they are so dirty, madden with rage they are so unfair like the Duke of Westminster and asbestosis. He seems to stand outside the dark tank of an aquarium full of weird cruel filthy comic fish, shining a light onto each in turn, explaining with humour but also with a touch of regret how greedy and wasteful they are. He never explains how he knows them so well, never talks about himself, but always about them, the others. Maybe he learned about them as he learned about Mum, Dad, the boss, by asking their daughters and employees. If asked about himself he gives a crisp reply in words that sound definite but say nothing definite. Ask where he lives.

"London, half the year, but which half is problematic. I go where the firm needs me: Scotland just now."

Ask where he is staying in Glasgow.

"I'm a guest of people who called in my firm. It's one of the ways I learn things, so I run away to you whenever I can."

Ask about Systems Analysis.

"We unstick things in businesses where things have got stuck. We also advise on mergers and acquisitions. It's all perfectly honest and above board. We're a registered company. Look us up in the directory if you don't believe me."

Ask what he does.

"At present I work mainly with newspapers – not for them, with them, because papers involve advertising, hence marketing. All very complicated."

Sigh, hating to be treated as an idiot. Ask if he works in accountancy, computer programming or time management.

"Yes, these are all part of it, but what I do best (and with considerable aplomb) is kick bums."

Ask if that means he sacks people. He chuckles and says, "Of course not, this is England! – I beg your pardon, Britain. Above a certain income level nobody gets sacked in Britain. My kicking simply shifts the bums to where they don't block things. If you want the details you should take a course in business management at London University, where I'll end up as a visiting lecturer if I'm not careful. My work pays a lot more than yours does, but in the long run is just as disgustingly boring. Perhaps more so."

Yet he is never short-tempered or depressed, always gentle, considerate, amusing, apologetic, letting no harshness or dullness appear, though it must exist. All folk have a nasty side which usually appears at the second or third meeting, if not the first. His appears on the fourth.

He calls at the bedsit between seven and eight and says with his usual humorous apologetic smile, "That dress won't do, I'm afraid."
Ask why.
"It looks cheap – doesn't suit you. Wear what you wore at the wedding. I insist."
Angry and cheapened, find no words to say no.
While undressing, redressing he sits watching closely. Know you are exciting him. Grow slightly excited. Before dressing is finished he stands and comes to you, makes love at once fast. Don't enjoy it much. He sighs and says, "That was our best time yet, I suppose you noticed?"
Agree. Finish dressing. Resignedly display yourself.
"Perfect! You suit the Cinderella look. Let's be different tonight. Where would you go for fun if you didn't know me? A disco?"

Take him to a disco where he dances a bit stiffly but well, considering his age. Like it that others (especially Tall Jenny) see him twisting before, around, beside in that well-cut suit, perfect shirt, tie flapping, fine blond hair flapping, and still the modest amused little smile.
"I'm whacked – need to stand still for a bit. But you're young – please go on dancing. I'm not a jealous type, I'll enjoy watching you dance."
Smile at him, pleased. Dance with a handsome gay in biker leathers. This is more fun as gay is better dancer and now have the pleasure of two partners, this Hunky Harry and him watching. Suddenly see him dancing nearby with Tall Jenny, most obviously attractive woman in the room. Are a little hurt but don't show it. Smile at them, twice, though they seem not to see. Never mind. Please go on dancing. Thanks mister, I will.

And suddenly enjoy it! For being with him (only notice this now) is a strain when not loving. Can never forget he is posh English, knows more about everything, is keeping a lot back so must think himself superior. Dance with boys who like dancing, like life without feeling superior. Have no shortage of partners, hooray for the ordinary! But while drinking a lime juice with a girl friend at the bar see him talking to Hunky Harry and laughing in a way that makes him look ordinary too, and much nicer. Stare at him, wanting him. He notices, stops laughing, comes over with his usual little smile and says, "Time to leave."
Am delighted. Truly delighted. Feared had lost him.

But both are quiet in the car as he drives to the Central Hotel, so something is wrong. Both are quiet because he is quiet, for it is always he who directs the talk or deals it out. Is he angry? Have done nothing wrong, unless it was wrong enjoying dancing with someone else. He is probably tired. Nearly midnight, now. Surprised the Central is still open.

Without a nod to the doorman he leads up broad shallow carpeted stairs to a lounge empty but for an elderly American-looking couple in a far corner. He tells a waiter, "This place seems quiet enough. Could you serve us a meal here?"
"Certainly sir, I'll fetch a menu."
"No need. This young lady wants nothing but a goodly selection of sandwiches and I will have **********." (French words.)
"I'm afraid the last is not available sir. The menu will show you what we can provide just now. We have ..."
"Get me the manager."
"The manager is not available sir."
"Don't pretend to be stupid. You know I want whoever is in bloody charge here just now."
He has not lost his temper, has not raised his voice, but

it has grown so distinct that the Americans look alarmed. The waiter leaves and returns with another man in a black dinner-suit who says, "I'm sorry sir but the situation is this: the day chef retires at 10.45 and the night chef ..."

"I did not come here for instruction in the mysteries of hotel management, I came because this used to be a good hotel, I happen to be hungry, and have a taste for **********, whose ingredients are now dormant in your kitchen. I mean to pay what it costs to have them expertly prepared. There is nothing to discuss. I am not going to explain, plead or bully you, so please don't use those tactics on me. Understood?"

He has not lost his temper. He looks at the head-waiter or under-manager or whoever this man is with a fixed half-smile containing no amusement or apology. The head-waiter or under-manager, his face paler than it was, says after a pause, "You are not a resident here sir?"

"No, nor ever likely to be. I promise this is the last time you will see me here, so do the wise thing and send up what I order?"

He says this softly, cooingly, teasingly, smiling almost sleepily as if at a joke the man before him is bound to share. The man before him, looking very pale, suddenly nods and walks away.

"One moment!" cries the Englishman – the head-waiter or under-manager turns – "I will have a bottle of ********** along with it."

Keep silent, though he watches sideways now. Was all that done to impress? Are chilled, embarrassed, disgusted, only glad the Americans have stopped staring, are leaving. Sigh. He looks away. A long silence happens. He murmurs as if to himself, "Sometimes one has to be firm."

The barman pulls down a grille over the bar, locks it and leaves. He murmurs, "They'll probably take hours, just to be awkward."

The waiter brings the selection of sandwiches. Have no appetite but nibble half of one, then leave it. Later, from boredom, slowly finish it and then all the rest. Eventually the waiter serves him with a plate containing slips of meat half sunk in reddish gravy with a sweet heavy sickly smell. He looks hard at it, murmurs, "I don't think they've spat in it," and eats. After some forkfuls he says, "Yum yum. Well worth waiting for."

Are driven home, arrive about one thirty a.m. bored, tired, disliking him. In the silence when he stops the car and smiles sideways you want not to invite him in tonight but are about to do it as usual when he says, "Listen, I'm sorry about tonight. It started the best yet but ended badly. Nobody was to blame. Perhaps we need a rest from each other. Anyway, tomorrow night I have to see people, and the night after. Suppose we meet the night after that? You choose where."

Suggest lounge of the Grosvenor.

"Fine! Half seven, then."

Go upstairs yawning and wondering (without much pain) if tomorrow night he will bed Tall Jenny or Hunky Harry, since obviously he can get anyone, anything he wants. Only wish had called off tomorrow before he did. But next day these ideas become a torment, why? Why care for someone so dislikeable? But he has usually been loving, gentle, pleasant, why dislike him? Is it bad to call out a hotel chef late at night if you pay the hotel enough to compensate for the extra trouble? When the bill came he glanced at it, grimaced slightly, wrote a cheque and gave it to the waiter without looking at him. And the waiter, glancing at it, became less stiff and expressionless, said, "Thank you very much sir," in a low voice, so he had been well tipped. One dull night after three lovely exciting nights is not bad, though he is far too obsessed with ragged jeans.

So here in the Grosvenor, ten minutes early, are dressed in a different high-heeled Cinderella way because that excites him, so slightly excited and hopeful too. Buy a lime juice, and for him a Macallan, the first thing you have ever bought him. Sit facing the door, whisky on table beside your lime juice and wait. And wait. And wait.

He arrives at half past eight, not smiling, and sits beside you muttering, "Detained. Unavoidable."
He sips the whisky, pulls a face, says, "What is this?"
Tell him.
"Are you sure?"
Tell him that was what you ordered.
"They've watered it."
Silence. Tell him something funny the boss did today. He nods twice and sighs. Silence. Ask him how his own work is going.
"Rottenly."
Say you are sorry.
"A woman of few words."
Ask why things have gone rottenly.
"I am sick of your unending probing into my personal affairs. If you have not already noticed I dislike that trait in women you are not just stupid, you are a cretin. A cretin may be good for three nights fucking in a filthy hole like Glasgow but three nights is the limit. Remember that."
He has not lost his temper. He stands and goes out, leaving the whisky almost untasted.

INTERNAL MEMORANDUM

TO : LUMLEY
FROM : LESLEY

The following will seem bad-tempered and in fact is. It says what I meant to raise at yesterday's meeting but my only chance came at the end when Phimister said, "Is there any further business?" and Henry Pitt (looking at me out of the corner of his eye) said, "No, I think that's everything," and suddenly I felt too tired. I seem the only manager in this firm who is allowed – indeed expected – to complain about practical everyday details. When I start doing it our directors exchange little smiles, stop listening and retreat into private dreamlands. They think everyday practical details are not their business but the business of Mulgrew the buildings manager and Tramworth the accountant. Nobody, not even Mulgrew, denies that what I ask to be done ought to be done, but only he and Tramworth can authorize it so it is never done. I have raised items on this list at meetings from last month to years ago. You joined us less than two months ago so the first and longest item on the list may strike you as an accident. I assure you that something of the sort happens every winter.

1 Heat. Monday was bloody cold. I asked Mulgrew to do something about this. He agreed to turn up the thermostat a little but not much because part of upstairs was already warm – the part where he and Tramworth have their office. Soon after 10 a.m. I noticed it was cold. When this happens I know others are freezing, so tried to find Mulgrew with the usual results. He had gone to the Sauchiehall Street depot, but when I phoned there he had just left it and nobody knew where he was supposed to be. By this time people

on my floor were asking me to do something about the cold and I actually met people from upstairs who were touring the building in search of heat. I phoned Mulgrew's office again and got Tramworth. He suggested I tell people to work harder or jump up and down in order to stay warm. I refrained from telling him this should be his job as it was his staff who were touring the building and on whose behalf I was trying to contact Mulgrew. I suppose people ask help from me instead of their own managers because I do not treat everyone with complaints as if they are troublemakers. Mulgrew appeared around lunch time. Either Tramworth did not tell him the problem or he ignored it. I caught him before he left the building a second time. He did go to the thermostat then and discovered it had been turned down from 30 to 16 degrees before he turned it up. Since only he can have turned it down how he made this mistake escapes me. During the afternoon the place slowly warmed. People were and are annoyed about this because:
(a) The discomfort stops them working properly, making them feel useless as well as frozen.
(b) Heating is decided by people who are outside the building, or cocooned in an office when in it.
(c) This has been going on for years.

2 The route to the emergency exit is as badly blocked as ever. Mulgrew is our fire safety officer as well as buildings manager, so draws an extra salary to stop that kind of thing happening. He can stop it by ordering new storage racks. I wish he was less friendly with the local fire precautions inspector. Mulgrew always knows when a thorough inspection will happen so the inspector never sees the usual state of the place. Sometimes, (like today), the inspector calls in without warning, but in that case (like today) he never looks at the emergency exit. God help us if we have a fire when a *thorough* inspection has not been scheduled.

3 The top tread of the stairs is still as loose as when Mrs Macleod tripped and fell down them. You may remember the doctor said she was lucky not to have broken her back. Senior management seem to think a handwritten warning notice has solved the problem for the foreseeable future, but one day we might have a short-sighted visitor. The other treads also need attention.

4 Nothing has been done about the window behind Helen Scrimgeour's desk. Its dangerous state was first reported a year ago.

5 Handrail on the spiral staircase is loose.

6 Radiators in the ladies' loo are not turned on.

7 Heatscreens. (Outstanding for two years.)

8 A light in the loading bay. (Outstanding for more than two years.)

Of course you know the reasons for the above. The directors' offices are in the George Square depot, so they are glad to spend as little as possible on maintaining and keeping comfortable a building never noticed by the general public. Yet most of the firm's employees work in this dirty old building, which houses the most profitable part of their business. Can Phimister and Henry Pitt not see that every hundred pounds saved on heating means that a hundred people do two thirds of the work they would normally do?

I realize this letter is not fair to you, Lumley. The directors and senior management have put you here to protect them from this kind of information. It embarrasses them to hear about staff problems from the mouths of the staff, they do not want to know about our problems at all. We are learning to handle the new computer which, properly used, should make us more efficient. While learning we must go on handling orders and dispatches in the old way, which makes us even less efficient. Since the directors and senior management know nothing about computers they thought everything would at once improve, not get worse, as soon as they bought one, so now they are trying to avoid paying for anything else. But why does Henry Pitt insist on handling all incoming mail and send every tiny complaint straight to my staff after marking it *top priority – attend to this at once*? They spend hours making sure that a garage in Stromness or Brighton gets a single free replacement while factories in the Midlands are kept waiting, though they have ordered 500 and paid for them in advance. Henry Pitt's grandfather founded this firm, he is a major shareholder and has been with it all his life, but his only management experience is with our depots. He should send all orders and complaints straight to me and Mrs Mcleod, who've been working here for fifteen years so know the priorities. The staff here sometimes feel that the directors and senior management are conspiring to STOP us doing the work they employ us to do. The idea is insane but that is what we sometimes feel, though they have probably just lost interest in us.

Or is it an insane idea? Henry Pitt is over sixty, must soon retire and has no children. Phimister has his Loch Lomond fish farm. It began as a rich man's hobby because he enjoys messing about in boats, but Mulgrew and Tramworth gave him a lot of help and a recent article in *The Scots Magazine* said it was now profitable. It also quoted him as saying, "I want a cleaner, fresher life for my children. Modern cities are becoming intolerable." If Pitt and Phimister sold the business they would make quite a lot. Since it is the only remaining firm of its kind in Scotland the buyers would almost certainly be southerners who would keep the depots but shut this distribution centre. Do you think we are coming to that, Lumley? It has happened with ship building, the car industry, textiles, steel, sanitary engineering et cetera.

I have had another idea. If they decide to sell us off could not a few of us (me, you, Mrs Macleod, Helen Scrimgeour, Colin Shand and maybe some others) put in an offer for the distribution part – this part – and buy it and run it for ourselves? We know how to do it. I would really like to talk to you about this. You are the only member of the senior management who listens to what I say and knows what I mean. Also, if a buy-out is being planned you will be one of the first to know about it. You also went to the same school as Phimister, so understand these things much better than I do.

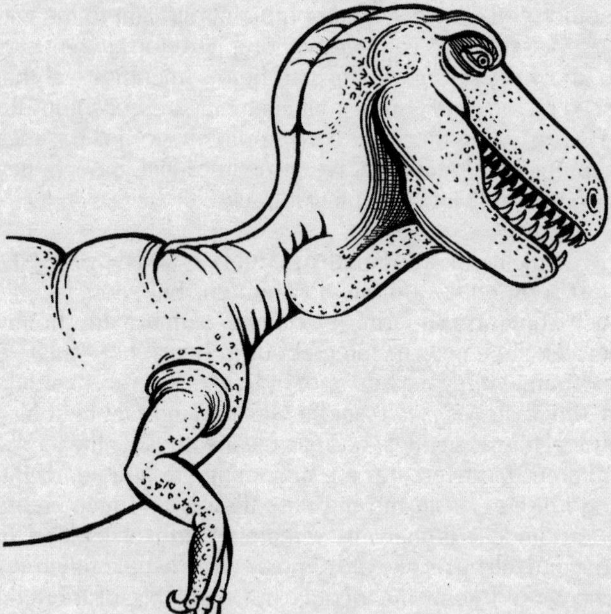

A NEW WORLD

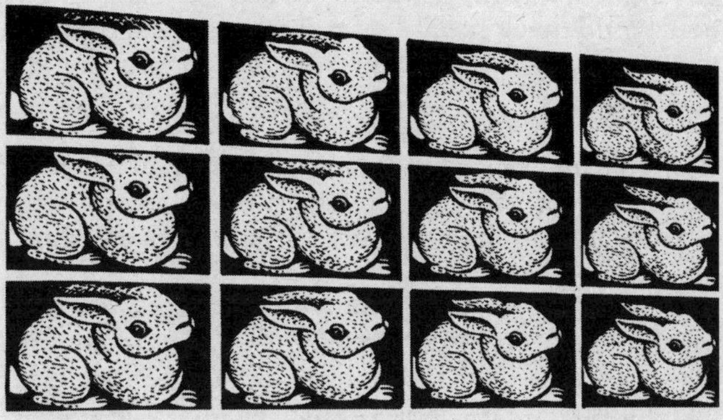

MILLIONS of people lived in rooms joined by long windowless corridors. The work which kept their world going (or seemed to, because they were taught that it did, and nobody can ever be taught the exact truth) their work was done on machines in the rooms where they lived, and the machines rewarded them by telling them how much they earned. Big earners could borrow money which got them better rooms. The machines, the money-lending and most of the rooms belonged to three or four organizations. There was also a government and a method of choosing it which allowed everyone, every five years, to press a button marked STAY or CHANGE. This kept or altered the faces of the politicians. The politicians paid themselves for governing, and also drew incomes from the organizations which owned everything, but governing and owning were regarded as separate activities, so the personal links between them were dismissed as coincidences or accepted as inevitable. Yet many folk

– even big earners in comfortable rooms – felt enclosed without knowing exactly what enclosed them. When the government announced that it now governed a wholly new world many people were greatly excited, because their history associated new worlds with freedom and wide spaces.

I imagine a man, not young or especially talented, but intelligent and hopeful, who pays for the privilege of emigrating to the new world. This costs nearly all he has, but in the new world he can win back four times as much in a few years if he works extra hard. He goes to a room full of people like himself. Eventually a door slides open and they filter down a passage to the interior of their transport. It resembles a small cinema. The émigrés sit watching a screen on which appears deep blackness spotted with little lights, the universe they are told they are travelling through. One of the lights grows so big that it is recognizable as a blue and white cloud-swept globe whose surface is mainly sun-reflecting ocean, then all lights are extinguished and, without alarm, our man falls asleep. He has been told that a spell of unconsciousness will ease his arrival in the new world.

He wakens on his feet, facing a clerk across a counter. The clerk hands him a numbered disc, points to a corridor, and tells him to walk down it and wait outside a door with the same number. These instructions are easy to follow. Our man is so stupefied by his recent sleep that he walks a long way before remembering he is supposed to be in a new world. It may be a different world, for the corridor is narrower than the corridors he is used to, and coloured matt brown instead of shiny green, but it has the same lack of windows. The only new thing he notices is a strong smell of fresh paint.

He walks very far before finding the door. A man of his own sort sits on a bench in front of it staring morosely at the floor between his shoes. He does not look up when our man sits beside him. A long time passes. Our man grows impatient. The corridor is so narrow that his knees are not much more than a foot from the door he faces. There is nothing to look at but brown paintwork. At length he murmurs sarcastically, "So this is our new world."

His neighbour glances at him briefly with a quick little shake of the head. An equally long time passes before our man says, almost explosively, "They promised me more room! Where is it? Where is it?"

The door opens, an empty metal trolley is pushed obliquely through and smashes hard into our man's legs. With a scream he staggers to his feet and hobbles backward away from the trolley, which is pushed by someone in a khaki dust-coat who is so big that his shoulders brush the walls on each side and also the ceiling: the low ceiling makes the trolley-pusher bend his head so far forward that our man, retreating sideways now and stammering words of pain and entreaty, stares up not at a face but at a bloated bald scalp. He cannot see if his pursuer is brutally herding him or merely pushing a trolley. In sheer panic our man is about to yell for help when a voice says, "What's happening here? Leave the man alone Henry!" and his hand is seized in a comforting grip. The pain in his legs vanishes at once, or is forgotten.

His hand is held by another man of his own type, but a sympathetic and competent one who is leading him away from the trolley-man. Our man, not yet recovered from a brutal assault of a kind he has only experienced in childhood, is childishly grateful for the pressure of the friendly hand.

"I'm sure you were doing nothing wrong," says the stranger pleasantly, "You were probably just complaining. Henry gets cross when he hears one of our sort complain. Class prejudice is the root of it. What were you complaining about? Lack of space, perhaps?"

Our man looks into the friendly, guileless face beside him and, after a moment, nods: which may be the worst mistake of his life, but for a while he does not notice this. The comforting handclasp, the increasing distance from Henry who falls farther behind with each brisk step they take, is accompanied by a feeling that the corridors are becoming spacious, the walls farther apart, the ceiling higher. His companion also seems larger and for a while this too is a comfort, a return to a time when he could be protected from bullies by bigger people who liked him. But he is shrinking, and the smaller he gets the more desperately he clutches the hand which is reducing his human stature. At last, when his arm is dragged so straight above his head that in another moment it will swing him clear of the floor, his companion releases him, smiles down at him, wags a kindly forefinger and says, "Now you have all the space you need. But remember, God is trapped in you! He will not let you rest until you amount to more than this."

The stranger goes through a door, closing it carefully after him. Our man stares up at a knob which is now and forever out of his reach.

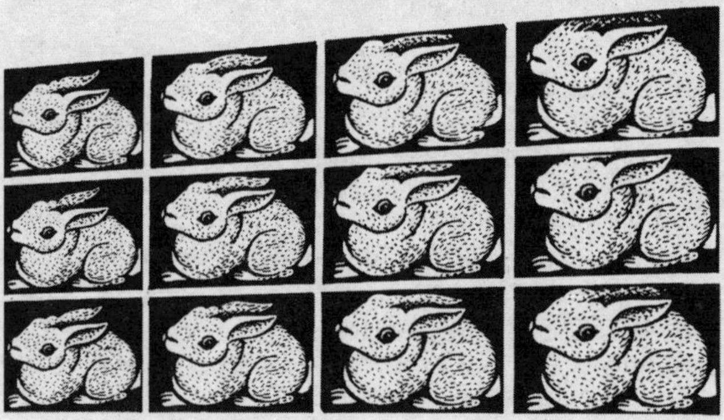

ARE YOU A LESBIAN?

THOUGH I SPEAK *with the tongues of men and of angels, and have not Love, I am become as sounding brass, or a tinkling cymbal. And though I have the gift of prophecy, and understand all mysteries, and all knowledge; and though I have all faith, so that I could remove mountains, and have not Love, I am nothing. And though I bestow all my goods to feed the poor, and though I give my body to be burned, and have not Love, it profiteth me nothing.' – Paul wrote this in his first letter to the Christians of …*

"Excuse me but I want to ask you one question, just one question. Are you a lesbian?"

"I am not a lesbian."

"That answer, if you will pardon me for saying so, is not satisfactory. For the last two Sunday mornings I have watched you stroll in here at five-thirty, wearing jeans. You order a pint of lager, bring it to this corner and sit reading a book and shrugging off every man who tries to start a conversation with you. Why act that way if you arenae a lesbian?"

"That is your second question. You said you would ask just one."

"Aye, all right. I take your point. Fair enough." *Paul wrote this in his first letter to the Christians of Corinth, less than twenty years after Christ was crucified. And now, a question.*

What do we need most in life? What, if we suddenly lost it, would make us both feel, and be, worthless? Some Christians will answer: their religion. They think their lives are given meaning by their faith in God who made and sustains the universe and became Jesus of Nazareth. Well, they are wrong. Faith in God can make us very strong – for centuries it has enabled Christians to suffer and inflict, prolong and endure hideous agonies for the most splendid reasons. But it is not what God wants. Paul tells us why: 'Though I have all faith, so that I could remove mountains, and have not Love, I am nothing.' 'Though I give my body to be burned, and have not Love, it profiteth me nothing.'

In many (not all) Bibles you will read 'charity' where I have written 'Love'. Paul used a Greek word meaning 'loving respect' – the deepest affection possible between people. Charity used to mean that in English, but has come to mean 'goodness to people who are badly off.' This sort of goodness can be a wonderful expression of Love, but is not Love itself. People have founded hospitals …

"Excuse me, I know I'm butting in again but I have something to say which will do you good if you will only listen to me and not lose your temper. There is only one reason why a man or a woman comes to a pub and it is not the booze. You could easily be drinking cans of lager in the privacy of your ain hame and it would be cheaper, for Christ's sake. So like everybody who comes to a pub you are here for the company, so why shut me out by sticking your nose in a book? I mean no offence, but you are a very attractive woman, in spite of wearing jeans and no being very young. I cannae be too plebeian nor too old for ye neither. You would have gone to a pub higher up Byres Road if you wanted posher or younger company."

"I will tell why I come here if you promise to leave me in peace afterward."

"Fair enough. Fire away."

"I have two daughters and a son in their late teens, and a homeloving husband who works in the finance department of the district council. They leave all housework to me but I enjoy keeping the house clean and tidy so can honestly say I do not feel exploited. I do voluntary work for Save the Children, and Amnesty International. I have no money worries, family worries, health worries and used to think I was one of the luckiest people alive. Nothing seems to have changed but my life is now almost unbearable. No doubt a doctor would blame the menopause and prescribe Valium. I think I've suddenly started seeing myself clearly after eighteen years of looking after other people.

"You see my father was a Church of Scotland minister and I loved him a lot – he was kind and distant and mysterious. Like most Protestant clergymen he was probably embarrassed by drawing wages to go about looking better than other people. The best clergymen get over their embarrassment by working hard – running soup kitchens, getting decent clothes for families who can't afford them, visiting the lonely. My father's church was in a posh suburb. Everybody in the congregation seemed prosperous so we never noticed the poor. He spent most of the time between meals in his study, writing sermons for Sunday. They were no better than other ministers' sermons but his elocution and manners were perfect, old ladies loved him, everybody admired what they called his *unworldliness*. I only noticed he was a fraud when I got to university.

"I enjoyed university because I believed I was becoming better – better than him. I took Divinity and was preparing for the ministry …

"Wait a minute! You were studying to be a Church of Scotland minister?"

"Yes."

"Since when has the Church of Scotland allowed women ministers?"

"Since the sixties. A woman applied for ordination and there was no law against it."

"Though not a churchgoer or a strict Christian I have strong Protestant sympathies, and women ministers just don't seem right."

"Then leave me alone."

"No no! I'm sorry! I mean go on and tell me what is wrong with your marriage. My own marriage is not what it should be. I will regard it as a great favour if you ignore my interruption and spill the beans."

"All right. At university I joined a lot of societies – The Students' Christian Union, The Iona Community and Christians Against the Bomb. I had lots of friends who knew the world should and could be improved, and worked at it. But I began to feel something essential was missing from our lives – God. When I prayed I never felt closer to anyone. When I asked my religious friends how it felt to have God beside them they got embarrassed and changed the subject. Why are you grinning?"

"I know a bloke who feels God is with him all the time. The two of them go along Dumbarton Road together having frantic arguments, though we only hear what poor Jimmy says. 'I refuse to do it!' he shouts. 'You have no right to order me to do it! You'll get me the jail!' It seems God keeps telling him to smash the windows of Catholic bookshops."

"Yes, anybody who hears the voice of God nowadays is deluded. God said everything we need to know through the words of Jesus. But many sane people have felt God's presence since Jesus died. I used to read their autobiographies, they made me envious – and angry too. Some were saintly junkies, hooked on the Holy Ghost like cocaine addicts to their dealer, passing miserable weeks waiting for the next visitation. I was not so greedy.

One wee visit would have satisfied me – I could have lived on the memory ever after. But if I became a minister of God without once feeling God loved and wanted me I knew I would end up a fraud like my father. The nearest I could get to God was in books, which were not enough. I lost interest in Christianity, fell in love with a healthy agnostic and married instead. It was easy."
"Do you know what I'm going to tell you?"
"Yes – that it was the best thing which could have happened to me. If you shut your mouth and listen as you promised I'll explain why it was not.

"I've always found it easy to give the people nearest me what they want. As a student I worked perfectly with busy, excitable, eccentric Christian Socialists. After marriage I perfectly suited someone who wanted a wife to give him polite well-dressed children and a home where he could entertain his friends and colleagues and their wives. So marriage completely changed my character and maybe destroyed part of it. Nowadays I want to hear people talk about the soul, and God, and how to build bridges between them. I can meet these people in books – nowhere else – but my friends and children and husband give me no peace to read. They can't stop telling me news and discussing problems which strike me as increasingly trivial. I can't help listening and smiling and answering with an automatic sympathy I no longer feel. They cannot believe my reading matters. If I locked myself for an hour in the bedroom with a book and a can of lager they would keep knocking on the door and asking what was wrong. Now you know why I come here to read."

Some have founded hospitals for the poor because they wanted popularity or fame or felt guilty about their wealth. That is why Paul says 'Though I bestow all my goods to feed ...'
"Wait a minute. Have you tried going to church?"

"Often. It was what I usually did on Sundays but the prayers now sound meaningless to me, the hymns like bad community singing, the sermons as dull as my father's. Two weeks ago, without telling my family, I came here instead. Nobody I know will ever come to this pub, and it doesn't play loud music. And I like the company, you were right about that."

"Eh?"

"Yes. I feel less lonely among people who are quietly talking and drinking – as long as they don't talk to me or lay their hand on my thigh."

"It won't happen again."

"Enjoying a pint and a read here is my Sunday service. Can I go on with it?"

"Aye. Sure. Of course. I meant no offence."

That is why Paul says, 'Though I bestow all my goods to feed the poor, and have not Love, it profiteth me nothing.' Peter says the same: 'Above all things have fervent love among yourselves.' John goes further: 'God is love.' And Jesus gave us a commandment which makes all laws needless for those who obey it: 'Love the Lord your God with all your heart and all your mind and all your soul, and your neighbour as yourself.' Remembering this, let us return to Paul.

Love suffereth long, and is kind; Love envieth not, and is not puffed up, doth not behave itself unseemly, seeketh not her own, is not easily provoked …

"Excuse me for butting in again but I've been giving some thought to your problem."

is not easily provoked …

"I think I see where the solution lies."

is not easily provoked …

"I know as well as you do that sex is not the reason for everything but …"

"YAAAAEEEE HELP BARMAN HELP!!!!"

"For Christ's sake …"

"Right, what's happening here?"
"Barman, this man nipped me."
"She's a liar, I never touched her!"
"Yes you touched me. I asked you again and again not to, but for twenty minutes you've sat here nip nip nipping my head like, like a bloody husband. Please get him off me, barman."
"Right you – outside. This is not the first time I've seen you at this game. Out you go."
"Don't worry, I'm leaving. But let me tell you something: that woman is a nut case – a religious nut case."
"Shut your mouth and clear out."
is not easily provoked, thinketh no evil; rejoiceth not in iniquity, but rejoiceth in the truth; beareth all things, believeth all things, hopeth all things, endureth all things. Love never faileth; but whether there be prophecies, they shall fail; whether there be tongues, they shall cease; whether there be knowledge, it shall vanish away.
"The old man who was pestering you has gone, Missus. You won't even see him in the street outside – he's slipped into the pub next door."
"Thank you. I'm sorry I troubled you but he insisted on pestering me."
"I understand that Missus, and I'm very sorry that now I must ask you to leave also."
"Why? *Why?*"
"Solitary women are liable to stir up trouble as you have just noticed. This is not your sort of pub. Try one nearer the top of the road."
"Will you allow me to finish my drink?"
"Certainly. Of course. Don't rush it, take your time. It's the last you'll be served here."

For we know in part, and we prophesy in part. But when that which is perfect is come, then that which is in part shall be done away. When I was a child, I spake as a child, I understood as a child, I thought as a child: but when I became a man I put away childish things.

For now we see through a glass, darkly; but then face to face: now I know in part; but then shall I know even as also I am known. And now abideth faith, hope, Love, these three; but the greatest of these is Love.

"I'm sorry Missus but you have to leave now, at once, whether you've finished your pint or not. We cannot have a woman weeping in a corner of the bar. It spoils folk's pleasure."

THE TRENDELENBURG POSITION

COME IN, come in, Mrs Chigwell. Sit down. My partner is sorry he cannot attend to you, as arranged, but there will be no complications. His wife was unexpectedly struck down by something this morning and though (thank goodness) she is not exactly at death's door he would find it hard to concentrate on your (thank goodness) smaller problem. His mind might wander, his hand tremble, so you are safer with me. His X-rays indicate two fillings, one of them a wee toaty tiddler of a job, and I am so sure of my skill that I promise you will feel no pain if I work without anaesthetic. But maybe you are nervous and want it, even so? No? Splendid. I am starting the motor – which lowers and tilts the chair – so easily and smoothly that your heart and semi-circular canals have suffered no shock or disturbance. The Trendelenburg Position – that is what we call the position you are in, Mrs Chigwell. This chair gets you into it, and out of it, in a manner which ensures you cannot possibly faint. I wonder who Trendelenburg is.

Or was. Rinse your mouth. Let me – keek – inside. Oho! And if you want to sneeze, gargle, hiccup or blow your nose just raise a finger of your left hand and I will stop what I am doing almost at once but here goes. Chigwell. Chigwell. An English name. Yes there are a lot of your kind in Scotland nowadays, but you'll never hear me complain. Do I bother you, talking away like this? No? Good. You probably realize I do it to stop your imagination wandering, as it would tend to do if I worked in perfect silence. There is, let us face it, something inherently sinister in lying absolutely passive while a stranger in a white coat – no matter how highly qualified – does things you cannot see to this hole in your head – between your jaw and your brain; inside this wee toaty cavity – I am opening – in a bone of your skull. Even the presence of Miss Mackenzie, my assistant here, might not stop your subconscious mind cooking up weird fantasies if we dentists, like barbers, had not a professional tendency to gossip. Which reminds me of a cartoon I saw in a bound volume of old *Punch* magazines: a barber says, "How would you like your hair cut sir?" to a bored-looking aristocratic type slumped in his chair who says, "In a silence broken only by the busy snipsnap of the scissors." Sometimes I hear myself saying ridiculous things, utterly absurd things, just to avoid that deathly silence, but if you prefer silence just raise two fingers of your right hand and silent I will be. But you like the chatter? Good, rinse your mouth again.

No, my worst enemy could never accuse me of being a Scottish Nationalist. I don't approve of Scotland or Ireland – both Irelands – or England, Argentina, Pakistan, Bosnia et cetera. In my opinion nations, like religions and political institutions, have been rendered obsolete by modern technology. As Margaret Thatcher once so wisely said, "There is no such thing as society," and what is a nation but a great big example of our non-existent society? Margaret had the right idea – DENATIONALIZE! PRIVATIZE! When all our national institutions are privatized the British Isles will no longer be a political entity, and good riddance say I. The USSR has vanished. I hope the USA and the UK follow its example. Last week (a little wider please) a man said to me, "If you

refuse to call yourself a Scot – or a Briton – or a Tory – or a Socialist – or a Christian what DO you call yourself? What do you believe in?"
"I am a Partick Thistle supporter," I told him, "and I believe in Virtual Reality."
Do you know about Partick Thistle? It is a non-sectarian Glasgow football club. Rangers FC is overwhelmingly managed and supported by Protestant zealots, Celtic FC by Catholics, but the Partick Thistle supporters anthem goes like this:

We hate Roman Catholics,
We hate Protestants too,
We hate Jews and Muslims,
Partick Thistle we love you …

My friend Miss Mackenzie is looking distinctly disapproving. I suspect that Miss Mackenzie dislikes my singing voice. Or maybe she's religious. Are you religious Miss Mackenzie? No answer. She's religious.

Fine. Rinse your mouth. Second filling coming up and I insist on giving you a wee jag, but you won't feel it. Did you feel it? Of course not.

My wife disagrees with me. She's a Scottish Nationalist and a Socialist. Can you imagine a more ridiculous combination? She's a worrier, that woman. She's worried about over-population, industrial pollution, nuclear waste, rising unemployment, homelessness, drug abuse, crime, the sea level, the hole in the ozone layer.
"Only a democratic government responsive to the will of the majority can tackle these problems," she says.
"How will it do that?" say I.
"By seizing the big companies who are polluting and impoverishing and unemploying us," says she, "and using the profits on public work, education and health care."
"You'll never get that," I tell her, "because prosperous

people don't want it and poor people can't imagine it. Only a few in-betweeners like you believe in such nonsense." (You have probably guessed she is a school teacher.) "By the year 2000," I tell her, "these problems will have been solved by the right kind of head gear. Even a modern hat of the broad-brimmed sort worn by Australians and Texans and Mexicans will protect you from skin cancer. Hatters should advertise them on television. TO HELL WITH THE OZONE LAYER — WEAR A HAT!"

Hats, Mrs Chigwell, hats. At the start of this century everybody wore them: toppers for upper-class and professional men, bowlers for the middling people, cloth caps for the workers. Bare headed folk were almost thought as shocking as nudists because their place in the social scale was not immediately obvious. I suspect that hats became unfashionablc because we passed through a liberty, equality and fraternity phase – or imagined we were in one. But we're coming out of it again, and by the end of the century everybody will have head gear. Their sanity will depend on it. Am I boring you? Shall I change the subject? Would you like to suggest another topic of conversation? No? Rinse your mouth out all the same.

The hat of the future – in my opinion – will be a broad-brimmed safety helmet with hinged ear-flaps and a mouth-piece which can be folded down to work as a mobile telephone. It will also have a visor like old suits of armour or modern welders have, but when pulled down over your face the inside works as a telly screen. The energy needed to drive these sets could be tapped straight from the action of the viewer's heart – it would use up less energy than walking down a flight of stairs. The difference between one hat and another will be the number of channels you can afford. The wealthy will have no limit to them, but the homeless and unemployed will benefit too. I am not one of these heartless people who despise the unemployed for watching television all day. Without some entertainment they would turn to drugs, crime and suicide even more than they're doing already, but these video helmets will provide richer entertainment than we get nowadays from these old-fashioned box TVs which to my eyes already look prehistoric – relics of the wood and glass age – BVR – Before Virtual Reality. You've heard about virtual reality? Yes? No? It's a helmet of the sort I've just described. You wear it with a kind of overall suit equipped with electronic pressure pads so that you not only see and hear, but feel you're inside the television world you are watching. Miss Mackenzie is pulling faces at me because she knows what I am going to say and thinks it may shock you since it refers to sex. But I promise that not one bad word will pass my lips. These helmet suits not only give sensations of life and movement in beautiful exciting surroundings. They also, if you desire it, give the visual and sensual experience of an amorous encounter with the partner of your choice. Perhaps Clint Eastwood in your case, Mrs Chigwell. Anna Magnani in mine, although it shows how old I am. Any professional person who remembers Anna Magnani in *Bitter Rice* is obviously on the verge of retirement. Or senility. And so, I am afraid, is she. Not that I ever saw her in *Bitter Rice* – a film for Adults Only. I only encountered the first love of my life through her posters and publicity photos. I wonder what Anna Magnani looks like nowadays?

Excuse me while I wash my hands. We are on the verge of completion. You're still quite comfortable? Good. Here we go again and remember I am talking nonsense, nothing but nonsense.

The hat of tomorrow – an audio-visual helmet with or without the suit – will not only release you into an exciting world of your own choice; it will shut out the dirty, unpleasant future my wife keeps worrying about. It will give marijuana or heavy drug sensations without damaging the health. Of course intelligent people like you and I, Mrs Chigwell, will use it for more than escapist entertainment. We will use it to talk to friends, and educate ourselves. Children of four will be fitted with helmets giving them the experience of a spacious, friendly classroom where beautiful, wise, playful adults teach them everything their parents want them to know. Schools will become things of the past and teachers too since a few hundred well scripted actors will be able to educate the entire planet. And think of the saving in transport! When the lesson stopped they could take the helmet off and bingo – they're home again. Unless the parents switch them onto a babysitter channel.

"All right!" says my wife after hearing me thus far, "What about homelessness? Your helmets can't shut out foul weather and poisoned air." "They can if combined with the right overalls," I tell her. "In tropical countries, like India, homeless people live and sleep quite comfortably in the streets. Now, it is a widely known fact that our armed forces have warehouses stacked with suits and respirators designed to help them survive on planet Earth after the last great nuclear war has made everybody homeless. But the last great nuclear war has been indefinitely postponed. Why not add Virtual Reality visors and pressure pads to these suits and give them to our paupers? Tune them into a channel of a warm Samoan beach under the stars with the partner of their choice and they'll happily pass a rainy night in the rubble of a burnt-out housing scheme and please rinse your mouth out. Don't chew anything hard for another couple of hours. The chair – is now restoring you – to a less prone position.

Bye-bye, Mrs Chigwell. The receptionist will give you the bill, and it might be wise to arrange an appointment in – perhaps six months from now.

Whatever the future of the human race
it is not likely to dispense
with dentists.

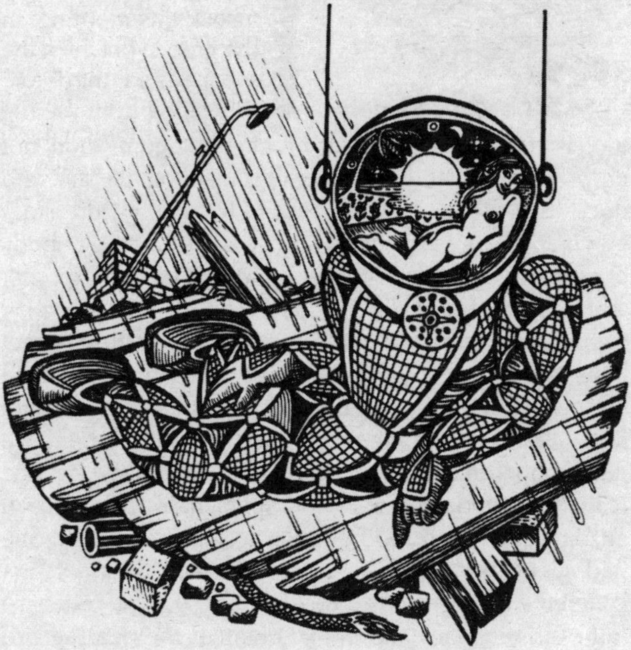

TIME TRAVEL

I DISCOVERED an odd thing about my left foot when about to pull on a sock this morning. In the groove between the second and third toe, reckoning from the big toe, is a small grey pellet of chewing-gum. I do not chew gum, or know or remember meeting anyone who does. I sometimes patter about this room in my dressing-gown and bare feet, but I never go out of it, and nobody comes here nowadays except the one who cares for me, who is Zoë I believe. And hope. Zoë would never play such a sly wee disturbing trick as putting a sticky sweet between the toes of a sleeping man. Her tricks were all bonny and lavish. I once came home to find that a friend had given her back money we had lent him, money we had stopped expecting to get back, though we needed it for food and rent. Zoë had spent half of it on food all right – we had food enough to last a fortnight. She had spent the rest on flowers. The bedroom floor was covered with vases, jugs, bowls, pans, basins, kettles so full of irises, lilacs and carnations that the bed seemed afloat in a small Loch Lomond of blue, purple and crimson petals. The scent nearly knocked me out. I had to be angry. I saw the loving goodness in that gesture, but had I encouraged lavishness we would have ended up homeless. She knew it, too. Once when I chose to be lavish she grew thoughtful, worried, then angry. She wanted me to be careful and mean so that she could be lavish, which does not explain how this chewing-gum arrived between my toes.

I do not believe in miracles. I believe the human mind can solve, rationally, any problem it recognizes and closely attends to. I decided not to finish dressing before I solved this one, though I usually earn my pocket-money and the right to stay here by working on the problem of time travel. I dropped the left sock on the floor (Zoë would pick it up) and from a sitting posture on the edge of the bed moved to a prone one on top of the quilt, which I must remember to call *a doovay*. If I do not learn to use the new words people keep inventing I will one day find I am talking a dead language. I decided to tackle the problem of the chewing-gum by a strategy combining Algebra, Euclidean Geometry and Baconian Induction; but feeling slightly cold in my semmit and single sock I first crept under the doovay and wrapped it round me because a snug body allows a clear mind.

GIVEN: M – Me who sometimes patter barefoot round this room. P – Pellet of gum stuck to the foot of M. UG – Unknown Gumchewer who is the source and prime mover of P. R. – Room that M never leaves and UG never enters. W – World containing M, P, UG, R and other items and events.

REQUIRED: To find the likeliest event or events which could move P from the mouth of UG to the foot of M while preserving these conditions:-
1. M and UG remain ignorant of each other.
2. M is ignorant of P before finding P between his toes.
3. UG is ignorant of P's movement after it leaves him, but not while it leaves him. (Chewed gum only leaves a mouth by being swallowed or spat or removed by fingers and flicked into air or removed by fingers and attached

to other item: all of which are conscious acts though soon forgotten.)

CONSTRUCTION! – Yes, I was now ready and able to set out the problem in geometrical space-time. I needed no pencil, paper, ruler or compasses. The decay of my organs and senses stops me doing or showing much to other people but strengthens my ability to see things inside. When completely dead to the world I expect to see it all perfectly. Without even closing my eyes I now visualize this:

The circles represent the world, the squares my room, the curved arrow the movement of the pellet into the room. Could I picture a single, simple event able to fire P for Pellet from the world outside onto the dark green mottled linoleum of this floor, from which the pressure and warmth of my foot later detached it? I pictured one easily.

Outside my window is an ash tree which looks insanely active, even when standing still. Three tall trunks diverge upward from the same root, and a few boughs or long branches fork from these in elegant curves, but most of them grow straight for a yard or more then, as if turning a corner, bend abruptly up or down or sideways, then undulate, zigzag, spiral, turn steep U-bends or suddenly explode outward into a lot of smaller branches, themselves as knotted and twisted as the tentacles of an arthritic squid. On the day I discovered the chewing-gum all these trunks, boughs, branches with their twigs and leaves were swaying, writhing, lashing about and reminding me they were rooted in a space of grass too smooth to be called a field, too rough to be called a lawn. I seemed to remember an asphalt path between the tree and window, but nearer the window than the tree. I easily imagined a stout sturdy man wearing boiler-suit, Wellington boots and cloth cap who strides along that path chewing a piece of gum which gets so flavourless that he fixes it to the ball of his thumb near the tip, bends his strong middle finger until the top edge of the nail touches the crease in the joint of his thumb then, using the thumb as a lock he builds up muscular pressure in the finger until, seeing an open window just ahead he mischievously aims his hand, unlocks his thumb and (without pausing in his stride) flicks slings catapults the pellet through onto the floor of the room, remaining as ignorant of me as I of him, at that moment. But the window is never open, so I must now seek a more complex though equally elegant solution to this problem.

Is? Now seek? This problem? I seem to be conducting my investigation in the present tense, though I certainly began it in the past. Time travel is unending. And I am sorry that the continually shut nature of the window has made that stout man improbable. For a moment I thought him a friend. I used to ask the one who cares for me (not Zoë, the other one) to open this window on sunny days, but he or she always said, "Sorry Dad no can do. It's against the rules. Why do you think we paid for air-conditioning?" I don't know why we paid for air-conditioning. I hate it. I learned to hate it in the 1980s when I was famous. I must have been, because people kept asking me how it felt to be famous. I always said, "Fine thank you, the perquisites are useful." The only perquisite I can now recall is flying from airport to airport all over North America, and sleeping in hotels, and appearing on platforms in conference centres. The airports, hotels and conference centres were very similar buildings with the same kind of furniture and windows which could not be opened because of the air conditioning. The air on the aeroplanes was fresher, though I could not open windows in those either. The only openable windows I saw in America belonged to cars speeding from one building to another, and would have poisoned me with exhaust fumes had I opened them. So I am used to breathing stale air, but it has damaged my memory. I do not know why people thought me famous, and asked me all over America, and why I went. It must have been a lie. When I was small, and passionately wanted to tell my mother something, and suddenly found I could not remember what it was, she always said, "It must have been a lie."

Wait a minute! I remember something said by a man who was introducing me to a big audience in Toronto or San Francisco or Quebec or Chicago or Montreal or Pittsburgh or Vancouver: *the most humane, far-sighted and lucid thinker the 20th century has known*, he called me. Yes yes. I travelled all over North America because I enjoyed the introductory speeches. This casts no light on the problem of the chewing-gum. I now know that UG could not flick or spit P for Pellet into this room. I am sure UG did not swallow it. Even if such a pellet could keep its colour, adhesiveness and integrity through a digestive tract, bowel gut and sphincter, its position after that would make its entry into my room improbable, whether UG defecated into a public sewage system or crapped behind a hedge. The following construction shows the likeliest chain of events. X represents a commonplace item in the world outside my room and later within it, having been brought from there to here by ... but the item itself will indicate who brought it, so *visualize*!

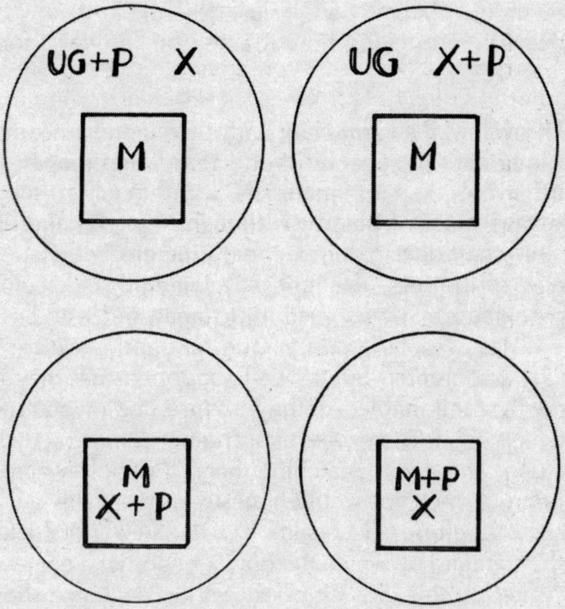

In this construction UG gets rid of P by casually sticking it onto X, which is carried into this room by Zoë, or by one of the other people who look after me, or by a visitor. But nobody has visited me for years so the fame did not last.

The problem had now been carried as near to a solution as this method allowed. I love the deductive method. No wonder its union of Greek geometry and Islamic algebra has seduced nearly every Continental thinker from Descartes to Lévi-Strauss. However, to identify X I needed the inductive method, the practical British approach devised by the two Bacons and William of Occam. I was making a list of everything in the room I could have trodden on when my attention was distracted by the queer behaviour of a chair I had known for years. It stands between my bed and the window, but nearer the window than my bed. I must describe how it usually appears before telling how it acted on the day I found the pellet.

It is a low, light arm-chair with a wooden frame, made not long after the Second World War when money was more evenly spread, materials were in short supply, extravagant use of them was thought wasteful and ugly. Yet this chair does not look cheap. The elegantly tapered curves of the legs, the modestly widening, welcoming curve of the arms owe something to Japan and Scandinavia as well as aeroplane design. The seat and back are not thickly upholstered but so well supported that they feel perfectly comfortable. All the furniture Zoë owned looks and feels good. There was once another chair exactly like this one, and a sofa matching them. If people wanted a standard arm-chair I would honestly propose this one, as James Watt proposed a healthy workhorse without defects as the standard by which the power of artificial engines is measured to this day. Or does that last sentence show I am living in the past? Have engineers stopped measuring the strength of engines in horse-power? Are horses as extinct as whales? Is the Watt no longer a unit of electrical force? Watt was an 18th-century machinist from Greenock who invented the coal-fired water vapour engine. Has Rudolf Diesel's compression fired oil vapour engine supplanted Watt's terminology as well as his machines? Don't panic. I suspect this is a word problem, a quilt-doovay problem, not destruction-of-Scottish-achievement-by-German-achievement problem. Unless I describe the usual colour of the chair the oddity of its conduct a week ago cannot be described.

The parts of the woodwork designed to be seen have been polished, stained and varnished to a medium chocolate colour that almost hides the grain. The upholstery is covered by a russet red fabric I found annoyingly bright before it faded. When in bed I view the chair in profile, like the chair Whistler's mother sits on, and see a tall narrow hole in the fabric of the back of the side, a hole through which at least twenty-four inches of pale unpolished unvarnished timber appear like a bone seen through an open wound. This hole has not been worn or torn open but shredded, as by a cat's claws – threads and shreds of fabric dangle down from the edges all round it. In the years when I rummaged in cupboards I found other evidence of a cat: a plastic feeding dish with FLUFFY printed on the sloping sides, and behind containers of Marmite Yeast Extract and Granny's Tomato Soup a tin of Whiskas Supermeat, Chicken and Rabbit Variety. Most sinister of all, behind the long-lost matching sofa I once saw a cardboard box more than two feet square with an arched hole like a door cut into one side, and crayoned over the sides and top a pattern suggesting brickwork, with the words CAT-PALACE, MOG-A-DEN and FLUFFY HOUSE. This writing was not in Zoë's hand. It suggested that before she helped me up from the pavement and brought me home here she loved another human being as well as a cat, somebody who enjoyed fishing. There was a wicker creel under the bed, an angling rod in the wardrobe, waders in the lobby press. I said nothing about these articles and one day I came home and they had gone. I said nothing, because out of sight is out of mind if I want it to be, nor did I mind Fluffy ripping at the chair. Cats invented themselves by clawing their way up and down tree trunks and scratching soil or grass over their excrement. Forbidding cats to scratch is like forbidding humans to cut their nails and hair. Also, the chair was not responding to Fluffy in the year I found the pellet. It was brightening and darkening. The dim russet fabric glowed and flickered, then leapt into dazzling vividness like when new, but with a moving pattern of leaves dancing over it in a very irregular way. This pattern (dull red on bright russet) was dove grey on creamy ivory over the exposed timber. For half a minute the chair persisted in this way then suddenly, like an exhausted dancer, slumped in two or three seconds back to its ordinary dull old colours. Had the chair been remembering leaves it had seen in earlier days?

Glancing through the window I noticed a remarkable coincidence. The leaves of the ash tree had the shapes and dancing movements of the pattern which had recently faded from the chair. And I saw another coincidence! Leaves, branches and trunks were flickering, lashing, swaying in the same direction and with the same turbulence as ragged whiteish-grey clouds in the sky beyond, clouds with shifting patches of blue and gleams of unpredictable sunlight between them. Without its underground roots every part of that tree would have flown off with the clouds, which shows the infectious force of a strong example. Had the air between the tree and clouds been visible I might have seen it rushing along too. For a moment I considered working out how the movements within the chair had been caused. People will pay a lot of money for objects that blaze and flicker, as television sets and games machines in public houses show. But I am too old to venture into show business. It is enough for me to passively enjoy the play of natural coincidences and actively enjoy the play of inward speculation. These two plays led to my famous discovery. Of course they did.

Einstein had died without establishing the unified field hypothesis, all the physicists had agreed the thing was impossible when I – a botanist – proved that every part and particle of the universe reflects every other part and particle and every past and eventual possibility inherent in each part and particle. My dissertation proving the identity of sense and motion in water lilies also proved the identity of sense and motion everywhere! And it cleared away all the paradoxes in Newtonian gravitation by showing that Kepler as well as Einstein had been right all along. Look at a star. Astronomers will say it is a distant sun or nebula, but even a moth can see it is a body of light. We know it gives light because we live inside the radiance of the gift – live inside the star. That twinkling little item is the core or central pip of a radiant fruit containing every other star and galaxy. My discovery angered many clever people, for by proving that loneliness is a convenient form of ignorance it left them nowhere to hide. "Nonsense!" roared the hearty pragmatists, "The light, heat, sounds et cetera given out by a body are not parts of the body, they are its excrement. Some bodies fling useful shit at us, some fling the dangerous kind so we need to identify the sources. The source you call a star is a mass of fissile material exuding beams essential to life and useful to navigators." People with this self-centred view cannot be faulted. They want to be nothing but cockroaches in the larder of the universe, so have no interest in the rest of the palace. There was more dignity in the wrath of a great French scientist who was also a practising Catholic, and so obsessed by the needless division between mind and body – so certain that only a God *outside* the universe could redeem what he thought was its horrible nature – that he would not see the regenerative side of my discovery.

"The silence of these vast spaces appalls me," he said, talking about the gaps between the stars. I told him these gaps were spaces between the bodies in a busy market where light was being exchanged so rapidly our eyes could not catch it. "Imbecile!" he cried, "Do you not know that whole blazing star systems are receding from us faster than light can travel, and will collapse into black cinders without a single ray or thought from them ever reaching the frozen cinder which was once our little world?"

I pointed out that while answering me his own mind

had overtaken these blazing systems, had survived their extinction and returned to our own extinct world, enlivening it with one ray of impossible light, dignifying it with an impossibly gloomy thought. He frowned and said, "You are playing with words. Words are an expression of thought, not a physical force." I pointed out that spoken sounds, though perhaps unable to open a closed mind, were as physical a force as dawn sunbeams that open the petals of daisies. But he so gloried in the faith he needed to face his appalling universe that he muttered, "Solipsist!" and turned his back on me. The Americans did not, or not at first. I expect they used me in propaganda for their space programme, or space race, or whatever the advertisers called it before the Russians made it pointless by stopping pretending to compete.

Having solved the universal problems I now need to exercise my brain with smaller matters like time travel, and where Zoë has been for the last two or three days, and Between Two Toes, or The Case of the Mysterious Pellet.

I cannot now say if I am solving the last of these problems in the present or remembering how I once solved it in the past but the time came (or has come) when I made (or will make) a list of items brought recently into my room from the world outside: food, cleaned clothes and towels, newspapers and letters. Then I made (or will make) another list of items on the floor of the room, items my foot could have pattered across: the linoleum, a fringed rug and things often dropped on these like food, clothes, towels, newspapers and letters. Items common to both lists should then be considered one at a time with great care, for one of these must be item X. And I have just remembered that letters and newspapers should be on neither list. Nobody has written to me for years, and I stopped taking papers during the last great miners' strike in the 1980s when I saw that Britain had again become a financial oligarchy protected by the ancient fraud of a two-party electoral system. But the lists are not needed because I now see the gum MUST have come from inside the sock I wore yesterday, a sock which like all my clothes is washed in a machine outside this room where the clothes of other people (one of whom must be the Unknown Gumchewer) are also washed. UG accidentally attached the P for Pellet to a cardigan or other woollen article. UG's helper (who is probably one of mine too) put it in the drum of a machine whose soapy solutions and hydraulic pressures dissolved most of the dirt but only displaced P for Pellet from the cardigan to the toe of my sock while the sock was inside out: its invariable state after I pull it off at night. Zoë or whoever else looks after me turns the cleaned socks the right way round at night before setting out a cleaned pair for me to put on next day. The fact that all my socks are grey like the Pellet would prevent Zoë or the other one seeing and removing it. Eureka!

I basked in the elegance of this solution for two or three happy and peaceful minutes. Since discovering the Pellet I had been rolling it idly between the ball of my right-hand thumb and forefinger. I was about to flick it into a pail-shaped metal waste-bin near the bed when something in its soft, plastic adhesiveness made me doubt if it was chewing-gum at all. It was very like a more recent invention called Blu-Tack, first marketed in the 1970s (I think) as a means of attaching paper notices and light pictorial reproductions to surfaces without puncturing or staining the notices, reproductions and surfaces. But there are no such things in my room. I don't need them. Zoë's chair in front of the window, the ash tree outside it give me all the entertainment and food for thought I need. Or have I forgotten something? Look suspiciously, carefully, at all nearby surfaces. Yes, there is something I forgot.

Beside my bed is a small metal wardrobe with wheels of a kind I have never before seen outside hospitals and homes for the chronically ill and disabled. On a side of this immediately opposite my face when I lie down is a paper document fastened by blobs of Blu-Tack at the two upper and the right-hand lower corner. This letter has a conventionally regal heading and a signature at the foot scribbled by Charles King number 3. The bit between signature and heading is very prettily printed or exquisitely typed, and congratulates me on attaining my hundredth birthday. Damn. Hell. F, no don't use fuck as a curse word. Remember what I wrote in that review of the 1928 edition of *Lady Chatterley's Lover*: "Lawrence has restored to tender uses what should be the tenderest word in any language." The *Glasgow Herald* sacked me for writing that review. I had guts in 1928. Perhaps that was my finest hour. But this letter which I tear down, crumple and fling into the waste-bin proves three unpleasant facts:

1. This is the 21st century.
2. Britain is still a damned and blasted monarchy.
3. I have not seen Zoë lately, or anybody else I know, because she and they died in the decade after Fluffy died, nearly twenty-five years ago.

I'm glad they left me Zoë's chair.
It makes time travel easier.

NEAR THE DRIVER

T**HIS** intelligent, kind old lady was once a schoolteacher, and it shows in her forthright manners and alert appearance. On the station announcement board she reads that the 11.15 Aquarian from Bundlon to Shaglow will leave from platform H, and this worries her. While aware that her memory is failing she is sure station platforms used to be numbered, not lettered, so why the change? And walking along the platform she sees the carriages have very small square windows with rounded corners. The last time she travelled by rail the windows seemed to be big long glass panels that stretched the entire side of each carriage with hardly any interruption. She also remembers when carriages were divided into compartments like the insides of stagecoaches, each with a door in the middle of either side, a door whose window could be raised or lowered by fitting holes in a thick leather strap onto shining brass studs. The handles of these old doors were shining brass levers. She stops and examines a door of a carriage near the front of the modern train. It has neither window nor handle, just a square plastic button in the middle with PRESS engraved on it. She presses. The door slides up like a blind. She steps through and it snaps down behind her.

She finds herself peering along a central corridor with rows of three high-backed seats on each side, all facing her. The backs of the six front seats hide all but the rows in front. Beside one window a sturdy old man sits reading a newspaper published by the British Orthodox Communist Party. The teacher nods approvingly, for though never a Communist she approves of radical politics. Beside the old man is a housewife with a worried expression, beside the woman a restless little child wearing a blue canvas suit. The teacher, proud of her ability to read character at a glance, decides these are three generations of a family belonging to the skilled artisan class. Beside the opposite window a middle-aged, middle-class couple sit bolt upright staring straight ahead. They seem to be ignoring each other, but with another approving nod the teacher sees on the arm-rest between them the man's left hand clasping the woman's right. The teacher sits in the empty seat beside this couple, saying to nobody in particular, "I suppose modern trains look like aeroplanes because they travel nearly as fast! I regret that because I hate air travel, but I'm glad our compartment is close to the bit that pulls – the bit we called the engine in the days of steam. I feel safer when I'm near the driver."

"My father feels that way too, though he won't admit it. Will you Dad?" says the housewife, but the old man mutters, "Shut up Miriam."

"I feel that too dear," murmurs the rigid lady to her husband who murmurs, "I know you do dear. Please shut up."

The teacher at once thinks of the married couple as Mr and Mrs Dear. Delighted to have started a conversation before the journey begins she says, "In most railway accidents the train is struck in the rear, isn't it? So statistically speaking we are safer near the engine."

"That's stupid!" squeaks the child.

The mother says, "Don't be rude Patsy," but the teacher says eagerly, "Oh please, I'm a teacher! Retired! But I know how to handle difficult children. Why is what I said stupid Patsy?"

"Because in collisions the front of one train always hits the front or back of another, so the safest place in a train is always the middle."

The old man chuckles slightly, the other adults smile. After

a moment of silence the teacher opens her purse, removes a coin and says, "Patsy, here is a bright new silver-looking five-pound coin. I give it to you because what I said was stupid and you were right to correct me."
The child grabs the coin. The other adults stare at the teacher and the conversation seems about to take a new direction when it is interrupted.

A melodious chime comes from the upholstery of the chair-backs then a quiet, firm, friendly voice saying, "Good day good people! This is Captain Rogers, your driver, welcoming you aboard the 1999 Aquarian from Bundlon to Shaglow, stopping at Bagchester, Shloo, Spittenfitney and Glaik. The Aquarian leaves at the end of this announcement, arriving at Bagchester exactly forty-one minutes later. Tea, coffee, sandwiches, will be served at half twenty-three hours, and in accordance with the latest stock-market reports, tea will be one point sixty pounds, coffee one point ninety-nine. Sandwiches are still last week's price and expected to remain stable for the duration of the journey. The bar is now open. British Rail trust you will have a comfortable trip. Thank you."
Through the window on her left the teacher sees a pillar supporting the station canopy slide sideways, then a view of slate rooftops and shining tower blocks turning indistinct and vanishing.

The other passengers are complaining about the price of tea. The teacher says, "But I'm glad they warned us. When is half twenty-three hours? It's a sign of senility for a retired teacher to admit this, but I can't grasp this new way of telling the time."
"Half past eleven, isn't it?" says the housewife uncertainly.
"A.m?"
"Yes, isn't it?"
The old man says abruptly, "Don't be daft Miriam. Half twenty-three hours is twelve from twenty-three and a half, which is eleven and a half, so half past eleven p.m."

"No no no!" cries the child excitedly, "Our headmaster says we shouldn't think about time in twelves because of computers and demicals. Computers can't count in demicals, so half twenty-three hours is half past twenty-three."

"Patsy!" says the old man in a low steady voice, "If you say one more word within the next ten minutes I shall remove the whole weight of my fist from the side of your jaw!" But the teacher merely sighs. Then says, "I wish they had let us keep the old noon with the twelve hours before and after it. But even the station clocks have changed. Instead of a circular face with all the hours and minutes marked around the edge, past AND future, we have a square panel with nothing in it but the minute we're at now. Nothing eight hours twenty minutes, then flick! – it's nothing eight hours twenty-one. That makes me feel trapped. Trapped, yet pushed at the same time. And I'm sure computers could be taught how to count in twelves, I hear some of them are quite intelligent. I hate that little flick when one minute becomes the next."

"I hate it too dear," murmurs Mrs Dear and, "So do I dear, please shut up," says her husband.

"Time and money!" says the teacher sighing again, "So much disappeared so suddenly: the little farthings with jenny wrens on them, thick brown threepennies, silver sixpences, the old ha'penny. Did you know, Patsy, that ha'pennies were once a whole inch in diameter, the size of the modern twopenny?"

"What's an inch?" says the child.

"Two point five three nine nine nine eight centimetres. And the old pennies were lovely huge lumps of copper, two hundred and forty to the pound, we shall not see their like again, with Britannia ruling the waves between a small battleship and the Eddystone lighthouse. Britannia was a real woman, you know. Not many people realize that. She was copied from a – a girlfriend of the Merry Monarch, not Nell Gwyn. The old pennies had room for so much history on them. They were history! Even in the sixties you still found coins with young Queen Victoria's head on them, and the old Queen was so common we took her for granted. Just think! Every time we went shopping we were handling coins which had clinked in the pockets of Charles Dickens and Doctor Pritchard the poisoner and Isambard Kingdom Brunel."

"It might interest you to know, madam," says Mr Dear, "that the weight of a modern penny, subtracted from a pre-decimal penny, left enough copper to construct circuits for nine hundred and seventy-three pocket television sets."

"But WAS IT?" shouts the old man so violently that everyone stares at him and Mr Dear says, "I beg your pardon?"

"The copper!" says the old man excitedly, "The copper saved by switching to a smaller currency was NOT used to make cheap television sets for the masses! It was used to build the circuits of an electronic nuclear defence system that cost the British tax-payer a hundred and eighty-three thousand MILLION pounds and was obsolete two years before it was finally installed!"

"I have no wish to discuss politics with you sir," says Mr Dear, looking out the window again. The old man snorts and concentrates on his paper.

The women are the most embarrassed by the ensuing silence. The mother sends Patsy to the buffet bar to buy a chocolate biscuit with her new coin, and in a low voice the teacher asks the mother the sex of her little child. The mother, also in a low voice, explains that she thinks there is too much sex nowadays, that her mother never mentioned it, that Patsy will make up her own mind as soon as he's old enough to choose. The teacher nods approvingly, but says in her experience children are grateful for a little guidance. The mother disagrees; says that all a child should learn from its parents is proper manners; says at least Patsy won't turn into one of these dreadful women's lib ladies – or a teddy boy. The old man surprises them by saying suddenly, "A cat."

"What's that Dad?" asks his daughter.

"Teddy boys were forties," he explains, "Beatniks fifties. Hippies sixties. Mods and rockers seventies. Punks eighties. And now they call themselves cool cats."

"Are you sure?" asks the teacher, "There have been so many strange names for young people – skinheads, bobby-soxers, flappers, knuts, mashers and macaronis – that I've started thinking of them as youths. The police reports always call them youths."

"And quite right too!" mutters Mr Dear, and would say more but again the musical warbling introduces the firm friendly voice.

"Good day good people – Captain Rogers here. We are making excellent time. On our left we are flashing past the reforested bings of the outer Bundlon slag depot, on our right are the soya fields of the British Golliwog Jam Corporation. I regret that a special stock-market news flash has obliged us to raise the price of coffee to two point forty pounds a cup –" (the passengers' cries of rage and disgust drown the announcement for a while) "– biscuits are expected to remain stable at least as far as Shloo. Passengers with an interest in transport will not need to be told that today is a special one for British Rail. In one and a half minutes it will be precisely the hundred and fiftieth anniversary of the exact moment when Isambard Kingdom Brunel –" ("Brunel!" gasps the teacher) "– tapped the last ceremonial rivet into the Grand Albert Royal Pennine Suspension Bridge: the first broad-gauge box-girder suspension bridge in the history of engineering. To honour the occasion we will now play you *The Railways of Old England*, orchestrated and sung by Sir Noël Coward. Through the length and breadth of Britain, in trains trundling through the lonely Pass of Killiecrankie or thundering across the Stockport viaduct, passengers are rising to their feet to hear Noël Coward sing *The Railways of Old England*."

There is a preliminary rolling of drums with a sombre yet challenging blast of trumpets. Mr Dear, Mrs Dear and the teacher rise to their feet and the mother seems about to do so when the old man hisses, "Miriam! Patsy! Stay exactly where you are."

"Excuse me sir," cries Mr Dear, "Are you not going to stand?"

"No I am NOT!"

"Oh please sh dear!" whispers Mrs Dear to her husband who cries, "Shut up dear, I will not sh! You sir, I gather are one of those left-wing militant extremists who yearn for a discredited Bolshevik railway system. Well the British railway system has no harsher critic than myself. I was sorry when they nationalized it, saddened when they axed off the branch lines and appalled by how long the government took to restore it to a responsible private company. But despite its grisly past our rail system was built by a combination of Irish brawn, Scottish engineering and English financial daring which made us once the foremost steam railway empire in the universe. Does this mean nothing to you?"

"Don't talk to me about British Rail!" yells the old man over Noël Coward's brittle patriotic tenor, "I worked all my life for British Rail. I was a fireman from the old LMS days to when they brought in bloody diesel! British Rail was destroyed by people like you – bloody accountants and lawyers and retired admirals on the board of directors –"

"That's ludicrous!" cries Mr Dear, and "Stop it Dad!" cries the old man's daughter, but nothing stops the flood of his articulate wrath: "– when they nationalized us the government said 'British Rail belongs to the people now' but who did we get on the new board of directors? Linesmen? Footplate men? Station-masters? Did we hell! We got the same old gang – stockbrokers, lieutenant colonels, civil servants with posh accents, the gang that eventually sold us out to the car manufacturers, the

building societies and the oil corporations!"
"I am not listening to you!!" cries Mr Dear.
"I never thought you would," says the old man chuckling and picking up his paper again. The music has stopped. The others sit down, Mr Dear looking as if he would prefer to do something more violent. There is another embarrassing silence, then the teacher slips across the aisle to Patsy's seat and tells the old man quietly, "I was to a large extent entirely on your side in that little exchange, even though I stood up. I like the tune you see, and old habits die hard. But the title was inaccurate. Our railways are British, not English." She slips back to her seat as Patsy approaches shouting, "Mum Mum Mum!"

Patsy, terribly excited, is closely followed by a tall, lean, mildly amused looking man who says, "Good day good people! Does this small person belong to any of you?"
"Patsy," says the mother, "Where have you been?"
"Wandering far too near the engine for anyone's good," says the stranger.
"How very naughty of you, Patsy. Thank the nice man for bringing you back."
"But Mum!" says the child excitedly bumping its bottom up and down on the seat, "Nobody's driving this train! The driver's cabin's empty! I looked inside!"
Mrs Dear gives a little gasp of horror. The mother says severely, "Patsy, that's not a very nice thing to say, not with that bad rail accident in America last week. Apologize at once."
"But Mum, it really was empty!"
"Dear, I'm terribly worried," Mrs Dear tells her husband who says, "Don't be stupid dear, the kid's obviously gone the wrong way and blundered into the guard's van."
The teacher points out that the stranger said he found Patsy near the engine, but "The child knows nothing about mechanics!" declares Mr Dear, "Hardly anyone knows anything about mechanics nowadays. It wouldn't surprise

me to learn that modern trains are driven from an obscure cabin somewhere in the middle."
"And it wouldn't surprise me!" cries the old man violently, "To learn that British Rail has sacked all its drivers and never told the public a word about it!"
The women gasp in horror, Mr Dear snorts, the stranger laughs and tries to speak, but the old man talks him down: "You needed a driver in the days of steam – two of them counting the fireman – tough men! Strong men who knew the engine and could clean it themselves, and grasped every valve and stop-cock like it was the hand of a friend! Men who felt the gradient through the soles of their boots and heard the pressure in the thrusts of the piston. But nowadays! Nowadays it wouldn't surprise me if the driver of this so-called train wasn't lying back with a glass of brandy in a London club, watching us on a computer screen and half sloshed out of his upper-class over-educated skull!"
"You're wrong and I can prove it," says the stranger. They stare at him.

At first sight there is nothing unusual in this man whose modest smile seems to apologize for his slightly taller than average height. The large pockets, the discreet epaulets of his well-cut, dove-grey jacket would look equally inconspicuous in a cinema queue or an officers' mess, yet he faces the six pairs of enquiring eyes with a relaxed and flawless confidence which so acts upon two of the women that they sigh with relief.
"Who the hell are you?" asks the old man, and the teacher says, "The driver – I recognize his voice."
"Correct! So you see, I'm not lying back in a London club, I'm here beside you. I really am one of you. May I join you for a moment?"
Taking a small metal frame from a pocket the driver opens it into a stool with a canvas seat, places that in the aisle and sits down facing them. Although his chin now rests on his steeply angled knees he does not look at all ridiculous.

Most of the company are impressed.

"I feel so safe," murmurs Mrs Dear, and "Stop scowling Dad, it isn't polite," says the mother, and Mr Dear says, "Excuse me sir, I have said harsh things about British Rail in my time ..." ("Of course you have," says the driver genially) "... but I have never doubted that our trains are the safest in the world and our drivers second to none – if only the trade unions would stop confusing them with promises of Utopian conditions."

"Thank you," says the driver.

"Train driving seems to have changed in recent years," says the teacher in a high clear voice.

"Excuse me madam," says the driver, "I'll gladly explain anything you do not understand after I've had time to ... to ..." (and suddenly he looks confused, embarrassed, almost boyish) "... you see it isn't every day I have a chance to speak to John Halifax!"

"Eh!" says the old man staring at him.

"You *are* John Halifax, the last of the steam men? Who took three whole minutes off the Bundlon to Glaik run in the great railway race between LMS and the LNER in nineteen thirty-four?"

"You know about that?" whispers the old man with a wondering stare.

"You are a legend in railway circles, Mr Halifax."

"But how did you know I was on the train?"

"Aha!" says the driver waggishly, "I'm not supposed to tell passengers certain things, but to hell with security. The ticket-office clerks are not the ignorant gits the public assume. They keep me informed. I used your grandchild's escapade as an excuse to seek you out, and here I am!"

"I see!" whispers the old man, smiling and nodding to himself.

"Please don't get cross, but I need to ask you a terribly personal question," says the driver, "It's about the last great railway race. Do you remember stoking the *Spitfire Thunderbolt* up the Devil's Kidney gradient with only

three minutes to reach Beattock Summit or the race would be lost?"
"Oh I remember!"
"Were you, on that heroic drive, exhausting yourself, torturing yourself, pressing out every ounce of your energy and intelligence merely to advertise the old LMS?"
"No, I was not."
"Then why did you do it? I know it wasn't for money."
"I did it for steam," says the old man after a pause, "I did it for British steam."
"I *knew* you would give me that answer!" cries the delighted driver, and Mr Dear says, "Excuse me, may I butt in? You see Mr Halifax and I kick, you might say, with opposite feet. He's left and I'm right. I didn't realize before now that we are essential parts of the same body. Captain Rogers has made me see that for the first time. Mr Halifax, I am no toady. When I offer you my hand I am merely demonstrating my respect for you as a man. I am apologizing for nothing. But here … is … my hand. Will you … ?"
Leaning sideways he stretches out his arm across the aisle. "Put it there!" says the old steam man and they shake heartily. Suddenly all three men are chuckling and the mother and Mrs Dear smiling happily and Patsy bumping boisterously up and down. But in a voice used to calling unruly classes to order the teacher says, "Perhaps Captain Rogers will now tell us why he isn't with his engine!"

The passengers stare at the driver who shrugs, spreads his hands and says, "I'm afraid, madam, the heroic age of engine driving went out with steam. The modern engine (we call them traction units nowadays) only requires my attention from time to time. Our speed and position are being monitored, at the present moment, from headquarters in Stoke-on-Trent. It's a perfectly safe system. All Europe uses it. And America."
"But in America last week there was a terrible accident …"

"Yes, madam, through a fault in their central data bank at Detroit. These big continental systems are all far too centralized. The British branch of the system has enough autonomy to prevent such accidents here. So you see, although I am not drinking brandy in a London club (I never touch alcohol – doctor's orders!) I look more like a Piccadilly lounge-lizard than like the legendary John Halifax here. My main task is to keep down the buffet prices and stop passengers bickering with one another. And I'm not always successful."

"I think you succeed splendidly!" says Mrs Dear enthusiastically.

"Hear hear!" says her husband.

"You're certainly good with passengers –" says the teacher, and, "You aren't the fool I took you for, I'll give you that," says the old man.

"Thank you John," says the driver gratefully, "With all due respect to the other passengers here, it is your opinion which counts with me."

The chiming is heard then the firm friendly voice says, "Good day good people, there is no cause for alarm. This is your driver Captain Rogers speaking. Here is a special message for Captain Rogers. Will he please proceed to the traction unit? Proceed to the traction unit. Thank you."

"Pre-recorded, of course?" says the old steam man knowingly.

"Quite right," says the driver, who has risen and pocketed his stool, "If the traction unit is empty when a message comes from HQ, the graphic print-out activates that announcement and – duty calls! I'm sorry I have to return to my cabin. I'll probably find a rotten stock-market report that forces me to raise the price of tea again. I hope not. Goodbye John."

"Goodbye, er … ?"

"Felix. Goodbye good people."

He departs leaving nearly everyone in a relaxed and social mood.

"What a nice man!" says Mrs Dear, and the mother agrees. Mr Dear announces, "He was informed – and informative."
The teacher says, "But the situation he laid bare for us was not reassuring. Nobody is driving this train."
"Utter rubbish!" cries Mr Dear, "There's a … there are all kinds of things driving this train, data-banks and computers and silicon chips all ticking and whirring in the headquarters at Stockton-on-Tees."
"Stoke-on-Trent," murmurs his wife.
"Shut up dear, the town doesn't matter."
"Well," says the teacher, "I find it disturbing to be driven by machines which aren't on board with us. Don't you, Mr Halifax?"
The old steam man ponders a while then says hesitantly. "I might have done if I hadn't met the driver. But he's an educated chap. He wouldn't take things so casually if there was any danger, now would he?"
"Madam," says Mr Dear, "We are actually far far safer being driven by a machine in Stoke-Newington. No thug with a gun can force it to stop the train, or divert us into a siding where terrorists threaten our lives in order to blackmail the government."
They sit in silence for a while then the teacher says firmly, "You are both perfectly right. I have been very, very foolish."

And then the chiming sounds and they hear that soothing voice again.
"This is your driver, Captain Rogers. We are cruising above the Wash at a speed of two hundred and sixty-one kilometres per hour, and the Quantum-Cortexin ventilation system is keeping the air at the exact temperature of the human skin. So far our run has gone very smoothly, and I deeply regret that I must now apologize for a delay in the anticipated time of arrival. An error in our central data-bank has resulted in the 1999 Aquarian from Bundlon to Shaglow running on the same

line as the 1999 Aquarian from Shaglow to Bundlon. The collision is scheduled to occur in exactly eight minutes thirteen seconds ..." (there is a brief outcry which nobody notices they contribute to) "... at a point eight and a half kilometres south of Bagchester. But there is absolutely no need for alarm. Our technicians in Stoke-Poges are working overtime to reprogramme the master computer and may actually prevent the collision. Meanwhile we have ample time to put into effect the following safety precautions so please listen carefully. Under the arms of your seats you will find slight metal projections. These are the ends of your safety-belt. Pull them out and lock them round you. That is all you need to do. The fire-prevention system is working perfectly and shortly before impact steel shutters will close off the windows to prevent injury from splintered glass. At the present moment television crews and ambulances are whizzing toward the point of collision from all over England, and in cases of real poverty British Rail have undertaken to pay the ambulance fees. I need not say how much I personally regret the inconvenience, but we're in this together, and I appeal to the spirit of Dunkirk ..." (the old steam man snarls) "... that capacity for calmness under stress which has made us famous throughout the globe. Passengers near the traction unit should not attempt to move to the rear of the train. This sound ..." (there is a sudden swish and thud) "... is the noise of the doors between the carriages sealing themselves to prevent a stampede. But there is no need for alarm. The collision is not scheduled for another, er ... seven minutes three seconds exactly, and I will have time to visit your compartments with my personal key and ensure that safety precautions are being observed. This is not goodbye, but *au revoir*. And fasten those belts!"

With a click his voice falls silent and is followed by bracing music of a bright and military sort, but not played loud enough to drown normal conversation.
"Oh what can we do, Dad?" asks the mother, but the old

steam man says gruffly, "Attend to the child Miriam."
The metal projections under the arm-rests pull out into elasticated metal bands with locking buckles at the ends.
"I don't want to be tied up!" says Patsy sulkily.
"Just pretend we're in an aeroplane, dear," says the mother, locking the belt, "Look Grampa's doing it! We're all doing it! And now ..." says the mother in the faint voice of one who fights against hysteria "... we're all safe as houses!"
"Dear, I ... I'm terrified," says Mrs Dear.
Her husband says tenderly, "It's a bad business, dear, but I'm sure we'll pull through somehow."
Then he looks to the teacher and says quietly, "Madam, I owe you an apology. This rail system is more inept, more inane, more ... altogether bad than I thought possible in a country like ours."
"You can say that again!" groans the old steam man.
"I want to get off this train," says the child sulkily and for while they listen to the quiet rushing of the wheels.

Suddenly the teacher cries, "The child is correct! We should slow the train down and jump off it!"
She fumbles with the lock of her belt saying, "I know our speed is controlled by wireless waves or something but the motor – the thing which makes the wheels turn – is quite near us, in the traction unit, could we not ..."
"By heck it's worth a try!" shouts the fireman, fumbling at his belt, "Just let me get at that engine! Just let me get out of this ... This bloody belt won't unlock!"
"Neither will mine," says Mr Dear in a peculiar voice. None of the seat belts unlock.
The teacher says forlornly, "I suppose they call this security."
But the old steam man refuses to sit still. Pressing his elbows against the chair-back he hurls his massive bulk forward again and again, muttering through gritted teeth, "I won't – let – the bastards – do it!"
Though the belt does not break it suddenly gives an inch then another inch as a rending sound is heard inside the upholstery.

Then somewhere a door swishes open and the driver is beside them asking smoothly, "What seems to be the problem?"

"Quick Felix!" says the old steam man, relaxing for a moment, "Get me out of this seat and into your cabin. I want a crack at the motor. I'm sure I can damage it with something heavy. I'll shove my body into it if that will let some of us off!"

"Too late for heroics John!" declares the driver, "I cannot possibly allow you to damage company property in that wanton fashion."

His voice is clear and cold. He wears a belt with a gun holster, and has his hand on it. He stands at ease but every line of his body indicates martial discipline. All stare aghast at him. The old man says, "You ... are ... insane!" and flings himself forward against the belt again but the driver says, "No, John Halifax! You are insane and I have this to prove it."

He draws his gun and fires. It explodes with a thud, not a bang. The fireman slumps forward though his belt holds him in the chair. Mrs Dear starts screaming for help so he shoots her too. There is now a dim, sharp-smelling smoke in the air but the survivors are too stunned to cough. They stare at the driver in a way which clearly upsets him, for he waves the gun about saying testily, "I have NOT killed them! This is an anaesthetic gas pistol developed for use against civilians in Ulster, does anyone else want a whiff? Saves emotional stress. A spell of oblivion and with luck you wake up in the ward of a comfortable, crowded hospital."

"Thank you, no!" says the teacher icily, "We prefer to face death with open eyes, however futile and unnecessary it is."

The chiming sounds and the familiar voice announces that this is Captain Rogers speaking, that three and a half minutes remain before impact, that Captain Rogers should proceed immediately to the guard's van. With a touch of his earlier, gentler, apologetic manner the driver says goodbye, and explains he is forced to leave them because someone must survive the wreck to report it at the official enquiry. The mother cries, "Oh sir, please unlock Patsy and take him with you, she's only a little child ..." but Patsy screams, "No Mum, I'm staying with you Mum, he's nasty nasty nasty!" so the driver says quickly, "Goodbye good people," and leaves.

When the door snaps shut behind him the mother says in a kind, careful, trembling voice, "You know The Lord Is My Shepherd, Patsy. Let's say it, shall we?" and together they murmur, "The Lord is my shepherd. I shall not want. He maketh me to lie down in green pastures. He leadeth me beside the still waters ..."

With a clang of metal sheeting the windows are blotted out by shutters.

"Pitch, pitch dark," says Mr Dear, "They haven't even allowed us light."

He is clasping his wife's body so that her unconscious head rests upon his shoulder, and he finds some comfort in this pressure.

"I know it is a small mercy," says the voice of the teacher, "But I'm glad that military band no longer sounds."

In the darkness the throbbing of the train wheels is more audible and the mother and child pray louder to be heard above it, but not much louder. They reach the end of the prayer, start again at the beginning and continue reciting till the very end.

"Do you remember," says the teacher suddenly, "When every carriage had a communication cord that any traveller could pull and stop the train?"

"Yes!" says Mr Dear with a noise between a groan and a chuckle, "Penalty for improper use £5."

"Once upon a time every small boy wanted to drive a train when he grew up," sighs the teacher, "And in rural communities the station-master played a rubber of whist on Sunday evenings with the schoolmaster, the banker and the local clergyman. I remember a bright spring morning on the platform at Beattock. A porter took a wicker basket from the guard's van and released a whole flight of carrier pigeons. I remember signal boxes with pots of geraniums on the sills."

Mr Dear sighs and says, "We had a human railway once. Why did it change?"

"Because we did not stick to steam!" says the teacher firmly, "We used to be fuelled by coal, our own British coal which would have lasted us for centuries. Now we depend on dangerous poisonous stuff produced by foreign companies based in America, Arabia and ..."

"You're wrong," says Mr Dear, "These companies aren't based anywhere. I've shares in a few. The people running them have offices in Amsterdam and Hong Kong, bank accounts in Switzerland and homes on several continents."

"So that is why we are driven from outside," cries the teacher, getting excited, "None of US is in charge of us now."

"Some of us pretend to be."

They hear the faint distant scream of an approaching train siren. It swells so loud that the teacher is forced to yell over it, "But nobody is really in charge of us now! Nobody is in charge of us ..."

She has braced herself for an explosion, but does not hear one, or hears and forgets it immediately. The train is no longer moving. The blackness enfolding her is so warm and snug that for a moment she dreams she is at home in bed. When she hears the voice of a child calling drowsily, "Mummy ... Mummy ..." she almost believes it is her own. The voice of a mother answers on a wondering note, "I think – Patsy – we're going to be all right."

A moment later the teacher, like other passengers on that train, hears the start of a truly huge and final explosion, but not
the end of it.

THE ENDS OF OUR TETHERS

FOR AGNES AND MORAG AGAIN

EDINBURGH 2003

PROPERTY

WHEN LONDON was advertised as the world's fashion capital – when The Beatles seemed the nation's greatest export – when a Conservative prime minister with a Scottish name said, probably truthfully, that the British people had never been so prosperous, two such people went for a weekend camping holiday in the Highlands.

They were building workers of seventeen and eighteen who lived with their parents in the town of Dumbarton. On Friday night after work they packed the panniers of their motorbikes, rode up the Vale of Leven, took the shore road by Loch Lomond to Tarbert, turned west to the head of Loch Long then zoomed over The Rest-and-Be-Thankful. As darkness fell they passed through the Highlands' only neat little eighteenth-century town and began looking for a camping place. There was a sea loch to their left, hedged fields to the right, and after a mile or two they saw a side road with a wide grassy verge. Here they stopped, spread a groundsheet, erected a tent and put the motorbikes inside. This left enough room to lay down sleeping bags with the panniers for pillows. Then they tied the tent flaps shut, walked back to the town and spent a pleasant evening in the bar of a small hotel.

There are many tales of Scottish country pubs serving drink after the legal closing time. This was one such pub. The boys, cheerfully drunk, left it after midnight and returned to the tent through a mild but sobering rain shower. They sobered completely on finding the tent flaps wide open and nothing but the groundsheet inside. They discussed returning to the town and phoning the police but gloomily decided that a Highland policeman might be hard to rouse at that hour, especially if the rousers were urban youths smelling of drink. They agreed to do nothing before daylight and spent a miserable night huddled in their leather clothes back to back on the groundsheet.x

At eight in the morning they were themselves roused by a man wearing well-cut tweed clothes and accompanied by a policeman. To the boys this man seemed very tall and fresh-faced, perhaps because they felt tired and dirty. He said, "You have insolently camped upon my land without asking my permission. What have you to say for yourselves?"

The elder boy said they didn't know that the roadside was not public, also that their motorbikes and other things had been stolen.

"Not stolen. Impounded," said the man, "I had them removed last night to the police station. You can thank your lucky stars that I was kind enough to leave you the tent. So now dismantle it, collect your chattels from the station and clear out. I do not object, as a rule, to visitors who behave properly and drop no litter. I regard this –" he indicated the tent – "as a form of litter. I have a friend, a very brave soldier who had similar trouble with a family of people like you. Well, he discovered their address, went with a friend to the municipal housing scheme where they lived and pitched a tent of his own in the middle of their back garden. They didn't like that one little tiny bit. Quite annoyed about it they were as a matter of fact."

The man turned a little and looked steadily out
over the loch, mountains, glens, rivers,
moors and islands that he regarded
(with the support of the police)
as his back garden.

PILLOW TALK

WAKENING HE TURNED HIS HEAD and saw she was still reading. After a moment he said, "About that e-mail you sent."

"I never sent you an e-mail," she said, eyes still on the book.

"Not before today, perhaps, but this afternoon you e-mailed me and said—"

"I repeat," she interrupted, looking hard at him, "I have never sent you or anyone else an e-mail in my life."

"But you did send one to the office this afternoon. I remember it perfectly – the heading stating it was from you to me and everyone else in the firm. Why did you have to tell *them*? You must have sent it from a friend's computer or one in the public library."

"You're still drunk."

"If you mean I was drunk when we came to bed you are wrong. We had only one bottle of wine with the evening meal and I drank only one more glass of it than you. I'm glad you're sorry you sent that message but you'll never persuade me you didn't."

"You're hallucinating. What am I supposed to have said?"

"That you want to leave me. Five words – *I want to leave you* – just that."

She stared at him, shut the book and said bitterly, "Oh, very clever. Cruel, but clever." "Do you want to leave me?"

"Yes, but I never told you so. I've never told anyone that – they think ours is such a *solid* marriage. You must have noticed it's a farce and this is your bloody cunning way of blaming me for something I never said and was never going to say."

"Blethers!" he cried, "I am *never* cunning, *never* cruel. I remember these words coming up very clear and distinct on the computer screen: *I want to leave you*."

"Then why didn't you mention it when you came home? Why didn't you mention it over dinner? Are you going to pretend you were brooding over it before we came to bed?"

He thought hard for a while then said, "You're right. I must have dreamed it before I woke a moment ago."

"I'm glad you've sobered up," she said and resumed reading.

After a while he said, "But you want to leave me."

She sighed and said nothing.

"When will you do it?"

"I don't suppose I'll ever do it," she murmured, still appearing to read, "I haven't the courage to live alone. You're an alcoholic bore but not violent and I'm too old to find anyone better."

"I'm glad!" he said loudly. "I don't want you ever to leave because I love you. My life will be a misery if you leave me."

"Then you're luckier than I am. Go back to sleep."

He turned away from her and tried to sleep. About half an hour later he heard her shut the book and switch off the bedside lamp. He got up and went to a room next door where he had hidden a bottle of whisky for this sort of emergency.

MY EX HUSBAND

I WAS NINETEEN when Colin and I met at a friend's party. He was nearly the same age and had a job in the navy. Though not in uniform and not remarkably handsome he was well dressed and carried himself handsomely without seeming arrogant. His conversation was good humoured, with a pleasant touch of shyness. He was also interested in me: the first to be interested since my father's death seven years earlier. We decided to marry. I had a good secretarial job. We raised a joint loan that let us buy a nice house in a pleasant street.

Shortly before the wedding I discovered he expected me to marry his mother too, so was terrified by the thought that our marriage might be a lasting one. In 1960s Scotland this was not an absurd idea. At that time the law made divorces too expensive to be usual in working-class districts where the few divorced men were widely pitied because they must now cook their own meals and wash their own clothes. The divorced women were thought easy meat by men and public dangers by other women. I hated the idea of a divorce but knew I could not live till death parted us with a man who expected me to eat with his relations. I had no mother, having been orphaned in my teens. My only relatives were two aunts who prided themselves on their intelligence and avoided me because I was cleverer than their own children. I was therefore shocked to find Colin expected us to visit his mother almost every night of the week and his married sister every weekend. He said the meals they made were more normal than mine. Here is an example of that normal.

Chicken Soup, made by boiling a chicken in water with salt but nothing else. The resulting liquid, ladled into deep plates, had a layer of chicken fat on top. I made a hole in this with my spoon and tried to drink the soup through it, but the layer of fat still kept the fluid underneath scalding. It had to be sipped slowly: so slowly that when the bird's carcass arrived as a main course it was nearly cold. As were the sprouts and tatties served with it. As were the tart and congealed custard that followed. The meal was also delayed by my mother-in-law or her daughter washing, drying and putting away the last course's cutlery before serving the next. They did that swiftly, but to enjoy some remaining warmth in the second and third courses we had to eat them at a gallop. Despite causes of delay I once shared a family Christmas dinner, with crackers and funny paper hats, where three courses and every sign of us having eaten them vanished in half an hour.

Perhaps that was the kind of food and way of eating Colin enjoyed at sea. I could not provide such normality and refused to eat with his family more than once a week. I tried persuading him to dine with me in Italian, Indian and Chinese restaurants, but he found them too exotic. I suppose our marriage lasted for years because he was usually at sea. When at home – I mean the home we shared – he usually watched television while sipping lager in our sitting room. We only quarrelled once. Friends had visited me on a local political matter. The television was playing at a low volume so I exchanged a few quiet words with them in a corner of the room. After they left Colin declared that, before inviting others in, I should have picked up and hidden the empty beer cans he had strewn over the carpet. I pointed out that I was a wage-earner like himself, not a house serf like his mother.

Soon after this he moved back in with her, having left the navy and found work in our town as a security guard.

She was certainly tidier than me. Divorce in Scotland was now as cheap and frequent as in other places, so we *681* divorced. I raised another bank loan and paid him for his *MY EX HUSBAND* share of the house. I heard later that he bought a flashy car, a Reliant Scimitar with the money, but never told his mother where he got it, so she came to think I had cheated him. That is my only grudge against him.

Thank goodness we had no children.

NO BLUEBEARD

BEFORE TALKING ABOUT TILDA I'll mention earlier wives. Wife 1 was an ordinary tidy home-lover. We met at secondary school and after leaving it she let us make love then refused to allow any more of that unless we married. So we married. Wife 2 was a bossy manager, wife 3 very quiet and messy. I married all of them because it made us feel more secure for a while and separated from them without fuss or fighting, so I am obviously no Bluebeard. Indeed, most of my life has passed in sexual loneliness which makes me hopeful when a new affair looks like starting, as happened a year ago.

In the park near my home I saw a couple stand quarrelling under a tree. No one else was in sight but they were yards away from me and I expected to pass without being noticed. Instead the woman rushed over to me saying, "Please help me, sir, that man is frightening me."
"Good riddance!" shouted the man and hurried away leaving us facing each other.

She was in her late teens or early twenties, big and beautiful in a plain undecorated way, with short brown hair and a determined expression that showed she was no victim. Victims don't attract me. Her clothes were of very good quality and conventional in a smart country-wear style, yet seemed slightly odd, either because they did not perfectly match or were more suited to an older woman. The silence between us grew embarrassing. I asked if she would like a coffee. She seized my hand saying, "Lead the

way," and I found us walking toward a hotel outside the park gates, gates through which the man who had shouted at us was rapidly vanishing without a backward glance. We walked side by side so easily that I thought she was leading me, though later I found she knew nothing of the neighbourhood. I asked her name. She said, "Mattie or Tilda, take your pick."
"Surname?"
"*That,*" she said emphatically, "is what they want me not to advertise. The less said about *that* the better you cunt."
Her loud clear voice had the posh accent that strikes most Scottish ears as English. I decided she was an eccentric aristocrat and suddenly, because I am a conventional soul, had no wish to take her to a hotel lounge or anywhere public. I suggested going to my place. She said, "Lead on," so I did.

We had not far to go and as we swung along she murmured, "Cunt cunt. Cunt cunt," very quietly to herself as if hoping no one heard. That excited me. My flat is a large bed-sitting room, workroom, bathroom and kitchen. She stood in the largest room and announced, "This is certainly more salubrious than that other man's place."
As I helped to remove her coat she whispered, "You cunt," which I took as an invitation to help her out of more garments. She muttered, "Right, carry on."
I led her to the bed. What followed was so simple and satisfying that afterwards I lay completely relaxed for the first time in years, almost unable to believe my good luck.
"And now," she said, lying flat on her back and talking loudly as if to the ceiling, "I want apple tart with lots and lots of cream on top. *Ice* cream."
"Your wish is my command," I said jumping up and dressing.

The nearest provision store was a street away. I

returned in less than fifteen minutes and found her in the middle of the floor, clutching her hair and dressed as if her clothes had been thrust on in panic. She screamed, "*Where have you been?*"

"Buying what you ordered," I said, displaying tart and ice cream. She slumped grumpily into a chair while I prepared them in the kitchen. Later, while eating, I asked what had made her hysterical. She said, "You left me alone in this strange house and I thought you would come back hours later stinking of whisky and wanting us to do it again."

I did want us to do it again but was not greedy enough to insist. I told her I was a freelance programmer who worked at home and I detested booze because my dad had been alcoholic. She looked pleased then said slowly and slyly, "Regarding the dad situation, ditto. Ditto but if disorder is confined to the family apartments others do not notice. And if you too detest alcohol and work at home like all sensible people it is possible, cunt, that you may be possible."

I laughed at that and said, "Possibly you are too. Where are you from?"

"I have already said they do not want me to say."

I explained that I was not interested in her disgustingly snobbish family but assumed she had not been long in Glasgow. She said cautiously, "Until the day before yesterday, or maybe the day before that, I occupied a quite nice caravan in a field of them. People came and went. Mostly went."

"There must have been a town or village near your caravan park."

"There was a village and the sea but neither was convenient. I ate in a hotel called The Red Fox. I met the man who brought me here in The Red Fox. He turned out to be most unpleasant, not my sort at all."

"Have you things in his house? Things you want to collect?"

"What things?"

"A nightgown? Clothes?"
"No. Certainly not. Not at all. Please don't be a ..." She hesitated then said quickly, "Cunt give me a glass of milk."
It is almost impossible to judge the intelligence of someone from an alien culture so I have never discovered exactly how stupid or mad Tilda is. She behaved as if she expected to live with me. I wanted that too so it was hardly a sign of *her* insanity. Lunatics are supposed to have delusions. Tilda had none. She said what she meant or expected in a few clear words that always made sense. Only secrecy about her family and her compulsion to say cunt were inexplicable at first, and from remarks she passed in the following two weeks I soon pieced together an explanation.

Her "people" (she never said father or mother) ran a residential hotel or nursing home for "people of our own sort". They seemed a pernickety sort because "everything has to be just so."
I asked what just so meant. She said, "Exactly right forever and ever world without end amen. Dinner was awful. We had to dress."
"In tuxedos and black ties?"
"Tuxedo is an American word. We British say evening dress. Female evening wear is less uniform than male attire but more taxing. Little hankies are an endless ordeal. I fidgeted with mine which is *not the done thing,* in fact *utterly wrong,* in fact *a rotten way to carry on* and I became quite impossible when I started (cunt) using (cunt) that word (cunt cunt)."
Tilda's use of that word had obviously been an unconscious but sensible device to escape from bullying relations. They had lodged her in a caravan park very far from them ("half a day's car ride away") and made her promise not to mention their name because "if word gets around it will be bad for the business and we aren't exactly rolling in money."

This made me think their business was a sanatorium for rich mental defectives whose guardians might have doubts about the establishment if they knew people on the staff had an eccentric daughter. I suspected too that Tilda's people were less posh than they wished. The few very posh people I have met care nothing for elaborate etiquette and swear like labourers. But Tilda's family had given her worse eccentricities than that Anglo-Saxon word.

Next day I arose later than usual, made breakfast, gave Tilda hers on a tray in bed and got down to business. At ten she came into the workroom wearing my dressing gown and sat on the floor with her back to the wall, placidly watching figures and images I manipulated on the screen. Shortly after eleven she announced that she wanted a coffee. I said, "Good idea. Make me one too." She cried indignantly, "I can't do that! I don't know how!"

"I'll tell you how," I said, treating the matter as a joke, "In the kitchen you will see an electric kettle on a board by the sink. Fill it with tap water and switch on the heat. There is also a jar of instant coffee powder on the board, a drawer of cutlery below, mugs hanging on hooks above. Take two mugs, put a small spoonful of powder in each, add boiling water and stir. Add milk and sugar to yours if you like, but I take my coffee black."

She stamped out of the room and shortly returned with a mug she slammed down defiantly on my worktop. It contained lukewarm water with brown grains floating on top. When I complained she said, "I *told* you I can't make coffee."

I found that Tilda could wash and dress herself, eat and drink politely, talk clearly and truthfully and also (though I didn't know how she learned it) fuck with astonishing ease. Everything else had been done for her so she stubbornly refused to learn anything else.

Despite which our first weeks together were very happy. She added little to my housework. Former wives had insisted on making meals or being taken out for them. Tilda ate what I served without a word of complaint, nor did she litter the rooms with cosmetic tubes, powders, lotions, toilet tissues, fashion magazines and bags of shopping. She hated shopping and refused to handle money. I gathered that "her people" had never given her any, paying the caravan rent and Red Fox food bills by bank order. She brought to my house only the clothes she wore, clothes passed to her by someone of similar size, I think an older sister. By threatening to chuck her out unless she accompanied me and by ordering a taxi I got her into the women's department of Marks and Spencer. Buying her clothes was not the slightly erotic adventure I had hoped as she cared nothing for what she wore and would have let me dress her like an outrageous prostitute had the garments been comfortable. But there is no fun in buying sexy clothes for folk who don't feel sexy, so I bought simple, conventional garments of the kind her sister had given, but more modern and in better-matching colours. I did not then notice that her attitude to clothes and making love were the same. She never restricted the pleasures I had with her in bed once or twice a night, so only later did I see she was indifferent to them.

Being together outside bed was also easy because we had no social life and did not want one. Since expulsion from her people's "rather grand place" her only society seemed to have been fellow diners in The Red Fox, and she would not have eloped with "that other man" if she had liked them much. My own social life once depended on friends met through my wives and a job in local housing, but during the last marriage I had become a freelance working at home, which perhaps drove away wife number 3. Since then I had managed without friends, parties *et cetera*. I like films and jazz I enjoyed in my teens. I play them on my computer and discuss them over the internet with fellow enthusiasts in England, Denmark and America so need no other society. An afternoon stroll in the park kept me fit. Tilda managed without even that. Apart from the Marks and Spencer's visit she has only left the flat once since entering it.

Our daily routine was this. After an early morning cuddle I rose, made breakfast, gave Tilda hers in bed, laid out her clothes for the day, put dirty clothes in the washing machine, started work. Tilda arose around ten, I made coffee for us at eleven thirty and a snack lunch at one. Then came my afternoon stroll and shopping expedition which she bitterly resented. I insisted on being away for at least ninety minutes but had to mark the exact minute of return on the clock face, and if I was a single minute late she got into a furious sulk. Then came a cup of tea and biscuit, then two or three hours of more programming, then I made the evening meal, we consumed it, I did some housework, internetted for a little and so to bed. And wherever I was working Tilda sat on the floor, looking perfectly relaxed, sometimes frowning and pouting but often with a strange little satisfied smile. I assumed she was remembering the people and place she had escaped from. I once asked what she was thinking about and she murmured absent-mindedly, "Least said soonest mended. Curiosity killed the cat."

I asked if she would like a television set? A Walkman radio? Magazines? She said, "A properly furnished mind cunt is its own feast cunt and does not need such expensive and foolish extravagancies."

But she did not often use the cunt word now and when she saw an arresting image on my screen sometimes asked about it. I always answered fully and without technical jargon. Sometimes she heard me out and said "Right", sometimes cut me short with a crisp "Enough said", so I never knew how much she understood. When someone speaks with the accent and idiom of British cabinet ministers and bank managers and company directors it is hard not to suspect them of intelligence. I sometimes think even now that Tilda might be trained to use a computer. Many undeveloped minds take to it easily, having nothing to unlearn.

But during our mid-day snack one day the entry-phone rang very loud and long. Tilda stared at me in alarm.

"A parcel delivery," I said to reassure her, but without believing it. Part of me had been expecting such a ring. A crisp voice on the phone said, "I am here to see Matilda and if you try to stop me I will summon the police."

I opened the door to a tiny old woman who looked nothing like Tilda except for the determined look on her terribly lined face.

"You are?" I asked, thinking she was a grandmother or aunt. She walked past me into the lobby saying, "Where?"

I pointed to the sitting-room doorway and followed her through.

Tilda sat at the end of a sofa where I had left her but her arms were now folded tightly round her body and she had turned to face the wall.

"Well!" said the little woman. Standing in the middle of the floor she drew a deep breath and thus addressed the back of Tilda's head.

"You will be *pleased* to hear, *delighted* to know, *ecstatic* to be informed that it has cost us a very pretty penny in private detectives to track you here. A small fortune. More than a family not exactly rolling in wealth can afford, you *ungrateful, inconsiderate, selfish, shameless, debauched* what? What shall I call you? Slut is too mild a word but I refuse to soil my lips with anything more accurate. And you, sir!" – she turned to me – "You cannot alas be sued for abducting a minor but we have lawyers who will make you wish you had never been born if you try to get as much as a farthing out of us. Not a chance. No dice. *Nothing doing sonny boy*."

I told her I had no intention of getting money out of Tilda or her family. She said, "Fine words butter no parsnips. Are you going to marry her?"

I said we had not yet discussed that. She told the back of Tilda's head, "Make him marry you. It's your one chance of security." She then strolled round my flat as if she was the only one in it, fingering curtains and furnishings and examining ornaments while I stared in amazement. Returning from an inspection of workroom, kitchen and lavatory she spoke as firmly but less fiercely.

"Matilda, I admit this is not the Glasgow hell-hole the detective agency led me to expect. Maybe you have landed lucky. This second cavalier of yours certainly seems more presentable than what I have heard about the first who picked you up. So marry this one. *We* don't want you. Having made that crystal clear I will take my leave. I have a car waiting. Goodbye."

"Come back!" I cried as she turned to go, for I was angry and wished to annoy her, "Come back! Your address please."

"What can *you* possibly want with *my* address?"

I told her I was willing to believe Tilda had been brought up so meanly that she had no personal belongings in what was once her home, but marriage had been mentioned. That would need copies of a birth certificate and notification of her parents' occupations and place of residence. The little old lady said, "Oh, very haughty. Very cunning."

She took a printed card from a purse, laid it on a sideboard and, scribbling on it with a slim small pencil, said through clenched teeth, "I am substituting – my name – for your father's, Matilda, because he died a fortnight ago of a stroke in his bath. Not a messy business thank goodness. This news *of course* holds no interest for you. All the affection was on *his* side, though it was not a very exalted form of affection and you might have done more to discourage him. I can leave now, I think."

She had been perhaps ten minutes in the flat but it now felt as if she had burned huge dirty holes with a flame-thrower in floor, walls and ceiling. I wanted to go outside and walk in the fresh air, but could not persuade Tilda to move or turn her face from the wall. I tried soothing words but she stayed silent. I laid my hand gently on her shoulder but she shook it off and sat where she was until long after nightfall. When she came to bed at last she would not let me cuddle her but lay as far from me as possible. Next day she did not get up and hardly touched the food I brought. I could not bear to leave her alone in the house that afternoon. At night when I came to bed I discovered she had peed in it. That made me furious enough to drag her out and wash her. While making a clean bed on the floor I told her I would send for a doctor if she did not pull herself together. She said nothing. I asked if she wanted me to send for a doctor. She said, "If you do I will scream."

I told her that if she screamed when a doctor came he would quickly whisk her into a mental hospital. At this she turned her face to the wall again.

"Tilda," I said, pleading, "I realise your father's death had been a terrible shock, but you mustn't just lie down and fall apart. Is there nothing I can do to help?"

She muttered, "You *know* what you can do."

"Honestly, Tilda, I don't know! How can I know?"

"Because she told you."

"Who told me?"

"My mother told you. Twice."

That our wicked little visitor was Tilda's mother had never occurred to me. I thought furiously back over her words then said, "If you mean, Tilda, that you want us to marry, of course I'll do it if that will restore us to being as friendly and loving as we were before *she* stormed in."

"Don't bank on it!" said Tilda bitterly between clenched teeth, sounding so like her mother that I felt the short hairs on my neck bristle. I tried to be reasonable and explained there was no point in marrying if it did us no good. She neither answered nor turned her head but I saw tears pouring from her eyes, saw she was shuddering with soundless sobs. What horrible training had taught her to weep noiselessly? The sight maddened me. The madness took the form of promising to marry her as soon as possible. At last I got her into the clean new improvised bed and we fell asleep cuddling again. Something had been regained and something lost. Tilda's mother had brought me to the same start as my previous marriages.

Several days had to elapse before the marriage. During them Tilda refused me the lovemaking I had once taken for granted, but we cuddled at night and steady cuddling has always nourished me more than the irregular pleasures of fucking. I was also fool enough to think that, despite the past, we had a honeymoon ahead and suggested visiting Spain, Greece or Barbados.

"Why?" asked Tilda.

I pointed to colourful pictures in a spread of travel brochures and said, "Bright sunshine. Blue skies. Warm sea. Soft sand."

"Foolish extravagance and a waste of good money. We aren't exactly rolling in it."

"The money is mine, Tilda, and I promise I have enough to easily pay for a trip."

"Nobody who knows anything about money *ever* has enough," she said contemptuously. I was glad she no longer seemed pathetic. Nowadays on rising she sat around the sitting room instead of joining me in the workroom. It was a healthy sign of growing independence, though I missed her silent company.

I wrote to tell Tilda's mother of the wedding, suggested one of her family should witness it, received in reply a card saying, "My brother-in-law will attend." We met him at the registry office: a big laconic man with an expression suggesting all that happened was his own very private little joke. I suspected him of being a highly self-controlled drunkard though he smelled of nothing worse than the tweeds he wore. The witness I had invited was Henderson, a freelance programmer whose character was like mine – we shared business when one of us had too much of it. After the signing I took the four of us for a meal at The Ubiquitous Chip despite Tilda muttering, "Do we have to do this?" She refused to drink anything but soda water and lime or eat anything but ice cream. For us men her uncle ordered preprandial brandies, wine with the food, and after the dessert an astonishingly expensive champagne with which he gave a toast prefaced by the words, "Be upstanding." He and I and Henderson stood holding fluted glasses with what resembled mist arising from them while Tilda sat glowering into her third dish of ice cream. Her uncle said, "Here's to the blushing bride. Here's also, more importantly I think, to a very honourable groom. You!" – he suddenly stared straight at me without the faintest trace of a smile – "You are a better man than I am, Gunga Din." He emptied his glass, said he must rush for a train and left. I am unable to regard him as a parasitic clown because later I found he had paid for the drink, which cost much more than the food.

Tilda and I went home, both entering the flat with sighs of obvious relief. Tenderly I helped her off with her outer garments and was about to undo inner ones when she said, "Don't be silly."

I shrugged and we sat facing each other across the hearth rug. Then she said slowly and firmly, "I *think*. It is *time*. I had a bed *of my own*."

I gaped at her for at least a minute before asking why. She said, "Why not? My mother and father sleep, no, *slept* you cunt in different beds, in fact different bedrooms. The best people do."

That thrust me into a confusion of thoughts and feelings from which the most definite to surface was the most mean and trivial: I regretted having thrown out the old

mattress and getting another, because if she insisted on sleeping alone she could have done it on the bedding she had wet. And she did insist on sleeping alone. I argued with her of course, at one point was on the verge of threatening violence when tears started from her eyes and I knew unbearable silent sobbing would begin if I persisted. I made a bed for myself on the sofa then decided to go for a walk and brood over this new, alarming development, but she screamed, "You can't leave me alone here *now*!"
And I couldn't. I saw that without me Tilda would melt down into nothing but helpless, terrible misery. I was trapped and could only break out of the trap by acting like a beast. I could not call a doctor and tell him that the woman I had married that afternoon was now certifiably insane.

I made myself a bed on the sofa. Without Tilda's body to snuggle against I was unable to sleep but found the situation oddly familiar. She was now rejecting me like three previous wives who began by liking me then found they could not. I had blamed neither them nor myself for that – a calm, uncomprehending acceptance had seemed the sanest attitude. It now felt like madness to try seeing why everyone I loved had rejected me, but I had nothing else to do. The simplest explanation was the old Freudian one that, like most men, I married women who resembled my mother, thus condemning myself to enact the same stupid drama with each. But my mother had been nervous and clinging, a type I avoid. Apart from strong wills and their wish to marry me wives 1, 2 and 3 had been as different from each other as they were from wife 4.

Number 1 had this in common with my mother: she expected and wanted to be a housewife. Before the 1960s most wives outside the poorly paid classes expected to be supported at home, because they were fully employed there. Before washing machines, good housewives scrubbed and wrung clothes for body and bed by hand – ironed and mended them – knitted socks and other woollen items – cut, sewed, embroidered garments, curtains, cushions and chair covers. Before vacuum cleaners they drove dust out of carpets by hanging them outdoors and whacking them with canes. Shopping was more frequent before refrigerators and freezers because foods had to be eaten near the time of purchase. Good wives baked scones, biscuits, cakes, tarts, puddings, made jams, jellies, pickles and an exquisite sweet called *tablet*, for which everyone had a slightly different recipe. They regularly cleaned and polished linoleum, glass, metal and wooden surfaces. Their homes were continually restored works of art, exhibited once a week at a small afternoon tea party for friends and neighbours who were similar wives.

Number 1 had looked forward to that life, though we acquired every sensible labour-saving appliance available in 1972 having saved up for them through a three-year engagement when we lived with our parents. She gave up her teaching job just before the wedding after making sure all our well-wishers would give us useful presents. We had a short honeymoon in Rothesay then moved to a rented flat in Knightswood, the earliest and, in the year 2002, still poshest of Glasgow's housing schemes. We were very happy at first. The washing machine, Hoover *et cetera* left her free to whitewash ceilings, re-paper walls and carry out many improvements I thought unnecessary, as previous tenants had left the flat in excellent condition. My job in a local housing department office let me walk home for lunch. On Friday nights we went to a film or theatre, at weekends had polite little dinner or bridge parties with other couples, and on most evenings found entertainment in television and a game of cribbage before the small snack we called supper. And so to bed.

I was pulling on a condom after undressing one evening when she suggested we should have a child. It had not occurred to me that her domestic activity was a form of nest-building. Perhaps because I was my parents' only child I dislike children, so suggested we wait a bit before starting to multiply ourselves: we should first get a bigger house, a bungalow in King's Park or Bearsden, which would be possible when I was promoted to head office and able to pay a large deposit for a mortgage. She said grimly, "If it's a matter of *payment* I'll go back to teaching and earn us more money that way. But you'll have to take your share of housework. I can't bring in a wage *and* do everything else."

I said I did not want her to go back to teaching; we were still young and had no need for impatience. She did not reply but refused to make love that night and (though my memory may be at fault – this was nearly thirty years ago) I think we never made love again. She returned to teaching, I started doing the shopping and would have made meals too, but she refused them. When I suggested that I could make meals as good as those my mother made she said, "That's why I'd find them inedible."

A month or two later I remarked that only a third of her weekly wage was being deposited in our joint bank account. She said, "That's because I do at least two thirds of our housework. You may think you do half but you don't."

I shrugged and said, "So be it."

She began going out once or twice a week with teacher friends. My promotion to head office came sooner than I expected. I began lunching in a snack bar with a colleague who also enjoyed cribbage and had a folding board we played upon. His system of marking was different from mine and more interesting. I explained it to my wife one evening while dealing the cards. She flung hers down saying, "If you're going to change the rules of this bloody awful game I'm done with it."

I realised that for months she had been pleasing me

by playing a game she detested and suddenly I felt for her a terrible loving pity. Had she told the truth at the start I could easily have done without cribbage because we had enjoyed so many other things together – meals and films and small polite parties and lovemaking. But maybe she had only pretended to enjoy these things too because she loved, not me, but a conventional marriage.

One evening she explained she was having a steady love affair with a colleague and wanted to divorce me. I took several minutes to absorb the shock of this.
"If," I said carefully, "you really need a child let us make one. Let us make it now. We don't need someone else to give you one of *those*."
She smiled mournfully and said, "Too late, you poor old soul."
I was only twenty-four but shrugged and said again, "So be it." In those days divorce by mutual consent was impossible under Scots law; one of the parties had to get it by proving the other's misconduct. She gave me proof of her misconduct, I passed it to a lawyer and paid for half the costs of the action. I moved to a boarding-house leaving her the flat with all its furnishings so she had no reason for a grudge against me.

Years later at an office party I danced with a very lively little stranger. She had huge eyes, a mass of thick black hair, a slightly transatlantic accent and told me she was Polish-Canadian. Contact with her was so exciting that I asked her back to my place. She rolled the pupils of her eyes upwards and murmured, "No, no, impossible tonight, Charlie is very jealous. But we will keep in touch." We did. I learned that both Charlie and her husband worked for the housing department. One morning the husband stopped me as we passed in a corridor and said, "You know my wife, I think. Has she told you I am divorcing her for promiscuity?"
She had told me but I denied it. He said, "Yes. For

promiscuity. Don't worry, you will not be cited in court, you are only her latest. Steer clear of her if you value your sanity."

I thanked him for the advice but was enjoying my casual affair too much to take it. That she had Charlie as well as me made it all the more casual.

One Sunday afternoon she arrived unexpectedly at my lodgings in a state of happy excitement. Early that morning she had discussed Charlie with a close woman friend who had burst into tears and confessed that she too was having an affair with Charlie.

"Guess what I did then?" cried number 2. "I calmed her and cheered her up then rushed round to Charlie's place and said, 'Sit down, I've news for you.' He went as white as a sheet. I told him I knew he'd been having it off with Sharon but I didn't mind at all because I've been having it off with you. So now we can all carry on with our new partners and everything will be fine! Isn't that wonderful? Now you can come and live with me!"

Though foreseeing she would almost certainly marry me I pretended to agree that this was wonderful.

Her home was beside the Botanic Gardens. She had her office there and was the first in Glasgow – perhaps in Scotland – to run a dating and escort business by computer and telephone. It was a profitable business. She ran it efficiently yet insisted on also doing everything good Scottish housewives did, refusing all assistance because she was sure only she could do such things properly. Luckily she wanted no more children, having two girls and a son in their teens who often visited her but preferred their father's house because, she said, "They think I'm too much of a bossy-boots."

She was certainly bossy. She both gave and was asked to many parties, and before setting out would glare at something I wore and say, "I refuse to be seen with you wearing that!"

"What's wrong with it?"
"It's years out of date. Ten or twenty years out of date."
"Male clothing doesn't date like women's does."
"That shows you know nothing about it." Yet she was generous and I had no objection to the new clothes she bought me: they always fitted well and were smart without being eccentric. But I was appalled when I came home one evening and found she had given all my former clothes to Oxfam, so appalled that I packed the few things I needed with the firm intention of leaving that house forever, though invitations had been posted for our wedding reception a fortnight hence. She had a master key and used it to lock me in. I managed to open a window and would have jumped out but her anger suddenly turned to a terrible storm of weeping and pleading. I had never before seen anyone in that state. I could not possibly leave her in it, so stayed and comforted her until we were friends again and got married after all.

Through number 2 I met people whose lives seemed jumpier and more erratic than I was used to: journalists, broadcasters, women who managed their own shops. All had children by former husbands or wives and lived with partners they seemed to leave or change without conspicuous fuss. Despite her ex-husband's warning I am sure number 2 was not promiscuous while we lived together. She enjoyed declaring her feelings too openly to hide them for long and in five or six years confessed only twice to having brief affairs with other men. These confessions were made partly to annoy me so I annoyed her back by saying I did not care what she did when I could not see it, which was true. Yet despite our main faithfulness to each other, and the lovely tricks and eccentricities by which she turned ordinary meals and events into pleasant occasions, every month came a huge explosion of grief and rage which made a hell of that marriage. They were provoked by trivialities that

I could never foresee and can now hardly remember. I think her love of drama was the main cause. While stooping to lift a fallen pencil at work I struck the corner of a desk with my brow and raised a small lump. When I got home she screamed, "What's happened to your face? You look horrible!"

I could not take that seriously and a week later referred to it as proof of how easily she was upset. She laughed and said, "I wasn't upset at all! I just felt wicked and wanted to annoy you."

But the longer we lived together the more explosive our quarrels became until I was pointing out, again and again, that the misery we gave each other was far greater than the comfort. But whenever I packed up to leave, again and again came appalling grief of the sort that had got me marrying her after seeing it was a bad idea.

She was fond of children, the younger the better, and was visiting someone with a new baby one evening when I decided to eat out alone. In the restaurant I met friends of number 2 with a woman I had never seen before. They invited me to join them, jocularly remarking that this was the first time they had ever seen me without a wife. I enjoyed that meal, drank more than my usual glass of wine and found the friends were leaving me with the stranger. "Don't worry, we won't clype," they said, pretending to creep away on tiptoe. So I spent that night in the stranger's home.

I call my wives by number instead of name to shield them from readers who may meet them, and I also disguise them with a few inaccuracies. With this in mind let me say that number 3 was a senior hospital nurse of a sort that used to be called matrons. She was as tall as me but so slimly built that she looked taller, with a delicate oval head and a thatch of blonde hair cut very short. More attractive than her beauty was her quietness. When not sleeping or sulking number 2 talked almost

incessantly, often with questions that needed highly detailed answers. Number 3 used few words, never gossiped and seldom asked questions. Being unused to long silences I found hers disconcerting at first and tried to fill them with entertaining chatter but she murmured, "You don't *need* to talk to me."
Before I left next morning we had come to one of the unexpected understandings that have changed my life.
"I want to live with you," I told her. "I am going straight home to tell my wife that. Have you room for me?"
"That depends on how much you bring with you," she said with a Mona Lisa smile.

She lived south of the river, not far from Queen's Park. Returning by bus I had plenty of time to plan what to tell number 2 and to imagine the hideous emotional explosion it would cause. My courage completely failed. I saw I hadn't the guts to be so cruel and ended by inventing a lie to explain my overnight absence. I found 2 moodily working at her computer. She did not look up or turn round when I explained to her truthfully how, the previous night, I had met the friends who said they would not clype on me, adding only that I had gone home with them for a nightcap and fallen asleep. But she knew the addition was untrue because very early that morning she had phoned them while phoning everybody else she knew in search of me. She asked if I had spent the night with a woman.
"Yes, but nobody you know," I said. The result was less violent than I had feared. She switched off the machine, bowed her face into her hands and in a muffled voice said she could do no more work that day, though it was Saturday, usually her busiest day. She behaved, and I acted, as if she was suffering from something like the death of a parent, something that left her too numb for outrage. I took her for a walk through the Botanic Gardens and up Kelvindale to the canal towpath. It was a mild, very pleasant spring day. We exchanged a few

words about unimportant things, dined in a pub near Anniesland Cross and were returning home before she said, "Do you want to leave me for this woman I don't know?"

"Yes," I said.

"If you had said no," she told me mournfully, "and begged and wept and pleaded like I sometimes do we could have gone on living together. But now I can't help seeing that you really don't want me, so it's goodbye."

She then wept a little, but very quietly, and that was the end of that because divorce by mutual consent was now as easy in Scotland as in England.

Number 3's home (where I still live) was the basement and former kitchen quarters of a large Victorian terrace house divided into flats. The front windows looked into a sunken area and a back door opened on to a long narrow garden, a garden number 3 looked after beautifully for she preferred gardening to housework. I never knew a woman who seemed to care less for her home.

It was sparsely furnished with few of the ornaments and knick-knacks most women accumulate. She had lived there fifteen years, long enough to pay off her mortgage on it, but wallpaper and linoleum had obviously been inherited from earlier tenants, while a cumbersome gas cooker and huge earthenware sink with brass taps seemed as old as the building. I wanted to pay for having the kitchen completely modernised but she said firmly, "No, I'll pay for that. I promised myself a new kitchen ages ago and I know someone who will do the job cheaply."

I refrained from saying that all jobs done cheaply are done badly. Instead I offered to put in double-glazed windows and have the whole place re-painted, re-papered and carpeted. She agreed to this and let me choose colours and patterns because she wasn't interested in these things. I was intensely interested because I had decided, with her permission, to make this flat the headquarters of a new business. I was tired of working for the housing department.

When I joined it in the early seventies Glasgow was still a partly socialist city state owning its own lighting, transport, water and schooling. It was the largest landlord of public housing outside London and proud of the fact, because John Wheatley, a Glasgow politician, had passed the act that made local government housing possible. By the 1980s central government pressure to privatise public property seemed irresistible, and Glasgow's ruling Labour party put up no resistance at all. Soon after it became legal for council tenants to buy their houses the council appointed a housing chief who publicly announced that Glasgow city council was the biggest owner of slum property in Britain. We in his department looked forward with great interest to his remedy. After a few months he resigned the post and started an agency helping private housing companies to buy local government property. Having had access to municipal housing records he knew, of course, the properties people with money would most want to buy. This would once have been thought a disreputable if not exactly criminal act, but now people in authority accepted such doings with a smile or a shrug, so I decided to do something similar. The department had retrained me in computer technology, so I knew it was now possible to run a professional consultancy without many filing cabinets and a secretary. Number 2 had also shown me that an office could be run from home. Number 3 had no objection to me setting up my desk and machine in what was then our living room.
"Since you own this house and pay the rates and go out to work each day," I told her, "I'll be the housewife and see to the laundry and cleaning *et cetera*."
At first she did not mind that arrangement and I was heartily pleased with it because her level of domestic

cleanliness was inferior to mine. All she had in common with my first wives was a determination to make the meals we shared.

Despite meeting number 3 through friends of 2, 3's closest friends were very different, being female hospital workers who called themselves The Coven, meeting at least once a week in a public lounge bar and once a fortnight for a party at one of their homes. Most had a husband or male partner who abandoned his home when The Coven convened there. Number 3, weather permitting, held barbecues in her garden, at which times I stayed tactfully indoors. Sometimes one of The Coven strolled in and we chatted. I gathered they preferred me to her previous lover, a doctor who had treated her "rather badly". They also seemed to think me a handy man to have around a house: which made what happened later more surprising.

Housework became the main source of tension between us. It was I who bought the foodstuffs, washed and dried dishes and put them away with the cutlery and cooking utensils so I naturally began arranging the kitchen cupboards and shelves as neatly as possible, throwing out old jars of spices and condiments on the verge of decay, replacing cracked insanitary crockery with clean, modern things. Instead of being pleased she accused me of trying to erase her. She said the same when I ironed her clothes, folded and put them neatly away.

"NOBODY irons clothes nowadays," she yelled, "NOBODY! Chuck them in the airing cupboard like I've always done."

She probably regarded home as a refuge from her highly regulated hospital life. I worked hard and unsuccessfully to stop my cleanliness and order offending her. I could do no kitchen work when she was home because what she called my "virtuous clattering" enraged her.

One day she returned from work frowning thoughtfully and when I asked why said shortly, "Nothing," and when I asked again the following night said, "Just a pain, it doesn't matter."

Strange that a trained nurse belonged to that large class of people who dread referring their illness to a doctor! Luckily she worked in a hospital. A phone call one day told me she had collapsed and was being operated upon for appendicitis with acute peritonitis. I saw her that evening when she had recovered consciousness and acquired an astonishingly young, fresh, new-born look. I sat silently holding her hand, feeling closer to her than I had felt since our first night together. A month passed before she was fit for home and I visited her at least once a day, would have done so twice every day but her bedside during visiting hours was often crowded with hospital friends so she told me to come in the evenings only.

"What present," I asked myself, "can I give her when she returns home? Of course! A new kitchen."

The renovation carried out by her cheap, quick friend had annoyed me by its awkward shelving, badly hung doors and an old cupboard space walled off with plywood. I imagined many kinds of rot, fungus and insect life burgeoning in there. "Nobody who has been ill," I told myself, "should return to a home with such a probable source of infection in it."

So I had the kitchen completely renovated, expensively and well, with the most modern and easily cleaned equipment, all electric instead of gas. I did not tell her this in hospital, perhaps fooling myself with the notion that she would enjoy the sight of it more when she got home, but of course she at once saw the new kitchen for what it was: a present to me, not her.

"Yes," she said, with a cold little smile, "you've erased me totally now."

I blustered a lot of explanations and apologies then

ended by saying that, alas, what had been done could not be undone. She disagreed, saying she could undo it by shifting to a house she could feel at home in – the house of a friend. *This house* was now only legally hers, so she would sell it and if I was the buyer she would subtract the cost of my new kitchen from a surveyor's estimate. I begged her to come to bed with me and talk the matter over next day. She made a phone call, packed some clothing and moved that night to the home of the friend. (I later learned he was the doctor who had been her previous lover.) Her last words to me, or the last words I remember were, "This hasn't been my home since you brought in that bloody machine so you're welcome to it. At a price."

She meant the purchase price of course, with the addition of her complete absence. Did this leave me desolate? Yes. Yes, with a mean little core of satisfaction that for the first time since leaving my parents I would possess a house that was wholly mine. But lying now in the dark with Tilda gently snoring less than two yards from me I started weeping tears I had never shed when number 3 left the house, and when number 2 told me to go to my new woman, and when number 1 said she was divorcing me for another man. I lay weeping for my whole past and could not stop for I suddenly saw what I had never before suspected: that I had lost three splendid women because I had been constantly mean and ungenerous, cold and calculating. Even my lovemaking, I suspected, had not been much more generous than my many acts of solitary masturbation between the marriages. I wept harder than ever. I crawled off the sofa, switched on a lamp and knelt on the floor beside the bed. Tilda stopped snoring, opened her eyes and stared at me.

"Please, Tilda," I said between sobs, "please just let me hold your hand for a while."

Her alarmed look gave way to puzzlement. She withdrew a hand from under the bedclothes and offered it almost shyly. I took it between mine, being careful not to press very hard, then her eyes opened wider as if she was only now clearly seeing me and she muttered, "Don't go away. Always be there."

Then I saw that she needed me, would need nobody *but* me while our lives lasted. With great thankfulness and great contentment, holding her hand, I fell asleep on the floor beside our bed.

BIG POCKETS WITH BUTTONED FLAPS

A MILD SEPTEMBER MORNING. A man no longer young strolls thoughtfully on a narrow footpath along a former railway line. Noises tell of a nearby motorway but brambles, elders and hawthorns on each side hide all but the straight empty path ahead until he sees a small clearing among bushes on his right. Two girls sit here at the foot of an old telegraph pole. He pauses, gazing at the top of the cracked grey timber pole. It has cross-pieces with insulators like small white jam pots from which broken wires dangle. He is aware that the girls are in their teens, look surly and depressed, wear clumsy thick-soled boots and baggy military trousers from which rise pleasantly slim bodies. One says crossly, "What are you staring at?"

"At the wires of that sad sad pole!" says the man without lowering his eyes. "A few years ago they carried messages from this land of ours to a world-wide commercial empire."

"A few years? It was yonks ago," says the girl scornfully. Without looking straight at her the man glimpses a stud piercing her lower lip and one through the wing of a nostril. He says, "Yonks. Yes. I suppose telegraphs were defunct before you were born."

He continues looking up at it until the other girl stands, stretches her arms, pretends to yawn, says, "I'll better away," and walks off through the bushes. Her companion still sits as she did before the stroller arrived.

A minute later he takes a folded newspaper from his coat pocket, unfolds and lays it on the grass where the departed girl was, then sits down with hands folded on the knee of a bent leg. Looking sideways at the girl (who still pretends to ignore him) he says quietly, "I must ask you a difficult question about … about the eff word. Does it shock or annoy you? I don't mean when used as a swear word, I detest swearing, I mean when used as a word for the thing … the act lovers do together. Eh?"

709
BIG POCKETS
WITH
BUTTONED
FLAPS

After allowing her a moment to reply he speaks briskly as if they had reached an agreement.

"Now I fully realise that a lovely young woman like you –" (she sneers) "– don't sneer, has no wish to eff with a boring old fart like me in bushes beside a derelict railway line. But I suppose you are unemployed and need money?"

"Fucking right I do!" she cries.

"Don't swear. This is an unfair world but I am no hypocrite, I am glad I have money you need. We should therefore discuss how much I am willing to pay for what you are prepared to do. I promise that a wee chat will probably give all the stimulus I need. I have never been greatly enamoured by the down-to-earth, flat-out business of effing."

"Ten pounds!" says the girl, suddenly facing him at last.

He nods and says, "Not unreasonable."

"Ten pounds now! Nothing without cash up front," she says, holding out a hand. From a wallet within his coat he gives her bank notes.

"Thanks," she says, pocketing them and standing up, "Cheerio."

He looks up at her wistfully. She says, "You're too weird for me as well as too old and you're right. This is an unfair world."

She goes off through the bushes. He sighs and sits there, brooding.

Then hears a rustling of leaves. The other girl has returned and stands watching him. He ignores her until she says, "I didnae really go away. I was listening all the time behind that bush."

"Mm."

"I don't think you're weird. Not dangerous-weird. You're just funny."

"Name?" he asks drearily.

"Davida."

"I thought the Scottish custom of making daughters' names out of fathers' names had died out."

"It came back. What's your name?"

"I'm giving nothing else away today Davida. Don't expect it."

But he is looking at her. She grins cheerily back until he shrugs and pats the grass beside him. She hunkers down slightly further away, hugging her legs with both arms and asking brightly, "What were you going to say to Sharon?"

"You too want cash from me."

"Aye, some, but not as much as Sharon. Forget about money. Say what you like, I won't mind."

He stares at her, opens his mouth, swallows, shuts his eyes very tight and mutters,

"Bigpocketswithbuttonedflaps."

"Eh?"

"Big," he explains deliberately. "Pockets. With. Buttoned. Flaps. At last I have said it."

"They turn you on?" says Davida, looking at her pockets in a puzzled way.

"Yes," he says defiantly, "because violence is sexy! These pockets are military pockets with room for ammunition clips and grenades and iron rations. On women they look excitingly ... deliciously ... unsuitable."

"Yes, I suppose that's why they're in fashion but they're nothing to get excited about."

"I enjoy being excited about them," he groans, covering his face with his hands.

"Were you a school teacher?"

"You'll get nothing more out of me, Davida ... Why do you think I was a teacher?"

"Because you're bossy as well as polite. Yes, and teachers have to pretend to be better than normal folk so they're

bound to go a bit daft when they retire. What did you want with Sharon's pockets that was worth ten quid?" 711
He looks obstinately away from her.
"Did you want to stick your hands in them like THIS?" she giggles, putting her hands in her pockets. "Did you want to fumble about in them like THIS?"

BIG POCKETS WITH BUTTONED FLAPS

"No more dirty talk!" orders a very tall thin youth emerging from the bushes, "How dare you molest this young lady with your obscene and suggestive insinuations?"
"ME molest HER? Ha!" cries the man and lies back flat on the grass with hands clasped behind head. He thinks it wise to look as relaxed and unchallenging as possible for he is now greatly outnumbered. Beside the tall youth is a smaller, stouter youth who looks far more menacing because his face is expressionless, his head completely bald, and beside him stands Sharon saying scornfully, "Big pockets with buttoned flaps!"
"You should have left us alone a bit longer," grumbles Davida. "He was starting to enjoy himself."
"He was starting to enjoy his antisocial fetishistic propensities with a lassie young enough to be his granddaughter!" cries the tall youth fiercely.
"Molesting two lassies in fifteen minutes!" says Sharon. "We've witnesses to prove it. He's got to pay us for that."
The man says, "I've paid you already."
"That ... is not an attitude ... I would advocate if you want to stay in one piece." says the tall boy slowly taking from a big pocket in his trousers a knife with a long blade. The smaller, more dangerous-looking youth says, "Hullo, Mr McCorquodale."

The man sits up to see him better and asks, "How's the family, Shon?"
"Dad isnae out yet," says the shorter boy, "but Sheila's doing well in TV rentals. She went to Australia."
"Yes Sheila was the smartest of you. I advised her to emigrate."

"I KNEW he was a teacher," says Davida smugly.
"You stupid fucking cretin!" the tall boy yells at the shorter one, "If you'd kept out the way we could have rolled him for all he's got, buggered off and nothing would have happened! We don't live round here, we've no police record, nobody could have found us! But now he knows you we'll have to evade identification by cutting off his head and hands and burying them miles away!"
He saws the air wildly with the knife. The girls' faces express disgust. The smaller youth says mildly, "Don't do that to old Corky, he wasnae one of the worst."
"Not one of the worst?" cries the ex-teacher jumping to his feet with surprising agility, "Did I not make my gym a living hell for you and your brothers? I also advise YOU," he tells the taller youth, "to put that knife away. You obviously don't know how to handle it."
"And you do?" says the tall boy sarcastically.
"Yes, son, I do. I served five years in the army before I took to teaching. Your combat training is all from television and video games. I have learned armed AND unarmed combat from professional killers paid by the British government. Davida. Sharon. Shon. Persuade your friend to pocket that bread knife. Tell him he's a fine big fellow but I'm stronger than I look and if he's really interested in dirty fighting I can show him some tricks that'll have the eyes popping out of his head. Tell him I gave Sharon nearly all the money I carry so if he needs more he'll have to come home with me."

And McCorquodale smiles rather
wistfully at the tall youth's
combat trousers.

AIBLINS

LONG AGO a college of further education paid me to help folk write poems, stories and other things that bring nobody a steady wage. I had applied for the job because I was in debt and needed a steady wage. The college also provided an office, desk, two chairs and flow of hopeful writers who met me one at a time. I must have talked to nearly a hundred of them while the job lasted but can now only remember:

(1) A shy housewife writing a novel about being the mistress of a South American dictator.
(2) An engineering lecturer writing a TV comedy about lecturers in a college of further education.
(3) Two teenage girls, unknown to each other, who wrote passionate verses against the evils of abortion.
(4) A dauntingly erudite medical student writing a dissertation proving, by Marxist dialectic, that Rimsky Korsakov's *Golden Cockerel* was a better forecast of mankind's political future than Wagner's *Ring*.
(5) The twelve-year-old daughter of Chinese restaurateurs who, led in by an older sister or perhaps mother or aunt, gravely handed me a sheaf of papers with a narrow column of small neat writing down the middle of each, writing that tersely described such horribly possible events that I feared they were cries for help, though of course I treated them as fiction.
(6) And Ian Gentle.

Ian was a thin student whose manner suggested he found life a desperate but comical game he was bound to lose. He gave me a page of prose telling how raindrops slide down leaves and stems, then join between grass blades in trickles that gradually fill hollows in the ground making them pools, pools steadily enlarging until they too join and turn fields into lakes. Without emotional adverbs and adjectives, without surprising metaphors, similes or dramatic punctuation, Gentle's ordinary words made a natural event seem rare and lovely. My new job had not yet taught me caution. I looked across the desk, waved the page of prose at him and said, "If I had written this I would strongly suspect myself of genius."

He smiled slyly and asked, "Can I sell it?"

"No. Too short. If you made it part of a story with the rest equally good *Chapman* might print it but Scottish magazines pay very little. Even in England the best literary magazines pay less for a story than a shop assistant's weekly wage. But this is a beautiful description, perfect in itself. Write more of them."

He shrugged hopelessly and said, "I can't. You see I was inspired when I wrote that."

"What inspired you?"

"Something I heard by accident. I switched on the radio one night and heard this bloke, Peter Redgrove, spouting his poetry, very weird stuff. I'm not usually fond of poetry but this was different. There was a lot of water in what he recited and I'm fond of grey days with the rain falling steadily like I often saw it on my granny's farm when I was a wee boy. I suddenly wanted to write like Peter Redgrove, not describing water behaving weirdly but water doing the sort of things I used to notice and like."

"If a short burst of good poetry has this effect on you then expose yourself to more. There are several books of Redgrove's poetry. Read all of them, then read MacCaig, Yeats, Frost, Carlos Williams, Auden, Hardy, Owens —"

"Why bother?"

"You might enjoy them."

"But what would it lead to?"

"If they inspired you to write more prose of this quality ... and if you persisted with your writing, and got some of it into magazines ... eventually, at the age of forty, you could end up sitting behind a desk like me talking to somebody like you."

He giggled, apologised and asked if nobody in Scotland earned a living by writing. I told him that a few writers of historical romance, crime fiction, science fiction and love stories earned the equivalent of a teacher's income by writing a new novel every year or two.

"Thanks," said Gentle standing up to leave, "I don't think I'll bother. But if it's genius you want read Luke Aiblins's stuff. It's as weird as Redgrove's."

"Is he a student here?"

"In a way, yes, but then again, in another way, not really."

"Tell him to show me his work."

"I will, but he's hard to pin down."

In the college refectory a week or so later a sociology lecturer walked over to me looking so grimly defiant that I feared I had offended her. She placed a slim folder with a bright tartan cover on the table beside my plate and said, "Read these poems. I typed them but they're written by Luke Aiblins, a truly remarkable student of mine."

"I hear he's a genius."

"He is, but needs guidance. Can I make an appointment for him?"

We made an appointment. She said, "I think I can ensure that he keeps it though it won't be easy. He's very hard to pin down."

She left. I glanced through the poems and saw they were beautifully spaced and typed. The first was titled PROEM. I read it with interest, re-read it with astonishment and a third time with pleasure. I then knew it by heart.

Bone caged, blood clagged,
nerve netted here I sit,
bee in stone honeycomb
or beast in pit or flea in bin,
pinned down, penned in,

unable to die or fly or be
any one thing but me,
a hypochondriac heart
chilled by the spittle of toads that croak
on the moon's cryptic hemisphere.

But yet, loft-haunter, tunnel-groper,
interloper among men,
I am the Titan & my pen
wet with blue ink or black
alone can tell them what they thought
and think and give them back
the theme, scheme, dream whose head
they broke, & left for dead.

Crown, King, Divinity: all shall be mine
to take, twine, make into a masterpiece
of fine thread, strong line.
Yes, let me write my life
ten volumes in one book
of good and bad friends, women who will
and will not walk with me,
the warped, harmonious, happy, sick & dead.
While I have eyes to look, so let it be. Amen.

All his other poems were equally resounding. I was now keen to meet him and quite unable to imagine him.

He kept the appointment and was a dazzlingly beautiful boy of eighteen or nineteen. His brown eyes and head of neatly curling brown hair harmonised perfectly with brown sweater and fawn slacks. Relaxation and eagerness don't usually blend but in him they did. He entered with the happy air of someone who has all the love he wants while looking forward to more; entered silently, sat down, folded his arms and leaned toward me with an enquiring tilt of the head and encouraging smile. Beauty in people makes me want to stare with my mouth open. In men it almost strikes me as indecent, yet I felt a pang of envy that I quelled by turning my chair a little so that I looked past, not at him. As I cleared my throat to make an opening remark Aiblins said, "Excuse the question: why don't you look straight at me?"

"I look straight at hardly anyone in case they think me rude. I suppose I'm afraid of most people but I'm not afraid of their writings. I like yours very much. You know that the rhymes of words inside a line matter as much as rhymes at the end. You know that the rhythms of lines in a verse can vary. You enjoy playing with the sounds of words and you make them entertaining for the reader."

"Right," said Aiblins, smiling and nodding.

"You have also learned from some very abstruse poets, Donne and Hopkins. Am I correct?"

"Eh?" said Aiblins.

"Have you read John Donne and Gerald Manley Hopkins?"

"No. Wait a minute. Yes. I once dipped into them but my work is original. I hear it inside this."

Aiblins tapped the side of his head with a finger.

"Never mind, Leavis says inspiration is often unconscious reminiscence. Now, creative writing teachers usually, and wisely, urge young writers to use the plainest, commonest words because many of the profoundest and loveliest and funniest ideas have been put into plain words. *To be or not to be, that is the question. I wish I were where Helen lies. So you despise me, Mr Gigadibs*."

"No," said Aiblins reassuringly.

"I was quoting Browning. Now these well-meaning instructors forget that the same great wordsmiths very often relax or ascend into sonorous complexities: *sharked up a list of lawless resolutes, and Eleälé to the asphaltic pool, each hung bell's Bow swung finds tongue to fling out broad its name*, (and here I flatter you) *a hypochondriac heart, chilled by the spittle of toads that croak on the moon's cryptic hemisphere*. That line of yours is absurdly pompous, grotesque, almost insane but!" (I started laughing) "It works! We are often depressed for reasons we don't understand but feel are caused by something huge, vague and distant, something ..." (I paused on the verge of saying *weird*, an Ian Gentle word) "... something uncanny that might as well be on the moon."

Aiblins, who had looked puzzled for a moment, smiled then said "Right."

"But I want to point out that these are the first poems of a very young writer, someone who is (please excuse the simile) like a bird flapping its wings to attract attention before launching into the air. You know that because it is your only theme. You should now—"

"Excuse me," said Aiblins quietly yet firmly. "Are these my poems?"

He lifted the folder from the desk, glanced inside then laid it back, shaking his head, smiling and saying, "Yes, my poems dressed in tartan. Women are incredible. What can you do with them? You were saying?"

"The theme of all your poems is the great poet you are going to be. It is a prologue to your life's work, a convincing prologue, but not enough."

"Why not?"

"Take the first poem, the best, and the first verse, also the best: *Bone caged, blood clagged, nerve netted* et cetera. You are describing a state of confinement and frustration everyone has sometimes felt, poets and housewives and schoolchildren and ditch diggers and college lecturers. Right?"

"Hm. Maybe," said Aiblins.

"Verse two. *Loft-haunter, tunnel-groper, interloper* et cetera. Here you state your feelings of being both above and below other people, being *an outsider* as we called ourselves in the sixties, so you're still talking for a lot of people, especially young ambitious ones. Right?"

"You're getting warm."

"Then comes *I am the Titan and my pen* et cetera. You now declare yourself a masterful figure like Prometheus, someone who will help humanity recover something fine that it has spoiled and lost: innocence perhaps, faith, hope, love – only God knows what. So you are not now speaking for most folk, you are describing what only very confident priests, politicians, prosperous idealists, teachers, artists and writers sometimes feel, while speaking mainly for Luke Aiblins." Aiblins smiled and nodded.

"Now look at verse three! *Crown, King, Divinity, all shall be mine*. What do these three words with initial capitals mean?"

"You tell me. You are the grand panjandrum, the salaried professor, the professional critic. I'm just a humble poet. You tell me my meaning."

"I think they mean that you feel sublimely smug because of your verbal talent."

"Do you think all my poems convey that?"

"I'm afraid so."

"Even the love poems?"

"Did you write any? Name one."

"OUTING."

Opening the folder I said "Let's hear it!" and read aloud the following.

This sunken track through the rank weeds
of docken, nettle & convolvulus
does not belong to us: only to me
whose nostrils gladly drank the stink
of vegetable sweat,
whose ears sucked in
the sullen whimper of the gnat's wing,
who gladly felt the wet sting of
smirr upon the cheek.

So do not talk, say no word to me
but walk in stillness on a path of moss,
a slope of trees upon our right hand side

and on our right the cluck & flow
of a wide stream.
I do not know what you see here.
I do not want to know.

For if each tries to see those things
the other sees
our probing eyes will shatter
the brittle matter of the other's dream
so each of us will be
inside a toneless, tasteless, aimless world of
mediocrity.

Walk in my dream and I will walk in yours
but do not try to share our separate dreams.
Two dreams can touch, I think,
but there's an end
of dreaming if we try to make them blend
for this can only be when both of us lie bare
and I have felt the ripeness of your flesh.

When bodies mix
then even dreams can melt.

"A love poem?" I asked, smiling.
"Why not?"
"It doesn't give the faintest idea of the companion it addresses, not even her or his sex."
"Shakespeare's sonnets aren't exactly portraits either."
"True, but it's clear the people he addresses are fascinating, and that he loves them. You tell your companion to shut up so that you can enjoy some very dull scenery, though at the end you seem to anticipate …"
I hesitated.
"Getting into her knickers?" suggested Aiblins.
"That's one way of putting it."
"Low marks for the start and the later poems. What about the last?"

"I'm glad you reminded me!" I said, greatly relieved, "At first its bathos didn't impress me but now I think it is your best piece of verse – truly objective – not self-vaunting at all. You emerge here at last from the shell of your ego. Yes yes yes, here it is—"

A SPELL AGAINST ENVY

Rascals whose energy made history
had splendid banquets, buildings,
songs of praise
they never made. Digestion, rot and fires
undid their solid things. The finest hymns
cannot outlive the language of their choirs.

Only the joy of making things anew
outlive the owners & the makers too –
those fabricators, songsters, cooks who give
web, honeycomb, nest, burrow, beaver dam,
house, clothing, story, music & tasty stew.

"Though lacking the gaiety Yeats thinks essential this is a highly successful Marxist version of his poem *Lapis Lazuli*," I cried, laughing.
"Never read it."
"Never mind. Perhaps you strain the last two lines by squashing into them every kind of animal and human maker you can think of, but it's still a good piece of serio-comic light verse. But the other poems resemble the efforts of a runner jogging up and down at the starting line before the pistol is fired."
"Another simile! And what are you reading these days?" said Aiblins brightly.
"Henryson's *Fables*."
"You enjoy that stuff?" said Aiblins, incredulously.
"Yes. When I concentrate I find it astonishingly good. I'm concentrating just now because I'm reviewing a new edition of them for *Cencrastus*."

"Hallelujah! Keep concentrating. I'm sticking to Shakespeare. Have you read *The Two Gentlemen of Verona*?"
"No. I've never even seen it acted."
"You should. It's great. Some idiots think he wrote very little of it but—"

For fifteen or twenty minutes Aiblins talked about *The Two Gentlemen of Verona* until I had no desire to read or see that play, then he looked at what seemed a new expensive wristwatch, apologised for having to leave now, lifted the folder, went to the door and paused to say, "Mark Twain."
"Yes?"
"Have you read his *American Claimant*?"
"No."
"You should. And don't blame yourself too much for the things you've just said. A couple of them made sense. Think on! I'll contact you when I need you. Cheerio."

I was left feeling horribly confused. Was he a genius? Was I an idiot? His damned *Proem* kept repeating in my head when I would have preferred to remember McDiarmid's *The Watergaw* or Hardy's *After a Journey* or even Lear's *Dong With the Luminous Nose*. Did that mean it was better than these? Impossible. But why could I not forget it? He had said he would contact me. A few weeks after seeing him I approached his sociology lecturer. She was chatting with colleagues in the staff club.
"Pardon me," I said, "Can you tell me how Luke Aiblins—"
"I can tell you nothing about Luke Aiblins except that he is mad, stupid, nasty and has, thank God, left this place for good." She turned her back to me.

The college changed its creative writing teacher every two years, perhaps to avoid paying a pension contribution due to regular teachers. I found similar jobs elsewhere, then had a book of poems published, then another. With an American friend I visited Edinburgh Castle and saw that an attendant in one of the regimental museums was Ian Gentle. I asked if the job bored him. He shrugged and said, "Not more than teaching, or punching railway tickets, or nursing in a mental hospital, or canning peas, which I have also tried. It's like reincarnation. You don't need to die to become somebody else. Have you read Schopenhauer's *The World As Will and Idea*?"

I had not and asked if he ever saw Aiblins.

"Poor Luke," said Gentle, "I'd rather not say anything about poor Luke."

I left the castle with a weird feeling that Aiblins would soon appear again.

Yet was unprepared when the phone rang and a voice said, "Luke Aiblins contacting you as arranged. Remember?"

"I remember you but remember no arrangement. It's years since you said you'd contact me."

"I'm doing it. I have a job for you. You're at home?"

"Yes, but—"

"I'll be there in ten minutes."

He hung up on me and arrived in four.

He was no longer beautiful because his nose was thickened and flattened except at the tip, which bent sideways. He was also haggard, with long bedraggled hair, and wore a shabby duffel coat and carried a duffel bag, articles I had not seen since my own student days. His manner was still eager but more tense. I asked if he would like tea or coffee.

"No thanks," he said, settling into an armchair with the bag between his legs. "Let's get down to business. You are at last able to help me because you are the king."

"What do you mean?"

"Poet Laureate of Dundee!" he said, grinning.

"I was born there."

"Honorary Doctorate from St Andrews University!" he said, chuckling.

"I was a student there."
"Winner!" he said, almost inarticulate with laughter, "Winner of the Saltire Award and a colossal Arts Council bursary for *Antique Nebula! Antique Nebula!! Antique Nebula!!!*"
"Have you read it?"
"Enough of it to see that it's crap, rubbish, pretentious drivel, an astonishing victory of sound over sense. You won't mind me saying that because you're intelligent so must know it's crap. I bet you often have a quiet wee laugh to yourself about how you've fooled the critics. Ours is a comic opera wee country with several comic opera imitations of English establishments. They're even thinking of giving us our own comic opera parliament! Our old literary crazy gang, MacDiarmid, Goodsir, Garioch, Crichton Smith *et cetera* were also crap but they've died or are dying and leaving your clique on top. You are now the boss and godfather of Scotland's literary mafia and at last in a position to help a real poet."
From the duffel bag he removed and handed me a thin, grubby folder with a tartan cover. I looked into it then told him, "These are the poems your teacher typed twelve years ago."
"Of course. You said you liked them, so prove it. Get one of your posh London publisher pals to print them. Tell them you'll write an introduction. Of course you won't know what to say so I'll write the introduction. It will appear under your name so you'll get the credit of introducing a great seminal book that won't give you any bother at all."
"Mr Aiblins," I said, "since you invoke the past let me remind you that I praised these poems for heralding much better work. Where is it?"
"Have you learned *nothing* in the past twelve years?" he groaned, then with an air of immense patience said, "The voice in my head says there is no point in dictating more poems to me before the first lot are in print, so to get the later poetry we *both* want, you must first get *these* published. Send them to Faber or Bloodaxe with a strong

letter of recommendation by registered post tomorrow. Phone regularly at weekly intervals and pester them till they've read it and offered a decent advance against royalties and a definite publication date. And remember to photocopy them before posting because then you can send single poems—"

I said, "Listen—"

"No! Last time we met I did the listening, now it's my turn to lay down the law. In the weeks before publication prepare for it by getting single poems published in *Stand, Areté, The London Review of Books, The Times Literary Supplement, Chapman* and *Cencrastus* beside good reviews of the book itself by well-known poets rather than academics. I suggest for England, Ted Hughes and Craig Raine; for Ireland, Heaney and Paulin; for Scotland, Lochhead and Duffy; for former colonies, Les Murray, Walcott, Ben Okri and Atwood. We have only one problem. My wife won't let me into our house, the people I'm staying with are trying to push me out, so for a while I'll have no contact address. Fear not, I do not plan to camp on your doorstep. I'll call here once a week for your report on developments at an hour *you*, not me, will choose. Make it as late or early as you please. Well?"

I said, "Mr Aiblins I am not the godfather of a Scottish literary mafia. There is no such thing. No firm will publish a book, no editor commission a review of it or print a poem from it because I order them. It is also many years since I was employed to show an interest in other folks' writing. I am now a selfish old bastard who cares for nobody's writing but his own. Please go away and tell that to as many other writers as you can. But you appear to be in poor circumstances. I am not. By a coincidence I refuse to explain I have seventy pounds in notes upon me. Here, take them. Goodbye!"

"You condescending piss-pot!" he said, smiling as he took the money, "But buying my poems won't get rid of me. I know they'll be safe here because your only claim to fame, your only hope of a place in world literature depends on them. So why postpone that? Your *Antique Nebula* will be forgotten long before critics notice where you got the few good lines in it."

"Are you suggesting that I have plagiarised you?" I cried, horrified, "I deny it! I deny it!"

"You sound as if you believe that," he said, frowning thoughtfully. "Perhaps you're unconscious of it. Perhaps most plagiarism is unconscious reminiscence."

"I am staring hard at that brass-topped coffee table," I told him, "because it is tempting me to lift it as high as I can in order to smash it down on your idiotic skull. But instead I will phone for the police if you do not take your poems and get the hell out of here."

"Dearie me, dearie me," he said waggishly. "I seem to have annoyed the poor old fat bald wee man. He must still envy me. I wonder why?"

He strolled with bag and folder to the front door, which I opened. On the doorstep he turned and said quietly, "One last word of advice. Publish these poems under your own name then try to live up to them. You'll fail, but the effort may make a real man of you, if not a real writer. And think of the fame you'll enjoy! I won't resent that because great poetry is more important than fame. Here, have it."

I closed the door on him. A moment later the folder, bent double, fell in through the letter box. My self respect felt as if it had been squeezed between the heavy rollers of a mangle. His poems were so strongly associated with this feeling that I could not bear to pick them up. Opening a cupboard holding gas meters I kicked them inside and locked them in. I so dreaded hearing from him again that I fixed an answering machine to my telephone and never took a call direct, but he never called again.

Time passed away. So did the Berlin Wall and the Russian Empire. In *The Times Literary Supplement* I read reviews of abstruse books by the former Marxist student who liked classical opera and now had a medical practice in Stuttgart. I discovered that the little Chinese girl who once visited me was now an award-winning feminist poet who wrote popular, very gruesome crime thrillers under a pseudonym. I read her works closely for signs of my influence and detected none at all.

One day I heard a friendly, eager voice say, "Hullo, how are you doing? What are you reading these days?"
I stopped and after a moment recognised poor Aiblins. He was completely bald with many bruises on his head and face and many unhealed cuts between them. He wore jeans, a leather jacket and shambled in a way I had not seen before, but his battered features had amazingly recovered the happily relaxed expression I had first envied.
"What happened to your face, Luke?"
"Oh, I had an argument in a pub with a man who glassed me so it became a police matter. I mean the police took me in and gave me a doing before turning me out. But it was all just usual reality, it doesnae matter. Have you read *The American Claimant* yet?"
"Not yet. Can I buy you a drink?"
I said this because we were in a street very far from where we might be seen by people I know.

After two unsuccessful attempts we found a pub that would serve him and sat with pints in a quiet corner. I admitted I had not yet read *The Two Gentlemen of Verona* and steered the talk away from literature by asking if he ever saw his wife nowadays. "Neither her nor my son. In fact she kicked me out before he was born because she hated the name I was going to give him – a lovely name it was too, a perfect poem in itself: *Tristram Pilgrim Aiblins*." He announced the name with great enthusiasm then repeated it slowly as if separately enjoying each syllable, then he asked if I knew what it meant.
"*Tristram* means *sadly born*," I said, "I'm not surprised the mother didn't want her boy called that."

"You've forgotten what Aiblins means. That makes a difference."

"What does Aiblins mean?"

"Look it up, wordsmith," he said, laughing. "Consult a Lallans dictionary, you antique Scottish nebula."

"But how did you know a son was coming before he got born?"

He tapped his brow saying, "I heard it in here."

I asked if his inner voice ever gave him poetry nowadays. He said, "I think it's trying to. Sometimes a good line gets through but never a whole couplet or verse because the government is jamming me."

"The government? How?"

"It keeps sending other voices into my head, loud ones that accuse me of terrible things I've never done, never even imagined doing. Why? Why should the government spend money on elaborate broadcasting equipment just to torture me with false accusations only I can hear? It makes no sense. It's a total waste of taxpayers' money." He did not say this angrily or miserably but with a kind of puzzled amusement.

I said, "Some people in high places must think you very dangerous."

"Yes, but why?"

"Tell me a line your inner voice has given you recently."

He pressed a finger to the side of his brow and after a while said, "*Since breathing is my life, to stop I dare not dare.*"

"I like that line. Any more?"

"Er ... *Great vessels sink, while piss-pots stay afloat.*"

"Better and better. Do you still think I'm a piss-pot?"

He grinned apologetically and murmured, "If the cap fits ... Oh, here's another coming through: *To die, to me, today, is like returning home from a war.*"

"That's the best line of all. You're still a poet, Luke, in a fragmentary way."

"The government must want to keep me fragmentary. Has your inspiration ever been broken up by outside broadcasting?"

"No."
On his discoloured, distorted face appeared a smile of pure childish happiness mingled with sly mischief.
"Your work isn't good enough to frighten them," he murmured and gave my shoulder a consoling pat.
"True. I must leave now."

I gave him money that he tranquilly accepted. I hurried away in a state very near panic. By pretending to share his world view I had almost been convinced by it. I was glad to learn later that the *dare not dare* line came from the introduction to John Lennon's *In His Own Write*, that the sunk ship and floating piss-pots were from a translation of a Gaelic proverb in one of MacDiarmid's most rambling monologues. I haven't found the source of the third, which may be a genuine Aiblins invention. But I am afraid to re-examine the verses in the creased folder in my lobby cupboard, afraid to show them to people who might judge them differently. It might emerge that I have driven a great poet insane by suppressing his earliest works.

For the same reason I fear
to destroy them.

JOB'S SKIN GAME

FOR GOD'S SAKE don't believe what my wife says: I am still one of the luckiest men who ever walked the earth. Yes of course we've had our troubles, like hundreds and thousands of others recently, and for a while it seemed impossible to carry on. I'd have paid a man to shoot me if I'd known where to find one. But I survived. I recovered. The sun is shining, the birds are singing again, though I perfectly understand why the wife has not recovered and maybe never will.

It was my father who had the really hard life, years and years of it: a joiner's son, self-educated, who after many slips and slides turned a small house-renovation firm into a major building contractor. Before he expired he was a city councillor and playing golf with Reo Stakis. He sent me to the best fee-paying school in Glasgow because "it's there you'll make friends who'll be useful to you in later life", and yes, some were. Not being university material I went straight into the family business and learned it from the bottom up, working as a brickie's labourer for a couple of months on one job, a joiner's labourer on another, a plumber's mate elsewhere and so on till I had firsthand experience of all those jobs and painting, plastering, slating, wiring, the lot. Of course the tradesmen I served knew I was the boss's son. He told them so beforehand and warned them to be as tough on me as on other apprentices. Some were, some weren't. Either way I enjoyed gaining manual skills while using my muscles. I even worked as a navvy for six weeks, and (under supervision, of course) drove a bulldozer and managed a crane. Meanwhile, at night school, I learned the business from a manager's standpoint, while calling in at the firm's head office between whiles to see how it worked at the costing and contracting level. So when the dad collapsed of a stroke I continued the business as if nothing had happened. My mother had died long before so I inherited a fine house in Newton Mearns, a holiday home on Arran and another in the south of Spain.

Is it surprising that I was able to marry the first good-looking woman I fell in love with? She was more than just a pretty face. In business matters she resembled my father more than me. I was less brisk than he in sacking workers when we lacked orders to fully employ them.
"You can't afford to keep men idle," said the wife. I told her that I didn't – that I found them useful though not highly profitable jobs until fresh orders arrived. "Maybe you can afford to do that but your wife and children can't!" she said, using the plural form though still pregnant with our first child, "You're running a modern business, not a charity, and seem anxious to run it into the ground."
I quietened her by signing the family property and private finances over to her on condition that she left the firm to me. It prospered! We sent our boys to the same boarding school as the Prince of Wales.
Being smarter than their old dad they went from there to Glasgow University, then Oxford, then one took to law and the other to accountancy, though both eventually got good posts in a banking house with headquarters in Hong Kong and an office in New York. Alas.

By that time I had sold the main business, being past retiral age. I kept on the small house-renovation firm my dad started with, more as a hobby than anything else. I had always most enjoyed the constructive side of business. Meanwhile the wife, on the advice of her own accountant (not mine) invested our money in a highly respectable dot com pension scheme which she said "will make every penny we own work harder and earn more".
I didn't know what that meant but it sounded convincing

until the scheme went bust. Highly respected traders had gambled unsuccessfully with the scheme's assets while spending most of the profits on bonuses for themselves. Clever men, these traders.

But when the fuss died down and the Newton Mearns house and holiday homes were sold, my wee remaining firm kept us from destitution. We shifted to a three-room flat in the Cowcaddens and without asking help from the boys had everything a respectable couple needs. If some of my wife's friends stopped visiting her she was better without them, I say. And our two highly successful sons in their big New York office were a great consolation to her until, you know, the eleventh of September, you know, and those explosions that look like going on forever.

Years ago I enjoyed a television comedy called *It Ain't Half Hot, Mum* about a British army unit stationed in Burma or Malaya. There was a bearded sage who spouted proverbs representing the Wisdom of the East. One was, "When a man loses all his wealth after contracting leprosy and hearing that his wife has absconded with his best friend, that is no reason for the ceiling not falling on his head." Or as we say in the West, it never rains but it pours. My wife never abandoned me though I sometimes wished she had better company. My efforts to console us drove her wild.

"You must admit," I said, "that compared with most folk in other countries, and many in our own, our lives have been unusually fortunate and comfortable. We must take the rough with the smooth."

"All right for you!" she cried. "What about the boys?"

"After nearly thirty-five very enviable years their only misfortune has been a sudden, unexpected death, and their last few minutes were so astonishing that I doubt if they had time to feel pain."

"They didn't deserve to die!" she shouted.

"Would you be happier if they did?" I asked. "The only

evil we should regret is the evil we do. As far as I am aware our sons' firm was not profiting by warfare or industrial pollution. Be glad they died with clean hands." She stared and said, "Are you telling me to be glad they're dead?"
There is nothing more stupid than trying to talk folk out of natural, heartfelt misery. I had talked to her like some kind of Holy Willie, so I apologised.

After a bath one morning I was towelling myself dry in one of these low beams of sunlight that illuminate tiny specks floating in the air. It let me see something like smoke drifting up from the leg I was rubbing and a shower of tiny white flakes drifting down to the carpet. Like most folk nowadays I know most dust around a house comes from the topmost layer of human skin cells crumbling off while the lower cells replace it. Looking closer I saw the lower layer of skin was more obvious than usual. It reminded me of the sky at night with a few big red far-apart spots like planets, and clusters of smaller ones between them like constellations, and areas of cloudy pinkness which, peered at closely, were made by hundreds of tiny little spots like stars in the Milky Way. Then came itching and scratching. The first is widely supposed to cause the second but in my experience this is only partly true. The first itch was so tiny that a quick stab with a needle could have stopped it had I known the exact point to stab. But this was impossible, so I scratched the general area which itched even more the harder, the more widely and wildly I scratched. This crescendo of itching and scratching grew so fiercely ecstatic that I only stopped when my nails had torn bloody gashes in that leg and the delight changed to pain.

Since then I have often enjoyed that ecstasy, suffered that pain. The disease spread to other limbs, torso, neck and head. I could no longer supervise work in houses under renovation. Dust from cement, plasterboard and timber maddened my itches to a frenzy that only the hottest of baths subdued. Under the pain of scalding water the skin also felt many wee points of delight, as if each itch was being exactly, simultaneously scratched and satisfied. I left the bath with my skin a patchwork of pink and red sores that I patted dry, ointmented with Vaseline, covered with clean pyjamas, every itch now replaced by dull pain. So I went to bed and slept sound by quickly drinking half a litre of neat spirits. Perhaps modern pills would have knocked me out more cheaply but I felt safer with a drug folk have tested on themselves for centuries.

So the main side effects of the disease are:

(1) exile from the constructive part of my business,
(2) exile from my wife's bed,
(3) her endless work to clean up my stained sheets and underclothes,
(4) greatly increased dependence on alchohol,
(5) a search for cures.

After a thing called A Patch Test my doctor explained that the disease was due to an inherited defect in the immune system defending my skin. A mainly serene and prosperous life had not strained it but now, weakened by recent emotional shocks, I was allergic to forms of dust that nobody could avoid. The origin of the allergy, being genetic, was incurable, but medication should reduce the symptoms. He prescribed a steroid cream to combat eruptions, an emollient to reduce the flaking, anti-histamine pills to ease the itching and (to be used instead of soap) a bath oil that also counteracted infection.

These helped for a while. The rashes healed in places and itched far less until the steroid cream ran out. My doctor was unwilling to prescribe more because continuous use made the skin dangerously thin. He prescribed a less potent antibiotic cream and arranged a consultation with a skin specialist who, because of a long waiting list, would see me five months later. My wife wanted me to jump that queue by paying for a private consultation. I refused for two reasons.

(1) I am a socialist who thinks our national health service is the best thing the British Government ever created, and is undermined by folk buying into a private system which can only exist because its doctors are also partly subsidised by ordinary taxpayers, and:

(2) I like saving money.

But while waiting for the appointment I noticed near my home an alternative medicine clinic, though not the sort using astrology and occultism. The consultation fee was not huge so I tried it. An ordinary looking youth weighed me, examined my fingernails, tongue and inner eyelids, asked questions about my eating and drinking habits, then delivered a small lecture.

Everyone must live by consuming more solids and fluids than their body needs, so our digestions, kidneys and liver help to excrete what cannot nourish us. With age these weaken and work less efficiently, especially in middle-class people like me who eat and drink too much. The excess not expelled through my bowels and bladder is retained in fat or expelled through the skin, damaging it on the way. I should therefore stop drinking alcohol, coffee and tea, apart from one cup of the last each day. I should daily drink at least three pints of pure water, should stop eating meat and poultry, but consume as much fish as I liked if it was not fried. I should also cut out dairy produce – eggs, milk, butter, cheese – also sugar and salt, but eat more fruit and vegetables, preferably organically grown. Two months of this diet would heal my skin if I also took more exercise: a brisk half-hour daily walk would be sufficient. When cured I could experiment by trying some things I had eliminated – wine with my meals or ham-and-egg breakfasts. If the disease returned I would then know what to blame. He also prophesied that any orthodox skin specialist I saw would prescribe a stronger kind of steroid ointment than prescribed by my general practitioner.

I left that clinic certain I had been told the truth and determined not to inform my wife. She would have adopted that diet for me with enthusiasm, especially the no-alcohol part; I would then have started tippling in secret and been continually found out and denounced. But I told her when I visited a Chinese clinic that sold me brown paper bags containing mixtures of dry twigs, fronds and fungus with instructions to boil the contents of one bag in water – simmer for half an hour – strain off the liquid – drink a cupful three times a day for two days then repeat the process with the next bag. My wife refused to do that so I did it myself, but kept forgetting to set the cooker alarm so twice ruined pans by boiling the vegetation into adhesive cinders. I realised that orthodox British medicine was the most convenient, even when the skin specialist prescribed what the nature healer had foretold. Luckily by then I had turned my bad skin into a hobby.

Explanation at this point becomes embarrassing because it requires a four letter word I hate. *Chamber's Dictionary* gives it several meanings but the relevant one is this:
Scab *noun:* a **crust formed over a sore or wound.**
I take a gentle pleasure in carefully removing most such crusts and have my own names for the main varieties:
Cakes and Crumbs. Black or brown lumps that form on the deepest scratches. Dried blood is a main ingredient. I try not to touch these because, picked off too soon, they leave a hole in which fresh blood wells up before clotting.
Hats. A cake or crumb may grow a crisp white border, as much part of it as a brim is part of a hat. This brim

overlaps the surrounding skin in such a way that the tip of a fingernail, slid beneath, easily lifts off the whole hat uncovering a moist but shallow and unbleeding wound. A few hours later other kinds of crust form over that. They also form over larger sores where topskin has crumbled off, flaked off or been scratched off.

Bee-wing. Pale grey and gauzy. It has white lines like veins on wings of bees, wasps and house flies, but more random looking. Minute red or brown spots sometimes suggest wings of more exotic insects. Bee-wing is so transparent that if laid on a printed page words can be read through it.

Parchment. Pale yellowish-brown, not gauzy, yet as transparent as bee-wing. It seems made by the drying of moisture exuded from raw skin beneath. I remove it by pressing a fingertip into the skin on each side and pulling them apart. The living underskin stretches, the parchment splits, its edges curling up like the edges of water lily leaves, making peeling off easy.

Moss. This yellowish-grey furriness seems an intruder, like the mould on rotten fruit. It grows in circular holes and narrow grooves made by accidental scratches in swollen, inflamed skin, but is so far below the skin's level that fingernails cannot reach it without doing more damage. I use fine-pointed tweezers to grip an edge of such growths and, since their roots must be intertwined, easily lift out the whole mossy mat or strip.

Paper. A splendid example of this lost me control of my remaining firm.

The board meeting in our Waterloo Street office consisted of secretary, accountant, lawyer, works supervisor and two major shareholders who were partners from the days when my father's firm had built housing schemes. As chairman I let the others do most of the talking, usually sitting with closed eyes and even dozing a little until silence fell. Then I would sit up, summarise the situation in a few crisp words, indicate the only sensible choices, hold a vote on them, then ask the secretary to announce the next item on our agenda. One afternoon, halfway through a meeting, I sensed that my left arm was in a very interesting state. I excused myself, went to lavatory, sat on pan, rolled up shirtsleeve. A big expanse of skin inside the elbow joint had withered into dry white paperiness, paperiness so brittle that it had cracked into little four-sided lozenges like an area of neatly laid marquetry. And it was NOT ALIVE. My first impulse was to set fingernails of my right hand in line and use them to rake that dead paper off with two or three sweeping strokes. It would have left an area of raw underskin with bleeding gashes in it and many wee triangular paper scraps standing up and not easy to nip off. So with the tweezers I delicately prized off each paper tile and placed it between the pages of my pocket book, leaving a raw but undamaged area on which I spread an ointment prescribed by the specialist – Betnovate or Trimovate or Eumovate, I forget which. Then I rolled down sleeve, washed hands, returned to meeting. While performing that delicate operation I was perfectly happy.

"Well, gents, what have you been discussing?" I said, having been absent for ten or twenty minutes. Only the secretary looked straight at me. The rest seemed too embarrassed to look at anything but the table before them, then they looked furtively at the works supervisor. He was the youngest, the one I most liked and trusted because I had promoted him from being a site foreman. He cleared his throat then explained that, though he did not wholly agree with the rest of the board, there was a general feeling that I should leave the firm's steering wheel and become more of a back-seat driver; my great experience would always be valuable but blah blah blah blah *et cetera*. I grinned as I heard all this and when he fell silent was about to quell the mutiny – could easily have done it – but was suddenly overtaken by weariness

with the whole business. It occurred to me also that someone had sampled the clear liquid in the tumbler beside my notepad and found it was not water but Polish vodka. I sipped from it, shrugged and said, "Have it your own way gents."
All but the works supervisor at once cheered up, congratulated me on my wise decision, said I would gain rather than lose financially because blah blah blah blah blah. So the paperish arm left me with nothing to enjoy but my skin game.

The nature of other crusts (**Lace, Fishscale, Snakeskin, Shell, Biscuit, Straw** and **Pads**) I leave to the imagination of my readers, but some cannot be classified by a simple name. From the shallow valley above the caudal vertebrae I have removed three discs of the same size but different textures: beewing, parchment and paper, joined at a point where they overlapped by a little dark purple oval cake. I have also detached something like a tiny withered leaf, intricately mottled with black and grey, glossily smooth on the underside but with a knap like Lilliputian velvet on the upper. Anything often thought about enters our dreams and I sometimes dream of more extravagant growths. One is like a thin slab of soft, colourless cheese, slightly wrinkled: it peels off with no physical sensation at all. Another lies under it and another under that. At last I uncover what I know is the lowest layer which I fear to remove, knowing that underneath lies nothing but bone wrapped in a network of naked veins, arteries, tendons and nerves, yet intense curiosity is driving me to expose what I dread to see when I fortunately awaken.

I reduced the bouts of wild scratching to once a week and between them carefully removed the crusts I have listed and the others I have not. The pleasure of this harvesting is twofold: *sensual* because the raw skin beneath feels briefly relieved, perhaps because it can perspire and breathe more freely; *emotional* because I like separating the dead from the quick, removing what is not the living me from what is. After each session I apply ointment then sweep up the dust, flakes and crusts with a hand-held vacuum cleaner of the sort used on car upholstery. Yet I do so with a kind of regret, feeling these former growths of mine should be *used* for something. I considered gathering the biggest in a porcelain jar as Victorian ladies gathered flower petals, but the scent would not have been sweet. So instead of that —

I switch a plate of the electric cooker to maximum heat and with the tweezers lay on it a little pagoda-like tower of the largest crusts. They catch fire, each glowing red-hot before, with a faint sizzle, darkening and merging with the rest in a small black wart or bubble that heaves as if trying to rise off the plate, then collapses into a smear of white ash while releasing a wisp of smoke. This wisp, inhaled, has a tiny but definite odour of roasted meat. Surely this sight, sound and smell are as near as I can get to enjoying my cremation while alive? The ceremony is performed, of course, when my wife is away from home, but it once engrossed me so completely that I did not notice she had returned and was watching.

"What are you doing?"

Lacking the strength to stay silent and the energy to lie, I told her.

"But why?"

"Because I enjoy it."

She arranged for me to see a psychotherapist.

He is a grave person not much younger than me. The following short summary of five politely laborious conversations makes them seem like comedy cross-talk with him the straight man, me the joker. A first person narrative makes such distortions inevitable.

I began by saying I had only come to please my wife and doubted if he could help me, as the skin game was

a harmless way of getting fun out of an incurable illness.
"But was the disease not caused by huge financial loss and the deaths of your sons? And have you not since become something of an alcoholic?"
I admitted that my illness had a psychological element. We then conversed as if it was the only element, because of course I was paying him to do that. He asked about my sex life. I said that like most faithful married men of my age and class and nation I had outgrown it.
"But has your wife? And do you not see that these obsessive scratchings and pickings are a regression to pre-adolescent infantilism?"
I agreed that I had reverted to infantilism but said I preferred the older name of second childhood, a condition to be expected in a man over sixty. My childish skin game perhaps blended narcissism, pre-masturbatory sado-masochism and a form of transferred coprophilia (I enjoyed coming back at him with big words) but it harmed nobody. I was sorry that my wife could not sleep with a man in my state but would not complain if she began visiting massage parlours or took up with a healthier lover, though in a woman of her age, class and nation this was improbable.
"Does it not occur to you that this narcissistic sado-masochism (as you agree to call it), this fast or slow flaying of your own epidermis – is a kind of self-punishment? What do you punish yourself for? Where lies your subconscious guilt?" I could not tell him so he told me.

At first he suggested I was subconsciously glad my sons had died, so felt subconsciously guilty of murdering them. I admitted that since their boarding-school days I had never felt at ease with the boys because (though they tried to hide it) they seemed to find my voice and manners too plebeian, but I was glad – not angry – that they felt happier with their mother than with me. Their deaths were surely depressing enough without making me a subconscious murderer.

Then he tackled me from the Marxist angle. I had once been nearly a millionaire and surely nobody innocently grows as rich as that? He was right, in a way. In the building trade a lot of contracts are won by private deals that bypass the advertised requests for tenders. Not many such deals involve the transfer of banknotes in plain envelopes. What outsiders call corruption is more a matter of people above a certain income level exchanging useful social favours, and certainly my father got business that way. I avoided these deals, which was not easy at first. A noted Lord Provost felt personally insulted when I ignored his hints that my bids for contracts would be accepted if submitted in particular terms on particular mornings. That was why I did not become a millionaire. I may have inherited some ill-gotten gains but had never resented paying income tax, and when that was reduced by Thatcher's government I more than made up for what I owed the human race in standing orders of money steadily paid to Oxfam, Amnesty International, Greenpeace and Scottish Wildlife. Despite a reduced income I still pay several of these orders. It is conscience money so I am at peace with my conscience.

The therapist could not believe that, so asked about my religion. I told him my mother had been a Catholic expelled from her local chapel when she married a Protestant, though my dad was not a church-going Protestant. His religion was money-making. To do so he congregated eagerly with Freemasons and Jesuits, Orangemen and Knights of Saint Columba. In Newton Mearns my wife attended a local Episcopalian Church, unlike me, though I had been friendly with her minister or vicar or whatever he was called: a decent man and one of the few Newton Mearns lot who still visited us. Like many non-religious folk I had a loose faith in a kind of God who was benign rather than punitive. I assumed God had the difficult job of managing the universe in ways that could not satisfy everybody. After all, He had made millions of microbes and insects that could only thrive by killing millions of bigger animals and we had given Him no good reason to prefer people to other forms of life. I was being deliberately provocative when I said that. Small signs had led me to think this soul-doctor, despite his Freudian jargon, was a Believer, though probably in a Jewish, Catholic or Protestant God rather than a Hindu or Mahomedan one.

"I have read," (I added) "that even in our cleanest buildings the carpets and the upholstery contain whole nations of wee beasts fed by the protein from old, discarded skin. I must have more than doubled the population of such beasties in my house. Their delight in the nourishment my eczema showers on them may compensate God for the pain it gives my wife."

With an effort my soul-healer kept his temper and said that many neurotic self-justifers made gods in their own image, but mine was the nastiest he had encountered. I disagreed, saying mine was a harmless image – nobody would kill or strike another in defence of it.

"But arguing about God," I told him, "is as futile as arguing with God. Let us agree that his mercy and justice are beyond any understanding. Goodbye and good luck."

That was a week ago and I'm not going back to him, though I feel our little chats did me good.

This morning I dreamed of wakening and lying naked on top of the bed, unable to move even a finger because my whole skin had stiffened into a hard rigid sheath. With a mighty effort I at last heaved myself up, feeling a delicious pang as the sheath cracked all over. Looking down I saw myself clad in a mosaic of parchment patches that began to move apart as their edges curled upward making them easy to pluck off. And what lay beneath was *not* raw cuticle but clean healthy skin. I awoke and found this was not so, but now believe that one day my skin will heal as unexpectedly as it diseased. Meanwhile my wee house-renovation firm, even without my controlling hand, is doing very well.

It will soon be quite a big firm again,
thank God.

MISS KINCAID'S AUTUMN

WHEN LOCAL NICKNAMES were common I grew up in a place we called The Long Town, a name not printed on maps or railway timetables. It had council houses where coal miners lived, a high street of properties rented by our shopkeepers and tradesmen, and several mansions and bungalows owned by so few professional folk that everyone in the town knew them. Conversations about local affairs usually mentioned Big Tam Kincaid the Free Kirk Minister, also his son Big Sam, schoolteacher and Labour councillor. I knew both by sight, the first as a gaunt striding figure in the streets, the second as a stout one crossing the school playground. I was never Big Sam's pupil but often heard his voice booming from an adjacent classroom. Joe Kincaid, a second son, was of usual height but in the merchant navy so hardly ever seen. Almost as invisible were Poor Mrs Kincaid and a daughter, Wee Chrissie, who were only mentioned in women's conversations. When I asked why Mrs Kincaid was Poor my mother said, "Her men need a lot of her attention."

I left The Long Town for university when television aerials had sprouted on most rooftops and the cinema had become a bingo hall. A job and a marriage kept me away from it but I often returned to visit my parents so saw the town change like the rest of Scotland. The railway and colliery closed. Cars and unemployment increased. Council houses took on a slummier look. At the edge of the town arose an estate of private houses, each with a garden and garage facing a circular drive. To discourage outsiders, it had only one way in, no through road and no shops, but it brought little extra business to the high street. The owners were commuters who mostly shopped in Glasgow or Edinburgh, where they worked. The wee shops of my childhood (baker, grocer, draper, sweet shop, newsagent, cobbler, clock mender) became mini-markets or shut forever.

I also heard that Poor Mrs Kincaid died, leaving Wee Chrissie as housekeeper. Big Sam became a headmaster, married one of his staff and brought her to live in the Free Kirk manse where his father was now a bedridden invalid. Soon after the wedding Sam's wife left him and a stroke paralysed his legs, events so close together that gossip differed on which came first. Though confined to a wheelchair Big Sam fought bravely to keep his jobs as headmaster and local councillor. Having many sympathisers he succeeded for a while, but misfortunes had destroyed the joviality that had made his bullying ways bearable. Former colleagues joined with enemies and forced him to resign from both jobs. These colleagues had been his only friends; he now regarded them as traitors. Then his father died, leaving Sam alone with Wee Chrissie in the former manse. I asked if she had no friends. "I never hear of Miss Kincaid having visitors," said my mother in a way that showed the nickname was not now appropriate, "though nobody dislikes her."

I got divorced and between jobs lived with my parents for a whole summer. Single women visiting Long Town pubs were looked at with grave suspicion. I dislike bingo so joined an evening class on modern Scots literature held in the public library. The lecturer was an enthusiast who tried hard to hide a conviction that the best things about his subject had been his meetings with the authors who wrote it. When he failed to do so I sensed that a straight-faced woman beside me was trembling. I glanced at her sideways. She gave me a smile that showed she was holding in tremendous laughter. I smiled back.

We left the library together, fell into conversation and I was surprised to learn she was Chrissie Kincaid, whom I had always imagined a poor wee timorous beastie. This woman was as tall as most of us who don't wear high heeled shoes. She was quiet and self-contained but keenly observant, with highly independent and broadminded views. Our parental homes lay in the same direction so I invited her back for tea. She sighed and said, "Alas, no. I regret my early training but it has made it impossible for me – a Kincaid! – to accept hospitality I cannot return."

"Then return it. I'll take tea in your house any day."

"No you won't."

"Why not?"

"I can't tell you because Kincaids never explain family matters to outsiders. Nor can we meet in a pub because female Kincaids don't drink alcohol in public. Nor can we meet in a tearoom or café because The Long Town hasn't one nowadays. But I hope you and I have another talk after the next evening class."

Curiosity drove me to see her sooner. I had offered to lend a book. Two days later I took it to the former manse, a solid grey stately Victorian building with a tall monkey puzzle tree on the lawn. A brass bell handle, pulled, made a distant dolorous clanging somewhere inside. Two minutes later Miss Kincaid opened the door and looked at me with raised eyebrows. I gave her the book and was saying something about it when a great voice from behind her said, "No whispering! No secrets from me, Chrissie! Bring your friend in."

It was a voice I remembered from childhood, booming but distinct and able to penetrate walls without yelling. Miss Kincaid shrugged her shoulders and ushered me in.

We crossed a dark lobby with a staircase and entered a very warm room of dark furniture with a bright coal fire. Beside it in a wheelchair sat Big Sam, now hideously fat, his legs covered by a tartan rug. A table at his elbow had books and papers on it, a jug of water, a glass and a decanter of pale golden liquid. He said, "Your name is? Valerio? Formerly Ferguson? Then your father had the excellent dry goods shop on the high street. I taught your uncles and your elder brother. Chrissie, offer our Mrs Valerio biscuits, cake and – tea? Coffee? Sherry? Why not sherry? I, you see, am a whiskyholic" – (he waved toward the decanter) – "but I never drink enough to become a total victim of my sister's ministrations. No. I am careful to keep my mind intact, my intellect in control."

I said I would like tea and Miss Kincaid left the room.

"Good!" he said on a more intimate note, "I am a crippled giant but not the ogre my sister has probably suggested to you. My sufferings derive from a strong intelligence diverted by those who hate me into the cul-de-sac of memory – a form of torture I assure you, Mrs Valerio. What a relief to meet someone with whom I can intelligently converse!"

He talked to me for a very long time. Miss Kincaid must have brought biscuits and tea but his flow of talk wiped out any sense of consuming them. He told me the social history of The Long Town in the lifetime of his father and himself, illustrating it with personal anecdotes, many of them interesting, but it is exhausting to be treated as an audience for over an hour by a single intense speaker. The more often I looked at the clock the more often he asked if he was boring me. I lacked the courage to answer truly but he was watching me far too closely to miss other signs of restlessness. They inspired him to talk faster and faster. Miss Kincaid must have learned not to hear Sam when not wanting to. She sat nearby calmly reading with a slight smile on her face that first struck me as mischievous then downright malicious until, after ninety minutes, she snapped the book shut, stood up and said, "Mrs Valerio has to visit some other people, Sam."

I stood up too.

"Goodbye, Mrs Valerio," he said, offering his hand. "I am at the mercy of a sister who is given to engineering these abrupt departures. My little holiday is ended but please visit the crippled giant again. Come again soon. Don't be a stranger."
I said I would come again. With something like a sneer he reached for the whisky muttering what sounded like, "I doubt it." Miss Kincaid escorted me to the front door murmuring, "Serves you right," but our later walks back from the evening class were as friendly as the first.

Years later I returned to The Long Town for my father's funeral, then for my mother's. Both had Church of Scotland services. The second was better attended because the Free Kirk congregation had by then joined ours, having become too small to maintain a separate minister of its own. I knew hardly any of the old people present so on leaving the church was pleased to see Miss Kincaid looking remarkably unchanged. I told her so and asked about her brother.
"Here he is!" she said, introducing a small compact man with eyes as blue and alert as her own. The complexion of his bald head and cut of his neatly trimmed beard showed this was Joe, the nautical brother. I asked how Sam was.
"As vocal as ever," she said merrily. "We've moved him upstairs. Come home for a drink with us."
So we three walked back to the old manse.

It was a chill November afternoon with occasional gusts of thin rain and I made a conventional remark about the weather. "Yes, a miserable climate," said Joe cheerily. "I've seen much worse weather but for sheer dull depressing misery a damp Scottish November cannot be surpassed."
He seemed highly satisfied with such Scottish Novembers.
"I disagree," said Miss Kincaid. "Autumn is Scotland's most colourful season. Fresh spring leaves look lovely but they don't look fresh for long. By the end of summer they've been tired and dusty for months. Then

comes September and they start withering into golden greens, deep purples and all the rich colours I've seen in reproductions of Gauguin's paintings. I'm sure they would damage our eyes if we saw them by the strong sunlight of Tahiti."

"Those don't look very dazzling," said Joe, pointing to the pavement. Adhering to the tarmac and almost as black was a thin carpet of rotten old leaves with some recent ones the colour of dung.

"But what an excellent background for those!" said Miss Kincaid, pointing to a couple of fallen chestnut fans further on. Each leaf was a glowing yellow that blended through orange into crimson at the tip, with a pale green streak along the central veins.

As we entered the manse lobby we heard from above a vocal hullabaloo. Miss Kincaid looked at Joe who said calmly, "Yes, it's my turn."

Without haste he removed and hung up cap and coat and went upstairs. Miss Kincaid led me into the room where I had last seen Sam, switching on bright lights that made the dark furniture look solidly comforting instead of forbidding. The air was pleasantly warm.

"Home," she said. "Home home home. Would you like a sherry? I'm having one." We sat sipping sherry and watching the flames in the hearth. She said, "They're gas flames now and no trouble at all. Sam loved the old coal fire, said the constantly changing flames were a more varied show than television. He also liked to see me poking it or adding coals every half hour. When Joe came home we outnumbered Sam. Our change to gas so enraged him that he retreated upstairs. We installed a lift attachment to the banister that can easily take the twenty stone of him up and down. Joe would gladly drive Sam and his wheelchair to the park or anywhere else he likes, but no. Sam says he will never let anyone see a Kincaid in a pitiable state, will never let Joe condescend to him, so he sticks in his room. Laziness masquerading as pride,

you see. Sheer obstinate idiocy in fact. Yet Sam used to be a better Labour councillor than most of them."
We had another sherry. She said, "Our father is to blame. He was a selfish monster who forbad us to play with other children. He damaged Sam most because Sam was his favourite so grew up like him, only happy with people he could bully. Thank God Joe and I had each other. We told each other all sorts of lovely stories and invented all sorts of exciting games when nobody was looking. Our affection made us quite unfit for matrimony. By going to sea Joe was able to sample other sorts of affection. He told me about them in letters because he knew I could never be jealous of purely temporary mates. He was living the life I would have led had I been a man, and I knew he would return to me at last. Another sherry?"

Joe entered and said, "Dinner-time. The Great I Am upstairs has grudgingly assented to oxtail soup, bangers and mash, tinned peaches with ice cream. What do you ladies want?"
We wanted the same. Joe prepared it and the three of us dined at the kitchen table with long chatty intervals between courses, the last of which was coffee with chocolates and liqueurs. Prompted by Chrissie Joe quietly recounted very entertaining comic or terrifying oversea adventures and every forty minutes he or she went upstairs and attended briefly to Sam. Sitting round the kitchen table was so agreeable that we ended the evening there playing Scrabble. My companions showed a relaxed pleasure in each other that I have sometimes (not often) noticed in recently married couples, but such marital pleasure is usually exclusive. I felt part of this Kincaid domesticity and had not felt so happily at home for years.

I told Miss Kincaid so when I was leaving. I think she replied that Autumn could be quite a satisfactory season, but being tipsy I may have imagined that.

SWAN BURIAL

I PHONE OUR ADMINISTRATOR and say that in ten minutes I will bring her the overdue assessments. She says, "Thank you, Doctor Gowry. And will you also bring the introduction to the new handbook?"

"That will take a little longer, Karen, perhaps another hour."

"Then don't bother bringing me all these things today. Leave the assessed portfolios and introduction in my front-office pigeon hole when you go home tonight. I'll process them first thing tomorrow."

"Thank you Karen, that would be much more convenient."

"I'm *Phyllis*, Doctor Gowry. Karen left three months ago."

"Haha, so she did. Sorry, Phyllis."

I finish assessing the portfolios on my desk, look for the others and remember I took them home three days ago. Never mind. I'll rise early tomorrow and bring them to the front office before Karen arrives. So now I tackle the introduction, though I fear this job is getting beyond me and I should apply for something less demanding. Which reminds me that I *have* applied for another job, with Human Resources, and must soon attend an interview for it. But first, the introduction. This should be easy. I need only bring the introduction to last year's handbook up to date by changing a word here or there.

But revising the old introduction turns out to be almost impossible. I wrote it only a year ago but the language now strikes me as long-winded official jargon, misleading when not practically meaningless. It was written to attract folk with money into an organisation I now want to leave, but surely that can be done in a few simple, honest sentences? I try and try to write them and have almost glimpsed how to do it when I see the the time is nearly four p.m.! My interview with Human Resources is at four fifteen! If I run to the main road and catch a taxi at once I can still be in time so *run*.

Rain is falling, every passing taxi is engaged, at ten past four I decide to phone Human Resources, apologise, blame the weather and if possible postpone the interview. I rush into a familiar pub and find the public telephone has been replaced by a flashing machine that gives the users an illusion of shooting people. I groan. A man I know asks why. I say, "No telephone."
"Use my mobile," he says, holding out what looks like a double nine domino.
"Thank you – thank you – but I don't know how to use such a machine."
"I'll dial for you. What number?"
I cannot tell him, for the number is in a diary on my office desk. He offers to dial directory enquiries but, suddenly full of black certainty that I have now no chance of the Human Resources job, instead I order a large whisky for each of us.

He says, "Thanks. Cheers. You seem troubled. Tell me your woes."
I do so in great detail, during which he buys us each another drink. At last he says, "Remarkable. Remarkable. But why apply to Human Resources? It doesn't even figure in the Dow Jones index. You're a metallurgist so you should apply to Domestic Steel. It died in the late sixties but a renaissance is due and your age and experience would make you a valuable link with the past."
I ponder these words and find that they also strike me as meaningless official jargon. I order another round of drinks and tell him I mainly regret losing my chance with Human Resources because of my wife. She feels my job with Scottish Arterial is killing me. The man says, "I suspect you need a total change of scene. Any plans for a holiday this year?"

I say, "Not this year," and explain that my wife hates leaving home, even for a few days, because she is sure we cannot afford it. She says such suggestions threaten our marriage and make her feel I am battering her. I then notice it is twenty minutes to ten, say goodbye and leave, but as usual nowadays I call for a quick drink at two or three other pubs on my way home.

I open our front door shortly after midnight and hear gentle snoring from the darkened bedroom. I undress without switching on the light but the window curtains are not completely drawn. By gleams from a street lamp outside I see a tumbler of clear liquid on my wife's bedside table. Is it water? Gin? Vodka? Does she drink as much alcohol in my absence as I do in hers? I refrain from investigating and slip in beside her. The rhythm of her snores alters slightly as she snuggles cosily against me. I lie basking in that cosiness. This is now the pleasantest part of my life; perhaps it always was. She mutters something that sounds like "I wish she had chosen a different star."
"Who are you talking about?" I ask. She is obviously talking in her sleep, but even then can sometimes answer questions. After a moment she mutters that they're burying the bird.
"What bird?" I ask, trying to imagine the dream she is having. After a while she says, "A swan."
Her dreams are as impenetrable as my own.

I continue basking in her warmth, dimly haunted by a feeling that tomorrow I should rise early and do something. I cannot remember what, but Karen will know. Karen is amazingly efficient and good at covering up for me; besides, nowadays in Britain no professional person as close to retiral as I am is ever sacked for inefficiency.

I wait patiently for sleep
to cover me all up
like a cloak.

SINKINGS

SUCCESS IS OVERRATED. The best proof of our worth is how we respond to failure. Herman Melville said that or something very like it. My marital partner still loves me, so do our children, I have recently retired with a cosy pension from a professional job which did some good and very little harm, so I have never been tested by really big failures. Yet the moments I remember with most interest are not my happiest ones, but those times when the ordinary ground under my feet seemed suddenly to sink, leaving me several yards lower than I thought normal or possible. This lower level did not prevent pleasures I had enjoyed at higher ones, but the pleasure never seemed to raise me up again. These sinkings (depressions is too mild a word for them) were never caused by irrevocable disasters, like the death of a parent. I am no masochist, but disasters on that scale stimulated and bucked me up. What let me down worst were failures of common decency, especially the first two.

My father was a businessman who died leaving just enough money for mother to send me to what was thought a very grand boarding school – the sons of many rich, well-known people went there. My immediate dislike of the place on arrival increased with time. The sons of the rich and famous were a social élite to which the teachers also belonged. Boys without much pocket money were excluded unless a brilliant appearance or talent for sport or clowning got them "taken up" by the smart majority. I belonged to a minority who were not physically bullied but usually treated as if invisible. I suppose if we had not existed the rest could not have felt so exclusive and fashionable. If we invisibles had united we would have formed a class more exclusive than the rest because smaller, but we despised ourselves too much to do that.

I had one friend among the élite, or thought I had: a senior military man's son. He enjoyed modern American literature as much as I did. We never noticed each other when he was with his fashionable friends, but on meeting apart from them in the school library we sometimes went walks together chattering enthusiastically about books whose main characters rebelled against social codes of a type that seemed to rule our own institution. Our form of rebellion was to identify various teachers and head boys with the deranged bullies and conformists of *Catch-22, Catcher in the Rye, Portnoy's Complaint*. Doing so often reduced us to fits of helpless laughter. Our homes in Glasgow were the only other thing we had in common. At the start of a summer holiday we exchanged addresses.

I phoned him a fortnight later and suggested we meet in town.

"I've a better idea," he said, "You come over here. Come this afternoon. I'm having a kind of a party ..."

He hesitated then added, "As a matter of fact it's my birthday."

I thanked him and asked if it would be a very smart occasion? He said, "No no no, just come the way you are."

He lived in Pollokshields, south of the river, and I arrived with a copy of *Slaughterhouse 5* in my pocket, a book I knew he would enjoy. I had never before visited a mansion standing in its own grounds. I pressed the bell and after a while the door was opened by an elderly woman in a black gown who stared at me, frowning. I said, "Is Raymond in?"

She walked away. It seemed foolish to remain on the

doormat so I stepped inside, closing the door behind me. The hall had a mosaic floor, a huge clock, corridors and a broad staircase leading out between Roman-looking pillars. I stood there listening hard for sounds of a party and could hear nothing at all. A tall man with a military moustache entered and said very gently, "Yes?"
"Is Raymond in?"
He said "I'll see about that," and went away. A lot of time passed. The clock struck a quarter hour. I sat down on the slightly rounded top of an antique ebony chest and noticed the time pass, feeling more and more bewildered. Fifteen minutes later the tall man appeared again, stared at me, said, "Why are you still sitting there looking so miserable? Get out! *We* don't want you." He opened the front door and I walked through it.

That was my first and worst sinking, also the end of my friendship with Raymond. I planned to studiously ignore him when our paths next crossed in the school library, but I never saw him there again.

The second sinking was a milder affair on my last day at that school. I stood with eight or nine other leavers, Raymond among them, in the Headmaster's study, pretending to absorb a flow of the man's brisk, facile, foreseeable, completely uninteresting platitudes. He ended with a firm, "Goodbye and good luck gentlemen. And Gilliland, stay behind for a moment."
He shook hands with the rest who left and I remained feeling rather puzzled, because this was the first time he had ever spoken to me. He sat behind his desk, clasped his hands upon it, looked at me sternly over them for a while then said, "Don't forget, Gilliland, that syphilis is an absolute killer. You can go now."
So I went.

Why did he talk as if *I* was a sexual maniac? Why was I the only school leaver he said that to? As in all

single sex schools for adolescents there had been discreet homosexual liaisons among us, but not among us in the invisible class – we were too demoralised to enjoy anything but the most solitary kind of sex. Was it possible that my slightly secretive walks with Raymond had been noticed disapprovingly by his other friends and reported to the teachers? Was our laughter over the antics of Portnoy and Yossarian overheard and interpreted as something sexually and socially dangerous? Was this reported to his father? And was keeping me behind to make that inane remark a headmaster's ploy to avoid shaking an unpopular pupil's hand?
I don't know, but if so Britain is
a very queer nation.

WELLBEING

I SAW A PLAIN strewn with marble rocks, the smallest higher than a man, the largest as big as a cathedral. They were pieces of a statue that had once stood taller than Ben Nevis. Groups of little people moved with horse-drawn wagons among these rocks. They were searching for a piece recognisably human yet small enough to carry away – the lobe of an ear or tip of a toe. Each group wanted to put such a fragment where they could love and pray to it, as it would prove there had once been power, beauty and unity that the world no longer contained. A group found a rock pierced by a beautifully smooth oval arch, part of a nostril. As they lifted it into their cart other groups combined to attack and rob them. This happened to all who found a good fragment, so none was ever carried away and love and prayer were impossible. I opened my eyes because my Japanese host was asking a question.

"In the second chapter of book ten you say *till all the seas gang dry, my dear*. My useful dictionary defines *gang* as a band of ruffians or criminals, a number of labourers working together. None of these definitions seems to fit."

I said that *gang* was also a Scottish transitive and intransitive verb meaning *go* and these words were a quotation from Robert Burns's greatest love song. My host murmured politely, "I believe Robert Burns's poetry is still sung in parts of North America."

I nodded. I was happy.

We were in the Smooth Grove, which had been the Central Station Hotel in days when Glasgow was joined to other places by railway. I felt the luxury of a good meal in my stomach, good wine on my palate, clean socks, underwear and shirt against my skin. They had been worth waiting for. Foreign translators, journalists and writers of dissertations always buy me new clothes before standing me a lunch – posh restaurants won't let me in without new clothes after I've slept a few weeks in ones the last foreigner bought me. Foreigners contact me through my bank. Ordinary pubs and all-night cafés accept me since I can pay for drink and food and can sleep in short snatches sitting upright.

I was not always dependent on foreigners for a smart appearance. I used to have several friends with homes and visited each of them once a fortnight. They gave me food and a bed for the night and put my clothes through a machine. Modern machines not only wash, dry and iron, they remove stains, mend holes, replace lost buttons and re-dye faded fabric to look like new. Or am I dreaming that? If I am dreaming such a machine it is certainly possible because, as William Blake said, nothing exists which was not first dreamed. Most of these friends steadily disappeared but were not, I think, stabbed or burned. People with homes still usually die of diseases or a silly accident.

My one remaining friend is now my first wife who pretends to be my daughter. I don't know why. I visited her a month ago. After enjoying a plate of her excellent soup I asked how Mavis was getting on in London. She stared and said, "I am Mavis. Cathy is dead – died twelve years ago, shortly after I came home."
"Nonsense Cathy!" I said. "You can't be Mavis because Mavis quarrelled with you and she was right to quarrel with you because you were not kind to her, though I was too tactful to say so at the time."

My host in the Smooth Grove was as ancient as I am and still used a notebook. Looking up from it he said,

"I hear there is now no middle class in Scotland and England. Is that true?"
I told him it was not true: the middle class are those who used to be called working class – they have jobs but no investments, and their only pensions are state pensions.
"But middle class implies a lower class. Who are they?"
I explained that thieves, swindlers, rapists, drug dealers and murderers are our lower class nowadays, many of them registered with the police. They have a place in society because without them police, lawyers, judges, jailers and journalists would be unemployed, and the profits of drug companies would slump.
"So in Britain everyone has a place in the social fabric?"
"Everyone but the homeless," I answered, trying to remember why I feel perfectly secure though I am one of these.

My host started writing again and to avoid disturbing thoughts I dreamed of a future state in which human police had disappeared because the rich no longer needed them. The rich never left their luxurious, well-defended homes except when visiting each other in vehicles moving at the speed of light. Each home was protected by a metallic creature the size of a kitten and resembling a cockroach. It hid under chairs and sideboards and was programmed to kill intruders. I was a low-class criminal who broke into the apartments of a rich young sexy woman, cunningly reprogrammed her police creature to serve me, then enjoyed a number of sexual acts which appeared to be drawn in a highly coloured, very entertaining strip cartoon of a kind which became popular in France at the end of the twentieth century and in Britain at the start of the next, though many British people then were still able to read. We had a very entertaining country in those days. I had been teaching abroad since the late seventies and every time I returned the changes struck me as so interesting that I wrote about them.

Yes, one year publishers sold my stories to a newspaper cartoon supplement for so much that I stopped teaching and brought my second wife home to Glasgow. She was from Los Angeles or Chicago, I think, and believed that life for prosperous people was the same anywhere, and indeed Britain was now very like America. The police only patrolled the streets of prosperous ghettos where householders had bought crime insurance. The police observed other communities through public surveillance cameras and had power to swoop in and uplift anyone on suspicion, but they mainly lifted unregistered politicians and folk who owed money to drug dealers. When people fell down in the street it was no longer etiquette to help them up or summon an ambulance. We hurried past knowing that next day they would probably be gone. I had a lovely home in those days. I lost it in a wave of inflation which suddenly made life *astonishingly* interesting. My wife returned to the USA. I stayed out of curiosity though British publishing had stopped. Not even newspapers were produced. Industries with a use for wood and rag pulp bought the remaining libraries. Some books are still used to give public houses an old-fashioned look. Boys' adventure stories from the 1910s predominate.

My host said, "Toward the end of your eleventh book you mention *no concurrency of bone*. What do you mean by that?"

All foreigners ask that question. I can now answer it without thinking. While doing so I closed my eyes and enjoyed walking on a grassy hilltop beside a tall, slender, beautiful young woman I had loved when I was fifty. Even in this dream I knew our love was in the past, that my virility was dead and that no beautiful woman would ever love me again. I told her this. She grew angry and called me selfish because I was only dreaming of her to cheer myself up. This was obviously true so I forgot her by staring at a hill on the far side of a valley, a Scottish hill soaring to Alpine heights with all the buildings I have ever known in rows between strips of woodland, heather and rocky cliffs. On the crest of the mountain I saw the red sandstone gable of the tenement where I was born in 1934, at the bottom I recognised the grey clock tower of the Smooth Grove where I was dining and dreaming. The scene delighted me by its blend of civilisation and wilderness, past and present, by the ease with which the eye grasped so much rich intricacy. Suddenly the colour drained from it. The heather turned grey, the trees leafless, but I still felt perfectly safe and remembered why.

Though still telling my host about the massacre of Glencoe and Ezekiel's valley of dry bones I remembered the death of Mr Anderson, a former radio announcer with whom I once shared a kind of cave, a very safe secret little hidey-hole, we thought, in a shrubbery of Kelvingrove Park. In those days I had not learned to sleep in small snatches while sitting upright so I slept by drinking half a bottle of methylated spirits. One morning I woke to find my companion had been stabbed to death and scalped. I did not know why I had been spared until several weeks or months or years later. Perhaps it was yesterday. I'm sure I did not dream it.

I stood on the canal towpath enjoying a glorious gold, green and lavender sunset when I was tripped and knocked down. I lay flat on my back surrounded by children of seven, eight or nine. Their sex was not obvious. All wore black jeans and leather jackets. All had skulls and crossbones painted or tattooed on top of heads that were bald except for a finger length of small pigtails all round. One poured petrol over my trousers, the rest waved bats, cutting implements, firelighters and discussed which part of me to bruise, cut or set fire to first.
"We are the death squad of the Maryhill Cleansing Brigade," explained the leader who was perhaps eleven or twelve. "We are licensed terrorists with a sacred

mission to save the British economy through a course of geriatric disposal. Too many old gerries are depressing the economy these days. If you can't afford to get rejuvenated, grampa, you should have the decency to top yourself before becoming a burden to the state."

I told him I wasn't a burden to the state, wasn't even a beggar, that money was paid into my bank account by foreign publishers and was enough to feed me though not enough to rent a room.

"You pathetic, hairy old driveller!" shouted the leader, goading himself or herself into a fury. "You're an eyesore! The visual equivalent of a force-nine-gale fart! You will die in hideous agony as a warning to others."

I was alarmed but excited. To die must be an awfully big adventure. Then a small fat person with glasses said, "Wait a bit, Jimsy, I think he's famous."

They consulted a folded sheet with a lot of faces and names printed on it. The fat person, who could read names, asked if I was Mr Thingumajig, which I am. They helped me up, dusted me down, shook my hand very solemnly one at a time, said they would remember me next time we met, said they would gladly kill any old friend I wanted rid of, advised me not to go near a naked flame before my trousers were dry, hoped I had no hard feelings. Honestly, I had none at all. My gratitude and love for these children was so great that I wept real tears. The leader got me to autograph the printed sheet. It was pleasant to meet a young Scot who still valued my signature. The sun had not yet set when they left me. I watched the gloaming fade, warm in the knowledge that I had a privileged place in modern Britain. Not only the children liked me but their bosses in the Cleansing Company or Social Security Trust or Education Industry or whoever had a use for children nowadays.

Yes, somebody up there likes me even though once I detested the bastards up there, the agents and consultants, money farmers and middle men, parliamentary quangomongers, local and international monopolists. My books were attacks on these people but caused no hard feelings, and now my books are only read in nations that lost World War Two.

My host spoke on a politely insistent note. "I suggest you visit my country. Your royalties there will easily rent a private apartment with housekeeper and health care. We are no longer a military nation. We revere old people, which is why they live longer among us than anywhere else."

I said I was happy where I was. He shut his notebook and bowed saying, "You are a true master. You have subdued your wishes to your surroundings."

This angered me but I did not show it. There are better ways of living than being happy but they require strength and sanity. The poor and weak are as incapable of sanity as the rich and powerful. Sanity in this country would drive the weak to suicide and make the rich distinctly uncomfortable. We are better without it.

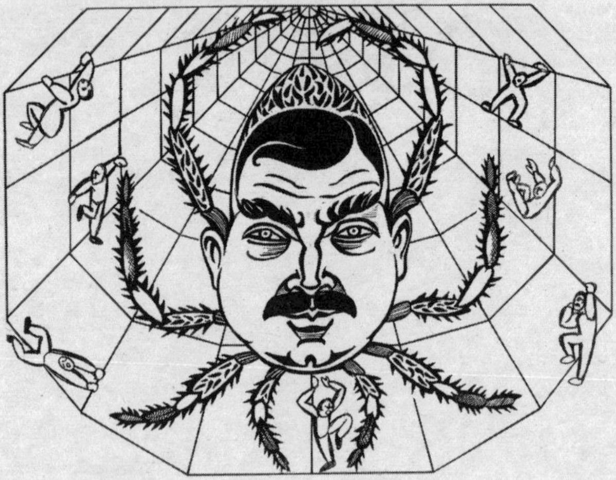

TALES DROLL & PLAUSIBLE

FOR THE TORY
AND LABOUR
CREATORS OF
MODERN BRITAIN

EDINBURGH 2012

EUSTACE

YOUR ROYAL MAJESTIES AND HIGHNESSES; your Holinesses, Eminences, Graces and Reverences; distinguished Prime Ministers, Presidents and Premiers of these our United Nations; my Lords, Ladies and Gentlemen! Never before in the history of **Great** Britain, and (here I repeat with peculiar emphasis) the history of *Great* Britain, have so many owed so much to one man, the modest individual at my side. Two weeks ago the whole population of our planet was threatened by the horror of an overwhelming social collapse. At the last moment his timely words and decisive action made that crisis seem less than the shadow of a cloud passing over a sunlit field. United in his genius we found the diplomatic skill of Knatchbull Hugeson, the hard smoothness of Scipio Todalini and the valorous marksmanship of Second Flight Lieutenant Wulfstan Tempest. I now call upon us all to drink a toast to our saviour *and* our friend, Eustace MacNulty."

"Eustace MacNulty!" cry the vast assembly and the toast is drunk, followed by a storm of hand-clapping and foot-stamping. The guest of honour silences them by jumping up and saying eagerly, "Comrades, how can I follow that introduction with anything that will please or entertain you? It cannot be done. I am very ignorant! So ignorant that I have never before heard the names of the three national heroes just mentioned…"

These words provoke sympathetic laughter which is prolonged with many cries of "Hear! Hear!" when the Queen of England calls out, "Neither have I!"

"Worse still," says the speaker desperately, "I cannot remember my own name, but it is certainly not Eustace MacNulty. And where are my trousers? Why am I naked?

I have never appeared in public before without wearing at least a necktie."

The speaker pauses, relieved to find he is clothed again and part of a queue in a familiar bank. At the counter he writes out a cheque to himself and places it in front of a teller who asks for proof of his identity.

"I have been coming to this bank for over thirty years," declares the customer, "and have never before been asked such a question. Surely the signature on my cheque proves my identity."

Says the teller, "Not nowadays sir. We now need something to confirm it. Your driving licence will do."

"I have no driving licence. I have no car."

"Then I need to see your passport or else two official documents addressed to you."

"That is absurd! I do not normally walk about with such documents in my pockets. Do you? Does anyone?"

Someone behind him in the queue says, "Excuse me for butting in but perhaps I can help. I can vouch for this man. I know him well. Everyone should know him well because he is Scotland's greatest living author, actor and architect. He is Eustace MacNulty."

"I am not! Not at all! This is my name – read it!" cries the writer of the cheque, holding it out for inspection. Then he notices that both his signature and the printed name beside it are Eustace MacNulty.

Again he finds himself naked, but in bed beside his quietly snoring wife. Switching on the bedside light he shakes her nearest shoulder until she opens her eyes and drowsily murmurs, "What's wrong?"

"Margaret!" he pleads, "Margaret who am I? Please tell me my name."

She says, "Shut up Eustace and let me sleep."

"If *you* think I'm Eustace I must still be dreaming," he whimpers.

"Then go on doing it," she advises,
turning her back to him.

WORKING WITH GIANTS

IN THAT WEEK WHEN ONE Scottish prime minister replaced another three people shared a table on an early morning train to London. A man and woman in the window seats were slightly younger than their companion reading *The Financial Times*. This so engrossed him that he gave no sign of hearing a word when, after nearly half an hour of silence, the younger man glimpsed machines digging a huge foundation pit and wondered aloud what the building would be.

"Probably another private hospital!" the woman across the table said bitterly.

"You disapprove of them?" he asked, smiling, and she replied with a torrent of words telling him, among other things, that she worked in a public hospital as a state-registered nurse. His sympathetic nods and murmured agreement encouraged her speech until it faltered, when he began supporting her main argument with so much detailed information about hospital funding that she asked if he too worked for the National Health Service.

"For nothing so useful," he said with a sigh. "I'm afraid I only work with giants."

She stared at him. He added apologetically, "I mean the big boys – the not very nice people in charge of British industry, or what remains of it."

"Politicians?" she suggested.

"God no! Politicians thrive on T.V. and newspaper coverage and all the publicity they can get. Most folk in Britain don't know the names of the big boys,"

"Why not?"

"Because they don't read the..."

He nodded sideways to the paper in the hands of their

companion. The nurse brooded on that till the man facing her said, " You see, England is different from the USA. The Yanks know they've been ruled by billionaires for centuries. A lot of folk here won't face the fact, hence the popularity of the Royal family."

"So how do you work with your giants? What do they pay you to do?"

"They don't pay me. I am usually paid (though not always) by companies or local politicians who want their support for some scheme or other. I'm what is called an entrepreneur – a middleman."

"Why do they need you to ask for their support? Can the people who want support not just write or phone to ask for it?"

"They would get no useful answers that way. Business is too competitive nowadays. The giants avoid putting anything in writing, and phone calls can be bugged and recorded. Most are nowadays, I believe. Surveillance technology has made tremendous strides."

"You make it sound very shady, very underhand."

"It is. Getting a straight yes or no from a big man (I never meet more than one at a time) is almost impossible. If he smiles after I've explained my client's proposition and says 'That would be risky,' the answer is probably no. If he frowns and says, "Of course it's not for me to decide, but say they can try it if they think it will work,' that probably means, Go ahead! Only if it goes pear-shaped will we leave you to the sharks."

"Sharks?"

"Investigation committees, journalists, those kind of sharks."

A loud speaker announced that the train was about to enter Euston station. The nurse said flatly, "And that's how you earn your living?"

"Yes, quite a good living, I always please those I work *with*, but not always those I work *for*. It's a balancing act."

He laid a small card on the table in front of the nurse

saying, "Sorry to cut our interesting conversation short. Phone me some time if you would like to continue it more privately. I must leave pretty smartly because I'm running late. Excuse me please."
The last three words were to the reader of *The Financial Times*, who carefully folded and pocketed it, then stood to let the younger man out. The entrepreneur took down a briefcase then hurried along the corridor past others taking things from overhead racks.

The nurse and older man avoided jostling by staying seated for a while. She looked at the card before her without touching it, remembering that the eyes of the man facing her had a hint of sexual appraisal. The older man startled her by suddenly saying, "There is no doubt that our talkative friend knows a lot about our National Health Service, probably because he is one of those working to privatise it. But I doubt if he knows many of the giants he referred to. Believe me my dear, the really big men never trust blabbermouths."

THE OFFER

A BIOLOGIST AND A LAWYER, he Swedish, she Korean, wait to meet the world's most famous living architect. Both are in their sixties but the lawyer's calm unlined face appears younger. Resting on a sofa she watches her colleague who stands before a window, staring gloomily down a long slope of villas among pines and many spires of those cypress trees which, to northern eyes, seem improbably tall and thin. The slope ends in a bright sea with sails of yachts near the shore, and on the high horizon the silhouette of an island that might be Monte Cristo.

The biologist looks at his wristwatch and sighs. The lawyer says, "The maestro always keeps visitors waiting."
"He, at least, should have grown out of playing childish games."
Their accents show both learned English in the U.S.A.
The lawyer says, "Yes, he is playful – tricks journalists into thinking him an alcoholic invalid and recluse who has retired from business. Three months ago he accepted a commission to design a village in Sri Lanka, and personally surveyed the site while carefully avoiding publicity. Surely you read that in the psychological profile they gave us?"
"No."
"Why not?"
"Psychology is too recent a branch of medicine to be an exact science. Only the master's achievements interest me. Everything he has done has been surprising, has shown the fertility of Lloyd Wright and Le Corbusier with the humane humorous detail of Gaudi and Mackintosh.

His work convinces me that my work may at last do humanity good."

"*Your* work?" she asks, with slightly mocking emphasis.

"Mine and Schoenenbacher's," he says impatiently, "and Hong Fu's and Glaister's. Yes, I am a dwarf standing on the shoulder of giants. Tomorrow I hand in my resignation and retire as soon as possible to my son's farm in Uppsala."

After two or three minutes the lawyer says carefully, "I advise you to stay on the Foundation's payroll as a consultant."

He turns and looks at her, saying, "Otherwise, despite all the confidentiality clauses I have signed, our employers may regard me as a loose wheel?"

She nods. He asks, "Which might shorten my life?"

She does not answer. He sits beside her, murmuring, "Then mine will be the sudden, unexpected death that Julius Caesar wanted, and got. But my post-mortem will attribute it to natural causes."

They sit a long time in silence, then a little girl looks in and tells them, "He can see you now."

The lawyer lifts a briefcase. They follow the child through a corridor and arrive in a big sunlit room with glass walls and a glass ceiling. Some dark blue panes ensure the noonday sun does not dazzle them. A little old man in pyjamas and dressing gown reclines in an invalid chair with a leg-rest exposing his thin legs and plump paunch. From a silky cloud of white hair and beard two sharp eyes look out above a potato-like blob of nose. The line of his mouth is shown by the lower edge of a moustache he seems to be sucking with tipsy relish. Waving to a couple of chairs he cries in a shrill falsetto, "Welcome! Be seated! What a pleasure, what a privilege to be visited by such eminences."

His fluent English has an Italian accent. The visitors sit. The child leans affectionately against the arm of the old man's chair. Placing an arm round her shoulders he tells them, "Yes, I am a paedophile. I love my grandchildren. Fourteen of them visit me in rotation. All are clever but Minnie is one of the cleverest. Minnie, give these nice people what they want to drink, and bring me a hock and seltzer in memory of dear Oscar Wilde."

He points to an adjacent drinks cabinet. The scientist wants nothing, the lawyer accepts a glass of sherry. Before sipping she says, "Maestro, I regret that our talk must not be overheard."

"Run away and play Minnie," says their host. "We are about to discuss indecencies."

The little girl curtsies to him and the visitors, and leaves.

The architect sips from his glass before saying in a surprising baritone, "You have asked for this interview without giving a reason. Let me save you the embarrassment of explanations. Your names were unknown to me before this morning when Minnie consulted the Internet. I now know that, in your very different professions, you are both internationally renowned, and work for the powerful but discreet Endon Foundation. After World War number two Endon absorbed the Blenkiron Trust, and twenty years ago took over some functions of the United Nations World Health Organization. I am right?"

The lawyer murmurs agreement. The old man nods twice, says, "So your immediate bosses are a clique I call the global employers' federation, which officially does not exist. I am still right?"

The lawyer, startled, looks at the biologist who cries, "O yes!"

Nodding twice again the architect says, "Years ago an American millionaire told the press that with the help of modern medicine he intended to live for ever. Is he a member of that clique?"

After a short silence the lawyer says, "No. He recently died of natural causes."

"Poor fellow! But I assume others as rich or richer need

not now die of natural causes. As an old Communist I think this a disaster. A few families (mostly American) command more wealth than the world's governments combined. Will the world from now on be ruled by a clique of plutocrats who will never let themselves be replaced?"

"No!" says the lawyer and "Yes indeed!" shouts the scientist with what seems hysterical merriment.

"Yes indeed," says the architect. "I now carry my deductions further. The alchemists' dream of eternal life has often been explored in fiction. The struldbrugs in *Gulliver's Travels*, Tennyson's *Tiresias*, the foetal ape wearing the Order of the Garter in Huxley's *After Many a Summer* are horrific portraits of people who cannot die. Shaw's *Back to Methuselah* and Wyndham Lewis's *Trouble with Lichen* describe jollier immortals. These hide their good luck from the majority who would also want eternal life – not possible on this over-peopled planet where most still die of malnutrition before maturity. So your ruling clique of billionaires, trillionaires, zillionaires must keep their happy state hidden, while sharing the privilege with scientists and supportive politicians who make it possible. You, my dear visitors, are members of this jolly club?"

The visitors look at each other. The architect says, "Ignore that embarrassing question. I continue. So many people now share this secret that it cannot stay a secret for ever. How can eternal life be made acceptable to a majority who will never have it? Obviously, by creating something like the Académie française, wherein folk made popular by their achievements in entertainment, science and medicine are made physically immortal too. The masters of our universe will start by admitting Nobel Prize winners like me –" (he taps his chest) "– and you!" He points to the scientist who says, "I am resigning from that club."

"I salute you," cries the architect, sitting upright and raising his hand in a smart military salute. "Tell me why."

"For personal reasons that have nothing to do with

the therapy. This will allow you, at least, many more centuries of good work. I am a Swedish Socialist who sees as clearly as you the evils of a self-perpetuating propertied class. I hope that a self-perpetuating academy of mankind's intelligent servants will counteract it, as the Christian church sometimes counteracted feudal warlords. That will be a long, weary struggle of which I am already tired."

The architect presses a switch that lowers his leg-rest, saying, "I must now furiously think in silence for a while. Excuse me."

He springs up and paces round the big room with bowed head and hands clasped behind back.

The scientist strolls to the drinks cabinet, lifts a sherry bottle, silently offers to fill the lawyer's half-empty glass. She refuses with a shake of the head. He fills a tumbler from a can of Pilsner lager and carries it to the longest window. This allows a larger view of the landscape he watched earlier, with tops of pines and cypresses visible through walls to left and right. The wall with the entrance door is a huge mirror reflecting the three window walls, so the room seems a magic carpet floating above the Italian Riviera. The architect halts before this mirror and examines his reflection like a zoologist studying a fascinating but repulsive beast. He asks, "Would this bloated belly of mine also be immortalized?"

Without turning the scientist says, "Eat less, exercise properly and you could be rid of it in a few months."

"Oho! So your therapy involves no grafting? No healthy young man of my blood group will be kidnapped and murdered and have his good organs replace my decrepit ones?"

"Of course not!" cries the lawyer, standing and refilling her sherry glass.

The scientist says, "The results of such therapy are too patchy to last. My therapy keeps restoring cells inherited at birth."

"Good! I have never believed that our intelligence and memory exist mainly in the brain. Lucretius knew our spirits are distributed through every part of our body. An architect's talent is gained by striding through lands and rooms while his eyes notice every kind of spatial limit, the nerves and muscles of arms and fingers learn skill in draughtsmanship. Like Leonardo I am ambidextrous, a fact I hid from my closest assistants, though not from my dearly beloved wives. I give you this secret in return for the dangerous secret you are offering me. If I understand rightly, I need not be rejuvenated? Need not forget the carefully, painfully learned experiences of a lifetime?"
"Not at once," says the scientist, "but in an eternal future you will only make room for new discoveries by forgetting more and more of the past. I predict that after several millennia immortals will have forgotten their childhoods, first marriages and children and probably the planet where they were born. I want no such future, but am not an artist, far less one who builds good homes for people who are not rich and privileged. Perhaps Goethe was right. He said artists have recurring puberties that keep returning them to a younger state before they advance to a new one."
"You compliment me," says the architect, now standing beside the scientist and watching the island that might be Monte Cristo, "but Goethe was an old bore long before his death, when he had just managed to finish writing the end of *Faust*. Remember what Schiller said on reading the start of that play thirty years earlier – it would be wonderful to see if Faust would be corrupted or win free of the Devil he employed. Goethe went on to make Faust a heartless seducer, murderer, warlord, an evictor of peasants and piratical millionaire who thinks he is liberating mankind when his grave is being dug. So Goethe sends his soul up to a heaven ruled by a female from Dante's *Paradiso*."

Behind them a harsh voice cries, "I must interrupt

this comradely swapping of cultural references. I reject the cynical reasons given by the maestro for our Foundation's offer, but the offer exists. Does he accept it? Maestro, please sign this contract."

She takes a sheaf of pages from her briefcase, goes to a map chest and spreads them on top saying, "Endon expects no payment for the therapy, which will be provided painlessly once a month by a doctor from the Foundation. All Endon requires in return is your complete silence about the matter."

"Nor will it change your character at first," says the scientist dryly, "though I think it will inevitably induce insane smugness toward all who have died or will die."

The architect goes to the chest, takes a fountain pen from the pocket of his gown saying, "I do not want to know the exact terms of this shameless document, but I will obviously be safer if I sign it."

"Sign each page separately and we will witness them," says the lawyer.

The architect asks the scientist, "You have signed such a contract?"

"Yes, years ago. It commits the signatory to keeping the therapy secret, but allows freedom to refuse or discontinue it, as I am doing."

"You have chosen rightly," says the architect. "I will stay as I am."

He carefully signs every page to which his guests add their signatures, then he asks, "Am I to have a copy?"

"No," says the lawyer, putting the sheaf into her briefcase. From a drawer in the chest the architect takes two cream-coloured papers with a small picture on each saying, "Thank you for this visit. Please accept a little gift as a souvenir. My latest hobby is the obsolete art of mezzotinting."

He carries the prints to a desk, lifts a pencil, sees that the point is needle-sharp, then carefully writes small words after his signature in the lower margins. He slips each print into a black plastic envelope, lifts a drumstick and strokes a copper gong with the padded end, making a noise like the roar of a melodious lion. He hands each visitor an envelope and shakes their hand as the little girl enters.

"Minnie," he says, "lead the fine lady and gentleman down to their car where a poor bored chauffeur has been languishing for nearly two hours. Goodbye my friends. This has been a pleasant meeting, productive of much thought. Tell your Foundation that I will keep their secret and stay as I am."

The child leads the visitors to a lift with glass walls. It takes them down a glass-walled shaft to a yard where they enter an old-fashioned Rolls-Royce with a screen dividing passengers from driver. As it speeds to the nearest airport the scientist asks, "Are we still being recorded?"

"What do you mean?"

"Yesterday Endon invited me to have a discreet chip embedded in my neck so that all the maestro said, and (of course) all we said, would be recorded. I refused. You will have received the same invitation. I assume you accepted?"

She turns her head and looks at passing scenery. He sniggers and says, "That question may be taken as proof that I am a loose wheel. You might say you are sorry for my imminent demise, if that would not compromise you."

She says sharply, "Your pessimism is absurd. Endon knows how trustworthy you are."

He murmurs, "A safely ambiguous remark."

A moment later he removes the print from the envelope he carries and studies it. The lawyer does the same with hers, then she says, "Talking of ambiguous remarks, was there no ambiguity in his, *I will stay as I am*?"

"None," says the scientist. "Read this."

He hands her his print. It shows the architect's house at night, the sky above and surrounding pine trees in a variety of velvety blacks and greys, contrasting with bright rooms within the glass walls. The biggest room has a little self-portrait of the architect in his chair, shown from behind. The other rooms are crowded with nearly nude women wearing long black stockings, and men in evening dress with horned heads and scorpion tails growing from their bums. After the architect's signature in the margin beneath is written in neat, forward-sloping letters the scientist's name and the words, *You have chosen rightly.* Having read this the lawyer hands his print back with her own. After her name in the bottom margin the biologist reads, in meticulous backward-sloping letters, \ accept Endon's offer.

THE THIRD MISTER GLASGOW

MR MACBLEANEY, SLIGHTLY FUDDLED, came home by taxi after midnight. A young woman helped him out, helped him up four steps to the front door and, when he started fumbling with his keyring, removed it, unlocked the door, gave the keyring back and pushed him into the lobby. He stood for a moment trying to remember an invitation he had devised in the taxi – "Come in for a drink dear, surely you won't leave an old man alone at this time of night?" – but before recalling these words he heard the front door shut firmly behind him, a distant car door slam and the taxi drive off. He sighed, trudged to the door of his apartment and fumbled in his pocket for the key until the lobby light went out. It had switched on automatically when the front door opened and was usually on long enough for him to unlock the door but now he could not see its keyhole. He trudged back in darkness to the front door, pressed the switch beside it and again there was light. With a pleased chuckle he noticed the apartment key on the ring in his left hand where the girl had placed it – silly of him to have forgotten it was there!

Back at the apartment door he carefully inserted the correct key, tried turning it left without success, then right without success, then jiggled it back and forward many times. For over a year this futile jiggling had lasted longer and longer each time he came home, always making him determined to do something about it, but when the lock yielded and door opened, the matter was no longer urgent. Tonight, after wrestling with the key for what seemed ten or fifteen minutes, Mr MacBleaney decided it would never turn: also his legs were tired. He sighed and leaned against the door, contemplating a rocking chair, the only furniture on the lobby's chequered marble floor. His wife had loved that chair. Its emptiness by the fireside brought her so painfully to mind that he had shifted it to the lobby, and even now was shy of sitting on it. He sat on a low step of the staircase to the upper apartments, pondering.

The apartment key must be worn out by too frequent use, since the copy used once a week by his cleaners gave them no trouble. He seemed to remember his wife had given a spare copy to a neighbour, but that was twenty or thirty years ago. So many neighbours had since come and gone that now all were strangers whose faces he could not remember. Of course they certainly knew him – the third Mr Glasgow – but why should Mr Glasgow know them? As usual, MacBleaney avoided thinking about a difficulty by remembering his fame.

The first Mr Glasgow had been Jack House, a journalist who knew more about the city than anyone else – he had written books on it, *The Square Mile of Murder*, *Heart of Glasgow* and *Pavement in the Sun*. Jack had represented Scotland in *Round Britain Quiz*, a famous radio programme when there were only three British broadcasting channels, none of them commercial. Then had come the second Mr Glasgow – Cliff Hanley, another journalist. He wrote *Dancing in the Streets* and a song that was likely to be voted Scotland's official national anthem by a large majority – *Scotland the Brave*! Or was it *O Flooer of Scotland*? Hanley's catchphrase on a comedy programme, "Sausages is the boys!", always raised a laugh – or had that been Jimmy Logan's catchphrase? Anyway, House and Hanley were both nice men, unlike B … (MacBleaney's mind recoiled from a name he did not wish to remember). Yes, House and Hanley had been nice friendly Mr Glasgows, he had cheerfully drunk and chatted with them several times during his three highly successful careers.

He had started as a footballer, and for two and a half years was Bully Wee Clyde's mightiest outside-left, almost in the Charlie Tully league, though he said so himself. Clyde was not one of Scotland's most famous clubs, but it was one of the most decent, unlike Rangers, whose followers were nearly all True Blue bigots – some of Celtic's Emerald Greens were almost as bad. But early retirement was forced on Bully Wee MacBleaney by a torn ligament too many. A bad time followed when he nearly killed himself with the drink – no wonder his first wife walked out.

The shock of the divorce did him good. He quit drinking. Through Alcoholics Anonymous he met a television producer who needed an adviser for sport reports. MacBleaney turned out to be exactly the right man for Independent Scottish Television. He was soon, as a football commentator, almost as famous as Arthur Montford, though he said so himself. Being younger and handsomer than Montford he had appeared on television commercials and newspaper adverts promoting a brand of shaving cream. He took up golf as a hobby and met his second wife. Their marriage was a big news story with photographs in all the dailies. "Mr Glasgow Weds!" said the *Daily Record*, and "Golfing Gloria Hooks Scotland's Most Eligible Bachelor". This brought an angry postcard from his first wife asking how a divorced alcoholic could be an eligible bachelor. His career as a sports commentator had ended very strangely. For a short spell he had replaced Archie Macpherson in Scottish BBC, then he too had been replaced without learning exactly why. British broadcasting works in mysterious ways.

But by then he had appeared in *Taggart*, the epic Glasgow television detective serial. An episode had a crime during a football game between clubs called Glasgow Rovers and Saint Mungo United. For this he had both advised the writer (who knew nothing about football) and played himself – Rory MacBleaney – the famous sports commentator who helped Taggart solve the murder in the directors' box of Hampden Park stadium. That episode had made television history, in Scotland if nowhere else. After that he had been given parts in several television films and one or two widely distributed London and Hollywood productions – small parts, admittedly, but when producers wanted the friendly sound of a good Scots voice they would often send for Rory MacBleaney, sometimes dubbing his voice onto a younger actor or a character in an animated cartoon. He had also been given a small important part in a film so horrible that, despite the low budget, every subsequent history of the cinema mentioned it. At the London showing a critic said to him …

Mr MacBleaney's memories had been making him feel warm and happy, but now he felt the hard, cold step under his bum and felt tired of life because the critic had said, "You were quite good, but of course they only employed you because they couldn't afford Billy Connolly."

A storm of rage brought him to his feet, stamping up and down the lobby. Billy Connolly was better known than Rory MacBleaney for bad bad bad bad bad reasons. Connolly and his what – partner? second wife? – had been pally with Prince Charles and Diana before the royal divorce, what claim to fame was that? Connolly was not a bad comedian – not as good as Jimmy Logan, though still quite good – but he was not an actor! In his biggest film, *Mrs Brown*, he had played Queen Victoria's Highland gillie with a Glasgow accent! It was the only accent he could do! The English and Americans didn't mind because they think every Scottish accent is the same, but every Scot in the world knew Connolly's voice

was wrong in that part. Connolly must have known his voice was wrong! So he had only taken the part for the money and the fame. How could he stoop so low?
"I could have played John Brown!" said Mr MacBleaney aloud. "Yes, my normal accent too is Glaswegian, but I'm enough of an actor to sound like a teuchter from Drumnadrochit when I want to, yess inteet to gootness Donalt, whateffer. Shimerahaa mahay!"

A fit of coughing made him sit on the step again, no longer happy, because directly or indirectly Billy Connolly was responsible for everything that had gone wrong with Scotland – small shops replaced by supermarkets, local schools and hospitals amalgamated into big central ones, and nobody asked to recall the old ways and speak for elderly marginalised folk. Newspapers no longer phoned the third Mr Glasgow for soundbites on politics and showbusiness; no wonder he had started drinking again. Gloria had foreseen that. When they knew she was dying she had not gone out of her mind (as he had) but calmly discussed their finances with an accountant and lawyer, and made him sign forms so that his home and finances were secure no matter how stupidly he acted. O yes, she had loved him. He wept for a while then began to cheer up again.

The indoors smoking ban had been wonderful for him! At first he thought it would kill him because smoking had made him drink more slowly. It still did because now he went outside to smoke, standing and puffing on pavements with other nicotine addicts. This had given him a new lease of life. Being now a persecuted minority smokers shared a liberty, equality and fraternity unknown to those who skulked in pubs until closing time. He had new friends because of the ban – older folk who remembered him as a footballer, sports commentator, actor, also younger folk who enjoyed his tales of those times. One of these usually brought him home in a taxi, often a woman, though it was hard to remember which – most women under fifty seemed the same equally attractive young woman nowadays. None had stayed the night, yet he still had hopes.

The cold step again reminded him where he was, then a sudden memory made him stand joyfully up. Gloria, in case one of them got locked out, had put a copy of the apartment key on top of the door frame. Being about three inches taller than him she could easily reach it by standing on tiptoe. They had never needed to use that key so it must still be there. A low box or stool was all he needed to reach it, but the hour was far too late to rouse a neighbour and borrow one; he must use the rocking chair. He pushed it over the marble tiles until the hind rockers and chair-back together touched the door, but this left the seat at an angle impossible to stand upon. He turned it round and put the front against the door, but now the back and arms stopped him climbing onto it, so he placed it sideways against the door. Holding onto the doorknob, he managed to kneel on the seat, which still rocked a little. Standing upright was a delicate balancing act. He did it by keeping hold of the doorknob with one hand, grasping the chair-back with the other, and cautiously raising his left leg until the foot was flat on the seat. That done, with equal caution, he began straightening the leg, then gradually raising his body while letting go of the doorknob and reaching upward to –

While doing this something happened so suddenly that he neither understood nor remembered it afterward. For a time he seemed comfortably at home in bed, in a darkness suitable to someone who has wakened in the early hours of a winter morning, yet he seemed to hear people overhead discussing him, though their words made no sense. That did not worry him, and soon he was asleep for good.

THE MAGIC TERMINUS

MY LIFE HAS CONTAINED VERY LITTLE PAIN. Even in childhood the worst I endured was boredom. My parents wanted dull lives because their own had been too exciting. They had belonged to an unemployed industrial class and lived in a slum in fear of having their dole money cut and in equal fear of sectarian violence. My dad's family were Protestant bigots, my mum's equally bigoted Catholics, and joined in matrimony were equally disliked by most of their neighbours. World War Two greatly improved things, bringing employment, fixed wages, regular meals at the price of some danger. Dad fought in North Africa, was injured by a fragment of shrapnel, then found a safer job in the army pay corps. Mum was directed into an underground explosive factory. When reunited after the war he started working in Clydebank for Singer Sewing Machines, she became a steady housewife. I was born when politicians of every party wanted Britain to be a Welfare State for everyone. Only those who had enjoyed great pre-war privileges found this boring, and young folk like me who had never known worse times. I matured before The Beatles were famous and being a teenager became exciting.

But the dull routines of home and school were made bearable by steady doses of art. There were two local cinemas within an easy walk from our home and half a dozen others a cheap tram ride away, so Mum and Dad and me saw three or four films a week – not unusual in these mainly pre-television days – and I saw more, being in the ABC Children's Saturday Film Club. I recently re-read *The Moviegoer*, a novel about a lawyer in New

Orleans who says the greatest moments of his life were not his love affairs, but when Gary Cooper straps on his guns and goes out to face the villains in *High Noon*, or when a cat runs across a dark lane, rubs herself against someone, and a spot of light briefly shows the sinister, slightly babyish smile of Orson Welles in the part of Harry Lime. My own best moments were when a whirling black tornado sucks the grey wooden shack of Dorothy's home up into the sky – when she sees through the window a cow bobbing past, two men rowing a canoe, a bicycle pedalled through the air by the nasty woman who stole Dorothy's dog Toto – when that woman and bike transform into witch on broomstick before the house crashes down – when Dorothy opens the door, and steps out of the grey monochrome bedroom into the full Technicolor land of Oz. In the local public library I found other exciting adventure stories, sometimes horrific but always safer than games played in the school playground. I am not a coward but have always avoided pointless risks. My favourite books had magic openings through which children not unlike me found wonderlands like those Alice entered through a rabbit hole and looking glass. I read Masefield's *Midnight Folk* and *Box of Delights*, also an Enid Blyton series about children finding secret passages into *The Valley of Adventure*, *Castle of Adventure*, *Island of Adventure*, *Mountain of Adventure*. I read several times Dan Billany's *The Magic Door* about an unruly class of primary school children with a silly teacher, Mr Rocket. One of the class finds a bronze doorknocker that, banged on any wall, creates a door into the past through which they meet Julius Caesar, King Arthur and prehistoric monsters. I would have enjoyed *The Lion, the Witch and the Wardrobe* but it was published when I had outgrown childish stories.

Visiting the library had an advantage over seeing films with Mum and Dad, because on the way home together we always cheerily discussed what we had seen, but never referred to erotically suggestive episodes that nowadays would hardly bring a blush to the cheek of the most innocent child. But they greatly excited me in ways I could only enjoy remembering when completely alone, so visits to the library were often more satisfactory. Here I filled my head with exotic fantasies whose only hero was me, daydreams so engrossing that I sometimes woke from them to find I had walked home with no memory of crossing roads busy with traffic. I would have been knocked down had a part of my mind not been unconsciously guiding me by noticing the traffic and traffic signals. It is commonplace for habitual actions to free our minds by becoming automatic, but the extent of my subconscious guidance was unusual, and I found it could be enlarged. Mum told me I had annoyed her friends by not answering their greetings and acting as if they did not exist when I passed them in the street. I promised this would not happen again. It did not. I still returned from the library in a complete daydream, but now unconsciously smiled back and exchanged conventional greetings with her friends.

Ever since I have enjoyed more and more imaginative freedom by making more and more conduct automatic. This meant deliberately learning the fewest words and actions that satisfy employers, after which I could forget and perform them in perfect intellectual freedom because I was truly living elsewhere in daydreams I absolutely controlled. At first their geography was banal and escapist with ancient castles, Oriental cities, Pacific islands, Tarzan jungles and Sherwood forests peopled by ruthless kings, mad scientists, American crime bosses and women who wore very little clothing. Between rising in the morning and undressing for bed at night, the minutes when I noticed what others thought *reality* added up to less than an hour, and only happened when occasional accidents required me to show initiative. I easily passed school examinations, automatically absorbing and regurgitating formulas I was given. Students who failed had either bad memories or a habit of thinking for themselves.

Life since then has been the maintenance of intellectual freedom through work needing no intelligent initiative. I found less than might have been expected in the army, when boys of eighteen were conscripted for two years of National Service. Obeying military rule and orders came easily to me. I must have been robust in those days because I hardly noticed the square-bashing that afterwards left other squaddies exhausted and cursing. This made me unpopular because they thought my indifference to what they most resented was a display of social superiority. Word got about that my father was a senior army officer I had quarrelled with, and that after this spell in the ranks I would enrol for Sandhurst. I became victim of practical jokes too painful to ignore. They stopped after I had thrashed two of the worst bullies. After that I was unpopular but generally ignored, however the continual forced intimacy of barrack life was often hard to shut out. One day I was summoned to an interview with an officer who suggested I apply for an officers' training course. I told him that giving orders would distract me far more than receiving them, and I would be as unwelcome in an officers' mess as I was among privates because I did not want friends to distract me. "Distract you from what?" he asked. He obviously meant well and seemed intelligent, so I explained the scope of my imaginary worlds at that time – a cluster of planets combining ideas got from H.G. Wells' *First Men in the Moon* and Lindsay's *Voyage to Arcturus*, along with some of my own. He listened carefully then passed me to an army psychiatrist who discharged me as unfit for military service.

I then trained as an engineer, mistakenly thinking that those who design machines can also work mechanically. This was partly true at the lowest drawing-board level where the main distraction was office camaraderie. I managed to ignore that, achieving a smooth efficiency that soon led to promotion. In the headquarters of a firm making hydraulic engines I found myself discussing with three others the best design for a casing that must (1) be securely attached by screws and brackets that would not interfere with an interior motor, (2) be easily opened when the motor needed serviced, (3) be easily cleaned, (4) and look good. The discussion of how to satisfy all these requirements was so trivial, boring and endless that I muttered, "Use a tough transparent plastic bubble. Stick it on with polymonochloropolytetrafluroethyline adhesive. When necessary the operator can smash it off with a hammer and stick on a cheap replacement."

I was joking so they laughed until the boss said, "Excellent! Our entire approach has been out of date. Your idea obviously needs refining but you are due for further promotion, my son."

So I left that firm and went north to Aberdeen and the oil rigs. Another mistake. Safety is impossible on these structures if you don't keep looking out for potential accidents. The only industrial jobs I found that paid steady wages for truly mindless toil were on assembly lines. The best was at a belt carrying chocolate biscuits out of a slot to where I tapped them with a little rod, changing their position so that they passed easily through another slot. A newer machine made that job redundant. For years I attached windscreen wipers in a car factory assembly line that eventually closed like every other productive Scottish business. And then I did what I should have done at first: trained as a teacher.

The subject I chose was Careers Guidance, for I thought my previous experience of several different jobs would be helpful. Wrong again. Everyone else on the course had entered straight from secondary school and were learning Careers Guidance without knowing any other career. But at last I have found the social haven

I always wanted. It is a small office in a vast secondary school serving a fifth of Glasgow. Single pupils arrive at twenty-minute intervals throughout the day, each leaving at least five minutes before the next. I ask automatic questions provoking predictable answers that I record by ticking boxes in a standard form. The outcome is always one of seventeen suggestions because there are only seventeen courses possible for people leaving this school. My desk contains a small larder and electric kettle so I need not visit a staff room during tea-breaks and the lunch hour, so apart from the Headmaster and his secretary hardly anyone else in the staff here knows I exist. I will tell you a secret. There is a cupboard in this office to which only I have a key. I have cut down a mattress to exactly cover the floor, where I can now sleep comfortably curled in a foetal position. Since travel to and from the office became pointless I gave up my lodgings, got rid of everything but a few essentials, brought these here and have since never left. I have keys that let me leave and return once a week with essential shopping. The janitor suspects I am here at unauthorised times but pretends not to know because I tip him well. Nothing – not even hostile applicants for careers guidance – interfere with my work of preventing old-fashioned catastrophes.

Many years ago, sick of fictional fantasy, my imaginary worlds became wholly shaped by real history and biography. I now know enough to travel back in time and, using no magic or miracles but my knowledge of the future and some basic physical science, give a few key people enough knowledge to prevent disease and warfare. Using freak tempests and tampering with his compass I stopped Columbus crossing the Atlantic and brought him to the coast of China, which he had set out to find. Europe learned of America in the following century when I had prepared the Mexican and Aztec civilizations to resist conquest by acquainting them with firearms and domesticated horses and vaccines that immunized them against European diseases. The rulers, alas, continued using human sacrifice as a means of limiting their populations, but no Native Americans were exterminated by foreigners and African slaves were never brought to the New World. I am currently preventing the miseries of the British Industrial Revolution by helping James Watt's son (a hitherto neglected historical figure who favoured the French Revolution) to develop clean hydro-electric power so efficiently that by 1850 coal furnaces, steam engines, gas lightings and black Satanic mills were banished from Britain. I have no time to say more about this, except that I am free to enter any room at any time in the past through any door I choose, and I am always welcomed as an entertaining and useful friend by many splendid people, mostly still famous nowadays.

But I must use great care to choose the right door when leaving any of these rooms in the past. I must summarise a short story by H.G. Wells to explain why. I read it when a child and it starts with a child, an unhappy little boy, an orphan lost in a dull London street. Here he finds a strange door admitting him to a sunlit garden where a lovely lady accompanied by tame leopards treats him wonderfully well, making him perfectly happy and at home. She then shows him an album with bright pictures of people who seem to be his parents with a baby which, as it grows older, becomes more like himself as he is now. She turns the pages until at last, fascinated, he sees the picture of himself in the street outside the magic door. She is reluctant to show him the next page but he insists, and when the page turns he *is* back outside in the street. That garden and woman become his most precious memory. He grows up into a man both rich and powerful, twice glimpsing the door again, but always in a wall he is passing on the way to a meeting that will advance his career or, if he does not arrive on time, completely damage it. Whenever he seeks the door after the meetings it cannot be found. He becomes a famous politician at the end of the 19th century when even these used the London Underground, and dies by stepping off a platform in front of a train for no known reason. The story suggests he thought he was stepping through the illusory door, and may have found his lovely garden and spiritual mother on the other side of death. Superstitious rot.

I always hated that end of a fascinating story. I did not want the garden to be an illusion. But when taking leave of a friend in the past nowadays – Jane Welsh Carlyle, William Blake, Charles II or Shakespeare – I usually find a door that is neither part of the room itself or the one by which I re-enter this office. It attracts me strangely though I know it leads to nothing, and when I go through
I will go completely *out* like
a candle flame.

MISOGYNIST

CHILDHOOD MAY CONTAIN everyone's happiest times, though it is hard to live without looking forward to better. That must be why many poor souls believe in heaven. When nearly all British homes were heated by coal fires, I would sprawl on the hearthrug at my mother's feet, warm and safe, playing with treasures from the Button Box while she knitted and read politely romantic stories in *The People's Friend*. The Box was made of solid wood, about a foot square and nine inches high, with a hinged lid. It held buttons of all sizes and colours, beads from broken necklaces, earrings and brooches of what seemed rich jewels but were really coloured glass. There were also dominoes that must have come from grandparents or uncles who died before my birth, since nobody in our house played that game. Some were wooden and black apart from spots of many colours. The rest were pale bone or ivory with black spots, though smaller and more numerous – they went up to double nines instead of double sixes. I arranged the dominoes like the walls of a castle with a city round it where I was king. To mark my royalty Mum pinned to my jersey three medals from the Box, medals with vivid ribbons given to my father for no special action but being in the British army from 1914 to 1918. I then put the brightest jewels in my castle's inmost rooms, and arranged the buttons in the streets outside, pretending they were admiring subjects and regiments of soldiers. Brass buttons were the officers, big coat buttons commanded enemy troops who, after battles, became prisoners in my dungeons or slaves in my factories. Amber and mother-of-pearl beads were princesses to be rescued, though after rescue I could not imagine what to do with them. These power games made me perfectly happy.

Late in the afternoon Mum would sigh, go to the kitchen and prepare the evening meal because Dad would soon arrive. I thought him a red-faced interruption with too loud a voice.

"Well!" he would say, entering and rubbing his hands. "How did things go today?"

Sometimes Mum mentioned a bit of gossip she had heard from a neighbour but usually she sighed and shrugged. Dad, looking down on my hearthrug, would say something like, "Well, General, what battles have you won today?"

I never answered. Over the evening meal Dad told us what he thought an amusing event from his work that day. He was a bookie when that profession was mostly illegal in Britain. Years later he and I became friends and I learned he had only told Mum the least interesting, most innocuous events that befell him. She disliked how he earned his money, though never complained of it. Dad was perhaps always slightly drunk when he came home, which added to Mum's displeasure but made life easier for him. When in bed at night I heard sounds from the living room that were mostly television noises, but sometimes his mumbling voice produced sharp exclamatory notes from Mum. I once heard her yell, "I will *not* see a doctor!", and another time, "I will *not* let you put me away!"

That was before I went to school, learned to please my teachers, make friends and play competitive games. Happy times became shorter but maybe more intense. Having no nostalgia for the old hearthrug game I found my mother's company more and more embarrassing. Education made me a man like many others. I was in the last generation of smart exam-passers who, though children of common labourers, tradesmen, or shopkeepers like Margaret Thatcher, went to university without getting into debt. In the 1970s such graduates were sure of good jobs, so (if by nothing else) I pleased my mother by getting one in local government. Her death soon after was no surprise. She had obviously been sick for years.

On leaving the crematorium I saw Dad did not share the general relief most folk at once feel after a funeral. We went to a pub and had a drink together. This cheered him so little that I blurted, "Why did you love her, Dad?" – a coarse question prompted by recalling no sign that Mum had ever loved *him*. He understood me and said, "Your mother was once a lovely wee girl, and witty, with a very funny sharp tongue. Of course marriage changed her like it changes us all. When you were born she had what they call post-natal depression, but hers never went away. Her life might have been better if a doctor had seen her. Diabetes isn't usually fatal nowadays, but doctors terrified her – she was afraid they would put her in hospital. She might have been happier if I had loved her less. Many women prefer the sort of men who don't like them much. My own dad was that sort. I hated him. Face the fact, son: women cannot help being miserable most of the time. Decent husbands don't complain. I'm no masochist, but I would rather be a hen-pecked wimp than a hen-pecking bully or a wife beater and –" (he showed signs of cheering up) "– my life has not been one long disappointment. I enjoy my job."

Dad's dismal home life may be why I postponed marriage till six weeks ago. Before that I was a serial monogamist with partners who tired of me after a year or two. When we started living together they soon complained that I no longer bought them meals in expensive restaurants, though all were wage-earners who never offered to buy such a meal for *me*. They were surprisingly proprietorial, making me buy new clothes because they said the ones I wore were unfashionable, but really (I think) because my older clothes reminded them of earlier partners. I submitted to this, but found it annoying because men do not need to be fashionable. They often became silent and dour because I had said or done something that I could not apologise for because I did not know what it was. If I begged to be told, they usually replied "There's no point in talking to you," and shrugged their shoulders, like Mum had done. Freud says all men are attracted by women like their mothers. My partners seemed nothing like my mum before they started living with me. They mostly left because they wanted children, for which I have no time. Their departure was generally welcome because they had turned into nags. I resolved never to marry until sure of better company, and meanwhile found satisfaction in a hobby that made me careful with my earnings, though the women called it meanness.

My work in local government brought me a sufficient wage, though I enjoyed it less than Dad enjoyed his. My department gave permission to demolish old properties and build new ones, delaying the process until applicants found discreet ways of bribing us. I intended to be honest at first, like the coal miner who the Labour Party made Lord Mayor of Manchester. He refused to take bribes and died in a common council house. In the 21st century local governments have legalized bribery by frankly saying that only those who pay extra money to the administration will have their business handled swiftly and efficiently. In my time civil servants were just starting to become property owners. Had I refused brown envelopes of banknotes I would have become an unpopular lad who thought himself superior to his colleagues, so would never have been promoted. I helped some poorer folk who could not bribe me, but my hobby needed the extra money. I was saving and searching for my ideal retirement home, a peaceful place in the country. A conversation had given this common British ambition an unusual twist.

A man seeking permission to make structural changes to his house invited me to discuss the matter over a meal in a posh restaurant, which suggested he had something to hide. The house had been the branch office of a bank, still had safety vaults in the basement, and he wanted planning permission to let a foreign firm convert these into deep-freezers – Swedish, Danish or American, I forget which. He wanted this done secretly because (he said) the cost of food is increasing faster than ordinary wages, so by laying in stocks of it now you will always save money in future. Yes, but why the secrecy? This came out as we relaxed with malt whiskies after an excellent dinner. A business acquaintance had recently flown him by private helicopter to a weekend in a remote country house. The house was protected by lethal security devices and a staff of well-paid servants with military training. The larders were stocked with enough frozen food to feed his host, guests and staff for a lifetime. My man said, "I'm not a millionaire but I want some of that security."

He told me that the world is heading for disaster, and powerful folk will do nothing to stop that, because it would make them poorer. They know that money will slowly or suddenly lose value as rising oceans flood the land and more disasters reduce food supplies, so when famine hits the cities, mobs of looters will take over. Millionaires are preparing for this. I said, "It won't happen in our lifetime!"

He said, "Perhaps, but it will come sooner or later."

I am no connoisseur of disaster movies but nodded and hid a smug little smile. I helped the man to get the refrigeration he wanted quietly installed, but knew that if starvation became general, nobody in a town could keep a steady, private food supply a secret from the neighbours.

I was sure civilization would not collapse before I did, but liked the idea of being self-sufficient as prices increased. I looked for a derelict building in an unfashionable district, large enough to be made comfortable but not conspicuous and at least a quarter-mile away from any other home, unless it was a farmhouse. It should have its own discreet source of energy in case electrical supply companies failed. Wind vanes are conspicuous, so water was the answer. At the start of the 20th century every community, large or small, had a mill to grind grain for flour. Robert Louis Stevenson (a great walker) said that leaving Scotland for England was leaving a land of mills powered by rushing streams for one of windmills clacking on hilltops. Imported grain put an end to all those mills, leaving *Milton* (from *mill town*) a frequent place name. I spent unhurried years searching for and listing old mill houses before discovering the right one in a wooded glen. A swift burn flowed past from a moor above, and (amazingly) a narrow steep country road ascended to it from the outskirts of the city where I lived and worked! In less than ten minutes a downhill bike ride could have brought me to a suburban shopping centre. Returning that way would have been nearly an hour-long slog, but by car only five minutes. This little road joined a motorway along which, on sunny weekends, thousands from the city drove miles to visit famous beauty spots, never guessing the quiet beauty so close to them. This was the place for me.

Gradually I had it re-roofed, made waterproof and rot-proof, had the inner walls plastered and painted. After linking it to the national grid I installed an undershot millwheel that, when connected to an electric turbine, could give all the light and central heating I might one day want. I brought my partners to see the place as I improved it, saying this would be my retirement home – an independent kingdom like those I had planned from the contents of the Button Box. They thought this an eccentric hobby, said they could never imagine living there, so I was womanless for two or three years before retirement. In that time I had the living rooms and bedrooms furnished with old-fashioned carpets and wallpapers, installed a modern kitchen and lavatory, filled big cupboards in the cellars with enough light bulbs, toiletries, shoes and other supplies to last if I lived to be a hundred. These stocks meant I would no longer be bothered by expenses or shortages, except in the matter of food. I did not start stocking my large deep-freezers with food because I was seeking a new, more agreeable woman partner than any I had hitherto known, and thought that (whoever she was) she might want a say in our choice of diet. I was sure that such a partner would not be hard to find if I gave the problem as much attention as the preparation of my final home.

Half a year before retirement, I saw that my secretary appeared to be holding back tears. This was surprising. Like earlier secretaries she had been so quietly efficient that I had seldom noticed her. As in most offices, females in mine were generally younger than the men, but for me work and sexual adventure were not connected – my female partners had all been met in pubs when I was slightly drunk. My reaction to my secretary's grief was unusual. I said gently, "Man trouble, Miss Harper?"
She murmured, "Something like that."
As easily as if I had drunk a couple of malts I said, "Come for a meal with me tonight. I'll try to cheer you up without asking questions about your private life, or telling you about mine, which hardly exists. We can talk about films or music or books or childhood memories, but silence won't embarrass me. What do you say?"
For a long moment she stared at me, obviously surprised, then nodded and said yes.
After agreeing on a restaurant and time to meet we completed our office work and separated as usual, but I was hopefully excited. Finding a woman I might marry in the office was like finding the house I had wanted so near the city where I lived. My partnerships with earlier women had started soon after we first bedded each other, as is frequent nowadays. I sensed that this love affair (if it became one) must advance more cautiously. At our meal that evening she left the talking to me, seeming quietly amused by what I said while maintaining a reserve I

respected. As I paid the bill she thanked me in a short, sincere-sounding phrase. I said, "Shall we dine out again next week?"
She replied, "Why not?"
We parted on a handshake, which is how we separated after more dinner dates until one night I asked about her man trouble. She said briskly, "No trouble at all."
"Has he come to heel?"
"He doesn't exist," she said, smiling.
I said, "You're better without him – I'm sure he never deserved you."
To change the subject I described at length the finding of my ideal home and the furnishing of it. She cried out, "I *see*! I *see*!" and giggled. I asked what amused her. She said, "I knew you must have some sort of private life, but this is the first time you've mentioned it."
She asked me more questions until I said, "The topic interests you so I'd better drive you there to see it some weekend."
Which I did, after going there earlier to prepare the place.

The day was bright and windy after a long spell of rain, so the burn was in spate, its gurgles mingling with the thrashing tree branches. The house surprised her. "But won't it be awfully damp?" she asked. I took her inside where the central heating had made the air pleasantly warm with no hint of dampness. I showed her all over, from the upstairs bedrooms to the store cupboards and emergency generator in the cellars, though it was not yet linked to my water wheel. This most aroused her wonder and amusement.
She said, "You seem to have thought of everything, how funny!"
The table in the kitchen above was set for two people, with glasses and a good bottle of wine. I removed a cold, cooked chicken and salad from the fridge saying, "I try to think of everything."
Being the driver I drank only one glass, which was all she

wanted. As we sipped coffees afterward in the living room I said, "Would you like to live here?"
She stared at me. I added, "As a married woman. This is a proposal of marriage."
After a pause she said, "I wouldn't like travelling so far to work in the morning."
I said, "You wouldn't need to work. I am an old-fashioned sort who will thoroughly support the woman I marry."
"Give me time to think about that. You'd better take me home now," she said, and I did.

Would I have escaped what followed if I had tried to kiss her then? Perhaps, but her reserve made such an attempt seem wrong. I drove her to the house she shared with a younger married sister. This was on Saturday. On Monday in the office she agreed to marry me. I will not describe our preparations and the registry office wedding. Neither of us wanted a public ceremony, despite the Victorian quality of our engagement. She never said there must be no sexual intercourse before the honeymoon, but that is what I assumed, and was charmed by such unfashionable modesty. It was passed on a luxury liner cruising the Mediterranean, the first foreign holiday of my life. She had been on trips with friends to Paris, Rome and Barcelona, so I was surprised and slightly hurt that she stayed on board when I went ashore to see Venice, Athens, Istanbul and Cairo, also when she said hardly a word to most of the other passengers. Her social confidence in the office had not prepared me for her lack of it with our dining companions aboard ship. Most were English, and richer than us, and perhaps she felt they would despise her Scottish accent. Yet they obviously found mine entertaining – one of them called it "charming". She made one friend, a younger, shyer girl travelling with a wealthy invalid granny. The granny spent most of the voyage commuting between her cabin and a deckchair. Our cabin had an ample double bed, but as a honeymoon the cruise left a lot to be desired. I hoped this was due to travel sickness, though her chilly remoteness was the only sign of it. But many couples have found their honeymoons less than ecstatic. I thought things might improve when we finally got *home*. "To travel hopefully is better than to arrive," says R.L.S.

Early one morning the ship berthed in Liverpool and I drove us back to the house where we had never lived before. We arrived in the evening of a pleasant summer day with the sun still bright in the sky. Leaving the car at the front door we entered and I was pleased to find thermostats and a time-switch had kept the air at skin temperature. She sat down in the living room and, sounding tired, asked for a gin and tonic. I served her, took the car round and down to the basement garage, unloaded our luggage and unpacked it. Back in the living room I suggested we go to our lounge on the top floor. She said, "Leave me alone for a bit," so I carried my own gin and tonic upstairs. The house is among trees, but their tops before the upper windows are pruned to allow a view of perhaps the widest valley in Scotland. I enjoyed it, sipping my drink until I thought she might have recovered a little from her tiredness. I found her sitting downstairs exactly as I had left her. I said softly, "There's going to be a lovely sunset sky. Come upstairs and see it."

She said, "I can't hear you."

I said the same thing more loudly. She said, "I still can't hear you when you mumble like that."

I said the same thing again loudly, so that she was bound to hear. She turned to me a face as rigid and pale as marble, and in a distinct, monotonous voice said, "As soon as you've got me trapped in this horrible lonely place of yours, you start yelling at me!"

Then she wept passionately, wretchedly, interminably, and I knew her antagonism was powered by a will as unyielding as my own, and
perhaps stronger.

GOODBYE JIMMY

IN WHAT IS BOTH A STUDY AND LABORATORY our Headmaster is contemplating an array of crystalline forms when one of his deputies arrives from a distant province. This visit has been long expected, yet the Head nearly groans before turning enough to give the visitor a mildly welcoming smile and say, "Hullo Jimmy. What brings you here?"

He has the mandarin voice of a working class lowland Scot unlocalized, but not Englished by a university education. His employee answers in a slightly plebeian Dublin accent, "You know well why I'm here. You've stopped answering my emails."

The Head says gently, "I know what they say."

"What use is that if you've no advice to give?"

The Head sighs with a slight shrug of his shoulders.

"Is that meant to be some kind of answer?" demands Jimmy. "Are you giving my wee place up as a bad job?"

The Head contemplates his crystalline models again but cannot shut his ears to the cry, "Then I'm giving it up too! Abandoning that nest of graceless, ignorant self-destructive creatures! Leaving it! Done with it!"

The outcry becomes wild sobs which slowly quieten and end.

After a pause the Head murmurs, "You can't leave that job. You've nothing else to do."

Then he suddenly adds loudly, "Unlike me!", grinning so impishly for a moment that the younger, careworn man seems faced by a mischievous child. A moment later the Head's old serene look returns, and to change the subject he says in a comradely way, "I have my own worries, you see."

"Life on other planets?" asks the visitor dryly.

"Yep!"

"Any luck with it?"

"Nope. I've produced a lot of the usual microbes in submarine volcanic vents, but changes in the chemical environment keep wiping them out before they can even evolve into annelid worms. A planet supporting much life needs a lot of water and some chemical stability. You can't get that without a near neighbour as big as Jupiter to hoover up the huge meteors, a satellite like your moon to grab most of the others. In this universe the chance of getting a planet like that are over a zillion squared to one against."

"But you got one!" says the visitor intensely. "Why turn your back on it – the only world rich with all kinds of life? Some with the brain to grasp your intention and I am not taking about whales!"

"Calm down Jimmy," says the Head kindly.

"I am perfectly calm and stop calling me Jimmy!"

"Do you prefer your earlier titles O'Lucifer? Son of the Morning? Prometheus, bringer of fire?"

The Head is joking. Jimmy says wistfully, "King of the Jews. Prince of Peace."

The Head wags a forefinger, says, "Prince of Darkness! Loki! Kali! Mephistopheles!" – his Scots accent broadens for a moment – "Auld Nick! Well, in my time I've been called a lot of funny names too."

"So why call me Jimmy?"

"It suits my accent."

"Why sound like a Scot?"

The Head sighs, looks gloomy, at last says, "I still get messages from that world of yours, messages from desperate people who want help. They demand help! These impossible demands ..."

He hesitates.

"They're called prayers," Jimmy tells him.

"You should stop them reaching me! These impossible demands ... are mostly from mothers."
"Mothers worry you," says Jimmy accusingly. The Head strongly counter-attacks.
"I cannot break physical laws that keep this universe running! I cannot stop fire or fiery chemicals hurting babies and wee kids because their skin is burned off by homicidal idiots obeying orders! When I answer ..." (he hesitates) "... prayers in a Scots accent they know I am not a loving father who will work miracles. They know they havnae a hope in hell."
"Then why not sound American? Like Dubya?"
There is a globe of the world within reach. The Head touches a northern continent upon it, saying sadly, "Don't depress me. I once had hopes of America."
"Why not sound," asks Jimmy brightly, "like a former Scottish Prime Minister? The war criminal who goes around claiming to be one of your greatest fans."
The Head covers his face with his hands, muttering, "Please don't sicken me. We supernaturals are only heard when we use other folk's voices. You sound Irish because you like to be liked and (IRA apart) the southern Irish voice usually does sound friendly to people outside Ireland. But God the Father must sook up to *naebody*! *Naebody*!"

After a pause Jimmy says calmly, "Do you sound Scottish to me because I haven't a hope in hell?"
"Yes!" says the Head looking straight at him. "But it won't stop you saying what you're here to say so say on, Macduff."
Jimmy holds out a sheaf of printed papers saying, "Read these emails you ignored."
"No. Bin them. I know what they say because I know everything. Everything."
"But you won't attend to everything so attend to these!"
The Head says patiently, "They say the world's richest governments have the power to kill everything bigger than

a cockroach, and are still buying even more destructive weapons to fight wars in any land that resists letting them take its natural resources. These governments still sometimes say their warfare defends democracy. They used to say it defended Christianity and free trade. All lies of course. What did you want me to do, O Prince of Peace? Intervene personally?"

"I do."

"That never works. I gave Moses a few good rules everybody should observe – Don't kill, don't steal, don't tell lies. Many mothers still teach that to their kids. But then came law makers with exceptions to my rules – You must kill when governments tell you to, and can steal from men, women and children when governments let you take their land, and must not tell truths when governments say truths are dangerous. Also adulteresses should be stoned to death. Had I said to Moses, *This I command thee, do what the hell you like!* human history would have been just as bloody."

"Nobody thinks your law against killing applies to foreigners," says Jimmy mournfully.

"You did your best to correct them about that, my …"

The Head hesitates. Jimmy looks hard at him until he goes on to say, "… my good man. Yes, you told them to love their neighbours as themselves and their enemies too. Don't fight the people who oppress you, but refuse to kill, steal or lie for them."

"Good words to spread," says Jimmy sadly.

The Head starts to speak, hesitates again then says in an embarrassed way, "There is something I've wanted to ask. When you were … hanging there …"

"I was nailed," says Jimmy flatly.

"Yes. And you told someone in the same state that he would go to heaven with you. Why?"

"He talked kindly to me," says Jimmy shrugging and spreading his hands. "I wanted to be kind back. Should I have told him there is as little justice in heaven as on earth? My body was in such pain that I forgot it was temporary. I

was delirious. Up to almost the very last minute I was mad enough to think you might save everyone who suffered unjustly, and save them ... through *me*!"
He gives a desperate chuckle. The Head assumes the manner of a schoolteacher and says, "If I only existed to give eternal sweeties to good folk and eternal beltings to bad, goodness would be cheap. There would be no decency, no heroism in it. I love heroism and you were a hero. I am proud of what you told people and what you endured for telling them."
"You didn't need heroism to be crucified," Jimmy tells him grimly, "the Romans did it to hundreds of thousands. From the start of history down to the present day millions of children, women and men have endured worse deaths for no reason at all – just because they were born in unlucky places."
Says the Head consolingly, "Your words comforted many unlucky people, especially slaves and women."
"O yes!" cries Jimmy. "And when my comforting words were made official by the Roman Empire and even policemen were christened, my Christians began murdering neighbours with different Gods and burning down their temples and synagogues. My Jesus was as big a flop as your Moses, which is why I want you to ..."
"Suddenly!" the Head interrupts, snapping his fingers. "Suddenly, simultaneously appear on every television and computer screen on the planet announcing, *You shall love the Lord your God with all your heart and all your soul and all your mind, and your neighbour as your self or You! Will! Be! Ex! Ter! Min! Ated!* They would treat me as a rogue virus Jimmy."
"You don't understand," says Jimmy shaking his head. "I *want* you to exterminate all the brutes."
"Say that again," says the Head, surprised.
"Exterminate all the brutes. Now."

The Head sighs, stares at his crystalline forms as if looking for help there, then mutters, "Michty me. Crivens.

Jings Jimmy don't be so damned biblical. I am not the genocidal lunatic described in Genesis. I never made a deluge that drowned everyone except a single family of each species. I did *not* burn Sodom and Gomorrah with fire and brimstone out of heaven."

"But you wiped out most of the dinosaurs and the saltwater plankton. You smothered Pompeii and Herculaneum in volcanic ash."

The Head says patiently, "A wholly stable planet is physically impossible. Even with Jupiter and the moon to shield it, an asteroid the size of Dundee is bound to hit the earth every thirteen million years or so. The dinosaurs lasted a lot longer than that. They had a fair innings. Six and a half million years will pass before the next meteoric disaster – plenty of time for folk to learn how to stop it. And it is not my fault when men build cities beside a volcano. Your job was to stop folk blaming me for things priests and insurance companies once called Acts of God – floods, earthquakes, plagues and epidemics caused by ignorance of safe cultivation and hygiene. And you cured that ignorance!"

"O yes!" says Jimmy bitterly, covering his face with his hands. "I encouraged Bacon and Galileo when ignorance seemed to be the main problem and good scientists were thought black magicians or heretics. And now natural science is triumphant."

"Exactly," says the Head, nodding. "Educated folk no longer blame you and me for everything bad. That is a definite step in the right direction. I refuse to wipe out life on earth because my agent there who should encourage it is tired of it."

"But I love life on earth! I want you to save it by quickly destroying only one kind of brute – the most selfishly greedy kind. Get rid of men, please, before they destroy every other living thing."

The Head smiles, says, "If mankind heard you now they really would think you ..." (he holds out both hands with his fingers curved like claws) "... Bee! El! Zi! Bub!"

"You know what I'm talking about," says Jimmy, again shaking the sheaf of printouts at him.

"Atmosphere overheating from diesel fumes," says the Head, obviously bored. "Glaciers, icecaps melting, sea level rising. Forests felled, land impoverished. Pure water tables shrinking or polluted. Drought increasing where forty per cent of folk suffer malnutrition and billions will die of famine and thirst."

"Primitive Christians were right," says Jimmy passionately. "Scientists *are* black magicians. Nearly all of them work for corporations tearing up the fabric of earthly life with the help of governments they have bribed. Half the animals alive fifty years ago are now extinct. Frogs and sparrows are nearly extinct. The bumble bees are dying. Some conscience-stricken biologists are freezing the sperm of threatened creatures so that they can be brought back to life when the earth is governed sanely. Mankind will never govern it sanely."

With a tolerant chuckle the Head says, "Aye, men have always been great wee extinguishers. Remember North America at the end of the last big ice age? A vast forest of deciduous trees with nothing dividing them but lakes and rivers and rocky mountains. It was the home of the biggest most peaceful vegetarians we ever achieved – titanic browsers, tree-sloths as big as elephants. The first men who entered that continent across the Bering Strait had never dreamed of so much easy meat. Killing bears and woolly elephants in Eurasia was dangerous work, but men easily took over America. The tree-sloths couldn't run away, couldn't run at all, didn't need to be trapped. Set fire to the trees and you had several roasted tree-sloths burned out of their pelts in a gravy of their own melted fat. The number of North American men expanded hugely – for two generations they were too busy eating to kill each other – they gorged themselves all the way down to Mexico!"

Seeing that Jimmy is staring at him in disgust he says, "Cheer up. That's how the prairies came about, with room for herds and herds and herds of buffalo."

"Which the white men slaughtered because the red men lived off them. But you know things are a lot worse now. Farmers are sowing genetically modified crops that die as soon as harvested, so they must buy new seed from companies that patented them, while plants folk used to feed on vanish for ever. Soon the only live creatures left on earth will be humans and the mutants they eat."

In a sing-song voice, grinning, the Head says, "Remember the viruses, Jimmy! They too are busy wee mutaters. People are great breeding grounds for viruses, especially people eating battery-farmed meat and mutant vegetables." With genuine regret he murmurs, "Croak croak. A pity about the frogs."

"Are you fond of the Barrier Reef?" asks Jimmy, desperately.

"My greatest work of art, one thousand, two hundred and fifty miles long," says the Head reminiscently. "A masterpiece of intricately intertwined fishes, plants, insects with the beautiful vivid colour variety of all the great pictures painted by Matisse and Dufy, and a refinement of detail greater than even Paul Klee achieved." He shakes his head in wonder at the thought of his own genius.

"It's dying," says Jimmy. "It'll all be gone in thirty years unless men die first."

The Head shrugs his shoulders, says, "Nothing lasts for ever," and turning, contemplates his crystals as if nothing else mattered.

"What use are you?" demands Jimmy suddenly.

The Head, amused, smiles at him kindly but does not reply until the question is enlarged: "What do you do while failing to develop annelid worms in submarine volcanic vents?"

"I'm preparing a better universe."

"Where?"

"Outside this one."

"How can you make a universe outside this one?"

This brings out the Head's schoolteacher side. Wagging a forefinger, with increasing enthusiasm he says, "If you subscribed to *Scientific American* you would know how other universes happen. Every universe is like a carpet with a gigantic draught blowing underneath, so in places it gets rippled up into peaks where energy and mass are so concentrated that BANG, a hole is blown in the fabric through which mass-energy pours, making another universe where physical laws can bend differently."
"What makes that draught?" says Jimmy keenly.
"Would you think me a megalomaniac if I told you it was my breath?" asks the Head, slyly watching him sideways.
"Yes."
"I have to use metaphors when describing universal processes," says the Head impatiently. "If you don't like breath-blown ripples call them ... call them labour pains if you like, but the result could be a universe where planets are this shape."

From a bench he lifts a variously coloured prism and hands it over. Jimmy looks at it then says unbelievingly, "A *pyramidal* planet?"
"You are wrong. A pyramid has five sides, with four isosceles triangles on a square base. This planetary model is a tetrahedron with only four triangular sides, four equal continents. Get the idea?"
"No."
"Look at it closely. Four glacial polar regions at the apex of each continent. Water trickles down from these to form an ocean in the middle of each surface – four Mediterranean seas of roughly equal size where life will evolve, and when it takes to land around the shores it will find none large enough for an empire to grow. All the nations that occur will be small and coastal, like Scandinavia."
Jimmy examines the prism closely then says, "I see some off-shore islands. The British Empire spread from an island."
"An island with a lot of coal and iron where James Watt devised the first commercial steam engine. In my new

world fossil fuel deposits will be equally dispersed. No gold rushes! The machines people invent will have to be powered by wind and water and oil from plants that can be grown, harvested and replanted."

Jimmy says, "The shape of this thing makes it gravitationally impossible."

"Only in this universe!" cries the Head. "I am preparing a liquid universe where heavenly bodies will be gravitationally formed by *crystallization*! Imagine galaxies of tetrahedral planets revolving round octahedral suns! A universe – " he ends by murmuring dreamily, "– with no big bangs and collisions."

"But how can a planet have seas in a universe full of liquid?"

"My universal fluid will be as light as air! In fact it will *be* air! I will make it air!"

Inspired by the idea he hurries to a blackboard with chemical formulae chalked on it, seizes a chalk and writes *N-78. 1%,* then heavily underlines it saying, "When my heavenly bodies have crystallized, these chemical constituents must remain."

He starts chalking down a new column of figures, muttering, "This universal ... solution ... will make flight between worlds easy. No need for people ... to blast themselves ... across light years of dreary sub-zero vacuum."

He flings the chalk down and contemplates the formulae with something like smugness. Jimmy says, "But ..."

"You are going to tell me, Mr Prometheus O' Lucifer, that air is largely oxygen exhaled by vegetation, and how can I grow enough plants to fill a universe with it? But my next universe will start with a big splash instead of a big bang, and the initial chemistry will be wholly different."

He sits down, folds his arms and looks triumphant. Jimmy, not impressed, turns the tetrahedral model in his hands saying, "Okay Mister Sly-boots Clever-clogs, I was also going to ask about this planet's angle of rotation." He hands the model back, says, "It will have to perform intricate somersaults if one of your triangular continents is not to be in perpetual twilight."

"That is certainly a problem," says the Head agreeably, putting the model back on the bench. "I am working on it."

"So how long will it take you to get this ... airy new universe up and running?"

"I have eternity," says the chief, smiling to himself.

"You will spend eternity dreaming up a Utopian universe while mankind destroys life on earth in a couple of generations?"

"That's nonsense Jimmy!" says the Head consolingly. "Men cannot destroy *all* life on earth, only themselves and equally complex creatures. In which case insects will inherit the earth while vegetation recovers and then ..." (he becomes enthusiastic) "... from the segmented worms you and I will evolve a wealth of new creatures with different organs and sensations and minds. I never repeat my mistakes. It was maybe a mistake to give big brains to mammals."

"Why deny intelligence to creatures who suckle their young?"

"Freud thinks it makes them unhealthily dependent and unhealthily greedy. Why not try hatching big intelligences from eggs? Birds, in general, seem happier than people. Tropical birds are as colourful as the organisms in my Great Barrier Reef, and the world will become a very tropical planet when men have made it too hot to hold them."

"But!" says Jimmy explosively. The Head swiftly interrupts him.

"You are about to say bird brains are too small for development because their necks are too thin, but owls have short thick necks and are notoriously brainy. One day you may fly up to me in the form of a dove with an eagle's wingspan and find me a gigantic owl ..." (he spreads his arms) "... with feathers as colourful as a parrot's. Pretty polly!"

"And is that the most comforting message I can take back to the few on earth who listen to me? The few who care for the future of life there?"

The Head says mildly, "You recently asked me to exterminate the human race and now you want me to send it comforting messages."

"Not comforting messages but useful messages. When I asked you to exterminate humanity I was trying to goad you into suggesting a new way of saving them." (He sighs.) "But of course you knew that."

"I did," says the Head, nodding. "But the only ways humanity can save itself is by old things that come in threes."

"Faith, hope and love," says Jimmy glumly.

"Yes, but these can only work beside liberty, equality, fraternity."

"Jesus, Mary and Joseph!" raves Jimmy. "What are you on about? I've been so mixed up with ... post-modern people that I've forgotten."

"Liberty is not having to obey other people because they are richer than you."

"Equality?"

"Is what everybody enjoys with friends, or in nations where everyone knows they need each other."

"Fraternity?"

"Brotherhood. The brotherhood of man."

"Exclusively masculine?"

"A good point Jimmy. Call fraternity love also, the love that still makes your earth the centre of the present universe."

"Don't talk shite!" yells Jimmy. "My wee world is near the edge of an average galaxy among a million million galaxies! I helped Galileo destroy the Jewish notion that the whole shebang was made for them. How can my wee world be a universal centre?"

The Head says patiently, "Wherever somebody opens their eyes is the centre of the universe and your earth is still the place where a lot of that happens. I hoped mankind would take life to my other worlds. They have the technology." (He shrugs.) "If they use it to destroy themselves we'll start again with another species. To-wit-to-woo. Pretty Pol."

Jimmy slumps down, looking defeated. Our Head rubs his hands together, goes to him briskly and claps him on the shoulders saying brightly, "Since we now see eye to eye I must waste no more of your valuable time. Tell folk the competitive exploitation of natural resources is a dead end. Nuclear power, used wisely, will give access to all the space, raw material and energy they need without fighting aliens for it. Less than five miles beneath the earth's surface is heat that, rightly channelled, will drive their machines without poisonous emissions."

Without appearing to use force he raises Jimmy and accompanies him to the exit saying, "Fossil fuels should be exclusively used as fertilizer, and housewives when shopping should use net bags instead of the plastic sort which add to the price of what they buy. Goodbye Jimmy."

"Nobody with wealth and power will believe me if I say that! They know the damage they are doing to the planet but they're still extending motorways! Making and selling cars! Nobody owning one will change to a bicycle! Nobody who can fly will go by boat! Owners of companies wrecking the ecosphere are buying self-sustaining bunkers where they and their like can survive when everyone else is poisoned!"

"They won't survive," says the Head, chuckling. "Only folk who want to save others too have a chance. Perhaps." Now he certainly propels Jimmy to the exit, adding with what sounds like mischievous encouragement, "Workers of the world unite! Remind them of co-operative Socialism! Owen, William Morris, James Connolly!"

"I'll be laughed at," moans Jimmy.

"Then all laughter will become screams of hysterical

despair. Send me all the emails you like but don't come here again for a millennium or two. Goodbye son."

"Son!" says Jimmy on the threshold. "I'm glad you … sometimes … admit I'm in the family."

"Goodbye son," says the Head, quietly for once, "and good luck."

"Which is not something you need, Dad," says Jimmy, and leaves.

The Head returns to contemplate the crystalline models and formulae on his blackboard, seeming almost despondent. He is sorry that it is so hard to show his love for those who love him most. The rest are not so demanding. And why does Jimmy think he needs no luck? Is it because, as Headmaster of all, there is supposed to be no greater power? He hums a little song to himself, "I'll give me one-o. What is my one-o? One is one and all alone and ever more shall be so."

After a pause he sadly says, "One is one and all alone and ever more shall be so."

In the place where he sits another presence becomes apparent, one that stands so much higher than he that its voice seems from above, a gentle, female, slightly amused voice saying, "You silly wee man."

"Mother?" he asks wistfully.

VOICES IN THE DARK

THE DARKNESS IS SO COMPLETE that only steady continual snoring suggests this is a bedroom. Then come muffled clicks, a sliding sound, thumps of someone coming stealthily through a window. A narrow beam of light pierces the dark from what can be dimly seen as a slit between curtains. The beam swings from side to side until it fixes on the foot of a big bed where the snorer lies, then explores sideways to light on a bedside table with many bottles on it. The source of the beam comes through the curtains. It is a torch in the hand of a black thin figure who advances carefully to the bedside table, crouches on the floor, then switches on a table lamp among the bottles before turning off and pocketing the torch. The light now, though not great, shows the head of the snorer half sunk in plump pillows. It is old and mostly bald, with clumps of white hair behind the ears. This man is called Rudi. Behind him is an elaborately carved bed head with a large letter F surrounded by a laurel wreath both under a layer of cracked gold leaf. The rest of the room also suggests palatial splendour down on its luck. The croucher at the bedside wears black canvas shoes, pants, anorak, woollen hood with eye slits and holds a gun pointed at the sleeper's head. With the other hand she pulls the hood off, and now is a tiny, haggard, desperate woman of any age between thirty and fifty. She listens carefully for sounds outside the room, but only those from the sleeper's nose are audible, so at last she reaches over with her free hand and pinches the nostrils shut.

His mouth opens and he starts breathing through it

noisily. She whispers fiercely, "Wake up!"

He does not. Releasing his nose she slaps him lightly on the cheek saying, "Wake up! Wake up!"

Even this has no effect. She slaps him much harder, says, "Waken you old fool!"

Not opening his eyes he mutters, "Um. Eh?"

"I have told you to waken."

"Impossible," he murmurs drowsily. "The sleeping pills I am given no longer work, it is true, but I reinforce them with alcohol. What time is it?"

"Three a.m."

"Well, before midnight, on top of my pills, I consumed a bottle of 90% proof absolute alcohol so you cannot possibly have wakened me at three a.m. Go away."

She prods his head with the gun saying sternly, "Open your eyes. This hard thing pressing your ear is the barrel of a revolver."

"Ouch," Rudi grunts, then adds thoughtfully, "Yes, it feels like one, but dreams sometimes contain strong sensations. I once dreamed I was eating a buttered roll, the loveliest experience of my life, a memory of the birthday present my mother gave me when I was two or three. That was during the German occupation. Everyone except the Germans were hungry then, even though the Jews and Gypsies had gone. My mother ..." (he sobs) "... my mother must have loved me a lot to have given me a whole buttered roll and not eaten half of it herself. Leave me alone."

He turns away from the light, trying to bury his head in the pillow, but she slaps his cheek so hard that he cries, "Huh!"

"Was that not more real than the dream of your mother's buttered roll?"

He says sulkily, "No. It was not."

She slaps again much harder.

"Yes!" he says, sitting up a little. "Yes indeed, that would almost convince me that I'm awake if this house were not surrounded by guards and alarm systems and all kinds of clever devices installed by Americans, the best people in the world for such contraptions. My dear, I regret disappointing you but you must be a hallucination. Nobody real could penetrate the impregnable security fence protecting me from—"

Loud knocking on the door is followed by a muffled voice saying, "Sir! Sir! Are you all right?"

Rudi sits up straight, showing he is unusually tall and unusually thin. He shouts, "Of course I'm all right! Can the President of Fredonia not enjoy a Shakespearean soliloquy and talk to himself without a God-damned bodyguard interfering? I have all the protection I need – in fact more than I want. Avaunt and quit my door. Vanish, abscond, absquatulate, begone. Shut up, pipe down, retreat and have a heart, as the Yanks say. Have peeety on your so-o-o-oul, as Dostoevsky would have said. Leave me in peace do you hear? Do you hear?"

The voice outside mutters, "Yes sir."

"But I don't *want* to hear you," yells Rudi. "Eff off, as the English say!"

A little later he cries, "Have you gone?", waits for half a minute, then chuckles and says, "Relax my dear. He's gone."

The visitor has been standing upright with legs apart, gun at arm's length pointing at the door. She now pulls a chair to the bedside, sits down and tells him, "You're a smart old bastard. You knew I'd have shot you if you'd called him in."

Rudi sinks back on his pillows, sighs, says, "Why should you not shoot me? I'm useless. Useless to myself, useless to my nation, useless to the world."

"But a tyrant to your people," she coldly tells him.

"You do me too much honour, my dear. I drove that servile security guard away because I was enjoying our conversation about appearance and reality. Do you know that in Western Europe and the U.S.A. nowadays, post-modern philosophy teaches that all external realities are mere opinions, all different but all equally valid?"

"Decadent bourgeois obfuscation," she says savagely.

Delighted he cries out, "I love these old Marxist phrases! After the Russians drove out the Germans I became the most dedicated Communist medical student in Fredonia. My speeches denounced Capitalist Lackeys, Neo-Fascist Warmongers, Bourgeois Hyena Cannibals and even (God forgive me) Unproductive Social Elements Deserving Elimination. I hailed the coming day when the Revolution would be Complete and The State Would Wither Away. These stale phrases rang in my ears like trumpets in the ears of Crusaders galloping out to exterminate infidels. Please tell me your name."

After a moment she says shortly, "You may call me Vera."

He begs softly, "Vera, join me in bed."

Astonished she cries, "You dirty old sod."

"Please don't mistake me my dear. I've been completely impotent since the People's Socialist Republic put electric currents through my testicles. The pressure of a friendly woman's body can no longer excite me, but it would soothe me. Nobody has soothed me since my arrest by the old regime. Time for another drink. Have some too."

She scornfully refuses. Rudi shrugs, grasps a bottle of vodka, fills a tumbler, sips, then says, "You must have a reason for breaking in. What is it, Vera?"

"I need to know why you betrayed us."

"Betrayed who?"

"The people of Fredonia."

He says mildly, "It is they who let me down – not the common people of course, who gained nothing from the collapse of the old regime but permission to say what they liked. But lawyers and businessmen, civil servants and local politicians, journalists and broadcasters seem happy with Grolsh in charge."

"Grolsh? Who is Grolsh?"

The president stares at her, says, "The man who runs Fredonia."

"Liar! The Mafia rules Fredonia."
"It could not rule us without local help, Vera. Grolsh and the Sicilian Godfathers co-operate like lock and key. Like many sadists he is a good family man, and knows it is unwise to be a well-known public figure. He never let the old Party bosses promote him above the rank of privileged State Security thug, so when the Communist regime collapsed, only those he had personally tortured ... people like me knew how vile he is and – and – and ..." (he shudders) "...we hate recalling that."
He tries to empty the glass down his throat, but his teeth chatter on the rim and half the drink spills on his pyjama jacket. Stretching a trembling hand to the nearest full bottle he begs in a whisper, "Please Vera. Please. Please."
She lays her gun on the table, lifts the bottle, sighs, takes the empty glass from his hand and pours in a small measure of vodka. Handing to him she says gloomily, "You should drink less."

Her action does him good. He stops trembling, smiles at the glass in his hand, sips very little then says, "You care about politics so must belong to some little party or other. Which?"
"We call ourselves The Decembrists."
"After the group who planned to assassinate the Russian Czar in 1825?"
She nods and explains, "We would have preferred a name recalling the great Soviet Revolutionaries of 1917, but their achievement went bad under Lenin, turned rotten under Stalin, collapsed under Gorbachev. So we chose the name of that earlier lot."
"Who also failed."
"Yes, but Pushkin nearly joined them and Tolstoy admired them."
Chuckling he says, "So you broke in here to assassinate the Czar of Fredonia! You nearly succeeded. I might have died of a heart attack."

"I did not *want* to kill you," cries Vera, distressed. "I once loved you. You were my hero when I was a tiny girl."

Seriously and sadly Rudi whispers, "O dear."

She tells him, "You gave hope to so many of us with that speech you made in the seventies. My mother and father …"

"Don't remind me," he begs but she raises her voice: "My mother and father listened to you on the radio with tears wetting their faces. You said the People's Republic of Fredonia would now take her own unique path to Democratic Socialism. All censorship was now abolished. Everywhere we would be allowed to say what we thought about *everything*."

She leans so far forward that her hair falls down to hide her face and she puts a hand on the bed to support herself. He pats it gently, quietly singing in a cracked voice a line of their national anthem: "Hail, hail Fredonia, land of the free", then switches to another song once popular with Socialists: "For all that, and all that, it's coming yet for all that, that man to man the wide world o'er shall brothers be for all that."

Vera sits up and says abruptly, "I am a woman."

"In a true democracy, women count as men."

"Then count me out."

"Why?"

"You retracted everything you said in that great speech."

"I was an idiot then, Vera," he mourns, "not a liar. I believed every word of that speech. Under Communism from time to time many leaders announced that the old rules were softening to let freedom in. Even Chairman Mao announced that a thousand flowers would be allowed to contend. Fools who acted on these announcements soon learned their mistake. I was a simpleton who believed what Khrushchev said about a thaw …"

"It was Brezhnev."

"So it was. I was then the Commissar in charge of National Health, and at once ordered that every political dissenter who had been registered insane should be released from our lunatic asylums. I declared this over the radio as a reason for public rejoicing. An hour later I was strapped to an operating table with electric wires attached to parts of me that – that – that I will not embarrass an attractive young woman by mentioning."

"You've already told me what parts."

"I must be senile if I told you that, but yes, it happened. Two days later I announced that my previous speech had been the result of a mental breakdown, and that I was retiring from politics for the good of my health. That was certainly true. I remained under house arrest until the Soviet Union collapsed."

"We all knew you had been coerced into taking back that announcement. And a man called Grolsh coerced you? And you handed power over to him when we elected you President?"

"Grolsh is not totally evil, Vera. He has more wives and children than he can support out of his private fortune, even with Mafia backing, so has not wholly dismantled our Welfare State. Single mothers still receive family benefits. Our health service is not wholly privatised. I am the doctor who mainly founded it in 1947. Surely some of it still functions, my little Decembrist?"

"Don't change the subject!" cries Vera. "You were elected President in 1990 because you were the only politician who had tried to defend Democracy under the Communists. We still loved and trusted you then."

"And rightly!" he cries, greatly excited. "I declared over the radio that Fredonia would become Europe's first democratic Socialist nation. Shops and small businesses and collective farms would be given to the folk working them. Big state businesses would become co-operatives owned and managed by their employees. Water, mineral resources, energy, newspapers, education and, above all, justice would be maintained for the people's benefit by the people working them with the support of their elected parliament. No wonder people cheered and cheered and cheered that speech."

"Fraud. Hypocrite. Whited sepulchre," says Vera. "Why did you go back on all that?"

"I never did. That is why they keep re-electing me."

"You must know the election results are faked," she states with huge contempt.

Sighing he says, "They must be, with old Grolsh in charge."

"But *why* is he in charge? Why has nothing you promised to do happened? Everything in Fredonia now belongs to global corporations and the international Mafia. More and more young people nowadays are drug addicts and vandals. Disease, crime, deaths in police custody are always increasing. The streets are full of beggars and most of us are poorer than we were under the Communists."

"True!" says Rudi nostalgically. "Under that regime there was widespread social equality for everyone who was not a Party member. It was equality of scarcity of course. Shoppers stood in queues for hours. Most folk had only four or five really satisfying meals per week. But we had no beggars and nobody starved because nobody was penniless. There was full employment because everyone without a productive job was paid by the state to spy on their neighbours."

"Are you defending the regime that scorched your balls off?"

"No," says Rudi, sighing.

"Then why has Fredonia got worse since you became our President?"

Rudi shakes his head in bewilderment and says, "I don't know. I signed documents making it legal for plumbers to own their own shops and farmers to own their own fields, and in swarmed middle men – brokers – there is an unpronounceable French name for such people ..."

"Entrepreneurs," Vera tells him.

"These entry-pruners swarmed in and asset-stripped the whole nation. I kept announcing that this should not be happening, but that did not stop them and nobody else I knew tried to. A President's speeches cannot change history when his lawyers, judges, civil servants with everyone else in his government *and* official opposition are being bribed by global companies while being openly paid out of the public purse. So I became what I am – a hollow figurehead, more useless than a scarecrow. Scarecrows at least keep predatory birds away from grain that is needed for bread. I am a sham, Vera. You are right to despise me, but …"

He is interrupted by music.

The opening chords of the Fredonian national anthem sound near, but muffled. Rudi says, "Excuse me a moment," takes a phone from beneath his pillow, presses a button on it, says, "Yes?" and presses another button which makes the caller's voice loud enough for Vera to hear. It says, "Rudi. Grolsh speaking."

"Why?" asks Rudi.

"I want a word with you."

"Say it."

"I must say it to your face. Now. At once."

"Why?"

"Rudi, there is a national emergency. Very serious. Very urgent."

"Oho! Where exactly are you, Grolsh?"

"Outside your bedroom door."

Vera, springing up, seizes her gun and again points it straight at the door. Rudi, amused, says, "At four in the morning? What a busy bee you are. But of course, that is the usual hour for security forces to grab a government's political enemies. I hear that the British police now arrest asylum seekers at this hour."

Grolsh says, "Please! I am not here to arrest you but please, we must now talk."

"I will call you in when I have adjusted my clothing," says Rudi merrily. Switching off the phone he tells Vera, "You can hide in bed with me or under it. I suggest in, on the far side."

He pulls his long legs up to make a tent-like bulge under

his duvet, then flings them back on the side opposite the bedside table. Vera frowns grimly for a moment, nods, goes round the bed and slips in with him. He covers her small body with the duvet without straightening his legs, then warbles in a loud sing-song, "Enter, Comrade Grolsh."

The door is opened by someone who enters and closes it carefully behind him. He looks like any European or American businessman, in an expensive suit that does not fit him very well. He approaches the bed and, sitting in the chair where Vera sat, clasps his hands between his knees and stares gloomily at the floor. Rudi, pleased to see him like this, says, "Care for a drink?"

Grolsh nods.

"Then help yourself."

Grolsh fills a tumbler near to the rim with vodka, swigs from it and says, "This building has been the President of Fredonia's residence since the time of Looper Firefly in 1933. Even then this was the President's bedroom. Did it never occur to you that State Security would have this room bugged?"

Rudi, chuckling, says, "Strange as it may seem, it never did."

Grolsh, sighing, says, "I know that Vera Zazulich, leader of the Decembrist group, is somewhere near with a gun she will shortly point at my head."

Vera, uncovering, sits up gun in hand as he predicted and tells him, "Yes, *Comrade* Grolsh, I have just learned that you are mainly responsible for the present state of Fredonia. If you call in your henchmen I will certainly put a bullet in your brain."

Grolsh shrugs and says, "Had I feared that I would have sent them in before me. A sudden clean death by bullet is the least I fear nowadays."

Laughing heartily, Rudi says, "The poor fellow must be in serious trouble, Vera. Who is after you, Grolsh? Will they attach electrodes to your genitals? Or work all over you with pliers and a blowtorch?"

"Don't joke!" says Grolsh, wincing. "Yes, I am in trouble, and a deal with you two may be my only way out of it. And I promise both of you will benefit hugely by playing ball with me because Grolsh is a man of his word."

"I am past playing ball games Grolsh, but go on! Go on! You are beginning to interest us. To your health Comrade!"

Rudi, stretching out, clinks his glass against that of Grolsh who glumly swigs from it, sighs and says, "I wish I had left Fredonia in 1989 but it was never easy to take currency out of a Communist nation. In the rest of the world any corrupt politician or businessman can open a big account in a Zurich bank, but left-wing regimes were notoriously stingy. Then came the Liberal Revolution that made you President, Rudi, and everything in Fredonia was for sale! I admit that went to my head. It was an intoxicating time. Never, in the history of Capitalism, has so much been sold to so few by so few. I sold land, factories, coal, tin and copper mines, power stations, reservoirs, schools, drugs, justice, everything. I lost count of what I sold and now alas, now it appears I sold some things more than once to different global companies."

Again Grolsh sighs. Rudi says cheerfully, "But Grolsh is a man of his word! He must know some way to compensate two or three world-wide companies for buying the same mines and power stations."

"It can be done," says Grolsh nodding solemnly. "There is a way of doing it that will delight you Rudi, and you too, Vera Zazulich. The Liberal Revolution, my friends, has now obviously gone too far. It hugely enriched a new middle class at the expense of the workers and the poor, but a trade recession is starting to hurt professional people too, so it is time for everyone to enjoy a New Deal. And working together we three can achieve this by seizing the reins of government and forming a new political party – the New Dealers Party!"

"What will it do?" asks Rudi merrily.

"It will make you more than a mere figurehead. You

will be able to keep some promises you made in your greatest speeches. You will at last achieve the Socialist Democracy you suffered by defending."

"He remembers my *sufferings* Vera! How *kind* he is!" snarls Rudi with a venom Grolsh ignores, jubilantly urging Vera, "While you! – leader of the Decembrists! – will openly represent all those young idealists who still have faith in liberty, equality, fraternity. We will put you in charge of education, broadcasting, culture, fashion, anything you like. You can be home secretary and create a Ministry of Feminism. And at last I will emerge into the limelight and manage boring economic matters that no high-souled people ever understand – things like trade and finance."

"And you think such an alliance will save your soul?" demands Vera scornfully.

"To hell with my soul!" cries Grolsh violently. "I fear for my body. I want to die painlessly of old age."

Rudi asks, "And what will our splendid new government do?"

"We will give Fredonia back to the Fredonian people!"

"How?" cry Rudi and Vera simultaneously.

"We three left-wingers understand Marxist historical logic do we not?" says Grolsh with a strained enthusiasm he obviously hopes will infect them. "Thesis! Antithesis! Synthesis! The state Communism that collapsed in 1990 was our thesis. It provoked the state Capitalism that is also starting to crumble. Our New Deal will renew Fredonia by synthesising both systems."

"Into Capitalist Communism?" asks Rudi, grinning, and "No! Communist Capitalism!" says Vera, also amused.

Grolsh says, "Exactly, exactly, exactly! We will re-nationalise all industry and public services that do not profit the present owners."

"Wonderful," says Rudi, "so the Fredonian tax payers will compensate the global corporations for the mines and railways you sold them, including those who paid simultaneously for the same ones."

"That must certainly happen," Grolsh tells them solemnly.

"Our new government will not last a week if it is distrusted by the International Monetary Fund."
The other two laugh heartily. Vera says, "Rudi, give me that glass – I'll have a drink after all."
He hands it to her and fills another for himself.
"What is this big joke you laugh at?" asks Grolsh grumpily.
"You," says Rudi.
"We don't believe in you," says Vera and Rudi adds, "You have lurked so long in the shadows, Grolsh, that you have become one. You are no longer solid but a phantom – a ghost of a mirage of an illusion."
"You are both terribly wrong!" cries Grolsh. "I still wield power, terrible power, and can prove it."
"Do you mean that the outré harpooners still trust you?" says Rudi.
"Yes! Because I am one of them. Also, I have international contacts of immense strength and intelligence ..."
Grolsh is interrupted by the first six chords of a famous national anthem.

Rudi and Vera, astonished, look around and see no source of the noise then notice Grolsh is cowering and that his face has gone very white. The chords are followed by an implacable voice saying: "This is the U.S.A. talking to European agent pee cue zero six nine otherwise known as Vladimir Grolsh. Agent Grolsh, you are in breach of the contract forbidding you to form new political alliances without previous C.I.A. clearance."
In feeble tones Grolsh cries, "I had no *time* to inform you of the useful alliance I have just proposed – I only conceived it half an hour ago – but I am delirious with joy that you know all about it now. Please congratulate the C.I.A. for wiring this room without my knowledge."
"We have not wired it. You are being addressed over a new satellite system which gives us total powers of surveillance and interference anywhere at any time. Ours is the only operating system of its kind in the world."
"No quite the only operating system," says a suave voice

with a Sicilian accent. "This is the Cosa Nostra speaking. Under clause 312 of the C.I.A. and Mafia International War on Terror Treaty, Cosa Nostra agents only need clearance from us. Our Fredonian agent Grolsh received clearance from us twenty minutes ago."

The room vibrates to the sudden boom of a heavily struck gong, and a new voice says, "But Agent Grolsh has not received clearance from the Chinese Central Intelligence Agency!"

"And if I might be allowed to put in a word ..." says an Oxbridge voice –

"You may not!" says the voice of America, but the Englishman continues pleasantly, "I realise the United Kingdom is a junior partner in our alliance, but the City of London is still the Western world's biggest money-laundering centre, and we feel Agent Grolsh is now a useful link between all of us, including the Muslims. Is that not true, Grolsh?"

"No deals with the enemy," says America.

"Surely," pleads Grolsh piteously, "surely in this free market world of ours a man may sell himself to everyone who can afford him? And the U.S.A., the Mafia, the U.K. and China are allies. You are not at war with each other!"

The gong booms once more and China announces, "Every nation must be prepared for every eventuality."

"You can say that again!" says America, so China says it again.

"You had better come back to Sorrento, Grolsh," says the voice of Sicily.

"No way!" says America. "When Grolsh leaves the President's bedroom he will be coshed, chloroformed, rolled in a carpet and sent for debriefing at Abu Ghraib."

Rudi, much amused by the conversation, has been quietly singing the Fredonian national anthem to himself, but a terrible wail from Grolsh silences him.

"Mercy, England! England, please have mercy! Surely your renowned sense of fair play will come to the aid of poor old Grolsh, your most faithful of Fredonian agents?"

"Sorry Grolsh old bean. Our prime minister is Scotch and has just given permission for your extraordinary rendition through Prestwick airport."
"Vera!" screams Grolsh. "You were going to put a bullet through my brain – pity me! Pity me and do it now."
In a girlish way Vera smiles on him and pleasantly says, "No."
"Then give the gun to me!" he begs, and she hands it over saying with a hint of apology, "There are no bullets in it."
"Rudi!" he yells, weeping. "Sanctuary! Sanctuary!"
Rudi kindly raises the duvet on Grolsh's side of the big bed. Grolsh grabs a vodka bottle, dives in and burrows as far down as he can while Rudi covers him up.

This little drama distracts all three from what the other voices are discussing, but that international squabble at last ends with the terrible boom of the Chinese gong.

MIDGIEBURGERS

STREETS OF BUNGALOWS are called suburban when part of cities, but exist in many much smaller British places. A wife sits in a bungalow beside an electric fire, knitting with the concentrated fury of one with no other outlet for her energies. A husband sits opposite, examining magazines received that morning with a bulky weekend newspaper. Discarding the one called *Sport* he leafs unhappily through *Lifestyle*, *Homes*, *Travel*, *Arts* and *Entertainment*, but every page seems to have colourful photographs of glamorous young people in richer, more exciting surroundings than his own. He leaves the magazines, goes to a window and looks out for signs of other life, but in the pale grey sky above the bungalows opposite not even a bird is visible. He says, "I can't make out what the weather is like."

"Where?" she demands.

"Outside."

"Go and look."

"No. I am insufficiently ..." (he thinks for a while) "... motivated. You're lucky."

"Why?"

"You can knit. Shop. Do housework. Retirement has made me ..." (he thinks for a while) "... an appendage. I should cultivate something."

"What?"

"A hobby perhaps. Friends perhaps."

"Friends are not cultivated," she tells him. "They grow naturally, like weeds."

"I bet I could cultivate one," he says with sudden enthusiasm. "This is a free country. I can go into any pub, see someone interesting, walk straight up to them and say: *Excuse me for butting in, but you look like a man of more than average intelligence and I need advice. Jim Barclay's my name, tax avoidance expert, retired, and I'm looking for a hobby to cultivate."*

He falls silent for a while, then says, "If I was American it would sound much better: *Howdy stranger. Jim Barclay's the name, and tax avoidance is the game. What brings you to this neck of the woods?"*

"Woods don't have necks," she tells him.

"Not around here, anyway," he says, sighing. Returning to the fireside he sits down again and at random opens a magazine at a page advertising an expensive gown. This looks like bunches of glittering rags not quite covering a glamorous, charmingly worried young woman in what seems the boiler room of an obsolete factory. He studies her wistfully for a while, then the doorbell rings.

"Somebody's arrived! Somebody's arrived!" he says exultantly, striding from the room, opening the front door and crying, "My God, it's you!"

"Yes, it's me," says someone modestly.

"Come in, come in, come in!" Jim says, ushering the visitor through and closing doors behind him. "Linda, this is old ... old ... old ..."

He snaps his fingers to encourage memory.

"Bill," says the newcomer pleasantly. He is the same age and professional type as his host, and adds, "I was driving north on business, saw I was near here and thought I'd call in."

"So you did! Linda, Bill and I were great pals when we worked for the old P.I.S.Q.S."

"You're wrong," says Bill pleasantly. "It was for the old S.H.I.Q.T."

"Are you sure?" asks Jim, surprised.

"Absolutely."

"Anyway, it was one of those hell-holes and you saved my life, I remember that clearly enough."

"It was my job," says Bill with a modest shrug. "I was in charge of security."

"Indeed you were, thank goodness," cries Jim. "This calls for a celebration. Have a seat."

"Only if you're having one yourself."

"Impossible. I'm too excited. But you *must* have one."

So Bill sits.

"Tea or coffee, Bill?" asks Linda, who has risen hopefully to her feet.

"Neither. Sorry," says Bill with a touch of regret, "my doctor won't let me."

Linda sits sadly down and carries on knitting. Her husband walks up and down, smacks his hands together, repeats, "This calls for a celebration. Orange juice? Beer? Gin? Vodka? Whisky? Drambuie? Tia Maria? Sherry? Port? Chateau Mouton Rothschild du Pape? I'm afraid we're out of champagne."

"Sorry," says Bill, "I'm a health freak. I only drink water, and stopped at a pub for a couple of pints ten minutes ago."

"O," says his host, sitting down and wondering what else to say.

And at last asks, "Care to talk about being a health freak? I mean, you might manage to convert us."

"No no," says Bill, "you'd find the topic too bloody boring."

"Ha ha ha, you're right there!" says Jim, then adds in an apologetic, quieter tone, "Sorry I can't ask you what make of car you drive, and tell you about mine and all the trouble I have with it. Linda finds the topic too bloody boring."

"Ha ha, she's right there!" says Bill. This leads to another long silence broken by both men saying simultaneously, "What are you doing these days?" after which both laugh until Bill says, "You first!"

"No, you!"

"You! I insist."

"Well, as a matter of fact I've ..." says Jim, but is interrupted by the first bars of *Do You Ken John Peel?* on a xylophone. With a murmured apology Bill takes a phone from his pocket, says to it, "Well?" and after listening for a moment tells it, "Listen, bitch, and listen good. There were no

witnesses to that promise you allege I made, pills are cheap so your bastard is not my concern. If you must whine, try whining to my lawyer. He'll land you in Cornton Vale jail without your feet touching the ground and women commit suicide to escape from that place. So get out of my life!"
Pocketing the phone he says, "As a matter of fact you've what?"
"Taken early retirement."
"But you used to be such a live wire."
"Yes, but the firm made me an offer I couldn't refuse."
"The swine," says Bill sympathetically.
With a shrug Jim tells him, "Business is business," then, struck by an idea, asks, "Have you noticed that every ten years since 1975 the number of millionaires in Britain has doubled?"
Bill nods. Jim asks, "Have you never wanted to be one?"
Bill says, "I am one."
Not quite catching this Jim says, "It's done by cashing in on the market whether it's going up, down or sideways. Jack Rotter of the Porridge Union is coming to everyone's neck of the woods next week so why not book a talk with him on *rotporridge @ slash dot crash dot wallop yahoo dot com* and get tips straight from the horse's mouth? All terms and conditions apply."
His wife, exasperated, looks up from her needles and says, "He's already told you he's a millionaire."
"Did you?" Jim asks Bill, who smiles and nods.
"Dear me," says Jim, "that ought to teach me something."
Linda says, "It should teach you to listen as much as you talk."
Not quite hearing her Jim murmurs, "Yes it really ought to teach me something," then sighs and adds, "But I wish they hadn't pushed me out of tax avoidance."
"I seem to remember you were damned good at it," says his friend.
"I was, but even accountants don't know everything."
"Maybe some don't, but mine at least is trustworthy."
"You may be living in a fool's paradise," Jim points out,

"because last year I was running to the seaside when the door of a parked car opened and smacked me into the middle of the road. I was left with nine broken ribs and a fractured pelvis."

"Tough!" says Bill.

Jim answers smugly, "Not at all. I got straight on to J.C. Pooter who will get me a cool million in compensation and a holiday in the Bahamas."

Bill says, "J.C. Pooter is certainly your knight in shining armour," so approvingly that Jim cheerfully asks, "What are *you* doing these days?"

"As a matter of fact I'm ..." (*Do You Ken John Peel?* is heard) "... Excuse me," says Bill, bringing out his phone.

After listening for a while he says, "They're rioting? We knew they would ... They've invaded the plant? We knew that would happen too. I hope they burn it down so the owners can claim insurance ... You're trapped on the roof? Phone the police to airlift you off." To Jim and Linda who have been frankly listening he adds, "Sorry about that. I was saying?"

"What you are doing these days?" says Linda.

"I'm a troubleshooter."

"You shoot troublemakers?" asks Jim, awestruck.

"No no no," says Bill, chuckling. "I never pull a trigger. I tell other people to do that."

"Which must take courage," says Jim, admiringly.

His friend, with a touch of regret says, "Not much. Hardly anyone gets killed. They usually see reason when confronted with the wee black holes at the end of Kalashnikovs."

"Does Russia still make those?"

"I'm not sure, but nowadays they can be picked up anywhere for a song."

"A song! That reminds me," cries Jim, "which of the following statements is untrue. Stoats are animals with almost human fingernails. For two centuries the Austro-Hungarian official language was Chinese. You can afford an Assassin Javelin Jeep with leather upholstery, an inbuilt

recording studio and all the trimmings. The Madagascar royal flag is an inverted hippo."
"Er … the inverted hippo?"
Jim says triumphantly, "They're all true! The most horribly abused single-parent pauper can now afford an Assassin Javelin Jeep thanks to an easy credit deal which lets anybody sell their children into domestic slavery."
"Do all terms and conditions apply?" asks Bill.
"Of course!" is the glad reply. "The best jeep in the world is now within everybody's reach, but I'd just like to put in another word for the Porridge Union …"

Linda has gradually stopped knitting and now flings down her needles and in a cold monotonous voice says, "Hell. Hell. Help."
Their guest stares questioningly at her husband who murmurs, "I think she feels excluded from … from …"
"From our discourse?" whispers Bill. "Yes, my wife sometimes feels that when a friend calls, so I know what to do about it." He coughs in an introductory way then says genially, "Here comes a very personal question Linda, but have you enjoyed the wonderful sensation of Gloria Vampa's new make-up remover?"
"I don't use make-up," she tells him stonily.
"Then maybe it's time you started! The surveillance society is here to stay, so why not wow the police watching you on closed circuit television cameras by looking like a new woman every day? And Maxine Hererra can make that easy."
"Maxine Herrera of New York?" cries Jim.
"Yes," says Bill, "Maxine Hererra of New York's heart-shaped love-box has a new lipstick giving you the choice of sixty-nine distinctly glamorous shades and ninety-six luscious flavours, and the cost is only …"
Linda says desperately, "Fuck cosmetic advertising."
Jim suggests, "Try something else."
After a thoughtful pause Bill says, "Money, Linda! Money. You know, the former Federal Reserve Chairman tells us

through the prism of the current situation we cannot turn a blind eye to the explosion of sub-prime mortgages, and the rapid growth of complex credit derivatives."

"Can't we?" asks Jim, astonished. "Imagine that Linda! What does it mean?"

"It means that history has never dealt kindly with the aftermath of protracted low-risk premiums, and the regulators will have to rely on counter-party surveillance to do the heavy lifting."

Through gritted teeth she says, "Monetary jargon and cosmetic jargon are equally disgusting."

Bill asks Jim, "Do you think she might join in if we discuss music?"

"Try it," says Jim glumly, so Bill announces that his favourite radio station is Classic FM. To explain why he says, "You cannot beat Classic FM for really smooth, relaxing music sponsored by the British Savings Bank which is currently celebrating the fiftieth anniversary of premium bonds …"

He falls silent because Linda is writhing in torment. Jim says, "Try health."

"You know there's nothing very clever about living with a hernia," says Bill gallantly, and Jim chimes in, "But operations used to be painful, took months, were often worse than useless."

"No more!" says Bill triumphantly. "And about time! Nowadays you can walk into the Universal Hernia Centre and walk out twenty minutes later with a brand new, state-of-the-art hernia and a life-long permanent kidney guarantee, and it won't cost you a – "

Linda screams. Jim clutches his hair. Bill, inspired, shouts, "I've got it! Science! Pure science. E equals MC squared. Poor Albert Einstein."

"Yes," says Jim, grinning with relief. "He never could get his head around quantum physics. *God doesn't play dice*, he said."

Bill, chuckling, says, "Remember what Max Planck told him: *Don't tell God not to play games.*"

"Was that not Niels Bohr?" asks Linda, who has resumed knitting.
"One or t'other," says Jim. "Einstein never understood that a unified field equation would only be possible in a steady-state universe that would be undistinguishable from an infinite Parmenidean solid."
"Schopenhauer showed how impossible that was."
"He did! He did! He did!" says Jim, and the two men are laughing happily when interrupted by *Do You Ken John Peel?*. With an apologetic shrug Bill tells the phone, "Hello? ... Okay ... Okay, the demonstrators have you spread-eagled naked and facedown on a tabletop with a funnel stuck up your arse. And? ... They are going to pour melted lead down it unless? ..." (his voice registers incredulity) "... Unless the government promises to nationalise their factory and reopen it? Why should the government do that? ... You're Gordon Brown's nephew? What's that got to do with it? Family loyalty is as dead as Socialism and the brotherhood of man. You've got yourself into a mess and there's nothing I can do to help." He switches off the phone and asks, "You were saying?"
"Schopenhauer showed how the definition of will as effect, not cause, depended on consciousness itself – a *reductio ad absurdum* that would reduce the gods themselves to helpless laughter. No wonder Nietzsche and Wagner loved Schopenhauer. I think Bruckner did too. In a peaceful wood, on a summer afternoon, one's mood is exactly conveyed by the almost inaudible vibration that opens his fourth symphony."
Bill nods, says, "Yes, the unity of art and science, hand and eye, is predicated by the past which is our only inevitability. did you know that Phoebe Traquair – evening star of the Arts and Crafts Movement – married a marine palaeontologist who specialised in the asymmetry of flatfish?"
Flinging down her knitting again Linda announces, "I can take no more of this pretentious shit," and folds her arms to prove it. Jim jumps to his feet points an angry forefinger and tells her, "O yes it's easy to sit at one side knitting

and nagging, nagging and knitting. I hate pretentious shit as you do but I loathe something else even more – that ghastly, brain-destroying silence in which people sit uselessly hating each other. Well, I give up. I'm tired of being the friendly host. I'm leaving Bill entirely to you."

Jim walks to the window and looks out, hands in pockets. Bill, not at all embarrassed, looks at Linda who smiles pleasantly back, sits beside him on the sofa and asks, "What brings you to this neck of the woods, Bill?"

He slaps his knee and says, "Ah, now you've got me really started. From now on you won't get a word in edgeways. I've been sent north by the S.L.I.C.Q.E. because—"

"Exactly what is the S.L.I.C.Q.E.?"

"Scottish Lice and Insect Corporate Quango Enterprises, which want me to—"

"Insects are disgusting," she tells him firmly.

"They are, they are, but from an industrial point of view midges—"

"The female flesh fly Sarcophoga Carraris," she says more firmly still, "lays young larvae in the fresh or decomposing flesh of almost any animal. Or in manure!"

"I know," says Bill patiently, "but why does a salmon as big as this ..." (he spreads his hands wide apart) "... leap out of a river to swallow a wee toaty midge as big as this?" and he not quite touches the tip of his thumb with the tip of the index finger.

And at that moment his phone plays *Do You Ken John Peel?*.

"Excuse me," says Bill bringing it out, but Linda grasps the wrist of the hand holding the phone and says firmly, "No gentleman should let a telephone interrupt a conversation with a lady. Switch that off."

Jim turns from the window and stares, amazed by an aspect of his wife new to him. *Do You Ken John Peel?* rings out again. Bill is too gentlemanly to wrench his wrist from Linda's grasp by force but the sound drives him frantic.

"I must answer it!" he cries. "If it's my boss I'll be sacked

if I don't answer! I have to be on call day and night! Day and night!"
"Is it your boss?" she demands. "Won't the phone tell you?"
"I don't know!" he exclaims. "Nowadays anyone who is computer literate can hack into my phone and make it say they're my boss. I'm bombarded by calls from an ex-employee I picked up in a Thailand children's brothel. I chucked her out a fortnight ago and now she rings me almost hourly! My life is a nightmare!"
The phone plays *Do You Ken John Peel* as he begs through tears, "Please let me answer. I'm drinking myself to death."
"With water?" she asks scornfully.
"Water can kill faster than alcohol. Please, please Linda – release me."
"Only if you switch it off, Bill. It's probably only strikers who want you to hear your colleague screaming while they pour molten lead into his bum."
"All right," says Bill, is released, and switches off the phone muttering, "I only pray to God that you're right."
"My my, Bill, what a full life you have!" says Jim, coming over and sitting down with them again. "Tell me, why do great big salmon leap out of rivers to swallow toaty wee midges?"
"Because of their adrenalin!" Bill triumphantly explains. "Every wee midge is a molecule of pure protein fuelled by an atom of adrenalin. That's why midges are able to stot up and down all day above rivers, lochs, cesspools, stanks and puddles in your back garden."
Linda tells them stonily, "Cephenorima Auribarbos is a rather flat parasitic fly whose shape and claws allow it to move quickly, crab-wise, across the soft hairy surfaces of ponies and suck their blood. The female gives birth to full-grown larvae, which at once pupate."
"Very true, Linda," says Bill, "but what would you have if all the midges infesting the Highlands and Islands were squeezed together into one huge dripping block?"
"What *would* she have?" asks Jim, fascinated.
"She would have a lump half the size of Ben Lomond and

containing enough adrenalin to start a Scottish subsidiary of International Pharmaceuticals, while leaving another half mountain of protein to be sliced and marketed locally as midgieburgers. The working class cannot afford to buy fish suppers nowadays; Scottish beef and venison are for export only, so midgieburgers are going to become Britain's fastest new food – our economy will depend upon it. And Scotland is in luck. Global warming is turning the Western Isles into the new Caribbean, so S.L.I.C.Q.E. is using lottery funds to shunt pension-less old age pensioners, *and* the unemployed, *and* the disabled, *and* criminals doing community service, into Highland and Island nudist camps where they do nothing but sunbathe and let S.L.I.C.Q.E. cull the midges they attract."

"Five of Scotland's worst social problems solved at a stroke. Wonderful!" says Jim, awestruck.

Linda, unimpressed, tells them grimly, "The deer botfly, Calliphora Vomitaria—"

"Sorry dear, but I have to interrupt," Jim tells her. "Bill is a troubleshooter. Exactly what trouble are you here to shoot, Bill?"

"The midges are not biting."

"Why?" asks Jim.

"Nudists are using midge repellents."

"Calliphora Vomitaria—" begins Linda but her husband talks over her.

"I'm sorry dear, but this really is important. You must know, Bill, that International Pharmaceuticals who want the midges also make the repellent sprays. They can make the sprays sold in Scotland ineffective by weakening the contents!"

"They've done that," says Bill, "but local chemists have stockpiled enough of the old effective stuff to repel midges for the next ten years."

Linda, trying again, says, "Calliphora Vom—" but Jim almost angrily says, "I told you this is *important* Linda. Listen Bill: the pharmaceutical companies must tell local chemists that the repellents that they've stockpiled may induce cancer because they've been insufficiently tested,

so will replace them with completely safe stuff free of charge."
Bill, shaking his head, says, "Too dangerous. If that lie turns out to be true, the pharmaceuticals will have no defence if people start suing them."
"So what can they do?"
"S.L.I.C.Q.E. have called in T.I.Q.T.S. who – "
"What," shouts Linda, "is T?I?Q?T?S?"
"My firm: Troubleshooter International Quick Termination Service," says Bill, modestly, and Jim asks, fascinated, "What will you do?"
In a low voice Bill asks if he can keep a secret. Jim quietly explains that he was once a Boys' Brigade captain, so never clypes. He is then told something in a voice so low that Linda cannot hear a word, and resumes knitting.

Jim is strangely affected by what he hears. Admiration contends with horror as he asks, "You can do that nowadays?"
Bill nods.
"But when Communist governments did such things everyone thought … I mean, in Britain, Europe and the U.S.A. most people thought … I mean, even the cheapest newspapers said that kind of thing was … er … wrong. Bad. Dirty. I think we even had laws against it."
Bill tells him happily, "We're living in a new age, Max."
Gently correcting him, Jim says, "Jim."
"I'm sorry?" says Bill, puzzled.
Treating the matter as a joke they will share Jim says, "I am not Max. I'm your old friend Jim Barclay."
Bill, thunderstruck, says, "You're … not Max Fenstersturmer?"
"No. I'm Jim Barclay, whose life you once saved."
Bill jumps up, cries, "Is this not sixteen Conniston Place, Strathnaver?"
"It is sixteen Denniston Place, Strathinver."
Bill responds in a new and strangely American-sounding voice: "No wonder nothing you've said to me has made

sense. O but you've been very very smart. I have to admire how you screwed what you did out of me."

Jim, slightly disturbed, stands up saying, "It's you who made the first mistake. I simply answered you as politely and agreeably as possible."

"But you didn't go out of your way to correct me, did you? Exactly who are you working for?" Bill asks on a note of naked menace, after which the quiet dignity of Jim's reply sounds unusually British: "I am not working at all. I am a tax avoidance accountant who took early retirement. My hobby is cultivating friendship and you are suddenly making it very, very difficult."

"They all make feeble excuses of that kind. I will now tell you what I came north to tell Fenstersturmer and you'd better believe it. If you're working for one of the other sides, come clean and we'll do a deal, because we can always do a deal with the other sides. But if you're a loose cannon you haven't a hope in hell. Get this. Everything you've heard, everything you know, everything you think comes under The Official Secrets Act, and if you breathe one word of it to a living soul you can kiss your ass goodbye. And if they come for me first I'll make sure that we both go down the chute together."

"Calliphora Vomitaria," announces Linda, "commonly called the deer botfly, deposits larvae in the nostrils of young deer. The larvae live in the nasal or throat passages, attached by their mouth hooks and living on the secretions of the host. When full-fed they are passed out with the deer's droppings and pupate on the soil."

During this Bill strides to the door, opens it and tells Jim, "Remember this, Fensterbacher! The crocodiles at the bottom of that chute have needle-sharp teeth and take years to make a meal of a man!"

Do You Ken John Peel? summons him from his pocket as he rushes out from the house, slamming the front door behind him.

Jim looks at Linda, perhaps hoping for an adequate comment. She sighs, shrugs her shoulders and resumes knitting, so he wanders around the room with hands in pockets murmuring, "Well well well," at intervals in slightly different tones of voice. At last he says, "I enjoyed his company before he turned nasty... I wonder if he was all he cracked himself up to be ... I'll know for sure if chemists' stockrooms start exploding. Linda! Should I phone the police and warn them about that?"

She says, "He was the police – a special branch of it."

"Not a troubleshooter for a private corporation?"

"That too. The police are half-privatised now, like most of the government," and she sadly adds, "I wish you were him."

"Why?"

"He and I nearly had a conversation before you butted in – almost the first intelligent talk I've had with a man since we married. Before that you sometimes talked to me. Never since. Not nowadays."

"Not now, no," he says absentmindedly going to the window and looking out. She stops knitting, looks at his back and says softly, "What if we – both you and me – were always listening – I mean really listening to the silence. Would we hear, – really hear and heed – the importance of waiting, – really waiting – for the right moment – to begin the song?"

There is a long silence, then without turning he asks if she said something. She says, "A poem I remembered."

He says, "For a moment I thought you were talking to me."

She resumes knitting. He resumes wondering about the state of the weather outside, and sometimes (as a result of his conversation with Bill) also worrying idly about the state of Britain.

WHISKY AND WATER

A PUBLIC HOUSE has been expensively refurnished and redecorated by owners who hope it will now attract a richer class of client, but while other pubs in the district are crowded as usual, this has only one customer. He sits at the bar, slowly sipping whisky while talking, though not conversing, with the barmaid. He wants a female audience to punctuate his monologue with agreeable sounds, and the barmaid does this easily while looking through a fashion magazine. Her most frequent sound is "mhm", a Scottish word of agreement which can be said without opening the mouth. The regular customer asks, "You know my brother the artist?"

"Mhm."

"He is more than an artist now. He is now chief arts administrator for the whole of North Lanarkshire. He has shagged nearly every woman in North Lanarkshire. Has he shagged you?"

"No."

"Where do you live when you're at home?"

"West Dumbartonshire."

"That explains it. He is also a property genius. He collects property like some folk collect postage stamps. You know the tenement at the corner of Boghead Road and Sheriff Irvine Smith Street? That's his."

"A prime site," says the barmaid, turning a page.

"Yes, a prime site. He has stuffed every room from floor to ceiling with old earthenware sinks, cisterns and lavatory pans."

"I've seen them through the oriel windows."

"You'll never see them again. Yesterday he had the windows white-washed on the inside to deter burglars.

Modern bathroom fixtures are mostly plastic. My brother thinks rich folk (not billionaires with gold-plated bathrooms but slightly poorer rich people) will soon want antique earthenware plumbing. When that kind of retro design hits the colour supplements he will unload his Irvine Smith treasury and make a killing, as we say in the Stock Exchange."

"Good."

"Do you know what, in my opinion, is life's best thing?"

She does not answer because an old man wearing a long coat and flat cap has entered and stands gazing round in dazed way. The barmaid asks if he is looking for someone. He says, "Whaur are the muriels?"

She tells him she knows nobody called Muriel.

"Ye've goat me wrang, misses," he says. "Am talkin aboot big wa' pentins, same as Michelangelo pentit a' owr the Pope's private chapel."

"This is a respectable pub in a respectable neighbourhood," says the other customer sternly. "Don't drag religion into it."

"What would you like to drink sir?" asks the barmaid kindly.

"A wee goldie, please miss. But whaur did the muriels go? Did Kelvingrove Art Gallery grab them?"

"When did you ever see a mural painting in this place?" asks the regular customer with contempt.

"At the time of the Upper Clyde work-in. A wiz a fitter in the yards *and* a shop steward. Jimmy Reid led us up this wie tae a protest meetin ootside the B.B.C."

"The B.B.C. building is south of the river," says the barmaid placing a small whisky on the bar. "Twenty pounds please."

"Twenty pounds for a wee goldie!" cries the old man, dismayed. He sadly lays down two ten-pound nickel coins, then sips his drink murmuring, "A great man, Jimmy Reid. Him and me wiz oot thegether in the 1950s apprentice strike. A great man for the Working Class *and* for Culture. That is why he broat me in here. 'This pub is whit every Scots pub should be,' says Jimmy, 'a livin centre of local community culture. Here the Scottish intelligentsia mingle with ane anither and with the common workin man. Hugh MacDiarmid! Jack House! The Wee MacGreegor! Wullie Joss of the MacFlannels! Duncan Macrae who appeared in *Our Man In Havana* alang wi' Alec Guinness and Noel Coward! And James Bridie, the Scottish George Bernard Shaw – Bridie who wrote that great London West End success, *Bunty Pulls the Strings!* And if they're no actually here today when we drap in, ye can still see them pentit on the wa's as large as life' and so they were. Aye, so they were. Mhm, so they were."

"Do you know how absurd you are being?" demands the regular customer.

The old man stares at him.

"Absurd and also obnoxious!" says his critic. "It is offensive to have a list of forgotten has-beens recited over us. Since the Upper Clyde work-in fiasco this pub has been completely renovated umpteen times by more managements than you've had decent breakfasts. You can bet your bottom dollar that soon after you saw them those old mural panels were chucked into a skip and taken straight to Dawsholm incinerator."

"Even the muriel of the novelists? Barke, Blake, Gaitens and Guy McCrone who wrote *No Mean City*?"

With sadistic relish his tormenter says, "They were the first to go."

The old man, stupefied, puts his empty glass on the counter and wanders out.

His departure seems to free the regular customer of a burden.

"As I was saying before I was so rudely interrupted," he tells the barmaid briskly, "do you know what the best thing in life is?"

"No."

"The kind of frank and friendly talk I am having with you."

"Thanks."
"Outside this pub I find it almost impossible to have a civilized conversation. Last night I was served in the Grosvenor Hotel lounge by a young chap, a very tight-lipped, taciturn, depressed chap. To cheer him up I told him about the wife leaving me, about the bills I had to pay and goldfish I had to feed. Do you know what he turned round and said to me?"
"What?"
"He said, *My friend, have you accepted Jesus Christ as your personal saviour?*"
"And had you?" said the barmaid, studying the astrology page.
"Had I what?"
"Accepted Christ as your personal saviour."
"For God's sake!" he cries. "Is every pub in this city staffed by religious fanatics? I refuse to tolerate fanaticism, fundamentalism or any form of bigotry. Every Protestant, Catholic, Muslim, Hindu or Quaker bigot should be hung, drawn, quartered, cut down while still living, buried up to the neck in the ground and stoned to death regardless of race, religion, nationality, political creed or—"
Someone breenjies in saying "Amen! Hear hear! Good thinking! I'm with you all the way on that!"

The stranger looks like a younger, happier version of the man he interrupts. He lays a wad of notes on the bar crying, "Drinks all round! For me, a large malt of the month. For you miss, whatever *you* like. For my pal here, whatever *he* likes."
"I don't drink at work," says the barmaid, pouring the malt for him.
"No more for me thanks," says the regular customer, quickly taking a newspaper from his pocket, holding it up and appearing to read closely. In one swig the

stranger empties his glass, slams it back on the counter and tells the barmaid, "Another. And keep them coming until that's used up."

He points to his money on the bar then asks the regular customer what he thinks of the weather.

"I don't discuss politics," is the short reply from behind the newspaper.

"O come come come!" says the stranger cheerily. "You used to be mad about climate change. You were a pal of Harvey Drambogie."

"I have never in my life known a man called Harvey Drambogie."

"But you shared a flat with him when you were students together. That flat was a hotbed of Greenpeace and climate-control freaks."

From behind the newsprint barrier a voice says distinctly, "As a student I once shared a flat with a lot of folk whose faces and names I cannot now remember and do not want to remember. Someone called Harvey was maybe one of them, maybe not. Even then I was staunchly unpolitical and am even more so now – a Tory, in other words."

"You can't possibly have always been so antisocial!" says the stranger, chuckling. "And Utopian politics were an innocent hobby in those days. There was no harm in you and Drambogie making pirate radio broadcasts, telling us the government should be throwing up dykes."

"You are mixing me up with someone else."

There is a long silence in which the stranger quickly drinks several large whiskies before saying coldly, "It is clearly time to remove my velvet glove and give you a touch of the iron hand. Look at this. Know what it means?"

He holds out a card in a transparent plastic envelope. The regular customer glances at it, sighs, says, "Yes," and gloomily lays down the newspaper.

"Let me spell it out in detail. This card gives me power to

arrest whoever gets on my tits and hold them indefinitely for questioning, without their family and friends being informed, and without access to legal advice."

"But I've done nothing. I'm innocent."
"You cannot touch pitch without being defiled," says the stranger implacably.
"What's that supposed to mean?"
"Do you deny that your brother has impregnated half the women in North Lanarkshire? And filled his Sheriff Irvine Smith Street flat with illicit unregistered earthenware plumbing? And white-washed the windows from inside without local community planning permission?"
"Why should that make *me* a criminal?"
"Because you cannot touch pitch without being defiled."

This conversation so interests the barmaid that she has laid aside her magazine. The regular customer cowers under the policeman's accusing glare, and begs humbly, "Don't arrest me please. Yes, Harvey Drambogie once inveigled me into voting for the Greens before I knew they were terrorists, but I've never voted since. I promise not to see my brother again as long as I live, and I'm very sorry I was so stand-offish when you first spoke to me. I admit that my manners to you then were deplorable so please, please, please accept my humble apologies and let bygones be bygones."
The policeman drinks the last whisky his wad has purchased and murmurs, "You're beginning to sound sincere."
His former cheerful manner suddenly returns. He extends a hand saying, "Apology accepted. Shake, pal."
They shake hands heartily, then the policeman says, "You will now prove your sincerity by handing over your wallet."
It is handed to him. He looks inside, removes a banker's card, hands the wallet back saying, "Without your personal identification number this card is useless. So?"
"Zero zero nine zero."

"Not a number I'll forget," says the policeman, going to the door. Before leaving he looks back and with a mischievous smile asks, "Would you like to know what will happen to you if you've lied to me?"
"Please don't tell me," the regular customer whispers. "I wouldn't dare lie to you."
"Wise man. See you around. Goodbye miss."

The door closes and the regular customer says gloomily, "That's the third banker's card a plain-clothes cop has pinched from me this year."
"I'm surprised you've any money left," says the barmaid.
"I've taken precautions. I have several bank accounts with small token sums in them and only carry one card at a time. My real savings are in a waterproof condom gaffer-taped to the inside of the U-bend behind my lavatory pan."
"Not much room in a condom."
"If I say that condom contains items to the value of nearly half a hundred million pounds, will you believe me?"
"No."
"It does. When I saw how galloping inflation was devaluing the currency I converted my capital into diamonds, pearls and a few well-cut multi-faceted amethysts, for which I have a weakness."
"I like a good amethyst too."
"Well you're not getting any of mine!" he yells in sudden parsimonious frenzy. "Don't expect it! I am not an idiot! Whit is mine is ma ain ye bitch, and whit's ma ain is nain o' yourn—"
The regression of his speech to a primitive level of dialect is abruptly cut short.

A tall dark brown man has entered wearing the traditional dress of ancient Gaelic warriors: rawhide pampooties on his feet, a tartan plaid upheld by a broad leather belt, a tweed waistcoat with voluminous linen sleeves. On his head is a white turban with a moorhen's tail feathers sticking up from a cairngorm brooch. There is a targe on his left arm, his right hand grasps a basket-hilted claymore which he lays carefully on the bar counter before saying in a soft, clear, Western Isles accent, "If you please, mistress, a small celebratory Inverarity."

He is paid no particular attention by the barmaid serving him. The regular customer has resumed reading his newspaper, as it is nowadays safer to ignore eccentricity. The Gael seems hurt by their neglect of his appearance. Having paid for his whisky he rotates the glass without tasting, then asks loudly, "Have none here heard the news?"

Without looking up from his paper the regular customer says, "You can save your breath if you want to tell us the Broomielaw embankments have burst and rising water is turning Glasgow into a cluster of islands. We knew that was bound to happen years ago."

"Indeed yes, it is happening, but that is not the *great* news."

The Gael lifts the whisky glass high above his turban, cries, "The Prince has landed — slanjay vawr," empties the glass down his throat and flings it to smash in a corner, so that no inferior toast may again be drunk from it. The barmaid looks annoyed. The regular customer says, "Exactly what Prince are you on about?"

"Prince Charles Windsor Xavier Sobieski Stuart the Tenth, our Once and Future King."

Says the barmaid, "I have more to worry about than politics these days."

In exasperation the regular customer flings his paper down and demands, "Exactly where did you dredge up that Prince?"

With a lilt in his voice the Gael says, "Charlie has been with us all his life, but kept from his rightful inheritance by treacherous politicians and a bad old mother wrongly called Elizabeth the Second of Britain. The first monarch of all Britain was Jamie Stuart the Sixth of Scotland! He came *after* Elizabeth the First of England. In 1714 a

German dynasty with Stuart blood in its veins was put on the British throne, blood of which Queen Victoria was rightly proud. And now Prince Charlie has extirpated his German taint by fully identifying with his Stuart ancestry. All Scotland must now arise to make him rightful King of Scotland, England, Ireland, Poland and North America!"

"If you asylum seekers had more sense you would keep your mouths shut," says the regular customer.

"Asylum seeker!" asks the Gael in a dangerously quiet voice. "Does that epithet refer to my complexion?"

"It stands out a mile."

In dignified speech that grows increasingly passionate the Gael announces, "I will have you know that I was born a subject of the British Empire. My father fought for it in two World Wars. In 1944, inside Buckingham Palace, King George pinned a medal to my father's chest in recognition of his conspicuous bravery. At the same ceremony he met my mother, a MacTavish of Jura, a nurse being honoured for her services to our troops in Malaysia. They married a week later and I was born twenty years after, since when I have farmed my people's ancestral croft with my own two hands. And now you – a Lowland Sassenach without land or ancestry – have the gall to call me an asylum seeker!"

"I'm glad the British Empire gave you a chance in life," says the regular customer, "but frankly, since the year dot, your sort have been diluting the purity of Scottish culture and enough is enough."

"What Scottish culture?" ask the Gael and barmaid simultaneously. The regular customer starts talking didactically but he too grows passionate as he tells them, "Scotland gave the world the Protestant Bible, steam engines, gas lighting, the bicycle, Tar Macadam, Macintosh raincoats, the electric telegraph, television, penicillin, Campbell's Soup, and McDonald's Burger King. Asylum seekers have been diluting that proud culture ever since 1890 when the Eye-Ties came here with their decadent ice-cream parlours, their corrupting fish-and-chips shops. Then came the Jews, Indians, Pakis, Chinks, Serbs and Croats. Every stupid nation we've helped by invading has brought us a new wave of asylum seekers destroying our native culture with filthy foreign cuisine until now …" (he chokes and sobs) "… now Scottish salmon, Highland venison, Aberdeen Angus beef, Forfar bridies, Finnan haddies, haggis, black pudding, shortbread and even my old granny's tablet is for export only."

By a strong effort he pulls himself together and announces, "Let us now change the subject."

The Gael, eager to speak, raises his hand but again finds himself neglected as the regular customer tells the barmaid, "The wife phoned me again last night."

"Mhm?"

"Said she still passionately loved me. She doesn't know what passion is. She's frigid. Never had an orgasm in her life. She was drunk of course. Alcoholic."

The barmaid says non-commitally, "I heard she'd sorted that out."

"Alcoholics never change. She sits at home seeing nobody, just boozing and making up her face and polishing her piano."

"She sees Senga Spotiswood."

"God knows why. What the hell's happening out there?"

From a great distance but growing swiftly louder and nearer is the sound of a big pipe band playing *Wha Daur Meddle Wi' Me?* The Gael seizes his claymore crying, "I told you! The Prince has landed!"

The regular customer raises his voice above the music of the pipes to ask, "Why should anyone pipe up for a second-rate no-user like the Prince of Wales?"

"Excuse me!" cries the barmaid. "That language is wholly out of order."

The Gael brandishes his weapon shouting, "You have been brainwashed, my friend, by the capitalist press which derides a man for loving trees, old architecture and a woman as unglamorous as himself – the only man fit to lead a second-rate nation like modern Britain! Come with me and help the last of the Stuarts redeem his nation!"

He departs, slamming the door behind him as the pipe music is suddenly quenched by torrential gurglings, but these are not loud enough to drown splashes that suggest the Gael is leaving the pub by wading upstream.

The two left behind watch a damp stain in the carpet advance slowly toward them from the foot of the door. The barmaid says sadly, "We'll have to leave soon."

"Mhm," says her last customer, "half the Scottish Lowland will soon be submarine. But let's have a whisky before our feet get wet. I'll pay."

The barmaid fills two tumblers saying, "These are on the house. Will you be moving to the Highlands?"

He says, "If there's room. The English have been buying houses there for years. I admire them. They're always a jump or two ahead of us."

She drinks deeply, choking sometimes but emptying the glass before giggling and saying, "You know, that is the first whisky I ever tasted. Why did our government not build dykes? The Dutch have had dry houses under sea level for centuries and Holland is still" – she hiccups – "safe."

"Dearie, the Scottish coast," he explains, distinctly pronouncing each word, to counteract a tendency to slur, "is so intricate that we have a longer coastline than most continents. And for centuries our taxes had to pay for us being the world's policemen. We could not afford to embank our coasts. Then the Yanks started policing the world and needed our armed forces to help save democracy from terrorists who do not share our values. So less, no I mean let us fish, no I mean finish, yes finish the blot, blot, blottle."

The lights go out. In total darkness comes a prolonged crash of falling masonry, then nothing is heard but rushing water.

MAISIE AND HENRY

MY PRIMARY SCHOOL TEACHER made every girl in her class knit the same size of socks and when I told her they were far too big for me said sharply, "You'll grow into them."

I never caused her trouble but she did not like me, perhaps because I questioned her occasional daftness. In my last primary year I was surprised and embarrassed to be the only one given navy blue wool to knit again more socks that would never fit me. Blue was the colour of the local academy uniform. Girls bound for junior secondary school were given maroon wool, those the teachers were unsure of received grey, so I was certainly going to the academy. This delighted my dad, a Communist shop-steward in the shipyards. He said, "Nowadays only an education for the professions leads to financial independence. Marriage won't give it."

Mum, a dependent housewife ever since marriage, agreed with him, so I despised girls who thought attracting men was life's main aim. Passing exams was more important. I was not very intellectual, so in my first university year missed parties to order to study harder than students who were, yet failed my first German literature test. I wrote that *Die Leiden des jungen Werthers* was not really tragic, that *Der zerbrochene Krug* was not much of a comedy. My tutor declared sternly, "These are German classics!" I replied that her exam paper had asked my opinion of these, so I had written what I thought.

"Are you here on an education grant?" she asked, though she knew I was. In those days even children of rich families got education grants, which was supposed to show Britain was now a classless society. The tutor said, "Students of your sort should know you are here to learn, not think." This shocked me until I saw that I need not study original texts if I regurgitated what tutors said about them. After that I easily passed exams and had time for parties. Some affairs before graduation taught me that lovemaking is enjoyable but not good for lasting partnerships, and that I could live without. Before the age of thirty I was managing the supplies department of a firm with bookshops in several universities. This meant interviewing folk who applied for jobs, which is how I met Henry.

He was young, tall and bony, thin yet not weak, polite and shy but not nervous, and he usually looked mildly amused. His voice was soft yet deep, his accent (like mine) academy-trained working class. His application form showed he had taught Maths for four years in a secondary school so I asked why he had left. He said, "I don't hate children but whole classes of them are too many for me. I want an easier job."

"You won't get one here," I told him. "You'll be constantly unpacking books from big boxes, then repacking them in smaller boxes. You'll be paid less than half what you earned as a teacher despite your first-class honours in Philosophy. That's a far better degree than I ever got."

He shrugged and said, "A philosopher who cannot teach may as well supply people with books."

"But a first-class degree from a good university should get you something better!"

He said he had been offered an Oxford scholarship but had to stay in Glasgow – his invalid mother needed him to look after her. That was why he had taught for so long, though hating it. He said, "She died last month so here I am. Please employ me."

He was obviously conscientious and truthful, so I did.

He arrived for work each morning before 8.30 a.m. when our place opened. It was my job to know he was

punctual, though I arrived after 10 a.m. because new orders seldom came earlier. To process them properly I worked later than everyone else, being able to concentrate better when my clerical staff were not pestering me with their problems. One evening when nights were growing darker, thinking myself as usual alone in the building, I went to the exit through the loading bay and saw Henry standing beside the door in his overcoat.
"Why are you still here?" I asked and he said, "There was still a lot of tidying to be done."
"You're not paid to work overtime," I pointed out.
"Neither are you."
"I'm paid a helluva lot more than you are, so it's worth my while."
He sighed then spoke slowly as if explaining something obvious to a child or an idiot: "This door leads into a very dark lane. This is a rough neighbourhood after most workers leave. The only people around are from council houses, many of them unemployed, so it is not safe for a woman to be alone here at night. Staying late doesn't bother me and my workmates leave the place in a disgusting mess. I hate messes and like tidying them up."
I said, "In that case I'll buy you a drink."
Neither of us had a car. I led him to a nearby pub where I often relaxed over a pint of lager after working late. Neither of us wished to seduce the other. I am a good judge of character, knew Henry was unselfish, knew he would have stayed late for any woman, old or young, married or single. Nor would he have made a pass at them. In such circumstances I think any single woman could have got him to marry her, for he thought it right to give women what they wanted if it would not hurt them. I had a proposal for him that was not romantic.

Over the lager I said, "If you insist on working late you can do better than tidy the basement."
The basement staff sent big consignments to shops all over Scotland. They also sent single books ordered by

customers up to my department, a smaller but equally important job that was not done regularly. The single books accumulated on a basement trolley for a day or more and often came up with invoices missing, causing me endless trouble. I had asked the basement foreman to send the trolley up twice a day. He grudgingly said he would, but never did as he hated taking orders from a woman. Our managing directors also disliked taking orders from women so would not speak to the foreman on my behalf, saying I should deal with him. I asked Henry to look out for the single books and bring them upstairs whenever he could. If this was not possible during normal working hours he could bring them to me after his workmates left. I said, "Manage that and I'll try getting you paid overtime, though the directors will likely say the firm can't afford it. They're very stingy with everyone who is not upper management and I'm only head of middle management."

"No matter!" said Henry cheerily. "Every business should be efficient."

From then on he made my life easier, and his only reward was the pint of lager I bought him afterward.

When the rest of my staff learned of this arrangement they decided we were lovers. The women all thought Henry "a heart-throb" because of his deep soft voice, and one said, "I honestly don't know what he sees in you."

Women who are not wee and chubby often wonder why men like me. At university one such man told me loftily, "Compact, manageable female bodies always appeal to the average male sensualist," though I never let him manage mine. My deputy (another heart-throbbist) said bitterly, "Henry knows which side his bread is buttered. Guess who will be promoted when the next vacancy occurs."

She was promoted when the next vacancy occurred. The directors employed whoever I thought fit but never promoted those I recommended, and certainly not

Henry. They called him "over-qualified". Six months passed before he and I knew each other well enough to be lovers, another month before we married, yet in all his time with the firm he was one of the worst paid despite (unlike some with four times his salary) keeping an essential part running smoothly.

We honeymooned on a Mediterranean coast where we did not know the language of the natives, so I forget if they were Spanish or Italian. We mostly met English holiday makers who seemed just as foreign, often dining with a couple from Felixstowe who seemed to like us. I once heard the husband say, not knowing he was overheard, "They're terribly *Scotch*, aren't they dear?"
"Very!" said his wife. "But quaintly entertaining."
He said, "You find them that, but I prefer the company of normal people."
We enjoyed the local food but never got used to the unrelenting sunshine. That was our first and last trip abroad. Since then Millport and Lamlash on the Firth of Clyde have been our holiday resorts.

The pattern of our evenings had changed long before our marriage. Henry still worked for almost eleven hours a day and I for over nine, so instead of visiting the pub we dined in Chinese or Indian restaurants. I hate making meals and other housework because Mum did these chores for me before I left home, and after moving to my own house I paid an agency to clean it, and for weekends bought meals that could be simply heated and tipped onto a plate. Henry preferred shopping for the ingredients of meals he cooked, having done that for his mum, so at weekends he did so for us, though I felt slightly guilty about that. But the real test of a partnership is how a couple manage together when not doing much. I am a television addict, Henry a thinker. After work and at weekends I relaxed watching a soap opera or reality show and he sat with me reading or thinking. The TV's noise did not disturb him because, he said, his parents had been television addicts in a two-room flat. The kitchen was the only room with steady heating so at first, when doing homework at night, he had shut out noise by putting fingers in his ears. But this annoyed his dad and Henry had learned to ignore noise by concentrating harder. When Dad died his mum offered (as I did) to listen to the TV on earphones, but he said there was now no need – he could ignore any amount of noise by concentrating.

"Concentrating on what? You've no school homework nowadays," I said, never having seen him read a book. Neither did I, partly because my university tutors had made them boring, partly because I worked all day with books. Henry said he needed no books now because he remembered enough of them, and the *Times Literary Supplement* told him how things were going.

"What things?" I asked and he said, "Things in general – things Victorians used to call The March of the Mind."

"How is it marching?"

"Badly. New discoveries in physics and biology are always happening but only do good to corporations who finance them. Humane sciences are at a standstill since Marx and Freud stopped being thought important, while linguistic philosophy – the watchdog of speech – is also out of date. So is Existentialism, the last school of philosophy relevant to human action. But I enjoy seeing how academics keep carving cosy niches for themselves and their friends."

That was not a conversation I could continue. Normally after discussing the daily events we shared he would start reading the *T.L.S.*, underline a word or two in an article, then sit looking into space for a long time with the unread journal open on his lap. When I asked what he was thinking once he jerked slightly as if waking from a dream then said, "Numbers."

"Mathematics?" I asked and he replied, "Not exactly. I ought to have said quantities – not quantities of things, just quantities in general. Even when very different – even

when seemingly contradictory – they still harmonise. Is this a law of nature? Or the result of quantities being human constructs, like language? I can't decide which."
"Neither can I. It's totally above my head," I confessed.
"You would understand me better if you were a musician," he said. Not being musical I returned to watching *EastEnders* while he resumed thinking about quantities or music with the little smile that some wives might have found annoyingly secretive. Not me. It showed my company was enough for him.

Our lives flowed very smoothly then because (I thought) we enjoyed safety and comfort that would last until retirement and beyond. Children do not guarantee future comfort, so though never discussing them we did without. One day I told my main assistant of our good time together and she said, "I suppose you get on well with him because he does everything you want."
"Perhaps," I said, "but I never want anything stupid or difficult."
"Good for you!" said she. "But I could never respect a man without initiative."
Almost angrily I said, "He has plenty of initiative! He keeps it for his hobby."
"He has a *hobby*?" she asked, incredulous. With hardly a pause I said, "Yes – quantity surveying."
"What on earth is that?"
Not knowing, I said, "I've no time to explain. Look it up."
Henry and I might have continued comfortably like that for years had I not hit him with a new idea.

One night I asked, "Have you noticed that the cost of dining out, plus paying the agency to clean this house, comes to more than your wage?"
"Yes," said he.
"So we would save money if you left the firm and did the … I mean became a …"

I hesitated before saying *househusband* because the word might offend him, and was still hesitating when he said, "Househusband. I wondered when you would think of that. But how will you manage at work without me?"
"As badly as I did before you came. But I would be used to it, and I hate you wasting your life emptying and filling boxes."
He sat silent and frowning for so long that I grew worried and asked, "Are you annoyed?"
Said he, "No. I was thinking that before financiers and politicians grabbed our economy it derived from a Greek word for housekeeping. So does ecology. Thucydides said the most satisfying economy was seen in rows of full pots arranged cleanly on shelves. Your idea is excellent. I will be a good housekeeper."

He was. After leaving the firm he rose each day at his usual 7 a.m., made breakfast for us both, and would have brought it to me in bed had not guilt made me rise an hour before my usual time and leave earlier for work. I never asked about his routines but the house was spotless when I returned. He put away clean clothes so neatly that I knew they had been ironed and told him housewives nowadays never bothered with ironing. He said, "They should. Clothes are better for it."
I had never much noticed what I ate but our meals now tasted so nice that I asked if he bought special ingredients. No, said he, the ingredients were cheap and local, but he was learning to properly cook them. He began baking bread and brewing ale. On a patio off the kitchen, in warm days of the brighter months, we enjoyed the ale while overlooking the back garden. My neighbours paid gardeners to keep their lawns and flowerbeds pretty, and had given me dark looks because I had left mine to the weeds. Henry planted our back with neat plots of potato and other root vegetables, built a glasshouse for tomatoes, dug a pit for compost and surrounded it with gooseberry bushes. On what had been the front lawn he planted a

herb garden with blackcurrant hedges. One evening at dinner he produced a bottle of wine saying the French believed that a meal without wine is not a meal.
"Is that why France has an alcohol problem?" I asked.
"Scottish alcoholism is worse than French," he said, "and French alcoholism is only rife among those who drink the worst and cheapest wines."
"So we are drinking *expensive* wine?"
"Just expensive enough to be good," he said, "and one glass each with a dinner won't impoverish us."
I enjoyed that dinner so much that I stopped arguing. Not since early childhood had home been pleasanter than my time at work. Work was getting more difficult, and not just because Henry had left.

The firm had been founded by a man who sold first editions of Burns' poetry, and had prospered and expanded until the late 20th century when I joined it. The owner was now someone I will call Sanker, who treated the business as a hobby he could leave to underlings. I thought him charming and aristocratic, partly because he made me boss of the orders department, partly from his eccentric terminology – he called me Mistress Maisie and pronounced John, Shon. Then he made someone I will call McGeeky the firm's general manager. McGeeky had been a good manager of our biggest shop but knew and cared nothing about ordering books, and was put in charge of the firm because he always told Sanker it was doing wonderfully. Since McGeeky was now in charge of promotion all the senior managers became folk who saw nothing wrong with the firm. McGeeky imitated Sanker's speech eccentricities, they imitated McGeeky's, and at meetings I was the only one who did not, and was the only woman. I privately called them The Smug because they tolerated me as a joke – a grumbler whose words could be ignored. Without consulting me The Smug began telling members of my staff to do small jobs for them immediately, then complained to me when this slowed delivery of big jobs.

Once I had overcome such problems by working overtime, but now the problems threatened to overcome me. New problems arose. The manager of technical book sales was put in charge of computerizing the firm and several hitches followed. He asked for and got two young assistants, each one of whom (I discovered) knew enough about computing to alone modernize the firm. That would have made their manager unnecessary, so he needed two assistants to play against each other, and the hitches continued. Then our works manager, though needed for heating maintenance, could seldom be found in his office or any of our shops. I suspected that, while paid by the firm, he was supervising the repair of Sanker and McGeeky's private properties. All this was reducing our profits so The Smug sent the rest of the staff on expensive re-education courses which improved nothing. Then from my office invoices for large sums began mysteriously vanishing. Nobody in our building, or even out of it (I thought), had anything to gain by these thefts which caused nothing but pointless delay. Continual frustration sometimes made me weep because I loved my work.

One night I was later than usual in the building and heard someone enter from the lane. That did not worry me because only members of The Smug had keys, but I was surprised when Sanker opened my office door. He paused, obviously surprised by the sight of me, though I was delighted by the sight of him. For years I had never had a chance to tell him what was going wrong with us, and now the chance was here! For maybe a whole minute he listened then in a wonderful, condescending tone interrupted with, "What you should do, Mistress Maisie, is see more of Shon McGeeky. If you acquired some of Shon's élan you would be a much happier woman. Goodnight Mistress Maisie."
With wide open mouth and eyes I stared at his back as he left the office, then realised why he had come. It was he who had been furtively destroying invoices that would let me quickly pay what the firm owed. I was now working for a collusion of liars. I did not run after Sanker and resign

my job then and there, because I had served the firm for twenty-five years – my whole working life – and could not imagine doing anything else.

Three days later, on Friday at half past four, a heavy cardboard box was carried in by the basement foreman and dumped on the floor by my desk. It held books flung in mixter-maxter, like a heap of bricks. I said, "Where's the trolley?"
He said, "How should I know? That ****ing works manager took every trolley away in a van ten minutes ago."
"Why?"
"For some ****ing reason that is not my business. My job is just to go on working in ****ing impossible conditions," he said and left before I could ask him to place the box on a table. Instead of asking for help I tried to lift it alone. A sudden dreadful pain made me drop it and fall on top, unable to move or feel anything but pain. Assistants sent for an ambulance that took me to hospital, and I slept after an injection that made cessation of pain the loveliest thing in the universe. Henry was at the bedside when I wakened, holding my hand and looking so afraid I grew terrified. Then a doctor arrived who told us not to worry – I had burst a disc in my spine, and for a few days would be practically paralyzed, but would completely recover if I lay still in bed for a couple of months, or perhaps three or four. Recovery would be complete if I never again tried to lift big weights without assistance. There was no reason to expect complications.
"Bed sores?" asked Henry, and was told I need not stay so still that those developed. Hating hospitals I asked when I could get home. The doctor said, "Probably the day after tomorrow, if you have someone dependable to nurse you."
"She has," said Henry.

That ended my last day with the firm, which survived my departure by not much more than a year. I doubt if Sanker or McGeeky tried to visit me in hospital, and I have since only seen them in bad dreams. Some correspondence must have ensured the pension due me so Henry must have seen to my side.

Our bedroom and bathroom had been upstairs so he bought and put into the kitchen (luckily a big room) a hospital bed with mattress that could be raised or lowered by pressing a switch. Each night before joining me in it he gave me a bed-bath which I enjoyed, for his handling was so gentle that even relieving myself in a bed-pan became pleasant. It was reassuring to have him working near me in the house or garden all day and I needed reassurance. The relief of freedom from an impossible job was mixed with rage that my whole working life had ended in wasted time. Nightmares in which I still grappled with McGeeky and The Smug bothered even my waking hours. Henry placed the TV set where I could see it but now what I saw on it enraged me. Presenters, newscasters and celebrities all seemed versions of The Smug or women they promoted for flattering them. To end my nightmares of the whole world being ruled by Sanker and his parasites Henry finally got rid of the set and I began reading the novels of Agatha Christie. She had written so many that at last I found myself halfway through one I had read a fortnight earlier. I switched to the less repetitive thrillers of Ian Rankin, Val McDermid and Louise Welsh, finally gorging on the anodyne novels of Alexander McCall Smith, who seemed able to write them faster than I could read. But the only really good times were after dinner when Henry, after spending half an hour with a computer in our old bedroom, sat beside me pondering over magazines with such names as *The Allotment Holder.*

Noticing one night that he hardly ever smiled in his old sly way, I asked, "Are you tired of the *T.L.S.* and The March of the Mind?"
Again he jerked as if wakened from a dream and said,

"Not exactly. I was thinking about shit. Ours, and where it went."

"Do you mean sewage?"

"Yes."

"Why should I know where it goes?"

"Everybody should. Do you remember sewage farms? Big open circular tanks with sprinklers revolving above? I haven't seen one for years. They used to supply farmers with manure. Farmers nowadays use artificial fertilisers, a bad idea. When you started using the bed-pan I fitted a chantie into the lavatory pan so none of ours is wasted."

"You are spreading our shit in the garden? Why didn't you tell me sooner?" I cried.

"I knew you would need time to get used to that wise and ancient practice," he said soothingly. "Chinese and Italian peasants have been doing it for thousands of years."

"Haven't the neighbours complained about our stinky garden?"

"Have you ever smelled it?" he asked, and I did not answer. On sunny days when he wheeled my bed out onto the patio I had smelled nothing odd. However, I promised that when fit to walk upstairs I would remove his chantie and shit straight into my own flush lavatory pan.

"A pity," he said musingly, then added in a voice that seemed to be quoting: "Soil should be dunged and dunged and dunged until it is the colour of my trousers." He had recently given up blue jeans for black corduroys. This was a conversation I neither could nor wished to continue, but he wanted to and said, "You enjoy the meals I make but don't seem to notice they are vegetarian. With a bit more land I could make us self-supporting in the way of food."

"Henry," I told him, "I am still not well, and don't think I will ever be well enough to discuss expensive new notions."

On that day he said no more.

I have never liked large breakfasts. Each day began with Henry bringing a cup of tea and saucer of fruit cut into thin little slices and arranged in patterns that became more and more fancy. "Why waste time making it fancy?" I asked. "Just tip the stuff onto the plate and I'll enjoy it just as much."

"I like making patterns and thought they would please you," he said.

"They don't. They're unnecessary – a waste of your time."

He shrugged his shoulders and said, "I'll stop making them."

"Good!" said I.

But next morning the fruit was arranged as fancy as ever. I stared at him. In a miserable voice he said, "I couldn't stop doing it. I tipped what you call *the stuff* onto the plate and the result affronted my sense of decency. I *had* to make a pattern of it."

"You did it to please yourself, not me!"

"Yes," he admitted, "but why let it bother you? Why resent patterns you destroy as soon as you start eating them? I expect you to destroy them. I want you to."

"I hate them because they show you are acting like a fool! Like a, like a, like a … like an artist!" I concluded, glad to have found the right word.

"O no!" he said, shocked, then added thoughtfully after a pause, "You're right. As a chef and gardener, yes, I am becoming an artist. Luckily. I used to be very miserable most of the time."

Hardly believing my ears I wept and wept and wept. He embraced me, said he was sorry, swore that before becoming a househusband he had never thought our marriage miserable because like me he thought it was normal, but now he had useful things to do and saw the past differently. He ended by saying with a touch of disgust, "I used to be completely selfish."

"Nonsense!" I cried. "You were the most unselfish man I ever met."

"You're wrong. I tried to be kind to everyone but apart

from that I just hung about feeling superior to them. I had no initiative."
"You think being unkind to me shows initiative?"
"I am not unkind! I am only telling the truth! And it is you who changed me! And I am grateful! Can you not see how much better we both are and be glad?"
"I am still very sick," I said, weeping, " and I wish you had stayed as you were."
He stared at me, then began trembling and shaking his head from side to side, then jumped up yelling, "This is impossible! You are making me impossible! Can I not be allowed to love you AND domestic economy?"
With clenched fists he began punching his head from side to side as hard as he could. In our four years together he had never raised his voice or acted madly. I screamed at him to stop, tried leaving the bed to stop him. He stopped at once, joined me in bed and we wept together. I promised I was sorry for having made a stupid fuss about the fruit breakfast, he said he was sorry for explaining things tactlessly. We became lovers and friends again. That was our first and worst quarrel and probably our last. I knew he would never be unfaithful to me, but I still worried about the future.

A week later he started talking as if in the middle of an argument with a beginning I had missed: "You see, the county of Fife was once a separate Scottish kingdom. Some Fifers have noticed it could be made economically self-supporting. So could Orkney. And Shetland. So could Aberdeenshire, if the farmers stopped turning fertile earth into beef for export by passing grass through cattle. Kitchen gardens are the most productive and sustainable way of turning soil into food. Factory farming is the worst way."
"Henry, I am not arguing with you," I said, but he continued vehemently as if I was: "I am all for Scottish independence but if people and governments keep depending on the Global Bosses' Federation things will go on getting worse."

"What is the Global Bosses' Federation?" I asked, exasperated.

"It prefers to be called the World Trade Organization. It rules the strongest nations and is out to grab all the resources of smaller ones. That is why Britain and the U.S.A. keep shooting and bombing folk in Islamic countries and why an Islamic clique destroyed the New York World Trade Centre. Global bosses don't need a single centre now, so their opponents are plotting to attack stock exchanges. A stupid idea. The bosses are financially insured against every kind of damage, and the plots only strengthen global armies and police forces they control. Global bosses can only be fought by taking Voltaire's advice at the end of *Candide*."

"Henry!" I cried, horrified. "Don't go into politics!"

"I will not, except at the grassroots level. Grass is an essential crop and should be properly cultivated, as I have been trying to explain."

After many of such complicated lectures full of irrelevant details I realised he wanted to start a vegetarian restaurant on land cultivated to supply it. I said I would never leave the home I loved and whose mortgage I had paid off years before meeting him.

"You will not need to leave it," he said. "When your health recovers I can commute."

"To Fife?" I yelled. He said he wanted to buy a patch of land within or near the Glasgow boundaries, perhaps one of those sharp triangles of ground that nobody wants because they are between intersecting motorways or railway lines. Before Old Kilpatrick there was a neglected strip of ground between the railway and the Clyde from which oil tanks had been removed. The ground was probably polluted so would be cheaper to buy or lease, and making it fertile by right cultivation would set a splendid example.

"What a crazy notion," I said. "But in the mouth of such a completely impractical man it should not surprise me."

"Why am I impractical?" said he. "What have I ever done that I did not do well?"
"You may have done things well but you've never been paid for them," I said.
"I had nothing better to do than tidy that basement," he said sternly, "and if I have not drawn a wage for being your househusband I have been sufficiently paid by your love."
It was hard not to laugh at that but I said, "But Henry you'll need a lot of money for a scheme like this, you've never handled any and you're getting none of mine."
"I neither want nor need yours," said he, "and you are wrong to say I have not handled money. I have handled it by saving what I earned as a teacher, added to what my parents left."
I knew that was quite a lot. His parents, like mine, had been very thrifty in the twenty years of full employment after the Second World War when the British working classes were better paid for their labour than before or since. He went on to say that through the Internet he had contacted folk interested in his scheme and willing to put money into it – architects, lawyers, civil servants, even a banker, all keen on gardening, all knowing that if our governments continued ignoring the Kyoto Protocol our children would either starve or be nourished by plankton from Scottish sea lochs, if not worms grown in bottles.
"We have no children!" I told him.
"Stop being selfish."
"Are you really planning to set up a commune?" I demanded. "They never work. They were tried in the 1960s and hardly outlasted them."
"Certainly not a commune. I am starting my own company and will be in charge of it at every level."
"If people invest in it your company will be a limited liability one – you will be a capitalist! Your investors will expect return for their money, shares of the profits."
"The return for their share, like ours, will be food or good meals."

"And how will I fit into this world-saving scheme? Remember the state of my back. I will never grub up weeds in your organic kitchen garden or chop onions in your kitchen."

"Clerical help will be needed when we get under way."

Once again I almost laughed aloud, seeing for the first time after four married years that Henry has no sense of humour and that mine, though a quiet one, would be needed in times to come.

My back has healed as the doctor foretold. Once again I flush my bodily wastes into the public sewage system, and have started applying for jobs in libraries and bookshops. All my applications have so far failed because I am (as they say) "over-qualified". My best chance of a job seems to be behind a supermarket counter and I have almost resigned myself to that. Henry's plan to reform the world by setting it a good example is not yet under way. He still runs what he calls "our domestic economy" perfectly, while spending more time on the Internet investigating land acquisition. He also talks to teachers and officials about his self-sustaining garden-restaurant giving work experience to local school children, though the locality is not yet decided. He works so hard over details of his scheme that sometimes I think it may work. If not, Henry will remain nothing but my dependable househusband. I do not know which outcome I most fear.

GUMBLER'S SHEAF

"AND," SAYS HARRY GUMBLER. His secretary types that then waits for some minutes until he says, "Delete that Sarah. No! Do not type *delete that*, delete *And*. I can dictate nothing more intelligent today so we'll tackle something else."

From a filing cabinet he removes a folder labelled *NOT URGENT* and from the folder takes a sheaf of letters. After gloomily examining the first he dictates the following.

"*Provisioning Visa*
Customer Experience Manager
Dear Mr Carter,

How dare you *compliment* me – a man you have never met – because your company's advertising campaign has chosen me to receive a card which will guarantee me no interest on any purchases I make for the next three months. Why should I or anyone expect interest on anything they buy in a shop? ... Can *you* explain why, Sarah?"

His secretary explains that many people without money use credit cards as a means of payment. Gumbler groans and says, "Delete the last two sentences, replace by: Why should I or anyone not desperately poor be tempted by an offer which is nothing but a bait designed to lure me into getting indebted to Barclay's Bank? A bait disguised as *a compliment*! Were I not professionally articulate your impertinent arrogance would reduce me to inarticulate rage. You should be ashamed of yourself. Yours truly et cetera. Now the next.

"*Excelsior Promotions*
Youth Encouragement Agency
Dear Egragio Heron,

I refuse to fill in and return your impertinent questionnaire, but will have the courtesy to explain why. Your pompous letter heading does not tell me if your organisation is a publishing house, a branch of a government education department, or a Quasi-Autonomous Non-Governmental Organisation (QUANGO for short). But your purpose is clearly stated: you are asking *celebrities* to explain the reasons for their *success* in a survey whose results will be used to encourage school children in their efforts to *succeed in life*. Let me ask you some questions.

1. Why do you think me a *celebrity*? Is it because some of my writing is in university textbooks and translated into Chinese?
2. Am I therefore fit to be among the rich usurers, politicians, research chemists, footballers, actors and popular entertainers who are 95% of the other *celebrities* your QUANGO is approaching? Are a few disinterested writers and artists needed to give other worshippers of the Bitch Goddess respectable company?
3. Are you prepared to tell the school children you seek to indoctrinate that many of the world's greatest people have died – like the majority of the world's poorest – in a state of miserable neglect? Jesus is the most famous example, tortured to death as a criminal by the Romans, his last words a despairing cry at his abandonment by the God of Love he had wished for all mankind. Herman Melville's first two books brought him early money and fame, but when writing *Moby Dick* – America's greatest novel – he told his wife's parents that this book would NOT succeed, and wrote into it that, **It is failure, not success, that tests the truly great hearts.** Melville died neglected and

forgotten by all but a few, not knowing that his last great work *Billy Budd* would ever be published. I will not add John Clare, Van Gogh and countless others who were treated as failures in their own lifetimes. Before he died even Leonardo da Vinci despaired of having finished anything worthwhile.

I make your firm a free present of this letter. If school children read it along with the other results of your celebrity questionnaire, I may not have written in vain.

"Yours truly et cetera. Email it Sarah. Here comes another.

"To the Manager of the Co-operative Bank,
Mingulay Street Branch, Glasgow

Dear Sir or Madam,

I opened an account with your bank in 1952 on receiving my first education grant through your Sauchiehall Street branch, a service I expected to enjoy for the rest of my life. I wish now to transfer my account to the Airdrie Savings Bank for two reasons, both connected with my hatred of banks and lawyers who advertise and tout for business like car salesmen, travel agencies and other greedy hucksters who nowadays pollute radio, television, film theatres, street hoardings and every other means of communication. In my youth British bankers and lawyers did not do such things. I liked the Co-op Bank because it was then part of a marketing scheme for the working classes created by nineteenth-century socialists. And I liked you declaring an ethical investment policy that would stop the Co-op Bank profiting from weapon and torture-instrument making, and from support of undemocratic governments. Here is why I have changed my mind.

1. You started sending me leaflets illustrated with the faces of handsome young men and women looking full of happy wonder and astonishment by the easy terms on which you were prepared to lend them money. I come from respectable working-class people who believed

that getting into debt was a crime that would lead to eternal damnation. I no longer share my parents' religious faith, but still share their attitude to debt.

2. At the same time other leaflets came from you without pictures, but in sober, even stately prose it suggested I invested my money in *close consultation* with a *Close Brothers Group* of *Wealth Managers* in the city of London money market, *Close Brothers* who promised to increase my money by investing it in safe ways not run by your less wealthy savers. I know as well as you and these *Close Brothers* that the only *safe* money market is managed by bastards who depend on warfare and drug dealing, and have invested the pension funds of our university teachers and probably most other institutions in them.
3. Moreover," says Gumbler, and falls silent. His secretary types that. After a while he says, "Delete marginal numbers and *Moreover*. Last paragraph coming up.

"I am therefore transferring my money to the Airdrie Savings Bank, founded in 1835 the only independent savings bank left in our disUnited Kingdom. When every other Scottish bank united with the Trustee Savings Bank and then floated on the London Stock Exchange, Airdrie did not. It survived obscure and local until 2010 when six merchant bankers each put a million pounds in it. They must have thought that a way to protect their money when the present capitalist system collapses in the near future. Yours truly, et cetera. Check these details with Wikipedia before sending it off, Sarah. Next letter."

"To the Rates Department
Glasgow City Council
Dear Sirs and/or Madams,

I have received your annual rates demand along with a leaflet headed *Pay Up For Glasgow,* which is quite unnecessary since for many years I have paid automatically by standing order. I write to complain about an even more useless pamphlet with a beautiful scenic view of a Scottish loch which turns out to be an advertisement for a private company now owning the Scottish water supply and which, through an international grid, also supplies England with water and, less directly, France. Glasgow civil servants (like our ruling Labour Party councillors) are likely too young and ignorant to know the history of our municipal water supply, which was once an inspiration to every intelligent citizen.

"Loch Katrine in the lonely heart of the Trossachs mountains became Scotland's main tourist attraction after Walter Scott made it the setting of his poem *The Lady of the Lake*. In 1859 Queen Victoria crossed it by the steamer *Rob Roy* to the mouth of a tunnel where she turned a handle. Water started flowing through seventeen miles of tunnel past Ben Venue and Ben Lomond to the great reservoir above Milngavie from which it descended to the whole city of Glasgow. This steady supply of pure water had been achieved by a Liberal local government against three sorts of Tory opponents.

1. Shareholders of private water companies who said a single municipal water supply would undermine their profits and the principle of free competition.
2. Prosperous citizens who found it cheaper to rent pure water privately than pay rates to a municipality that would supply everyone cheaply.
3. The British Admiralty who, because Loch Katrine's overspill was a source of the River Forth, feared the Firth of Forth might silt up, thus depriving the Royal Navy of its most important dock and harbour north of the Humber.

On the other side the Liberals argued that:

1. The steam engines Glasgow exported needed more pure water than private companies could supply. Muddy water in a workman's tubes might kill him, but labour was cheap. Muddy water in an engine's tubes could break it down, and machines were dear.

2. Typhus, typhoid and cholera epidemics began among the overcrowded poor who could seldom pay for good water, so maybe God was punishing them for that, but the diseases often spread to respectable householders.
3. The Admiralty was wrong.

So Glasgow became the industrial city with the best municipal water supply in the United Kingdom and escaped the 1866 cholera epidemic that attacked the rest of the country. For decades a local Liberal government made Glasgow the world's foremost city in public water supplies, public lighting, transport, libraries, hospitals, almost everything except housing. Only when the Scottish Independent Labour Party got a place in the London parliament while also taking over Glasgow were the first and best local housing schemes created.

"You have grown up in a completely privatised world, but as public servants you have no right to be distributing an advertising brochure for a private company that has grabbed all of Scotland's great municipal heritage. Your only job now is to police it and ensure it is providing the public service you have relinquished. Do you really think the brochure *proves* the company is doing its job well? Are you fools who don't know that EVERY private company pays smart agencies of copywriters and artists to persuade most of us of its wonderful achievements, while blinding us to its crimes and failures? Or are you scoundrels with shares in Scottish Water? I am eager to be informed. Yours et cetera.

"Do you think that letter will have more impact, Sarah, if I address it to Glasgow's Lord Provost instead of the rates department?"
She says, "I think it will all come to the same thing Harry."
"In that case leave it. Fifth letter. You will have to consult the internet to find the address of this firm which is either in Austria or Germany."

The Business Manager
Rotring Pen Company
"Dear Sir,

Since my days as an art student I have used, and come to depend upon the use, of your once excellent pens, which I was delighted to see never changed their style of manufacture for over half a century. Twenty five years ago you made pre-filled ink cartridges available, but I ignored these, finding it both cheaper and more convenient to fill the interior reservoir by hand. Whenever a pen was lost or a nib damaged I had no trouble replacing these from one of Glasgow's two main artist-supply shops – until recently, when the shopkeepers started spending more and more time searching through drawers for what I needed. I attributed this to modern shop servants knowing almost nothing about what they sell.

"Recently I bought an 0.5 nib which stopped working after my first session of using it. Neither weak solvent (hot soapy water) or stronger (refined spirits of turpentine) unclogged it so I bought another, which seems to be the last in Glasgow. It too stopped working. I feel bereft of an old and useful friend. Can you advise me on this matter? Yours truly et cetera. Please find the maker's address. I think it is in Germany."

After some Googling his secretary pointed to the screen and asked, "Is that the pen you like using?"

He peered at an image and said "Yes indeed."

"They're still making it. Perhaps the last two you bought had been lying a long time at the back of a drawer. I can order some more online."

"But where would I pick them up?"

"They would be delivered by post."

After a long pause Gumbler said gloomily, "Abort that letter. Please order three Rotring Isographs with 0.3, 0.5 and 0.8 nibs. Last letter.

"*The Sales Manager*
Serious Reading Lamps
Dear Madam,

I was pleased by your reaction to my phone call last week when I explained that the standard lamp I had been using for a great many years had failed for no explicable reason, since the bulb lit up when transferred to other lamps. You told me your firm would replace it with a new one, if I returned it to the courier in the box wherein the new was delivered. On receiving the new lamp yesterday I was delighted, had the old lamp removed, as agreed, so was flabbergasted last night to discover the plug would fit no standard socket in my house! The prongs are far too large, and instead of being metallic, seem composed of a thick white plastic. I find it almost impossible to believe that your firm expects every user of your most recent lamps to have the electric sockets of their homes renewed to fit. Such a requirement is commercialism gone mad and cutting its own throat…"

"Excuse me Harry, but could you show me that plug?" says his secretary.

"Why not?" says Gumbler grumpily. Leaving his chair he brings the lamp over from a corner and hands her the plug. She removes the white plastic sheath covering the metallic prongs, drops the sheath in a wastepaper basket and hands the plug back. Gumbler sighs deeply three or four times then says, "I see. I see. Thank you. My problem is being too old. There is no point in sending the other letters either."

LATE DINNER

SHORTLY BEFORE MIDNIGHT only two tables are still occupied in this small expensive restaurant. At one table a couple sip coffee and liqueurs and the man says, "It will be a stormy meeting tomorrow. All kinds of people will be trying to wriggle off hooks."

"That won't be our problem," says the woman, and he agrees with her.

At a nearby table set for two, a woman with a glass of wine beside her is reading a magazine. A waitress tells her, "I'm sorry, but the chef will be closing the kitchen in ten minutes if not told to start the meal you ordered. Surely you've waited long enough?"

"I certainly have," says the woman, closing the magazine. "My friend has never been as late as this before so tell the chef to – no – wait a bit, Mr Big is finally arriving."

A quiet, penetrating voice reaches them before the speaker saying, "And Starky was hanging about your office today. Why? Sorry I'm late Proody. That last remark was not for you, Mrs Russell. You want to get to bed as it is near midnight. I am about to order a late dinner, first tell me why you let Starky natter to MacLeod for nearly twenty minutes."

Mr Big is over six feet high, handsome, middle-aged, with a convincingly young manner. He sits opposite the woman he calls Proody, listens to his phone then says, "I see. You did not like to interrupt Starky and MacLeod because they are old friends. That's bad, Mrs Russell. MacLeod is useful, Starky a waste of time which is why I fired him. When you don't interrupt a chat like that you too are wasting my time. From now on I'll be watching

you. This is a friendly warning. Go to bed and sleep on it. Goodnight."
He pockets the phone and murmurs across the table, "Sorry Proody. Tough days don't bother me but this one has been very tough. I must shut my eyes for a bit."
He leans back in the chair and does so. The waitress, interested by his performance, looks questioningly at Proody who begins to say that the kitchen is soon closing, but he interrupts her without opening his eyes: "Tell them I want the main course you're having, with absolutely no starters."
"Certainly sir," says the waitress. "Another risotto of summer greens, Grana Padano, truffle oil. Anything to drink?"
"Tell her," he murmurs to Proody. "Give her the recipe."
She tells the waitress, "A black velvet please – half pint of Guinness with an equal measure of champagne in a tankard or tall glass."
"But that means opening a bottle of champagne!"
"He'll pay for it and may drink the rest later," says Proody, exchanging an *O these men* look with the waitress, who leaves. Proody reads her magazine again.

Voices at the other table become audible. The man says, "There is no real backlash against audit. The backlash is against terms that audit employs."
"Yes," says his companion, "but there must be such a thing as real information about issues that need to be addressed. Am I wrong?"
"Not wrong, but how can you get the right people to address issues on a local level when they are fed nothing but fashionable trends from the upper level?"
"Who are the right people?"
"Those who have most impact on the public services."
They are startled by a groan from Mr Big, but resume their conversation more quietly after staring at him, for his laid-back figure gives no sign of having heard them. A distant cork pops. Soon after the waitress arrives with

a tray and places the contents on the table saying, "Your black velvet, sir. The amuse bouche tonight are smoked salmon with crème fraiche and lemon purée."

"I distinctly said I want no starters!" says Big, sitting up and glaring.

"Amuse bouche are not hors d'oeuvres sir. They are a free gift from the management for which customers are not charged."

"Don't try to blind me with your French," says Big. "There is no such thing in the world as a free gift. This unasked-for rubbish will not con me into thinking I am getting something for nothing. The management makes customers pay for it by increasing the price of what they really want. Remove this trash."

"I'll keep mine thank you," says Proody, closing her magazine and taking a fork to a small plate as the waitress removes the other. Big tastes his black velvet, looking brighter and more wide-awake for his outburst.

"Are you always rude to underlings?" asks Proody in a pleasant way.

He answers pleasantly, "Only when they don't give me what I expect. I'm not rude to people I trust."

"Were bosses rude to you when you were an underling?"

"The efficient ones were, at first. As I climbed the company ladder they saw it wasn't necessary."

"I've decided to leave you," she says.

He murmurs, "Ah."

They are silent for a long time. The main course is served and they start eating.

At the next table the woman says, "There is surely such a thing as real information, information on a national basis."

"I don't deny it," says the man, his voice growing loud again, "but we are not really making things change because we have not pulled the right levers. What we do in a detailed way should depend on a better understanding of topic selection. Until you have the right concept in place you are basically incapable of setting up an effective hub."

"So where, practically speaking, are we coming from?"

"Hard to say. We used to have the Institute for Improvement and Development behind us, but it was disbanded a month ago."

"But *somebody* must be responsible for improving things, surely?"

"Yes. Us."

"Us? That's a terrifying idea."

"Because we lack a concept of a new hub of values that will respond to levers we can actually, basically, handle."

"Bullshit!" says Big loudly for the first time. "They're drowning us in the stuff."

"Are you talking about us?" the other man demands fiercely.

"No. Only about you," says Big. "After a hard day's work your drivel (which I could not help hearing) is intolerable. In my business words have precise meanings. Your jargon is more destructive of sensible thought than the noise of a pneumatic drill or a modern pop group."

"You know nothing about my business," cries the other, "nothing about what we were discussing."

"You are obviously something in local government," says Big, "someone with no real power nowadays, so you try to hide the fact with meaningless speeches. You can't admit that the levers controlling Britain are handled by real businessmen like me. Every year we buy hundreds of you. M.P.s and local councillors and the police cost most. The rest of you are comparatively cheap."

"Are you suggesting that I and my friend are corrupt?" demands his victim.

"Certainly not!" says Big with a sudden cheerful grin. "Your jargon makes it clear you have so little power that you aren't worth bribing. I am sorry to hurt your companion's feelings, because she seems keen to understand things ..." (the woman at the other table seems near to tears) "... so let us all talk more quietly now."

"Bring me the bill!" the other man tells the waitress. "I will never set foot in this restaurant again, and will make sure none of my friends do either."
He pays. The couple leave. Before reaching the door the man tells Big, "You are a right bastard."
Big chuckles and resumes his meal.

Without obvious blame Proody says, "You enjoyed humiliating that man."
"It relieved my feelings," says Big pleasantly. "You must admit that he talked a lot of shit."
"Did you hear me say I was going to leave you?"
"Yes."
"Anything to say about that?"
"No. I knew you were going to leave me."
"Since when?"
"Since we became lovers."
She stares at him until Big feels an explanation is due.
"You're very attractive Proody," he says, "attractive and intelligent. I find it easy to charm women like you at first and can keep doing it if they don't see much of me. But when the sex thing starts they do see more of me, and start not liking what they often see."
"A bully," she tells him.
"If you say so," he answers humbly.
They stop eating. After a while she almost begs, "Since you know yourself so well, can you not change?"
"I've tried. I was married you know, with kids and apologies for not remembering anniversaries and politeness to in-laws who bored me stiff. I kept forgetting how much hypocrisy marriage needs to keep it going. I employ more than forty people, some of them with smart ideas of their own. I can only control them by being what you call an bully. I am not a Mr Hyde or Ebenezer Scrooge at work who could *completely* become Dr Jekyll or Mr Pickwick in the bosom of my family. Maybe that was possible in pre-mobile phone days, but now folk with thriving businesses can never lose touch with them. My wives

couldn't understand that. Luckily I can afford to support them, being one of those fat cats people complain about."
They are silent for a whole minute then she says, "So from the start you knew our affair was an episode? An emotional dead end?"
"That's an ugly way to describe some very nice times we've had, Proody."
"From now on my name is Prue or Prudence."

They are speaking too quietly for the waitress to hear. She comes to remove the plates, saying that the kitchen is closed but she can serve coffee or anything else they wish to drink. Big says, "Bring me—" but Prue or Prudence interrupts saying, "Nothing for me. I'm leaving. Make out a bill for the risotto and my glass of wine."
"Please don't leave like this dear!" he begs. "Can't we part like friends?"
"No. I will lose all self-respect if I stay with you another minute."
She follows the waitress to the bar, pays and receives her coat. He stares forlornly after her, but she leaves the restaurant without a backward glance.

Putting an elbow on the tabletop he rests his chin on the palm of the hand, sighs deeply and groans quietly. Seeing the waitress approach he groans more theatrically and announces, "I may not seem a tragic figure to you, but once again a good woman has rejected, dumped and done with me, having discovered what a selfish, exploitative bastard I am. I have never got used to this, no matter how often it happens."
Unimpressed, she asks, "Do you want the rest of your champagne?"
"You are a clever girl, Maggie. I must indeed soothe myself with plonk before leaving, but not with the plonk in my black velvet which, though tolerable mixed with Guinness, was obviously your cheapest. Bring me a bottle of your most expensive."

"My name is not Maggie."
"You astonish me. What is it?"
Almost surprised into smiling she says, "None of your business. We have Moët et Chandon 2003, seventy-three pounds."
He pleads pathetically, "Please don't leave me to drink it alone. For a short time before leaving here I need a good-looking, intelligent woman to sit here pretending my company is bearable. I will not try to make you drunk. Please invite the chef to drink with us too."
"He's gone home," says the waitress, looking at him thoughtfully.

There is no record of how their conversation ends.

THE PATIENT

WITH NO MEMORY OF ANYTHING PREVIOUS he found himself sitting up in a hospital bed wearing a hospital nightgown while a young woman checked his pulse, temperature, tested his reflexes then asked, "How do you feel now?"

"Perfectly all right," he said because that was exactly how he felt. She made notes on a clipboard while he wondered if she was a doctor, a highly trained nurse or something between the two. His main experience of hospitals had been half a century earlier, when everyone's rank in a hospital was shown in the clothing. Doctors had white coats, usually open to show suits worn by most professional people then. Ward matrons and the nurses they commanded wore crisp linen aprons over blue dresses, with the matrons' superiority asserted by a linen headdress rather like the wig of a sphinx. He thought about changes that had altered most things he once took for granted until a young man in a green T-shirt and trousers came and began checking his pulse, temperature et cetera. The patient said, "This has been done already."

"Yes," said the man, "but we like to make sure."

The patient thought about asking what was wrong with him, and how he had come there, but felt that admission of ignorance would demean him. Instead he asked (for the thought had suddenly occurred), "Where is my wife?"

"She's staying overnight in a hotel. We'll probably let you out tomorrow, but had better keep you here till then in case complications develop."

The man went away and the patient took stock of his situation.

His clothes, neatly folded, were on a chair beside the bed with his shoes on the floor beneath. A window behind showed total darkness outside so the hour was very late or very early in the morning. He was in a square ward with a bed in each corner. The bed facing him was empty. The other two beds, on each side of the ward's entrance, had curtains pulled round them with two or three people inside talking in low voices. This was certainly an Accident and Emergency ward, but what had been the accident and where was the hospital? There was no ache in any part of his body and no stiffness in any joint, but on top of his skull where hardly any hair now grew he felt a mound like half a hard-boiled egg without the shell, sore when pressed, and with what seemed a gritty groove across it. How had that happened? Margaret and he had gone to a conference at Edinburgh University. His speech had received the usual friendly applause, and in a staffroom afterwards they had stood eating wee sandwiches and sausage rolls from cardboard plates, gossiping and sipping wine. Or was it whisky? Or both? Both were possible. Had this led to him falling down? But he had no hangover. He really did feel perfectly well and (he suddenly noticed) hungry.

After a while he got out of bed and went between the curtained beds to the entrance. Here he met the young man in green clothes coming in with a piece of medical equipment and asked him, "Can I have something to eat?" "Certainly. Soon. Soon." said the man, going behind the curtains around a bed. The patient went back, lay down and after a while decided that the Emergency staff had more important things to do than feed him, so he would go out and buy a supper from the nearest fish and chip shop. Without removing the hospital nightshirt he tucked it into his trousers, put jersey and jacket on top, strapped on his sandals and went out into the corridor. Following EXIT signs with pointing arrows he passed through several corridors without passing anyone who noticed him, then arrived at a big doorway and went through. There was no street outside, only an acre of tarmac with a few parked cars and on the far side the black silhouettes of treetops against the slightly less black night sky. Then he remembered that Edinburgh City Hospital was no longer beside the University with nearby shops and pubs. This modern hospital was obviously miles from a fish and chip shop. With a sigh he went back inside. Seeing some seated men who seemed to be ambulance drivers he asked if there was a place where food could be got.

"You'll find a vending machine through there," said one of them, pointing. He found a big waiting room with nobody but himself there, and beside an empty reception desk a big glass-fronted cupboard containing many shelves. On the upper shelves packets of differently flavoured potato crisps were displayed, on the lower shelves those sweets that Americans call candy bars. Each was identified by a number and a letter of the alphabet beneath it on the shelf. A bar of chocolate interested him but could only be acquired by pressing buttons on a small switchboard at the side and putting money into a slot. He had not used a slot machine for years so had not realized they had become as bafflingly intricate as modern telephones, wireless sets and the latest models of probably everything else. He went back to the Emergency ward, again without anybody appearing to notice.

On the locker by the bed was a sandwich in a plastic wrapper and a cup of tea that was still warm enough to drink. Whoever left it there had perhaps assumed he was in the ward's lavatory. It was a cheese and tomato sandwich. He ate it and drank the tea with great pleasure while sitting on the bed, then removed his sandals, stood up to undress, then saw that what had been the empty bed opposite had now a woman in it who was much younger than he. She was watching him with an absence of expression that somehow made him feel apologetic. Before pulling the curtains around his own bed he told

her, "I'm doing this because I'm going to get undressed." She said, "Don't worry – I won't jump on you."
He pulled the curtains round his bed, undressed, got in and slept.

And awoke to a new day because there was a bright sky outside the window. He got up and dressed. The bed opposite was empty again. The two beds beside the entrance were now uncurtained. One was empty, the other contained a body he did not look at closely because of the low distressing sounds it made and the many tubes running into it. A clock on the wall showed the time was 8.20 a.m. National Health Hospitals had certainly changed a lot. Until the 1970s or perhaps later he remembered all patients being wakened soon after 7 a.m. by nurses serving breakfast. Then he heard a familiar voice from the corridor saying a sentence ending with the words, "... my husband."
He stood up and went to her saying, "Here I am."
"So he's all right? I can take him home?" she asked the man in green who was obviously still on duty.
"Yes, take him home. If any of the symptoms described on this sheet occur, send for your GP at once, but if he takes things easy for a few weeks and avoids booze for a fortnight, I think he'll be fine."
As they walked hand-in-hand to the exit he asked, "What happened? How did I get here?"
"We were going down some steep steps into the Old Quadrangle. I needed help and got it. You thought you didn't, and tripped, and would have fallen on your face had you not twisted sideways and banged your head instead. I thought you were dead – it was a nightmare. The ambulance came quite quick and the doctors here said it was a simple case of concussion, and I needn't worry, but how did I know they weren't saying that just to calm me? We are not going back to Glasgow by train. We're going by taxi the whole way, no matter what it costs."
And they did.

BILLY SEMPLE

LEANING HEAVILY ON A STICK and walking with great difficulty, a man came into the pub where I usually drank a few years ago. The pub has since been gentrified out of existence. I did not think the man leaning on the stick was drunk, but the barman refused to serve him. The man said, "I'm Billy Semple, I used to play for Rangers. My legs are all shattered."
"You still have to leave here."
"How?"
"The way you came."
Both were silent for a while, then the barman asked if he should phone for a taxi. Semple nodded.

While the barman phoned I helped Semple to the door and stood outside with him, though standing seemed as hard for him as walking. I also noticed he was, in a quiet way, very drunk indeed. I know nothing about football, so to make conversation said, "Not easy, eh?"
He muttered something like, "You never know how things will end."
The taxi arrived, but when the driver saw Semple he said, "Not in my cab," and drove off. I returned into the pub and asked the barman to phone for an ambulance. He did, then came outside. The three of us waited, and when the ambulance came the ambulance men also refused to take Semple. I had not realised that our public health service now rejects helpless invalids for being drunk, but of course the world keeps changing all the time.
"Nothing for it but the police," said the barman going back inside.

When the police came they lifted Semple into their van and drove off.

End of story. Maybe they charged him with being drunk and disorderly, maybe they took him to where he lived, or maybe both. I asked a football enthusiast if he had heard of Billy Semple. He said, "Yes. Used to play for Rangers. Definitely a name to conjure with."

Maybe the man was lying about his name but he convinced me.

ENDING

HAVING BEGUILED WITH FICTION until I had none left I resorted to facts, which also ran out.

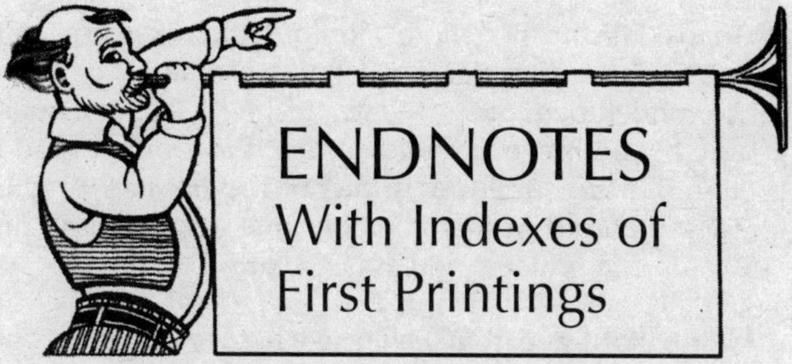

ENDNOTES
With Indexes of First Printings

AT THE MOMENT OF HIS GREATEST TRIUMPH Captain Hook falls into a melancholy that is perhaps familiar to many old Etonians. He then and there decides to give his dying speech, in case the inevitable tick-tocking crocodile leaves him no time for it later. The same vanity has made these endnotes tell more about my life as a fiction writer than I first intended. An astute critic said my last book would bore many readers by its repetition of passages printed elsewhere. Many sentences that follow have also been printed before.

INTRODUCTION

Wordsworth is right to say the younger we are the brighter our world appears. I was born in a pleasant home, a flat in a newly built Glasgow housing scheme with gardens, trees and skies as good as anywhere else, but when these had grown familiar by the age of two I wanted extravagantly different experiences. My parents satisfied this want. I cannot remember not knowing Cinderella, Aladdin and the adventures of other weak or exploited folk helped to happiness and wealth by magic gifts. I then came to enjoy the cosy fantasy of Pooh Corner with its soft toy inhabitants, and the dangerous, more challenging worlds of Hans Anderson. From him I learned that even in magical lands people like me could come to grief and die, and I felt like the main character in every interesting tale, even the Little Match Girl. Fabulous tales free us from immediate, everyday suffering but also prepare us for it. The talking animals known to Dr Dolittle and Toad of Toad Hall are not more fabulous than Aesop's, but Aesop's fables (like Beatrix Potter's) promote common sense, undeluded, Stoical views of life. I was not such a stoic as the Brave Tin Soldier, much as I pitied him. I preferred the unemployed soldier of *The Tinder Box* who murdered an old woman then became a spendthrift, an abductor of a princess and at last a king.

It is a small step from feeling like heroes or heroines of other peoples' stories to swaggering through stories of our own imagining. Most children take that step, instinctively editing what they hear, read and enjoy in films and comics into daydreams of the sort Dr Freud called (when sleepers had them) wish-fulfilment dreams. Experience mostly changes our childish daydreams into what we adults hope and fear for our future. My serial daydream of having a magic gift granting extraordinary power is the basic plot of *Superman* and must have inspired several presidents of the USA. Most American comics came to Britain at the end of World War Two, fascinating me by their competent outlines, lavish colour and pictures of damsels in distress, but my serial fantasy was active before that war started, and was so satisfying that I sometimes resented its interruption by adults, but not often. Mum, Dad, my sister and me were close together most evenings of the year because only our living room usually had a warm fire. Mum had given me fairytales. Dad showed me *The Harmsworth Encyclopaedia*, *The Miracle of Life* and other books with pictures proving there were, or had been, or could be, wonderful realities outside our douce housing scheme that also fed my fantasies. To make these more real I needed an audience and my sister Mora became that. I told her my fanciful adventures as we walked to school, then later as we lay in adjacent bedrooms with the doors between open. Like most parents Mum and Dad put us to bed earlier than we thought right because (they said) we needed a good night's sleep. They may also have wanted more time to themselves. They never interrupted my serial story by shutting the bedroom doors. Mora did not interest me as a person, being two years younger and a girl, but until I was thirteen or more I needed her as much as I have since needed a public for my books.

The world outside my fantasies imposed itself. The 1939 war evacuated us from Glasgow. For a few years I enjoyed a privileged childhood in Wetherby, a Yorkshire market town where I explored the countryside, climbed trees and played with other boys. Our main game was finding or making dens – secret places in bushes, up trees or in odd huts or buildings where none suspected us. I recall nothing remarkable done in our dens or even stories associated with them, apart from one. I discovered a den by myself in an isolated outhouse, one of several in the munition workers' hostel where Dad was manager. It must have been an auxiliary furnace room, to be used if one of the hostel's other power sources was damaged. I could not open the door or window but found at ground level a low shutter – a hatch through which fuel could be raked from an outside heap of coke – and slid it up far enough to let me crawl under. Within was a cement floor, bare brick walls, the cold furnace and a secrecy I much appreciated, for I had a notebook in which I meant to write a story of my own. It was inspired by a booklet in a series, *Tales for the Young Folk,* each of which cost thruppence, and were often so puerile that I easily imagined improving on them. Why did I want secrecy to write this one? To discourage exhibitionism my parents never praised my writings and drawings, but I knew they approved of them – Dad had typed silly verses I had written under the inspiration of A.A. Milne. I suspect my version of this tale gave it a cruel twist Mum and Dad would dislike. I now recall nothing of the story I attempted, but in that outhouse came a glorious conviction that one day I would write a book that many would read. After that I think every interesting story or experience was regarded, often consciously, as potential material for fiction. This happened when I was eight or nine, because for what seemed years after I meant to astonish the world with a book completed when I was twelve – the first of my many failed literary projects.

Life seemed more confined when we returned to Glasgow after the war. Dens could not be made in our back green or the nearby public park. My schoolmates' outdoor games were kicking balls about, which I did not enjoy. Riddrie Public Library became my second home, visited at least four times a week as I often read a book in a few hours. Many males graduate to maturer fiction through tales about sportsmen, detectives, cowboys, soldiers or spies licensed to kill. I could not imagine dominating events by violent action so kept to tales of magic most children lose interest in earlier, finding slightly more adult forms in Conan Doyle's *The Lost World*, Rider Haggard's *She*, novels by H.G. Wells. His early science fiction shows impossible worlds in such intelligently imagined detail that they are excellent social criticism, no more escapist than *Gulliver's Travels*, *Brave New World* or *1984*. One summer morning when ten or eleven I stood in a shop among a crowd waiting for a delivery of morning papers to Millport on the Firth of Clyde island where my family was on holiday. On the counter I saw a little paperback book with no author's name or picture on the cover. In 1945 such booklets were the only non-periodical literature sold in newspaper and tobacconist shops, the contents always being highly sensational, popular, out of copyright stuff. Nearly all the tales I had so far enjoyed had been illustrated, so only boredom led me to open this booklet and start reading *The Pit and the Pendulum*. With the first few sentences the surrounding friendly crowd seemed cut off from me. I believe my pulse and skin temperature changed. The adjacent talk seemed a distant hum or buzzing, as the voices of the inquisitors sounded in the ears of the narrator condemned to die by torture. This was my first experience of being badly frightened by a story, if I ignore a few chilling episodes in Disney's *Snow*

White and *Pinocchio*. It was not my last. Back at home in Riddrie I found my parents had a little set of books, one of them Verne's *20,000 Leagues Under the Sea,* one of them Kipling's *From Sea to Sea* and one of them Poe's *Tales of Mystery and Imagination.* Alone in our comfortable home one sunny evening after returning from school I read *The Fall of the House of Usher*, and for a while grew afraid to look behind any familiar article of furniture, from fear of seeing something dreadful.

Which shows I was in tune with Edgar Allan's weird verbal magic – and was a good reader. Though keen to be an author I gladly submitted to the power of others, which is how best to learn authorship. Milton describes the process in rhyming epitaph to Shakespeare, where he tells the playwright that his impressive lines:

... our fancy of it self bereaving
dost make us Marble with too much conceiving

– meaning Shakespeare's words can make us briefly more like statues of Hamlet, Falstaff or Cleopatra than like ourselves. This loss of our person in another author's character strengthens our critical power if we read closely and widely. For years my critical powers stopped me writing every fiction I started after two or three pages. Despite good marks for school essays, despite filling notebooks with details and ideas, I saw that each false start was obviously in the voice of a child or (later) of a self-obsessed adolescent. But before leaving secondary school I started identifying most strongly with potential writers or artists in fictional worlds more like mine – David Copperfield's Victorian England, Paul Morel's Nottingham, Stephen Dedalus's Dublin, and the 1938 Bankside, London, of Gulley Jimson, the disreputable old mural painter in Joyce Carey's *The Horse's Mouth*.

UNLIKELY STORIES, MOSTLY

The first story in this book was written in the last summer holiday with both my parents on the island of Arran. This has been called Scotland in miniature, having a jaggedly mountainous north and to the south lower hills, some farms and sheltered woody hollows. The villages and houses nearly all face the sea across a coastal road. For two or three years our holiday home was the last house in Pirnmill, a row of houses with primary school and post office on the quietest side of Arran. In long summer holidays there I often regretted having no friend of my own age and sex, yet enjoyed long walks accompanied by my imagination. On the three or four miles of road between Pirnmill and Lochranza the only houses are a low white terrace nicknamed the Twelve Apostles on Catacol Bay. Just before Catacol the coast road is pinched between the sea cliff and a boulder bigger than a house, steep sided but easily climbable by any boy who likes feeling king of a castle. The top had bushes and turf where I lay one sunny afternoon feeling elevated and private, and here I imagined *The Star* in a gust of what seemed inspiration.

The critic Leavis suggests that inspiration is unconscious memory, because well made phrases only come without effort when authors intuitively adapt words by earlier writers. At least twenty years passed before I noticed that *The Star* was inspired by H.G. Wells' story *The Crystal Egg*, in which the hen-pecked owner of a grubby curio shop finds consolation in a lens through which he glimpses life on another planet. He dies while hiding it from a potential customer and his rapacious wife. *The Crystal Egg* is about a dozen pages long; my tale of a young boy dying to keep a magic gift is barely two. I did not know the end before describing the teacher demanding the gift, which resembled one of those coloured glass balls Scots children call bools, jorries or jinkies – English children call them marbles. I did not want the reader to think it was just a cheap glass toy made magic by the fancy of a deluded child. I disliked stories equating imaginary worlds with delusion, which the *Alice* books miraculously avoid, despite their stories being dreams. I was pleased and astonished at finding three last sentences that left the star a reality.

Four years or more passed before I wrote four stories following *The Star*. *The Spread of Ian Nicol* and *The Cause of Recent Changes* were stimulated by a chance of publication in *Ygorra*, a facetious magazine published annually by Glasgow University students and sold for charity. For two years the editor was Alan Fletcher, a Glasgow School of Art student whose talent and intelligence led him to design the covers, give it cartoons, print articles and work by Frank Bowles, Reid Moffat, Malcolm Hood and me, his fellow art students. My illustrations to two stories, slightly improved, are now on pages 10–11 and 17 of this book. I also wrote *The Comedy of the White Dog* at art school, but the climax is bestial sex so could not be published before the permissive 1960s. *A Unique Case* was written for *Cleg*, an art school magazine of which the only edition was conceived and edited by my friend James Spence.

I was a student supported by my parents and the British Welfare State education grants when I wrote these early fables. Then came two years of part time uncertificated teaching, as little of it as possible while I tried and failed to earn money by my visual arts. With another education grant I then trained as a full time teacher; the only short story written in this glum period was *The Answer*, a likely story which, though told in the third person, tells how another trainee teacher, without fuss or harsh words, showed she was tired of me. James Joyce had shown me how everyday happenings could be as much the stuff of fiction as miraculous fables. For many years after that I was too busy combining the familiar and fabulous in a novel to write anything shorter, apart from a spoof lecture, *The Crank that Made the Revolution*. To tell how more unlikely stories came to be written I must speak of that novel, *Lanark*.

When half finished in 1970 an excellent English literary agent, Frances Head, showed *Lanark* to three London publishers who agreed it might become something saleable, but as it would be very long, and eccentric, and the author was unknown, it might be a very expensive flop. Each was willing to publish it as two books of average length, which could easily have been done because it combined two narratives – one of them fabulous, a modern *Pilgrim's Progress* greatly influenced by Kafka, one a *Portrait of the Artist as a Young Man* set in Glasgow instead of Dublin. I refused that offer but one of these publishers, Quartet Books, offered £90 for the right to accept or refuse it on completion. I gladly accepted that money from Quartet, which was then worth at least five times what £90 buys now, forty-two years later. I continued writing the novel, confident that Frances Head would find a good publisher for it on completion, even if it was finally rejected by Quartet. But Frances Head died of lung cancer shortly before the novel was completed in 1977, and Quartet Books rejected it because of the length. Without much hope I sent it off to Canongate Books in Edinburgh, a Scottish publishing house so small that I doubted if *Lanark* would ever be published. My income had largely come from television plays commissioned through Frances. These stopped. I failed in a miserable effort to teach again. Thoroughly depressed, I decided to waste my talent by writing a book that would make money, a pornographic novel full of fantasies I had been suppressing since the age of four or five. But despite trying to write it for weeks, I was so unlike the Marquis de Sade that I kept losing interest.

Very few authors, even good ones, can live by their writing, a fact that has driven some to suicide. B.S. Johnson was infuriated by publishers earning good money by selling the work of authors who had to feed themselves by teaching or some other distraction. The British Welfare State tackled that problem by creating Arts Councils, and the Councils made life easier for some authors by paying universities to take them as Writers in Residence. University literature departments in those days taught nothing but criticism. For two years a resident author could receive a good salary to help the few students trying to write fiction, poems or plays for themselves. The authors chose their hours for this work and otherwise did as they pleased. I applied to become Glasgow University's third resident writer, on the basis of my radio and television plays. The selection committee was headed by Professor Peter Butter, a Shelley specialist. When he asked what I would write if I got the job, I said a modern version of *Prometheus Unbound*, the lost play by Aeschylus that Shelley had attempted, unsuccessfully, I thought. With time for research I hoped to do better. That my friend Philip Hobsbaum was also on the selection committee may also have helped me get the job.

From 1977 to 1979 I earned my first steady wage for enjoyable work. My office, in the top-floor south-west corner of Glasgow University, had a big desk, two padded chairs, a bookcase and, through the window, a downward view through treetops of the river Kelvin and beyond them the towers of our art galleries and museum beyond. Here for two and a half days a week I easily helped willing people with their writings in one-to-one tutorials, and otherwise was my own master. *Prometheus Unbound* proved an impossible play to finish. I had no ideas for writing anything else. Deciding to further my education by more reading I bought *The Road to Xanadu* by Livingston Lowes, and a thick book of all Ezra Pound's *Cantos*.

The Road to Xanadu surveys the old travel and history books that inspired Coleridge's fragmentary *Kubla Khan* poem and his *Rime of the Ancient Mariner.* It excited me by recalling every book about lost or hidden worlds I had enjoyed in adolescence. Ezra Pound's verses about good and bad monetary states confused me with their far-fetched, detailed quotations until an unexpected line from his Chinese *Cantos* made excellent sense:

> *Moping around the Emperor's court, waiting for the order-to-write.*

Order-to-write was hyphenated because (I thought) it translated one ideogram – one Chinese letter that was also one word. I suddenly imagined a man being trained from infancy to be a great poet, yet prevented from writing anything until the government told him what it wanted. Thinking this travesty of my university job might fill an amusing page or two I wrote –

Dear mother, dear father, I like the new palace. It is all squares like a chessboard. The red squares are buildings, the white squares are gardens…

– and started inventing a world of my own. Livingston Lowes' account of what went into Coleridge's *Kubla Khan* – the artificial paradise of assassins in the Atlas Mountains, the happy valley where Abyssinian kings grew up, a source of the Nile described by the Scots explorer James Bruce – went into *Five Letters from an Eastern Empire*, my best and longest short story, quickly written in two or three weeks. Years later an Irish friend told me he had heard a Chinese and a Japanese scholar discuss which of their nations my empire most resembled. Some hints of the real Orient may have come from my early reading of a Chinese anthology and the comic *Monkey* epic in Arthur Waley translations, but I think my empire resembles Britain today as much as any other land.

Several months had passed since I posted my novel to Canongate. Shortly after writing the *Five Letters from an Eastern Empire* a letter came from Canongate's reader, Charles Wilde, saying he was only partly through reading *Lanark* but was already determined to see it published, despite its great length. He thought the Scottish Arts Council would help Canongate by subsidizing the printing. This greatly revived my confidence and an old plan for a second book containing all the short prose I had written, both fabulous and realistic. Apart from the *Five Letters* my fables were short and few, but for years I had scribbled down ideas for others and now had time to write them.

The *Axletree* tales were inspired by a reproduction of Bruegel's great *Tower of Babel* painting in the head art

teacher's room of Whitehill School 25 years earlier. It had looked so capable of reaching heaven that God's desire to prevent that by disuniting the human race seemed quite natural. Like other trainee teachers at Jordanhill College I had been told to deliver a monologue, and gave a spoof lecture suggesting the Tower of Babel provoked the Deluge. In Genesis Babel was built after, not before Noah's flood, but I did not mind revising Genesis. My lecture had none of the political and historical details that came to me when a Resident Writer. I had also imagined inventing the diary of an aristocratic scholar who never doubts the eccentric theories he promotes, and which might be made entertaining for their own sake, like de Selby's theories in Flann O'Brien's *The Third Policeman*. In Glasgow University Library I found Sir Thomas Urquhart of Cromarty's pamphlets reprinted by the Roxburgh Society and knew HE was the aristocrat I wanted. I invented his diary by rewriting much of the story in his own words, edited with additions of my own. I used my failure to write a modern *Prometheus Unbound* by giving the poetic fragments I had achieved to a highly intellectual French dwarf. He too (I imagined) could not complete them, being frustrated by his inability to seduce a woman activist during the 1968 failure of the student revolt. This story drew much from my own failure to seduce (by letter!! by letter!) a feminist met only once through my friend Joan Ure. Altogether I now had five new fables:
The Start of the Axletree about civilization's imperial and religious origins.
Five Letters from an Eastern Empire about the poet as totalitarian state bureaucrat.
Logopandocy about the poet as Scots Renaissance aristocrat.
Prometheus about the poet as French 1960s democrat.
The End of the Axletree about the downfall of greedy civilizations.

Canongate had arranged to publish *Lanark* jointly in the USA with Lipincot, an old, well established American

firm. But before publication Lipincot was swallowed by Harper and Roe, an equally old well established firm, which slowed publication. *Lanark* was printed in 1981 after a four-year delay enabling me to enlarge the Epilogue, add a verse to the end, and design the book jacket and five interior title pages. It sold so well that Canongate gladly agreed to publish my second book, *Unlikely Stories, Mostly*. This would also contain:
A Report to the Trustees, a true account of how I had used a travelling scholarship between the years 1957 and 1958;
Portrait of a Painter, about my friend Alasdair Taylor;
Portrait of a Playwright, about my friend Joan Ure; and
The Story of a Recluse, a speculative completion of a story Robert Louis Stevenson left unfinished. In 1982 all these had been written. I had only one more story to add, a realistic one.

I scribbled the opening and closing sentences when, as a University extra-mural lecturer, I had often visited Paisley, Dumfries and Moffat. The tale would be the monologue of a tradesman whose job took him all over Scotland, working automatically in an almost continual alcoholic stupor because he hated himself. The main inspiration was the story by Dostoevsky whose title in one translation is *Notes From Underground*, and in another *Confessions of a Cellar Rat*. I first happened upon this story on a ship going to Gibraltar in 1958, and found it so upsetting that I never read it to the end nor looked into it since. I knew such men existed because I was sometimes one, and thought I could make this unattractive chap interesting for a page or two. But on setting out to complete this tale I had postponed writing for nearly twenty years I saw my man's sex life must have shrunk to mere masturbatory fantasies, and decided to spice his tale with bits of my failed pornographic novel of four years earlier. James Joyce wrote that a true work of art makes in the reader or viewer an attentive trance – makes us conceive it so completely that (as Milton said of Shakespeare's plays) it bereaves our fancy. Only improper arts, pornography and propaganda, excite movement in beholders, said Joyce. I agreed with him, and was astonished to find my imagination accelerating and expanding a story containing not just pornography but also my outrage at the way Britain is now governed. It also used many real and moving events that had befallen me and folk I loved – materials which had not gone into *Lanark*. I had meant *Lanark* to be my only novel, and was now writing another! The story had to be divided into chapters and whenever one was finished I believed there was only one more to go, but found I was wrong. I had never written so quickly before, yet after ten chapters I ran out of money and had to stop, being no longer a writer-in-residence. But I was sure *1982 Janine* (so called because it was begun and half written that year) would be in many ways a better novel than *Lanark*.

I gave a copy of the first half to Stephanie Wolfe Murray, owner and director of Canongate, asking if the firm could give me £1,000 advance against royalties to write the end, but Canongate was too poor to do that. She sent the copy to Harper and Row in the United States hoping to raise money by selling the foreign rights but that firm's reader rejected it. Meanwhile we worked to complete *Unlikely Stories, Mostly*.

Stephanie suggested that *Unlikely Stories, Mostly* would be more harmonious without the realistic prose which might become the nucleus of a later book. Agreeing to this I designed it as a compact pocketable volume with the print sufficiently big, with broad margins and many illustrations. Many were needed to make the book enjoyable throughout, since the contortuplicate 16th-century prose of Sir Thomas Urquhart would bore most readers unless the appearance of the pages amused them. To make pictures and text fit each other perfectly, I worked for many days with Jim Hutcheson, excellent typographer and designer, in his Edinburgh office. Relaxing one afternoon with our work almost finished, I lamented that *Unlikely Stories, Mostly* must now lose its third word, leaving the first two lame and alone. We then talked of personal matters. Jim mentioned that a woman he loved had recently rejected him in a perfectly friendly way, answering his plea that their relationship should continue by saying, "Jings, you take everything very seriously." This gave me the idea for two last realistic stories, each five lines of dialogue long, with a picture to preserve the book's original name.

Unlikely Stories, Mostly was as successful a book as *Lanark,* having been translated into almost as many foreign languages. *A Unique Case* and *The Answer* were not in earlier editions because I had forgotten writing the first, and had excluded the second for its realism. I remembered the first when a friend found *Cleg* (that rarest of magazines) in a second hand book stall. By including them here, all my short fictions from 1951–1983 are now printed in their order of writing, with the exception of *The Problem*. Its short length made it fit better among the shortest early stories.

WHEN AND WHERE FIRST PRINTED

The Star in the May edition of *Collins Magazine for Boys and Girls*, 1951.
The Spread of Ian Nichol – Ygorra, 1956.
The Cause of Recent Changes – Ygorra, 1957.
An Exceptional Case – Glasgow Art School magazine, *Cleg,* 1957.
The Comedy of the White Dog had the first half in *Scottish International*, 1969, the whole of it in *Glasgow University Magazine*, 1970.
The Crank That Made the Revolution – The Scottish Field, 1971.
The Origin of the Axeltree – Collins Scottish Short Stories, 1979.
Five Letters From an Eastern Empire – Words Magazine, 1979.
The Answer – Words Magazine, 1980.

LEAN TALES

In 1983 Liz Calder of Jonathan Cape advanced the £1,000 I needed to finish writing *1982 Janine*. Before publication in 1984 I gave a reading to students of St Andrews University, staying overnight in the home of the lecturer who had invited me. I thus met his wife, Jennie Erdal, who worked for Quartet Books. She said that since the success of *Lanark* Quartet regretted having refused it, and asked if I had ideas for another book. I told her of the writings Stephanie Wolfe Murray had thought might be the nucleus of a new book, but I was sure could never be, as I had no ideas for more stories so I could never fill another book. She asked if I would consider putting what I had into a collection with other writers. "Certainly!" said I, expecting *her* to suggest the others, but she asked what other writers I would like. "James Kelman and Agnes Owens," I said, these being excellent Scottish authors and friends of mine, whose first novels had just appeared. That is how *Lean Tales* came to be published in 1985, though not by Quartet.

My third of this book contained the writings excluded from *Unlikely Stories, Mostly*, plus a new a six-page story, *The Grumbler*, suggested by a manic phase following the publication of *Lanark*; also a three-page story *I Own Nothing, I Owe Nothing*, given me in a dream; and a one-page story, *Decision*, about a girl discovering too late the connection between sexual intercourse and pregnancy – a true tale told me by my lawyer friend, Angela Mullane. By adding a handful of tales that were even shorter I nearly made my number of pages close to those of Jim and Agnes. The last one, *Ending*, was a single sentence. I have now made this the last story in *this* book. The Quartet editor dealing with *Lean Tales* was not Jennie Erdal. She liked all my co-authors' stories and most of mine, but thought *Portrait of a Painter* and *Portrait of a Playwright* unsuitable because they could not be read as fiction. I understood why she did not want them, but having nothing to replace them with I asked Liz Calder if Cape would publish *Lean*

Tales as I wished. Cape did. Here is the blurb I wrote for it.

The three writers of this book live in a British region containing the world's largest number of unemployed Scots, the biggest store of nuclear weapons in Europe, and lovely great tracts of depopulated wilderness. Lean Tales *brings together a fine selection of short stories by James Kelman, Agnes Owens and Alasdair Gray who all write as if poverty is normal, but poverty is no more their theme than a fixed income is Jane Austen's. What else they have in common readers may discover and enjoy for themselves.*

Lean Tales sold well enough to be reissued twice as a paperback, and I think would have stayed in print and been popular if ordered for use in Scottish secondary schools. The stories of Jim and Agnes are not in this book, being reprinted a few years ago in other collections of their tales. I have removed the two *Portrait* appreciations and my *Report to the Trustees* because they will be better in a book of essays. To stop this *Lean Tales* section being absurdly thin I have fattened it with four stories from a book that is wholly out of print (*Mavis Belfrage, A Romantic Novel with Shorter Tales*, Bloomsbury 1996). I have also added four tales from later collections in this book whose absence will not be noticed. I will only comment on two of them here. *The Marriage Feast* was written as a counterblast to Kingsley Amis' unfairly dismissive remarks about Dylan Thomas. *A Reality Show* is also a tribute to Danish democracy, because the Royal Family there supports public education by sending their children to state schools instead of those rich private ones falsely called Public in Britain.

WHEN AND WHERE FIRST PRINTED

The Grumbler – *The Fiction Magazine*, 1984.

The Marriage Feast (entitled *Jesus Christ*) – *The Sunday Independent*, 1991.

Fictional Exits – Ten Tales Tall and True, 1993.
Money – Scotlands, 1994.
Edison's Tractatus – New Novel Review, 1995.
Mister Goodchild – Mavis Belfrage with Five Shorter Tales, 1996.
The Shortest Tale – Madam X, 1996
Inches In a Column – Unlikely Stories, Mostly, Canongate Classics Edition, 2001.
Moral Philosophy Exam – The Ends of Our Tethers, 2003.

GLASWEGIANS

Between the publication of *1982 Janine* and *Lean Tales* Scottish newspapers occasionally mentioned that Alasdair Gray had abandoned Canongate, the small Scottish firm that had made him famous by publishing his first two books, and was now enriching by his talents Jonathan Cape of London. That was not the exact truth but it seemed true enough to worry me. Having no ideas for another novel I thought of turning my first television play into one and giving that to Stephanie Wolfe Murray. I did so and Canongate published *The Fall of Kelvin Walker* in 1985. This example was useful to me later.

In 1986 I told the American author Kathy Acker that I was unlikely to write another story, because I had noticed that all mine described men who found life a task they never doubted until an unexpected collision opened their eyes and changed their habits. The collision was usually with a woman, involved swallowing alcohol or worse, and happened in the valley of the shadow of death. My novels and stories so far had been made in the faith that each was an adventurous new world. I now saw the same pattern in them all – *Lanark* used it thrice. Having discovered how my talent worked it was almost certainly defunct. Imagination will not employ whom it cannot surprise. Kathy Acker asked if I had thought of writing a story about a woman. No, I said, that was impossible, as I could not imagine how a woman felt when by herself.

The announcement that I did not expect to write more fiction was truthful but not wholly honest. I hoped my talent was only as dead as Finnegan, and would leap from the coffin and dance a new jig if the wake got loud enough. Meanwhile I arranged a show of paintings, began collection of English vernacular prologues, worked with Sandy Johnson to make a film script of *Lanark* (so ambitious that no financier would look at it) and came to owe my bank a sum oscillating between a few hundred and a few thousand pounds. This was not poverty. Most professional folk live in debt nowadays. Banks and building societies encourage it because debts make them richer. My state only depressed me because my parents had been working class folk who, though not religious, avoided debt like the devil. I too could have avoided it by renting a smaller flat, using public transport instead of taxis, eating at home instead of restaurants, drinking alcohol four or five times year instead of nearly every day. Alas, I felt nostalgia but no desire for the decent carefulness which had bred and educated me. I *wanted* to be a middle-class waster, but a solvent one.

In Queen Street station one morning I glimpsed a girl stepping jauntily through the crowd in high heels and a leather suit which fitted her so snugly in some places, and left her so naked in others that it seemed a preliminary to lovemaking. Soon after or soon before I began imagining how a woman might feel when alone. This came from accompanying a friend on a shopping expedition. Some women – even women who know what looks best on them – enjoy a man's company when buying clothes, though the man stops being a distinct character to them. He becomes an audience, or rather, a small part of a vaster, more satisfying audience in their heads. I penetrated *What Every Woman Wants*, *The House of Fraser*, and *Chelsea Girl* with the guilty reverence I would feel in a mosque, Catholic chapel or synagogue, yet the odour was familiar and friendly. I had sniffed it as a small boy in my mother's wardrobe. I was fascinated by women pondering sombre or vivid or subtly pale colours, fingering husky or frail or soft or sleek fabrics, holding loosely or crisply or tightly tailored second skins to their bodies. I felt a long slow sexual ache in these shops, a sad ache because no earthly coitus could satisfy all the desires and possibilities suggested by the many garments. The ache, of course, was mine, but I was sure many women felt it too and perhaps felt it stronger. Most women have fewer devices than men to divert them from affection. I imagined a woman whose world was full of that ache, whose life was years of ordinary frustrations patiently endured before a chance suggestion led her further and further away from the familiar things she normally clung to. The woman need not have been beautiful or her adventure perverse, but these notions brought my imagination to life again. While writing the first chapter of this book I enjoyed a prolonged, cold-blooded sexual thrill of a sort common among some writers and (I suspect) all lizards.

At that time I thought *One for the Album* (then called *Something Leather*) a short story. On completing it I imagined more adventures for June, but the first episode had internal order and was a thriller of *The Pit and the Pendulum* sort, ending when the reader was likely to be most intrigued. Believing it could be popular I sent it to a famous London literary agency, suggesting they try selling it to an expensive glossy magazine with a transatlantic circulation: *Vogue* or *Esquire* or better still *The New Yorker*. After a few weeks I learned it had been sent to a couple of British literary magazines whose editors, though friendly acquaintances of mine, had not embraced it with cries of "yes please".

In 1987 Tom Maschler, Chairman of Jonathan Cape Ltd, asked if I had ideas for a new novel, a question he had asked me more than once since Cape had published my second novel three years earlier. I was in danger of mounting a literary treadmill. Most writers of saleable books can get money from publishers to write another as an advance against future royalties. Years of reprinting in paperback and foreign translations may pass before writers get money from royalties. I had not yet received royalties for earlier books because, though *critical* successes, they were not bestsellers. Critical successes are reviewed at length in literary magazines and lectured upon in universities. This hardly ever happens to bestsellers. Conscious of the economic treadmill ahead I sent Tom Maschler my story, suggesting it might be the first chapter of a novel for which, had I been truthful, I would have said I had not enough ideas. He replied with the enthusiasm of a publisher who suspects he may be about to get a bestseller from a critically successful author. I had never haggled with a publisher for money and did not do so now. Publisher's contracts usually offer the writer a third of the advance on signing the contract, a third on their receipt for the book and the last third on publication. I asked for an advance of £40,000, over four times any of my earlier advances. Some days earlier that sum had come up in a discussion of money worries with my friend Bernard MacLaverty, who said a good publishing house should give me £40,000 a year to write for them anything I liked. I asked Cape to give me £20,000 on signing the contract and the other half on receiving the full text, if they received it not later than two years after signature. This agreement gave me nearly three years of financial comfort with only one problem: making a lightly pornographic short story into a novel.

Lanark had been planned as an epic and written carefully over many years; *1982 Janine* was a sudden inspiration, and if not delayed by poverty would have completed in 1982 when it was started. I easily imagined a lesbian sado-masochistic orgy following *One for the Album* – such fancies come easily to me, but I cannot take them seriously for long having employed so many in my second novel. The story had now three main characters – June, Senga and Donalda (Harry had not yet occurred to me). I imagined June's seduction giving her an aggressive social confidence she had hitherto lacked, and using her work in a local government office to seduce, entangle and corrupt (with the help of Senga and Donalda) Scottish legislators. I wrote nearly a chapter along these lines but stopped on the verge of being unconvincing. Powerless to imagine a way of carrying the plot forward I thought of using that meaningless label, POST-MODERNISM, to enlarge the book in any way possible, and looked at old television and radio plays that had once been my livelihood. In the 1970's *Dialogue* was a half hour play broadcast by Scottish BBC radio, then networked on television by Granada, then performed in theatres by the short-lived Scottish Stage Company. I prosed it into the present tense, called it *A Free Man with a Pipe*, and easily believed my free man was June's unsatisfactory ex-husband, trying to forget her by failing to seduce someone else, with her voice on the telephone at the end finally demolishing him. This suggested a new form for the book.

Having shown Senga and Donalda seducing June in the late 1980s (the fashions in the streets give the date) each chapter would show in earlier years one of the women involved with men who failed them, starting with Senga's schooldays. While recycling these past dramas I began wanting to show more than the local Scots who compose today's Britain. My first and longest book had tried to do that, but lacking the knowledge to show (as Dickens had in *Little Dorrit*) Britain's oligarchs in a plot involving slums and slum landlords, the jailors and the jailed, I had hidden my ignorance in *Lanark* with fabulous metaphors. But a book of episodes showing the lives of three women converging over twenty-five years might describe, without fantasy, shifts and dependencies between many believable people. How could I bring a representative English oligarch to Scotland? In 1990 it was the turn of a British city to be the culture capital of Europe. Margaret Thatcher's government gave the job to Glasgow, which suggested a richer past for Harry.

I had invented her for the *Class Party* chapter, because a quartette allowed more permutations than a trio, but she said little because I had no idea where she came from or what job she did when not playing perverse games. I knew she was a rarer social type than my other women. It helped the plot for her to be rich, and it was a useful economy to make her almost speechless. I did not bother imagining a past for her, except to think she might have been made administrator of a large hospital with the job of closing it down. I had often thought about what makes rich people different from others, especially the rich whose wealth is a habit of mind due to a big unearned income. I had met a few and got on well with them because they had not been snobs – Francis Head had been one – but occasional remarks had astonished by showing how foreign to me they were. The owner of a big private garden told me how he had devoted it wholly to trees and shrubs because plots of flowers gave his gardener too much work. I asked if he grew vegetables. He said, "Once I did but it wasn't worth the trouble. You can get them in a shop for a few shillings."

I had also known a young woman who disliked everyone her parents knew, saying she preferred "ordinary people". She sulked when expected to make a cup of Nescafé for herself, explaining that she could not possibly do that, and proved it by floating a spoonful of the powder in a mug of lukewarm water. These people were individuals, not types, but as Scott Fitzgerald said at the start of his story *The Rich Boy*, "Describe an individual and you may end with a type; describe a type and you are likely to end with – nothing." It occurred to me that perhaps the very rich, after leaving boarding school, found it hard to take others seriously because they could easily replace or escape from whomever they did not like. That might explain why some were astonishingly unaffectionate towards their young. Brooding on this I suddenly imagined Harry's mother saying at her birth, "Oh God a fucking little gel," and began conceiving my distant cousin of a queen. The speech rhythms of this class (devoid of swearwords) had resounded through all the homes where I lived from babyhood. The BBC had been created by Lord Reith, a Glasgow minister's son, but most broadcasters had the dialect of posh English boarding schools. I had also met that class in the pages of Wilde, Firbank, Hemingway's *Fiesta*, Denton Welsh and Evelyn Waugh.

I did not expect to write much about Harry at first. I planned to shift her in one chapter from her nasty Scottish nanny and chilling mother to a boarding school, thence to the Warburg or Courtauld Institute, thence to being an arts administrator in Scotland. But the boarding school acquired a distinct geography where small details developed active bodies to support them. *Amanda's kid* and *new money* had been phrases I invented to show what a snob Harry's mother was. In the shrubbery the two phrases became Hjordis with The Fortress, Linda with the speech and character she is evicted from. I grew so attached to Harry that I made her an artist and took three chapters to move her north. From the gnat in *Alice Through the Looking Glass* I got the idea that the almost speechless Harry, after finding her voice in Glasgow, would talk in a smaller typeface than other people.

This list gives the dates of my women's adventures between the early 1960s and 1990.

CHAPTERS	YEARS	HEROINES
One for the Album	1989	June, Senga, Donalda
A Distant Cousin etc	1963	Harry
The Proposal	1965	Senga
The Man Who Knew etc.	1967	Donalda
Mr Lang and Ms Tain	1973	June
In the Boiler Room	1977	Senga
Quiet People	1971	Donalda
The Bum Garden	1963–1989	Harry
A Free Man etc.	1989	June (off stage)
Culture Capitalism	1989	Harry, Senga
Dad's Story	1989	Donalda, Harry
Class Party	1989	June, Donalda, Senga, Harry
New June	1989	June, Harry, Donalda, Senga

When June returned to the leatherwear shop where the novel started I realized my book had reached its natural conclusion, which is how I have left it in the foregoing short-story collection.

It was published as a novel entitled *Something Leather* in 1990. Most blurbs I write for my books are tampered with by editors who believe that unstinting praise of their publications is needed to sell it. The following blurb I wrote for *Something Leather* was printed as I wished:

> *SOMETHING LEATHER is about the love lives of June, Senga, Donalda and a distant cousin of the queen from 1963 to 1990. Also in it are unhappy children, a dangerously liberal headmistress, a tobacconist's family, a student, night watchman, pimp, businessman, boilerman, policeman, ex-serviceman, quiet couple, tinker, nurse, commercial traveller, arts administrator, former Lord Provost, Glasgow comedian, worried civil servant, brilliant but unstable politician. This is the first British fiction since THE CANTERBURY TALES to show such a wide social range in such embarrassing sexual detail, yet no characters are based on real people, not even the Glasgow comedian. The inefficient Scottish Office department in the Epilogue never existed – since 1967 its work has been efficiently done by the office of the ombudsman. The story starts near the end, has ten earlier starts, a crisis, a catastrophe and a moral. Unlike Alasdair Gray's earlier books, SOMETHING LEATHER has no fantasy and combines the amenities of a novel with the varieties of a short-story collection.*

The book was dedicated to Flo Allen, who had typed all my publications from the last chapters of *Lanark* onward. I knew she would not be shocked by my pornographic passages, of which I was slightly ashamed, with good reason. Most critics have agreed that *Something Leather* is my worst novel. Since chapters 1 and 12 are exploitive sex fantasy they have not noticed the very different writing between these. Despite exciting publicity this book did not become the bestseller Tom Maschler expected and Jonathan Cape never recovered my unusually big advance against royalties. I believe 9 to 11 inclusive are among my best stories in the realistic genre established by great German, Russian, Irish and American authors, French Maupassant, English Kipling and V.S. Pritchett, most of Chekhov and Joyce's *Dubliners*. That is why *Something Leather* has here been retitled. Anyone curious to read the sexual fantasies removed from *Class Party* may buy a first-edition hardback of *Something Leather* (in which it is printed uncensored as Chapter 12) from Morag McAlpine's online bookshop for £12.95. The rarity of this book is maintained by the only acceptable payment being in Sterling cheques.

WHEN AND WHERE FIRST PRINTED

One for the Album appeared in *The Fiction Magazine*, a brave attempt at a new Scottish quarterly launched in 1988, which expired after two or three issues.
With slight changes it was printed with the others in *Something Leather*, 1990.

TEN TALES TALL AND TRUE

This collection of stories was printed in 1993 by Bloomsbury instead of Cape, for complicated reasons starting years earlier.

William Smellie was a publisher who belonged to what has since been called the Scottish Enlightenment. One of the first to print Robert Burns' poetry, he also conceived and mainly collated the first edition of *The Encyclopaedia Britannica*, which he called "a scissors and paste job". He also wrote *A Philosophy of Natural History*, published in Edinburgh in 1790. Early in the 1980s a descendant of Smellie – the surgeon Campbell Semple – lent me that book. The preface to it began with these words: *Every preface, beside occasional and explanatory remarks, should contain not only the general design of the work but the motives and circumstances which lead the author to write on that particular subject. If this plan had been universally observed, a collection of prefaces would have exhibited a short, but curious and useful history both of literature and authors.* This suggested a history of literature made by arranging prefaces by their authors to great poems, plays, novels etc in chronological order. The result would be a history of English literature by those who had made it best, and seemed such a simple job that I was amazed to think nobody had yet done it, and I signed a contract for the book with Canongate. I started work on it and in less than a year had spent the publisher's advance against royalties, and found the work looked like taking almost as long to write as *Lanark*. It would have to be subsidized by other writing.

In 1992 Xandra Hardie was my English literary agent. I sent her some short stories made by turning short plays **not** used in *Something Leather* – correction! In *Glaswegians* – suggesting these would be the core of a new short story book if she could get me an advance for it from Jonathan Cape. She was slow in doing so because Tom Maschler, whose enthusiasm had inspired my last book, had left Cape and been replaced by David Godwin. Then a number of English publishers came to Glasgow and gave a party for their Scottish authors, since they now had several of these. Here I met David Godwin. He said he believed his firm was considering a new book of my short stories. I told him I needed an advance on it as soon as possible in order to complete my *Anthology of Prefaces*. He asked about that book. I told him about it. He said, "Are **we** getting it?" meaning Cape. I explained that it was going to Canongate, because I had to alternate my books between my Edinburgh and London publishers, to not seem ungrateful to the Scottish firm that had made my first books well known, while keeping an English publisher that could pay me what I was owed. David Godwin seemed to accept that explanation.

Next day Xandra Hardie phoned and said brightly, "Alasdair, I think it would be a good idea if we offered your new book of stories to Bloomsbury. Liz Calder is in charge there now, and she likes your work." I said that seemed a good idea, because I regarded Liz as a friend. Xandra said, "But please don't tell Liz that you want the advance in order to finish your anthology for Canongate. I had David Godwin on the phone this morning saying he didn't see why he should give a f****** advance for a book of stories to a f****** writer who needed the money to write another f****** book for a different f****** publisher." I told her I was surprised at Godwin's childish attitude, and knowing Liz Calder was thoroughly adult, amused her by telling her the whole story. Bloomsbury has been my London publisher from then onward. But I dedicated *Ten Tales Tall and True* to Tom Maschler, Xandra Hardie and Morag McAlpine (whom I had recently married) because I felt they were all partly responsible for the book.

Not all the tales derived from my early plays. *You* came from the anecdote told to me by Joe Mulholland, former journalist and antique dealer, about a late meal bought for him in Glasgow's Central Station Hotel by a rich and powerful man, though I changed the sex of his guest. *Internal Memorandum* was based on an internal memorandum my wife sent to one of her bosses when she worked for a Glasgow bookselling firm, founded in the late 18th century, which mostly expired in the early 21st. *Are You a Lesbian?* derives from a question she was asked in a local pub, though the woman I describe reacting to that question – daughter of a Church of Scotland minister – is nothing like Morag, and the original question was "Are you a fucking dyke?" *The Trendelenburg Position* was first written for an English film-making firm who wanted a talking-head monologue of the sort Alan Bennett had written for the BBC. I had greatly admired a couple of these, not least because his speakers were talking to the world at large – to nobody in particular. Unable to imagine anyone like that, I thought of a garrulous dentist working on a helpless patient. My own dentist, Mr White, is not garrulous, but when asked for information to help my monologue, said dentists' chairs were designed to support patients in the Trendelenburg position. Freidrich Trendelenburg, a German surgeon, had devised the position to support bodies with the least possible physical strain.

But when working on these stories I had a dream which I have spoken of so often, and written about at least once (though I forget where) that I will not describe it. Believing the strange atmosphere of the dream might be put into a story of two or three pages I started what once again grew quickly into a big novel, *Poor Things*, which some have found my most enjoyable. This is perhaps because the three main characters are all good natured without being bores. This novel grew so quickly that Liz Calder published it a year before *Ten Tales Tall and True*.

WHEN AND WHERE FIRST PRINTED

Homeward Bound – New Writing, Spring 1992.
Loss of the Golden Silence – Bete Noir, Christmas 1992.
You – Casablanca, May 1993.
Houses and Small Labour Parties – Living Issues, August 1993.
Time Travel – The Review of Contemporary Fiction, USA, 1993.

THE ENDS OF OUR TETHERS

The Book of Prefaces I had promised Canongate gained me an advance that was spent long before I completed the Chaucerian period of this *History of the English Language by Those Who Wrote It Best*. It was a complex editorial job that I could only do properly while sitting with the typesetter. My efforts to get the job done drew in my friend Angel Mullane. She financed Dog and Bone, a new wee Glasgow publishing house which would typeset the book for Canongate. Her husband Chris Boyce supplied the laptop technology and a friend was our typesetter. A good start was made. The typesetter left us without warning. Dog and Bone became impossible. I offered Canongate a new novel if they would release me from my *Book of Prefaces* contract. They thankfully agreed. I gave them *The History Maker*, a futuristic science fiction tale made from a rejected 1960s television play. I then signed a contract with Bloomsbury for an advance of £1,000 a month for three years, and a different monthly payment to my part-time secretary and eventual typesetter. The complete text was to be delivered in 1998, with illustrations. I delivered it in 1999. This did not surprise the editor, Liz Calder, who said it had been worth waiting for.

On publication in 2000 it was splendidly reviewed. By this time royalties for two of my early books that were still in print had overcome their original advances. Some were occasionally translated into other languages, so once a year I received cheques from Canongate and Bloomsbury. This steady income was not enough to stop my wife Morag (no longer a wage earner) fearing she might have to save us from poverty by selling her home (which was now mine) if I fell ill. Luckily my friend Bernard MacLaverty suggested I apply for a Royal Literary Fund pension. I did, and was granted it. A year later I got a steady income from being Professor of Creative Writing at Glasgow University, a job shared with Tom Leonard and James Kelman. The three of us resigned from it in 2003 for academic reasons too complex to mention here, but during that time most of the stories in this collection occurred to me, nearly all of them about folk with not much left to live for. This had increasingly been the theme of earlier stories, yet I was not miserable when writing them. Tragedies would not be popular if there was no exhilaration in facing the worst.

No Bluebeard sprang from ideas about marriage derived from women I have known, but none I ever married. The non-Bluebeard who tells it, like all my narrators, is a form of myself but in many ways different, I hope. The story *Aiblins* was certainly suggested by being a creative-writing teacher, though I met nobody like Aiblins when I was a professor. I gave him three of my own poems. *Proem* and *Outing* were written in my teens and luckily never published before I saw how bad they were. *My Ex Husband*, *Sinkings* and *Property* are based on real occurrences told to me by friends, and which nagged me ever since until I made short fictions from them. *Job's Skin Game* was conceived as a monologue when eczema recurred to me after an abeyance of nearly forty years. I connected that with the Book of Job when Lu Kemp, a Scottish BBC radio director, commissioned a story from me derived from a book in the Bible. It was broadcast in January 2003. *Well Being* derives from a nightmare I had about the future of Scotland when writing a pamphlet.

WHEN AND WHERE FIRST PRINTED

Well Being – Why Scots Should Rule Scotland (a political pamphlet), 1997.

Big Pockets with Buttoned Flaps – New Writings 9, 2000.

Job's Skin Game – Prospect Magazine, 2003.

TALES DROLL AND PLAUSIBLE

Once again after completing a book – *The Ends of Our Tethers* – I had no intention of writing more fiction and felt another publisher's advance need never again attract me. In 2003 I began a job I had wanted since my art school days: painting the ceiling and walls of a great building with no deadlines and sufficient payment. The job would last for years (it is not finished yet) but while working on it I would always earn a good weekly wage. Colin Beattie, the Glasgow pub owner, was converting the former Kelvin and Botanic Free Church (derelict for years) into an arts and entertainment centre called the Óran Mór – Gaelic words meaning the Great Music. I decorated the ceiling of the auditorium before the Óran Mór opened to the public, then decorated lower auditorium walls when this did not interrupt the concerts, banquets and conferences which were the hall's main source of income.

In the autumn of 2004 the Óran Mór's lunch hour theatre, A Play, A Pie and A Pint, occupied the auditorium floor on most days between 12.30 and 2 p.m. I was then painting walls of the gallery behind and above the audience's back, so had no need to stop work, and thus heard several times several performances of new one-act plays commissioned from Scottish authors by Dave McLennan. With no funding but Colin Beattie's support, Dave still directs this small, successful theatre. Eight years later, in 2012, he has commissioned 38 new plays, thus encouraging more new authors in a year than any other theatre, even those with the support of Creative Scotland (formerly the Scottish Arts Council) and more than all of Scotland's broadcasting networks joined together. A Play, A Pie and A Pint revived my interest in playwriting, as it also offered a chance of production. From 2006 to 2008 it staged: *Goodbye Jimmy*, *Midgieburgers*, *The Pipes! The Pipes!* and *Voices in the Dark*. I gave these a longer life by turning them into stories, only changing the title of *The Pipes! The Pipes!* to *Whisky and Water*. I then added them to other new stories that had accumulated when I was not painting. *The Offer*, *Misogynist* and *The Third Mr Glasgow* were written as entries for competitions suggested by Canongate Books or my London agent (they did not win). *The Magic Terminus* was commissioned by Tot Taylor of London's *Riflemaker Gallery*, Soho, to accompany his show of Francesca Lowe's richly fanciful paintings. Six stories were written in the year it was published.

Gumbler's Sheaf came from a folder of annoying letters received over several years but never before got round to counter-blasting. *Eustace* happened because in April 2012 Dan Kitts MBE sent me a copy of his new publication, *Military, Naval and Civil Airships Since 1783*. Here I read that in October 1916 the last Zeppelin destroyed over England had been shot down by Second Flight Lieutenant Wulfstan Tempest. He at once joined two splendid names I had been unable to forget or use for years: Knatchbull

Hugeson, an obscure Victorian literary gent, and the sculptor Scipio Tadolini. I invented a vaunting speech to combine that trio, and a love of anticlimax led to the sad state of Eustace McNulty. I thought that a good way to start these late tales. *Working with Giants* came from words I heard – or misheard – spoken by a man opposite me on a London underground train when I visited that city to see the big Hockney exhibition in May. *Late Dinner* also came from eavesdropping on a train, sometime in 2011. I heard a man pontificate about his work in such empty clichés, that I had to invent bullying Mr Big and to give his vacant words a context. *Maisie and Henry* used some of my wife Morag's experiences when young, with later memories that we now hold in common. The longer we live together the more her past haunts me. Maisie is therefore slightly like Morag, but also as different as I am from Henry, that efficient gardener. *The Patient*, however is almost purely autobiographical.

The four drollest tales near the end of this book derive from four short plays I wrote this century; but droll or plausible all of them are class bound. Though not about comfortable folk, they are nearly all folk with enough money. So *Billy Semple* is my concluding tale, if not the ending. I had met him in Studio One, a mildly sleazy local pub in the early 21st century, since gentrified out of existence. I described that meeting soon after it happened because (**A**) it reminded me that nobody can be sure of their end and (**B**) it mentioned social changes for the worse that surprised me when they happened, and which many younger folk take for granted. This I now see is the theme of all my later tales.

WHEN AND WHERE FIRST PRINTED

The Third Mr Glasgow – Prospect, 2007.
Magic Terminus – Riflemaker Gallery Catalogue, 2010.
Midgieburgers – New Writing Scotland 30, 2012.
Billy Semple – The One O'Clock Gun, 2012.

THE ILLUSTRATIONS

Pictures in *Unlikely Stories, Mostly* had some details copied from work by Paul Klee, Michelangelo, Raphael, Piranesi, G. Glover, W. Blake, E.H. Shepherd and a Japanese artist whose name has no phonetic equivalent in Roman type I am aware of. Drawing is a way of keeping the appearance of folk I know. The last page of my first Unlikely Story shows the face of my son in his teens and the last two Likely Stories show Doreen and Russell Logan when I first knew them. I will not name other friends used in that book. The original *Lean Tales* by James Kelman, Agnes Owens and me had a picture of each author before their part of the book, so now it has only mine as I was in 1985. The vignettes of merry or glum horned heads are a recent addition. In *Glaswegians* the initial capitals contain portrait drawings (not wholly in the following order) of May Hooper, Morag McAlpine, John Purser, Eddie Linden, Agnes Owens, Bethsy Gray and Carole Rhodes. A childish pun suggested the illustrative scheme in *Ten Tales Tall and True*. The frontispiece to *The Ends of Our Tethers* is based on its 2003 jacket design. The horned skulls were also in that. Other work left me no time to illustrate *Tales Droll and Plausible* so I enriched them with vignettes scanned from a book of plays by Philip Massinger published by Ernest Benn Ltd, London, and Charles Scribner, New York. Though undated it is obviously late Victorian, and though the artist who designed the vignettes is not named, their style belongs to an even earlier century. Most surviving art is by forgotten artists.

A G RAY
BY JAMES Bliss
29.5.1990